THE PIRATE SHIP

Also by Peter Tonkin

The Iceberg
The Bomb Ship
The Leper Ship
The Fire Ship
The Coffin Ship
The Journal of Edwin Underhill
Killer

THE PIRATE SHIP

Peter Tonkin

Copyright © 1995 Peter Tonkin

The right of Peter Tonkin to be identified as the Author of the Work has been asserted by him in accordance with the Copyright, Designs and Patents Act 1988.

First published in 1995
by HEADLINE BOOK PUBLISHING

A HEADLINE FEATURE hardback

10 9 8 7 6 5 4 3 2 1

All rights reserved. No part of this publication may be reproduced, stored in a retrieval system, or transmitted, in any form or by any means without the prior written permission of the publisher, nor be otherwise circulated in any form of binding or cover other than that in which it is published and without a similar condition being imposed on the subsequent purchaser.

All characters in this publication are fictitious and any resemblance to real persons, living or dead, is purely coincidental.

British Library Cataloguing in Publication Data

Tonkin, Peter
Pirate Ship
I. Title
823.914 [F]

ISBN 0-7472-1242-2

Typeset by Keyboard Services, Luton, Beds

Printed and bound in Great Britain by
Mackays of Chatham PLC, Chatham, Kent

HEADLINE BOOK PUBLISHING
A division of Hodder Headline PLC
338 Euston Road
London NW1 3BH

For Cham, Guy and Mark,
and in memory of my father
Wing Commander F. A. Tonkin, OBE, C.Eng., FRAeS,
RAF 1919–1994

PIRATE SHIP: A vessel employed in piracy or manned by pirates. First used 1600.
Oxford English Dictionary.

PIRACY
1.4
   Attacks on vessels by armed thieves in the South China Seas have been reported in 1982, 1987 and 1988. These attacks are usually made from fast motor boats approaching from astern. Laden vessels with low freeboard are particularly vulnerable.
China Sea Pilot, fourth edition 1978 (revised 1987), updated 1991.
Admiralty Charts and Publications. Crown copyright.

The South China Sea is the worst in the world for maritime robbing and hijack. Since 1992 the International Maritime Bureau . . . has logged over 120 pirate attacks in South East Asian waters, where there is a tradition of piracy centuries old.
Focus Magazine, November 1993.

ONE

SULU

O Captain! My Captain! our fearful trip is done,
The ship has weather'd every rack, the prize we sought is won,
The port is near, the bells I hear, the people all exulting,
While follow eyes the steady keel, the vessel grim and daring...

                Walt Whitman. *Oh Captain! My Captain!*

Chapter One

When he judged that they had come far enough south, Huuk raised his right hand from the stock of his AK74 assault rifle and extended his arm straight up above his head in the agreed signal to the other boats. At once they all swung due west and he lowered his hand again. The old gun lay across the low pulpit in which Huuk was standing like a slight, slim figurehead and it vibrated against the teak rail as the motors rumbled up towards full throttle. The long magazine curled out over the still waters of the South China Sea and the warm, oiled mechanism of the chamber pushed back gently and reassuringly into the pit of his stomach like the muzzle of a pet animal.

Unconsciously, for he was concentrating absolutely upon his lookout, Huuk took a deep breath and held the cool, damp, shadowy air in the depths of his lungs until his ribs began to hurt. The action of breathing in pulled the thick wool of his balaclava into his mouth and he tutted mentally at the anxiety which had made him put it on too early. Left-handed, he pulled the rough wool up over his short nose and high forehead until it sat on the top of his skull like a cap. Only then did he breathe out, stroking the stock of the gun with his right hand as though it were a good-luck charm. Behind him, his five-man crew sat silently, all of them, like him, cradling their weapons and keeping keen watch. Away on either hand, slightly astern in an arrowhead formation, two more launches kept pace, each of them also packed with well-armed men on the lookout.

They were running in under the last of the night, skimming west as though racing the first great beams of dawn light down the rolling curve of the earth. Already there was enough brightness to cast shadows dead ahead onto the silvery surface of the sea and colour was bleeding into the scene with insidious inevitability.

Huuk's newly naked cheek was unnaturally sensitive and so it picked up the first kiss of the dawn wind an instant earlier than usual as it puffed from the south, given extra impetus by the threat of a storm running up from down there. Huuk knew that if he glanced north and perhaps a little east now he would see just the very tip of the Peak aflame like a volcano. No sooner had he thought this than there, like a fallen star, low on the starboard quarter, came the light of the Wenweic Zhou. The point of brightness was so startling that Huuk was tricked into speculating whether, if he continued to watch in that quarter, he would be able to see the distant Fortaleza da Guia light at Macau.

He stroked the stock of the AK74 and dragged his dazzled vision back. His fine-featured countenance remained as tranquil as the sea but within he was seething with anger. What was making his usually disciplined mind run on such trivialities? What childish forebodings were these which made him almost nervous of completing this mission? What spirits were moving among the last of the darkness warning of terrors to come? What sort of a leader would the men think him if he was not the first to sight their target – and the first to board her, and the first to draw blood? This was the pride which had put him here, at the cutting edge of the bloody business, keeping lookout without using his binoculars.

The slightest stir behind his left shoulder alerted him that one of the others had sighted something and he glanced south, turning his still-sensitive face into the cool, charged oil-tainted wind. There, away on the dull, threatening, smoke-grey horizon, sat a freighter such as the one they were hunting, her long hull almost invisible in the shadows and her upper works seemingly ablaze. Huuk shook his head once, decisively. No. This was not their quarry. Too far south; on the wrong course; moving too fast. The intelligence out of Aberdeen had been precise about their quarry's course and disposition at least. Huuk knew exactly what he was looking for, and precisely where it was going to be. Position and movement were, after all, of paramount importance. He narrowed his eyes and faced forwards once again.

And there she was! Bow on, dead ahead, seemingly dead in the water, there was the ship they sought. Huuk let go of his AK74 for a moment and raised both his arms straight up into the air before gesturing forcefully forward, chopping both hands down like axes with the hard edges of his palms downwards over the hissing water, as though he was delivering two kite strike karate chops to the inoffensive air. This was also an agreed signal. The motors reached a new pitch of snarling frenzy and the three slim launches leaped forward as one, slapping through the still water, kicking up foaming bow waves as they went.

Huuk looked, mesmerised, foreboding like a stone upon his slight chest. The ship came up towards them as though miraculously rising out of the water, still, silent, apparently deserted. There was no pale wave at her slim bow at all as she drifted north-eastwards into his territory just as the mysterious information had led him to expect.

With her hull still a shadowy shape and her lines cloaked by a dull purple-grey mist, her superstructure glimmered spectrally as though given some kind of foul luminosity like meat beginning to rot. The square of her white-painted bridgehouse shone dully behind the black bars of her deck gantries, like something caged. As Huuk watched, narrow-eyed, the first great bolt of sunlight smashed against the equipment in the crow's nest atop the stubby mast which stood above her bridge. The light seemed to shatter as though it was red-molten gold and spattered downwards like a firework, raining dazzling brightness. The tops of the hard-edged black gantries caught fire like candles, tall flames leaping forward in series along the main deck towards the speeding launches. The stormy dawn wind rumbled and thudded, as though echoing the sounds which ought to have accompanied the blinding pyrotechnics.

That was just what they needed now, thought Huuk more happily. The freshening wind would cover the sounds of the racing motors as effectively as the waterfall of light would hide their long, shark-like shapes from the watchkeepers aboard – if there were any, which he had been led to doubt.

He glanced down, past the lateral shape of the AK74, to the neatly coiled rope with its three-pronged boarding hook lying between the gleaming whiteness of his Reeboks. The trainers were expensive and, rarely for this neck of the woods, they were the genuine article. The Levi 501s were far more suspect, purchased cheaply like much of his clothing, in the night market on Temple Street. He knew for a fact that his shirt was not made by Yves St Laurent as its label claimed, and that his watch had never been anywhere near the Rolex manufactory in Switzerland. But he was a neat dresser and came well turned out even on a job like this one. Still, when push came to shove, his life could well depend on the steadiness of his stance, the swiftness of his step and therefore on the grip of his footwear, so his shoes and his equipment were the genuine article at least. He patted the butt of the AK74 one more time for luck, pulled down his balaclava and looked up.

The mottled, varicoloured three-dimensional jigsaw of the deck cargo was alight now, glowing between the columns of brightness which were the main deck gantries or samson posts. The top of the superstructure, too, had risen into brightness and the long window across the front of the bridge gleamed ruby in the red dawn like the wound of a cut throat. Huuk looked away from the light again; the time for watching was well past now. As the prow of his launch came in past the sheer bow, still seemingly cloaked in the last of the shadows here at sea level, he slung the AK74 over his right shoulder and lifted the grappling hook, swinging it with an easy, practised motion, looking up.

The side of the ship reached out to a slight overhang here at the bow. The metal near the water was mostly plain, rusty black but here at the forefoot there were white lading marks and the hint of red beneath the surface. Above, there was a slightly old-fashioned flare, painted white, where the side became deck rails round the forecastle head. Just below the white line, above and behind the rusty double hook of the anchor, also in neat white, the name was painted: *SULU QUEEN*. The light bludgeoning across the deck reflected out across the slight mist, giving the upper reaches, for an instant, a disturbing glory. The whole of the ship seemed to waver as though some unimaginable explosion was taking place within her. Even the bright solidity of her name seemed to tremble on the verge of dissolution. Then the light altered and reality settled back into place again.

As they came aft of the name, Huuk threw up his boarding hook, tugged on the knotted rope to ensure that the hook was holding firmly, and swung up out of the safety of his launch. As he scrambled up the slippery, clammy side, he could hear the hiss, clatter and twang of half a dozen more hooks being thrown and when he scrambled over onto the deck itself, he was relieved to see five more hooks bedded safely in series. He looked up.

Everything was different up here. The change was so absolute it was almost incapacitating, as though he had clambered onto a different plane of existence, into a different world. In the absolute daylight, the deck stank of metal and the air, already humid and hot, was filled with further smells from the metal sides of the high-piled containers and, more subtly, mysterious hints of whatever they contained. He had his back to the sun which smote down upon his shoulders through the spurious Yves St Laurent shirt. The containers hulked above his left shoulder and the wind muttered through the spaces in between them as though the ghosts of all his forefathers were there, trying to warn him about something too terrible to be discussed full voice. When he moved, the sole of his Reebok screamed and he jumped, shocked to find that he was sweating.

By the time the first of his men swung themselves aboard, Huuk was down at the far end of the line of hooks. Stationed between them and the silent bridge, with his eyes darting everywhere and his AK74 cocked and sitting ready on his hip, he waited while the rest of them scrambled aboard and the last pair hauled up the two boxes of extra equipment. In a matter of minutes they were ready and he was able to give the signal. Still without a word having been said, the whole gang of them ran down the deck, keeping close to the shelter of the containers, in covering pairs out of sight of any invisible watchkeepers on the bridge towards which they were heading.

Action blanked Huuk's mind to the intensity of sensation and the whirl of worrying, slightly superstitious speculation, as it always did. He was a natural leader, a combination of imagination and bloody-minded courage, of sensitivity and brutality, of cold calculation and explosive action which made his men worship him. They called him *Tuan*, Lord, in a way which was as impressive as it was old-fashioned, foreign and inappropriate.

He arrived at the main door into the port side of the bridgehouse and paused. The heavy metal portal stood invitingly ajar and there was not a whisper of sound or breath of motion, but that meant nothing. This would be the first place Huuk would have mounted a trap had he been in command of the *Sulu Queen*. He flattened himself against the white-painted outside wall, eased the AK74 until it lay across his silently heaving belly, and waited.

His men were up beside him within instants, fifteen of them, with himself the sixteenth. Two carried the boxes brought up from the first launch. The rest of them were armed with an assortment of automatic and semi-automatic weapons. They were dressed in an array of jeans, trousers or shorts in various states of cleanliness and repair, and in a range of shirts likewise. They all wore balaclavas or face masks, leaving uncovered only their long dark eyes, ablaze with the prospect of action.

Huuk's right hand chopped a series of silent orders and the first pair separated off. In a silent explosion of action they hurled themselves in through the innocently gaping door and were down in a crouch at once, their weapons sweeping from side to side, ready to lay down arcs of fire. Then they were gone and the next pair followed – one high, one low. Huuk stepped through with the last man in and stood, fully erect, with his own AK74 swinging from side to side covering their backs.

Silence. Stillness.

Not a whisper of sound. Not a flicker of movement.

The still air settled, stinking of iron, redolent of something else – something putrid. A lone gull screamed in the distance and its cry set off a cacophony of calls accompanied by the beat of wings like distant thunder. And just at that moment, under that faraway disturbance, Huuk suddenly felt the short hair on his neck stir. For he had the strangest feeling that there was someone there, just out of sight, hidden away close by, watching. Waiting. Then the feeling was gone and the gulls' cries whispered into silence.

Huuk looked around the faces of the team crouching along the narrow alleyway in front of him. Their eyes met his one by one, each with the faintest shake of a head. None of them registered anything. He stepped back, leaned out through the doorway and gestured the others in. Still in silence, they trooped in through the door. At once the lateral alleyway was crowded and Huuk led his men swiftly down to the main companionway where they could spread out up and down the steps. Here a rapid series of gestures and clicks split the men into their assigned teams. The first of the black boxes was opened and Huuk handed the leader of each group a Motorola PRC 319 two-way radio. These had been set and tested earlier and needed no further checking now.

Huuk snapped his fingers once again and despatched one team down to explore the engineering decks below, another to check out the accommodation and the navigating areas above, and left a third, fiercely armed, to guard the boxes here. The men went as ordered, some of them frowning now, for they clearly could not see the need for combat readiness and continued silence aboard this drifting, abandoned hulk. But their orders were clear and, for all they looked like a Triad street gang from the Wanchai, their discipline was absolute.

As the brooding silence persisted to the point of monotony and his own radio stayed stubbornly silent, Huuk shook himself into action and crossed to the companionway leading up towards the bridge decks. Then, uncharacteristically hesitant, he changed his mind and returned. He handed his AK74 to one of the men guarding the boxes and bent to snap the second one open. There was a bundle of green material on the top and he lifted it out. As he swung it upwards, it unfolded, revealing padded sides, and by the time he had shrugged it over his slim shoulders it stood revealed as an ancient, almost threadbare, bulletproof jacket. He reached back into the black depths of the box and pulled out something else. This was a gun, but no gun like the old AK he had handed to the nearest guard. Where that had been slim and reassuringly fashioned with a light stock and a scimitar-shaped ammunition clip, this was squat, brutal and black. Its stock was skeletal, its barrel short, wide and gleaming obsidian. When he pulled it up to point at the deckhead above and sat it on one slim hip, it still looked more like a grenade launcher than a rifle; and even the open flap of the venerable flak jacket, swinging wide as he moved, could not conceal the brutal power of the thing. With his left hand he caught the tight neck-piece of the balaclava and wrestled it up over his short nose and high forehead until he was able to pull the thing off altogether and cast it impatiently aside.

The man with the extra AK narrowed his eyes as he watched *Tuan* Huuk. He watched as the slight figure hunched forward, vibrant with concentration, head moving from side to side like a radar dish – or the head of a hawk in search of its prey. He watched as the bantam-weight body rocked up and forward onto the balls of its feet and was gone up the companionway like a wraith. The guard exchanged a glance with his nearest companion. A ghost of a nod was all that passed between them but it was enough. They knew that while the rest of his command was searching through this idle, abandoned derelict as it drifted across the South China Sea towards distant Hong Kong, *Tuan* Huuk himself was hunting.

Huuk crept up the companionway onto the lower bridge deck with every muscle taut, as controlled as a hunting cat. At the top of the stairway he hesitated, glancing left and right along the narrow alleyway on either side of which, he knew, the crew should have been housed. Everything was as silent and still as it had seemed when he first broke into the bridgehouse a mere ten minutes earlier. He paused again, calculating. He was certain that there was someone aboard, shadowing his men and watching. He was unsure what precisely was going on here. He didn't entirely trust the information he had been given and in any case the situation as described had been all but incredible to begin with. That anyone would leave a fully-laden cargo ship of more than 20,000 tonnes adrift and abandoned just outside Hong Kong territorial waters, ripe for the picking, was more than even the most gullible of Huuk's men could believe. And yet here it was, apparently exactly as described. It was all far too good to be true.

'*Tuan!*'

It was the first word which had been spoken since Huuk and his men came aboard and, in spite of the fact that it was whispered, it was enough to make Huuk's lithe body lurch and jump with shock. The stubby black barrel swung towards the source of the sound and threatened one of his men who was frozen in the open doorway of the nearest cabin, his face the colour of old ivory, made pale with the depth of his shock. Huuk pulled the barrel of his new gun up until it was pointing at the deckhead immediately above him again. Once again he frowned, concerned that the tautness of his nerves should have frightened one of his men like that.

But all too soon it became apparent that the man had not been frightened of the gun but had been sickened by what he had found. Huuk stepped through the door and found himself in a double cabin exactly of the sort he would have expected two crew to occupy or one officer to use as an office. And, indeed, just beyond the flip-flops of his own pale man there were the cabin's occupants. They lay face down, side by side. Their hands were tied behind their backs. Huuk noticed this fact before he registered the pool of blood that they were lying in. The pool of blood congealed upon the linoleum flooring led Huuk to pay closer attention to the backs of the dead men's heads. He hissed with shock and then at once, almost without thinking, he switched in his iron self-control. Three steps brought him to the edge of the black-red pool. Brutal brightness broke in through the forward-facing porthole with all the dramatic clarity of a spotlight. It played across the backs of the dead men's heads, revealing the bullet holes, placed execution-style, dead centre. The power of the light was such that it penetrated the rough circles in the black matted hair and the sharp bone beneath to reveal bruise-black swells of ruptured brain looking as though the ravaged skulls had been packed with ripe black-berries. Without taking a conscious breath, Huuk stepped forward and placed his almost priceless Reebok into the red-black circle and reverently nudged the side of the nearest dead face. It rolled over just enough to reveal the horror beneath. As it lifted, there came the loudest noise to disturb the brooding air aboard the *Sulu Queen* so far – the long, clear sound of a cotton bedsheet being torn in two. It was the sound the dead man's face made as it was lifted off the floor.

Clearly the man had been placed face down on the linoleum and then been executed by the discharge of a heavy-calibre gun immediately behind his head. The bullet had smashed through the head, rupturing the man's brain and exiting through his face exactly between his eyes, tearing off much of his visage, making the eyeballs themselves explode and shattering the bridge of his nose. The floor was made of steel, covered with linoleum. The bullet had exploded against the metal and released its terrible energy into heat. Shattering, it had bounced back in a perfectly circular wave of molten pieces which had brought the instantly liquefied linoleum with it. Around the edges of the crater which was all that was left of the crewman's face above the jaw, long strings of rubbery linoleum were indistinguishable from the thickening threads of hair, skin and brain matter. The circle on the floor, lifted like risen dough by the bubbles within the half-melted material, was speckled with bits and pieces of various sizes and colours and covered with the thick red semi-liquid ooze of dried blood. The whole mess reminded Huuk irresistibly of an obscene pizza and he had to be very careful not to vomit. Instead he looked up, his narrow eyes almost invisible behind the slits of speculation. Standing opposite him, beyond the bodies, was his armaments expert Tse Ho.

'What do you think did this?' he asked in a scarcely audible whisper of Mandarin.

'Something very big. Forty-four Magnum maybe. Something far bigger than anything we're carrying.'

Huuk's hiss of indrawn breath was still lingering on the air when his radio spat into life. *'Tuan.'*

At least the Vietnamese corpses had faces, but that was more or less all that could be said for them. There were six of them – four women and two children – and they lay naked but reverently arranged in the cold storage. Except that, since the ship's power was down, there was nothing to keep the cold storage cold. From nearby areas it was possible to smell putrefying meat of all sorts as the domain of the chief steward and the chief cook slowly went rancid and rotted away. The bodies were beginning to bloat quite badly but it was still possible to see that three of the women had been young and one had been middle-aged. One child had been a girl of about ten years and the other a baby. Without a close examination it was impossible to be sure, but it looked as though they had all been raped. In spite of the obvious care which had been taken to clean them before laying them out, there were certain signs which could not be overlooked, for the acts seemed to have been brutal – and repeated. There was no doubt that they had all been murdered: their throats were cut. The three younger women had been subjected to further mutilation – hopefully after death – and various pieces of them were missing.

Huuk looked down on them, his mouth a thin line. He was beginning to get a very bad feeling about this; a very bad feeling indeed. His information had described a drifting derelict, ripe for piracy, heading into his waters; it had made no mention of corpses, and here were seven already. At least these five were innocent of the gaping wounds such as bullets from a .44 Magnum might make.

His radio hissed. '*Tuan!*'

In the library on the boat deck immediately beneath the bridge were twenty more. They lay frozen in a disgusting shambles of blood and books, viscera and videotapes, seemingly covered in a soiled snowdrift of shredded paper. There had been, it seemed at first, no organised executions here – they had all been crowded in among the bookshelves and then hosed with automatic fire. High-velocity bullets had tumbled through jumping, writhing, spurting bodies and then torn through the volumes around the walls making everything explode as though tiny grenades had been detonated within. Bullets had ricocheted off the iron-hearted ceiling, bringing down showers of broken glass from the light fittings. Bones had shattered as the bullets passed, starting out through already cooling flesh; plastic had shattered, spewing long loops of brown. Everywhere was splattered with great gouts of blood. In each body had been eight pints of bright red liquid. In each body there had been a pint or so of urine. In each body there had also been at least a pint of faecal matter, made liquid in most cases by shock and terror. Careful observation made clear what a first glance might have missed, that most of these people were wearing only light sleeping attire. Certainly very few were clad in anything substantial enough to soak up or contain any of the various liquids.

On the floor of the library, therefore, in amongst the wreckage of books and videotapes and half floating bodies, there lay nearly thirty gallons of liquid, most of it still fluid. For some reason best known to the naval architect who had designed the *Sulu Queen*, even the internal doors on the upper-deck corridors had sills as though they were bulkhead doors opening to the outer weather deck. In this instance that was fortunate. There was nearly a foot-deep of stinking liquid on the library floor which otherwise would have flooded down the alleyways and companionways – and out through the scuppers or down to the bilge.

Huuk stood outside the door with the toes of his Reeboks pressed up against the sill looking in across the still sea of blood and body fluid at the corpses frozen like the companions of Captain Scott at the South Pole. Able and experienced commander though he was, it proved difficult for him to remain in control faced with this horror. Nevertheless, there was worse to come. As his vision cleared, he began to make out one or two larger craters amongst the smaller bullet wounds. He had been wrong. The .44 Magnum had been at work in here after all. He raised his right foot, preparing to sacrifice his Reeboks by wading in for an even closer look, but his Motorola stopped him.

'*Tuan!*' whispered his radio, and he knew at once from the sound of the voice that there was something even more terrible to see.

The rest of *Sulu Queen*'s crew were on the bridge but these men had not only been shot. Huuk's wise eyes swept over the carnage allowing his mind to reconstruct what must have happened. What must have happened not just here but everywhere aboard.

At least one man who had done this must have been amongst the crew already. There was no sign of anyone having come clandestinely aboard, though the corpses of the Vietnamese gave him cause to wonder. Whoever had done this, for whatever reason, there had been no attempt to take the crew captive, no thought, apparently, of holding officers or men while searches were made and questions asked. There had simply been a concerted, lethal attack whose objective had been to get rid of everyone aboard as swiftly as possible. An attack whose technique had varied only between frenzied assault, callous mass murder and cold execution.

And, seemingly, it had all started here, on the bridge, in a silent rush. At least one man, armed with a pistol and a panga, had come silently onto the bridge. He had begun with the watch officer and he had used the panga in order to maintain silence and surprise. The first blow had opened the back of the man's head and must have knocked him out but it may not have killed him for the frenzied chopping must have continued as he rolled onto his side, pulling himself into a foetal position, trying in vain to escape from the blade which was hacking through his chest and torso like an axe. At some time, probably later, to make assurance doubly sure, someone had put a pistol to his ear and pulled the trigger. That was probably why there was so much brain matter sprayed out across the floor behind him – with the clean outline of a pair of footprints in it. The steersman had been next, in all probability dispatched while the watch officer was dying. One blow had been enough for the steersman. A lateral one across the back of the neck. Now his body lay where it had fallen on the deck beneath the tiny helm and his head stood on the shelf above it, nose against the clearview, wide eyes keeping eternal watch forward down the deck.

The dress of the corpses in the library had already told Huuk that this brutal attack must have happened in the middle of the night. Last night? The night before? There was no way of telling at the moment. Even so, in the middle of the night, there had been yet another man out on the bridge wing. On seeing or suspecting the attack, he had rushed in and actually caught hold of the murderer. There had obviously been a brief wrestling match but it was one-sided and had come to an inevitable end. The murderer had been carrying a heavy panga and a gun. He had blown a hole in the unfortunate officer's side. The entry wound was black-ringed with powder burn and the exit wound showed where a rib had been torn wide and a kidney blown free. The shock of impact had thrown the officer back into the watchkeeper's chair by the bridge wing door and here he had tried unavailingly to protect his head and shoulders with his forearms from the panga. One hand lay on the floor, severed. It was the left and there was a pale band on the clean-cut flesh of the wrist where a watch should have been. But there was no watch. The left arm itself now hung down as though reaching to retrieve the hand. The right arm lay curled within the lap, a mass of chopped flesh and white splintered bone. The thorax, chest and shoulders were in the same state. Huuk found himself hoping with unusual piety that the victim had been unconscious at the very least before the brutal attack had finished.

And yet here too, to make assurance doubly sure, some time after death, judging from the footprints in the blood beside the left hand on the deck, a heavy-calibre handgun – the .44 Magnum, he was sure – had been pressed to the dead man's left breast and it had done to his heart what it had done to the watch officer's brain.

Perhaps to keep him a little distant from these atrocities, Huuk's mind was still calculating – recreating the probable sequence of events. With the bridge taken, the ship was at the mercy of the madman with the gun and the panga. It would have been easy enough to surprise the rest of those aboard. Anyone who resisted would be tied up. The rest would be put in the library. The bound men were executed as soon as everyone was secure. And finally, those in the library were simply hosed with automatic fire. They would have stood no chance. Huuk had detected no sign of a concerted rush among the pyjama'd bodies but even had someone tried to get to the man at the door, any kind of automatic weapon, from the AK74 onwards, would have been pumping bullets into the confined space at such a rate that they would simply have been chopped down, blown backwards, destroyed with all the rest.

No, concluded Huuk, turning away and beginning to prowl back down the corridor towards the companionway. One man could easily have achieved all this. Then it occurred to him to wonder why he was thinking in terms of one man in the first place.

Because, he realised, he was convinced there was still one man alive aboard. One man who was moving from place to place concealed, silent as a ghost, coldly observing Huuk and his men, watching and waiting for his chance to act. The man with the .44 Magnum. Perhaps the man who had done all this. Huuk's hair stirred at the thought and the hot, fetid air suddenly seemed to contain chilly little drafts.

No one else seemed to suspect the presence of the mysterious observer, but Huuk was not concerned with what his men could or could not sense. That was why he was in command. A series of monosyllabic orders spat into his radio caused his teams to fan out and change the pattern of their search. Within moments they were all spread like beaters at a hunt, driving their quarry to the hunter, and Huuk himself was like a spider at the centre of the web of their careful movements. Or rather, not quite at the centre of the web; not here, not yet. Silent as a hunting tiger, he began to pace down the companionway. The only sounds he made were the whisper of his flak jacket against the painted panels of the walls and the occasional unavoidable squeak of his moulded Reebok soles upon the stair. He knew where the stranger would be. He had made the men guarding the black boxes join the other teams and he knew the silent watcher would be tempted to them. No matter how well armed, how calculatingly sane or how foamingly mad, the watcher would be tempted to check out the boxes.

Huuk's mouth stretched unconsciously wide as though he was screaming. His jaws ached but he didn't notice. He concentrated on moving with absolute silence, breathing through the gape of his throat with utter voicelessness. He was a hunting cat. He was a soundless spectre. He was a shadow with a gun.

Huuk swung round the corner of the companionway leading down from the lower bridge deck where the two dead crewmen lay, swinging the squat barrel of his big black gun into position as he moved. And there, crouching over the boxes, was the apparition he had been hunting. Huuk got the impression of a tall, thin body dressed in white overalls smeared with blood. Shod with blood and red to the knees. A burning glance from wild bloodshot eyes. A flash of movement in almost superhuman speed of reaction. A big square automatic coming up. Light grey and boxy. One of the new Smith and Wessons. A .44 Magnum, just as Tse Ho had said. It was the speed that caught Huuk by surprise. He had aimed his own gun at the centre of the scene – at the centre of the twisting body. He pulled the trigger at once, jerking the weapon sideways with such force that even the massive grip of the Reeboks gave way. Huuk slipped down on one knee as the gun bellowed. Like the hardened professional he was, Huuk did not blink in spite of all the sound and movement and so he saw the tall, bloodspattered figure flip backwards as the bullet took him not in the chest but on the temple. The wild figure spun away as the brutal impact added to his own twisting movement and as Huuk rolled clumsily down the half-flight of steps to land jarringly beside his precious boxes, the last living crewman of the *Sulu Queen* flew backwards down the next companionway, crashing away into the engineering sections.

Huuk was at the fallen man's side in seconds, thrusting his fingers under the angle of his jaw, feeling for a pulse. As he did so, he silently cursed his luck. The anti-personnel round should have hit the man in the chest, dropping him instantly but relatively safely. Instead the squat rubber bullet had hit him in the head doing heaven alone knew what damage. And this fall down two flights of stairs could all too easily have broken his neck or his back. After a frenzied search, however, Huuk found enough to satisfy him that the unconscious man was alive and so he called his men back and went on to the next stage of the carefully-prepared operation.

He pulled the Motorola from the shoulder of his flak jacket and thumbed the open channel. 'This is Captain Huuk here,' he said. 'I am on board the motor vessel *Sulu Queen*, currently adrift and without power in Hong Kong territorial waters.'

He paused, but there was no reply. 'I have one man down and thirty people dead,' he continued, for he knew there were people monitoring his call. People in Prince of Wales building, in HMS Tamer on Stonecutter's Island and in RAF Sek Kong at the very least. He gave the ship's precise co-ordinates, and ordered, 'Send in the choppers at once.'

Chapter Two

The lone survivor from the *Sulu Queen* opened his eyes. He was lying on his back and he looked straight up at a featureless white ceiling. The fact that it was a ceiling seemed important, somehow. Now, why was that?

His head hurt.

He lay for a little while before allowing his gaze to wander further. He was thinking about dreams. He decided he had not had any before he woke up and he wondered about that. And he wondered, in a vague way, about the pain in the side of his head.

After a few moments, he moved his gaze a little down and left. A long fluorescent light fitting came into view. It was switched on and the ceiling was very bright. It was a brightness intensified by the fact that everything was painted white. This in turn gave the room an atmosphere which was pleasantly cool against the sensitive flesh of his cheeks and forearms. Cool enough to make him grateful for the slight weight of the blanket covering him from his chest to his toes.

Idly, he rolled his aching head to one side, allowing his gaze to follow the light across the ceiling to a Venetian blind whose edges were etched with an absolute darkness which spoke of a window open to black night. The fact that it was a window seemed important too.

But the movement made the pain in his head intensify until the room swam as though it had suddenly been plunged underwater. He blinked his eyes for the first time and felt hot tears trickle down his cool temples towards his ears. Before they moved more than an inch or two, they soaked into the bandage binding his head.

A bandage! It came as a terrible shock to realise that his head was bandaged and yet, somehow, he felt that he had known about it all along. Certainly, the pain in his temple was intense enough to warrant a bandage. Still, the surprise was powerful enough to jerk his right hand up to his forehead and his fingers explored the padded gauze. The movement of one hand seemed to liberate the other one as well. He lifted it and brought it close to his face. At first he simply examined the back of it, noting tanned flesh, skin containing patterns of veins and lightly furred with black hair. The fingers were long and broad-knuckled, beginning to peak here and there with incipient arthritis. The nails were strong and square cut. Round the wrist there was a band of paler flesh where a watch had protected the skin from the sun but there was no watch to be seen. He turned the hand and continued to examine what he saw like a trainee palm-reader. The palm was paler than the back but still pink-hued. There were yellowish callouses at the bases of fingers and thumb. The lines were manifold and meandering but they defined strong, muscular areas. He tensed the muscles, turning his fingers into fiercely hooked claws, watching the way the skin behaved and the play of muscles beneath. Then he let the hand fall back listlessly onto the counterpane at his side as his eyes explored the rest of the room.

Individual impressions fell into patterns now as though the shock he had given himself about the bandage had kicked his brain into gear. He was lying on a white-painted, iron-framed bed. There were big, soft, crisp-starched pillows under his head and shoulders. Beyond the foot of the bed there was a plain white wall with a picture on it and a door in it. The picture showed three tigers romping in snow. The door was made of wood. It looked solid and it was shut.

At the other end of the wall was a chair of moulded grey plastic, which occupied a corner. The second wall which made the corner behind the plastic chair was the wall which had the window in it. The Venetian blind covering the window been adjusted to exclude whatever view there might have been. On the wall opposite the window there was a second picture, this time of a fearsome dragon. The reflection of the Venetian blind in the picture glass made it seem that the dragon had been put in a cage with thick white lateral bars.

The man in the bed wondered whether the strong teak door was locked. Slowly, thoughtfully, he lowered his hand from the bandage to the crisp, starched linen sheet on his chest and lay for a moment more, deep in thought.

Of course this was a hospital room. He had known that right from the start. He didn't need to examine the standard hospital equipment all around the bed-head behind and beside him to realise that. The whole room could only be a hospital room. Everything about it spoke of hospitals. There was even, on the still, silent air, that smell of disinfectant which you find in hospitals anywhere in the world.

Anywhere in the world, he thought. *Where* in the world? He found he had no idea at all. He frowned.

He glanced across at the bedside cupboard on his left side, looking for clues. There was water, there were plastic bowls, jugs and beakers. Nothing else. He moved his left hand, twisting his arm and shoulder almost painfully until he could pull open the cupboard itself. It was empty apart from a book. He picked the book up and examined it, opening it. It was a Bible, in English. It seemed new, unused.

'And the sea gave up the dead which were in it,' he read idly, 'and death and hell gave up the dead which were in them; and they were judged every man according to their works.'

He closed it and put it back. On a panel behind his bed was a pair of earphones. On the table by his right side was some kind of remote control. He held the earphones to his ear and fiddled with the control but no sound came out. No national radio; no hospital channel.

Well, he decided, he wasn't going to find out very much just lying here and wondering.

When he moved, it was with an explosion of energy, instantly controlled, as though he were a robot. He moved in slightly jerky movements, each one complete before the next was begun, as though he was incapable of doing more than one thing at a time. He sat up straight. He closed his right fist on the tangle of sheet and blanket at his waist and pulled it back. He paused, looking down. The pain in his head made his vision swim again but that was not the reason for his hesitation. It was the sight of his white hospital gown. If he was wearing a hospital gown, he reasoned, then his own clothes should be close by. Suddenly he very much wanted his own clothes.

He swung his legs out of bed and slowly, stiffly bent his knees until his feet were firmly on the thick carpet. In the wall between his bedhead and the window there was a light door made of overlapping strips of wood. It looked like a cupboard door and this was where his clothes seemed most likely to be. He stood, again stiffly. Once up, he paused again, waiting for a nauseating giddiness to pass. Then he moved. Three firm, purposeful strides took him to the wardrobe door. He hesitated for an instant with his right hand on the handle, then pulled it wide with unnecessary force. The wardrobe thus revealed was utterly empty except for half a dozen wire coathangers. He could hardly believe his eyes. He stepped in and confirmed what he could see by touching the vacant shelf, sliding numbed fingers along the empty horizontal column of the clothes rail until the coathangers chimed like distant bells.

'What is this?' he asked himself, aloud in English.

As though the sound of his own voice had liberated him from some magic spell, he swung round, pushing the wardrobe door closed behind him as he did so, and strode across to the big teak door. He closed his hand round the big brass handle, twisted and pulled. Nothing happened. He twisted again and pushed with all his might. The door remained absolutely firm.

'It's locked,' he told himself bitterly, and slapped the wood as though it had insulted him.

Full of decision and energy now, he strode across to the window and pulled up the blind. He saw a massive darkness etched against distant constellations. The stars in the lower galaxies were white and red and yellow and green. Some of them moved in a multitude of ways and some did not move at all. He stood there, blinking owlishly until his vision cleared.

His first impression was one of height. He was in a room on an upper floor of a tall building. The feeling of height was emphasised because there was some distance between this building and the next. He was overlooking a black-shadowed area of grass and trees but around the edge of this panorama was a jagged light-specked wall of tall buildings which glimmered and wavered in the night heat. Beyond the buildings he could see the sea, a sparkling surface over a black heart through to nothingness in the far distance. He knew this scene. He recognised it – not exactly, for he had never been in this room before. But he knew this place. He knew where he was.

A jumbo jet laboured by slightly below his line of sight and he felt, disturbingly, that the passengers whose pale faces he could make out all too clearly would be able to see into the room. Then the massive plane settled down behind the nearest of the buildings and he thought it must have crashed into the city or the sea until he realised that there was a runway stretching out across the bay; there was an airport down there.

But, almost inevitably it seemed to him, his eyes were dragged away from the airport and out over the anchorage again, straining to see past those maddeningly familiar buildings down to the familiar sea. There would be something down there in that jewel-bright sparkle or that utter velvet blackness which he knew, which would make it all click back into place.

Such was the survivor's concentration on the scene below him that he did not hear the quiet grating of the key in the lock, but the swish of the door opening made him swing round at once. There were three men hesitating in the doorway, apparently surprised to see the bed empty. When their eyes fell on him, they seemed taken aback, almost nervous.

One of them, a bird-like figure in a loose white coat, bustled forward. 'You should be in bed!' he chided with a surprisingly light tenor voice. He was familiar. The straight black hair; the ivory coloured, angular face, the burningly intense, almost-black slanting eyes, the quiet, compelling Oxbridge English tones. The survivor remembered having talked with this man at some length. That was perhaps the most important of all of his disturbingly imprecise memories.

The survivor stood where he was, looking past the doctor to the two men who had accompanied him. Both wore uniform. Both, like the doctor, were disorientatingly Oriental. One was a wiry young man with an open, almost boyish face. He wore a uniform which was familiar, Naval. The other was a taller, older, fatter man. His uniform was also easy to recognise. He carried a briefcase and wore the unmistakable uniform of a police officer. The policeman, like the doctor, was familiar.

Even when the doctor took him by the arm, the survivor refused to move. Something about their demeanour told him that the doctor was almost redundant here, in spite of the fact that this was a hospital. It was the policeman and his youthful associate who were important.

The fat policeman crossed to the bed and placed his briefcase on it. He moved with stiff precision, as though on parade. Leaning forward, with his back ramrod-straight, he snapped the locks up and lifted the top open. He pulled out a buff folder and crossed towards the window, opening it as he did so. The survivor watched the man's face and eyes, not his hands. The eyes were rounder than the doctor's, but not much. The skin quality was different – less refined. There was perspiration in the folds which ran from behind the policeman's neat ears down to his collar and the bulge of his double chin. He looked like a Buddah and barked like a boatswain. 'Any of this material familiar?' he snapped, stumbling over ls and rs as he offered the folder to the survivor.

The survivor took the folder and looked down as it fell open before him. He found himself looking at a glossy ten- by twelve-inch photograph of a blonde woman with bright eyes and an engaging smile. He turned the photograph over. There was nothing written on the back, no clue to the identity of the subject. Thoughtfully, he placed it face up on the windowsill and turned his attention to the next. It showed two children, a boy and a girl, seemingly about the same age, perhaps twins. They bore more than a passing resemblance to the woman so he put their picture on top of hers. Then there was a ship. That was more familiar, but he still couldn't put his finger on why it seemed so important. He squinted at the forecastle, but the name had been blanked out in the photograph. He put it beside the pictures of the woman and the children, shaking his head in mild perplexity.

For some reason he hesitated before looking down at the last picture. It showed a head and shoulders portrait of a man. The colours were a little too garish, perhaps, and made the face seem larger than life. The eyes in particular gleamed with an unsettling blue intensity. The black hair seemed unnaturally glossy, seeming to contain also a glint of blue. The long nose, broken slightly out of line, was etched against the long, lined cheek. The mouth was straight but full and with the slightest hint of an upward curl at its corners emphasised by the crows' feet stretching back from eye corners to grey-flecked temples. The chin below the mouth was square and strong. The survivor's eyes were drawn back almost against their will to the blue dazzle of the photograph's hypnotic gaze. For the first time, the survivor seemed to flounder uncertainly as the suspicion came over him that there was something deeply, unsettlingly wrong here. He put the whole manila folder down with a decided slap. 'Who are these people?' he rasped. 'What is going on here?'

The boyish Oriental in the Naval uniform reached into the policeman's case and crossed the room decisively. He handed the survivor something and the man took it before he realised what it was. It was a mirror; a long oval mirror set in wood with a wooden handle. Holding it, the survivor looked around the room again, shocked that he had missed such an obvious fact. Two pictures; no mirror. It had been important and he hadn't even noticed. The survivor raised the little mirror and looked into it. Looked at the man in the fourth photograph. The hair in front of the ears was greyer and what little could be seen of it beyond that was dishevelled. The chin was grey with stubble and the mouth had no upward curl to it. But there was no mistaking the patrician line of that nose, broken slightly awry. Nor was there any escape from the hypnotic glimmer of those burning blue eyes.

'It was me,' said the survivor, stunned. The last picture was a photograph of me!'

'You are certain?' asked the young Oriental officer. 'You are *sure*?'

'Of course. But I—'

'And me?' the Oriental man interrupted gently. 'I am Captain Daniel Huuk of the Royal Hong Kong Naval Contingent. Do you not remember me?'

'Not your name . . . Your face . . .'

The police officer stepped forward and interrupted as though his Oriental colleague and the survivor had not been speaking at all. 'In that case, sir,' he began, then paused to clear his throat with a mixture of formality, pomposity and nervousness. 'In that case, I have to inform you that you are Captain Richard Mariner of the Heritage Mariner shipping company of London, England. Your registered domicile is Ashenden, South Dean, East Sussex, England.' He stopped. Drew breath.

'I have further to inform you that I am Commander Victor Lee of the Royal Hong Kong Police Force. I formally arrested you earlier this morning, at five past midnight when you where last conscious. At that time you signed the form waiving your right to legal representation. I now charge you with the wilful murder of Charles Macallan, chief engineer of the motor vessel *Sulu Queen* and of Brian Jordan the first officer. And, Captain Mariner, you should be aware that further charges concerning the murders of thirty-seven other crew members aboard the *Sulu Queen* will be laid against you in due course.

'You were formally cautioned and told your rights earlier this evening. I must formally re-caution you now but presume you do not wish to say anything in the circumstances.'

Chapter Three

Robin Mariner had no sense of foreboding at all as she wrestled the big Monterey round the last turn of the drive and up to the front door of Ashenden, her home. She was too tired and far too angry to have any chance of entering the psychic plane. She was tired because it had taken her nine solid hours to get down here from Cold Fell, her father's house outside Carlisle, a journey usually accomplished in six hours at the most. She was angry because the twins, William and Mary, six and a half years old, had taken leaving their beloved grandfather and ending their short holiday very badly indeed and had been murder for every blessed inch of the M6, M5, M40, M25 and A22 on the way down here. And not one service station, not one bloody toilet, between the back end of Manchester and Stratford-upon-Avon and *then* not another one until Sevenoaks! And all those accursed roadworks: mile after mile of three-lane traffic jams. It was enough to make a saint enraged.

But most of all she was angry with her errant husband Richard.

They had arranged this holiday – a fortnight away over the May Bank holiday – so that they could all be together for a change. They had planned it so carefully and booked it so hopefully and it should have been perfect, their little family and Nurse Janet in a perfect little holiday home just outside Portree on the Isle of Skye. She had arranged to take the Monterey all the way up and back, using the Cal-Mac ferry from Mallaig and breaking the journey each way at Cold Fell where Richard was due to catch up with them on the outward journey, but had she imagined in her wildest dreams that Richard would have been called away to Singapore on the very day of their departure, she would have refused point-blank to go.

It had been a disappointing holiday without him. She was as good a sailor, as intrepid a fell-walker and as knowledgeable a bird-spotter as he; she read – and told – as mean a story and played an equally cutthroat game of Monopoly, but she lacked something of his boundless zest for life. She had missed him bitterly and so had the twins. 'It isn't as much fun without Daddy,' had been their endless, irritating cry. And, secretly, she had agreed with them.

The weather had been stunning, the sea surprisingly warm and perfectly set for sailing and bathing. The fish had been plentiful and easy to catch – except for the trout – and delicious. The wildlife had been spectacular and endlessly fascinating. The local people had been warm, welcoming and cheerfully courteous. There had been beaches, cliffs, caves and wild places aplenty. They were returning, tanned and wind-blown, from what should have been a perfect family holiday and yet here they were, tired, dissatisfied and at each other's throats. And all because Richard hadn't been there!

And the rotten so-and-so hadn't even bothered to write, though he should have been able to get a letter or two from Singapore to Skye. There had better be some good ones on the mat inside the door – and some long messages on the tape of the answerphone.

Still, they were home now, safe and sound, she thought as they came round on the pebbled forecourt outside Ashenden's big black oak front door. She braked too hard even for the four-wheel drive, skidded a little and stopped with a lurch which threw them all against their seatbelts and started the twins whining again.

'Here we are!' she announced, with fierce brightness. 'Let's get you two into a nice warm bath while Janet and I rustle up some supper. Then it's bedtime for all of us, I think.'

As soon as I've unloaded the Monterey, she thought to herself, tempted beyond bearing just to drive it into the garage as it was and deal with it in the morning.

But as soon as she opened Ashenden's front door she knew things were moving rapidly from bad to bloody worse. She had to push the heavy door because of the great pile of letters, papers and junk mail packed behind it in the hall. How could such a massive pile of rubbish arrive in only a fortnight? she wondered. The twins danced and whined that she was taking too long because they were bursting to go to the toilet and she ended up shoving the black wood so hard that she tore much of the paper piled behind it – including, she noticed grimly as she stooped to pick it all up, at least one airmail letter postmarked Singapore. She looked at the screwed-up mess of flimsy blue paper, hoping fervently it contained no important news: it would be impossible to read it now.

The twins thundered past her, racing each other ill-naturedly for the same toilet, a fight obviously brewing between them. Janet came past her more slowly, lips thin, ready to wade in beside Robin when the fur began to fly, pausing to hand over the keys to the Monterey. 'I've locked it up for the time being,' she said, and Robin nodded; good idea. The Scottish nurse had enjoyed the holiday with the depleted family very much and her presence had gone a long way to making up for Richard's absence. The two women were more like old friends, or even sisters, than employer and employee; certainly they were of an age and were not dissimilar in appearance. More than one hopeful islander had tried flirting with the pair of them during the last two weeks. To no avail whatever.

'It's gey cold in here though,' distantly observed Janet whose language had become markedly Scottish up in Skye.

Robin followed her down the passage, still clutching the pile of bright, torn and crumpled paper. Janet was right. Hell's teeth! she thought. Now what? But she knew well enough. Mr Patterson, the retired chief petty officer handyman from Friston, the nearest village, had promised to pop in and get the heating on, both the immersion heater and the oil-fired Raeburn. And to pick up the pile of mail from behind the door before it grew too large! But it was all too obvious that the usually reliable CPO Patterson had let them down. If she had been thinking clearly, the pile of mail behind the door would have told her that before the cold air of the hall confirmed it. A wave of bitterness washed over her. At least one letter from Richard gone beyond recall. No hot water. No central heating. No oven or hob. 'We'd better get the kettle on and look for something to microwave,' said Robin as the pair of them came into the cavernous, chilly kitchen. She put the bundle of papers onto the kitchen table and crossed to the inner door, thinking to go up to the landing and get the immersion heater on at once. The Raeburn, like the unpacking, would wait until the morning.

At the moment she opened the door through into the main house, the fight began in earnest and the immersion was forgotten as she tore up to the bathroom to find her children, each with their jeans and pants round their ankles, locked in mortal combat under the porcelain overhang of the toilet bowl. She stooped to grab the pair of them by the scruffs of their necks and dragged their squirming bodies up by main force. *'Will you two stop this NOW!'* she bellowed in her terrifying captain's quarterdeck voice, shaking them like rats.

They both burst into tears at once and she let them go, feeling unforgivably brutal. Janet appeared by the door. 'I'll look after Mary,' she said soothingly.

'I'll take William downstairs,' said Robin and led the sobbing child off. He went down the stairs on his bottom, refusing to pull his jeans up past his knees, and Robin let him, still feeling guilty over her outburst. She paused on the landing and switched on the immersion heater while he waddled away from the foot of the stairs below like a grumpy little penguin.

Robin returned to the kitchen and filled the electric kettle. Sod the children, she thought; this was for a cup of tea. Janet and she had more than earned it. Automatically as she did so, she glanced across at the kitchen clock. Nearly nine. The twins should have been in bed hours ago: no wonder they were so fractious. As she glanced down from the clock, her eyes fell on the crumpled remains of the blue airmail letter and she thought of Richard again. Her thoughts of him became a little more forgiving as she waited for the kettle to warm up. She pulled out the teapot and the tea. By the time the tea was brewing fragrantly under its cosy, she was almost in charity with her errant husband again.

She ran out of charity with her son, however, two minutes later. She came out of the kitchen in search of him as soon as the cosy was on the pot. 'It's brewing, Janet,' she called up the stairs as she crossed to the downstairs cloakroom. No sign of William there. She crossed the hall and popped her head into Richard's study where William often liked to play. No sign. Nor in the dining room. Where had the little monster got to? she wondered indulgently, opening the door into the great, broad sitting room whose wide windows gave a panoramic view of the Channel. A secretive flurry of motion told her she had found him – and that he was up to no good. 'William!' she snapped. 'What are you up to?'

She reached over and switched the light on, revealing her son and heir crouching, with his jeans inexpertly adjusted, over the answerphone.

'William! What are you doing? That is not a toy! You know very well—'

'I wanted to talk to Daddy!' he wailed. 'There was a message from my daddy for me . . .'

'Oh, William!' She crossed the room and hugged him to her. He had always been Daddy's boy and that was all there was to it. Whenever the twins had a fight or whenever Mummy or Janet told them off, William always ran to his daddy while Mary sulked and plotted dark revenge. She should have known that the exhausted boy would come in here after the fight and the telling-off. She led him back into the hall and across to the kitchen, too preoccupied to register the whirring and clicking sounds which came from the machine by the phone.

Robin and Janet had a nice cup of tea. Mary and William had beans on toast which they loved. Then the twins went to bed. Janet and Robin tucked them down and their mother switched on the tape recorder with their Beatrix Potter tapes. They were too exhausted even to squabble over whether it should be *The Tale of Jeremy Fisher* or *The Tale of Peter Rabbit*. Robin herself thought that *The Two Bad Mice* would have been the most appropriate, but she said nothing and kissed them goodnight and turned down the light.

As soon as there was quiet, the women went back downstairs and had a stiff whisky each. After the first sip of hers, Robin remembered about the Monterey and popped out to slip it into the garage. She would unpack it in the morning after all. There was no reason to worry about it, the garage was built like Fort Knox in case anyone got any idea about stealing Richard's E-type Jaguar.

Robin and Janet had another whisky and then they also had beans on toast which they loved. Janet went off to bed at ten and Robin at last got the chance to look through the rest of the mail and give her father a ring.

Idly, leafing through the crumpled pile, she walked through to the sitting room. The light was still on and she collapsed on the big overstuffed sofa beside the phone table. As soon as she was seated, she thought of Richard. This was the time of night he always phoned, wherever in the world he was, whatever time zone he was passing through. And she would always be sitting curled on the overstuffed sofa looking out through the French windows across the garden and away across the Channel beyond, waiting for his call.

But it never came. As she waited, she checked through the letters in more detail, separating the junk from the rest, the business from the social. She read his hurried, apologetic missives – two postcards, one posted from Heathrow on his way out, the next from Singapore on his arrival. The promise of a letter soon. The destroyed airmail letter. Nothing more from him. Perhaps if she put the flimsy pieces back together in the morning she would be able to decipher the tiny, impenetrable scrawl he reserved for one-sheet airmail letters such as this. She flicked through the rest. Even the letter from Phylidda Gough with its familiar Budleigh Salterton postmark was put on one side. She would catch up on the adventures of the Wallys, father and son, and of her old friend, their wife and mother, in due course. She was too exhausted even to think straight now.

By ten thirty she knew he was not going to call tonight. But she knew what to do about that, too. She would do what William had done and let the tape do the talking. But when she switched the machine onto Playback it only hissed at her. Hissed and whispered wordlessly. She got up and looked closely at it. The message counter read zero. Any messages which had been there were gone now. It made no difference what knobs she pressed or what dials she twisted, there was nothing on the message tape but a quiet, static whisper.

She returned to his letter from Singapore. She spread it out. With considerable effort she just managed to make out one side, only to find it was just their address. Turned it over. Pored over the other side thinking that if she could make out the outside, she might risk cutting it open and try for the inside – if she could work out which bits had been the edges and where they needed to be cut. The back gave the name of the hotel he was booked into, the Raffles, where he always stayed. But it took her so long to work it out she decided that, like everything else, the next step had better wait until morning.

In the meantime, there was still some action she could take. She knew where he was: she could give him a call. She walked through into his study and looked the number up on the big Rollerdex he kept on his desk. Singapore 337 8041. She dialled.

But the man on the reception desk of the Raffles Hotel, Beach Road, Singapore, informed her that Captain Mariner had vacated his executive suite nearly a week earlier. And no, he had no idea where the captain had gone after that. And no, there were no messages. And no, he could help no further at all; he was sorry. Would the caller like him to refer her to the night manager?

She phoned her father, but Sir William had received no recent news of Richard either.

She phoned Heritage House, but no one at Heritage Mariner's headquarters had any news either. It was as though her husband had vanished off the face of the earth. Even the twenty-four-hour secretariat at Crewfinders were surprised to learn that Richard was not at the Raffles. He was out of touch with them for the first time in twenty years.

In the end she gave up and went to bed on the verge of tears. Now, in the quiet dark with the faintest whisper of the sea climbing the cliffs in the night wind, Robin did begin to feel a sense of foreboding. It grew to nightmare proportions as she fell into a restless sleep.

But not even the worst nightmare imaginable could have prepared her for the phone call which came through direct to her bedside from the Heritage Mariner office on the fourth floor of Jardine House, Connaught Road, Central District, Hong Kong, at half past midnight BST next morning.

Chapter Four

The ringing of the telephone insinuated itself into Robin's nightmare and in her dream she answered it only to find that it had become a snake which was trying to choke the life out of her. As well as hissing, the suffocating serpent continued to ring insistently. When she could breathe no more, she tore herself awake and echoed in real life the action of her dream, reaching for the shrilling handset.

The earpiece was icy against her ear.

'Hello?' she said, her voice still rusty from the effect of the choking snake.

The line hissed and her hair stirred. This was the noise the creature in her nightmare had made. Adrenaline began to pump through her exhausted frame. Her mind tried to batter its way through the suffocating residue of her disturbed slumber.

'Who is this?'

Deafening crackle. Distant connection, bringing a voice rushing through a one-sided conversation which seemed already to have begun. 'You do not know me. I am John Shaw, office junior at the Heritage Mariner office here in Jardine House, Hong Kong. Please excuse someone so junior for disturbing you like this but I thought it best under the circumstances. It is early morning here and I have arrived first at the office to complete an assignment for my manager Mr Feng. But instead I have read of this occurrence in the *South China Morning Post*. We have had no warning. There has been no announcement. *Sulu Queen* has not even been registered as missing. I do not understand how this could have occurred.'

'Who is this? What are you talking about?'

Silence. Then 'Excuse, please. This is Heritage Mariner office, London?'

'This is Captain Robin Mariner, of Heritage Mariner, London. Who is this?' Already her blood was running cold. Her respiration was speeding up. In a moment she would find it hard to breathe.

'This is John Shaw, Heritage Mariner office Hong Kong. I have urgent report concerning motor vessel *Sulu Queen* and Captain Richard Mariner. This has not been verified, you understand. It is a report from the *Morning Post*. We have not been notified here.'

She breathed in. How thick the air seemed. How cold! What time was it? 'What report, Mr Shaw?'

'The Hong Kong authorities are towing *Sulu Queen* into port. She was discovered drifting without power out in the South China Sea at dawn yesterday and Hong Kong Naval officers went aboard. All her crew are dead. Murdered.'

The darkness seemed to be smothering her. She reached across clumsily with her left hand and turned on the bedside light. She knew the name of the ship well enough. Some of the new cash which had come into Heritage Mariner from the affair of the iceberg codenamed Manhattan by the United Nations had been invested in a small shipping line with two freighters working between the Philippines, Malaysia, Hong Kong and Japan. It was called the China Queens Line and she had reason to remember its existence clearly – it had been on China Queens business that Richard had gone to Singapore ten days ago. The captain of the *Sulu Queen* was Wally Gough the elder, husband to the Pyllidda whose letter lay unopened beside the dead answerphone downstairs.

The shock of that realisation jerked her awake like a douche of cold water.

The Chinese-accented voice from the Hong Kong office was still relaying to her the contents of the newspaper report: '. . . a terrible scene. Wholesale slaughter with guns and knives. This is according to what the reporter has learned from the officers who boarded her, you understand. No one else has been aboard. It is understood that the ship will be impounded in a secure dock, searched in every detail and then held until the trial.'

'The trial?'

Her question brought the flow of words to a stop, but only for a moment. 'That is why I phoned through at once. I waited only for the international operator to get me through. I do not have the direct dialling numbers here, you understand. These are in the manager's office and Mr Feng will not be here until after eight o'clock on normal work day but today it is Saturday and I do not think he will be in at all so I thought . . . Under the circumstance . . .'

'What? What are you trying to say? What trial? What is going on, for heaven's sake?'

'It is the captain, Captain Mariner. He was the only man left alive on board the *Sulu Queen*. It reports in the paper that he has been charged already. He will be put on trial as soon as possible, they say, accused of the murder of the whole ship's crew.'

She sat curled in her bed waiting for her breathing to steady, her heart to slow and her mind to clear. It was one o'clock in the morning and she couldn't work out who to call first. Obviously John Shaw, the clerk in the Hong Kong office, had come through directly to Ashenden because of a mistake made by the international operator but that made no real difference. If he had got straight through to Heritage House, someone would have phoned her anyway. Her father was retired now and increasingly out of touch with the business he had set up. Heritage Mariner's chief executive Charles Lee, himself from Hong Kong, was in Beijing at the moment, negotiating contracts for the company in the days, so close at hand now, after Hong Kong was returned to Chinese control.

Helen DuFour, the other senior executive, was in Moscow, still negotiating with the Russians and the independent republics of the old Soviet Union for the official, controlled shipping and the proper, safe disposal of the weapons grade plutonium, lithium and tritium resultant from the decommissioning of their nuclear arsenal. These were negotiations which she had been holding for some years now, ever since the SALT agreements; but the fissionable material, together with the triggers and mechanisms used in weapons preparation, seemed to be haemorrhaging away into the Mafia-controlled black market. Almost none of it was being disposed of properly. For Heritage Mariner this meant a dangerous loss of potential revenue; what it meant for international security was much more difficult to calculate.

No. As things stood, John Shaw's terrible news would have come through to her in the end. But what should she do about it first?

Check it out, of course.

She pulled her stiff limbs into the baggy old track suit which often served as a dressing gown and pattered downstairs barefoot into Richard's study. All the contact numbers he possessed were on a disk for his neat PC and Robin was as computer literate as anyone, but for some reason she chose to turn to the Rollerdex tonight. Perhaps it gave her some kind of security.

The first number under 'Hong Kong' was the Tourist Board at 125 Pall Mall. She dialled without further thought but there was no reply. Not at this time of night! Stupid. She wasn't thinking clearly at all.

She sat back and took a deep breath. The Hong Kong numbers were the usual hotchpotch of personal contacts (but not too personal or they would be filed under names), hotel reception numbers, offices. She looked at her watch: 01.10. Hong Kong was eight hours ahead of GMT, seven ahead of BST. It was coming up for 08.15 out there. Eight fifteen a Saturday morning. Even Government House would still be closed.

Who was it that she really wanted to talk to? Newspapers for further information, someone in authority for confirmation, lawyers for advice and action. But if she could get through to the right lawyer, he could do the checking on the scene while she got into action...

She hunched forward and punched in the familiar number of the twenty-four-hour line at Heritage House.

Musical tones of almost instantaneous connection.
One ring.
'Good morning. Heritage Mariner. Claire speaking. How may I help you?'
'Claire, this is Robin Mariner. I need some information urgently. Can you access the memory banks for me?'
'I would need a current company codeword for anything confidential, Captain Mariner.'
'This won't be confidential. I need the home telephone number of the Heritage Mariner legal contact in Hong Kong.'
'Let me see ... Hong Kong ... That would be the firm of ... Balfour Stephenson, 116 Johnston Road ... Yes. Here it is. Contact Andrew Atherton Balfour. He lives in Repulse Bay. His number is ... Have you got a pencil, Captain Mariner?'

The phone rang three times and there was a click. Robin's heart sank. A stilted mechanical voice like that of a Scottish robot said, 'Hello, this is Andrew Atherton Balfour. I cannot answer the phone at the moment. If you need my professional advice you may contact my office on 8246444. Otherwise, please leave a message after the tone.'
'Mr Balfour. My name is Robin Mariner. I am very much afraid that my husband Captain Richard Mariner of Heritage Mariner may have been arrested in Hong Kong. I have information that he may be involved in an incident to do with the motor vessel *Sulu Queen*—'
'Hello? Hello, Mrs Mariner?'
'Mr Balfour?'
'Aye, I'm sorry, yes ... You caught me still in bed, I'm afraid. There was a bit of a party at Government House last night.'
'Have you heard anything about the *Sulu Queen*?'
'Nothing at all ... Look, it's still early here, but I can start checking—'
'Do you have a newspaper delivered?'
'I do indeed. Well, the maid brings it in. The *South China Morning Post*.'
'Could you look at the front page for me, please?'
'Well ... Yes, of course. Just a moment, please; I'll just slip into a dressing gown and grab the walkabout ...'
The line went dead. Robin waited, her eyes unfocused. She didn't know it, but she was chewing her fingernails, a habit she thought she had broken more than twenty-five years ago.
'*Wai!*' The unexpected Cantonese greeting made her jump. 'Still there?' Balfour's gentle Scottish tones flowed smoothly on.
'Still here.'
'Right ... Just bear with me for a second ... *Jou shan*, Su Lin, *mgoi*.'

There was the chink of a teacup and Robin remembered that *mgoi* meant 'thank you'. 'Right . . .' A rustle of paper.

Inconsequentially, Robin wondered just how much British Telecom would be charging her for the privilege of listening to a Hong Kong solicitor the better part of ten thousand miles distant say 'good morning' to his housemaid Su Lin, accept a cup of tea and unfold his morning paper.

Then idle speculation was shattered. 'My God!' said Andrew Atherton Balfour, his voice horrified. 'Sweet Christ!' And Robin had formed the firm opinion that this was not a man who approved of blasphemy under normal circumstances at all. 'I'll get onto this,' he said, as though she could see the paper as clearly as he. 'I know just the man to ask about this. Jesus. Captain Mariner himself. It's incredible.'

'I'm on my way,' she said.

'What?'

'I'm coming out myself. At once. Book me a suite for tonight. From tonight, open-ended. No. Look for a leave flat, just in case.'

'Mrs Mariner—'

'Get the suite at the Mandarin if you can. I haven't been out for some time but it used to be my favourite. Or the Peninsula if Kowloon side is better. Someone will be in contact later with my arrival details. And don't forget the leave flat if it looks as though it'll be a long-term thing. Would you mind?'

'Well, no, of course. Only too happy, but—'

'I have to be with him. Can you see that?' The intensity of the words shocked even Robin and the massiveness of the truth almost overwhelmed her.

Richard was in trouble. Bad trouble, by the sound of it. She had to be there at his side, no matter what. Nothing else mattered at all.

'Look,' she drew out the vowel sound making the word lengthen as she fought to control her voice. 'I'll start to move at once but I'll check with you later myself. If push comes to shove I'll call through from the departure lounge at Heathrow or Gatwick. You can advise me then.'

'And if my advice is to stay at home?'

'Then I'll take it under consideration, Mr Balfour.'

A very slight hesitation. A very slight change of tone. 'Please call me Andrew, Mrs Mariner.'

I'll take that under consideration too, Mr Balfour, she thought, and hung up.

She was back on to Heritage Mariner in a matter of moments, her mind racing in the grip of a whole sequence of shocks, not the least of which was the realisation that she was actually, really, on her way to Hong Kong. 'The current company codeword is *Conrad*,' she rasped. 'When I get to Heritage House I want a complete print-out on everything to do with the China Queens Company, and everything to do with Heritage Mariner's involvements in Hong Kong, China, Singapore and, let's see . . . Russia.

'Then I want to be on the first flight out to Hong Kong. I have to be there later today, if not sooner. And I'll be at Heritage House before dawn.'

'Certainly, Captain Mariner,' said the friendly, calming voice of the massively competent Audrey on the far end of the connection. Then the family atmosphere upon which Heritage Mariner prided itself took over. 'And what are you going to do with the twins?' Audrey asked.

It was Batty Fothergill who proved the life-saver.

Since they had bought Ashenden when the twins were still a large lump inside her, before Richard got caught up in the Gulf War, Robin had been a mother more than a master mariner, and although she was forever rushing up to Heritage House, she was nevertheless also an active member of the local scene down here in Sussex. Inevitably, she had made a wide circle of friends and acquaintance simply by being what she was and who she was.

Batty was the den mother to all the local girls. She had been an auxiliary nurse and doubled as midwife occasionally still. She and her ex-Army husband had owned their rambling mansion outside Westdean since the war, and lived in it since Charlie had retired nearly fifteen years ago. Batty had been one of Robin's first visitors and soon became one of her fastest friends, in spite of the age difference between them. Perhaps this was because Robin had lost her mother early and Batty had lost her only daughter early too. 'Any panic, any problem, call us any time; the colonel and I don't sleep much these days so that's a day or night offer.'

Robin was chary of taking the offer up in anything other than *extremis* because, quite apart from anything else, a certain measure of spiritous liquors was likely to have been consumed in the Fothergill household by bedtime and she didn't want to risk calling either Batty or Charlie out at night if they were likely to be over the limit. On the other hand Batty was just the girl to help Janet get the twins organised in the morning to oversee the clearing of the Monterey and the laundering of its contents and to help with the transport of the twins back to their doting grandfather for an unexpected extra holiday at Cold Fell; and Charlie was just the man to contact CPO Patterson and close down the house again until this matter was settled one way or the other.

Robin took a deep breath and began to dial.

There was one ring, as there had been at Heritage Mariner. 'Fothergill. Hello?' The voice was clear if husky, and sounded alert even at this hour.

'Hello, Batty, it's Robin . . .'

Janet answered Robin's first quiet knock. She sat up wide-eyed and awake, the instant Robin crept into her room. 'What is it? Is it the children?'

'No. But it is an emergency, I'm afraid. I have to go to Hong Kong later tonight. I've arranged for you and the twins to pop across to the Fothergills for the rest of the night. Mrs Fothergill will help you clear the cases and everything out of the Monterey and then she'll wash it all in the morning. When its all sorted out, she and the colonel will bring all the holiday stuff back here and close Ashenden down. I don't know when I'll be back. I'd like you to take the Monterey, firstly across to Westdean and then, tomorrow, up to London, with the twins. Sir William will come down and collect them. They'll go up to Cold Fell for the time being. You can go with them or you can take yourself off on a holiday somewhere. You've certainly earned a proper break and we'll be happy to foot the bill.'

Janet nodded, but in fact she had been hardly listening to the latter part of what Robin had said. 'Sir William and I will take them to Cold Fell tomorrow.'

'Or the next day. The company flat in Heritage House is empty in the meantime.'

'Fine. Shall we get them dressed now?'

'No. We'll pop them in the Monterey in their pyjamas. The Fothergills will have beds ready and will simply carry them in. With any luck they won't even wake up.'

Janet nodded again, dark blonde curls bobbing over steady eyes. 'Its something urgent, then. Is it Captain Richard?' She had called him Captain Richard ever since she had nursed him back to health after the Gulf War, before she had become another kind of nurse to the twins.

Robin gulped, her eyes suddenly burning. 'I think he's in terrible trouble,' she said. 'I've got to go to him.'

Nurse Janet nodded again.

It was only as she watched the taillights of the Monterey vanish round the first bend in the drive that Robin realised she had sent almost all her summer clothes away with her babies. She turned back and walked blindly in through the great double door of the garage, tears streaming down her face. She was still crying when she reached Richard's study and picked up his phone for the last time. Again, she punched in a number from memory and listened to the sound of the connection clicking through.

'Good morning. This is Crewfinders. Audrey speaking. How may I help you?'

'Audrey, it's Robin Mariner here. I'll be on my way up to Heritage House in a moment. Anything in particular I need to sort out for a visit to Hong Kong?'

This was not an unusual question for the Crewfinders personnel. The agency had built its reputation on being able to transport any ship's officer or crew member from anywhere in the world to anywhere in the world within twenty-four hours, and they were consequently expert in advice about any odd requirements en route. For an old hand like Audrey, Heritage House to Hong Kong should be a breeze, but her good work could all too easily be negated if Robin did not have the correct paperwork – especially after the plague scare in India a couple of years ago, and the Ebola outbreak in Africa.

'I've got my passport. Any jabs?' They had a company doctor on twenty-four-hour call, ready to administer any injections required for immigration.

'I'll check. Anything else?'

'I'll be bringing basic baggage – very basic.'

'We'll see about topping it up. Still size twelve?'

'Yup.' Nobody had any secrets from Audrey.

'And off to HK. Only the *Sulu Queen* due there. Are you going aboard her?'

'Nope.' This was no time for further explanations, even to Audrey. 'I'll be ashore. I just need enough to keep me going until I see about getting kitted out.'

'I see,' said Audrey, though she plainly didn't see at all. 'I think we can help you out, Robin. Everything you need will be waiting here, together with the information you requested under the *Conrad* company codeword – unless you'd like to start from Gatwick?'

'I'll be driving up in Richard's E-type.'

There was a brief silence as this sank in. No one ever drove Richard's E-type except Richard himself.

'You'd better bring it here, then Robin; we'll put it in the high-security section of our underground garage, beside Sir William's Mulsane Turbo, just to be on the safe side.'

Chapter Five

Just taking the cover off the thing terrified her: what if she should scratch it? Richard would be livid! A woman who had commanded great ships in the most extreme and dangerous of circumstances quailed before the thought of scratching her husband's beloved toy, just as the gawky sixteen-year-old had been terrified of the dashing young sea captain when she first met him all those years ago. It was ridiculous, she told herself firmly. She had grown out of that tinge of girlish awe the better part of twenty-five years ago, when this exquisite creature had been rolling off the production line at Radford or Brown's Lane. But even so, she checked its gleaming paintwork for the faintest suspicion of a scrape.

Feeling a little like a thief, she slid the key into the silver circle of the lock in the driver's door, hooked her fingers under the cool chrome handle and pulled it open. Surprised alike by the unexpected weight and the elegant balance of the long door, she swung it back and forth twice, feeling it wanting to hesitate halfway as the catch clicked past; then she pushed it wide and stooped to look inside the cockpit. The fragrance of leather washed out, contained – concentrated – by the combination of hard-top and cover. She breathed it in as though it had been created by Chanel, then she straightened. Mentally she berated herself. She was not here to indulge in sensuousness. And yet that was what the exquisite car seemed to offer: sensuousness, almost sybaritic indulgence, quite apart from the heady promise of naked power such as she had never experienced before – at least, not on wheels. Giving herself a mental shake, she put her small kitbag down on the garage floor and swung her long body in. The sill was incredibly wide and she felt herself stepping over and decidedly down into the cockpit. But for all that, when she had settled into the seat she was well up and perfectly positioned to look over the lateral grilles and along the seemingly infinite curves of the bonnet. She was nowhere near the right position, however, and she had to reach down, relishing the sound of the soft leather grumbling against the cotton of her jeans and the silk of her travelling blouse, to slide the seat forward almost to its furthest extent before her feet were comfortable on the pedals.

She sat for a moment, summoning up the willpower for the next action. It suddenly occurred to her that since nine o'clock yesterday morning – a time now seventeen hours distant – she had left Cold Fell, driven for nine hours, had a fight with the kids, a plate of beans, two whiskies, one hour's sleep, and ninety of the worst minutes of her life so far. Exhausted, she reached out across that massive sill and hefted her kitbag over her lap into the passenger's seat. Then she pulled the driver's door shut and slid the key into the ignition.

She took a deep breath, adjusted the rearview and rocked the gear lever to check it was in neutral. She studied the black dashboard and made sure she was clear about where the dials and rocker switches were positioned. The car had been under cover for only a couple of weeks and the weather had been warm: probably no need for any choke, she calculated. I hope she's got a full tank, she thought, rested her hands on the big black leather steering wheel, snuggled back into the bucket seat, rested her head against the headrest, depressed the clutch, prepared to tap the accelerator and reached down to turn the key. The massive V12 engine purred into life and the whole car throbbed. Each vibration of that perfectly controlled power pumped a little energy and excitement back into her. She checked the dials: full tank; battery powered up, water and oil OK. She flipped the switches and brought up the lights. Then she slipped the gearshift into first and eased her foot up off the clutch. The rev counter hardly stirred and the engine engaged. The black car rolled forward, more alert, more utterly at her command than anything she had ever controlled before. It required an effort of will to brake after a couple of yards and jump out to close the garage.

This time when she slid back in behind the wheel she paused for a moment longer while she made closer acquaintance with the accelerator. Thoughtfully, she tapped it hard enough to bring the needle or the rev counter up to 45 a couple of times, listening to the purr change timbre into a roar, aware of the gaze of the cat's face on the steering-wheel boss. She wanted to be confident about that particular pedal and this particular dial because she was acutely aware that the speedometer beside it was calibrated up past 160 miles per hour. As she tested the accelerator and watched the needle on the rev counter, she fastened her seatbelt and automatically eased it to a comfortable position.

This time when the E-type rolled forward it did not stop. It slid like a black shark out into the utter dark of the southern Sussex lanes and roared away along the tunnel of light laid down by the headlight beams as though exhilarated to be out of the confinement of Ashenden's garage.

The first corner caught Robin by surprise and she was lucky to come through it unscathed. She had just slipped the gear lever up into second – second was plenty for this corner in the Monterey which pulled past 20mph in second – when she felt herself skidding and realised she was moving at more than 40 already. She stamped on the brake a little more fiercely than she meant to and discovered the hard way just how efficient the split surface ventilated disc breaking system was. The skid compounded and the car turned round once in the middle of the road, tail-heavy like all of its kind. Then she found that the Adwest power steering system was just what she needed to get herself straightened up again. Thank God the road was empty, she thought. At least she hadn't stalled the thing.

Five minutes later, Robin gingerly came onto the A259 and headed west for Brighton. She soon mastered the first three gears, but she felt she really needed a long, straight dual carriageway, or better, before she put the car into top and let it go. At Newhaven she swung carefully onto the A26. Here for the first time she experimented with top gear but she approached the roundabout south of Lewes very carefully indeed. She was not really happy with things until she swung off the roundabout onto the dual carriageway section of the A27. Even here she did not let the monster under the bonnet loose, but snarled and grumbled along at 70mph, holding the car in check as she got to know it.

She slowed again at the Brighton bypass but prepared to give the car its head as she swung onto the A23 and headed up through the increasingly frequent dual carriageway sections towards the M23. At Bolney her right foot pressed down with more confidence and, in spite of the fact that she was coming up quite a steep hill, She watched the needle on the speedometer leap rapidly past 70mph. She came over the brow of the hill and the road lay bright and straight ahead of her, stretching across the sleeping Sussex Downs towards the gilded gleam of the motorway and the distant amber blaze of Gatwick Airport.

'What the hell, old girl,' she said. 'Let's go!'

She skidded across the roundabout with the B2115, very lucky indeed that there was no traffic about, but even that signal warning that she should be careful how she judged very high speeds did not dampen her elation or slow her down. Quite the reverse, in fact; she went under the bridge at Handscross at 100 and entered the M23 at 120, speeding to the rescue of the man she had loved for more than three-quarters of her life.

She remembered the first time she had ever seen him: at the anchorage in St Tropez the New Year after Mummy died when he had moored his little yacht *Rebecca* beside theirs unaware. How vividly she recalled the opulent after section of her father's ocean-going cruiser, open to the unseasonably clement night. Herself, little mere than a teenager in awe of her fantastically beautiful elder sister Rowena; Daddy, still with the last of his youthful energy clinging about him, beginning to come out of mourning at last.

And Richard, tall, slim, dazzlingly good-looking, totally oblivious of their presence and of her gaze. Lonely and disconsolate, he had opened a bottle of champagne to celebrate the arrival of the seventies and the cork had flown across the tiny gap between the boats to hit Daddy on the head. The accident had led to apologies, mutual recognition, formal introductions and a night of lively conversation which had brightened the moment and changed all their lives. Richard had been a captain for some time by that stage even though he could have been little more than twenty-five years old. He had knocked about a bit and was looking to settle down. And Sir William Heritage had been looking for a senior captain to groom for executive office in Heritage shipping. It had all been perfect, except for the existence of Rowena.

Robin remembered how dashing Richard had looked at his wedding to her elder sister, and how she had walked down the aisle as bridesmaid in floods of silent tears. It had been a miracle that she managed to complete any 'A' level studies, such had been the power of her unhappily thwarted love.

She remembered all too clearly the look of shock and horror on his face when she had cornered him at her twenty-first birthday party three years later to inform him that her big sister, his wife, was using his time away at sea as an unrivalled opportunity to sleep her way through the younger, better-looking sections of Burke's Peerage.

She preferred to forget the conversation she had with her father soon after, and the sight of Rowena going sulkily aboard Richard's new command, her father's new tanker flagship which even bore her name: *Rowena*.

That had been the last time Robin saw her sister alive and the last time she saw Richard for five barren years. *Rowena* had exploded and sunk. Rowena had gone down with her. Richard had been lucky to survive and his service with Heritage had ended.

In the time he was away setting up Crewfinders, Robin completed her studies at the London School of Economics, completed a Masters at Johns Hopkins, and finished her studies for her officer's ticket. Had she been anyone other than her father's daughter she would have stood no chance of achieving the wide range of qualifications she now held, but all her hard work had been more than amply rewarded when she had managed to get the position of third mate on *Prometheus* which Richard had crewed and then commanded after a terrible industrial accident.

Within a year of completing that horrific voyage on the coffin ship *Prometheus*, the pair of them had been married. Heritage Shipping subsumed Crewfinders to become Heritage Mariner and a legend had been born.

During the last fifteen years, in the face of the collapse of the British merchant marine, they had seen tanker traffic boom and dwindle. They had faced terrorism in the Gulf. They had moved into leisure boating with the fabulously successful *Katapult* range of multihulls. They had become involved by accident in the shipping of dangerous waste and had opened the North Atlantic to routes for the specially-designed waste carriers *Atropos* and *Clotho* – though here, too, they had faced a new kind of terrorism: La Guerre Verte.

Richard had faced his own kind of war in the Gulf, while she had been pregnant with the twins. Almost single-handed, he had pulled the great iceberg Manhattan to the war-torn state of Mau in West Africa, and then become involved in another sort of war as he and all the others fought to deliver the water Manhattan represented to the people who needed it the most.

And now he deserved a rest; a holiday. He was over fifty tears old, for crying out loud. He should have been with her and the twins relaxing on Skye, not rushing off to Singapore. He should be safe at home in bed at Ashenden, not sitting accused of murder in Hong Kong. It was too much! It was just too bloody much!

Robin was extremely fortunate that, even at 2.35a.m., the traffic moving north between Gatwick and the M25 was heavy. Rather against her inclination, with half her mind occupied by thoughts of Richard, she slowed the E-type to a much more reasonable pace and consequently sailed across the M5 intersection perfectly safely, managing to bring the long black car almost sedately onto the single carriageway of the A23, though she did not actually come anywhere near the speed limit until she stopped for petrol in Coulsden, wondering vaguely where the tank-full she had started out with had gone to.

After Coulsden came Purley and she speeded up going up the hill towards the old Croydon Airport. It had been there, she thought – as she always did on this route into town – that Monsieur Hercule Poirot had unravelled the mysterious fatality in *Death In the Clouds*. Between Croydon and Streatham there was a large number of roundabouts and so she rarely got up out of third and hardly ever exceeded 60mph. She did not exceed the national speed limit again, in fact, until after she had slipped round the south circular and came hammering down Lordship Lane towards East Dulwich, heading for the Elephant and Castle.

The roundabout at the Elephant is big and complicated. At 2.44a.m. it was empty so Robin's speed and lane-positioning were of only academic importance. She shot through like the Wrath of God swinging a little wildly into Newington Causeway heading for London Bridge – and not even the sight of the law courts slowed her down. She had to slow through Borough, however, for there was a long series of traffic lights now and only true lunacy would have taken her through them on red. She went under the railway viaduct and out onto London Bridge itself at ten minutes to three. She went past the Monument less than a minute later, roared into narrow Gracechurch Street like a thunderstorm, jumped the lights at the Fenchurch Street intersection and swung into Leadenhall at 3.00 on the dot.

It was 3.10 by the time she had the E-type positioned to the mutual satisfaction of herself and the Heritage Mariner's garage night-security man. For one nightmare moment it seemed possible that she would use her husband's Jaguar to scratch her father's Bentley and upset the two most important men in her life at once. But everything was settled satisfactorily before Robin ran out of patience and she was in reception at Heritage House by 3.15.

The security man had warned Audrey the moment the distinctive oval grille thrust itself out of the dark like the snout of a cruising shark and she was waiting with another case for Robin. 'There's all the information you asked for under the company codeword,' Audrey said quietly. 'There's a full itinerary too,' she added as she handed over case and tickets. 'Now, let me see, what else was there? Oh yes, there's the most up-to-date information we can get on the situation in the Crown Colony during the last weeks before it goes back into Chinese control. There are no jabs needed urgently, you'll be pleased to hear, but there are no flights allowed from City Airport at this time of night, I'm afraid, and we can't use the heliport for another couple of hours either, so it's back on the road for you.'

'That's OK. Do I have time to check what's in the slop chest here?' It was an old joke – and one that Robin would have avoided except that she was truly exhausted now that she no longer had the exhilaration of the wild drive to keep her going. Audrey and her staff were meticulous in the selection of clothing to cover emergencies such an this but everyone always made a game of assuming they packed emergency cases with cast-offs and secondhand clothing like the crew's slop chest on a boat.

Audrey smiled. 'Fraid not. But look on the bright side.' She reached into the ticket folder and pulled out a Gold AmEx card. 'You have the power to put things right. Now, how are you with trains and tunnels?'

Chapter Six

She had promised to phone Andrew Atherton Balfour from Heathrow or Gatwick. She called him instead from the new Eurostar rail-link departure area at Waterloo Station. The Paris express would be departing at 3.45 a.m., due at La Gare du Nord at 6.30 a.m. The sleek, still futuristic shape of the Eurostar train stood behind her, all gleaming power, taut with the promise of massive speed. Robin had been welcomed by the train's guard already and her seat was safe. She just had time to check in as promised.

Andrew had had time to do some checking too. 'It looks bad, Captain Mariner. There's no mistake and the HK police aren't fooling around. They have charged him with two counts of murder but I understand they are only specimen charges. They mean to accuse him of murdering the whole ship's crew.'

'But that's fantastic! Insane! What does Richard say?'

'I haven't been able to see him yet. I should have the same right of access as I would in the British system, of course, but there's something else going on I don't understand yet and they won't let me see him. They have him in a private room on the top floor of the Queen Elizabeth Hospital but I don't know what's wrong with him. It can't be anything too serious or they wouldn't be playing it the way they are. But I can't be certain what's up until I speak to him, or the arresting officer or someone in authority. They're stonewalling me at the moment. Most unusual.'

'I have to go at once if I'm coming out...'

'Oh, you must come, Captain Mariner. As fast as you can. I've booked you a suite at the Mandarin, by the way.'

'I'll be there at eight your time tonight, Andrew, if everything goes to plan.'

'But that's impossible!'

'Nothing's impossible for Crewfinders and British Rail!'

The train pulled out at 3.45a.m. on the dot and Robin settled back into the comfortable, softly moulded support of her seat, fully intending to sleep, but her mind would not rest. The situation had come about so suddenly. It was so impossible to believe. Richard charged with murder – soon to be charged with the murder of an entire ship's crew. Her

Richard. Her gentle, considerate, kindly Richard. It was simply beyond belief. But so much about this whole situation was so strange. Why had Richard really been called out to Singapore so suddenly? Why had he gone aboard the *Sulu Queen*? What had happened to the *Sulu Queen* and her crew in the dangerous waters of the South China Sea? If everyone else was dead, how had Richard survived? What grounds were there to accuse him of any murders, let alone all of them? And why, oh why had he not contacted Heritage Mariner or the Hong Kong lawyers or Andrew Balfour himself? Why had he not contacted *her*?

But of course he had. She thought of that ruined, indecipherable airmail letter crushed beneath the door and thrown so bitterly away. Of the tape on the answerphone wiped clean by the accidental actions of an angry child wanting a word from his absent daddy. Perhaps – her heart wrenched within her – perhaps he was waiting for her to act upon some instructions lost with the paper and the tape. Perhaps he was waiting for her to do something of vital importance which would resolve everything. As her mind dwelt on these thoughts, her weary eyes began to drift out of focus and her lids began to close. The vibrato whisper of the Eurostar hurling down through the southern suburbs of London and out into northern Kent began to lull her to sleep.

The train thundered through Sevenoaks, jerking Robin out of her reverie and she shook herself. If Richard was waiting for her to do something, then he would tell her about it tonight and she would get it done tomorrow. If it was something which could be done on a Sunday in Hong Kong.

Well, no matter what, she decided grimly, if she wasn't going to sleep then she might as well look at the limited access company documents Audrey had found for her under the codeword *Conrad*. The carriage was surprisingly full of passengers heading for Paris even at this time in the morning, but Robin still had a little unit of four seats and a table to herself. She put the briefcase on the seat beside her and was arranging the files it contained in a neat pile on the table when the guard came by to check her ticket. 'Still on time?' she asked. She had an important connection to make, she knew.

'Bang on time, Captain Mariner,' he answered. 'We should be pulling into La Gare du Nord at six thirty on the dot.'

Robin nodded once, and the guard went on down the train. No one else disturbed her until the concession trolley came past and she bought two cups of strong black coffee, filled them with as much sugar as they would hold and drank them one after the other, pausing in her reading as she did so to admire the dazzle of lights which sped past and were snatched away as the train plunged into the tunnel itself.

The atmosphere changed subtly as they sped underground, the sound, the rhythm of the movement, the pressure and odour of the very air all changed. Robin dismissed the sensation and went back to her reading. Her head did not come up again until an exact reversal of the process of atmospheric change in the carriage announced their arrival in France. She was courteous in return to the courteous questions of the French Customs official who came down the carriage as they came fully into French jurisdiction, then she had two more cups of sweet black coffee as the Eurostar exceeded 200kph, accelerating breathlessly across the broad, dark fields of Normandy. And she read, and read, and read.

Facts from the files fitted against each other like the pieces in a jigsaw, revealing the breadth of Heritage Mariner's plans for the East and the Far East. Much of it was familiar to her and she skimmed it rapidly; some of it was newer, and she studied it with more care. And there were sections of it – and implications arising from it – which were quite new to her and required much frowning, concentrated thought. Facts, observations, long-held beliefs all became related to each other in new, sometimes surprising ways. Things which seemed to be discrete and utterly unconnected suddenly seemed to attain some kind of relationship, giving Robin chimeric glimpses of truths which came dazzlingly into view and then vanished like mirages in the desert. This was particularly, disturbingly, true if you placed Hong Kong in the centre of things and looked at it all from that new perspective.

Take Canada, for instance. Heritage Mariner were closely associated with an East Coast company in Sept Isles, on the St Lawrence. They were in full co-operation with the Sept Isles Toxic Waste Disposal Company, and together they ran the two great ships *Atropos* and *Clotho*, specifically designed for the safe transport of nuclear waste across the North Atlantic and its disposal at the Thorp reprocessing plant in England and the Canadian facility in Quebec. But in order to explore the possibilities of taking that business west – especially since Helen DuFour's visits to St Petersburg and Moscow had established that much of the fissionable material resulting from the Russian decommissioning of their nuclear arsenal under the SALT agreements was flowing towards Archangel and not Murmansk – both companies had opened offices in Vancouver. Heritage Mariner's office was staffed by expatriate Hong Kong associates of Charles Lee; and it was located beside the new offices opened by Jardine Matheson when they had moved their corporate headquarters out of Hong Kong Central.

Even their association with the West African coastal state of Mau which had originated with Richard's commissioning by the UN to tow the great iceberg Manhattan to that troubled country seemed to have led inexorably Eastwards, for it was the profit from that epic enterprise that had financed the purchase of the China Queens Company. Their offices, so recently taken over by Heritage Mariner, were located on the fourth floor of Jardine House in Hong Kong Central, and it was their ship, *Sulu Queen*, that was currently being towed into Aberdeen Harbour to be impounded by the Hong Kong authorities.

Some refocusing of their business towards the East had been inevitable after Charles Lee had taken her father's place as chief executive of the company after Sir William's near-fatal heart attack four summers ago. Charles's family were Hong Kong boat-owners from way back. They had pirated and smuggled their way to and through many fortunes in their time but Charles's father had insisted on the latest generation getting a proper education and so young Charles had been sent West and gone through the best business training available. But, back in Hong Kong to take Lee Shipping into the twenty-first century and the big league, he had become involved with the student protest movement in China. After Tiananmen Square, the Chinese government had realised that the young Hong Kong businessman had simply been trying to suborn the next generation of Chinese intellectuals so that after 1997 he would have a power base of increasing influence in Beijing. The Lee Shipping Company would not survive the return of the Crown Colony to Chinese influence, he was informed. And so he had gone West again. He was a dynamic, powerful chief executive and although he and Richard had often clashed, the pair of them were expanding the business rapidly.

Pragmatic to the last, and used to negotiating with worldly, pragmatic men, Charles Lee was currently in Beijing negotiating with the Chinese government on Heritage Mariner's behalf – and doubtless mending fences on his own behalf as well. That fact, combined with the current catastrophe, made her blood run cold for some reason. It was a little strange that this should be so – and she put at least some of the feeling down to tiredness – for she liked Charles personally very much indeed. He was a worldly-wise, cynical, drily witty man of enormous personal charm. She knew him very well, believed she knew him as well as any Occidental could know an Oriental. They had much in common, for they had received almost identical educations for almost the same reasons and they had many friends in common at Johns Hopkins and the London School of Economics where they had almost been contemporaries as students. She had been closely involved in the headhunting, vetting and appointing of the new chief executive and had kept close social contact with him as well as the inevitable business contact.

And yet, now she thought about it, if Charles were less of a friend than she believed him, how well placed he was now to dispose of his co-executive and rival and move the whole weight of Heritage Mariner into his own city, to replace his own lost little family business. If the Chinese were serious about making the whole province a special economic zone for the next fifty years, then there was a serious vacuum waiting to be filled there. The business done in the past by Jardines, Swires, Sime Darby, Hutchinson Whampoa, Wheelock Marden and Inchcape, not to mention the Hong Kong and Shanghai Bank, would still need to be done, and Heritage Mariner could do it as well as any other and better than most. If the Chinese were serious, then there was a fortune to be played for here, which was almost beyond computation. And Charles Lee was at the heart of things in Beijing. The man with the knowledge; the man with the contacts. The man with all to play for and nothing much to lose. The thought of it made her head whirl. And that was while she was still looking at the blue legitimate business files and the beige personnel files, dealing with above-the-board elements of the situation; long before she opened the red intelligence files and began to get some kind of a grasp on the manner in which the Mafia in Russia and the Triad organisations in Hong Kong and China might be involved. Not to mention the professional pirates in the Chinese Navy and the Philippines.

Chapter Seven

Robin was still reading the US Navy's five-year-old warning advising American ships in the South China Sea to beware of renegade Chinese Navy units working as modern-day pirates as the Eurostar express eased itself into the long platform of the Gare du Nord terminal. She threw the varicoloured pile of files into the briefcase and rose stiffly. She shrugged herself into her light travelling raincoat, pulled her heavier overnight case out from between the seats and slung the long strap up over her right shoulder. As the doors hissed open, she was there, ready to step out, her eyes already busy looking for the contact she knew would be waiting to whisk her away to Orly.

The platform was empty and her heart sank. She stepped down onto the concourse and as she did so it abruptly became bustlingly busy as the train's other passengers did likewise. Straightening her back, she strode up at the head of the tide of travellers towards the ticket barrier. Her escort would be in the main part of the station, of course; she had been silly to be worried. But no; she came through among the first into the great echoing vacancy of the main area of the Gare du Nord. It was still well before dawn, and the only people there were other passengers from the Eurostar, all of whom seemed to be hurrying out towards the taxi rank.

She hesitated, like a tall yacht with the wind taken out of her sails. The fatigue which she had been keeping heroically at bay washed over her with disorientating force. Her footsteps faltered and her shoulders sagged. Her eyes lost their focus and her ears filled with the roaring which comes with sheer exhaustion.

So it was that she did not at first hear the announcement on the tannoy. 'Will Captain Robin Mariner, a passenger recently arrived from London, please report to the Enquiries Office...'

Had the message been relayed in anything other than those cut-crystal English tones, she probably would not have heard it at all even though her French was fluent and idiomatic.

The taxi driver was gruff and monosyllabic. One of the old school: he wore a beret and a Gitane as inevitably as his round shoulders and hangdog expression.

'"Jour."
'*Bonjour. Orly?*' She copied his spoken delivery and decided against asking him to take her cases.
'*Orly*,' he confirmed.
'*Alors. En avant.*'

His eyebrows rose and the corners of his eyes crinkled. '*Bon.*' He led her out onto the station forecourt under a bright clock displaying the time 06:35, past the long, desperate-looking queue of passengers beside the empty taxi rank, across the gleaming cobbles to a smart, powerful-looking silver Citroen Xantia. Silently he opened the rear door for her and held it almost gallantly as she piled her cases onto the back seat. 'I wish to sit in front,' she said in French. 'Is that OK?'

He shrugged: OK.

She strapped herself in and it was well she did so. The Xantia was a powerful car and the driver was a great deal less laggardly than he seemed to be. He approached *le périphérique* as though it was Le Mans. She was incapable of sitting there silently, however, and so she seduced her taciturn companion into conversation as they sped out through the sleepily stirring city towards the airport. His name was Henri and he was originally a Marseillaise. His wife was Parisienne and, against the tradition, he had come to her home town instead of making her come to his. They had three sons, all married now, and a daughter. The sons were a teacher, an accountant with a firm in Aix-en-Provence, and a sailor. Henri was currently saving every *centime* he could towards his daughter's looming nuptials. And all the brothers sent in what they could as well. It was the eldest, Henri, his favourite, who had gone to sea. Henri *fils* was third officer on a liner cruising the Mediterranean and he loved the life. Oh yes, the Henris *père et fils* knew all about Heritage Mariner. Did the captain think simply *quelqu'un* would be selected to drive a person such as she? Even among the drivers who worked regularly for Crewfinders, he, Henri Le Pen, was considered to be the most reliable.

This revelation reduced Robin to silence, but the quiet did not last long for Henri Le Pen was exceeding the speed limit by a considerable factor and Orly was rising up towards them, a blaze of light just beginning to lose its lustre in the brightening dawn.

After parking, Henri did indeed take Robin's cases – rather to her surprise – and led her swiftly and purposefully through the massive terminal. She had checked her itinerary and her tickets in the London taxi travelling between Heritage House and Waterloo and so it came as no surprise to her that Henri was plunging doggedly towards the increasingly exclusive environs of the international departure gates and finally to the Concorde lounge. It was inevitable, really; there was only ever one mode of transport which could get her more than halfway round the world within a twenty-four-hour period. She had no clear idea why Concorde was actually flying out to Hong Kong today, but she was very glad indeed that there was just one spare seat in the long, needle-shaped fuselage, and that she was now in possession of the ticket that went with it.

She handed over that ticket to the smart young receptionist at the Air France counter and was whirled into a silk-lined, velvet-gloved, luxurious world at once, hardly having time to retrieve her luggage and to say *au revoir* to Henri.

While her weekend case was whisked away and her briefcase was put through standard security checks, she was led down a series of thick-carpeted corridors by that same svelte, blue-uniformed receptionist. 'The flight departs in a few minutes,' this young woman informed her. 'You have arrived at the last possible moment.'

'I came on the Eurostar express train from London,' said Robin, as though this was an extenuating circumstance.

'*Dieu!* I do not think I would enjoy to travel through the tunnel beneath la Manche. Give me an aeroplane every time!'

'I enjoyed it. It was convenient, comfortable, fast and efficient. Very like a plane in many ways, I thought.'

The blue-clad shoulders in front of her shrugged eloquent disbelief, as though Robin had suggested that English wine was superior to French.

Conversation was at an end.

Their footsteps echoed hollowly, suddenly, and it became obvious that they were walking across an enclosed bridge. They turned a corner and there was a doorway immediately in front of them with the Air France girl's identical twin – except that she was in a BA uniform – standing waiting for them, holding Robin's briefcase. She offered it with a smile and Robin grinned wearily in return, secretly hating the young woman's bright-eyed tirelessly pleasant demeanour, her perfect make-up and her bouffant hairstyle with not one gleaming golden fibre out of place.

Inside Concorde's main passenger cabin there was a quiet hum of expectation as the better part of a hundred very superior men and women readied themselves for departure at this cripplingly antisocial hour. The blue-uniformed air hostesses passed between them solicitously, ensuring that everything required and requested was done for their comfort. Robin's seat was by the window halfway along the narrow aisle to the right, just below the mid-cabin display designed to show what speed they were doing. At the moment it read MACH: 0.00.

The hostess gently disturbed a young man in shirtsleeves wearing exquisitely tailored suit trousers and red and black silk Mickey Mouse braces which looked like something left over from the yuppy eighties. He rose accommodatingly, offered to put her briefcase up in the overhead rack and grinned understandingly when she refused. He sat

51

silently when she was settled and did not strike up a conversation until after she began to talk to him.

But she did not begin that particular conversation until they were climbing towards five kilometres up in the air, the display above her head was reading MACH: 0.95, and breakfast was being served.

'Do you like scrambled egg and smoked salmon?'

'Rather!'

'Would you like mine? It's a bit rich and I'm feeling a little delicate.'

'I say! That's jolly decent! Can I swap anything for it? Want my croissant? Can't say I'm too keen on croissants. Think they'll have any toast and marmalade?'

'I'd love your croissant, thank you. And yes, I'm sure they'll give you toast if you ask.' She broke open the flaky crescent of honeyed gold pastry and reached for her knife. A little butter, some apricot *confiture* and some thick, black coffee was just what the doctor ordered. If only the coffee cups weren't so small!

'Champagne, Captain Mariner?' asked the hostess.

'No . . . Yes, please,' she said, watching the foaming nectar and her companion both at once. As soon as the hostess was gone, she resumed the conversation. 'I'll swap you if you like . . .'

For her, it was exactly like being back at boarding school, as it was for him, she guessed. They made a good team, always accepting everything offered and then bargaining so that both of them got a lot of what they wanted instead of a mixture of palatable and unpalatable alternatives. Like Jack Sprat and his wife.

It was a ridiculous game to play in this situation where either of them could have had exactly what they wanted simply for the asking, but it was a diverting amusement, if a childish one, and they both enjoyed it. It became a little like an innocent flirtation after a while and they were confederates and friends long before they got round to proper introductions. The introductions were simply information about first names in any case because he knew she was Captain Mariner from what the hostess said in the same way as she knew that he was Dr Maxwell.

The game had the unexpected effect of isolating them a little from everyone else aboard. Even had Dr Maxwell not been there, Robin would probably have taken little notice of the other passengers as, more than seven kilometres up in the still, sun-filled spring air above the eastern Mediterranean, they hurtled eastwards at more than twice the speed of sound. She was preoccupied, unaware that there might be anyone aboard whom she knew, and insensitive to the atmosphere which surrounded her. Had she not been so tired – so overwhelmed – she would have thought to wonder about the flight, its timing, its destination and its occupants.

'Your doctorate. Is it in medicine?'

'Economics, I'm afraid. So I hope you're not feeling unwell.'

'No. Why?'

'What you said about feeling delicate. And you do look all in, if you don't mind me saying so.'

'No. I'm just tired. I've had a pretty bad day, I'm afraid.'

'Anything I can do to help?'

'I shouldn't think so.' She said it automatically, hardly thinking about the actual meaning of his words, certainly not looking beyond their apparent simple civility.

'Well, I won't be in HK for long but I'll be networking like hell from the moment we touch down. We're just going in to oversee the handover, you see, but they'll have to let us have pretty wide access even in Government House. The legal team will have a broader brief than us economists, of course, but we'll still be there on the pulse. Look...' He reached down under his seat and pulled out his jacket which had been beautifully folded. He started sorting through the pockets, turning the perfectly arranged material into something which looked like a dishrag. Robin watched him, not a little dazed. At last he wrestled a business card out of an inner pocket and handed it over with boyish pride. She looked at it. 'ADAM STAMFORD MAXWELL, DOCTOR OF ECONOMICS,' it said. 'COMMITTEE FOR THE OVERSIGHT OF POST-TREATY HONG KONG, ECONOMICS SECTION. Room 101, Government Offices, Government House, Hong Kong.'

'It's a bit of a misnomer really,' he said a little sheepishly. 'We're not really going to be there *post treaty*, really; we're just there to observe the handover for the House and report back in detail. There are a lot of government people very nervous about the whole thing, you see. We won't be able to do anything *but* observe, I shouldn't think, but we've got to report very fully on the Basic Law and the functioning of the Special Administrative Region and the Special Economic Zone. That's my specialist area, of course.'

She looked down at the card again. There in the corner was the seal of the House of Commons. She slid the pasteboard into the breast pocket of her blouse and relieved him of his wadded jacket. As he continued to talk, she shook it out expertly and refolded it with her practised sailor's fingers until it fell into razor creases as though it had just been pressed.

'So this flight is full of economists and lawyers all getting ready to report to Parliament on the final handing back of Hong Kong?' she asked, on the verge of bewilderment.

'Not quite. I'm sorry, I thought you knew. No, they wouldn't waste Concorde seats on small-fry like me if it was just a question of getting us out there. You know Prince Charles is already out there, of course? Now we're bringing out the Foreign Secretary and some big wallahs from the Foreign Office. It's for the opening of the new airport just off Lan Tao Island, called Chek Lap Kok.' He looked at his watch. 'What's the time? What time zone is this?'

'I don't know. Lunchtime?'

'We're due there to be part of the opening ceremony tonight sometime.'

Robin sat in silence for a moment. Her forehead slowly creased and her grip on reality began to slip. 'If half the Foreign Office is on board, why on earth didn't the flight start from Heathrow?'

'It did. But we had to drop off a couple of Mandarins and pick up fuel and flight crew in Paris. That's how you got that seat, I suppose. I thought you'd have known. I mean, you're Heritage Mariner, I thought you'd have been bang up to date with all of this. Someone somewhere must have pulled strings without number to get you on this flight. If you're not swanning out to the Chek Lap Kok opening with the FO Buy British team or joining the diplomatic roller-coaster for the next two months, then what are you doing here?'

She took a deep breath. 'Well, Adam,' she said, 'I'll tell you ...'

An hour later, as the hostess cleared away the last of the lunch things, Adam said, faintly, 'And this is what you call a bad day?'

'Yup.'

'I'd hate to see what you would call a disaster.'

They sat in silence for a while then, 'Robin?' he said.

'Yes?'

'Look, I don't know anyone on this plane, but you must. I mean even if you haven't met the Foreign Secretary, then you or your husband must have met some of his team. Can't you get some of them busy on this?'

'I've been thinking about it, yes.'

'But?'

'No buts.' Robin pressed the button to summon the hostess.

'Yes, Captain Mariner? What can I do for you?'

Robin looked up. This was another woman, older than the hostess who had brought breakfast and lunch. She was tall, well-groomed, of indeterminate age. But she was perfectly turned out and exquisitely made up. Even her eyebrows seemed to have been combed. And she had *Security* written all over her. Robin racked her memory for the most likely names to be accompanying the Foreign Secretary. Who did she know at the Foreign Office who might be up at the front of the plane? No names would come.

'Yes, Captain Mariner?' The cool tones had a touch of asperity now, just a hint of impatience. The perfectly-rouged lips thinned.

'Can you give me a list of the other passengers aboard?'

'I'm sorry, Captain, but that would be out of the question.'

'In that case,' Robin hated sitting down here looking up at the woman, it put her at such a severe disadvantage, 'I would like to speak to the senior security officer aboard, please.'

'You are, Captain. Now what can I do for you?'

'I would like to speak to the Foreign Secretary.'

The perfectly curved eyebrows rose fractionally.

Robin's nose went up by exactly the same degree and an icy hauteur swept over her. 'We know each other,' she said. 'Socially.'

The senior security officer hesitated an instant longer. 'I'll tell him you're aboard, Captain,' she said, and was gone.

'My God!' said Adam and pressed the button again. This time the original hostess appeared. 'Whisky, please,' croaked the economist.

As the drink came, the cabin announcement system chimed. The captain of the aircraft advised them that they were just about to begin their descent into Bahrain International Airport where there would be a refuelling stop of one hour. The cabin tilted, pitched. The tiny canals within Robin's ears which registered level and pressure began to warn her that they were diving increasingly steeply down towards the distant curve of the world. She found herself relieved that her stomach contained nothing particularly heavy.

Waiting for an answer to her message, Robin found herself looking dreamily out of the window. They descended swiftly through a skim of high cloud and down until the ground became visible. It was the old, familiar terrain of bare gold rock and brick-dust desert. There seemed to be a wind down there, blowing a skim of sand, not enough to be called a sandstorm, her wise eyes registered, just enough to keep the edges of all the land forms blurred and to make the shadows scurry across the landscape which was itself hurling past below disorientatingly as though the plane itself were still and the turning of the earth were visible.

She knew Bahrain well – the way it had been when it was an island state. But the bridge was there now, striding across from the Emirates, and the contact with the mainland, by all accounts, had made quite a difference. Lazily, she strained for the first sight of the old, familiar Gulf.

As things turned out, there was no opportunity to leave the plane as it stood on the apron and was serviced. Robin looked at the distant airport buildings as they danced in the haze of the Bahraini afternoon like a mirage just about to dissolve. She was never so glad of anything as she was of the fact that the toughened glass through which she was looking kept out the heat which she remembered so well. The last time she had been here she had been pregnant with the twins and the fearsome heat had knocked her out like a mugger's cosh.

She looked vaguely at her watch which told her mendaciously that it was three hours earlier than the sun outside thought it was. Idly, she wondered whether to correct it, but that would be pointless. In three hours' time she would be in HK and then she would need to go through the process all over and move it forward another four hours. The weight of all those extra hours crushed down upon her and she was asleep when the elegant length of the Concorde accelerated down the runway and swooped up into the air above the iridescent water of the Gulf.

She was awoken an hour later by a decided movement at her side. There was no disorientation – the catnap had refreshed her enormously and she knew exactly where she was. Adam Maxwell was pulling himself up out of his seat and an impatient figure loomed restlessly beyond him. Robin recognised the newcomer – with no particular pleasure. It was StJohn DeVere Syme. Of all the names she could have called to mind in the Foreign and Diplomatic Services, his ranked among the lowest. He was not particularly senior in the Foreign Office but had every intention of going far. His presence here was proof that his ambitions were being fulfilled, she supposed. He seemed clever enough – he had a First in Classics and was a member of the First Division Club – but he was coldly ambitious and arrogantly scornful of concealing it. He was over-precise in his movements, pedantic in his speech, fussy in his dress, and obviously an extremely lucrative customer for the Personal Toiletries counter at Harrods. Whenever they talked, Robin could never get rid of the idea that she was being interviewed by Lady Macbeth or one of King Lear's elder daughters.

Syme perched on the edge of the seat vacated by Adam, brought his knees together, eased the trousers until one could have shaved with the creases, flicked a little lint off the cloth and rested his long, pale hands precisely on his kneecaps. The subdued light of the cabin gleamed upon his fingernails. 'Mrs Mariner,' he said. 'How nice.'

'Not really, Mr Syme,' she said with a touch of asperity. 'I'm on my way to Hong Kong to try and find out why my husband has been accused of mass murder.'

Syme's pale eyes flickered. He was used to innuendo, not directness. 'While we were in Bahrain, we took the opportunity of contacting HK ourselves,' he purred. There was an instant of silence as he paused for a response. But the words had taken her breath away. 'Your husband, Captain Mariner, is in fact, it seems, being held in a secure area of the Queen Elizabeth Hospital. There is indeed a warrant for his arrest naming two victims. I'm afraid I can tell you no more than that at this stage. The Foreign Secretary—'

'Is there anything you can do to help?'

'With what?'

'With getting him out. Helping him. Finding out—'

'The matter is absolutely beyond our jurisdiction. The Foreign Secretary—'

'Names then, who do I talk to?'

'I should start with the police or the Navy. The Foreign Secretary asked me to explain some points briefly to you which you might not have quite appreciated.'

'Who do I talk to at Government House?'

'I'm afraid you will find that everyone at Government House will be extremely busy. As you will readily appreciate, the Treaty runs out in a matter of weeks. We are extremely active in overseeing the handover of the Crown Colony to the representatives of the People's Republic. It is at the top, the absolute top of all our agendas to ensure that the transfer does not damage the institutions or economic standing of Hong Kong. The Foreign Secretary—'

'But there must be someone in Government House I can speak to who will help me arrange for Richard—'

'My dear Mrs Mariner, you do not seem quite to have grasped the point. It is the Hong Kong authorities which have made the charges. There are forms and provisions, of course, but it is just as if he had been accused of murder in London. You cannot go running to Government House as though it were an embassy in a foreign country. There is no one there who can be of particular help except that they might be able to recommend a good local lawyer. Hong Kong is, effectively, England in this instance – until the Basic Law is instituted when the Chinese officially take over on the first of July, of course.'

He had hit her with this fact as though it was a weapon and the shock of it was like a slap in the face. She was reduced to stunned silence for a moment as he proceeded as smoothly as a greased steamroller. His eyes dwelt with apparent fascination on the glitter of his gold cufflinks and the absolute white of his folded shirt cuffs. 'The Foreign Secretary has asked me to ensure that you have a clear view of this situation. This is a position for the Hong Kong authorities. There is nothing that anyone on this aeroplane can do to help you. It is absolutely crucial that you understand that we can do you no good at this time and in this instance but you can do a certain amount of harm to us. We are proceeding at twice the speed of sound towards what the tabloid newspapers call a "media circus", I understand. The Prince of Wales will be there. The Foreign Secretary will be there, of course. The Governor will be there, needless to say. Senior representatives of the People's Republic will be there. And the world's press will be there. It is absolutely vital that you do not do or say anything inappropriate. And not only tonight, either. Only a dunderhead would suppose that your husband's case will not arouse a great deal of publicity, given its background, placing and timing. It is a situation fraught with incalculable dangers, you see, and we cannot afford to have a hysterical woman running around in the middle of it. My personal recommendation would be that you see your husband, talk to the authorities, arrange for a defence if necessary and then go home to look after those charming twins of yours.'

'How dare you, Mr Syme!'

'Ah now, Mrs Mariner—'

'Just who the hell do you think you are talking to?'

'This is just the sort of reaction which we feared—'

'Let me see if I'm following your logic clearly.' Robin's voice trembled with the effort of regaining some kind of control over her flaming temper. 'Hong Kong is just about to be handed back to Chinese control so it is high on the Foreign Office's agenda. No doubt there is an awful lot of political, and financial, capital to be protected. We are just about to attend the opening of a new, extremely costly airport by the Prince of Wales so it is high on the press's agenda too. And you think I'm going to charge hysterically into the middle of the ceremony begging the Prince to help me defend my husband. And then you think I'm going to rampage around the Crown Colony for the next few weeks, grabbing headlines and damaging the political process of the handover.'

Syme studied his signet ring and allowed this to wash over his perfectly coiffured head. When he moved slightly, the light emphasised the absolute straightness of his white-floored parting. His blonde locks gleamed like a helmet of oiled gold. 'Then please explain to me, dear lady, just exactly what you *do* propose to do.'

'You must be joking!'

'I beg your pardon?'

'After the conversation we have just had, Mr Syme, a man of your acuity must readily understand that you could roast in hell before I told you one word about my plans.'

He shook his head slightly and tutted like an irritated schoolteacher. The signet-ringed hand rose palely to adjust the tiny, tight knot of his tie, lingering briefly on the dark and light blue striped silk. 'Then there is really no point in continuing this conversation,' he purred regretfully.

'Nor, I assume, of having a similar conversation with anyone else on your team,' she snapped.

'Or, indeed, in Government House, Mrs Mariner,' he persisted. 'Unless you are simply following the normal procedures, of course.'

'I see,' she said. 'I see very clearly indeed.'

'I am most gratified,' he drawled. He rose and hesitated, obviously wondering whether to offer her his hand. But then he realised he was unlikely to get it back unscathed. 'So nice,' he said again, vaguely, and wafted away leaving a lingering cloud of something expensively spicy.

It was a positive relief when Adam dropped back into the seat in something akin to a sprawl and overpowered Syme's lingering scent with Imperial Leather soap, the odour of Scotch and a hint of honest perspiration. 'You move in exalted circles,' observed the economist. 'Syme is what they call a coming man.'

Robin grunted. She was tempted to deliver her own estimate of Syme but she didn't know Adam Maxwell well enough yet and so she held her peace.

'Bad news.'

Robin thought it was a question referring to her conversation with Syme and was about to answer when Maxwell continued.

'Well, it might be bad news. They're not sure yet.'

'What?' she asked, pulled away from her own concerns for a moment.

'Air hostess just told me. The typhoon warnings are out in Hong Kong. The Number Three signal is up already,' he said glumly. 'If it gets any worse they'll have to close the airport.'

Chapter Eight

Robin had vivid memories of flying into Kai Tak – as did everyone else who had enjoyed the experience, she suspected. She remembered really believing that the jumbo's wing tips were going to brush against the high-rises as the massive plane came round between the mountains capped with mountainous blocks of flats. She remembered how the washing on the poles outside the windows flapped in the slipstream, how the greenery in the plant and vegetable boxes extending from the sills bowed and danced, how the gardens on the rooftops rocked as though in the grip of typhoons and the *tai chi* schools practised with the precision of marionettes and did not to look up. How life behind the windows just went on regardless. She had bright memories like picture postcards of scenes she had seen, for ever frozen: the mahjong games; the family meals; the rows caught in snapshot, angry faces and violent gestures frozen; the relaxed bodies sprawled in front of the television, almost always on the floor; occasionally people in various states of undress, at their ablutions or partway to or from their beds; and once (perhaps it was just as well) a pair of beautiful, golden, naked bodies wrapped passionately in a kind of rictus of love. The pictures were terrifyingly clear proof of just how close the planes came to the buildings on final approach to Kai Tak.

Such was not the case with Chek Lap Kok; and Robin was quite certain that Kai Tak must be closed now because of the severe weather. The wind buffeted the Concorde's long fuselage from side to side and up and down. Rain spattered against the window as though fired from a series of shotguns close by, and had been doing so ever since they dropped below the cloud base. The silence with which the fuselage had stabbed through the thin upper atmosphere was replaced by the thunderous noise of the thick wind down here. Darkness seemed to be painted against the outsides of the windows; even the skim of rain and spray stood out only because it was illuminated from inside the cabin as it appeared and disappeared across the glass past the shadow of Robin's head.

Suddenly and distantly there came the gleam of a light away on the right. Robin, the mariner, automatically racked her brain. There was a light at Tai O village, on the north coast of Lan Tao Island, she remembered; that was more or less where they were, surely. What was it? A fifteen-second flash time? While she waited for the light to return, she found herself thinking that at the Tai O police station they displayed storm warnings too. There would be a storm warning up at the moment, she thought wryly. They would be waiting for the Hong Kong coastguard to warn them that Number Three should be replaced by Number Four or even Five. The light flashed back and she was surprised that she had to look so far back in order to see it. The bright beam stabbed out, giving a depth to the night and revealing the scurrying sheets of rain. As her eyes focused upon it, so they cleared sufficiently to see the pale outlines of storm-shuttered buildings on the sloping, hilly coast. The whole vista seemed to shiver in the grip of an earthquake and the thunder of the wind came again. She glanced across at Adam whose eyes were closed. He was white and seemed to be regretting after all the smoked salmon with scrambled eggs, champagne, whisky and all the rest. Now, she thought, was just the moment to reset her watch.

It was not until she was actually inside the new building of Chek Lap Kok International Airport that the cold reality of her situation hit her. The Foreign Secretary and all the others were whisked away. She herself was isolated by the requirements of Customs and Immigration which the diplomats did not have to undergo. Even Adam, with his House of Commons cards, got an easier ride than she did. But she did not really care. Her one desire was to get to Richard. She was certain that the pair of them were on their own. That humiliating conversation with StJohn Syme had established that they could expect little or no support from the establishment for the time being. Especially as Syme's point was well made: it was the authorities here which were accusing Richard in the first place.

As she thought these dark thoughts, everything in the great, plush building seemed to become increasingly sinister. All officialdom seemed to be taking longer, looking more closely, becoming more threatening than she had ever experienced before.

It began with the Immigration Service. She was alone when she reached the high desk. She had to wait while a plump Chinese official came out of a small office, leaving the door ajar. He walked slowly to the desk, sat behind it like a Buddha and held out his hand. She handed over her passport. He looked at it and looked at her. He did so slowly, frowningly. Then he pulled himself back up onto his short legs and went away with it, walking silently, rudely, through that doorway. Robin waited, her nervousness adding urgency to her impatience. The first man came back into the doorway accompanied by another, a Westerner. They both looked at her, silently, suspiciously, sinisterly. They went away. Abruptly she found herself wondering whether Audrey's advice of nine hours earlier had been inaccurate after all and she was about to be deported straight back to England – or slammed into custody as a illegal immigrant. Anything seemed possible to her exhausted, stress-hyped imagination. Never had she felt more alone, more under threat. It was like something out of one of Kafka's novels, and yet here she was in the hands of fundamentally British officialdom. It was ridiculous.

Typically, she began to get angry.

But before her temper was put under too much strain, her passport was brought back. The Chinese immigration official sat behind the tall, forbidding desk. Just as though he had not already examined it at some length himself, and then again with the security man in the office behind, he opened her passport wide for the third time and studied it. 'What is the purpose of your visit, Captain Mariner?'

'I have come to see my husband who I understand was arrested yesterday for murder.' This was the fifth or sixth time she had said this. Why should the reality of it hit her so powerfully now?

The official looked up at her. His bland, round face betrayed no emotion at the sight of the tears on her cheeks – if he felt any.

'And how long do you propose to stay?'

'I really have no idea. It depends on what happens with regard to my husband's case.'

The official gazed stonily at her for a moment longer. 'Mariner,' he said. '*Sulu Queen*.' He gave a single nod. 'You may be here some time.' He stamped the passport and gave it back to her. 'You will need to visit our offices in Immigration Tower at 7 Gloucester Road at the earliest opportunity,' he said. 'You will need to talk your situation through with someone there. The telephone number is 824-6111. Straight through to the baggage hall.'

Robin was absolutely alone in the baggage collection hall. There weren't even any baggage handlers. No need for any, she supposed. The Foreign Secretary's luggage would hardly come through here. Nor Symes' or even Maxwell's, she thought glumly. Handlers would only have been an unnecessary security risk, what with the Prince of Wales, the Foreign Secretary, the Governor and the representatives of the People's Republic all out there somewhere. There was a distant babble of voices interspersed with the popping of camera flashes as the official opening ceremony got under way in the main hall.

As she waited, alone, Robin had leisure to consider the efficiency with which the other passengers – the VIPs – had been whisked away and their baggage disposed of. It would have been so easy to treat her single little case with the same consideration. Ah well, she thought, that's what you get for upsetting the Foreign Secretary's lackey. The thought, and the anger it stirred against Syme whom she blamed for all of this, failed signally to make her feel better. Against the tall windows above the baggage collection hall, rain and wind thundered suddenly, like a waterfall. It drowned out the sounds of the ceremony in the next hall. The power of the noise emphasised how small humanity's efforts were, how insignificant she was, and how alone. Her overnight bag, when it finally flopped onto the carousel, looked unutterably forlorn.

She didn't bother with a trolley, she just slung the strap over her shoulder and walked through into the Customs hall. There were the familiar lanes and she chose the one marked in green as she had nothing to declare. The Customs officer who stopped her halfway along it was another Chinese. He was a slim, bird-like man whose high forehead and thin neck made his whole head seem far too big for him. When he asked to examine her luggage she almost told him to get lost. But she controlled herself and placed the case and the briefcase side by side in front of him with a brittle smile.

The officer opened the overnight bag and rummaged through it comprehensively. He kept moving the case and his slim body in such a way that it became obvious to her that everything he was doing was being monitored by the security camera over his seemingly fragile shoulder. Thank God, she thought, that the personal items were all new. It would have pushed her over the edge into the hysteria Syme apparently feared had those busy little fingers been sorting through anything which she had actually worn herself, revealing it to whoever was watching through the camera.

She no sooner welcomed the thought into her weary head than the officer opened her wash-case clumsily and half a dozen tampons fell out onto the floor.

He took out each file from her briefcase and examined it in detail with the sort of concentration which someone displays when looking at something utterly beyond their understanding. The manner in which he looked at each document made it obvious that they were also being checked by whoever was behind the security cameras. A wave of helplessness swept over her and she hoped that the information in those limited access company files would not fall into the wrong hands. But the thought that it might do so made her go cold again. It was worse than the moment when they had taken her passport away.

But then it was over. The bags went through the X-ray machine just to double-check, she supposed. And she went on through the body-scan. She had half expected the machine to set off the alarm but it did not do so. There was a female officer waiting for her at the other side, however, and her stomach clenched with an absolute terror far worse than anything so far. Her steps faltered as the nightmare possibility of a body search flashed into her mind. For an instant, she was on the verge of panic flight, absolutely certain that she was going to be stripped and given a full, intimate examination; by the Chinese woman, in a private room, no doubt, but still in front of those sinister security cameras.

But then a single thought came. One thought which straightened her spine and steadied her nerve. The thought of why she was here. Even a strip-search, even that she would have borne to get to Richard's side. She met the woman's gaze and stepped out firmly. On her third step, the bird-like officer joined his colleague and each one handed her one of her bags. With almost regal calm she accepted them and then turned towards the apparent freedom of the gate. So, with the briefcase again in her right hand and her ill-packed overnight case thumping her left thigh and dragging on her shoulder, she walked through into the reception hall.

It seemed that she had missed the ceremony. The noise and the flashing lights she had seen from baggage collection were gone now and all that was left to show what had been going on was an empty podium, a large number of vacant chairs and an enormous amount of photographic equipment being busily packed away. With this as a background, a broad young man was standing, looking anxiously towards her. A beautifully tailored suit contained the body of a rugby prop forward by something akin to a miracle. The anxious face was square and freckled and, to chime with the body, presented a snub nose which might have been squashed in a lively scrum and a pair of ears with just the most distant hint of the cauliflower. The hair swept back above the broad forehead was bright copper and crinkled like live fuse wire. 'There you are, Captain Mariner!' he called as his blue gaze fell on her. He strode forward at once, his movements lively and forceful, his broad face breaking into a welcoming grin. 'Thank goodness. I was becoming concerned.' He shoved out a hand towards her and caught the weekend case off her shoulder before she could object. He swung it up onto his own shoulder. 'Security has been incredibly tight tonight. I'm extremely surprised you managed to get through!'

'You're not alone there.' She was beginning to come out of the near-shock which had been an inevitable result of her fears, if not of her actual experience. She registered more than his bright eyes and ruddy hair. His voice held the softest ghost of a lilt which made her think irresistibly of crofts and peat-scented malt whisky. But then, she had been on the Isle of Skye less than fifty hours ago, and his accent brought it all back too vividly.

'And I must admit that I'm absolutely flabbergasted that you managed to get here today at all,' he persisted. 'Was it only this morning that we were talking on the phone? And you were calling from Waterloo Station! It seems impossible. You are absolutely amazing, if you don't mind me saying so.'

'How's Richard? Have you seen him yet?'

'I'm afraid not, Captain Mariner. They won't let me anywhere near him.'

'But you're his legal representative! Surely they can't stop you if you insist?'

'It's certainly very odd,' he admitted.

'I have to go to him at once,' she said.

'We've got to leave before they close the bridge,' he warned. 'They put up Warning Four just after you touched down and the typhoon warning system only goes up to Six. They cut short the opening ceremony because there was no sign of an improvement – that's why the place was so empty when you came out of Customs. If they put up Five then we're here for the night.'

Robin suddenly realised that the noise she had been hearing in the background was going on immediately outside. 'What is this?' she said desperately. 'This is May, for heaven's sake! It's far too early for typhoons.'

'Nobody seems to have told Tin Hau,' he observed wryly. 'God, but this is bad joss,' he added angrily.

And Robin really knew she was back in Hong Kong.

Andrew Atherton Balfour's car sat all alone in the multi-story car park, mercifully close to the lift doors. The power of the wind was apparently intensified by the building's construction and they seemed to be battling a full hurricane as they hurried across towards it. The fierce gusts were quite warm, however, and although there was spray aplenty, no rain actually penetrated. There was far too much going on for Robin to pay any attention to what type of car it was, though she had an impression of brutal power in the muscular squat of its shape. 'Sling your stuff on the back seat,' he yelled, swinging the passenger door open for her. This was easier said than done, for the pale hide seat-backs were high. But he managed to get her overnight case in, so she gave the briefcase a hearty shove and hoped for the best.

Then they were both in, side by side, gasping for breath, with the car doors tightly closed and the massive solidity of the automobile reassuringly close around them. 'Right!' he said after the briefest respite. 'Let's get this show on the road!'

He shoved his key into the ignition and turned it. The starter crashed into life and the power of the storm was reduced to size at once in comparison. He hit the lights then wrenched the big gearshift into reverse. While she was still reaching for her seatbelt, he slammed the car into violent motion. She rocked forward, as though going to kiss the dashboard. Her briefcase thumped down onto the floor behind. The car crouched back, like a panther about to spring. Balfour reached for his own seatbelt and strapped it on while Robin, silently, was doing the same. Unobtrusively, she eased herself down and pushed her hips forward until her feet were firmly on the floor in front of her. Something made her suspect that they were in for a bumpy ride.

He was very good to begin with. They hardly exceeded 20mph inside the building. Both acceleration and brakes were tested to the limit at the exit barrier, however, and then they were out on the open road onto Lan Tao Island.

Conversation was impossible while he was thundering up through the gears, apparently with his own *tai fun* somewhere just behind the dashboard. The blaze of the airport fell away on their left, seemingly sailing off across the agitated ocean, while they sped along the new highway up the steep hillsides which were the backbone of the long island. Hong Kong itself remained invisible, concealed behind the sharp peaks of the skyline, until they came to the watershed and the massive car seemed to leap over the sharp crest and the whole breathtaking view spread out dazzlingly in front of them.

The swirling storm clouds whipped by above their heads and ran – almost as agitatedly as the surface of the sea below them – to break against the tops of the sharp peaks across the bay. Beneath them hung chains of rain which seemed to whip in the grip of the wind and glitter in the reflected brightness of the red, green and broad bright yellow lights. The lights themselves seemed to run down the hillsides with the rain to gather in bright pools hard against the sea. Straight ahead lay the New Territories, scarcely twenty kilometres away, the slopes below the whirling clouds falling precipitately from sheer darkness concealed by driving rain to increasing jewelled brightness extended by a bright aura of driving spray.

Pointing straight towards the invisible Tai Mo Shan peak at the cloud-capped summit of the Territories, the great span of the new road bridge reached out like a golden arrow beside its darker twin railway bridge. Footed on Ma Wan Island, they stepped across more than three kilometres of rough water, and even as Robin looked down in breathless wonder, another fierce gust seemed to make both structures tremble.

To the right of the road bridge's span, behind the bulk of Tsing Yi Island, the bright glow of the mainland coast followed down past the Kwai Chung container terminal towards the low hump of Stonecutter's Island, and the Kowloon Peninsula beyond. Even as she looked at the gaudy brightness plunging like a golden waterfall between the streaming sky and the foaming sea, she saw the lights of a jumbo jet sailing steadily down behind the hillsides, settling towards the runway at Kai Tak. 'Kai Tak's still open,' she called with some surprise.

'Not for long, I'd say,' he answered. The massive car swung downwards, plunging towards the bridge. The movement was to the right as well as down. The whole of the peninsula swam into her view, with the glitter of the bay and the brightness of the lights on Central, Wanchai, Causeway Bay and North Point of Hong Kong Island itself. It was a breathtaking view, one of the wonders of the world. The beauty of it buoyed her up; simply being here fed her the extra energy she needed, even though in terms of her body's time it was just coming up to twenty-four hours since she had pulled the Monterey to a halt outside the front door at Ashenden.

On this side of the hill there was a wind shadow which cut down the sound of the storm, but the grumbling snarl of the huge engine just ahead of them continued to dominate the airwaves. 'We have to go straight there,' she called.

'One step at a time. Let's get across the bridge. I warn you, it could still be closed. If Number Five is up—'

'No! You don't seem to understand. We have to go straight to the hospital.'

'We'll talk about it when we get past Boundary Street. At least if we get there we know we're not going to get moved off the road and into the nearest shelter by the police. But until we do get there, it's too soon to worry. We could get pulled up at any time. Really, Captain, we have to take it one step at a time. Let's get across the bridge first. Then let's get in out of the New Territories. Then we'll decide what to do. Fair enough?'

She sat back, silenced by the logic of his words.

The car sped down the hillside along the eight-lane highway like a thunderbolt. Robin glanced around again, craning to see out of the high, narrow windows, but the position of the car and Balfour's square body combined to eclipse most of the city. That fact made her think about her companion as though his position in front of the view triggered the obverse of the old saying 'out of sight, out of mind'. There was nothing else to look at and nothing else to think about – except for the constant agony of thinking about Richard. But that, like the plan for action, needed to be put off for the time being. So she began to wonder about Andrew Atherton Balfour. And the instant she did so, she realised how selfish she had been.

'You should have been there!' she said suddenly.

'I should have been where?' he asked, obviously failing to follow her logic.

'At Government House! At the reception for the Prince and the Foreign Secretary, with all the rest of the local bigwigs!'

He gave a bark of laughter. 'I'm sorry to disappoint you, Captain Mariner—'

'Call me Robin, please.'

'Thank you. I'm sorry to disappoint you, Robin, but I'm no *tai pan*. I would have been there, though; I have to admit that.'

'Then this is particularly kind of you,' she said.

'Not really. I'm not very good socially. I prefer the quiet life at home, if the truth be told.'

'Then you must be unique in your profession.'

'Ah now, don't confuse us poor solicitors with our flamboyant associates the barristers.'

Now it was her turn to bark with laughter as she thought, This from a man driving an Aston Martin. The grudging sound was brought about by recognition of the truth of his observation. The one barrister she knew really well was called Maggie DaSilva and Maggie was as flamboyant as they came. 'Even so,' she said, 'this has to be one of the highlights of the recent social season.'

'Perhaps, but I think there will be an even bigger party in seven weeks' time. When the Chinese arrive full force.'

'Or no party at all. What do you think?'

'It's difficult to tell. There has been an enormous brain-drain and a massive movement of companies and capital outwards. But what if the Chinese come in like a lamb rather than a dragon? What if they are serious about the Special Economic Zone and are willing to put up with rampant consumerism in order to establish the window into the capitalist world that they need? They have to realise that Marxism is dead as a social system; I mean, since the collapse of the Soviet Union...'

'Yes. If?'

'Well, it's something I must admit has been exercising my mind recently, though I'm not an economic expert.'

'And? So?'

'Well, it does seem to me that, even if the government of the People's Republic is largely composed of senior and conservative, not to say elderly, men, it is nevertheless probable, perhaps certain, that it will soon become obvious to them that Hong Kong could be really important to them. I mean *really* important. What if they want to follow the footsteps of post-Marxist Russia but don't want to make any of the mistakes? What if they could use Hong Kong like the valve on a pressure cooker to channel solid currency in – dollars, marks, pounds, gold, for heaven's sake – and let the product out. You see, if they do it carefully, they won't need to deal with the industrialised West on equal terms at all: they have an infinite supply of the ultimate machine – people. They have an effectively infinite workforce capable of producing damn near anything, and they control the wages and the costs! Forget Japan. Look at South Korea; look at Samsung and Hyundai.

'The system seems to work just the same as it did in the sixties but on a far larger scale. They've already started producing the cheap and easy stuff – the fake St Laurent shirts, the Reeboks, the Rolexes. That spat they had with the USA a couple of years ago showed how good they are getting at copying the more advanced stuff – the videos, laser discs, CD Rom packages, bio-programmes and genetic stuff. They're even pulling ahead with the legitimate stuff – the extruded plastic toys, the simple electrical goods. Look in any of the Hong Kong markets, look in any high street back home! They can earn millions by keeping on with that sort of product, like the Philippines, Taiwan and South Korea used to do.

'But then they'll use those millions to buy in extra expertise. They'll use Hong Kong as a combination leisure facility and test bed at the same time as they are using it as a conduit and a shop window. Don't you see? If automation is the way to go, then they'll get the leading people in from the West and they'll put them up at the People's Mandarin Hotel and they'll have meetings in the People's floating restaurants in Aberdeen and they'll buy in advice and expertise and suddenly some factory up in Shenzhen will be automated to hell and beyond and the bottom will fall out of the cheap TV market. Or the cheap car market. Or the personal computer market.

'The Chinese already produce massive amounts of this stuff. It already comes out through Hong Kong, or most of it does. They have a winning formula, tested for them by every successful local economy from Japan to South Korea. They know that it works perfectly well, as long as you keep firm control of the workforce when the good times arrive. They know that we've effectively lost that control in Europe and in the States with our minimum wages and guaranteed benefits, our longer holidays and restrictive work practices. They know that the only way the West can compete nowadays is to out-automate or out-invent them. On every other level they have to wipe the floor with us as long as they continue to play the game their way. Why should they change it?'

Robin looked across at him. 'There was a young man on the plane beside me I think you should talk to,' she said. 'An economist called Adam Maxwell. Sounds to me as though you and he would have a good deal to talk about.'

'One of the Government House Parliament wallahs,' said Andrew. 'I'll look him up, if I get the time.'

The massive car snarled out away from the last of Lan Tao Island and swept up onto the span of the new bridge. At more than three kilometres in length, even allowing for its footings on Ma Wan and Tsing Yi Islands, it was the longest bridge in the world. Although obviously still open, the bridge was empty. Andrew drove in the left-hand lane although the car was travelling well in excess of 100mph now. From Robin's perspective, looking left, it was disturbingly similar to being in Concorde as she sped out across the stormy reaches of the South China Sea – except that the rail bridge ran parallel to it, like a shadow. The road bridge was lit, however, so there was more to see – more rain and spray and distant, seething foam. But the set of the sea was confused; the waves sharp and nasty-looking but little more than bad chop. There was none of the long, deadly storm swell which the wind might have led her to expect. Perhaps this was it, she thought idly. Perhaps it wasn't going to go to Five after all.

Suddenly, as it had been on the Concorde, her eye was taken by a bright light far away. She frowned. She should know the distant coast, by reputation if not by experience. She was looking across the mouth of the Brothers Separation Zone towards Brothers Point. Beyond it she could just make out the glow of the desalinating plant. Nearer, the coast bowed towards them with the bright snake of the Tuen Mun Highway winding sinuously along the dark edge of it, joining the individual jewels of the villages into a bright necklace. The bridge seemed to step up again and they were flying over the Zhujiang Kou waterway. She realised that the single, oddly placed light she could see was on a big freighter heading doggedly in towards Hong Kong harbour. Vividly, she empathised with the sailors aboard and wondered that the captain had not run for any of the nearby typhoon shelters. He would have instruments aboard and constant contact with the coastguards and the local weather stations which would tell him precisely what to expect from the weather – and perhaps, like her instinct, they told him things would not be getting any worse after all.

The Tuen Mun Highway reached down the coast towards them until the almost ballistic arch of the bridge bounced over Tsing Yi and began to fall towards the big new junction on the mainland. Robin's heart began to pound with excitement at the thought that soon she would see Richard. The car swung round the new roundabout without losing any appreciable speed. Thinking of Richard, Robin was reminded of her wild ride in the E-type. Had she cornered at this speed, she would have lost the rear end, she knew. 'Exactly what sort of a car is this?' she asked, as much for something to say as to satisfy the tiny prickling of curiosity.

'Aston Martin Vantage. Hell of a machine, isn't she?'

'Amazing.'

'What do you drive yourself?'

Oh great, she thought, a car nut. I thought he was too good to be true. 'Monterey.'

'Family car. What about your husband?'

'Jaguar,' she admitted grudgingly.

'Gosh!' he said enthusiastically. 'Don't suppose you know what sort?'

'Nineteen sixty-nine vintage six-litre V12 E-type. Black with silver trim. Detachable hard-top. Ventilated disc breaking and Adwest power steering. That's about all I can tell you, I'm afraid. If you really want the details then get in to ask the man himself.'

'Gosh,' he said again. There was a bit of a pause. Then, 'Yes, I must do that,' he said, and lapsed into a thoughtful silence.

Unconsciously, his foot went down a little harder on the accelerator and the Aston Martin came round the head of the bay into storm-shuttered Tsuen Wan like doom. He stuck to the coast road and to begin with the land sloped up on the left, hulking steeply into the clouds, while the sea reached away on the right over the little strait to Tsing Yi Island. But soon the sea receded. One bridge leaped right, towards the island, then another, and the great bulk of the Kwai Chung container terminal loomed. The road swung left then right again, then it sped straight through Cheung Sha Wan and Sham Shui Po. She knew this road. It was Lai Chi Kok Road. As the familiar districts sped past, her excitement mounted even further and her desire to speak grew too strong to be controlled.

'Where is everyone?' she said, as much to herself as to him.

'Typhoon parties, if they've got any sense.' His voice was preoccupied. Driving conditions were not easy, even though the road was straight and uninhabited. Buildings began to loom on either side. The highway narrowed.

She sniffed. 'That's pushing it a bit! I'm sure the wind is moderating. They probably won't go to Five, or close the bridge, or close Kai Tak.'

'You're an old salt,' he said. 'I'll take your word. I'll bet they're glad they decided on Government House for the reception, though, rather than the Royal Yacht.'

'That was it!' she said abruptly, glancing left. She knew it because it cut across Lai Chi Kok Road at an odd angle, running exactly east/west while all the others came and went at precisely ninety degrees.

'What?' In spite of the desultory conversation, he had been concentrating on driving, and hardly surprisingly. The road might have been straight but it was narrow, bounded by highsided buildings and, now that they were in the city proper, full of a kind of blizzard of windborne rubbish. Cross streets hosed more detritus into the air from either side, depending on the vagaries of the squalls within the steady gale. Boxes, cans, the odd bigger bin danced and hopped and rolled in front of them. Everything might be closed and shuttered but the electricity was still switched on and the street lighting was supplemented by a bright array of shop signs which swung and vibrated, flickered and flashed, filling the whole street with an unsettling, unpredictable array of shadowy movement. Out of the restless shadows the occasional surprise leaped out: a pram – thankfully empty; a streamer of gaudy canvas stripped from a roadside stall; a banner blown from a pole somewhere, painted with a long green and gold dragon, weaving through the air head first in sinuous flight, apparently alive.

'What?' he said again, wisely refusing to take his eyes off the empty, busily restless road ahead.

'Boundary Street! That was Boundary Street. We're nearly there!'

He seemed to jump out of a trance at her words and slammed the brakes on, pulling over to the side of the road at once. He left the lights on and the engine turning over. He put the big square gearshift in neutral and pulled up the handbrake.

He looked at the clock on the dashboard. Checked it against his watch. 'Look, Robin,' he said. 'Let's look at the reality of this situation here. It's coming up to midnight. Everywhere is closed and storm-shuttered. We're in the middle of the first typhoon of the season and the tightest security situation the Crown Colony has seen in fifty years. Everybody is uptight to the point of paranoia. Nobody is going to let you into an only partially secure section of a public utility to visit a man accused of mass murder.

'Even if the sergeant of the guard refers it up to his inspector, the inspector is almost certainly going to be unavailable because he is involved in the security guard watching Government House. In the unlikely event that there is an inspector available and in a fit state to make a decision, then that decision will be to refer the matter up to the chief superintendent. And I can tell you for a certain fact that the chief superintendent is at Government House himself. I can tell you that he will not be available because he is at the reception and has his Do Not Disturb flag up. And in the highly unlikely event that he will come to the phone, he will ask the inspector how he has the brass-balled gall to disturb him while talking to the Prince of Wales. And if the inspector actually tells him, then he will certainly tell the inspector to drop dead at bloody once and the inspector will tell the sergeant and the sergeant will tell you. Honestly. Believe me. This is what will happen.'

'If it happens, then it happens, Andrew. I'm not made of porcelain. I won't chip or crack. I've been told to drop dead before. But if you don't try then you won't succeed. Let's go.'

Wordlessly, Andrew Atherton Balfour shoved the gearshift into first, checked the mirrors and released the brake. The Aston Martin rolled forward, past the end of Prince Edward Road and into the Mong Kok Tong. Still wordlessly, he swung into Nathan Road and went up through the gears as the Vantage powered more purposefully southwards. He was thinking about the woman beside him and the thoughts were tinged with awe. He was a man used to working and living alone. He was an important cog in an influential machine and he got on very well with his colleagues and his friends, and their friends too. But the fact was that he had not been unduly disturbed to miss the opening ceremony and the reception at Government House, and, he now suddenly realised, he would rather be here with this extraordinary woman, playing Sancho Panza to her Don Quixote, than chatting with the Prince of Wales.

Her eyes remained on the shopfronts, shifting right and left almost aimlessly. To the right, the roads ran down for a few yards and then opened to the Yaumatei typhoon shelter with its bobbing mass of boats, most of them apparently as shuttered as the shops. But it all simply flowed by – and over – her. Only the familiar front of Chung Kieu, alone unshuttered, caused her eyes to focus for an instant. The great shop, packed with its gaudy wealth of Chinese native luxury produce, stirred her, the bright, embroidered silks, gleaming pearls and intricately carved jade reminding her forcefully of Andrew's words on Lan Tao Island as they swept down towards the new bridge. Perhaps this was the future for Hong Kong.

But then she put everything else out of her mind again as they came under the bridge and he began to signal his upcoming left turn. As he turned into Gascoigne Road, Andrew caught his breath and mentally berated himself for having come this way.

Perhaps because of the sound he made, Robin turned in her seat as well and found herself looking left and upwards at the squat building which stood immediately in front of the bright tower of the hospital. 'Convenient,' she said. 'Do you think that's why he's in the Queen Elizabeth?'

'No. It's just coincidence, I'm sure.'

On the corner of Nathan Road and Gascoigne, immediately in front of the hospital which could only be approached after another two left turns, stood the South Kowloon Law Court building. 'They're probably joined by some sort of tunnel,' she said gloomily. 'They're certainly close enough together. Practically back to back.' There was a road up beside the courthouse which led to the hospital. Andrew decided to take the next one instead. The buildings fell away and they found themselves almost disorientatingly plunged into the great pool of relative darkness around the hospital to the north and the Gun Club Hill barracks to the south. Straight ahead were the more distant, darkened buildings of the polytechnic and the railway station, then the bay and, even more distantly, far across the water, the lights of Kwun Tong.

Andrew swung into Wylie Road and began to climb uphill again, through the dark open areas towards the bright loom of the hospital. Robin moved almost convulsively and he glanced over and down at her. Granted that she was illuminated by the backwash of the headlight, her face was stark white and lined with absolute shadows. She looked like someone in the grip of a seizure and he was genuinely concerned that she might be having some kind of attack. 'Are you all right?' he asked. No reply. 'Robin, are you all right?'

'I'll survive,' she said. 'Just get me there.'

He swung the Aston Martin's brutal snout to the left for the last time and pulled up by the bright entrance of the hospital. Suddenly he felt more like Little John or Virgil Earp than Sancho Panza. 'We're there,' he said and killed the engine.

Chapter Nine

To Andrew's surprise, Robin didn't jump out of the car and rush into the hospital. Instead, she reached back and wrestled the top of her weekend case open. A moment's rummaging brought out a flat little vanity case which she placed in her lap. 'I need some light,' she said. He hit the courtesy light without hesitation then watched in fascination.

The light and the open lid revealed a pale, lined, exhausted face beneath a windswept riot of curls reflected in a square make-up glass. 'This won't do. I look like someone's grandmother recently deceased and that will not help the cause one little bit – even here.' She reached into the case and began to pull out various bits and pieces which he eyed with bachelor ignorance and not a little suspicion. In a very short time indeed, however, Robin was performing a kind of magic which simply deepened his awe of her. That stuff must be what they called foundation, he thought, with only memories of amateur dramatics to help him. And that must be blusher – hadn't Mother called it rouge? And lip gloss. But what in God's name was that sparkly powder stuff? It looked like Tinkerbell's magic powder from *Peter Pan*. That brush looked big enough to shave with!

'Hold this,' she ordered. He obeyed, and found himself in possession of the shaving brush covered with magic dust. 'Don't sneeze,' she said. Immediately he felt a desire to do so. His nose crinkled.

She was putting some kind of edging round the lip gloss with swift, deft movements. Then she picked up a small palette full of colours and a long black pencil. The colours went on her eyelids and the pencil outlined her eyes. Her lashes and brows needed no attention. She looked at herself while he held his breath with the brush trembling. As soon as she took it back, the desire to sneeze vanished. She brushed the soft bristles over her face with a swift series of movements then put the top back on the powder box. 'Right,' she said and pulled out something which looked like a lengthy little bottle brush. She dragged this roughly through her curls twice and the windswept mess was transformed. 'One last thing. Hope you don't mind. I won't get it on the leather, I promise.' She took out a tiny phial of amber liquid and twisted it open. For the first time in its existence the Aston Martin's interior smelt of something other than premium hide.

'What is that?'

'Chanel.'

'Oh.' He should have guessed.

She clipped the vanity case closed and tossed it onto the back seat. Then she was out before he could move. He reached up to turn off the courtesy light only to find her head and shoulders thrust back into the cockpit as she reached back for her briefcase. Their noses almost touched and he faltered in his normally decisive movements. The transformation was astonishing. The pale, exhausted creature who had staggered half fainting into his life an hour ago was gone. In her place was a cool, confident, dynamic ship's captain and senior executive with irresistible decisiveness surrounding her as potently as the scent of Chanel.

'Let's go,' she snapped.

He strode off at her shoulder, not even glancing back to check the thud of the central locking or the chirrup of the alarm engaging. The wind battered his back but not hers. Rain spattered onto his suit shoulders but her raincoat shrugged it off. She was right, he thought. The weather was calming down. He just hoped she was right about their ability to pull this off. She was certainly giving it one hell of a go.

He leaned forward as she swept into the light and put his fingertips on the door which was already yielding to her automatically. There was a small foyer, empty, and a teak reception desk at the far side of it. Robin Mariner, every inch the captain now, strode across and slammed her briefcase onto the wood. The noise she made obviated any necessity to ring the bell. The door behind the desk opened at once and a young Oriental orderly in white came out, frowning. 'We're here to see Captain Richard Mariner,' snapped Robin.

'Sorry, is not possible,' said the young man with massive calm.

'Don't be ridiculous. I am his wife. This is his solicitor.' She punched the locks on the briefcase and slammed the lid open. Her hand went in and out with the speed of a conjurer performing a trick. A blue book appeared between her fingers. 'This is my passport. You have no power to stop us seeing him.'

'Is not poss...' The young orderly turned and vanished into his refuge.

Robin tossed the passport into her case and slammed it. She whirled away from the desk, jerking the case after her. Andrew followed automatically, wondering whether his heart was fluttering with nervousness or excitement. She was heading for the lifts.

'What floor is he on?'

'Top.'

'Is not possible! Missy! Is not!' called the orderly.

Robin hit the lift button and the doors began to open at once. But suddenly there was a scurry of feet and the young Oriental was there in front of them, his arm thrust across the open door holding the snarling mechanism still as he said, frowning with concern, 'There is an armed guard. You understand? An armed guard.'

His long eyes flicked up to the companion lift display and back. They followed the direction of his gaze and saw that the other car was on its way down. 'Stand back, please,' said Robin, and the young man obeyed.

Andrew slammed his own hand against the door until first she then he had stepped in. She hit the top button and the DOORS CLOSED button at the same time. The doors closed and the car was in motion at once and for the first few moments of its motion they could hear the sound of the other car arriving, its door opening, someone stepping out and an angry gabble of conversation fading.

With almost boyish excitement, Andrew looked across at his companion in adventure, but that one glance sobered him at once. He thought he had never seen a face more grimly determined in his life. Irrespective of her sex, here was a person taking a desperate gamble in the full knowledge of the terrible magnitude of the stakes. There was a kind of gritty heroism here which even the carefully applied make-up could not conceal. He breathed in, stretching his ribs until his sides ached, unconsciously making himself larger, like a threatened animal.

The lift car stopped with a jerk. The door wheezed open.

Still slightly inflated, Andrew stepped out, his shoulder and side eclipsing his companion protectively. He took three steps along a long corridor and he stopped. Four doors down on the right, a man in uniform sat at attention outside a doorway. He held a square black gun which Andrew did not recognise as a Heckler and Kock SP5 across his lap. At the sound of the lift doors opening, the man looked down the corridor and Andrew found himself the subject of a cold, unmoving stare. When Robin stepped round him he felt an almost uncontrollable urge to hold her back, but he failed to move fast enough.

'We are here to see Captain Richard Mariner,' she said crisply in an unexpectedly loud, carrying voice. 'Please let us in at once.'

The uniformed guard stood up, lifting the gun into prominence simply by moving it across his chest into a sort of 'slope arms' position. In spite of the fact that he was armed, he was not obviously threatening. He did not seem to be undecided, thought Andrew; he was simply waiting for something else to happen. The solicitor hurried a little, trying to keep up with the human dynamo in front of him.

'Captain Richard Mariner,' she said again in that piercing, carrying voice. Abruptly Andrew realised she was calling to him, asking him to reply, to alert them to his whereabouts. 'We are here to see Captain Richard Mariner.' The last near-bellow drowned out the sound of the second lift door opening, but as it echoed into silence, there came all too audibly one word and a metallic *click*. The guard sprang to attention and suddenly his gun was no longer simply across his breast. It was pointed at them. There came another *click* as he, too, flicked off the safety.

There was a moment of absolute stillness. Then, from behind them, came a quiet, beautifully modulated voice which carried effortlessly over the hiss of the closing lift doors.

'Captain Mariner, Mr Balfour,' it said. 'My name is Daniel Huuk. I am a captain in the Royal Hong Kong Naval contingent and I have been detailed to guard the accused Richard Mariner tonight. Captain Mariner is not available for interview at this time, I'm afraid. May I escort you back to the foyer?'

Robin held herself in check until he turned back onto Gascoigne Road, heading south towards Tsim Tsa Tsui Tong East, Hong Chong Road and the cross-harbour tunnel. Then she simply started to shake. Andrew did not look at her, feeling terribly deflated – defeated – himself, suddenly at the verge of exhaustion, extremely worried about losing concentration and doing something silly with the car. 'It's been a bad day,' he said, soothingly, desperately keen to give her something to cling to.

'Let me tell you, Andrew Atherton Balfour,' she said, her voice thick and husky with tears. 'Let me tell you about my day.' She fell silent, and he risked a glance, fearing she was losing control of herself. The bright signs directing them to Kai Tak illuminated her face, making it seem to be made of marble. It was set, still, apart from the twin floods of liquid glistening on her cheeks. With that vision in front of his eyes, he looked back at the road, signalling the right turn and pulling into the right lane for the feeder into Hong Chong Road and preparing for the near U-turn down between the polytechnic and the railway station to the Kowloon entrance to the tunnel.

'Let me tell you about my day,' she repeated, clearly taking herself in hand. 'Since the last time I enjoyed a decent night's sleep, I have driven down the full length of England with two irate six-year-olds in the back seat. I have had a fight with my son, destroyed a letter from my husband and discovered that all his telephone calls have been wiped off the answerphone. I have had a plate of beans, a glass of whisky and two hours' sleep. I have received the most terrifying phone call of my life. I have arranged for my children to be sent back up the full length of England and then driven my husband's E-type for the first and last time in my life.' She took a deep, shuddering breath. 'I have ridden in the Eurostar express to Paris and caught the Concorde. I have talked to one nice man and one exceedingly nasty one, eaten two croissants and one rather chewy salmon steak. I have consumed, I guess, six cups of coffee. I have been subjected to what I believe you called "tight security" and I have come through a typhoon. All for no reason. I have had three hours' sleep in forty-eight. I have eaten beans, croissants and a sliver of fish. I have come halfway round the world. All for no reason at all.'

They had rumbled down into the tunnel long before she had finished this monologue, and Andrew was driving with owlish concentration by the time they came out of it up into the restless air past the Yacht Club and, aptly, the Police Officers' Club. All he could think of was that he had to get her to the Mandarin up on Connaught Road Central. He guided the Vantage onto Gloucester Road through Wanchai and, for the first time in his life found that he had the windblown thoroughfare all to himself. It was fortunate that this was the case, for he would never have managed the one-way system round onto Connaught Road had his not been the only vehicle involved in the manoeuvre.

It was with something akin to surprise that he pulled up outside the Mandarin and found himself looking up at the expensive frontage of the exclusive hotel. 'Here we are,' he announced cheerily.

No reaction. Except, perhaps, just the faintest snore.

'Captain Mariner . . .' He leaned across and shook her gently.

The wind thundered in past Jardine House and he wondered briefly whether she had been correct in her weather forecast after all.

He leaned across and said with fatigue-slurred urgency, '*Robin!*'

No reaction. She was dead to the world. Catatonic; as good as.

'*ROBIN!*' he bellowed.

There was no reaction at all.

Andrew slumped back into his seat and looked from right to left. On his right was one of the most exclusive hotels in Hong Kong. The doors were closed. He would have to summon the night porter in order to get in. The thought of turning up at that forbidding door with an insensible blonde draped over his arms was more than he would readily face. He took Robin by the shoulder and shook her with such energy that it would have had him sent off a rugby field for inappropriate use of force. She snored. She did not stir.

He sat back with the impression that his mind was racing, though in fact he was thinking with almost drunken sluggishness. OK, he thought. He had a comatose woman whom he wished to get into her suite in the Mandarin Hotel. There were only two ways in which he was going to achieve this. He would have to carry her to the door and then into the reception area, or he was going to have to get a night porter to carry her. That was it. Those were the alternatives. It was difficult for him to calculate which would be more dreadful.

'I'm sorry, Robin,' he said, loudly and seriously, 'I'm going to have to take you home. But don't worry,' he added bracingly, 'I know you're going to love Repulse Bay.'

As he guided the Aston Martin Vantage back across Central and then out through Wanchai, past Happy Valley and on up the hill, heading south through Magazine Gap and away into the stormy night, Andrew Atherton Balfour tried to work out what he was going to do. Robin Mariner and her mysterious husband had rather turned his life on its head, and all at an amazing speed. He would have to talk things through as a matter of some urgency with his senior partner Gerry Stephenson. He would have to start making detailed arrangements to lean on the police and the Royal Navy very hard indeed. There had better be very, very good reason for the armed guards and the continued refusal to allow access to his client. Then he needed to start looking into the background of the case as a whole and find out just what the hell was going on – what had already gone on aboard the unfortunate ship the *Sulu Queen* and, perhaps most importantly, what would go on in seven weeks' time if the case toppled over into the jurisdiction of the new Chinese Basic Law.

Put at its most simplistic, the nightmare scenario was this: there was a distinct possibility that a man found guilty of murder on 30 June could expect to be deported to England and put in prison there; but a man found guilty of the same crime on 1 July might expect to be taken to Beijing and executed.

As though she could read his mind, Robin stirred and groaned. It was the saddest sound he had ever heard. 'Robin?' he called.

No response.

He shook himself, suddenly aware that he had been bowling along the road at the better part of a ton effectively sound asleep. The wind tore a rent in the hurrying cloud cover and a low, bright moon lit up the countryside all around him. The wet slopes glinted as though the hillsides were covered with ice or snow. Ma Kong Shan gleamed precipitously on his left, its top chopped off by the Aston's low roof. Far behind, Jardine's Lookout glimmered spectrally in his rearview mirror, then vanished with the moonlight. Andrew hunched forwards and followed the tunnel of the headlights down to the southside coast.

It was after 1a.m. when the Vantage grumbled into Repulse Bay. Andrew swung it left, up the hill towards the little enclave where his house stood overlooking the restless sea beside that of his senior partner and wife. As the massive car pulled up the steep hill, it moved more and more slowly. This was not because of any failure of power but because of a mixture of various types of confusion in the mind of its driver. His own, relatively modest, residence stood shuttered and dark at the end of a short drive on his right. The much larger house owned by Gerry and Dottie Stephenson stood on the left, with bars of light blazing round the edges of the storm shutters and reaching out like odd-shaped searchlights, given body by the last of the rain. The contrast between the houses gave Andrew pause for thought. The broad wheels rolled to a stop and Andrew pulled up the handbrake as he calculated what it would be best to do.

The problem was this. His *amah* Su Lin did not live in. She would arrive with the Sunday papers in less than seven hours' time. She was a lively and intelligent woman but he knew from past experience that she was also an inveterate gossip. No matter how innocent the actual explanation, the discovery of a strange woman asleep in his bedroom while he camped on the sofa would give Su Lin untold licence for sexual speculation. It was a little like something out of a French farce, but he was all too well aware – as who in his profession was not – that there are not many laughs in sexual misunderstandings in real life. Especially as Su Lin's brother was a stringer for the *Standard* newspaper and several Chinese language dailies. He could just see the headlines: 'BLONDE WIFE OF MASS MURDER SUSPECT DISCOVERED IN LOCAL SOLICITOR'S BED'. And that was just the way the conservative English-language papers would put it. What the Chinese press would say went beyond even his lurid imaginings. No. If Gerry and Dottie were still up, then he had better impose on their good nature a little.

Gerry and Dottie Stephenson were more than up, they were in the middle of a rave-up. The weather was a perfect excuse for the first typhoon party of the season, and the Stephensons were throwing it.
 Andrew, all unaware, drew the car onto their forecourt, left the lights on and ran through the spitting rain and the jumble of other vehicles to their front door. He pushed the bell and then hammered on the wet wood. The wind grumbled up from the bay but it was no longer powerful enough to drown out the thunder of music from inside. The big solicitor frowned and began to look around, the penny slowly beginning to drop. Too late. The door burst open and there was Gerry, hair awry, in his shirtsleeves with his collar wide and his tie at half mast. 'Why, it's Andrew! Come you in, my boy, come you in!' He waved Andrew inwards a little unsteadily with a hand holding a tumbler full of whisky. Behind him, the Stephensons' hallway seethed with bodies pushing through from the sitting room to the kitchen and back. The stairs rose up like the terraces at Twickenham packed for the Oxbridge match. Warmth rushed out and the wind rushed in. Knowing he was going to regret this, Andrew went in as well. Gerry at once draped himself affectionately round Andrew's shoulders and bellowed, 'What'll it be?'
 Long experience had taught Andrew that abstinence begat argument in the Stephenson household, so he said, 'Carlsberg, if you have...'
 'See what I can do,' said his host cheerfully and plunged left to the bar in the kitchen. Andrew pushed right, nodding and waving to everyone he knew – which was almost everyone there. He found Dottie by the piano surrounded, as always, by her boys from the Cricket Club. 'Andrew,' she cooed, her voice carrying over the hubbub after years of practice. 'Darling, where have you been?'

'Dottie, I have to talk to you. It's an emergency, I'm afraid.'

'Should you be telling this to Gerry, darling?'

'Not that sort of emergency. Look, can we go somewhere?'

'I say, Balfour, old man, are you still driving that beast of a Vantage?' asked one of the Cricket Club, a slight, whip-strong man who was a demon wicketkeeper.

'Yes, I am, Jeremy. Look, Dottie, *please*, I'm sorry but I need your help.'

'Of course, darling. Follow me.' Dottie caught up her glass with one hand and her cigarette holder with the other. She waved the Cricket Club aside with an imperial gesture, then she plunged through her guests and he followed in her wake. Jeremy the wicketkeeper tagged along behind unnoticed.

Out through the sitting room door they went, Andrew pausing only to reach across and relieve Gerry of the lager glass he was waving, down through the hall and to the door of the cloakroom beside it. They jumped the little queue waiting there and Dottie slapped the door with an open hand until a sheepish girl in a rumpled miniskirt came out and then the pair of them crushed into the tiny room and closed the door behind them, unaware that Jeremy the wicketkeeper had gone on out to look at the car. Andrew pressed his back against the mass of coats dripping against the wall and took an extremely welcome pull from the glass. Dottie put the lid down and perched on the loo. 'Now,' she said, 'tell me all about it, dear.'

He had only just begun when everything outside suddenly went absolutely still. Wind thundered loudly, but all music and conversation stopped dead. 'Now what?' snapped Dottie, pushing past Andrew to open the cloakroom door.

Her action revealed the packed hall, with everyone facing the stairs. And it revealed, halfway up the stairs, Jeremy the wicketkeeper with his hands wide and his face white.

'Swear to God,' he was yelling at the top of his voice, 'swear to God and I kid you not. Balfour's got a strange blonde in his Aston Martin, and I do believe she's dead!'

Chapter Ten

Next morning, Robin was awoken by a combination of sunlight striking through pink silk curtains and the gentlest of knocking at a door. She looked around herself with profound disquiet, for the last thing she remembered was falling asleep in Andrew Balfour's car on the way to the Mandarin Hotel. And this was not the Mandarin Hotel. This was nowhere that she recognised at all. This was not a bed she knew. This was not a duvet she had ever seen before. And, perhaps most worryingly, the nightdress she was wearing was not one she knew either.

She sat up, looking around. The room was reassuringly feminine and a little cluttered. Her cases were piled on an armchair, both closed. Her coat and travelling clothes were neatly folded on them and her underwear was still in place beneath the peach chiffon of the strange nightie.

The knocking was repeated and a slightly plummy, husky voice called, 'Mrs Mariner, are you awake?'

'Yes,' she answered. 'Please come in.'

A middle-aged woman in a beige wool suit, pearls and a neat little hat came in followed by a younger, Oriental woman carrying a tray. At once the fragrance of brewing tea filled the air and Robin's mouth began to water. 'I'm sorry,' she began, more in confusion than actual apology.

'I know, my dear, you have no idea who I am or where you are. You're worried and I can't blame you.'

The tray went onto a little kidney-shaped vanity table and the lady in the beige wool suit perched on the bed while the tea was being poured. Robin noticed that she was wearing tan kid gloves. At no time did she stop talking.

'My name is Dorothea Stephenson but everyone calls me Dottie. My husband is Andrew's senior partner and you are in the spare room of our house in Repulse Bay. One lump or two?'

'Just a little milk, thank you. I—'

'Andrew brought you here last night when he couldn't wake you up. I don't think he was particularly concerned about that, you understand, though we did ask Dr Towne to look at you after that idiot Jeremy announced that you were dead. No, it was quite obvious that you were simply exhausted. But I'm afraid the thought of carrying you into the Mandarin in that condition was simply too much for the poor boy...'

Robin accepted the tea and sipped it. Her expression was one of absolute concentration, but she let Mrs Stephenson's words wash over her, content to pick out one in ten and think her own thoughts.

She was in Repulse Bay. That was no good at all. She had to be back in Central where she could get to the police and the navy and pop across to Kowloon if need be. She had a name now: Daniel Huuk. She wanted him for a start. And she wanted the name of the man who had put armed guards on Richard's door. That would have to be a senior police officer, the man in charge of the case. And she wanted the name of, and an interview with, whichever doctor in the Queen Elizabeth Hospital was treating Richard.

The Stephensons were off to church apparently and that was why she had been woken up by a woman so obviously ready to go out. Andrew would normally be going with them, the woman continued, but he was at Robin's service this morning. When she had got herself up and ready, she only had to give him a ring. He was just next door. His house was easily visible from the window...

The Stephensons, Dottie concluded, would be back just before lunchtime and she was very welcome to stay. She was to treat the house as her own. Anything she wanted, just ask the *amah* whose name was Ann Chu.

'You've been most kind, Mrs Stephenson...' Robin was overwhelmed to the point of being acutely embarrassed, but Dottie Stephenson was genuinely the soul of goodness and hushed her as though they had been friends for many years. 'It's nothing, my dear, nothing at all. I'm just so happy that Andrew thought to bring you to us. I'm sure we'll become the best of friends and look back on this as quite a little adventure! Now I must run, my dear, the Reverend Chan is quite a timekeeper, and gets so *grumpy* if one is late...' She leaned forward and gave Robin a peck on the cheek, and then she was gone, leaving Ann Chu hesitating with the teapot.

'You're going to have to stop waking me up like this,' said Andrew, a little less that an hour later. Then he gave a half-grunt of laughter. 'God, Robin, was it only *yesterday morning*?' He hesitated for an instant, then he said, 'And what mischief do you want to get up to today?'

Against her better nature, Robin found herself frowning at his over-intimate assumption of friendship. She almost wondered whether to call him Mr Balfour and put him in his place a little. But she could not bring herself to do anything so mean, for she did stand in his debt – and was likely to have to ask for more favours in the near future, though to do so went against the grain. And anyway, she was probably just being over-sensitive after being kissed like a girl by Dottie Stephenson.

She reached across the table for another piece of toast and Ann Chu pushed open the door from the kitchen with yet another pot of that delicious tea. 'I was just calling,' she said, 'to tell you that you don't have to get involved in today's adventures at all if you don't want to. I've just finished talking to reception at the Mandarin and they're very happy to send one of their limousines down for me.'

'Oh, I say...' His voice sounded deflated, a little disappointed. She found herself smiling indulgently and realised it was her first smile since she got the news about Richard.

She stopped smiling at once, but a little warmth lingered in her voice as she said, 'Look, Andrew. Today I propose to do the following things. Drop my bags off at the Mandarin, then go the Heritage Mariner Office in Jardine House. That's just across the road so I can walk.'

'Well, yes, good, but...'

Robin rode over him easily and the warmth rapidly drained out of her voice as she continued, 'Then I propose to go to the police headquarters on Harcourt Street and if I can't find out what I need to know there, then I'll go on down to the Police Officers' Club beside the Yacht Club. I'll need to get a car for that but it won't be too much trouble and they'll help me get a taxi at the Mandarin. That will make it easy to pop across to Kowloon and the marine police HQ opposite Star House there on the corner of Canton and Salisbury, where I shall start to ask my questions about Captain Daniel Huuk. Then, while I am Kowloonside, I thought I'd pop back up to the Queen Elizabeth and see if they still have armed guards outside my husband's room. On the assumption that they do, I will come back to the island side but on the way back to my hotel I thought I'd see if the Supreme Court on Queensway is open for business so I can get some kind of an injunction and at least start the process of getting to see Richard as soon as I possibly can!' By the end of this speech she was in tears again and that fact was obvious to the man on the other end of the connection.

The instant her surprisingly knowledgeable tirade came to a halt, he said, 'Look, you can't do all that on your own, you know. Don't bother with a saloon, I'll take you up; and if you don't want me tagging along after you all the time, I'll go into the office and clear my desk a bit. I rather think you're going to be my concern exclusively for the next few weeks.'

'Right,' she said, never at her best while crying. 'I'll get my things. Twenty minutes?'

'Oh. Ah... Yes. Fine. I mean... Fine.'

As she broke the connection, she heard him call, a little plaintively, 'Su Lin, forget breakfast. No time, I'm afraid...' She felt guilty, but the simple fact was that if she was still here when Dottie and her husband returned then she would find it impossible to escape without actually being rude to them.

She munched on her last piece of toast and sipped her last cup of tea. Thanked Ann Chu for the meal and asked where she could find pen and paper. She wrote a short thank-you note and grabbed her cases.

It was an easy walk down the Stephensons' forecourt, across the top of the little road and over to the side of the British racing green Aston Martin Vantage, but it took her longer than it should have to achieve. The reason was a combination of the weather and the view. Last night's near-typhoon was gone as though it had never been, except for a litter of leaves and rubbish strewn across the ground. The air was limpid and the sky high and clear. This thrust of the precipitous hill overlooked the bay uninterruptedly over Tin Hau's temple across to Lamma Island nearly three miles away and then beyond to the curve of the world. The water between the sharp, green-flanked, high-sided juts of land was calm and achingly blue. The breeze brought scents and spices to her nose and a gentle rustle of greenery from the nearby trees and bushes. The sun was coming up towards the meridian and its rays smote down upon her hair with almost as much force as the rain had done last night. She put her bags down beside the fat front tyre of the brutal car and turned until she could lean her back gently against its warm side, then she looked away until her eyes ached, beyond the island, into the still, haze-veiled distances in the quiet heart of the South China Sea.

When he said, 'The Mandarin first, then?' from immediately beside her, she jumped with surprise. She hadn't heard him approach at all.

The staff at the Mandarin were quietly courteous and gently concerned in the way for which they were famous. Andrew, watching how they swept Robin into their bosom, began to suspect that he could, in fact, have got away with carrying her in here last night. He looked idly round the decor of the reception area as she went through the check-in procedures, impressed by the understated luxury of the black marble walls and the tasteful gilt statues. This was not a place with which he was overly familiar, though he had eaten in the Mandarin Grill like most of his acquaintance, but he could see exactly why Robin had asked him to book her in here. It was almost as welcoming an institution as was Dottie Stephenson's. '*Grazie*, Giuseppe,' said Robin quietly to the solicitous concierge. 'Please just send the weekend case up. I'll take the briefcase myself. We'll be out for most of the day.'

The tall, distinguished Italian bowed over her with an almost paternal air and spoke in respectful whispers.

'No, she answered patiently, 'I don't think I'll be doing much business this time. I see no probability of eating in the grill or the major public rooms. Any meals I cannot have in my suite, I will take in Man Wah. We will discuss it in more detail later. Thank you again.'

Outside, it was coming up to lunchtime on a bright early summer Sunday. All the warm and quiet air in Hong Kong seemed to smell of dim sum as the *amah*s took their days off and sat around in social groups eating the food they had purchased from kerbside hawkers. Robin could not bring herself to get back into the Aston Martin, and there was no need. The Heritage Mariner offices were less than one hundred yards from the Mandarin, across Connaught Road and down towards the Star Ferry Pier.

They lingered for a moment at the corner of the square, brown building while the entire Hong Kong Filipino community seemed to be bustling in Statue Park behind them. 'Do you want to split up?' Andrew asked. 'You go up to your office – I expect you've some phoning round and reporting in to do – and I'll go down to the police headquarters. I can get more accomplished there than you could on your own in any case. We could meet in the Supreme Court building if you'd like. The only place I know where you can pick up a good bargain and a life sentence under the one roof.'

'No, I don't think so, Andrew. I'd prefer to stick together – to begin with, at any rate. I'm not going to be doing anything you can't know about, and I want to be there when you talk to the authorities. There is something going on here which I don't understand, and it's not just something to do with my husband or our company. It's something to do with shipping and with ships. You don't know about that side of it. Except for Captain Huuk, nobody I've met so far knows anything about it. But I do. And I want to be there for every second that this is all discussed. There may be nothing there, but then again . . . You never know, do you? You just never know. Let's go.'

Five minutes later, side by side they swung in through the bustle on the concourse outside the tall, pale building with its distinctive round windows. 'The House of a Thousand Orifices' the Chinese call it, though they do not always use the word 'orifices'. After a few moments more, they were striding between the sloping supports and up to the glass doors of the main entrance. Even on Sunday, the reception area of Jardine House was staffed and security guards were well in evidence. Robin crossed to the lift doors and punched the UP button.

The Heritage Mariner offices were at the front of the building, just far enough up to look over the top of the General Post Office building, over what little was left of the old Blake Pier and away across the harbour towards Kowloon. The view through those concrete-sided portholes was breathtaking. As they entered the main office, they discovered a slight Oriental man in a well-pressed grey suit, enjoying the view in solitude. Beside him stood a desk piled high with files and papers. A chair behind the desk stood with its back to the view and on the seat of the chair lay a folded pile of Sunday newspapers. Hearing the door open, he turned and the effulgent light etched the fine lines of his face. His eyebrows rose and, seeing them, he turned so that he was behind the desk – obviously his accustomed position. Robin strode over towards him with her hand held out. 'John Shaw?' she said. 'My name is Robin Mariner. You called me on the telephone yesterday morning, and I'm so very grateful.'

He took her hand. 'Yes, Captain Mariner, I am John Shaw,' he said. 'I am so very sorry. Have you more news of your husband please?'

'Not at the moment, no. This is Andrew Atherton Balfour of Balfour Stephenson, our solicitors. May we be seated, please?'

John Shaw bowed and gestured. Robin waited until the young man had moved the newspapers from his own chair and then they all sat together. Andrew was reminded forcefully of the way in which she switched so easily into Italian. She understood the language of Oriental courtesy and face also, it seemed.

She waited until John Shaw was seated and then she asked, 'Now, Mr Shaw, have you any more news of our ship?'

John Shaw was an office clerk and very much lower in the order of existence than the people sitting opposite him, except that he was of the Middle Kingdom and they were *gweilos*. But, he thought, as had Andrew, the woman understood courtesy better than any other barbarian he had met. Therefore he would be happy to help her. 'The *Sulu Queen* is moored off Stonecutter's Island at the moment,' he said with quiet courtesy and a certain amount of pride that he was in possession of the information she required. 'The bodies have been removed, I believe, and whatever papers that could be found. The various authorities are aboard now, I expect, going over it from stem to stern.'

'Thank you, Mr Shaw. I'll need to get aboard as soon as possible myself, Andrew.'

'That may be difficult to arrange,' warned Andrew.

'It may be, but it will be vital. Now, Mr Shaw, do I need to see Mr Feng in order to get into the private office?'

'No, Captain. Mr Feng was in yesterday afternoon and will be in again later today. He, like myself, has been extremely busy on your behalf in this matter.'

'I am impressed and grateful for your dedication. I hope the regrettable incident has not caused you or Mr Feng any undue concern or embarrassment.'

'I regret to say that we have much work to do, for the authorities say they will impound the cargo as well as the ship. We have a lot of customers to contact, a lot of explaining and apologising. This is bad joss, Captain Mariner. It will hurt our face and do our business much harm.'

'This cannot continue, Mr Shaw. We must save face at all costs. Andrew, add that one to the list. We have to get the cargo out of bond at least. Mr Shaw, I hope you will stop apologising for a moment and see if you can get us another ship and crew.'

'People will not like to take—'

'I know, Mr Shaw, so it will cost us more. But if we pay them enough then someone will do it. And we, who caused it to happen, will gain face and be seen to have good joss after all, perhaps.'

The Chinese nodded once, decisively. The meaning between her words was not lost on him: he would be arranging the replacement ship and he would be spending the extra money. He would be seen to be a man of great face and power. If his employer kept dealing with matters through this office in this decisive manner, it would do untold good to the reputations of himself and Mr Feng, whom he admired and respected. He was so pleased that he almost forgot that the employer in question was a *gweilo* woman.

'Where is *Seram Queen*, Mr Shaw?' she asked, calling him back to himself.

Mr Shaw rose, crossing to a large chart on the wall. At once Robin was also on her feet, just behind the young man, apparently eager to see what he was desirous of showing her. '*Seram Queen* is currently in T'ai-pei,' he said, gesturing up to the northern point of Taiwan. 'She has just discharged a full cargo of electrical parts, circuit boards and computer sections from Japan. She is due to start loading a cargo of completed computers, video machines, televisions and other electrical equipment which has been awaiting her arrival.' His hand began to move across the Luzon Strait, following the course that the ship would take, and his voice lost a little of its formal businesslike edge. 'Within the next few days she will set sail for Manila. Her cruising time on that part of the route is about ninety-six hours, so, depending on turnaround, she should be ready to leave Manila with a full load of clothing and household goods bound for Mindanao in about a week. We have a regular run around the edge of the South China Sea, as I am sure you know. From port to port, depending on the cargoes, it takes each ship two months to complete the circuit.'

'Thank you, Mr Shaw, that is very clear to me now.'

Robin spent half an hour in Mr Feng's office while John Shaw started ringing round for a replacement ship and crew. Fortunately Andrew had thought to bring his personal phone out of the Aston Martin so he was not left hanging at a loose end either: he started ringing round everyone he could think of who might give him some idea of how soon he could get *Sulu Queen*'s cargo out and onto another ship. He found it increasingly hard to concentrate, for as lunchtime loomed, it only served to emphasise the fact that he had not had breakfast this morning or, indeed, dinner last night. But he had underestimated his employer yet again, for after that half-hour, she popped her head out of Mr Feng's office and said, 'There'll be a knock on the door in a moment. I've ordered up lunch from the Chiu Chow Garden. Mr Shaw, I thought we might need a working lunch so I took the liberty of ordering sufficient for three. I hope you are not offended. Please start without me.' She vanished again, and Andrew's eyes met John Shaw's. The communication between them was eloquent, if silent. Not offended, either of them; awed, both of them.

'That was one of the best meals I've ever had,' said Andrew an hour later as they walked briskly towards police headquarters. 'That tea is incredibly powerful, though. What do you think?'

'That's why they call it Chiu Chow, because of the tea,' she said, preoccupied.

There was no end to the stuff Andrew Atherton Balfour was learning today.

But it was his turn to take the lead as they entered the police headquarters. Both of them knew that, although he was aware it would cost Robin quite a lot to keep quiet and let him work. The longer she had been on the phone in Feng's office, the unhappier had sounded the tones of her voice coming wordlessly through the door. It seemed to him that this was not the only place where she was meeting stone walls. But he didn't ask for any details when she came out and picked moodily at the feast the restaurant had sent them and he knew better than to ask for any now. She would tell him what he needed to know. And, oddly – for he did not often trust his clients absolutely – he knew in his heart that she would tell him everything he needed to know the moment he needed to know it.

Police headquarters was a building given over to the policing of the whole Crown Colony and New Territories. In its upper levels it contained security sections, intelligence sections, anti-terrorist sections, anti-drug sections, and organised crime sections, but inside the main door at street level it was just like any other police station. Side by side they walked through the little reception area under the silent eye of the security camera, approached the desk with its security screen and waited while Andrew buzzed for attention.

The sergeant who answered his summons was even leaner that John Shaw. His face had a darker colour and his eyes were long, black and disturbingly intelligent. 'Yes please?' he said.

'This lady is Captain Robin Mariner. You are holding her husband Richard on a warrant for murder.'

'And you are, sir?'

'I am Captain Mariner's solicitor. My name is Balfour.'

'You are solicitor for Captain Robin Mariner or for Captain Richard Mariner?'

'Both. I'm the solicitor for both of them.'

'I see. Please wait here, Mr Balfour. Captain.'

They eyed each other as they waited. 'Well,' she said grudgingly, 'it's a start, I suppose.'

'We'll get there,' he promised.

'This afternoon. I have to see him today.'

'I can't promise, Robin.'

'I know you can't, Andrew. But ... Oh God...'

A door nearby was opened and the thin sergeant said, 'Please come this way.'

He led them into a corridor with doors all along one side. At the third door he stopped, then he opened it and showed them into a small interview room. There was a table and a selection of wooden chairs. 'Would you like tea?' he asked gently.

He brought them tea himself, hardly keeping them waiting at all. It came thick and dark in big porcelain mugs. The sergeant put the mugs on the table, arranged some milk and sugar, and left.

'One extreme to the other,' said Andrew, thinking of the thimbles the Chiu Chow tea had come in. Robin said nothing. Her control was so obvious and so clearly costing her so much to maintain that she could almost have been screaming at the top of her voice. When he looked at her, Andrew thought that she seemed to be shaking and he remembered the way she had shaken last night after the incident in the Queen Elizabeth Hospital. She is really absolutely extraordinary, he thought to himself. I wonder what this chap Richard Mariner is like? He must be quite something to have a wife like this one. And he found to his surprise that he felt a little jealous of his client.

The door opened again and the sergeant was back. This time he was carrying a pile of paper. 'If you don't mind,' he said quietly, sitting down, 'I have a few questions I must ask you.'

'Is this necessary, Sergeant?' demanded Andrew, tempted far beyond his normal boundaries by his empathy with Robin.

The sergeant looked across at the solicitor with an absolutely expressionless face as his hands arranged the papers neatly and then reached up to his pocket for a pen. 'It is the procedure,' he said quietly. 'You know that Mr Balfour.'

He unscrewed the top of the fountain pen and then turned slightly towards Robin. 'May I have your full name, please, Captain Mariner?'

They were partway through the third form when the door opened and a round, Buddha-plump man in full blue uniform with commander's insignia and a side arm stepped into the room. Andrew looked up and hoped that his face betrayed nothing. But there was no concealing the mutual recognition. This was Commander Victor Lee and he was a very important officer indeed. 'That will be all, Sergeant Ho,' said the commander and the sergeant came to attention at once, turned and left the room without even putting the top back on his pen.

The commander replaced the sergeant and looked at the uncompleted forms. He seemed to be arranging his thoughts, or the words in which he was going to couch them. But Robin had run out of patience.

'When can I see my husband?' she asked.

Lee's long eyes flicked from one Western face to another.

'Whenever you like, of course,' he said.

'Now!' She leaned forward, almost incandescent. 'I want to see him at once.'

'Naturally. I think we can arrange an interview in almost no time at all. Of course you will want your solicitor there and, at the first meeting, we will also want observers both from the Royal Hong Kong Police and the coastguard authorities and the hospital, if that is acceptable.'

'Now wait a moment, please,' said Andrew. 'That is most unusual. What is going on here, Commander?'

'One step at a time, Mr Balfour. Has Captain Mariner any objections?'

'What if I have?'

'Then this interview is at an end and I look forward to dealing with your fully completed forms when they reach my desk in due course. Next Wednesday, let us say, or Thursday.'

Andrew actually gasped. This was blackmail! The commander must be desperate about something if he was willing to run the risk of holding this conversation in front of a solicitor.

But Lee had underestimated his opponent. 'You have accused my husband of murder,' she said.

'I have. I did so thirty-six hours ago.'

'There is a strictly limited time before you are required to allow him to see a solicitor. You will certainly have to allow him to see a solicitor long before the middle of the week.'

'Captain Mariner has not asked to see a solicitor.'

'What?'

'Nor has he asked to see you, Mrs Mariner. He has shown no desire to see you at all, and has signified in due form that he does not require legal representation.'

'No!' She was half out of her chair. But once again, that enormous self-control held her back.

Andrew thought he saw a logical explanation. 'If he's insensible,' he said, 'if he's in a coma . . .'

The commander looked at him with a slight narrowing of his eye. 'Captain Mariner is wide awake,' he said shortly. 'How else could he have signified anything? But we are wasting time. I will allow you both to see him this afternoon, under the conditions I described. Or you can put your request through normal channels. It is up to you.'

Given that the Commander Lee was obviously up to something, and playing a very risky game indeed, Andrew was surprised that he let them ride up to the hospital together. Until, made a little paranoid by his deep distrust of the officer, he suddenly wondered if he had had the Aston Martin bugged. But no; surely even the police would have found it impossible to get through the vehicle's defences, plant a bug and then get out again without a trace in the time. Wouldn't they? Andrew decided to keep it in the back of his mind at least. The Aston Martin rolled out into the solid traffic crawling like cool tar up Connaught Road towards the distant tunnel entrance.

'What do you think?' he asked.

'Isn't that why I'm paying you? To tell me what to think?' There was enough of a smile in her voice to rob the words of offence.

'All right. In that case you think Commander Lee is up to something.'

'What sort of thing is he likely to be up to?'

'With Lee, so I'm told, you never can tell.'

'What do you mean?'

'I'll tell you when you need to know. Right now we need to concentrate on this interview.'

'OK.'

'Look, Robin, I've got to start with this. Why are you so desperate to see him?'

'Because I love him. What would you do if someone you loved was accused of mass murder?'

'Academic question with me, I'm afraid. But OK. If you love him so much, how come you know so little about what he was up to? Was he cheating on you?'

The possibility was so remote she didn't even get offended. 'No. And anyway, he did get in contact. It's just that the messages got lost.'

'All right.' Andrew didn't sound all that convinced. 'Then why didn't he report in to Heritage House in more detail?'

'No idea. He'll have had his reasons, though I am surprised. He's always been so careful.'

'Could he be protecting you, then?'

'What from?'

'From whatever he's got involved in.'

'But he's not involved in anything!'

'He is, Robin. He's involved in mass murder at the very least. He may not have done it but he is involved in it.'

'Yes. That's true. But you don't understand.'

'Don't understand what?'

'You don't understand Richard. He's not the sort of person things just happen to. He makes things happen.'

'All right. Let's say that he was at least partly in control of things to begin with. He can't have been in control of things at the end, can he?'

'No. No, you're right, he can't.'

'So how will he have reacted to that?'

'In what way?'

'Look, Robin, we have to consider this. Could it be that he hasn't contacted you or asked for legal representation because . . . I don't know . . . because he's had some kind of breakdown?' He rushed on in case his words were too painful for her. 'You know, he could be going through some kind of rejection or something, refusing to face reality, I don't know . . .'

'I suppose it might be possible. But that's not the man I know. I can't imagine anything hitting him that hard.'

'Not even forty deaths.'

'Not even that.'

'All right . . .'

'He was involved in the Gulf War, you know.'

'No, I didn't. I haven't had time to check.'

'And in the civil war in Mau.'

'Really?'

'He knows about death. He does. It wouldn't have broken him.'

'Then what do you think is going on? What do you think he is up to?'

'I don't know!'

It was at this point that they turned down onto the tunnel approaches. The traffic congestion eased at once and their speed picked up considerably. Andrew checked all around him as best as he could but he could see no cars which looked anything like a police car. He was fairly certain that, unless there was a car in the tunnel near enough to tape their conversation, they could not be overheard, even had the sinister Commander Lee managed to place a bug aboard somehow.

As the tunnel entrance closed over them, therefore, he took his foot off the accelerator slightly and began to speak more rapidly. 'Look. They can only be doing things this way because they want to shock you into saying something unguarded or because they want you to shock Richard into saying something unguarded. Were you being absolutely honest with me when you said he was always absolutely honest with you?'

'Yes, I was.'

'You're certain he couldn't have got himself caught up in anything clandestine?'

'Nothing of his doing.'

'Ah. So he might consider doing something less than legal on someone else's behalf?'

'Not illegal, no. But he is an absolute friend. Once he makes friends with someone then it's one hundred per cent. I suppose he might have got caught out doing someone a favour.'

'But nothing illegal?'

'No. Nothing.'

'All right.' He drew breath. 'Right!' he said again, thinking at feverish pace. 'Look. If they aren't hoping to shock Richard into making any revelations, then maybe they're hoping to shock you. Had you thought of that?'

'No, I hadn't,' she admitted.

The opening of the tunnel was showing in the distance. Andrew was thinking at fever pitch. 'Who do you know in Hong Kong?' he asked. 'Hong Kong or China? Who do you know?'

'Well, no one, really . . .'

'You don't sound too certain.'

'Well, it's odd.'

'What?'

'I only really know two people in this neck of the woods. And both of their names came up today.'

Really? Who?'

'Well, Charles Lee. He is a senior executive with Heritage Mariner. He's in Beijing at the moment. He's from Hong Kong.'

'Charles Lee. I see. And the other one?'

'It was that sergeant. Sergeant Ho.'

'Yes?'

'We have a senior steward, retired a couple of years ago from our tankers at Heritage Mariner. He was from Hong Kong. His name was Ho.'

'First name?'

'I don't think we ever knew it. We just knew him by his nickname.'

'Oh yes. That's not unusual. What was the nickname?'

'Twelvetoes.'

The Aston Martin actually swerved off line. Then it swung back again, heading for the growing circle of white light. 'You know Twelvetoes Ho?'

'Yes, I do. He's an old friend.'

'My God! You do realise . . . Well, you just stay on your guard, that's all.'

'What? Andrew? What do you mean?'

'Nothing! It's not germane now. I'll explain later. Just stay on your guard, that's all. Twelvetoes Ho! My God. Really! I mean it. Stay on your guard.'

Even as he said this, the Aston Martin came out into the daylight at the point where they had plunged southwards little more than twelve hours earlier. Robin sat up, preternaturally aware of the change in conversation he had risked while they were in the tunnel. 'Is there anything else I should be careful of?' she asked.

'Please,' he said, *'please* try not to say anything unless I sanction it. You never know.'

'No,' she said. 'You never know.'

* * *

Commander Lee was waiting for them in the reception of the Queen Elizabeth Hospital, bouncing up and down impatiently on the balls of his feet. His whole demeanour bespoke impatience, but the more overbearingly fussy he became, the more slowly and carefully did Andrew react, and Robin was careful to follow her solicitor's lead. His words in the car had not been as well-chosen as he would have liked, she suspected, but wisely she tried to clear her mind of the half-comments and innuendo which had arisen during their conversation in the tunnel, and the speculation these gave rise to. She focused instead on the very clear series of warnings he had given to her, like a drunk concentrating on walking a line. And the comparison with a drunk was not ill-founded, she knew, watching herself with as much detachment as she could summon. Even though the catatonic sleep of last night had done much to restore her, her body was still playing dangerous tricks on her because of shock and fatigue.

The lift door opened and the three of them stepped in, Commander Lee tutting quietly to himself in such a pantomime of frustration that Robin began to wonder whether the plump police officer was indulging in some kind of double bluff and really wanted them to slow down further for some dark reason of his own.

'We were lucky with that typhoon,' observed Andrew, oozing calm and confidence.

'Yes,' she said, a little breathlessly. 'I thought it would get stronger and stay longer.'

Silence.

'It's certainly a beautiful day today,' she continued a little desperately. 'What do you think, Commander?'

From the manner in which he looked at her, Commander Lee clearly thought she was going insane. Desperately, she tried to think of a stratagem which would begin to break down that chilly reserve. Some tiny, unexpected point of etiquette such as she had exercised on John Shaw. But, calculating consciously, especially under these circumstances, only made her mind go blank.

Andrew tried. 'It is unusual for an officer of your seniority and reputation to be involved in a case of this sort,' the young solicitor essayed.

Lee's long eyes glinted. 'You are making an insinuation?' he snapped.

Andrew had failed.

The lift arrived and the doors hissed open. Robin was finding it hard to breathe now. Her cheeks were burning and her head throbbing. She was seeing slight bright flickers at the outer edge of her vision. She had not suffered a migraine since her late teens. God, she hoped she wasn't starting to have one now.

There were two armed guards on the door this time, perhaps Commander Lee warranted more back-up than Captain Huuk. They slammed to attention as soon as they saw him, and the effect was not lost on either Robin or Andrew. He pushed past them fussily and rapped smartly on the door. He waited for a count of three and then opened the door. Andrew took Robin by the left arm and they walked in side by side. Andrew's grip was more for restraint than support, but in fact neither was needed. There was nobody in the room at all.

It was a simple little interview room, more like the room they had just left in the police headquarters than a room one would expect to find in a hospital. There was a table with a set of chairs on each side of it, a door behind them which they had just come through and a door in front of them which remained closed. On the right was a window with a Venetian blind which was closed. And that was all.

'What is going on here?' said Andrew, clearly sinking out of his depth.

Robin felt as though she was drowning. With an increasing sense of unreality, she looked across at her solicitor and registered the concern and confusion on his open, almost boyish face. She looked across at Lee who stood like an amber Buddha, hard, cold and inscrutable. She suddenly realised that Richard must be dead. That was all that could make sense in the circumstances. They were breaking all the rules because the rules didn't matter any more. They needed to take no care over their preparation for the case because there would be no case. Because there was no accused any more. She turned back to Andrew and her movement broke his grasp on her arm at last.

'Richard's dead,' she said with absolute certainty. 'That's the only explanation. Richard's dead.'

As she said it, the door opposite opened and Richard came in. He was wearing a hospital gown which came down to his knees like an old-fashioned nightshirt. He had flip-flops on his feet which were far too small. He was wearing a white gauze bandage round his head and his hair stuck out over the top of it in black spikes threaded with grey. His long face was lined and pale. His lantern jaw was almost black with stubble. His eyes gleamed like sapphire flames. Behind him came Captain Daniel Huuk and a short man in a white doctor's coat, like a couple of pilot fish following a great shark, but neither Andrew nor Robin really saw them. Richard filled the room, easily dominating it, even in this state.

Robin stepped forward, literally entranced, and Andrew was too slow to catch her. She only stopped when she reached the table and even then the force of her impact against it made it judder noisily on the linoleum floor.

Richard's blue eyes fell on her then and he stopped moving too. Just for a moment they stood there, looking at each other in utter silence, while the others in the room, each with his own personal agenda, looked on.

Then Richard said, slowly, 'I know you. You are . . .' and he stopped, frowning with concentration, his eyes fastened on her pale and desperate face. Then he smiled, with dazzling self-congratulation. 'You are Robin. You're my wife . . .' The smile faltered. 'Aren't you?'

Chapter Eleven

Robin was in the Mandarin suite, on the corner of the twenty-fourth floor with one balcony looking north past Jardine House over the top of the multi-storey car park and away over the busy harbour towards Kowloon and the hills beyond, and another looking west across Statue Square to a new high-rise where the old Hong Kong Club once stood. The weather that afternoon was still warm enough to allow the use of both balconies. And that was just as well, thought Andrew, because he would have found it almost impossible to keep Robin caged in the rooms of the suite itself. For nearly an hour now, ever since their return from the Queen Elizabeth Hospital, she had been pacing from one part of the suite to another in a frenzy of restless frustration.

In through the quietly furnished magnificence of the reception room like a *tai fun* herself she had come. Savagely sliding the burwood furniture out of the way so that she could pace in long straight lines. Carelessly slopping tea from the pot brought so solicitously by the concierge himself with an enquiry as to the state of play and an instant offer of help. Throwing open the door into the honey-pink marble bathroom to dash some cold water into her face. Jerking wide the double door into the main bedroom with its great teak double bed. Jamming back the French windows so that she could stride outside – which she did with such dark purpose that at first he was scared she was thinking of throwing herself down.

And all the time talking, talking.

'God in heaven, the bastard, the absolute bastard! He knew. That Commander Lee, he knew it would be a shock to both of us. He was counting on that, wasn't he? He had a suspect almost catatonic with amnesia and he just sent us into the same room with no warning to see whether I could shock him out of it. Using me to try and incriminate Richard like that. The bastard. And that doctor letting it happen. Just standing there and allowing it to carry on. What was his name?'

'Dr Chu.'

'Yes. Dr Chu. I want him too. I mean I know they don't actually take the Hippocratic oath, but even so, that doctor must have owed a duty of care. I want him sued for neglect. I want him struck off. And if he works for that hospital then I want them sued too. And if he's a police doctor working with that *creature* Lee, I want them sued as well. And I want the Royal Hong Kong Police in court anyway just as quickly as you can arrange it! By God have they picked on the wrong man here. They are going to regret this by the time we've finished with them!'

'We'll never get that many suits to court in seven weeks!'

'Right. Doesn't matter. They're British subjects – I bet every sleazy one of them has a valid UK passport so I'll take out personal suits against them in the British courts. This is a Crown Colony, after all.'

'Well—'

'But first things first. We need our own doctors in there as soon as possible. We need someone who specialises in memory loss. Whoever. Wherever. We need them here now. And we'll need a silk, won't we, for when the case comes to court. We'll need the best silk in the world. Better get someone booked PDQ. What do you think?'

'Yes—'

'Good. Now what else? Enquiry agent? Do we need our own detectives on the case or are you happy to work with whatever evidence gets thrown up by Lee's investigation or by that man Huuk?'

She stopped then, framed in the French window looking into the room with Kowloon hulking brightly and distantly over her shoulder, jade peak reaching to lapis lazuli sky.

'Huuk. What did you make of Captain Huuk, Andrew? He didn't seem to fit to me. He was out on his own there. He isn't under Lee's command, which might explain it, and the coastguard are probably independent of the police in any case, but he was there for a reason and I don't know what it was. What was Huuk up to?'

'We have to find out more when he's traduced and transferred.'

'What's that?'

'Richard has been duly charged so he will have to be traduced before the Magistrates Court. If what Commander Lee said was true, and I must say I believe him, the two charges so far are only specimen charges. Richard will have to be taken before a magistrate within a certain period of time and all the charges will have to be put to him, and, in all probability, some idea of the basis on which those charges are founded – though they will only have to establish enough of a case to warrant transferral to the High Court. And it's at the Magistrates Court that the questions of officially appointing a defence and of bail or police custody will come up, but with a charge like this, bail will be academic. He will be remanded in custody until the trial date.'

'So when will this be?'

'As soon as they can.'

'We have to be there.'

'I certainly do. I've never come across a case like this one and I'll check with Gerry first thing and try to chase up some case law on it. But I suppose it's even possible that the court could appoint someone else to the defence if Richard makes no specific request to retain me. And that's quite possible because he has no idea who I am any more.'

'I know how you feel!'

'Robin, don't get bitter. It's not his fault. He was wounded in the head, for goodness sake. It could have happened to anyone. He'll remember soon enough, I'm sure.'

'You're right. I'm sorry. So, this transfer.'

'I'm not sure it would be a good idea for you to be there. It may get pretty bad.'

'I've had *bad* before.'

'Not like this. I warn you. These will be specimen charges but they'll choose the easiest to prove, and if they hold it in open court, then the press will have a field day. And there are so *many* of the press here, with the Prince...'

'Then you'll have to stop them. They'll have to hold it – what do they call it? – *in camera*.'

'Yes. Yes indeed. We'd better see about getting right onto that,' and that was the moment Andrew really thought he had better at least try to get some sort of a grip on this situation. 'Phone?' he asked.

'Behind the teapot,' she answered, still hesitating in the French window.

'I see it,' said Andrew and crossed to it at once. The handset was warm from the heat of the pot. 'Hello, switchboard? Hello? Yes, I'd like 812-0392... Hello, Dottie? Pretty bad, I'm afraid... Yes... Oh, holding together, you know... Listen, Dottie, is Gerry there?... He is? Good. Can I speak to him, please?... Hello, Gerry? Listen...' He glanced across towards Robin, saw that she was still watching him, turned his shoulder a little to shut her out and dropped his voice. 'Listen...'

Robin turned away and crossed the balcony. Clearly Andrew needed privacy at this point, though she had a feeling he was only protecting her feelings. She leaned on the warm rail of the balcony and looked down at the pedestrian area. She would probably have been less happy about doing so on a weekday, but on Sunday sections of this area were closed to traffic. She took in a deep breath and held it. There was so much emotion within her and it needed to be sorted out before it overwhelmed her entirely.

She supposed that her reaction to this situation over the last terrible days had shown her where the centre of her world was. Like any mother, she had played mind games with herself wondering whether, if she ever had to choose between them, she would surrender her husband or her children. She had always assumed that she would stand by the twins. And yet here she was in Hong Kong having dropped William and

Mary into her father's arms again. When it had come right down to it, she had left her darlings and come after Richard.

Which made the pain of his rejection even harder to bear. And it was a rejection. No wise words from Andrew could alter what she felt. She felt he no longer loved her.

How could anyone love someone they couldn't remember? If he had really loved her he wouldn't have forgotten her in the first place. No. He loved his company and his ships and his sailing from one romantic place to another; he was happy enough to leave his wife and his babies at home. And sometime during the time he was away from them he had ceased to love them. Ceased to love her. That was all that made sense; there could be no other explanation. Somewhere along the line, on some day she had never known about or noticed, the steps had become complete: out of sight, out of mind, out of heart. Out of love.

There was a sharp pain in her breast and vaguely she wondered whether she was having a heart attack. That would be just perfect, she thought bitterly. What would happen to the children if her heart gave out now? With a mother lying in the middle of Connaught Road and a mass murderer father who didn't even remember them, what would her darlings do?

She should go back to them. She should go back to them at once!

The decision made, she forgot all about her heart and her husband and stepped decisively back through into the room to find that Andrew was waving at her with some desperation. He was still glued to the phone and there was someone knocking at the door. She crossed to the door at once and opened it wide, expecting a member of the hotel staff to be waiting to take the tea things.

The police sergeant from police headquarters was there. The sergeant called Ho. She looked at him, her body utterly still as though he had struck her. He looked at her with the dark length of his eyes burning with fearsome intelligence. She opened her mouth but he raised his hand. She flinched, actually expecting a blow because the gesture was so sudden. But no. He was holding his hand level with her eyes so that she could see the corner of paper clutched between his closed fist and his thumb.

Slowly, as though performing some kind of *tai chi* exercise or kung fu move, he lowered the fist and pushed it towards her. Numbly, she took the white corner of the paper and he released the rest of it into her grasp. He smiled. His face was transformed. He turned on his heel and marched off down the corridor, moving with absolute silence.

Robin stepped back into the room and closed the door. Before turning back into the room, she looked at the piece of paper closely. It was white rice paper, clean cut. It was about five centimetres square. It was not folded. There was a combination of writing and printing on one side. The writing and printing were in black ink. The writing was in

English and seemed to be written with a brush. The printing was in black also and looked to be a *chop* – a personal signet or seal. And that was all.

Robin turned. 'Andrew,' she said. 'Andrew, look at this...'

Andrew looked across at her and stopped in mid-flow. There was a pause lasting hardly longer than an instant. 'I'll call you back,' he said. And he hung up at once. 'What is it, Robin?' he asked.

'This. It's just come. What d'you think?' She held it out and he took it.

He squinted at it.

'The English writing says "Golden Star, 5 p.m.". What does the *chop* say?'

He looked at her, frowning. 'What do you know about *chops*?' he asked. 'You know, you seem to know one hell of a lot about this place. It's amazing...'

'Is it a Triad *chop*?'

'There are a lot of people who would like to know the answer to that. Starting, I suspect, with your friend Commander Lee.'

'What does the *chop* say?'

'You can work it out for yourself. Look. This is the Chinese character for foot. And these dots are toes.'

She took it back and looked at it as closely as he. She saw the character clearly. And the dots, the toes. There were twelve.

'So, what is it?' he asked.

She handed it to him, suddenly filling with excitement. 'It's a message,' she answered insouciantly. 'A message from an old friend.'

She walked back to the French window and he saw that there was a new swing to her movement, a new bounce to her step. His heart clenched. He put the paper on the table without looking at what he was doing. It fluttered down onto the tray beside the cups and the cold teapot. 'You're not going?' he said, aghast.

She stood silently, looking down across the car park to the bustle of the Star Ferry terminal. 'What time is it?' she asked, almost dreamily.

'Four on the dot,' he answered. 'You're not going,' he repeated and this time it was an order, not a question. He crossed to her, suddenly very much afraid. 'I can't let you go,' he told her. 'It's far too much of a risk.'

His hurried movement across the room caused him to brush against the tea table making the fine cups chime against each other like prayer bells in the sudden silence. And the tea spilt earlier soaked through the little square of rice paper, making it spread and dissolve into pale slime on the tray.

Chapter Twelve

The *Golden Star* left from the right-hand pier at five that evening. In fact, the voyage and turnaround were so quick, it left every twenty minutes, but the note said five and that was the voyage Robin wanted to be on. 'You're mad,' huffed Andrew, deeply concerned, as they walked briskly down towards the ferry terminal from the exit of the underpass across the plaza outside Jardine House.

'He's an old friend.'

'He's a pirate.'

'I'd trust him with my life.'

'That's exactly what you are doing. And with my life too, come to that.'

'You don't have to come if you don't want to.'

'*Jesus wept.*'

They came past the taxi rank and joined the crowd going into the ferry terminal. She took his arm placatingly, feeling a little guilty about all sorts of things. 'Got three dollars?' she asked.

'Of course.'

'What more do we need?'

'The return fare,' he said glumly, but he said it to himself. She was already at the nearest $1.50 counter, speaking to the ticket clerk. 'Tsimshatsui,' she said, holding up two fingers with a smile. Not that the ferry went anywhere else in any case.

The clerk put two tickets in front of her as Andrew came up with the money.

'*Mgoi*,' she said, taking them and smiling.

'*Hou wa*,' said the clerk with unusual courtesy. Then he silently took the money from Andrew, obviously thinking *gweilo*!

The ferry was nestling restlessly beside the pier and Robin almost ran through the slow stream of people moving down the pier side, all but jumping aboard into the shade of the white awning which served the green-sided vessel as a roof. Andrew followed as closely as he could, keeping his eye fixed on her tossing golden curls. He had paid for upper deck but that did not mean that she would stay up here. If he lost sight of her now there was no telling where she might end up. This was one hell of a way to spend a weekend, he thought, and stepped aboard in her wake, just as the boat began to move.

This time on a Sunday the ferry was perhaps at its quietest. A certain number of Hong Kong natives sat, their noses buried in papers or daydreaming as though bored with the view, while the ferry began to pull away. A far larger number of tourists stood, awed by the view on the upper deck, talking excitedly in a range of languages and accents and using up roll after roll of film.

The waters of the harbour across which they were beginning to push were at their quietest as well. There would be more of a surge of traffic later, perhaps, when the crystal evening began to close down, but now it was a slack time. There were only half a dozen junks spreading their great red sails in the forlorn hope of a wind and hardly more than twenty sampans crawling like energetic black beetles across the surface of the water. A great freighter piled high with containers lay moored to an SMB and for a stomach-churning moment Andrew thought it must be *Sulu Queen* before he remembered that she was tied up further out near Stonecutter's Island.

And it was during that moment, while Andrew stood looking at the freighter, that he lost sight of Robin. When he turned back, she was gone and an extremely large black-haired gentleman with long dark eyes was standing immediately at his side. The gentleman smiled, displaying a large number of extremely straight, white teeth. The peppermint odour of chewing gum swept over Andrew as the stranger began to speak. 'Hi. I'm Joe De Santos from Portland, Oregon,' he said in a thunderous bass, sticking out a hand the size of a ham. 'Would you mind taking just one or two photographs of me and my wife Annie here while we stand at the front of the ship?'

Robin walked down the companionway onto the lower deck. Here there were more Hong Kong people, all very obviously minding their own business, and no tourists at all. Some might come down later – if the term 'later' could be applied to something less than five minutes away – when they began to pull through the last of the shipping and into Kowloon. She walked purposefully along the deck towards the stern of the little boat, looking straight ahead of herself, back across the widening gap of water, towards the tall spear of the Jardine building.

When the tall, black-clad figure fell in step beside her she did not vary her gait but walked on until they could lean against the rail together and look out from under the awning as the first shades of early evening began to climb Saan Deng, the Peak.

'*Neih hou ma*, Twelvetoes?' she asked gently, using up almost all her Cantonese.

'I am well, Little Mistress,' he answered just as gently in English. 'But how are you?'

'I feel as though I've lost a leg; an arm; a heart.'

'It is a bad, dark business.'

'Can you tell me what is going on?'

'I do not know. My people do not know. Yet.'

'My people don't seem to know much either.'

'Give them time. They will learn.'

'They haven't done much so far.'

'Early days. Be patient if you can.'

'It is so hard, Twelvetoes. I have been here less than twenty-four hours and yet I am out of patience with them already.'

'Patience was never a strength with you, Little Mistress. You have chosen well with this advocate, though. He is a good man. Give him time. Let him work. Trust him.'

'Trust him? He came on board against his better judgement simply to protect me. And he's lost me already!' Her voice was mildly scornful.

'You know better than that,' chided Twelvetoes indulgently. 'He is a greyhound, not a bloodhound. There are horses for courses. Trust him.'

Almost the whole of the harbour now stood between them and the far pier. They would be pulling in to Tsimshatsui in a moment. 'Is that all you wanted to tell me?' she asked. 'Trust Balfour?'

'The messenger was also the message,' he said.

'God, I'd forgotten how you love to be cryptic. Is he your son?'

'We are related.'

'And everyone must know.'

'They know what they choose to know and believe what they choose to believe.' He stirred as the ferry slowed, ready to come into its Kowloonside berth. And she knew that now would come the true point of their meeting. 'Would it amuse you to see over *Sulu Queen*?' he asked.

'When? How?'

'The last sailing tonight is at eleven thirty. Be there one hour earlier. This time come alone.' He stepped away from her and she turned, looking down the length of the boat as she pulled into the terminal. His tall form hesitated. 'Wear something dark,' he said almost inaudibly and then moved on.

As Ho reached the foot of the companionway, Andrew came down it at a rush. Their shoulders almost touched, then the lawyer came puffing down the deck obviously relieved to have Robin in plain sight again. He had not even noticed the tall old Oriental in his traditional black clothing with his pink newspaper tucked under his arm. She switched on a dazzling smile and walked up the deck to take his arm. Solicitously listening to his affronted story about importunate American tourists, she led him back up the companionway and off onto the Kowloonside dock. When she was in a position to look for Twelvetoes again, he had vanished, one old Chinese invisible amid the milling crowd streaming up the pier towards the bus station.

'Well, that's that. No mysterious Twelvetoes Ho after all. What do we do now?' he said when they reached the ticket office with no further incident.

She looked up at him, pleased that the adventure with his American tourists had so perfectly disguised her own adventure. So perfectly, it made her wonder... 'If you've got another three dollars, we ride back,' she said. 'If you haven't, then I'm afraid we'll have to swim.'

Chapter Thirteen

There was only a skeleton command at HMS *Tamar* that night because the Prince of Wales, for whom the barracks and the great broad-shouldered building beside it were named, was entertaining the command aboard the Royal Yacht, currently moored off the new base on Stonecutter's Island. The senior service stretched to the normal guard at the entrance, supplemented by two of the colony's shrinking Gurkha contingent, but no guard at all on the good ship *Sulu Queen* moored well out in the roads. It seemed that no one either at Tamar or at police headquarters was worried about the number of people in the harbours close by who might be expected to come aboard her for a little clandestine exploration, for they had even left the accommodation ladder down. This apparent carelessness was less stupid than at first it might have seemed, for it was taken for granted among the authorities that the events on the ship would have given her such a fearsome reputation among the notoriously superstitious Orientals that only the most foolish would dare go aboard.

Only the most foolish – or the most desperate.

It was just approaching 11p.m. when the long prow of Twelvetoes' sampan nudged silently against the metal hull beneath the ladder's bottom step. Robin would have gone up first given half a chance but she was in the waist of the boat beneath the little thatched shelter with Twelvetoes himself and there were two strapping young men crouching in the bow as well as the two oarsmen in the stern with the long oar held between them.

'We go slowly, with dignity,' said Twelvetoes in a voice softer than the flutter of a moth's wing. 'And with flashlights, among other things,' he added drily.

She did not ask about the 'other things', but took a torch when it was offered.

They did not switch the torches on at once. *Sulu Queen* might be unguarded but she was unlikely to be unobserved. They crept up the rocking sampan and clambered up onto the first step. Here they paused until a tiny flash of movement above summoned them onwards and upwards. They could hardly go side by side and so Robin went first and Twelvetoes came up close behind her. One of his men was waiting for them at the top of the ladder. He waved Robin inboard as Twelvetoes came silently up beside her and then he motioned them onwards.

Up on deck here, even beside the high-piled deck cargo, there was more than enough light to see by. The moon was almost full and hung like a lantern above the Peak. The stars were low in the clear sky, and the only thing which kept them from adding many candle-powers of light themselves was the overpowering glow which came from every side, multiplied by the quiet water all around. Such was the brightness that the bridgehouse seemed to glimmer as though it was luminous. Somehow Robin was surprised and vaguely offended that there was no barrier against their entry to the A-deck corridor. Perhaps she had seen too many American police films, but she had expected to find yellow-and-black striped tape with 'POLICE: NO ENTRY' written on it. It was as though the lack of such an injunction was an insult to Richard: were they taking this case as seriously as they ought to do?

Such thoughts were driven out of her mind the instant she entered the bridgehouse itself. It was the smell that did this. Not so much the smell, as the stench. After the cool, stormy Saturday, today had been summer-hot and obviously all the doors and portholes had been left closed, if not locked. The atmosphere in the bridgehouse was so fetid that at first it was difficult to breathe. The darkness itself seemed to wrap round her face and try to suffocate her. She started to cough but choked herself into a wheezing silence and breathed through clenched teeth from then on, trying to let no air onto the sensitive planes behind her nose. Even so, the air in the rooms and corridors seemed to coat the back of her tongue with rancid fat.

As soon as she stopped choking, she switched on her torch and, as though they had been waiting for her with some obscure Oriental gentility, the others switched theirs on too. There were three others now: Twelvetoes and his two young men. Each of them had a torch, and Twelvetoes at least also had a personal radio. One of his array of 'other things', Robin supposed. Like a cast of extras from a kung fu movie, the three black-dressed men and the indigo-attired woman in white training shoes moved off into the shadows. It would have been laughable had it not been for the slaughter-house stench on the air and the absolute seriousness of the situation.

During the next half-hour the four of them unknowingly retraced the steps of Huuk and his men. They found everything that Huuk found except the bodies. The first thing they found was the pizza-like linoleum in the first officer's day room. Speechlessly, they knelt beside the little volcano shapes, frowning until they worked out what they were, then flashing their lights briefly around the rest of the little room and pushing on. The library was next, awash with congealing slime. Then they found the chopped wreckage on the bridge, the crisp trail of congealed blood on the shelf above the helm where the helmsman's severed head had stood.

But no clues. No leads. Nothing at all worth adding to the defence's case; or nothing obvious, at least. It was hard, disgusting work, checking through all the blood-soaked areas with nothing but torches and fingertips and Robin was in a blind fury at so much terrible risk and wasted time, and all of it for nothing, when they arrived up on the bridge. They were there when Twelvetoes' walkie-talkie buzzed.

Standing by the helm, as though he was going to guide the stricken ship to some safe haven himself, he raised it to his ear and answered, '*Wai!*'

The walkie-talkie yammered in an unintelligible jabber of static-bound Cantonese.

But Twelvetoes understood: '*Haih!*'

Again, the overpowering torrent of Chinese words. Robin thought she understood '*Deui mjyuh*' – I'm sorry. But she could have been mistaken.

'*Bin-douh?*' he demanded.

Where? she translated numbly.

The walkie-talkie screamed.

'*Gei yuhn?*' he asked tensely – how far?

Again, the babble. No words made sense to her, but her pulses were beginning to race by now.

'*Gei-do?*' How many?

Again the babble, but this time, this last time, she thought she heard '*Bou ging?*' Report to the police?

'*Mhaih,*' spat Twelvetoes. No!

The walkie-talkie whispered; the channel open and empty.

Twelvetoes turned to Robin, his face a mixture of angular planes and deep shadows. 'There is a launch coming out towards us,' he said calmly. 'It seems to be full of officials of some sort.'

'We'd better get off,' she said.

'No, I'm afraid it is too late for that. The launch will be here in a matter of moments. And there are quite a few people aboard it.'

'What do you think is going on?' asked Robin, although she had already come to a firm conclusion herself.

'I think they are going to move the ship,' answered Twelvetoes.

'That's what I think. That means they have a skeleton crew of trained seamen aboard whatever is coming out.'

Twelvetoes gave a nod of agreement, although there was little that an ex-chief steward was likely to know that a practising ship's captain did not in the matter of skeleton crews and moving freighters.

'They won't move her with less than ten men. They need deck officers and engineers; proper watchkeepers in this lot. And they'll all come out from Tamar, so they'll be Navy men.'

Twelvetoes nodded again, with just the faintest sign of regret, and Robin suddenly realised that he might be planning to make a fight of it.

'Send away the sampan,' she hissed. 'We have to hide.'

He hesitated.

'The bridgehouse is huge,' she insisted. 'And they'll only have a skeleton crew, I'm sure. They'll never even know we're here.'

'But we won't know where the ship is going to!'

'They can't be moving her far. Just to somewhere they can tie her up in a dock so the forensic teams can come and go easily, and maybe where they can get the cargo off.'

'Kwai Chung!'

'That's where I'd take her, especially if they have a secure dock there so that they can impound her and hold her safely until the trial. Yes. It has to be. The container terminal at Kwai Chung.'

As though the realisation of a likely destination was a spur to action, they were off at once. They split into two pairs. Ho spat some orders in Cantonese which Robin could not translate but she guessed that the two young men were being directed to remove all traces of their entry here before hiding. All four of them set off at once, the younger two moving quickly and purposefully, she and Ho staying together, with Robin very slightly in the lead.

She was not running aimlessly. She had an idea. It was nothing advanced enough to be called a plan, but it was a combination of suppositions which suggested an outcome which would kill several birds with one stone. She was heading for the first officer's day room. First, she had noted that they had stopped at the craters of expanded linoleum on the floor as though they were some kind of a barrier – and she suspected that anyone else would too. And that was important, because the standard layout of the bridgehouse dictated that, just beyond that psychological barrier, the room went into an L shape which was not obvious from the door. At the foot of that L shape, invisible unless you came right into the room and looked round the corner, would be the first officer's work area. If they could get there, she estimated, they might well find something worthwhile.

In order to move the ship, the skeleton crew would have to start up the alternators. The alternators would restore light and power. Light would allow them to search the first officer's desk. Power might do even more, for Robin had noticed that *Sulu Queen* was well supplied with computer equipment, not just on the bridge but dotted all around the bridgehouse. It would be strange, therefore, if the first officer did not have a computer in his work area. With a computer and a little luck, Robin could access almost all the ship's records, for the first officer was the lading officer and would hold detailed records of the cargo; he was the ship's medical officer and would hold medical files on all the crew. If they were very lucky, the computers were in a network and the network would hold all the ship's information including restricted access logs and records; perhaps even the captain's private logs. And if the codewords were company standard and current, then Robin knew them all.

With light and power, a computer terminal and a little time, Robin reckoned she could find out everything there was to know about the last cruise of the stricken *Sulu Queen*.

They arrived at the door to the first officer's day room at a flat run, all too aware of the sounds one deck below made by men coming up the weather deck and preparing to enter the bridgehouse. The voices were speaking English so individual words and phrases could be distinguished without too much trouble and complete conversations were audible as the skeleton crew came into the A-deck corridor and split into watchkeepers and engineers. The watchkeepers came up the companionways towards the bridge, some of them actually going past the door into the day room unaware that it had closed silently just the instant before it came into their view.

They were complaining bitterly about the hour, the duty and especially about the smell. It was by no means only those who spoke with Chinese accents who were worried about ghosts and curses. But it was a pair of Chinese-accented voices that complained most poignantly – the others were the ship handlers, these two were the permanent watch.

Among the rising and falling of the English voices came two Chinese words which gave the secret listeners cause to smile with relief: Kwai Chung. When she was powered up and under way, the ship would be going to the container port, just as they had predicted.

Using their flashlights with care, the pair of them crept round the corner into the first officer's work area. It was bigger than might have at first been supposed. As well as a table laden with a computer and a printer, a number of books, files and folders, there was a comfortable sofa, a drinks fridge and a bookcase with family photographs on the top of it. Above the bookcase, all along the wall itself, were more bookshelves, piled with a higgledy-piggledy range of things. There was nothing else to do until the lights came on so they sat side by side on the sofa, switched off their flashlights and waited.

They did not have to wait long.

It was the sound which came first, a distant, apparently subterranean rumbling. The sound translated itself into a vibration which gave birth to a series of little whisperings all around them as things which had sat still for so long began to stir to the rhythmic pulse. 'Not long now,' whispered Robin.

The air-conditioning coughed into action and draughts like ghosts crept over them, adding to the stirring and whispering, rumbling and fluttering. Then the lights blinked on and dazzled them for a moment or two. Finally, over all the restless noise around them, came a crackle and a hum as the computer sprang to life. Robin was half out of the seat heading across towards it when the tannoy system barked, 'All hands to position please. All hands,' and nearly gave her a heart attack.

She pulled out the chair and sat, her hands poised over the keyboard and her eyes on the screen.

Looking for an operating system, it said. So much for the network, then, she thought. Unless the network crashed when the power went off. Which was quite likely if, like this machine, it had been switched on at the time.

'All right,' she said, talking to the terminal as though it were alive and conversing with her. 'Let's get your operating system.'

There were two disk-drive ports labelled A and B, for little 3.25-inch disks. The left port, A, was empty, but there was a disk in port B. It was in there, but it was not engaged. She pulled it out and looked at its label. 'Bingo,' she told the machine. She put the disk back in port B and pushed it until it clicked. There was a whirring noise and the machine took over.

Loading ... it said, and then the screen went blank for a second before lighting up again, displaying a series of boxes.

'Good girl,' purred Robin. 'Now, let's get down to business.' She hit the keys needed to open some text files. The word-processing function came up. But there were no text files on the disk. Leaving it on WP, she popped the first disk out and reached across with the merest glance for the next one.

'Let's start with the cargo,' she suggested to the machine as she slid the disk into the port and hit the keys.

CREW said the screen.

'Hello,' said Robin, quietly to herself. She popped the disk out and reached for the next. '*This* one should be Crew ...' She pushed it in as she spoke. The machine whirred.

STORES said the screen. Robin reached out automatically, still lost in thought, but then she hesitated and sat back. 'Twelvetoes,' she whispered, 'take a look at this.'

The desk was not that of a tidy man, yet everything seemed to have its place. Robin's experienced eyes swept over the piles of books and papers, noting the dead officer's simple system. It seemed to her to be the desk of an untidy man imposing on himself rigid rules about organisation. Or, more likely, an extremely busy man too often run off his feet for fetishistic neatness who nevertheless needed to know where to put his hands on things at a moment's notice. Richard's desk was a lot like this, she remembered, her eyes prickling dangerously. 'You see his system?' she asked, her voice husky.

'Yes. It's very consistent.'

'Then why, do you think, does it break down here?'

Between the grey box of the computer and the pile of fat black files labelled *CARGO* was a small fan-file designed to contain computer disks. It was wide, and the little pockets gaped, each labelled in neat English writing. From back to front, the pockets were labelled in the same order as the piles of papers on the desk, clockwise, starting with the machine itself.

But the disks were not in their right places.

'Do you think it's important?' mused Robin.

'It could be. I'll write down where everything is, and then sort them into their right places, see if anything is missing.'

'Good idea. I'll go into the *CREW* file, as I know which one it is.'

She popped the *CREW* disk back into the machine and called up the directory. It came up on the screen as a list of ship's officers and crew, starting with *Captain* and working down step by step to *GP seamen*, then with a special section entitled *SUPERNUMERARIES & PASSENGERS*.

As she did this, the whole ship seemed to lurch and swoop. The sound of the alternators was joined by the much more powerful vibration of the engines. The ship was in motion.

'That was quick,' whispered Robin.

Twelvetoes nodded tensely.

Robin called up *Captain*, and as she did so her heart skipped a beat. What if it should come up with something about Richard after all? But no:

Captain: Walter John *Gough*	DoB: 28-10-1935
Home Address:	
Scrimshaw	NoK: Mrs Phylidda *Gough*
Marine Drive	Rel: Wife
Budleigh Salterton	
Devon	
England	Tel: B/S 712903

NBNB All Professional Correspondence to:
    Miss Anna Leung
    Company Secretary
    China Queens Company Limited
    74 Kandahar Street
    Singapore 0924   Tel: 2210922

NBNB: From 01.04.1996: Heritage Mariner, Heritage House, London.

Passport No: 272734 R (British National)   NAT INS No: AA 319437 A;
DIS. A. No: R 561593;   B.S.I.C. No: BS 371828;

This was all on the first page of the document except for an index of what was contained in succeeding pages (detailed personal description and further family notes; qualifications with dates; company employment history; general employment history; medical history; etc.) and cross-references to the actual papers held in the files of the ship's records, many of which seemed to be on the desk.

Robin saved it back down and sat for a moment, wondering where to go next. There were obviously far too many files here for her to look at now. The small double-density disks would hold about 100,000 words of information and she would need a great deal more time if she was to go through them properly. The fact that Singapore was mentioned was of interest, though. She thought of Richard's card from there, with the beautiful picture of Raffles' white statue.

It was with this thought in mind that she punched up the only other file likely to have information of immediate interest and importance: *SUPERNUMERARIES & PASSENGERS*. She had rather expected a long list of names, although she had no idea how far back the record would go nor what the China Queens Company's policy was with regard to passengers and supernumeraries. Here, however, was the most likely place to find a record of Richard. He had been found aboard, so he must have come aboard. If he came aboard, he must have done so with a purpose, and either as a supernumerary or a passenger. But, frustratingly, there was only one name in the file:

Miss Anna Leung
China Queens Company Limited
74 Kandahar Street
Singapore 0924
Tel: 2210922

Miss Anna Leung, secretary of the China Queens Company, had been aboard twice a year, in March and October, for the four years back that the records stretched.

'There,' said Twelvetoes, his quiet whisper calling her back to herself. 'That's as many as I can find.'

She looked up and his elegant hand was gesturing to the little plastic fanned file. The disks were obviously in the correct places now, but there were several gaps. Slowly, concentrating as hard as she could, certain that this was very important, she slid the file across to the centre of the desk and placed it immediately in front of the space bar on the keyboard so that it obscured the keys marked C, V, B, N and M.

It was at once obvious to her which files were missing: BRIDGE LOG; ENGINE LOG; ACCIDENT LOG. Why the first officer should keep copies of these was a matter for Captain Gough, but there were spaces for them all in the file and there were no disks to fill them.

Even more interestingly, right at the front, even before the space, now duly filled, labelled START-UP, there was an empty space labelled NWK BOOT. 'Let's have a good look around,' she said to Twelvetoes. 'I think there's a network disk somewhere in here and if we can find it, it could get us some more information.'

'Right. In the meantime, do you need any of that?' he gestured to the screen.

'I don't know. We'll take all the disks we find. Dare we risk printing some of this information?'

'Why risk it if you're going to take the disks anyway?'

'Yes, the printer might be noisy, which could be dangerous. Better not, then.'

They began to search the room, hampered by the fact that they did not know whether the tiny disks they were searching for had been hidden, dropped, scattered or removed. 'What I don't quite understand, though,' she said as they searched, 'is why put the disks back? I mean, why were the disks in the file at all, let alone in the wrong order? If the first officer was the last one to use them he would probably have taken them out one by one and put them back in the correct place.'

'So, it wasn't the first officer.'

'Right, but if not him then who? Who would need to look at them, be careful and tidy enough to want to put them away again, but not know where they should go?'

Her question was enough to reduce them both to thoughtful silence as they worked. The feeling that the ship was moving with a purpose now made them want to work faster themselves. The container terminal was no great distance away and they had no real knowledge of the speed of which the ship was capable. The great RB211 engines in the Heritage Mariner nuclear waste transporter *Atropos*, for instance, could bring her up to speed with smarter acceleration than many a speedboat. Now that they were moving, their time might be limited indeed.

'Someone looking at them in the dark?' suggested Twelvetoes after a few minutes. 'That would explain it.'

'Power on but lights out? So they couldn't see where the disks belonged? It's possible, I suppose, and I sure as hell can't think of a better explanation.'

She was still working through the desk as she said these thoughtless words. Her concentration was on the piles of papers and the bundles of files. Her heart had gone out to the beleaguered first officer when she found his desk reminded her of Richard's, and the more she explored it, the more she felt an ache of sympathy with the dead man. The only items on the desk which seemed out of place were the personal things, the photographs of the woman and children – his young wife and daughters, she guessed. There were photographs aplenty on the bookcase beside the desk, but it was as though he was not happy unless he had some one of them in view at all times and so they overflowed onto the desk. The wife looked to be in her mid-twenties and the two little fair-haired girls about six and four. They would never, she guessed morbidly, look as happy again as they did in the photograph on this desk. Betrayed alike by her femininity, her motherhood, her loneliness and her sympathy, she picked up the family portrait from the desk and the disk labelled *ACCIDENTS* fell out of the back where it had been carefully hidden.

And just as this happened, Twelvetoes gave a grunt. 'Here.' He handed her a beautifully-wrapped little parcel slightly larger than a paperback book, covered in Mickey Mouse designs. Her fingers recognised it at once as a video cassette. She flipped over the gift tag, Mickey in a striped blazer and a straw boater. It said in square, boyish writing on the back: 'To: Fiona From: Daddy. Happy 6th Birthday, Darling. June 1st, 1997.'

Frowning, with her heart twisting fit to break, she looked up at Twelvetoes and he pointed to the side, where the paper overlapped. The overlap had been Sellotaped closed but there was space to slide something below the tape, beneath the paper. Something flat and square, the size of a computer disk. Feeling as though she was desecrating something almost holy, Robin prepared to rip the paper wide. But she found she simply could not do it. It would have been too much to destroy the poor child's last-ever present from her father. Instead, she angled the package, patiently and painstakingly widening the seam of the overlap by peeling the Sellotape off Mickey Mouse little by little until at last the disk slid out to land on the table, label side up. *NWK BOOT* said the label.

Slowly, deliberately, almost as pleased to have preserved the one as to have found the other, Robin put the present down and picked up the disk. Without further thought, she removed the *SUPERNUMERARIES & PASSENGERS* disk from port B and slipped in the *NWK BOOT* disk in its place. Nothing happened.

'Oh . . .' she said, with quiet desperation.

She punched the button and pulled the disk out. She checked it but could see nothing wrong with it. She looked up at Twelvetoes but he was continuing to search through the books on the wall. 'Oh well,' she said to herself and put the disk back in. This time in port A.

The screen lit up like a firework display.

'Got it!' she exulted.

Welcome to Sulu Queen's *Network*, it said. *Your Network Manager is the First Officer. If you have any trouble, please see him. PRESS ENTER TO PROCEED.*

Robin pressed ENTER.

The following files are available for general access, it told her. *Please use your F keys to select then press ENTER to proceed.*

She scanned the list. It was low-grade stuff: crew names; crew responsibilities; duty roster; dates of current voyage; useful addresses in the next port of call. Against F10, however, it said *Enter company code to proceed.* She tapped F10.

The screen went blue. A line of dots appeared across the middle. Above it were the words ENTER COMPANY CODE TO PROCEED. The red square of the cursor flashed insistently on the first dot.

'Now,' said Robin, quietly. 'Let's hope the Conrad codes are in place or I'm sunk.'

The lowest current company codeword was JIM. Like all the others it was derived from the title of a book, but not obviously so. The idea was that although there was an obvious pattern for senior executives who knew the central code, the associations between the lower codes remained obscure enough to foil all but an impossibly psychic hacker. The central code was CONRAD – all the codes derived from his books. Next time it might be DICKENS or DOSTOEVSKY – or MELVILLE for that matter, they tried never to be consistent or predictable. She typed in JIM.

The list of F prompts came up again. But this time the files offered were not for general access. Names and addresses of company agents; lists of cargo of particular worth or needing particularly careful handling . . . and again at the bottom F10 *Enter company code to proceed.*

'We haven't much time, I'm afraid,' prompted Twelvetoes.

She tapped in F10, waited and typed in GUARD, the next code up. Then, hardly bothering to scan the screen, she tapped F10 again, waited and typed in LOCK.

'One more to go,' she said, 'then we're in to the most secret files.'

'What sort of information will there be?'

'Could be anything. Anything from all the previous levels of file that is too personal or important to be left open. It could be stuff not recorded anywhere else.' She glanced across at her old friend. 'One of our captains uses the MOST SECRET for the recipes he collects all over the world then takes home for his wife. Sounds stupid, but you should go to their place for dinner!'

She hit the last F10 and when the blue screen came up she typed in CONRAD and sat back, waiting.

The whole screen went red. *MOST SECRET*, it said, *NO ACCESS.* The letters were large and black.

'What is this?' gasped Robin, all her confidence slipping rapidly away. 'This should not be happening. My God!'

The screen went plain red for a second then the letters changed.

EYES ONLY MRS ROBIN MARINER, HERITAGE MARINER LONDON.

'I don't understand! I simply don't understand!'

The screen went plain red again.

'What is going on?'

PLEASE SAVE THIS FILE AND SEND IT DIRECTLY TO MRS MARINER.

'God . . . Oh God . . .'

Robin pressed ESCAPE S.

The screen went blank. Black. Then, in red letters: *ERROR – FILE NOT SAVED.*

'Not on the network disk,' she yelled to herself. 'Put another disk in, you silly woman!'

Twelvetoes whirled away up the little room to stand behind the door, listening. 'Too much noise!' he hissed in warning.

She caught up the nearest disk, the one labelled *ACCIDENTS* and swapped it for the disk in drive A. She hit ESC S again and the screen went blank. The machine hummed and clicked. The screen switched back to blue.

Welcome to Sulu Queen*'s Network*, it said in white lettering across the middle. *Your Network Manager is the First Officer.*

'I think I've got it!' exulted Robin breathlessly. 'I don't know what the secret file is, but I think I've got it.'

'*Ssssshh!*' hissed Twelvetoes. 'Someone coming!' As he spoke, he reached into the fold of his jacket and pulled something out. Robin hardly paid any attention to him. She was too busy pulling the *ACCIDENT* disk out of the computer and looking feverishly around for somewhere to hide it.

Footsteps echoed down the corridor, coming closer. Lent a touch of genius by the pressure, she slid the disk back into the parcel where the *NWK BOOT* disk had been and popped the brightly wrapped little present back where Twelvetoes had discovered it. Then, with the room exactly as they had found it except for the *BOOT* disk lying on the desk beside drive A, she walked towards the door. It was only as she did so that she registered that Twelvetoes, standing immediately behind it, was holding a very large and dangerous-looking Gurkha's panga.

The door handle turned and the tall Oriental tensed. 'It's all right,' called Robin, a little shrilly. 'You've caught me.'

The door swung wide until brought to a halt by Twelvetoes' foot. Immediately inside it stood Robin and she found herself looking out into the cool, calculating eyes of Captain Daniel Huuk. Into his cool eyes and into the cavernous barrel of the black gun he was carrying. Its skeletal butt pressed hard against the shoulder of his bulky bulletproof jacket. His finger on the trigger was pale, almost white, and trembling slightly.

'It was the computer, wasn't it?' she said quietly. 'The network gave me away.'

'What are you doing aboard?'

'Looking for clues. It didn't occur to me until after I put the disk in that all the computer terminals would probably light up at the same time.'

'Are you alone?'

'And it was a bit of a give-away. "The Network Manager is the First Officer."'

'Are you alone?'

'A bit like saying "Here I am, come and get me". What took you so long?'

He looked at her for a moment longer, then lowered the gun fractionally. He took a deep breath, breathing in and out through his nose making the sort of sound an angry parent makes before forgiving a wayward child. He reached up and pulled a walkie-talkie off its Velcro shoulder attachment. He thumbed SEND. 'Captain?'

'Yes?' answered the walkie-talkie.

'All clear down here. It was just a computer glitch.'

'I might have known,' said the walkie-talkie. 'Bloody machines. Carry on, Huuk.'

Huuk put the walkie-talkie back on his shoulder and gestured her out of the room. She came out obediently and closed the door gently behind her like a good girl.

'We'll be docking in Kwai Chung in a few minutes,' he said. 'I'm going to put you in the officers' lounge until then. There is only one other officer aboard, the captain, and it's off limits to everyone else, then I'm going back to check through the first officer's quarters and secure them. I'm working on the assumption that you have brought nothing out of there with you. Am I right?' As soon as he started speaking he was in motion herding her down towards the proposed destination as he talked. She walked just in front of him, picking her way carefully, very aware of the manner in which the brutal-looking gun extended his arm.

When he asked her the question, she paused, looked back and met his gaze. 'I've brought nothing out,' she said earnestly. 'I swear.'

He nodded, then continued to talk quietly as they proceeded. 'You will be safe in the officers' lounge. No one will disturb you and if you are quiet no one else will ever know you came aboard. How did you manage that, by the way?'

'I have friends in low places.'

He grunted, not much amused. They arrived and she opened the door. He let her walk in and loitered for a moment longer in the doorway. 'If you try to hide or escape I will find you and arrest you and take you directly to prison, where you will be held until Commander

Lee decides whether to charge you sometime tomorrow. Then you really will make some friends in low places. Be warned. If you stay here I will arrange to let you go. When we have docked I will be the last off except for the skeleton crew, and I will take you with me. We will be in Lai King by twelve thirty and I will put you on the MTR to Central. You should be back well before the system closes at one.'

'The MTR? Will that be safe at that time of night?'

'You choose a strange time to worry about safety, Mrs Mariner. But you will be quite safe, I assure you. The MTR is not the London Underground.'

Robin could hardly contain herself during the next three-quarters of an hour as she felt the ship pull into dock and tie up, heard the engines slow and stop; heard the main crew come grumbling down the corridor and get off; listened as Huuk gave his orders to the skeleton harbour watch immediately outside the lounge door; then sat watching the slow crawl of her watch's minute hand until he came to get her. With every occasional scurry of footsteps or measured pace of boots outside the door she expected Twelvetoes to appear. Equally nerve-racking was the constant expectation of gunshots. But neither thing happened, and when the door handle turned, she knew in her heart that it was Huuk come to get her as he had promised. And so it was.

There was no secret scurrying, such as there had been when she came aboard. Instead he just took her firmly by the upper arm and led her straight down the corridor to the A-deck door. He pushed the heavy door open with the ghost of a grunt and supported her over the step out onto the deck as though she were a contessa stepping into a gondola. The deck rail was open immediately outside the door and they walked straight across three metres of deck and stepped up onto the gangplank. At the far end of the plank, parked on gleaming cobbles, was a new Honda Accord. He opened the door for her and she slid into the passenger seat. He climbed into the driving seat and pushed the key into the starter.

'Nice car,' she observed.

His long eyes observed her narrowly and she realised that their relationship, such as it was, was one in which everything she said was going to be mistaken, misinterpreted, or misunderstood, almost wilfully. He switched on the engine and hit the lights. The headlights came up and the beams cut across the terminal, revealing great square mountains of containers. He gunned the motor, engaged the gears and they were away.

They paused only briefly at the gate for a word with the security guard who, Robin was sure, did not even realise that she was there. Then it was a little like a replay of last night's fatigue-blurred memories as Huuk's Accord drove her across roads which Andrew's Aston Martin had driven her along, until they reached the MTR station at Lai King. He pulled up on the bright street, busy even at this hour, and ablaze with garish neon signs. 'The MTR is just down there,' he said, pointing.

'I know where it is,' she said, 'but I'm afraid I don't have ten dollars.'

He gave a bark of laughter. 'No, of course you don't,' he said. 'Well, never mind. I got you into this, I'll get you out of it.'

The bitterness with which he said this really made her sit back but when she looked at him she could see nothing but a slightly self-mocking smile.

Her thoughts went far beyond the usual calculating, diplomatic approach to face; she really, genuinely wanted to thank this man. It was an impulse undermined only by the fact of his involvement in the arrest of her husband.

At this point she was not aware of his responsibility for Richard's current state; at no stage so far had anyone informed her that it was Huuk who had shot her husband.

'No, Captain,' she said, her voice ringing with absolute sincerity, 'I got myself into this situation and I'm very, very grateful to you for getting me out of it.' She stopped, embarrassed, and then added, 'What is it Shakespeare says? "I am a spirit of no common note, and I do thank you..."'

'It is kind of you to say this, Captain Mariner, but you do not have to thank me. Here.' He passed to her a crisp $10 note and she took it thankfully. He held onto the end of the note, however, while he pointed out, 'Shakespeare in fact allows Titania to say, "I am a spirit of no common rate. The summer still doth tend upon my state, and I do love thee."' His deep, smooth voice dropped with just a tinge of extra emphasis on '*love* thee'.

Perhaps it was a corrective against her incorrect quotation; she could nor be sure, but she found it unsettling. She pulled the note free. 'I owe you,' she said and reached for the door handle.

Even at this time in the morning, the street was filled with the odour of cooking. The smell brought saliva to her mouth for she had eaten nothing since she had picked at the Chiu Chow lunch she had ordered. And the saliva reminded her of other liquids elsewhere within her; but there was nothing she could do about any of it now. She had to catch the last MTR train or she was walking home. There was no eating allowed on the MTR and there were no toilets down there either.

The concourse was quite busy but she had no real trouble in getting to a ticket machine. She fed in her $10 note and pushed the button marked 'Central'. The ticket came out at once and she took it. The ticket itself was like an extremely thin credit card, complete with black stripe on the back. Even had she never ridden the MTR before, the automatic barriers of the London Underground would have prepared her for the system. She joined the quiet queue for the nearest entrance and shuffled forward with the rest. She fed her ticket into the automatic barrier and walked through when it opened, collecting her ticket as it was spewed out at the other end.

Down on the platform, there was only the briefest of waits before the big silver train pulled in. The doors opened and she climbed in. Luckily there was a space on the long polished steel bench and she got to it first. She half-sat, half-collapsed beside an extremely fat woman – and then all but arrived in her lap as the train pulled away and she found herself sliding helplessly down the seat. She shrugged apologetically and received a long cold stare. Then she settled back and tried to order her thoughts.

She was too tired for logical thought, however, and all that would come was a swirl of images, dominated by Richard's stare as he looked at her with no spark of recognition in his eyes at all. That was really terrifying. That upset all her preconceptions and turned her whole life on its head at a stroke. It was as though she had found him dead after all. It was as though she had found him with a mistress. She had never doubted him before. She had always taken for granted his strength and his love. And now they were not there any more. Or, if they were there, then they were buried somewhere under an experience or a medical condition so terrible or so severe that no one could reach them. But that was what she was here for, to reach into Richard's damaged mind and pull his strength and his love back up into his eyes. Doing that was even more important than establishing his innocence.

It did not occur to her in her depressed state that establishing his innocence might in itself rebuild his memory and reawaken his love. Instead she found herself glumly rehearsing of Hamlet's self-pitying lines, 'The time is out of joint; oh cursed spite that ever I was born to set it right . . .' But *no*, she thought, as Huuk's long, inscrutable eyes leapt disturbingly into her mind; she had quoted more than enough Shakespeare for tonight.

As the train pulled through the stations past the Hongs and Tongs of Kowloon towards Tsimshatsui and the tunnel to Hong Kong Island, the people around her came and went, but greater and greater numbers of them stayed. And the age of the other passengers began to fall, and their gender to become dominated until she found herself not only the one Westerner visible in the carriage, but one of only three women. All the other passengers seemed to vary in age from late teens to late thirties. They were dressed in an assortment of clothes but the majority favoured plain slacks and bright shirts with open collars. One or two of them had long hair dragged back into pony tails but most of them wore a kind of short-back-and-sides which spread rapidly into wide mop-like overhangs of thick, lustrous black hair. One or two of them were fat, with cheerfully rubicund faces, but most of them were lean, angular, intense and slightly predatory. They seemed intensely self-absorbed, but even so they were never still. They sat and fidgeted, with hands and knees jumping, elbows tucked in and long yellow fingers frenetically busy. Fiddling with their tickets, endlessly turning their tickets, rubbing their tickets and flicking their tickets.

It never occurred to her that this was the inevitable result of a total ban on smoking on a network in a city where almost everybody smoked. It did occur to her that almost all crime in Hong Kong was performed by young men aged between their late teens and their late twenties. That almost all of it was related to the vicious Triad gangs who were known for their ruthless brutality, and that the rest of it, with quite an overlap in the middle, was performed by addicts desperate to buy drugs. By the time the train plunged down into the tunnel beneath the harbour, Robin had convinced herself that the nervous ticket-flicking which the MTR board worked so hard to discourage was in fact a kind of code which allowed the young men all around her to plan the robbery and murder they would execute upon her at the earliest opportunity.

By the time the train pulled into Admiralty, Robin had frightened herself so badly that she was seriously considering making a run for it; but she knew that Central was next so she stayed in her seat and tried to make a plan instead. The seat she was in was near the doors. This fact made her decide to try to get out first and make a break for it. If she could keep ahead of them, she calculated, she stood a chance of getting up into the street. In the street she would summon help if she still felt threatened. Even at this time of night, the streets of Central were likely to be busy, and protection should not be too difficult to come by. It wasn't much of a plan but it was better than none. As the train began to slow, she tensed. The minute it rolled into the bright station she was in motion.

She was the first person to the door but it was slow to open and she could feel the weight of people behind her before it parted. More frustratingly, she could see the tide of people from the other coaches begin to thicken and coagulate at the ticket barriers. She half fell out onto the platform and used the stumble in order to give herself a running start. Once she started to run, however, it was much more difficult for her to see things clearly and it became impossible to plan any further. It also became difficult for her to distinguish any sounds other than her breathing and the beating of her heart, but as she began her flight she thought she heard a sharp cry of surprise and the scuffle of running feet at her back. She ran down the platform, along the line of turnstiles, looking for the shortest queue. The furthest had three people waiting and she chose that because there was nowhere else to go. By the time she joined it, there were only two ahead of her. Then there was only one. She danced with impatience, covering her actions in the eyes of the curious by giving a perfect impersonation of someone with a bursting bladder. The scurry of feet closed in behind her just as her turn came. She slid her ticket into the barrier and waited for the barrier to move in an agony of suspense. There was the sound of laboured breathing immediately behind her but she would not look round. She tried to keep her fists from beating against the recalcitrant barrier. But then it moved. She was in motion at once, dancing through, feeling with enormous relief the shutter close behind her. She looked back over her shoulder as she ran to the escalator, just in time to see the man who had been behind her have his ticket returned as the machine calculated that he had paid too little and the barrier remained closed.

Beginning to shake with relief and reaction, she walked briskly across the concourse and began to climb up towards the street. Her plan had worked perfectly after all. She was among the first out; and she was certainly the first – the only – person on this escalator. Taking more time now, she looked back over her shoulder down into the busy concourse. People were oozing through the barriers like trickles of oil. No one was looking at her. No one was following her. There wasn't even any undue ripple of movement among the bodies surging slowly across the concourse towards the empty escalators endlessly uncoiling behind her and beside her. What else did you expect from people coming exhausted off the last train of the night? 'You stupid woman,' she said to herself. 'Scaring yourself for no reason!'

And she stepped up into the street and collided with a tall, solid man. He turned towards her and there was something shockingly familiar about his face. Before she could turn away his hand fastened onto her arm and she felt herself being swung bodily out of the bright crowd. Her breathing stopped as though she had been winded. She opened her mouth to scream but no sound would come. And in any case, the street was empty and the nearest person to her was still not even on the escalator yet. She tugged her arm fiercely, but he did not slacken his grip. Instead he reached into the folds of his jacket. An instantaneous vision filled her mind: Twelvetoes' hand coming out of the fold in his jacket, clutching that massive, deadly panga.

She found that she could scream after all. And she did, at the top of her lungs. No words, just a throat-tearing, terrified animal sound.

He let her go and she staggered back, falling to her knees on the ground. She did not stay there, she scrabbled feverishly onto all fours, hoping to make a sprint start and get away still.

'*Deui mjyuh*,' he said in a guttural gasp. '*Deui mjyuh!*'

Something clattered onto the pavement beside her but she paid it no attention. All her mind was concentrated on the absolute need to get enough grip beneath her feet to run away as fast as she could. She slipped and fell to her knees again, shouting with frustration.

'Missy,' came a gentle voice, a woman's voice, from close beside her. 'Missy, you arright?'

The sounds which a crowd of people might make suddenly swept over her and she realised that she had been joined on the street by all the other people who had been on the train with her. A group of them were standing around her looking down with lively concern. A young woman with masses of long dark curly hair was crouching on one knee beside her. 'Missy?' she repeated anxiously. 'You arright?'

'I,' said Robin, fighting for breath and self-control, 'I slipped.'

'Ah.' The girl nodded wisely. 'You take care.'

Robin pulled herself to her feet and stood, testing her ankle and knee joints. No damage. 'I'm fine,' she said. 'I'm fine really. Thank you. Thank you all.'

She looked around. There, hardly any distance away, was the bright tower of her hotel with 'The Mandarin' in bright neon at its peak. She began to walk down the crowded street towards it, but once again a hand fell upon her sleeve. She jumped and gasped.

But it was only the girl. 'You drop this, Missy,' she said.

'No, I . . .' said Robin automatically.

The girl held it out towards her and the light fell on it.

'No, I . . . Yes. Yes I did. Thank you. Thank you very much indeed.'

And she took it and hugged it to her heaving breast, holding it as tight as tight while she walked back to the safe haven of the Mandarin. It was a package slightly larger than a paperback book, neatly wrapped in paper covered with pictures of Mickey Mouse.

Chapter Fourteen

Giuseppe Borelli was still on duty when Robin rushed into reception a few moments later, and her breathless request to borrow a laptop computer caused nothing more than the raising of an eyebrow. The condition of her clothes and person would have raised rather more than that, however, if she had allowed them to; but she was not to be sidetracked by his obvious concern. She must have a laptop computer immediately. Could he oblige her with one at once?

Of course there was a range of laptop computers available to the Mandarin's guests. Would Captain Mariner perhaps like to avail herself of the twenty-four-hour secretarial service also?

'No, just the laptop,' she said with unaccustomed rudeness, dancing with impatience.

'Of course, Captain,' he capitulated, still frowning with lively concern. 'Do you have a preference?'

'No.' Her tone was a little uncertain as she realised that she might in fact have a preference – for a machine compatible with the disk hidden in the package in her hand. 'But it must take three and a quarter inch microdisks,' she added.

'And what operating system do you prefer?'

'I don't know. Anything IBM compatible...'

'We have quite a range. Most of the hard disks come pre-programed with works or windows. Unless you want the Apple or the Orange – or the Apricot ranges. The program best suited to your requirements depends on what you are trying to access, of course...' Giuseppe paused, his eyebrow still raised slightly, his face now expressing the most innocent enquiry.

Paranoia swept over Robin in a disorientating wave. What did she really know of the charming Italian or of his true intentions? Just because he had a Western face, there was no guarantee that he was honest, trustworthy, uninvolved. She hesitated, her tired mind a whirl, trying to think what to say. She was all too aware that her own expression was changing, losing the open confidentiality which usually characterised it. She began to act – and hoped her performance was convincing. Donning a mask of confusion, she shook her head. 'I really don't know,' she faltered. 'I just want to access some of my notes and things. It's whatever system we use at Heritage Mariner...'

'And that is?'

'I really have no idea.' Not much of a lie there: she really did have no idea.

'A word-processing program then. Not a graphics program or a spreadsheet. I will give you a range of word processing programs and desktop publishing systems on microdisk. Follow the instructions. They will all vary and you will need to pay close attention, as I'm sure you realise. I'm sure one of them will be familiar almost at once and then it will be plain sailing from there on.'

Giuseppe's pious hope was ill-founded, Robin discovered during the next hour or so. The laptop computer he had given her turned out to be an unfamiliar make when she lifted it out of the black zip-top case. She sat it on the table and followed the instructions about how to plug it in. She raised the top and switched the screen on. It offered her a disorientating list of alternative programs and it took her a full fifteen minutes to work out the sequence of commands required to get out of the hard disk and into the mode for drive A. And it was here that her problems really began.

Robin was as computer-literate as the next person. She did not have the deep passionate knowledge that Helen DuFour possessed. Helen's desk was a great moulded plastic complex of processors, modems and databases – almost a supercomputer itself, and intimately linked to the Superhighway. Robin's desk was Victorian, mahogany. But, that said, she used the company's computers confidently and regularly, taking for granted the kind of programmes and systems which had allowed her into the *Sulu Queen*'s network. But, although she could use them, she had no idea how they were set up or how to make them work from scratch. She was a confident, accomplished driver; now she was being asked to build an engine. She soon found that she didn't really know where to start. And Helen was in Moscow, effectively out of reach. Robin could think of no one at home in the office to check with further. And, now that she had lost her trust in Giuseppe Borelli, she found that she was also suspicious of international telephone lines in any case. So she plunged on alone and unadvised.

The disk from the *Sulu Queen*, designed to function as a part of the ship's network, not on its own, contained no program that would allow her access to the information hidden within it. She established that fact first. Then she proceeded doggedly, from bad to worse. Giuseppe had given Robin ten disks which he said contained the most common word processing and DTP programs. All she had to do was find the one which worked on the dead first officer's network and she would gain access to the information on his disk. Each one she loaded and accessed, however, presented her with unfamiliar screen formats and irritatingly complex instructions. The more she concentrated and the harder she tried, the more exhausted she became and the sillier and sillier the mistakes she made.

Time and again, Robin stopped, horrified, as some utterly unexpected result arose out of a carefully-thought-out sequence of actions and instructions, suspecting for terrifying minutes that she had ruined the whole system and wiped the disks clean by accident. It became clear to her at last that only someone who knew more about computers than she did, or someone who knew the name of the word-processing program she was seeking, could help. But the most obvious sources of that knowledge were all, like the first officer and network manager, dead. Too tired to think clearly or to plan further, she owlishly ensured that the disk from the *Sulu Queen* was separate from the other disks Giuseppe had given her and slid it back into the wrapping paper. Then she stood, irresolute, in the middle of her bedroom, prey to another bout of paranoia, wondering where she could hide the precious thing.

Andrew Atherton Balfour's call to arms caught up with Robin in the Landmark at ten thirty the next morning. She had gone there to get some necessities, starting with clothing, but when she actually heard her name being called, she was looking longingly at a display of the latest computers and thinking of the dumb little disk in the birthday present from a dead officer to his daughter who would not be six for another couple of weeks.

Robin had finally surrendered the precious parcel, and the priceless disk she could feel through the paper, to the night porter at 12:25a.m., able to think of nothing else to do with it; and he had placed it immediately in the hotel's safe. Then she had turned forlornly away, exhausted, defeated, starving, but too sleepy to think of anything beyond a relaxing bath and bed. Just one look at her had been enough to disturb the porter and soon after she arrived back in her room a gentle knock on the door alerted her to the fact that the Mandarin's fabled family atmosphere was wrapping her in its gentle arms. Leaving the bath running, she wrapped herself in the fluffy white robe hanging behind the bathroom door and crossed the reception room. 'Yes?'

'It is Lao Sung the night porter here, Captain Mariner. I thought perhaps you would like a cup of tea.'

'Oh, that would be heavenly!' She opened the door and the night porter brought in the tray at once.

'I will bring up some sandwiches in a few moments,' he told her paternally. 'I will leave them immediately outside the door so as not to disturb you again.' He placed the tray gently beside the laptop on the teak table in the middle of the room.

'Thank you, Mr Sung,' she said, although she felt that the words were scarcely adequate.

'Also,' he said, hesitating slightly, 'I observed when we talked just now that your clothing may require a little care. The concierge also expressed some concern upon that point when I took over from him.'

'I fell over,' she said, again, inadequately.

He tutted. 'Would you like the hotel doctor to examine you?' he asked solicitously, pouring the tea.

'No. I am not hurt. Thank you.'

He glanced up at her. 'Milk and sugar? It is Darjeeling tea.'

'I'll do that myself, thank you. And I would love some sandwiches. Meat, please, of any kind.'

He straightened and smiled. 'I had thought beef, with a trace of English mustard on one side and some Burgess's creamed horseradish on the other.'

'Are you psychic, Mr Sung?'

'Concerned, Captain Mariner. I will go now, before your bath overflows. We have a Malaysian prince immediately below you and I know he would not like to be disturbed at this time of night. Your sandwiches will be here within ten minutes.'

Fortunately the sandwiches were covered with damp paper, for it was the better part of an hour before she could bring herself to drag her stiff body out of the scalding bath water. Then, wrapped in the hotel's cotton-wool cloud of towelling robe, steaming gently in the cool air, she snatched the sandwiches in and had a midnight feast sitting in the middle of her bed at the better part of two o'clock in the morning. And the next thing she knew it was 9a.m. on Monday morning.

She found she had to ferret around in her suitcase for something clean to put on, and as she lifted out the underwear, thinking about the hands of the Customs official sorting through the silk and nylon, it became most forcibly borne upon her that it was time to get some proper clothes for herself. Her travelling outfit was still in the hotel's laundry and dry-cleaners so it was only the fact that her outfit from last night had been sponged, pressed and returned by the night staff that allowed her to dress to her own satisfaction.

But as had been demonstrated quite forcefully several times during the last thirty-six hours, there was one item she needed even more urgently than decent clothes: Hong Kong dollars. But even here, the forethought of the staff pre-empted her. As she approached the reception desk on her way out into the bright morning half an hour after waking up, the door into the concierge's office opened and Giuseppe Borelli stepped out, apparently by coincidence. 'Ah, Captain Mariner,' he said, falling in step beside her. 'We could not help but observe that since your arrival yesterday you have not had the opportunity to pick up any local currency. It may be that you have other plans, but we were wondering whether five thousand dollars would meet your immediate needs. Of course it would be added to your account at the current rate of exchange...'

'In actual fact, Giuseppe, it would be an absolute godsend,' she admitted quietly. 'It will save me a lot of time, mean I can skip a visit to the Hong Kong and Shanghai Bank, and allow me a great deal of freedom of action at once. I can't thank you enough. Now, would it be possible for me to have a regular supply of local currency or shall I set up matters with traveller's cheques?'

'Of course we will be happy to supply cash on a regular basis, duly accounted of course, but we might find ourselves hard put to supply large amounts at short notice.'

'I understand. Perhaps if five thousand was held for me on a regular basis until I have a chance to clear things with my bank?'

'Of course. Your cash, Captain.' He reached across the desk and the reception clerk handed him an envelope. 'I trust you will have an enjoyable day.'

Twenty minutes later Andrew's call came through to the Mandarin's switchboard. There was no reply from Robin's suite, and the switchboard operator was just about to ring off with regret when the concierge became involved. When he heard who was calling and who the call was for, Signor Borelli decided to take it himself. 'But no, Mr Balfour, I regret that Captain Mariner seems to have gone . . . shopping, I believe . . . No, I have no idea. She did not mention what time she expected to return . . . An emergency, you say? Well, in that case . . . No do not worry. If it can be done, then rest assured . . . No thanks are necessary, sir, she is a valued client.'

Signor Borelli hung up the phone. 'Now, where will she have gone?' he mused.

'Des Voeux Road?' wondered the receptionist.

'I think not. She has no coat, remember; she is more likely to remain under cover. And in any case, I have not observed her coming back through reception. Have you?'

'No.'

'Then she must have gone through the walkway into Prince's Building. We will start there.'

Robin came out of the Swire Building at ten twenty and crossed Des Voeux Road towards the towering bulk of the Landmark, her mind still miles away and her hands still empty. Somehow, shopping had become a very difficult thing to do. The fact that she had the equivalent of several hundred pounds sterling in cash and a limitless Gold AmEx card on her only seemed to make things more difficult still. There was almost nothing on show which, one way or another, she could not afford. But to purchase anything but the practical necessities seemed to be so petty, so pointless, so self-indulgent, somehow. All she wanted was some plain clothing at a reasonable price which would do her when she got back home to Ashenden.

She came into the Landmark's main concourse and her dull eyes swept over the fountains, the golden trees, the crowded escalators, the balconies and the bazaar of shop fronts. She was surrounded by the calming, expensive sounds of running water, piped music, hushed conversation. Her nostrils twitched with the scent of the fresh flowers round the fountains, almost inundated by the less delicate smells of expensive fragrances and polished leather. She began to walk around here in the same way as she had walked around the Prince's Building, Alexandra House and Swire House. It seemed to her that all she could see were Gucchi, Konrad, Klein, Courreges, St Laurent, Armani, Issey Miyake, Nina Ricci and Chanel.

'Haven't these people ever heard of Marks and Spencer's?' she asked herself, and then she saw the computer display and crossed to it, all thoughts wiped out of her mind other than the urgent speculation as to how she was going to find out what was on that disk without running the risk of letting someone else into the secret – or of wiping the secret message out altogether. Was it another computer she needed, she wondered, or a computer expert? Who would know the name of that elusive program? If there was no one from the *Sulu Queen* any more, then surely someone aboard her sister *Seram Queen* – or someone at the China Queens office. What was the name of that woman? Anna Leung. Yes! Either company secretary Anna Leung or *Seram Queen*'s first officer. Hope welled within her. All she needed was a phone...

'Captain Robin Mariner,' said a gentle, cultured voice in soft yet piercing tones. 'Will Captain Robin Mariner please report to the information desk in the foyer?'

On the second repetition she realised the announcement was for her and, frowning, crossed to the desk. 'I am Robin Mariner. You have a message for me?'

'You are Captain Mariner?' The receptionist's eyebrows rose slightly. No doubt she had been expecting a more masculine figure. Perhaps someone in more fashionable clothing.

'That's right. Captain Robin Mariner. You have a message for me?'

Had it been a matter of parting with anything other than information, Robin felt, she would probably have been required to present identification. As it was, the receptionist gave her a brittle smile and said, 'Will you please contact reception at the Mandarin Hotel? Apparently there is an urgent message.'

She did so at once and the switchboard told her to call Andrew Balfour at his office.

All thought of calling Anna Leung or the *Seram Queen* was driven from her mind for the time being. 'Andrew? It's Robin. What?'

'Robin. Thank goodness we found you. Can you be at the Magistrate's Court building at one o'clock? At reception, just inside the main entrance?'

'Of course. What's going on?'

'Apparently they're going to traduce him then. Listen.'

'Yes?'

'We've retained a local silk who will stand up for us for the time being. He's very good. And, look . . .'

'Yes?' she was concerned by his hesitation. There was something he did not dare to say to her, and it sounded like something bad. Had Twelvetoes Ho or Daniel Huuk let something slip about last night's adventures? Was it something about Richard? 'Stop beating about the bush, Andrew. What is it?'

'Well, it's your clothes. I mean the magistrate's court is hardly high fashion, but you simply cannot be wearing trousers and—'

'Listen, *buster*, if you had any idea of the trouble I'm having finding *anything* to wear . . .'

'Sorry, sorry.'

'Do you know of a decent shop where I can get an off the peg suit or twin-set which wasn't made for an anorexic schoolgirl closely related to the Sultan of Oman?'

'Ah. Right. Um, I'll just ask Gerry. He might know where Dottie gets her . . .' he stopped dead, realising that Robin might want to pitch herself somewhere between a teenage millionaire fashion victim and Dottie Stephenson.

But after a certain amount of bellowing back and forth across the office, he came back uncertainly, defensively, with, 'Look, is Jaeger any good? Gerry says it's where Dottie sometimes—'

'Jaeger? You wonderful man, you know where there's a Jaeger?'

'Yes. It's in the Landmark, actually, Gerry says. Now where are you?'

But she had hung up already and was turning to the supercilious young woman at the information desk.

By one o'clock, it was impossible to guess that the calm, collected, perfectly turned-out Englishwoman in her Jaeger suit, silk blouse (she had found a Laura Ashley in the Prince's Building on the way back) and Bally shoes entering the magistrate's court was breathless with trepidation. True the clothes made her feel more confident, but the vertiginous suspicion that everything was going to slide downhill very fast indeed from this point was overpowering.

It was the stark reality of her situation which was doing it. Whatever she did, whatever little task she set herself to complete, whatever little obstacle she overcame, once in every couple of minutes she would look up mentally and there would be the terrifying enormity of her true situation standing like a giant before her. Richard, *her* Richard, was effectively in jail now. He was going to stay in jail and nothing she could do would get him out. She doubted whether there was even anything she could do to ease his situation. He would remain beyond her help, beyond her love, physically as well as mentally, for months at least, and there was nothing in the world which could alter that. Until he came to trial. Then what? What then indeed?

And, in the meantime, what could she tell the twins? The family? Their friends? Their business associates? The world?

Oh God in heaven, what was she going to do?

With these thoughts clamouring in her mind, Robin glided into the magistrate's court building, turning heads unconsciously as she went, like a model just stepped out of the London edition of *Vogue*.

Andrew was waiting for her inside the main entrance and he swept her along as soon as he saw her; and, after all the fuss he had made, he didn't even bother to mention her clothes. 'Right. Welcome. Perfectly timed. We're just down here. Richard's up before Stipendiary Magistrate Morgan. I don't know anything else at this stage. The police will be applying to have Richard remanded in custody until they can complete their case. Then of course they'll be looking for a transfer to the High Court. The Crown Prosecution Service, the Lord Chancellor and the Lord Chief Justice don't work here quite in the way that they do in Great Britain; Mr Morgan will rule on whether there's a case to answer and we'll go from there. If there is, then the prosecution will have to present it to him *prima facie* within eight days, he'll decide on the transfer and that's when we can really go to work. I know I've told you this before but I don't want you to have any unpleasant surprises . . .'

It was such an ordinary door; Robin couldn't get over how ordinary it was. Just a plain, painted door such as might lead into any kind of a room, even a little room. It opened with just the hint of a creak and she walked in behind Andrew into the courtroom itself. It was a small, slightly shabby room, very different from the High Court setting Robin had expected.

As Robin looked for a seat, her open, clear-skinned face folded into a frown. The court was crowded. There was very little space indeed for Andrew and her to sit in. The front few rows were unoccupied, but it was clear that these were for court officials of one kind or another. Behind that the rows were increasingly packed. She looked at Andrew, her face a picture of wonder. He shrugged. She looked back up at the people sitting in the court. She did not recognise one face. They were all strangers to her. But it seemed from the increased buzz of speculation which built up as she stood there that some of them at least recognised her. She stood, riven by the horror of her unexpected situation, until a young man took her by the sleeve and pulled her into a seat he had obviously been saving for her. Andrew sat immediately in front of her.

'Andrew,' she said, leaning forward. 'What are all these people doing here?'

'Word must have got out,' he said sheepishly. 'We'll apply to have the court cleared as soon as . . .'

'What?'

'I don't know. Robin, I have to tell you I've never been in a position like this before. I can't guarantee what is going to happen, I'm afraid.'

'*Now* you tell me.'

'No! I mean that we can't find a case like this in any of our Hong Kong records. Of course we're going through English case law as well, but I'm not sure that we've even been legally retained. Only Mr Morgan will be able to tell us that, and I think he'll be ruling on it himself.'

His words were cut short by the arrival of a slim man in a dark suit. 'Well Andrew,' he said. 'You didn't tell me it was going to be a circus!'

'I didn't know. Can we have the court cleared?'

'We can ask. If the magistrate will speak to us.'

'This is Captain Robin Mariner,' said Andrew. 'Captain Mariner, Edward Thong, your counsel. We hope.'

'I know he's *my* counsel,' snapped Robin. 'I thought our problem was whether he is Richard's counsel!'

'I say,' said Edward Thong with a mixture of surprise and approval, 'that was very well put.' He reached out a long, slim hand and his angular face broke into a dazzling smile.

'All rise,' came a voice from the front. 'All rise.'

The magistrate, Mr Morgan, was a tall, angular man and there was nothing soft or self-indulgent about him. He bustled in apparently preoccupied with bitter personal reflections and sat as though he had noticed none of the other people there. But he had. 'The prisoner is not here,' he observed and his voice was full of disapproval.

Commander Victor Lee stood up. 'The prisoner will be here in an instant, sir. There was a last-minute hitch, an unforeseen circumstance. We could find no clothes to fit him.'

'I beg your pardon?' snapped Morgan. 'No clothes?'

'At the time of his apprehension, sir, he was wearing a ship's overall which has subsequently been retained for forensic analysis. It was heavily bloodstained. Since he was formally charged, he has been a patient in the Queen Elizabeth Hospital where he has been wearing a hospital gown. It was not until . . .'

Lee's voice droned pompously on. Robin rocked back, paying no further attention to it, very near breaking point. She had spent this morning making sure that she was properly attired and had not spared even one thought for her poor Richard.

How dare they! How dare they take even the clothes from his back! She burned with outrage and hatred of the unfeeling system which could have done this to Richard. Wisely under the circumstances she turned the guilt she felt at her own oversight into rage against the system. It kept her going. It turned maudlin self-pity into fierce fighting spirit; and Richard needed one much more than he needed the other.

Chapter Fifteen

The sole survivor of the *Sulu Queen* walked briskly along the underground passageway between the two uniformed guards, wondering vaguely whether he should be more concerned than he was. He understood what was happening to him in much the same way as he remembered the last few days, as though this was some kind of dream. But the last few days were all he could remember still, so he had no real yardstick against which to measure his current confusion. He was suspicious that more was going on than he clearly understood, that perhaps more had actually happened than he clearly remembered. It was very disorientating. But it was not really real.

Far more real, overpoweringly so at times, was the immediacy of simple sensation. He could smell the cologne worn by the guard on his left and the fact that the other guard would have benefited from wearing it as well. The echoing of the tintinnabulating footsteps seemed to redouble once the sound got inside his head. He could taste, on the air washing through his nose and mouth, the dusty brick, the thick, oily paint; the sharp, citrine steel all around.

But it was what the survivor could *feel* that was almost too much to bear. The throbbing in his temple and at the back of his head as the unaccustomed effort of walking drove blood through damaged tissue. The itching of the bandage maddeningly tight round his head. The feeling that his skull was going to explode because of the constriction of the shirt collar round his neck. The tightness of the shirt round the bruised barrel of his chest compounded by the equal tightness of the jacket which pulled across his shoulders like a strait-jacket and cut into his armpits almost as painfully as the too-tight trousers cut into his crotch. But the discomfort there was as nothing compared to the agony of size twelve feet in size ten-and-a-half shoes.

It was ironic, really, when you considered that his favourite and most comfortable suit had been made for him by Kiam Sin down on Des Voeux Road.

The memory popped into his head and was gone again in a flash, so swiftly that he hardly registered it but he was still frowning with the disquiet it engendered when they arrived at the door which gave onto the magistrate's court itself. The underground passageway became a corridor in a building and the overpowering wave of sensation varied in its content but not in its impact.

His face was bland but closed as he came at last into the shabby courtroom. He followed the guards down to the dock and stood there, concentrating on the sensations of light and sound from the windows and the crowd. The metal edge of the dock itself was warm and almost oily beneath his hands. The black hairs on the back of his hands stirred as the skin tensed and relaxed, reacting to the change in atmosphere. Words echoed around him and he looked up, trying to sort them out of the background noise into some kind of sense and relevance.

Almost by chance, his gaze fell upon a golden-haired woman in French blue twin-set and pearls. Recognition hit him like a thunderbolt. He knew her! He strained with superhuman effort to follow that golden thread of recognition back into the jumbled maze of his memory. If he could just recall, he knew, one series of memories in which this lovely woman had featured in the lost days before he awoke in the hospital, then everything would click back into place.

But no. All he could remember was the look on her face when he had come into the little reception room in the Queen Elizabeth Hospital and found her there yesterday afternoon. And, on the same shallow level, he recognised the big, square, red-headed man at her side. His attention began to wander again and he looked around the courtroom wondering why there were so many people here. Wondering who they all were. Wondering who the beautiful blonde woman in the twin-set and pearls with the red-headed rugby player by her side actually was.

Robin sat, numbed, watching the recognition die in the eyes of the man she loved. And yet this was not the man she loved at all. This was his shell, perhaps, but it was not *him*. She watched his attention wander and become subsumed into near vacancy, and for the first time she began to wonder if his brain had been damaged permanently. She found it hard to breathe suddenly; the room began to waver. Had she not been sitting, she would undoubtedly have fallen. Her hands and feet went numb and icy cold. A humming filled her head and it required the greatest effort of will not to slip away into the darkness just beyond her dazzled vision. Even so, she found herself leaning on Andrew's broad shoulder, very close to fainting dead away. But the buzzing in her ears was more than her incipient faintness; the whole court was astir with speculation, which faded into silence as the magistrate asked around, his face set in lines of almost dyspeptic disapproval. 'As this case seems to have aroused a great deal of speculation already,' began the magistrate in a voice as thin as his hair, 'I should remind all those present, especially anyone representing a newspaper, that I have no intention of lifting standard reporting restrictions on this case. The name and residence of the accused, and the crime of which he stands accused, are the limits of what may be reported at this stage – if, indeed, we proceed to an indictment. Mr Po, I see you are learned counsel for the prosecution. Can we please establish who the defendant is and of what he stands accused?'

A slight, almost boyish figure stood up. So slight and boyish was Po Sun Kam, in fact, that he had been all but invisible up to this point, his meagre frame obscured by the bulk of Commander Lee. 'Sir,' he began in a quiet voice which nevertheless carried to the furthest reaches of the silent court. The accused is Captain Richard Mariner of Ashenden, South Dean, East Sussex in England and he stands accused of the murders of Charles Macallan, chief engineer of the motor vessel *Sulu Queen* and also of Brian Jordan, first officer of the *Sulu Queen*.' He paused for a heartbeat, then proceeded. I should inform you, sir, that these stand as specimen charges at this time. It is the Crown's intention to prove that on or about midnight on the night of Thursday 8th May of this year, 1997, Captain Mariner, either alone or in confederacy with a person or persons unknown, wilfully and with malice aforethought murdered all the officers and crew of the motor vessel *Sulu Queen*.'

'The Crown expects to proceed on specimen charges of murder against Captain Mariner. The Crown has proceeded with only two specimen charges at this time because of the understandable difficulty of formally identifying forty deceased persons dressed in night attire, none of whom were carrying any form of identification. But I am assured that the ship's records and company records will allow the Crown to check passports, fingerprints and dental records against the deceased persons in question, many of whom seem to have been either shot or chopped to pieces.'

Stipendiary Magistrate Morgan once again quelled a buzz of speculation with a cold stare. 'If there is any further disturbance, I shall order the court to be cleared,' he warned, his voice a nasal, sheering drawl. 'One step at a time, please, Mr Po. Has the accused admitted his identity?'

'In the presence of Commander Lee and of another naval officer, as well as of Dr Chu of the Queen Elizabeth Hospital, the accused admitted that a photograph of Richard Mariner was in fact a photograph of himself at the time of his formal arrest at the Queen Elizabeth Hospital at thirty minutes past four on the morning of Saturday 10th May.'

The reply was so guarded that, had he not already been aware of the unusual circumstances surrounding the case, Mr Morgan must have grown suspicious now. He swung round and looked steadfastly at the prisoner. 'Captain Mariner,' he said more urgently. The accused's wandering gaze slowly focused on the magistrate and even then it was by no means certain that the tall man in the over-tight suit was actually paying attention. 'Captain Mariner,' said Mr Morgan again, 'do you formally admit that you are the Richard Mariner referred to in the charge?'

The accused frowned, clearly fighting to follow the legalistic wording.

'Are you Captain Richard Mariner of Ashenden, South Dean, East Sussex?'

'Oh yes. That's me. Mariner. Ashenden.'

The magistrate hesitated, obviously calculating whether this child-like affirmation, such as might have been elicited from a well-tutored three-year-old, constituted a formal admission of identity.

'Captain Richard Mariner,' said the accused again, with more force and certainty. 'Yes. That's me all right.'

The magistrate nodded. 'And do you understand the nature of the charges against you?'

'Yes. They say I killed Chas Macallan and Brian Jordan. They say I killed them all. Everyone on the *Sulu Queen*.'

'I see, Captain Mariner. And how have you replied to this accusation?'

'Sir.' Learned counsel for the Crown was trying with some energy to attract the magistrate's attention.

'I know, Mr Po. This is thin ice. I shall skate with the utmost care and I will avoid any possibility of dismissal at a later date through incorrect procedure now. Now, Captain. How did you reply when you were arrested by Commander Lee?'

'I don't remember.'

'You do not remember how you answered the accusation Commander Lee put to you?'

'I remember that. I said that I don't remember whether I did what they say or not. I don't remember anything before I woke up in hospital last Saturday morning.' He looked around the court with a slight frown, like a man uncertain whether or not he was behaving properly in a strange situation. Like a guest not sure which knife to use at dinner with the Queen.

Robin's heart twisted in her breast so poignantly that for a terrible moment she thought it was going to break. Tears started onto her cheeks. She wished with all her being that she could run across the dusty, stuffy little room and fold him in her arms and comfort him. It was a feeling familiar to her, but she had only ever felt such an intense sensation when preparing to fly to the protection of her babies. She had never before seen Richard in this light and it came as a disturbing shock to her that the husband whose intellect, leadership, decisiveness and strength she had always idolised should be reduced to this child-like state. At once, and not for the first time, she wondered with something close to terror whether she herself had the strength and resolution to set things right. And this time there was no cosy distancing from the reality of things through an apt Shakespearian quotation. When she breathed in, the shuddering sound she made was so striking that the magistrate looked narrowly at her. His face set in lines of absolute disapproval, thin lips turned down.

'Captain Mariner,' said Mr Morgan after a moment's hesitation, 'please let me be clear about this. You say you have no recollection whatsoever of anything that happened to you before you woke up last Saturday morning in the Queen Elizabeth Hospital?'

'Yes. That's right.'

'I make no comment as to the common nature of pleas of amnesia such as yours in cases involving extremes of violence, but I would like to be absolutely certain in my own mind. You say you have no recollection whatsoever of the events which occurred on the *Sulu Queen* during, let us say, the forty-eight hours before midnight on Thursday, 8th of May?'

'That's right. I don't remember anything.'

'Of course this must be entered as a plea of not guilty. You are aware of this fact, Mr Po?'

'Indeed, Sir, the Crown is fully aware—'

'And, while admitting again the thinness of ice beneath me, I must observe that unless you can find a way round absolute amnesia, you may find it difficult to establish the full *actus non facit reum nisi mens sit rea.*'

'The Crown is confident, sir. We can produce *prima facie* evidence in a matter of days.'

'I see, Mr Po.' Stipendiary Magistrate Morgan's watery blue eyes stared apparently casually over the assembled onlookers, dwelling, perhaps, on the familiar faces of one or two well-known reporters. 'I rule that the accused, Captain Richard Mariner, be detained at the Siu Lam Psychiatric Centre for a time not exceeding eight days while the Crown prepares its case.'

'Sir?'

'Commander Lee?'

'The . . . ah . . . Crown requests, sir, that the prisoner be remanded to the secure rooms in the Queen Elizabeth Hospital where he has been held so far.'

'Very well, Commander. The court assumes that the charges at the Queen Elizabeth will be no more expensive than those at the Siu Lam facility, either for holding the accused or for his treatment.'

'That is the case, My Lord.'

'Very well. Take him down.' Morgan's long pale fingers flashed to his thin lips, and then away again.

'Excuse me, sir,' Even as Robin's lips parted to protest the casual order, so her barrister was on his feet and addressing the magistrate. All movement, all sound, ceased.

'Mr Thong?' purred Morgan, this time speaking round the slight obstacle of a cough sweet. 'You represent Captain Mariner, I assume?'

'Quite so, sir.' The barrister paused and rearranged the papers before him a little fussily. 'I have been retained to act in this case though I understand that when the matter comes to trial I might not actually lead—'

'You intrigue me, Mr Thong. I must ask how a defendant with no memory nevertheless has the presence of mind to acquire the services of learned counsel.'

'I have been briefed, My Lord, by the accused's wife and company.'

'His wife, Mr Thong?'

'Indeed, My Lord. In that the Crown has been so assiduous in establishing the identity of the accused, they have, by definition, also proved his antecedents and relations.'

'A good point. And so?'

'So, My Lord, I stand before you on behalf of Captain Mariner's wife and company to request—'

'Not bail, Mr Thong. Not bail in the matter of the mass murder of some forty unfortunate souls, surely.'

'No, My Lord. Access. My clients request access to the accused, whether in Siu Lam or in the Queen Elizabeth Hospital. Access for themselves and for such officers as they might appoint.'

'Officers, Mr Thong? That is a matter for the authorities.'

'We have in mind, My Lord, the accused's defence and such medical experts as that defence shall call, My Lord.'

'Early days, Mr Thong. Surely this application would be better made in eight days' time?'

'Even so, My Lord, we are anxious to establish right of access, even under these highly unusual circumstances. It may be, for instance, that in eight days' time my clients will wish to see Captain Mariner coming to court wearing clothes that actually fit him, My Lord.'

'Point taken, as I believe the Americans say, Mr Thong, point taken. Very well. I so rule. The court recognises you as Captain Mariner's defence and accords you the usual rights of access. Now, is there anything more?'

The barrister glanced down at the solicitor and launched into a speech which was obviously carefully prepared – the first part of a carefully prepared plan. 'Sir, the crown has admitted that they can provide a *prima facie* case in a week. We waive all formal time limits, therefore, and apply to proceed to transfer as soon as possible. We would agree to a formal transfer to the Crown's specimen charges, in seven days, if that is agreeable to you, sir.'

It was nearing four o'clock in the afternoon by the time Robin reached the Heritage Mariner office in Jardine House. She was, she discovered, too late to make the acquaintance of Mr Feng the manager who normally returned to the bosom of his family soon after 3.30p.m. She didn't, for the moment, care. All she wanted was Mr Shaw, his telephone and some contact numbers for Anna Leung at the China Queens office in Singapore or, failing that, for the *Seram Queen* wherever she was beyond the island of Taiwan in the western reaches of the China Sea. Having seen Richard again and having agreed plans to gain access to him and to ease his plight as soon as possible, she was full of decisive energy and certain in her heart of hearts that today was a good day when nothing was likely to go wrong.

Such was her fierce good humour that she was not cast down teo discover that Miss Leung apparently kept the sort of hours favoured by Mr Feng. There was no answer from the China Queens office in Singapore. 'Right, Mr Shaw,' she said, hanging up on the dreary, unanswered ringing tone, 'please give me the number I need in order to contact the *Seram Queen*. No, wait. Have you a copy of the current crew list? I'd like to have an idea of the names at least of the men I'm going to talk to.'

Mr Shaw obliged with a flimsy fax which proved that the two offices did occasionally contact each other, in spite of the working habits of the people controlling them. Robin took the ill-printed paper and pored over it with some interest. But it was simply a list of names and titles. No one aboard was familiar. She frowned, all too aware of the dereliction this realisation revealed. Heritage Mariner owned this vessel. She was a director of Heritage Mariner, a company which prided itself on the family atmosphere it fostered. She should at least have recognised the names. Still, she shrugged, she had enough to worry about without getting sidetracked now. She began to punch in the numbers which would put her through to the radio room aboard the distant ship. Why worry about the crew of a vessel she had never been aboard? When was the last time she had given any serious thought to the wellbeing of her children? She should be calling Cold Fell, not *Seram Queen*! What sort of a mother was she, for crying out loud?

The unbidden thought brought an unexpectedly constricting lump to her throat, so that when the voice came on the line without even the simple introduction of a ringing tone, she found it impossible to answer.

'Hello? *Seram Queen*. Who is calling, please? I say again, this is *Seram Queen*. Who is calling please?'

'Ah ... This is Captain Mariner, calling from the Heritage Mariner office in Hong Kong. Could I speak to the first officer please?'

There was a pause; the line went absolutely silent. There was not even the faintest whisper of contact. Then, 'Say again please. This is *Seram Queen*. Who is calling, please?'

'This is Captain Robin Mariner, calling from the Heritage Mariner office in Hong Kong. Can I talk to the first officer?' There was something of a whiplash in the tone of her voice.

The line died once again. She looked across at John Shaw who was courteously observing the view rather than her discomfiture. Then the distant voice came back again. 'Can I just check that please, caller? Could you hand the phone to Mr Feng the manager for confirmation?'

'Mr Feng has gone home for the day. I can hand you over to Mr Shaw for authentification or I can give you the current company codeword.'

The line died again and she realised the person at the other end was pressing the SECRET button and asking for advice. She frowned. She did not like being treated like this. 'Could you please hand the phone to Mr Shaw for confirmation. I say again...'

'Mr Shaw!' There was still enough of a snap in her voice to jerk his head round as though he had been slapped. She saw resentment in his dark eyes and, had she had the leisure, she would have regretted it. Instead she thrust the handset at him. 'Please confirm my identity to the *Seram Queen*.'

John Shaw took the handset and turned away from her slightly so that his shoulder concealed the lower part of his face. '*Wait?*' After that the conversation became impenetrable to her. So much so that she did not even recognise his no doubt courteous farewells and it came as a surprise to her when he handed the phone back with a smile. 'Thank you, Mr Shaw,' she said and took the instrument. 'Hello? *Seram Queen?*'

'Hello, Captain Mariner? So sorry, this is Radio Officer Yuk Tso. How may I serve?'

'I would like to speak to the first officer, please. First Officer...' She consulted the flimsy fax with frowning concentration, a grim devil at the back of her mind observing that her memory was little better than Richard's. 'First Officer Lau. Chin Lau. He is network manager as well as first officer, is he not?'

'Yes, Captain, but no, Captain, I regret——.'

'I beg your pardon?'

'Captain...' There was a sound at the far end of the line and a new voice replaced Yuk Tso's. A harsh, impatient voice which made Robin's hackles rise even at this distance. 'Yes? This is Captain Man-wei Sin. Who is this? What do you want?'

'I am Captain Robin Mariner. I am a director of Heritage Mariner, the company which owns your ship, and I wish to speak to First Officer Lau at once!'

'Chin Lau is sick. Malaria. Bad fever. He may die, I don't know. He cannot speak to you. I will help. What do you wish to know?'

'All I want to know...' She took a deep breath and looked to the ceiling as though it could lend her patience and tact. 'All I want to know is the name of the wordprocessing program on the *Seram Queen*'s computer network.'

There was a stunned silence followed by a bark of derisive laughter. 'You expect that I can tell you *that*? Captain Mariner, you are a very foolish—'

'Captain Sin! If you can't, then perhaps Radio Officer Yuk Tso will...'

But the line was dead.

And, when she dialled again, engaged. She stayed in the office until after six o'clock, going through all the records she could find, looking for the information she so urgently required, but every time she called Singapore there was no reply and every time she called the *Seram Queen* the phone was off the hook. Which was quite a trick, she thought bitterly; it meant closing the whole radio room down.

Chapter Sixteen

At five thirty, Robin managed to get Andrew lingering late at his office and she asked him about the best way to get some decent food and comfortable clothing to her husband. Andrew agreed to check about access for such things but warned her that he was unlikely to get permission to send anything in tonight. She nodded, as though he could see the action at the far end of the line, and hung up. It was then that she decided she would go shopping tonight so that she could at least have pyjamas and slippers in his size ready to send in in the morning. Just after six, Andrew called back to say that he had been referred to Commander Lee and had invoked PACE. They would have access in the morning. What was she going to do tonight? Andrew enquired.

Go shopping, she replied.

He broke the line, satisfied, thinking of her returning to the secure environs of the Landmark, or maybe taking a stroll along Des Voeux Road. He had yet to learn that it was a mistake to judge her against other women he knew.

At six thirty, Robin gave up trying to get through to either Anna Leung or the *Seram Queen*, hung up, and sat back wondering what to do next. Her stomach growled, dropping a hint. 'I'm going down to get something to eat,' she announced. 'What about you, Mr Shaw?'

'I have *mai* at my home, Captain Mariner.'

'Is there anywhere local you would recommend?'

'You go your hotel. Man Wah very good. Very safe.'

'That's good advice, Mr Shaw. But I'm not in the mood for formal dining tonight. There's too much to do and not enough time. I want to go to the night market in Upper Lascar Row later and I wondered whether there is anywhere you could recommend on the way.'

'Cat Street market? You go Cat Street?' He gave the old market its Hong Kong name with something akin to horror.

'Yes. I want to buy some presents for my husband and I'll be able to get some good stuff up there for my children too. If memory serves, they have the best ranges of electronic games and equipment at the lowest prices.'

'But Cat Street! It is not proper you go to such place alone!'

He sounded so much like a patronising, over-bearing Victorian paterfamilias that her temper flared and caused her to miscalculate. And as is often the case with face and its loss, one wrong step led onto a path from which there was no hope of returning.

'If you're so worried, Mr Shaw,' she snapped, 'then perhaps you had better escort me yourself!'

He drew in his breath with the slightest of hisses. Did this *gweilo* bitch know what she was asking? he wondered. Well, perhaps. She was unusual for a foreign devil. She seemed almost civilised at times. But now she showed the natural arrogance of the round-eye. How dare she order a person of the Middle Kingdom in such a way? Did she not understand the depth of the impropriety in what she was suggesting? Why, even were she his mistress, he would hardly . . .

Perhaps that was what she was suggesting! His mind raced. She had bought him food and shared it with him even before the *gweilo* lawyer. Her man was locked away from her. And it was common knowledge that all westerners thought about was sex. John Shaw had been brought up to understand that what passed in Western society (though to say that *gweilos* had a society was a joke of course) what passed for philosophy was the supposition that everything was based on sex. Lust for power, money, position, all the destructive forces which shaped the sad ways of these people were based on their frustrated desire to make the beast with two backs.

The thoughts rushed through John Shaw's head in an instant, long before Robin even registered that her anger had changed her relationship with her clerk. He even had time to imagine her naked and speculate upon the possibility that her body hair was the same dazzling colour as the curls on her head – something he had been careful not to do after the first five minutes of their acquaintance, as a sign of grudging respect.

By the best of joss and through the good offices of several generations of deceased ancestors, it so happened that his modest flat was up on the edge of the mid-levels at the end of Conduit Road. No distance at all from Cat Street. He wondered whether it would excite her to see his collection of photographs, all of them cut from magazines, some of them even cut from *Playboy*, and all of them of blonde *gweilo* girls just like her.

'Suit yourself,' she said, breaking into his thoughts and clearly taking his brief silence as a negative response. His eyes flew to the clock and registered with relief that the speculation he had just enjoyed had filled mere seconds.

'No, missy,' he said automatically – and thankfully she was still too preoccupied to notice the patronising reference, 'No, Captain. You cannot go Cat Street alone. Of course I will come. We will buy food, perhaps, from the street vendors. Very good, very cheap, very quick.'

Robin mellowed. 'What an excellent idea!' She pulled herself to her feet. 'But I can't go dressed like this. This is not an outfit suited to strolling around Cat Street eating with our fingers. It took too much trouble to get hold of to empty soy sauce down the front of it.'

They locked up and walked out of the building into the bustle of the plaza outside Jardine House. Neither of them heard the telephone in the Heritage Mariner office begin to ring. Neither of them heard the answerphone click on. Neither of them heard Andrew's voice, dripping with concern, call, 'Robin, are you there? No, Gerry, she's gone, I'm talking to a machine. What do you think. Is it important enough to call the Mandarin and ask them to warn her? She's going shopping, she said. Yes, quite safe I should think. I mean ... Oh!' He realised he was still talking to the answerphone and hung up abruptly.

John Shaw waited in the reception of the Mandarin while Robin ran upstairs to change. For once Giuseppe Borelli was nowhere to be seen and the desk clerk simply glanced across at the young clerk and returned to his work without any flicker of interest. In his ill-cut but carefully tended work suit, John was not too badly out of place, but he could hardly be said to have been comfortable either. He sat on a huge sofa and lit a cigarette. A moment later he noticed the 'No Smoking' sign and rushed to put it out. But there were no ashtrays and so he had to give up his comfortable seat, cross to the reception desk and ask for help. 'No,' said the receptionist, with no obvious sympathy or interest. 'We have no ashtrays. It is forbidden to smoke in here. You had better throw it into the gutter outside.'

John Shaw crossed to the main door to take the receptionist's advice and risk a heavy fine by dropping the smoking stub outside in the street. No sooner had he returned than the concierge himself appeared. 'May I help you, sir?' the tall Italian asked austerely in nearly flawless Cantonese.

'No, thank you,' answered the clerk defensively. 'I am waiting for...' He hesitated while his mind rather wildly sought a word which was utterly without double meanings or overtones. 'I am waiting for a guest.'

'Really?' said the concierge. 'And who might that be?'

'Captain Mariner.'

An instant's hesitation. 'May I enquire as to the reason?'

'She is my employer... I am the clerk at Heritage Mariner across the road. She wishes me to escort her to the night market.'

'Really? And may I enquire which market?' A momentary silence. Shaw's eyes narrowed and his lips turned down. Another inquisitive *gweilo*, he thought. Why should I answer? The Italian saw the expression and recognised it. 'It may be that someone important might wish to contact her urgently. You are aware of her position? And that of her husband?' The concierge emphasised the word 'husband' slightly but sufficiently.

'Yes... Yes, of course. The captain wishes to visit the Cat Street market and I have offered to escort her.'

'I see.' Giuseppe turned away with icy hauteur, more impressive than any emperor.

It was with the most lively relief that John Shaw saw his employer returning. She was dressed in tight blue jeans and a loose plum-coloured silk blouse with a light fawn raincoat draped over her shoulders. 'Ready?' she asked. He nodded, and they were off.

Cat Street was a little less than a kilometre away. In East Sussex this would have been an invigorating stroll, but here the roads were steep, congested and seriously polluted. John supposed that they would take a taxi – the woman was very rich, after all. But no. She set off at a spanking pace and he followed, regretting at once his forty-a-day habit and the fact that he could not sit in the safety of a taxi and negotiate with the driver for permission to smoke. He was badly out of breath by the time they got to the end of Hollywood and swung left past the temple up on to Ladder Street. The humid heat of the evening and the acid thickness of the rush-hour fumes acted together to make his thin chest heave with almost consumptive pants and he felt perspiration beginning to stain all the most intimate seams of his precious work suit.

The *gweilo* bitch had better be worth all this, he thought bitterly. But the thought had no sooner entered his pounding head than she came out of her dark brown study and seemed to notice him for the first time since they had left the hotel.

'Mr Shaw,' she said solicitously, 'I do apologise. Here I am, charging ahead, leading my guide by the nose. That was so rude. I am sorry.' She moderated her pace at once and they strolled on upwards side by side. Now that she had registered his presence properly, she fell into easy conversation with him, establishing that he was a bachelor who lived alone. I would hardly be so happy to be guiding you around Cat Street, he thought, if I had a wife and children awaiting my return at home. At the thought of his home, he glanced up towards the frowning building which housed him, just one more of the grim grey clifftops high above. She continued the one-sided conversation with more solicitous questions which he answered in breathless grunts until he regained his wind and was able to communicate properly.

By the time John Shaw was able to use consecutive words and sentences again, they were just on the point of turning into Cat Street itself. The long thoroughfare was a blaze of light in the shadows of the peaks and the tall buildings which clothed them. It was a great bustle of sound and movement, dazzling to the eye and numbing to the mind.

Robin was swept up into the simple excitement of it at once. The buildings on either side of the road were open-fronted at ground level and glass-fronted above. For the most part they were bazaars offering a gaudy, noisy, bewildering range of wares, each shop reaching upwards, floor above floor, but spilling its goods out over the thronging pavements too, as though mere buildings could never hope to contain their breathtaking variety. But the pavements offered not just the wares from the shops. Tiny traders with one specialised range on offer jostled with stores seemingly the size of Harrods. Between the square sides of the commercial giants, garish neon signs demanded the attention of passers-by for smaller concerns of every sort from herbalists to handbag shops, from potters to porn shops, from saltfish sellers to strip clubs. In the gutters – clean, for all the jostling of the multitudes here – stood the braziers of the food vendors with a mouth-watering range on offer – roasting, toasting, frying, boiling, baking, steaming, hot or cold.

Under John Shaw's direction, parting with mere pennies each time, they picked their way through the food on offer, starting with savoury clouds of *dim sum* and proceeding from vendor to vendor, speciality to speciality, through a complete gourmet meal. As they ate, they chatted like old friends and surveyed what was on offer, but Robin did not really begin to shop until they had finished eating and wiped their sticky lips and fingers with fragrantly steaming cloths.

Then she went in search of silk. John Shaw cheerfully followed her from emporium to emporium and tailor shop to tailor shop. Robin didn't realise it, but her escort thought there was a fair chance that she was shopping for him.

Robin proceeded, in blissful ignorance, her mind full of her husband and her darlings; shopping as therapy, she called it, and it was working. She knew that there was little chance of actually finding pyjamas big enough to fit Richard, but she estimated that she could have some run up within twenty-four hours or so, and for pyjamas a fitting wasn't so important. The same was true of socks and underwear. Shirts and suits would be more of a challenge. But pyjamas and a dressing gown, and a pair of leather flip-flops, come to that, would be an easy start. She had better see about some towels and toiletries too, she thought. But then she remembered that Cat Street was not the best place to pick up expensive cologne; the bottles were unlikely to contain what the labels and packaging promised.

An hour later, she had selected material and left precise orders with an obliging tailor. She had purchased the largest pair of leather-soled flip-flops she could find and placed them in a bright plastic bag beside a leather sponge bag full of soap, toothbrush, flannel, shaving tackle, and a bottle of aftershave which did, in fact, smell something like Messrs Roger & Gallet might have produced. It was the only one which she had been allowed to test and it was, therefore, the least likely to be a fake.

Talking of which . . . She stopped and stooped. On one stall, in among a range of electrical wares and an enormous variety of tapes, audio and video, blank and pre-recorded, there was a familiar name. She picked it up and looked at it more closely. Yes. The cover looked perfect. She opened the box and took out the tape. It was wrapped in cellophane through which she could see the holographic image which was supposed to guarantee authenticity. To all intent and purposes she was holding a perfectly legal VHS tape of the new Walt Disney cartoon *Sinbad*. The pictures were all there, beautifully produced, the printing – 'with the voice of Sir Anthony Hopkins as the Sultan of Deriabar'. An oscar-nominated performance, she thought inconsequentially, remembering the massive pre-publicity, and looking at it with something akin to awe. William had been going on and on about this. He would rather have gone to see *Sinbad* than accompanied them to Skye. And, by all accounts, it was a fantastic experience, putting even *Aladdin*, *The Lion King* and *Pocahontas* in the shade. But it was only just out in the cinema in London. How on earth could it be on video here already? She knew the answer to that one: it was a pirate version. She had the grace to feel a twinge of conscience as she asked the vendor, '*Gei do chin?*'

'*Yih-sahp man.*' The vendor held up both her hands, fingers and thumbs spread, closed them into fists and opened them again to emphasise the point.

John Shaw took over before she could reply. '*Yih-sahp man?*' he spat with vivid disbelief, and within seconds they were locked in a bout of bargaining which went far beyond anything she could have managed. But, truth to tell, she would not have minded being fleeced a little for the video. It would have salved her conscience slightly. She was all too well aware, as who in shipping was not, that the traffic in this sort of merchandise was a running sore in the side of legitimate business, giving illicit rewards comparable to the drugs trade and doing a great deal of damage.

John Shaw came back to her, a little grimly. 'She won't go below fifteen dollars,' he said. 'It's very expensive, but she says it is extremely rare. It's the only one in town. She's only just got it in.'

'I'll take it, thank you, Mr Shaw.' She handed him a twenty dollar note.

As he paid, she turned away; and her gaze was suddenly captured by an unexpectedly familiar figure. It was St John Syme, except that the elegant man she remembered so vividly and unpleasantly from Concorde was no longer dapper and well turned out but dressed, almost shockingly, in jeans, T-shirt and a leather jacket. He was with a young Chinese man and they were in such intimate conversation that neither of them had any idea that she was there. They were forcing their way urgently through the crowd and Robin, almost without thought, followed. It occurred to her at once that these two were lovers. But almost immediately the two men turned into one of the garish strip joints. Syme paused in the doorway to look beadily up and down the street and Robin turned back so that he would not see her and found herself face to face with John Shaw, so close that they might have been about to kiss.

'What is that place?' Robin asked. 'Do you know?'

'Which?' he was confused by this unexpected turn of events, She was so close. She looked so excited.

'That place,' she pointed, 'the one called Bottoms.'

'I have no idea,' he lied. By a combination of chance and proximity this was his nearest strip joint. It specialised in graphic and exotic shows. In many ways it was the most unusual strip joint in Hong Kong, and he was a frequent visitor. 'It is probably a girlie bar,' he added weakly.

'Really?' She seemed surprised. 'Well, let's go in and see.'

'But . . .' John Shaw was stunned. Was this some kind of come-on? One could never tell with *gweilo* women – well, that's what he had been told, anyway. Even so, a sense of decency he had not realised he possessed made him warn her, 'This is not suitable for women such as you, Captain Mariner.' But Robin was already hurrying towards the place.

He followed her through a narrow doorway into a short passage which opened out into a dim reception area. Here an extremely large gentleman demanded an entry charge which more than put the pirate video of *Sinbad* into sharp perspective. Had she not brought the full $5,000 out with her – and spent so little, though promised so much – entry would have been difficult and the first drink out of the question. Robin's mind was still reeling from the shock of having to pay a cool $500 to get the pair of them in when the waitress informed them that drinks were $100 a glass.

Slowly, Robin began to take stock of their surroundings. They were in a big room, probably a cellar. It was ill-lit and full of packed tables. Between the tables moved waitresses who were all Chinese or Oriental. They all wore the same uniform of tight and minuscule shorts made of what seemed to be black leather, and earrings. The earrings were suspended, not from their earlobes but from their nipples. From what Robin could see – and she was not looking closely – the ornaments were all long and weighty. It was fortunate for most of the girls that they were young and their breasts were pert. What someone with a large chest would look like, with the weighty ornaments abetting gravity, heaven alone knew. Robin was put forcefully in mind of the generously proportioned Diana Dors's famous observation of the sixties: that if she joined Womens' Lib and burned her bra she would be knock-kneed within a week. The humour, weak enough, with which Robin sought to distance herself from what was going on around her was inadequate, however, and inappropriate. Although she was slow to admit the fact to herself, this was a serious situation.

And she was rather more at risk than she realised. John Shaw was at a peak of excitement. Here, as far as he knew, was a woman who might well have featured honourably in his personal collection of erotica; paying large amounts of money to entertain him to the most graphically pornographic show in Hong Kong. Fortunately the bustle of the clientele and the blare of the music made talk impossible so that he never managed to say anything even faintly inappropriate, in spite of the nature of his thoughts and suppositions.

Robin moved from initial disgust into a mode of total concentration, using those eyes which had impressed the most experienced of watchkeepers to quarter and search the dim recesses of this ghastly place. Syme was at one of the most distant of tables, down near the clear space which Robin reluctantly recognised to be a stage. She leaned across towards John Shaw, her eyes never leaving the civil servant's oiled gold helmet of hair. 'Is there some kind of show?' she asked.

'Yes indeed! It is most—' John Shaw stopped, aghast, sharply aware of how much he might inadvertently be giving away.

'Any idea when it begins?' Robin had not noticed anything untoward.

'At nine. So I believe.'

Robin glanced at her watch. It was an old-fashioned Boy Scout's watch with a useful bevel and vivid luminous figures. 'Five minutes,' she observed, her eyes still on Syme; just beginning to wonder what might be coming up.

Not in her wildest dreams could Robin have guessed what was going to come on as a floor show at Bottoms. Even the name of the place failed to warn her, though in her years as a full ship's captain she had come across a broad range of predilietions, on videotape and in glossy magazines, if nowhere else. Whatever dark motive masquerading as curiosity had driven her in here on the heels of the foul StJohn Syme, Robin had seen more than enough and broadened her experience far beyond her wish within moments of the floor show's beginning. What the information about the civil servant's unnatural erotic interests would be worth – if she ever dared admit to having followed him into such a place and to have witnessed such a show – was beyond computation. It was not worth putting up with any more of this disgusting spectacle to further her understanding of the man or to glean more information about his peculiar predilections. 'That's it!' she said. 'Let's go.'

Hoping against hope that their ultimate destination would be his flat, John Shaw was happy to oblige. Hot on her heels, he followed her out into the Cat Street market. Here she hesitated for an instant, as though uncertain where to go next, and he was within the merest instant of taking control and directing her to his tower block when one of the stall-holders called out raucously and unexpectedly. It was a woman who specialised in newspapers and magazines in a range of Chinese dialects, and she had evidently just received a range of Chinese newspapers. 'It's her!' screamed the harridan. 'The *gweilo* woman – the wife of the mass murderer who was in court only this morning! Her photograph is in all the papers! It is her, I tell you!'

Robin heard the commotion but had no idea what was being said or that she herself was the centre of attention. It was John who warned her first. 'Missy,' he called, regressing again 'Captain . . .' He caught her by the sleeve with such force that she was shocked. 'We better go! These people, they know you ... The newspapers ...'

Robin pulled away, her mind refusing to accept what was going or around her. It was a nightmare. The very instant she came creeping out of a pornographic show in a market she had never visited in a city she had been away from for years suddenly she was the centre of attention, the cynosure of all eyes. And not merely of all eyes. The old woman who had started the commotion burst out from behind her meagre stall brandishing a pink newspaper with a grainy but vivid black and white picture of her on the front page in the midst of a black sea of Chinese lettering. The newspaper was thrust like a kind of mirror into her face, and suddenly she was at the centre of a small knot of strangers, all calling out and grabbing. Her arms, her shoulders, her back, her hair. John Shaw's hands were trying to pull her free with bruising force, but his were not the only hands pulling at her now. Wasn't there a movie, she wondered for a horrified moment, where someone got torn to pieces by an uncontrollable mob? She pulled away with mounting terror, thrusting herself towards John Shaw but he was no longer where she thought he was. Wherever she turned, there were only twisted, Oriental faces and mocking monochrome pictures of herself. 'Shaw!' she screamed. 'John Shaw!'

And John Shaw came back to get her. He was not alone; Andrew Atherton Balfour was at his shoulder and they came in through the crowd of hysterical women, shoving bodies this way and that, like a fly half and a prop forward tearing down a rugby pitch, until they had her safe and could lead her back to the great green Aston Martin Vantage parked at the end of the street.

'Just listen to this,' ordered Andrew, his massive frame given an excess of restless energy by the adrenaline still coursing through it in the aftermath of the rescue.

Robin sat, almost prostrate, in his office, gripped by whatever chemicals had the opposite effect of adrenaline. 'Listen to what?' she said pettishly, gracelessly, as though she was angry with him for coming to her rescue. As, in fact, she was.

'It came in late this afternoon, after six. Well, after I called your office in Jardine House. I went out for a bite to eat. I checked back before returning to Repulse Bay and there it was. I called the Mandarin to tell you about it. The Mandarin told me where to find you. End of story.'

'What is it, Andrew?'

'Listen. Just listen.'

He turned up the volume on his answerphone and the tape hissed as it moved across the heads. '... Atherton' it cut in suddenly and loudly enough to make them both jump a little. Just that one word, the consonants like rocks in the speaker's mouth, the 'r' teetering dangerously close to an 'l' sound, was enough to establish a Chinese accent. 'You want see what happen *Sulu Queen*'s cargo, you go Ping Chau tomorrow night.' There was a click and the caller hung up.

Andrew switched off. Rewound. The voice repeated, clearly, in its Chinese accented English, '...Atherton. You want see what happen *Sulu Queen*'s cargo, you go Ping Chau tomorrow night.'

'What do you think?' he asked.

'*Sulu Queen*'s cargo is at Kwai Chung,' she said.

'Maybe, maybe not.'

'Come on, Andrew. It's where the ship is. It's where the cargo is.'

'Maybe not all of it.'

Her eyes narrowed. 'All right,' she said quietly. 'Let's say I go along with that. Maybe there was something being smuggled on *Sulu Queen*. Where does that get us?'

'Closer to an explanation as to what was actually going on?'

'Possibly. Now, what is this Ping Chau?'

'It's an island. A ghost island. It's way, way out in Mirs Bay, so far north and east of here that it's only a swim from the mainland.'

'From *China*?' Andrew had Robin's full attention now.

'Yes. China. Po On District, as a matter of fact.'

'What do you mean a "ghost island"?'

'It has villages, near enough a town or two. It used to support thousands of people. But they all left. Went to England, most of them. Only two people live there now. Two people to open it all up for the tourists when they go out there for day visits, and close it all up again at night. Whole island. Couple of kilometres long; maybe a kilometre wide. Two people.'

'You could hide a lot of stuff on an island that size.' Against her better judgement, she was intrigued.

'Do you think it's conceivable that *Sulu Queen* could have been carrying contraband? Smuggling?'

'Who knows? I'd need to see the full manifest. I don't suppose whatever we're looking for would be mentioned, but we could total actual capacity against the volume of cargo carried. If the two figures don't match, then maybe...'

'Any way you can check?'

'*I* can't,' she said slowly. 'But I think I might just know a man who can.'

'You get on to him, then,' said Andrew, 'and I'll see about booking a boat.'

'No, wait,' she said. 'If my man agrees to help us, he can probably supply a boat of his own.'

Chapter Seventeen

Daniel Huuk stood at the point of the cutter's bow, looking northeast across Mirs Bay towards Ping Chau Island which was heaving itself out of the calm grey water like a vivid green sea monster coming to the surface. It was mid-morning on Wednesday, 14 May. The island would be deserted except for the two watchkeepers and the cutter's crew. The sun broke through and glinted on the slopes of Dragon Fall Hill.

'Oh, that's lovely,' said Robin, standing just behind his shoulder. 'What is it called?'

He turned his head just enough to see the loom of her right shoulder, clad in plum silk and covered, as though by a cloak, with her light fawn raincoat, and told her.

Huuk was in two minds about this expedition. He was not particularly impressed by the solicitor's tape, and it seemed hardly likely to him that even the most intrepid smuggler could get into Kwai Chung, past the men guarding the cargo of the *Sulu Queen*, remove a couple of containers without anyone noticing, and then bring them out here. Why should they? What for?

And yet ... And yet ... There was a niggling doubt. Enough of a doubt to get him out here to check for himself, independently of the fact that Commander Lee, his effective boss at the moment, wanted to keep Andrew Balfour sweet, and Huuk himself was by no means averse to obliging Robin Mariner.

This was not the most convenient time for him to be taking a jaunt out here looking for ghosts and mysteries, however. There was the cargo of the *Sulu Queen* to be catalogued in detail; there was every inch of her hull to be thoroughly searched. The Hong Kong police were doing that, of course, but Huuk and his men provided assistance and naval knowledge which could be vital. The men from the coroner's office were establishing individual causes of death and matching up corpses and ship's records surprisingly quickly, and Huuk knew that Lee wanted to proceed to formal indictment as soon as possible. There was just too much publicity in this case for anyone to be laggard or derelict. On the other hand, nobody wanted to risk anything being overlooked.

Ultimately, that was why they were here. It had not required the razor sharp legal mind of Prosecutor Po to make them all understand that it was going to be very difficult to establish intention and motive. Although it seemed quite clear that Richard Mariner had gone berserk with at least one gun and killed everyone else on board – except the Vietnamese, who had already been dead – there was very little evidence as to why he had done so.

Involvement in some kind of smuggling operation would further blacken Mariner's name, undermine his reputation in the eyes of judge and jury, and provide enough of a motive to strengthen the prosecution case just where it needed most support, when the inevitable transfer was made from magistrate's court to High Court.

Robin, however, was in no doubt that discovery of smuggling activity centred on the *Sulu Queen* could only help to establish Richard's innocence.

She stood just behind Huuk's right shoulder looking up over his uniform epaulette towards the island. As they neared, she began to make out the gleam of houses clustered at the waterline and to discern the patterns they made mounting the steep green hillsides. The sun came and went behind a thin overcast which kept the surface of the sea a dark blue-grey, like certain types of clay. Beyond the bright island, the sky seemed to curve down into a misty grey backdrop as it met the distant hills of Po On District on the mainland. 'It is close,' observed Robin quietly. 'I hadn't realised.'

'Not as close as Shenzen,' he grunted. He turned until the boat's pulpit rail held his back like a friendly arm and leaned back. Framed against the misty hills and the vivid, verdant island slopes, he made a dashing figure in his whites, but he was not posing for effect. 'If I were smuggling anything out of Kwai Chung into China,' he said gently, 'I'd slip it over the border at Man Kam To and take it up into the Special Economic Zone.'

'Lots of border guards. Customs. Witnesses,' she commented.

'All right,' he said slowly, warming to the debate. 'I'd move it across the marshes south of Lok Ma Chau, then I could even slip it up the river if I wanted.'

'Only if it was fairly light and easy to handle, and . . .' she paused as a new thought occurred to her.

'And?' he prompted.

'And if I hadn't taken it off earlier in any case.'

'What do you mean?'

'Before it got to Kwai Chung.' Her voice was guarded now, for the new thought might be an important one and if it was then it had much better be put to Andrew Balfour rather than Daniel Huuk. She glanced back towards the wheelhouse where Andrew was standing talking to the helmsman – and keeping an eye on Robin.

'How long before?' Huuk asked silkily, recalling her to their conversation. 'My men and I were on board for the twelve hours before she came into Tamar. Could it have been taken off then, do you suppose?' He was daring her to accuse him of criminal complicity but in doing so he let slip a piece of information he would rather have kept secret from her.

'No, of course not. It was a silly idea. I'm sorry.' She looked up at him suddenly as the penny dropped. 'You were aboard for twelve hours before the *Sulu Queen* came in?'

'Yes,' he answered shortly.

'So...' She drew out the word gently and he could see her mind racing behind those still grey eyes which were so exactly the colour of the distant, beautiful hills.

Huuk turned away again before she could ask the next, inevitable, question. He was certain that she did not realise that it was he who had shot her husband in the head and injured him so badly. And, for all sorts of reasons, Daniel Huuk did not want her to know; certainly not yet. 'We're nearly there,' he said. 'That's Emperor Point, where we dock.'

Both the islanders were there to greet them, two wizened, elderly-looking men who nevertheless moved with great energy and seemed to be bright and lively. Certainly, they escorted their unexpected guests into the eerie, deserted village with every sign of boundless enjoyment and jabbered full, detailed answers in impenetrable, machine-gun-fire dialect to Huuk's questions. The six of them – Robin, Andrew, Huuk and three sailors from Tamar – sat down and were given fragrant tea in cups like eggshells and tiny, honey-flavoured cakes as the interrogation continued. But for all their enthusiasm to discuss with each other and with their interrogator every possible answer to each question Huuk asked, his final summing up, in English, was short enough: 'They know nothing.'

Andrew's eyes swept up the forested hillsides rising abruptly above them and stretching away to the south for more than a mile. 'We'd better get busy then,' he said, 'if we're going to earn our keep and have a good look round. With just six of us it'll take a good while.'

'We only have to walk round the coast,' said Huuk. 'I don't think anyone is suggesting that anything is smuggled in or out by air, are they? And these two have heard no helicopters recently. No. If there is anything here, it must be within easy reach of the sea.'

'And,' added Robin grudgingly, 'it can't be of any great size either. Unless there is a deep-water inlet somewhere, you won't get a ship of any size anywhere near the shore.'

'Back to my river boats?' asked Huuk, with just the slightest teasing edge to his voice.

'Perhaps,' she conceded. 'But at least you could use a fleet of them out here and nobody would notice. Anyway.' She gathered her fawn-coloured raincoat about herself and said, 'Let's go.'

They split into two teams. Andrew and Robin took one of the sailors with a walkie-talkie and Huuk took the two others, also with a walkie-talkie.

Robin's team struck directly south, straight down the coast. Huuk's team would go north to the furthest point and then swing down the far side of the island. They would meet halfway round and compare notes. Then, if need be, each team would continue and double-check the territory already covered by the other. They would meet again back here when they had finished their tour. At most, each team would walk little more than two miles and the exploration should not take long. Certainly, they had no intention of staying on the island for the night. None of them took the message on Andrew's answerphone that seriously

Turning southwards meant that Robin and her team had to walk through the rest of the town to begin with, and that experience set the tone for much of what was to follow. The two islanders waved them away cheerily enough and vanished at once – no doubt to do the washing up. Isolation closed round the three of them like a fist. The houses seemed to crowd around them, their walls, eaves and roofs bright with stone, shale and shells, making the windows and doorways in contrast unnaturally dark. Above, etched black crosses of gulls wheeled against the restless overcast, screaming like lost children, and soon a wind sprang up. It was a strange wind, by no means blustery or stormy, hardly even forceful at first. But it was regular and persistent. It began to whisper and mutter in the empty dwellings all around them. As it gained force it began to whine piercingly and caused unexpected explosions of sound as doors, windows, shutters slammed. Sand, blown up from the beaches, slithered and hissed against edges and corners. Chimneys whimpered. Courtyards howled eerily. The cloud thickened and the noon light came and went, liberating a disturbing army of shadows to dance mockingly in the corners of their eyes.

'I say,' said Andrew after a while, 'this is a pretty lonely spot, isn't it?'

'Putting it mildly,' agreed Robin. 'But it'll be better when we're out of the town, I expect.' She looked across at the sailor Huuk had detailed to accompany them. 'Are you all right?' she asked him.

He nodded cheerfully. 'Arright,' he said.

The roadway they were following tended more and more steeply uphill, and as it rose the houses began to fall back and separate, revealing between their walls and over their flat roofs increasingly broad vistas of the sea. At last, they stood on a high promontory with a cliff at their feet and a breathtaking view away westwards towards Crooked Island before them. At their backs was a hillside reaching further up into Dragon Fall Hill which stretched down the middle of the island like a spine. On their right, the path they had just climbed meandered back down into the deserted town. On their left, the terrain sloped down and back into a shallow bay before turning through nearly forty-five degrees and gathering itself up into an even higher cliff which, Robin guessed, must look due south past Tai Long, down towards Brunei more than two thousand kilometres distant. The path down into the shallow bay was narrow and overgrown. There was no obvious path leading up the steep shoulder of the next slope. 'This may become hard going,' observed Robin, glad of her jeans and stout travelling shoes in spite of the heat and humidity. 'Are you up for this, Andrew?'

'Yes,' he said, though he didn't sound all that certain. 'As long as there aren't any snakes or venomous insects.'

'Are there?' Robin asked Huuk's sailor.

'Arright,' he said.

In fact the going was not that bad. The slopes further inward and upward were heavily wooded, but they managed to stay on the outskirts of the forest where the vegetation was low, thick grass and thin bush. The wind now made less disturbing noises. It was content to whisper, sigh and hiss. In any case, it would have been hard put to it to undermine the cheery whirring of the cicadas choiring their lunchtime songs. The wind was given occasionally breathtaking form, too, by clouds of bright yellow butterflies which seemed to leap from bush to bush ahead of them like peripatetic blossoms. In the groin of the little valley, however, the woods thrust down towards the sea in a wall and they had no choice but to push their way between the trees. Inevitably, they found a stream at the heart of this dim green tunnel and Robin stopped, standing on a low flat stone in the middle of the chuckling brook to look away down the last of the valley to the broad spread of shallow water washing across a rocky beach into the silvery ripples of the sea. As it went, it washed past a brown wall of seaweed piled along a high waterline. Almost inconsequentially, Robin found herself wondering about the tides in this region.

The view from the top of the next cliff was simply breathtaking and their position, more than forty metres sheer in the air, put all thoughts of tides out of Robin's head. Like a child about a summer holiday adventure, she went to the very edge of the cliff and lay down on her stomach. 'I say, look out,' called Andrew from some way back.

'Oh Andrew, don't be so pompous,' she called. 'It's quite safe.' His stick-in-the-mud concern brought out the worst in her and she wormed forward into a position which was, in fact, bordering upon the dangerous. With her hips right at the last safe point of grass-pillowed ground, holding onto a firmly-rooted bush with her right hand, she hung over the cliff edge, looking straight down. Below her, she saw the dizzying expanse of black rock falling as sheer as a wall. At its foot, a jumble of rocks littered a deep shelf which reached out into the foam, all covered with green swathes of weed and bright splashes of yellow salt-loving lichen. Lying there, for a moment it was almost as though she was back on Skye and none of this had happened. The thought was so soothing that she was happy for it to persist for a while and she lost herself in the great sway of the sea as it thrust in at the cliff foot to crash among the black rocks and then whirl back out in long claws of foam.

Had she not been lying in such an unwise position, she would never have seen the odd variation in the pattern of the waves, both coming in and washing back. And, had she not seen that odd pattern – though to begin with she paid little conscious attention to what she could see – she would not have allowed her eyes to follow that strange pattern on the water to its source, far down on her left. But she did all of these things and suddenly she was snapped out of her reverie into wide-eyed wakefulness. 'Hey!' she yelled. 'Andrew, there's a cave down there.'

'What?' His footsteps thudded on the turf behind her, then stopped.

'Take my legs and hang on tight.'

'Robin, I—'

'Come on, Andrew, I just want to get a clear look. It might be important.'

She felt him kneel beside her feet, then he took firm hold, thrusting his chest between her ankles and tucking her feet into his armpits. Safely anchored, she wormed her way a little further forward and was rewarded with a much clearer view. There was a deep cleft in the black rock, perhaps as wide as three metres where it met the cliff foot, thrust back like a knife wound into the side of the cliff. And there was the darker outline of a cave mouth like an ink stain running down to the waterline. As she watched, Robin saw a bright drift of seaweed – torn loose, no doubt, by the storm on the night she arrived. She watched it as the waves gathered it and guided it into that wide gap. 'Just a little longer,' she called back, her eyes fixed on the seaweed raft. With surprising rapidity, it was thrust up the narrow channel and thrown – no, *sucked* – in though the side of the cliff. And, as she watched, straining all her senses in absolute concentration, she heard the deep, telltale thunder of surf running in through subterranean caverns and the whole cliff top juddered slightly.

'Pull me back,' she called and Andrew obeyed with a will. In an instant she was back on terra firma, with her hair wild and her face flushed. 'There's a bloody great cave down there,' she said. 'No access from up here, but well worth checking out. We'll warn Huuk that we might need to take a closer look in the cutter later.'

Huuk was not overly impressed. Even over the radio link they could almost hear him shrug and his tone was little more than dismissive. But the discovery galvanised Robin. As the little team walked easily down the far side of the cliff, turned the corner at the rock's southern point and began to come back up the China-facing side of the island, she regaled Andrew with excited stories of her childhood holidays in Devon and Cornwall when caverns exactly like the one she had just found had been the haunts of smugglers since the day that import duties were invented. She quoted Kipling so loudly, repetitively and often, that Andrew was soon able to join her in the chorus of 'The Smuggler's Song'.

'Four and twenty ponies, trotting through the dark,' they sang in unison as they walked briskly along the lower slopes above the white breadths of beach with Huuk's sailor watching them from an increasing distance as though they had gone dangerously insane.

They paused here, contacted Huuk, and then recited the whole poem right through one more time as they examined the way in which the next headland gathered itself up and thrust itself out into an easterly-facing point which was extended by a series of snaggle-toothed rocks.

Then they began all over again.

'Brandy for the parson, baccy for the clerk,' they bellowed as they rushed up the slopes onto the crest of that other cliff beetling over the China side of Mirs Bay, the twin of the one with the cavern at its heart.

'Them that asks no questions isn't told a lie,' Robin concluded at the topmost point of the east-facing cliff, and she cast herself down again, paying no attention to the breathtaking view over not-so-distant China afforded by her position, preferring to wriggle forward and hang over the edge once more.

'So watch the wall, my darling...' continued Andrew, falling to his knees behind her, ready to take her ankles again, unaware to begin with that he was speaking alone. Then he stopped.

'I'll be damned!' she said.

'What?' He took her ankles and tucked them into his armpits.

She wriggled forward another metre and repeated, 'I'll be *damned*!'

'*What?*'

'It's the same. Exactly the same, but bigger!'

'What are you talking about, Robin?'

She jerked and rolled so actively that for a moment he thought she was falling. But no. She came in and curled round until her face was less than a metre from his own. 'There's another cave down there. Another smuggler's cave.'

'Really?' He was much struck by the coincidence, and not a little carried away by her obvious excitement.

'Except,' she continued, wriggling further inland towards him so that she could grasp him by the shoulders and pull their faces into almost intimate proximity. 'Except that it looks much bigger. And I think there's a way to get into it without a boat.'

From the next beach along, it was clear that the cliff thrust out towards China in such a way as to achieve something of an optical illusion. Only from the very top, and even then only if one was looking very carefully indeed, could it be observed that there was not one point but two. They were the better part of a hundred metres apart – and there was a cavern in the hidden section which reached inwards like the cavity in a rotten tooth.

Robin actually ran back across the beach until she was able to scramble up onto the jumble of rocks at the low cliff foot. Here she waited for Andrew to come puffing up beside her. 'Look,' she said, as he pulled off his shoes and emptied the sand out of them. 'You see what happens out there? The rocks give way to a solid platform which stands just above water level. If we can get onto that platform it will lead us round the point and back into the cave mouth!' She folded up her raincoat and dropped it onto a convenient rock.

'Are you sure?' Andrew asked sceptically.

'Certain. I saw it all from the top of the cliff.'

'OK,' he said. 'Can't argue with a confident woman.'

And they were off, with Huuk's sailor lagging unhappily behind.

It was exactly as Robin had said. The jumble of pool-filled rocks that they were clambering over soon gave onto a solid rock ledge which stood like a shelf out above the quiet water. With Robin in the lead, they pushed out onto this ledge. Only because she was by nature intrepid and by situation desperate did they proceed round the point. The sheer cliff loomed over them and at the very point, the ledge apparently stopped dead. The snaggle-toothed rocks which were apparently a straight line beginning at the cliff foot itself were revealed to be a narrow-based arrowhead, the nearest of which stood in a dangerous-looking welter of foam three metres distant. Too far to be of any help in an emergency but near enough to present a very real danger as the waves tore around it into a deadly welter.

'I don't like this,' bellowed Andrew.

'Hold my hand,' ordered Robin. 'I'm going round.' He obeyed, but less than wholeheartedly. *'Tight!'* she snarled, sounding just as dangerous as the foam. He closed his hand round her right wrist as though her arm was a rope in a tug of war. She swung out, stepped round the massive point of rock and stopped, spread-eagled. He could only see her right arm to the shoulder and her right thigh, calf and shoe, so sharp was the corner she was going round. Her right arm shook violently and he suddenly realised that she wanted him to let go. With a sick feeling in his stomach, he obeyed, and she was gone.

A glassy green heave of wave came thundering inwards, shattered on the nearest rock and washed up over the narrow pathway to the great black knife-blade of rock. Andrew stepped back automatically to protect his shoes. And as he did so he realised that he would never voluntarily step forward again. Nothing in the world would make him take his life into his hands and follow Robin into her cave. Almost desperately, he looked back to the point where the ledge was lost in the jumble of rocks at the groin of the white-sand beach. Here Huuk's man was waiting and watching. Andrew waved. The sailor gestured. The solicitor took one last, forlorn glance back to the terrible place where his client had vanished. 'Robin?' he called, but there was no reply.

'*Robin?*' he yelled, in the voice he normally used when cheering his team to victory.

'*ROBIN?*' he screamed, so loudly that he felt his sides and vocal chords begin to tear.

No reply. There was the calling of the gulls and the thundering swell of the sea. But there was no reply.

Then, deflated, defeated, and suddenly full of deep foreboding combined with not a little naked terror, he began to inch back toward the pale, forlorn square of Robin's folded coat, towards the sailor – and the walkie-talkie.

Robin stood with her back to the sheer, icy rock wall and watched the foam slide past her toe-tips as though it was full of lethal sea serpents. She had taken one step, turned to face outwards and flattened herself against the wet stone like a limpet. There was no thought in her mind that Andrew might be coming round after her. It was immediately clear to her that only a suicidal lunatic would have come round in the first place and she did not really expect Andrew to put himself in such idiotic peril. Crucified to the safe solidity behind, she took stock of her situation, her mind, as always, a swirl of conflicting sensations and emotions. She watched the deadly green thrust of the water, cloaked in illusory webs of foam, wash past her toes with sinister, muscular vigour and plunge into the absolute darkness on her right. All too vividly aware of the sudden chill and the way it combined with the clammy dampness of the place, she raised her eyes to look across the cave mouth which was rapidly losing light and heat because it faced east and it was well past midday.

Away on her left, out of the brightness of the early afternoon, waves washed with deep, dark purpose and almost limitless power through the arrowhead of rocks as though they were the teeth of a drowning dragon. Into the throat of this hidden cave, on the China side of a ghost island, they surged as though the place was breathing. Past her toes they rolled, splattering her shoes with brine, down into the throat of the cave as though the place was drinking them in.

What terrified Robin and added to the dankness of the place, tensing her nipples into flinty points poking against the plum silk of her blouse, was the suspicion that the back of the cave closed down into a wall pierced only by a narrow gullet which would let nothing but the great waves in.

Well, there was no going back, she thought, and only one way to check her route forward. With a terrified, unseeing glance right, she began to edge along the tiny shelf, deeper into the cave.

At about this time, Andrew reached the waiting sailor. 'Captain Huuk,' he yelled. 'Get me Captain Huuk.'

The sailor smiled. 'Arright,' he said.

In a moment, the solicitor was in contact with the irritable captain. 'Huuk?' he faltered.

'Yes?'

'Ah ... Captain Mariner ...'

'Yes?'

'Captain Mariner has gone into a cave between the beaches here.'

'*What?*'

'I think you'd better come at once.'

By the greatest of good fortune, the throat at the back of the cave did not close down. As she moved gingerly through the gathering shadows, Robin was able to see with increasing clarity that there was a tunnel here. It was half flooded to be sure, but its roof was high and the ledge became, if anything, wider. It was difficult to be certain, but it seemed to her that the roof of the tunnel never came much below three metres above the restless water, and the distance between the rock faces was scarcely less. Indeed, no sooner had she become accustomed to the claustrophobic feeling brought on by the closeness of the rock than it opened out into great, cavernous spaces and utter darkness. The wall at her back tended away from her and the rumble of the waves gathered as they plunged across shallow beaches on either side of that surging central channel.

After a few more blind steps, Robin stopped. Because her legs were beginning to tremble so terribly, she eased her back inch by inch down the running, icy wall, feeling her thighs fold up against her breast, until her numb buttocks hit the horizontal security of the ledge. With her heels stuck tight to the outer edge and with no intention of allowing her feet into the grasping swell just beyond them, she sat, hugging her knees to her juddering jaw and wondered what to do next.

As the moments passed, Robin became aware of just how much light was coming in through the cave mouth, following the weave of the water in, as though channelled along a massive fibre-optic line. Her eyes began to clear enough for her to make out the outlines of the cave in whose portal she was sitting. The restless, verdigris light revealed, half by looming, restless shadow, half by disturbing, gleaming luminescence, a space almost as large as St Paul's Cathedral in London. By dint of concentrating absolutely on the rock ledge to her right, she slowly realised that there was a passable pathway stretching back to the edge of a broad, gravel-bottomed beach which she could reach by the expenditure of just a little more effort. The only problem with following that course was that she could not quite see what lay beyond the tideline there. And she could not trust her legs to support her. Like a child cheating at musical chairs, she began to slide along the ledge, never letting her nearly senseless bottom part company with the icy rock.

It was not until she had actually arrived at the black shingle beach and destroyed her good new shoes by wading through the surf in them that she began to regret the fact that she did not smoke. The air around her was restless, for it washed through in waves driven by the waves of brine below it, but even so she reckoned that she could have got a match or two to light and stay burning long enough to let her look around. As things were, she was effectively blind. There had never been any question of exploring by night or underground, so she had no torch. And without a match or cigarette lighter to give the faintest illumination, there was no hope of detailed exploration. The light coming in through the green-glowing mouth of the cave was like the luminescence of her Boy Scout watch: vivid, green, and useless as a torch beam. Beyond the weirdly luminescent water, and the odd glimmer in the vast, echoing distances, it gave no direct light at all.

Time cleared Robin's eyes a little more as the near-absolute darkness stretched her pupils to the uttermost limit, but there was never any chance of her seeing anything in detail. Wading up through the surf whose pebble-grating rumble echoed almost painfully, she could see nothing but the largest of nearby objects. And not their real shapes, just their silhouettes against the slightly more Stygian blackness beyond. Most of these shapes were natural, near-organic and rounded through centuries of erosion by the South China Sea. As she slopped unsteadily up the heaving, rolling beach, however, Robin began to discern less natural, more angular shapes. She stopped, staggering forward and backwards a little in the suck and wash of the surf, scarcely able to believe her all but blind eyes. There were boxes in here. No, not boxes – *containers*. She stood with the busy foam frothing in and out past her knees, looking at the square shadows of a whole series of ship's containers standing along the shoreline.

Able to do little more than stagger, Robin pulled herself up the treacherous slope towards the black-shadowed boxes. Concentrating on what she could see so absolutely that she hardly felt her shoes beginning to yield and slip on and off as she walked, she pulled herself into the restless cacophony of the shallows and went onto her hands and knees as the support of the water fell away. At the top of the pebble-beached slope was a tiny cliff before the shelf she had followed in here returned, wide enough for a series of containers to be perched like cardboard boxes in a kitchen cupboard. Too cold, too exhausted, too overwhelmed to think clearly, Robin hauled herself up beside the containers and sat on the edge of the rock shelf, shivering uncontrollably, with her feet dangling and her shoes half off.

How long she sat there she did not know – or what she planned to do with what she had discovered, or how on earth she proposed to get herself safely back outside again. The first thing that forced itself past the chilled exhaustion of her brain was the increasingly insistent lapping of the wavelets on the back of the steadily rising tide at her dangling toes. It was that which made her glance up, unwrap her arms which she had thrown like a warm scarf round her trembling shoulders, and think about looking for some more secure position. As she felt the water rising, it came to her that she had no notion of how the tide stood, and no idea of how high within the cave it would come. Clearly it could not fill the cave to the roof, even at high tide, or the containers would have been washed away. But in the dark with nothing but chilled fingers to guide her, she found that it was impossible to estimate how far up the sides of the containers the cold wet tide had come.

Stiffly, as though all her joints were rusting up, Robin forced herself to her feet and began to explore further like a woman struck stone blind. She was guided only by the vaguest of outlines between the restless shapes and the utter dark. She explored slowly and carefully through the placing of her dull fingers and her near-senseless hands, all too well aware of the damage which might be done by splinters, sharp points and razor edges to these precious, nerveless, extremities. And she was guided to a certain extent by her sense of smell, though her nostrils were already awash with the metallic stench of brackish weed and of well-washed stone, so that the odours of waterlogged ply and rusting metal were hardly distinguishable. Her ears were so full of the restless thrust and hiss of the water all around her that she might just as well have been deaf too.

In the event it was her eyes that agonisingly told her of impending rescue. As she was hesitantly, painstakingly feeling her way along the rough and slimy side of the nearest of the great containers, a shadow – as of absolute, utter, interstellar darkness – swept through the place. It was there for a moment, making Robin catch her breath and choke on a fluttering scream. Then it was followed by the brightness of concentrated lightning. But instead of dying in a flash as lightning had always done in her past experience, this brightness persisted unbearably until it smote her to her knees with its torturing, incapacitating effulgence. And, out of the heart of it, Daniel Huuk's voice quietly, calmly, said, 'Please wait just where you are, Captain Mariner, and I will come ashore to get you.'

'No! Wait!'

'We have no time. The tide is rising rapidly.'

'A moment. Just a moment!' She almost broke her nose trying to dash the white-hot tears out of her eyes. 'Look!' she continued, almost mindlessly, unable to believe that the containers she had discovered were not an important clue. 'Look what I've found! What are they?'

'They are containers,' Huuk's calm voice admitted somewhat wryly. 'Five ship's containers.'

'Do they have any distinguishing marks or numbers?'

'None that I can see. Mr Balfour?'

'None. They are all absolutely plain, Robin. I'm sorry.'

Robin put her hands to her face and pressed her fingertips into the pits of her streaming eyes, trying to stem the flood of incapacitating tears. When she took her hands away from her blinking eyes, she could see the outlines of the great angular boxes. They stood two metres high by two metres wide by three metres deep. All of them were marked to almost half their depth by water. All of them stood open and empty. She plunged out of the brightness of the cutter's searchlight into the shaded interior of one container after another. But there was nothing to be found.

'Please be quick, Captain Mariner,' called Huuk with increasing urgency. 'If the tide gets any higher we'll all be trapped in here.'

Robin scrabbled on the floor of the last container, unable to believe that all this had been for nothing.

'Captain Mariner!'

Of course, she thought. There was no point in looking below the waterline. 'You imbecile!' she spat at herself and rose to her full height, looking up above her head. And, sure enough, the dampness of the atmosphere was causing some of the seams to swell and part. And in one of the swollen cracks was the tiniest strip of paper. It wasn't much, but it was enough to make her feel vindicated. She pulled it out with the utmost care, folded it and slipped it into the tiny key pocket at the waistline of her jeans.

'*Captain!*'

'Coming,' she called and clambered out of the echoing box.

At once she saw that Huuk's concern had not been misplaced. The cutter was nudging against the ledge already so that she was able to scramble straight aboard without doing further damage to her already ruined shoes. Two strong pairs of hands caught her, Huuk's lent extra impetus by his anger and Andrew's by his lively sense of guilt. As Robin allowed herself to be bundled down the cutter's little foredeck, the pitching vessel swung round and surged back out beneath the steadily falling guillotine blade of the cavern's lintel.

A couple of moments later she was down below the wheelhouse in the tiny twin-berthed cabin which lay under the two and a half metres of the foredeck. Here it was stuffy, cosy; blessedly warm.

'Well?' barked Huuk, sounding, for the first time in their acquaintance, very much like a captain. 'Was it worth it?'

Robin looked up a little guiltily from her place in the growing puddle on the cutter's shallow port-side bunk. 'No,' she admitted sheepishly – it sounded more like 'Doh' to her – and she sneezed.

'Did you find anything?' he rasped.

'Doh,' she lied forlornly and, shivering convulsively, lay back on the pitching bunk.

After a couple of minutes he eased the sopping shoes off her freezing feet and left her. When she was sure she was alone, she checked that her key pocket, and the precious piece of paper it contained, were dry. By something akin to a miracle they were, so she turned until the pocket was uppermost and curled her shivering body protectively round it.

Half an hour later someone came into the tiny cabin and solicitously pulled out the damp blanket from beneath her. He then took a warm, dry blanket from the bunk on the opposite side and tenderly tucked it round her. 'Thank you, Daddy,' she said, almost sound asleep. She never knew which one of them it was.

Chapter Eighteen

The ringing of the telephone insinuated itself insistently into Robin's sleeping head but she simply would not wake up. It persisted, however; stridently, commandingly. Unavoidably. She groaned, rolled over reluctantly, and reached for it.

'Yes?'

'Reception here, Captain Mariner. We have a Mr Balfour who insists upon speaking to you.'

'OK, thanks, put him through... No wait. What time is it?'

'Nine a.m., Captain. Shall I put him through now?'

'Yes, thanks.'

'Robin? Robin? Are you there?'

'Andrew, this had better be good. I've only had, what, six hours' sleep.'

'It's good. You've got to move like lightning to get everything arranged as you want it. We're on in two hours' time, in front of old Morgan again. God alone knows how Commander Lee put it all together in the time. Oh, and it's Friday. You've had nearly thirty hours' sleep.'

'Jesus Christ,' she yelled, coming out of the bed as though the duvet was on fire. Her wild movement jerked the phone off the bedside table and sent a silk-shaded lamp flying.

'Robin!' There was shock bordering on outrage in his tones – but that could have been to do with the volume, not the blasphemy.

'What do I do first?' She hopped naked around the room trailing the main part of the phone with her to the limit of its cord as she looked for clothes and necessities.

'What we discussed on the way back in from Ping Chau.'

'I know but what do I do first? Come on, Andrew I've only been awake five seconds, give me a break here.'

'Get up to Cat Street and pick up the clothes you ordered on Tuesday. The police will allow you a short interview in the courthouse holding cell so that you can hand over his new clothes. Remember, don't try to give him anything else, and no pointed conversations. They'll be monitoring things pretty closely.'

'Any recent news? God, Andrew how could you let me sleep a whole day?'

'Nothing new. Calm down, for heaven's sake. And anyway,' he added rather huffily, 'I tried to wake you several times but short of coming in and shaking you till your teeth rattled, I stood no chance. And of course Signor Borelli wasn't going to let me anywhere near you without your express permission. In triplicate. Countersigned. In blood. My blood.'

'All right, all right, I apologise. I'm sorry.' She dumped herself on the bed as though her body was a sack of washing. Then she caught sight of what she looked like in the mirror and modified her posture somewhat. 'So I pick up the clothes from Cat Street and go straight to the courthouse?'

'Yes. Quickly.'

'And they'll let me in to see him? I won't need you there?'

'Should be fine. You won't need me until he comes up into court. Well, not then, really. But we'd better be there. I've got Gerry geared up, and young Thong.'

'Look, Andrew,' she said, watching the whole pink and white expanse of her body tense as she said it, as though she had been suddenly douched with cold water, 'is there any chance this whole case will just get chucked out of court at this stage? That the prosecution will fall at the first fence and Morgan will throw out the cast and let me take Richard home?'

'No,' said Andrew. 'There is no chance at all that that will happen. You've got more chance of winning the Lottery. Really. Truly. I kid you not. So put it right out of your head and get up to Cat Street.'

This time Robin did use a taxi, though it might have been just as quick to walk. The cabbie waited cheerfully as she rushed into the tailor's shop where she had left Richard's measurements, and then, laden, dashed into the nearby shoe shop where, miracle of miracles in this place, a pair of English size twelve black lace-up shoes awaited her. They were suede, but what did that matter now? Then the cabbie took her straight to the courthouse where she paid him off.

Feeling out of place with her plastic bags full of shopping, she ran up the steps and into the great cool foyer. She crossed straight to the inquiries desk and crisply stated her business, oozing a confidence she was very far from feeling. An expressionless young police officer regarded her with long, dark eyes, picked up a phone, punched in an extension number and conducted a brief unexpectedly animated conversation, like a robot that had suddenly developed a fault. Then he hung up. 'You wait a moment, please,' he said. 'One come soon.'

Robin looked around for somewhere to sit but there was nowhere available. The clothes had been folded carefully into the bags and she was unwilling to put them down. She stood, feeling slightly foolish now, as well as out of place. The Chinese policeman looked her up and down, his face as expressionless as an ivory carving. She felt hot, frowsy and dumpy. Foolishly – comically – over-laden and almost slatternly. Apple-cheeked, frowsy and glowing with perspiration. She felt as though she should be blowing up at an errant curl out of the side of her mouth. Letting air out of herself like a slowly deflating balloon. She felt as though she should be adorning some thirties seaside postcard. 'The Guest Who Omitted To Book Ahead.' Yes. That was just about her speed today.

'Captain Mariner?' a soft voice just behind her said. Commander Lee had come himself. In full uniform, complete with swagger stick. There was an air about him of a man about to deal with the most important business imaginable. 'May I assist?' he enquired urbanely, the soul of Oriental charm and courtesy.

'No,' she said gracelessly and stupidly. 'Thank you.'

He smiled a minuscule smile and gestured with his left hand, almost – but not quite – bowing. They crossed to a door which led into a corridor not quite wide enough for them to walk down side by side. The door opened inwards and he managed to hold it for her and then to move away so smartly that he was still in the lead. Robin followed him, looking right and left at the series of open-barred doorways into old-fashioned holding cells which resembled something out of a cowboy film. Halfway down, however, there were full doors with sliding panels at eye level. At the first of these Lee stopped and rapped with the end of his swagger stick. The eye hole slammed open and then closed. There came a rattle of keys on the far side. The door opened and a young policeman stood at attention. Lee brushed in past him and Robin followed.

Richard was sitting at a table, dressed in the ill-fitting clothes he had worn for his first court appearance four days ago. When he saw them, he stood up. In direct opposition to Lee's almost fussily precise movements, his actions were a slow, almost lazy, unfolding limb by long limb.

'Richard,' said Robin, still so flustered that she almost forgot the position they were in. 'I've moved heaven and earth to get you these. I hope to God they all fit.'

She placed the bags on the table before him and he turned the piercing blue-white brightness of his eyes down towards them. How massive his hands were, she thought; but how gentle. He slid the charcoal suit out of its bright bag so gently the tissue paper didn't even rustle. He lifted out the boat-sized black shoes, tutted quietly to himself and lifted the black cotton roll of the socks. He picked up the white silk of the shirt and shook it with one violent gesture, suddenly, like a bullfighter with a cape. Both Lee and his constable jumped at the movement and Robin suddenly realised how nervous of him they were.

Naturally, she thought. They believed he had killed forty people late last week.

'I don't like these,' said Richard, utterly unexpectedly. He was holding up silk boxer shorts.

'I know, darling,' answered Robin without thinking. 'But they didn't have any Y-fronts in your size.'

'They'll have to do then,' he said with resignation.

Then it hit her. They had just had a perfectly normal conversation. Domestic and personal, but all the more normal for that. 'Richard,' she squealed, leaning forward over the table. 'Richard! It's me. Robin.'

With startling speed Commander Lee wrenched her back and she staggered until she collided with the constable by the door, her left hand smashing agonisingly against the butt of his holstered pistol.

Everything stopped for a moment. Richard was frozen in place, holding the boxer shorts and staring at them with utter vacancy, his eyes as flat as glass, like doll's eyes.

'Captain Mariner,' rasped Commander Lee, no longer quite so urbane.

Robin looked at her burning hand. The knuckles were skinned and beginning to bleed. 'I'm sorry,' she said, and brought the knuckles to her lips. She sucked at the blood thoughtlessly, like a schoolgirl. All of her attention was on Richard. 'But I . . . he . . .'

Then Richard was in motion again, putting the underwear beside the rest of the clothes and folding himself silently back into the chair.

'I thought he was back. I am sorry. I couldn't help it. I thought he was better.'

Commander Lee nodded once. 'He does that sometimes. Just for a second. Then he's gone again. The psychiatrist says—'

'He's seeing a psychiatrist?'

'Of course, Captain. What do you think? The man is unwell, he must be treated; we have a duty of care. And anyway, it is also in our interests that he should get his memory back.'

'But what if he remembers that he had nothing to do with the deaths?'

Again that minuscule smile. 'In our experience, when the memory really returns, they all remember that they did the crimes of which they stand accused. That's always what they were trying to forget, you see.'

The sole survivor of the stricken *Sulu Queen* stepped carefully into the silk boxer shorts, his face set like stone. He had forgotten that he did not like boxer shorts, but he was acutely aware that he hated performing intimate functions under the eyes of police guards. He settled the cool silk round his lean waist and crossed to the table, falling into one of those routines so old that it needed no conscious exercise of memory.

He unrolled the socks and hopped like an ungainly stork on one leg and then the other as he put them on. The shirt was a joy, loose, billowing and the correct collar size. He would rather have had cotton than silk – now who would have bought him a silk shirt? Still, never mind. He shook out the trousers, stepped into them and pulled them up. He met his first problem as he did them up. They were a good deal too loose for him. He frowned. There were no braces. Now what... After a moment's hesitation, he took the black tie from the ill-fitting outfit he had just removed and knotted it round his waist. He looked at the guard. 'Needs must,' he said. 'But I look as though I'm off to play cricket.'

The guard smiled once, the expression switching on and off like a facial tick. There was a sheen of sweat on his skin, although it was quite cool in here. The survivor wondered what the matter was, never guessing that the man saw him as a homicidal monster and was terrified of him.

The survivor did not know it, but he was only able to enjoy this much freedom and to move about unrestrained because the guard was a crack shot, with orders to kill at the first sign of trouble. There was also a squad of his colleagues, equally lethal, on the far end of the video link which monitored every move, waking or sleeping, day and night. In blissful ignorance, he reached for his shoes and slipped them on, lacing them carefully and double-tying the knots. 'Not really the thing,' he burbled on mindlessly. 'But what can you do?' He pulled the rich but conservative tie out of its box and knotted it expertly in a full Windsor. He tucked the thin tail into the label behind the thick face of the tie and smoothed it down his stomach, looking around for a mirror. There were, of course, no mirrors. He tutted thoughtlessly and straightened the knot by using the backs of his fingers and thumb against the wings of his shirt collar. Then he slipped on the suit jacket and buttoned it. 'There,' he said. 'Can't see the tie holding my trousers up now. This suit is pretty big, though. Think I've lost weight lately?'

The guard stood silent.

The survivor shrugged. 'Well, I'm ready,' he said, cheerfully. 'Now, where is it I'm actually going?'

'Captain Richard Mariner,' read an official, quietly but clearly, 'you stand accused that on or about midnight on the night of Thursday, 8th May, you murdered Brian Stanley Jordan. How do you plead?'

Silence. Not a whisper, not a breath in the crowded courtroom.

'Let it be recorded,' said Stipendiary Magistrate Morgan quietly, 'that the prisoner made no answer to that charge. And let that be entered as a plea of not guilty to the first count of murder.'

'Yes, sir.'

'You may proceed.'

'Captain Richard Mariner. You stand accused that on or about midnight of Thursday, 8th May, you murdered Charles William Macallan. How do you plead?'

This time the silence lasted for only an instant.

'Let it be recorded that the prisoner made no answer to the charge. And let that be entered as a plea of not guilty to the second count of murder.'

'Yes, sir.'

'Proceed.'

'Captain Richard Mariner...'

Let this not be happening. Oh God, let this not be happening. The words were bad enough on their own but even in the legalistic phrases they brought with them pictures . . . more than pictures . . . smells, sounds, the feelings of that night . . . the terror, the horror, the helplessness . . . the madness . . . the horror, the horror . . . How could this be happening? Where had it begun? Where would it end? How much more destruction was there still to come? Oh God . . . Oh God . . .

Robin sat rigid, her eyes brimming with unshed tears. Beside her, Andrew Balfour tried to impart strength and control to his extraordinary client through his square, solid shoulder by a kind of osmosis. It would get much worse later on and he was saving his brotherly grip for then – he had calculated he might need to hold her hand in due course and would probably need to support her from the court and the building in the end. He had asked her to listen to the charges – there might be a clue there that only she would notice. But he had warned her and warned her again to try and avoid using her imagination. If she began to visualise the acts described, and to visualise Richard doing them, she would be incapacitated and useless. But she was taking it hard, he could see that. And there was much worse to come. She closed her eyes and the first tear trickled down her cheek. It was time, Andrew thought, to take Robin by the arm. There would be crowds in the street outside, he thought, and where there were crowds there would be cameras.

'Now that we have the charges, Mr Po, and a full list of all the deceased discovered aboard, do you think we could proceed, please?'

'Certainly, sir. The prosecution would first call Captain Daniel Huuk of the Royal Navy, liaising with the Royal Hong Kong Police Force in the matter of coastguard duties.'

'Captain Huuk.'

Daniel Huuk stood in the witness box, the soul of calm reliability and utter professionalism. He calmly gave a statement which detailed how, on the early morning of Friday last, 9 May 1997, he had been contacted at his office in HMS *Tamar* by an unknown informant who had warned him in vague but urgent terms that all was not well on the *Sulu Queen* inbound from Singapore and, in consultation with his police liaison officer, he had determined to check on the ship. He had approached the vessel in disguise, aware that his information might not be genuine – or innocent. As the ship, apparently derelict, had drifted into Hong Kong waters and into his jurisdiction, Huuk had led his men aboard . . .

As the captain's calm voice detailed the exploration through the stricken vessel, describing everything he found there, Robin suddenly jerked into convulsive action, like a marionette in the hands of a child. She pulled out a notepad and started writing feverishly.

Andrew leaned forward. 'It's all right,' he breathed. 'You don't need to make notes. We'll get a full transcript of all this.'

She shook her head and continued writing. But only for a moment. She wrote only two words and showed it to him: WHERE'S WALLY?

He frowned. Shook his head. He did not understand. He wondered for an instant whether she had gone a little mad. Not surprising, under the circumstances.

By way of answer, she underlined the simple question with such force that the paper tore.

Andrew shrugged.

She moved to add some explanation, but her movement was arrested by Daniel Huuk's admission that, confronted by the prisoner, blood bedabbled and wild, he shot him on the left temple with an antipersonnel round and blasted him backwards down a full flight of metal-edged steps to land on the back of his head. 'When I got to the bottom of the steps,' Huuk admitted calmly, 'I was extremely surprised to find Captain Mariner was still alive.'

Andrew's grip on Robin's arm stopped being supportive and became a fierce restraint as he felt her begin to move. Shuddering, she subsided. The little pad with its cryptic message fell onto her lap and lay there, forgotten.

Daniel Huuk described how one team of his men had got the ship under power again and rendezvoused with a helicopter from RAF Sek Kong. He detailed the manner in which Captain Mariner, still not expected to survive, was loaded in. Under the direction of the police liaison officer, he had moved none of the dead bodies but rather left them in place until the ship tied up at a buoy off HMS *Tamar*.

Huuk came to the end of his statement and was replaced by Commander Lee. The policeman detailed the manner in which he had called together the best-qualified forensic team he could find in the Crown Colony, and had proceeded to examine, record and ultimately to remove all the victims from the ship. And how he and his team had spent the better part of a week doing nothing but establishing identity, circumstance and cause of death. He described how the stricken ship had next been moved to Kwai Chung where another two teams of experts had gone aboard, one to detail, move and hold the ship's cargo, the other to examine the scene of crime – the most extensive scene of crime in the history of the Crown Colony's police force – and to gather the last of the clues which would go towards the construction of their *prima facie* case in preparation for this hearing. 'Sir,' he concluded, 'I feel that you should be aware that, because of the scale of this enquiry, there is a range of details still under investigation. What we have here, are the broad brush-strokes, so to speak. As you will understand, I am sure.'

'We shall see, Commander Lee, in due course.'

Next came the pathologist who had carried out the post-mortem examinations. His evidence was a summary of much detailed work, but it added nothing new to the proceedings except to describe how the victims died, and when. The only exception to this was his introduction into the case of the five Vietnamese who had died some days earlier than anyone else, and whose bodies, although extensively ravaged at some earlier time, had more recently been treated with reverence and respect.

Last came an expert witness whose name Robin did not hear. He was a tall, stooped Westerner of professorial bearing and sibilant, nearly silent, diction. He had been called in, he stated, to examine the weapons used in the incident aboard the *Sulu Queen* and to establish whether there were any links between the weapons and the clothing, persons and environs of those people, living and dead, who were involved.

'I was presented ,' whispered the professor, 'with a range of clothing for examination. It was all tagged but not assigned. It was all stained and soiled with a range of bodily fluids, most notably blood, and it varied between two broad sorts: standard nightwear and equally standard seafarers' overalls. There was also some footwear, equally varied. I was also presented with a range of weaponry, rather more unusual. There was an M14 automatic weapon, caked with a range of bodily fluids. There was a Smith and Wesson .44 calibre automatic handgun with three rounds of Magnum strength remaining in the clip. And there was a basic panga, again caked in bodily fluids, mostly blood. This was especially true of the handle, which was effectively a rag wrapped round the metal tine at the base of the blade. The rag had been bound with adhesive carpet tape.

'I was required to examine all these articles in order to establish whether, at the basic level, there were any attributable fingerprints. I was required to examine the articles further to establish whether the blood and bone fragments could be assigned to any members of the ship's crew on an individual basis. Finally, I was asked to examine the firearms in particular, in order to ascertain whether it was possible to establish whether any individual person had been murdered with those weapons or could be proved beyond a reasonable doubt to have fired them.'

'Yes?' Prompted Morgan gently, as though the professor was as frail as he looked to be. 'And what did you establish, Professor?'

'Among the range of facts I established, the following seem to me to be germane.

'First: on the smooth surface of the carpet-tape handle of the panga which certainly executed the helmsman Win Chau as well as the two officers found on the bridge, there was only one clear set of fingerprints. These belong to the accused, Captain Richard Mariner.

'Secondly: on the Armalite M16 assault rifle, discovered in the ... ah ... fluids on the floor of the ship's library where the vast majority of the victims were later found, once again there is only one set of identifiable fingerprints. Those of the accused, Captain Richard Mariner.

'Thirdly and finally: with regard to the Smith and Wesson .44 calibre Magnum automatic handgun. It was to be expected that Captain Mariner's fingerprints would be on it as a witness has given in evidence that he saw the accused holding it. However, I was able to establish that this gun, with the captain's fingerprints on it, was the gun used in the execution-style killings of two of the officers on the bridge and of the first officer and the chief engineer. Further, there was one – and only one – set of clothing and footwear which was uniquely stained with blood and fragments of soft body parts and bone such as could only occur, in my submission, if the wearer was closely involved in the murders in question. This clothing was also stained by the residue of a range of burns and deposits such as could only be consistent with the repeated firing of the Smith and Wesson .44 calibre handgun held by the police if it was loaded with a Magnum load, such as was discovered in its half-empty clip.

'All of this clothing was, as I discovered later, the clothing worn at the time of his apprehension by the accused, Captain Richard Mariner.'

Richard was transferred half an hour later when Stipendiary Magistrate Morgan ruled that there was indeed a case for him to answer. Again, as planned, Edward Thong rose and agreed that the situation was in many ways unique. Because of the exceptional situation, he said, the Captain's defence team requested that the trial date be set as soon as possible. With no very good grace, Morgan agreed that he would see whether it would be possible for the trial to be heard at the Supreme Court in five weeks' time, during the final days of Crown rule in the colony. He also agreed, with some surprise, to waive reporting restrictions.

Richard's face was still wreathed in the utter unconcern which had characterised it so far, like a man totally unaware of the danger of his position and deaf to the increasing cry of vilification being hurled against him from every quarter.

Robin was not so deaf or unaware. As she rose, she found herself in urgent need of Andrew's supportive arm. Indeed, as they walked out of the courtroom into the corridor outside, and then immediately into the wide, cool reception hall of the Magistrate's Court, Andrew thought that his client might very well be going to faint. He had worried about her face going red and blotchy, now he was much more worried by its absolute pallor. She was as white as a corpse, and in his job he had seen a good few corpses.

As they crossed the reception hall, surrounded by such a crowd that it was out of the question to pause or to turn aside, Andrew looked down at her, wishing strength and life back into her with all his soul. And she seemed to respond to his desperate thoughts. Some colour flooded back into her cheeks, albeit livid and in sharp contrast to the greyish tinge of most of her face. Life flooded into the shaded pools of her eyes. 'What are we going to do?' she whispered. 'What in heaven's name are we going to do?'

On the threshold, hesitating against the outward pressure of the milling crowd around them, holding everything still with almost superhuman force while he dragged her back to life, he hissed in answer, 'We fight! For the next four weeks we work every hour God sends and then some. We pray the publicity *alerts* someone somewhere. We build a team, we come to court as fast as we can and hope to get this settled before the Treaty runs out and we make a case; we destroy their evidence item by item and point by point and we fight for all we're worth to get him acquitted, exonerated and free!'

Then, side by side, they moved out onto the steps, up to the howling crowd and into the headlines of every news programme, newspaper and news magazine in the world.

TWO

SERAM

But O heart! heart! heart!
O the bleeding drops of red!
Where on the deck my Captain lies,
Fallen cold and dead.

Walt Whitman. *Oh Captain! My Captain!*

Chapter Nineteen

Lata Patel had enjoyed a sheltered upbringing, and her only really serious vices had all involved sweets.

As the wildly indulged, only daughter of a hard-working family which owned a series of shops in the West End of London, she had attended an exclusive private school and put aside all thoughts of popular music, boyfriends and parties as she struggled to gain the best possible grades at GCE and 'A' Level. At Girton College, Cambridge, she had eschewed male society and other temptations equally assiduously, hoping to graduate at the top of her law class. And, now that she was in chambers, junior to one of the most flamboyant of the barristers in the Queen Elizabeth Building of the Middle Temple in London, she found she was far too busy to bother even with the most eligible of men.

Taking all that for granted, then, it came as something of a shock to Lata when she began to suspect herself of harbouring unnatural thoughts towards a woman.

The woman in question was her colleague, Magdalena DaSilva. The moment at which the shocking suspicion slithered into Lata's innocent bosom was on the afternoon of Tuesday, 20 May 1997. It was unnaturally warm, as the whole winter had been, and the Old Bailey courtroom had become unbearably hot. The barrister, in her wig and heavy robes, had found it increasingly difficult to work, Lata had observed sympathetically. And when the judge had called for an early lunch, Maggie had fled home as fast as possible to her little flat in Fetter Lane, not to eat but to shower. The case was at a critical point and so Lata had accompanied her boss, laden with papers which they were searching through for that one vital inconsistency. Maggie had taken the case at short notice because of an illness and the papers had just arrived in reply to her request for disclosure.

Going to Maggie's flat was not an unusual occurrence for Lata, but Maggie herself was wound up tighter than usual by the case, in a massive rush, and standing on no ceremonies. As soon as the two women arrived in the hallway of the flat, she was kicking off her shoes and shrugging off her jacket. Lata went through to the tiny kitchenette and put the pile of papers on the table. 'Would you like a drink?' she called through.

Maggie popped her slightly tousled head round the kitchen door. 'I need cool water,' she said. 'Outside and in.' She was pulling the hem of her blouse out of the waist of her calf-length black skirt as she spoke and by the time Lata handed her a glass of Ramaloosa from the fridge, she had all but unbuttoned it. 'We haven't much time,' said the barrister decisively. 'Bring the new papers through.'

Lata arrived in the bedroom in time to see Maggie stepping out of the skirt. She left it like a puddle of black ink lying on the floor, and began to pull down her tights. Lata looked around for somewhere to sit, more than a little amused by the mess which characterised the room, and no more embarrassed yet than a girl in a girls' dormitory. Maggie swept through into the shower room and Lata followed again. Here she found a little wicker stool with nothing but a cushion on it. She sat and arranged the papers on her lap, focusing her extremely intelligent concentration upon it. Distantly, she heard the roar of the shower going on, but her nimble mind was engaged in the intricacies of the case.

'It seems to me,' she called, raising her voice automatically to compensate for the noise of the water, 'that it all turns on whether we can prove that the victim, Horton, did actually make improper advances towards the accused, William Perkins.'

'Yes, I can see that,' called Maggie from the shower stall. 'The letter in blood, the black magic paraphernalia and the Dennis Wheatley books are all irrelevant.'

'If we allow that the jury will see that, then it comes down to whether Horton cornered Perkins in an empty street at midnight and frightened the life out of him by demanding his wicked way there and then,' said Lata. 'It would be enough to frighten me. Horton was an enormous man. And we know there were questions as to his intellectual competence.'

'So the fact that the murder weapon was a sacrificial dagger made of a goat's foot is completely incidental . . .' Maggie broke off, knowing that her junior would pick up her thought and run with it as though they were members of a rugby team.

'And the prosecution have miscalculated by emphasising the occult aspects. This isn't a ritual slaying by a crazed Devil worshipper . . .'

'It's a simple case of self-defence by a frightened, unworldly boy, threatened by a six-foot red-headed predatory homosexual in an empty street at midnight, fighting back with the first thing that came to hand,' concluded Maggie, her voice rising as though the matter were settled now.

'If we can prove that Horton was that way inclined,' warned Lata, as careful as always.

'And can we?'

'Well . . .' Lata temporised, sorting through the pile of papers which had recently arrived, 'There's a letter here . . . Its from a young doctor.

He wrote to the police but they never followed it up. It's no wonder they've been sitting on this!'

'What's it say?'

'That the doctor, returning late from a party along that same street the night before our incident was cornered by a six-foot tall redheaded predatory homosexual male and was lucky to get away intact.'

The door of the shower slammed back and Magdalena DaSilva emerged, running with diamond-bright drops of water. 'Got them!' she exulted. 'Lata, you're a genius!'

Lata sat, simply awed, until Maggie, too excited to notice the effect she was having on the girl, said, 'Pass me a towel, there's a darling.' And laughed like a silver bell when Lata spilled all the papers over her *café-au-lait* toes as she reached across to do so.

Back in the bedroom five minutes later, Maggie was still in devastatingly expansive mood – and absolutely nothing else. Having cast the towel on top of the mess which hid her bed, she was rummaging around in her underwear drawer.

'Will we need to contact the doctor?' asked Lata trying to keep her mind on the business in hand and off the fact that she had never seen anything quite so elegant as the manner in which Maggie's milk-chocolate back flared creamily outwards past her hips and then curved in secretly towards thighs which were almost the colour of toffee.

'We certainly will!'

Maggie swung round, holding some tiny pieces of white lace. She dropped them on top of the chest of drawers. Impulsively she crossed the room towards Lata who found herself actually shrinking back a little and trembling. Her shoulders hit the top edge of another tall chest of drawers and she was trapped. Maggie reached out towards her and Lata found herself falling helplessly into the golden depths of those great cat's eyes of hers. 'There one rule you've always got to remember,' said Maggie, softly, intimately.

'Yes?' said Lata.

'Fragrance first!' And Maggie stepped back, holding the great amber bottle of Obsession she had picked off the chest behind Lata's shoulder.

The room looked like hell but smelt like heaven ten minutes later when the two women exited. Lata had regained her pile of trial papers – and some of her composure. Maggie remained innocently oblivious of what had gone on in the quiet junior's mind, too excited at having discovered the fatal flaw in the prosecution's case.

As they hesitated at the door, the telephone began to ring. 'I'll get it,' Maggie decided at once. 'Always answer the telephone, even if you're in the bath. Never miss an opportunity. Hello?'

Maggie stood silently for a moment or two as the instrument chattered urgently, and all the laughter drained out of her face. Lata stood watching, speculating on how deeply tragic the telephone message could be. Maggie was silent for a second or two after she hung up and her eyes had a distant, almost dreamy look which Lata had never seen in them before. Then the flamboyant barrister shook herself, like a tiger after a swim. The life came back into her face. 'Let's go and crucify the prosecution,' she said. 'And then . . . How would you like a couple of weeks in Hong Kong?'

The Special Forces officer handed Tom Fowler the handset with some difficulty because he didn't want to put down his rifle, just in case.

'Direct line, sir,' he said. 'There's another one from the main communications vehicle; that will be used to monitor things so this is just for your use. Push the button to connect. Release the pressure to break off again.'

Tom took the handset and looked down at it without pressing the button, his mind racing. He had an habitual air of absent-mindedness which he fostered. It went well with his professorial image and, more importantly, it gave him extra time to think, in a world where too many people too often spoke too quickly too soon. Often with fatal results.

'You've got to speak to him, sir,' said the Special Forces officer, turning his head only slightly as he spoke, so that he would not loose his view of the main door down the barrel of his high-powered rifle.

'People tend not to do things just because they're kept waiting for a moment,' said Tom gently. 'People tend to do things because they're pushed; because of what is said, not because of what is unsaid.'

'You know best, sir,' said the soldier in his best 'Sod You' tone. 'But he's got the whole family in there and he's got five pounds of commercial explosive strapped round his waist, all set to go.'

'Then why is he sitting there waiting to talk to someone on the phone?' asked Tom.

The soldier opened his mouth to reply but Tom pressed the button and put the handset in position. 'Hello, Mr Thomas? It's Tom Fowler here. What can I do for you?'

Hoarse breathing.

The man was obviously terrified, Tom thought. He looked along the quiet, almost domestic street. Five police cars. Two armed police units. Bomb disposal squad. Fire brigade as back-up, just in case. Special services vehicle. That was unusual – the nearest people with sniper rifles, probably. Execution squad, nevertheless. And all there because a young man, apparently a builder, with various bits of wood and equipment had walked unexpectedly into a quiet terraced house and then phoned the police. If I was him, I'd be bloody terrified, Tom thought.

'I seen you on the telly...'

'So they said. Now what can I do for you?'

'You talked the guy in the plane down.'

Tom had accidentally stepped out of contented, relative obscurity at the Maudsley Hospital in South London when he had talked down a self-appointed terrorist with a flying licence, who was threatening to crash his Cessna into one of the terminals at Heathrow last Easter. The pilot wouldn't tell them which terminal was his target; wouldn't tell them anything other than that the Cessna was packed with explosives. He had been telling the truth too. And Tom had talked him into making a safe landing. He had been a Special Forces man, Tom remembered; retired, of course.

'So you want me to talk you down, Mr Thomas? What's your first name? Stanley? May I call you that?'

'Christian name. Stanley's me *christian* name. You believe in Christ, Mr Fowler?'

'Ah ... um ... Well now ...' There was a trap here. This was very disturbing. The man was supposed to be so desperate that he was begging for a shrink to talk him out and yet here he was playing games and laying traps. As a matter of fact, Tom Fowler did believe in Christ. He went to church every Sunday, read the lesson once a month and had even done a bit of lay preaching in his time; and his steady baritone was the backbone of the choir. But this wasn't anything to do with the God Tom Fowler worshipped.

Still, in for a penny ... 'Ah, yes, I think I do believe in God, Mr Thomas. In my own way.'

Again the hoarse breathing.

'Yeah. They said so on the telly. Lay preacher. Funny thing to be looking down on such a good man.'

More hoarse breathing.

He isn't scared after all, Tom decided. He's unafraid, in control and upstairs. What, apart from fear, makes a man breathe like that? Exertion. Pain. Excitement.

Apparently idly, seemingly in a world of his own, Tom Fowler began to spread out such information as had been supplied to him about the people in there with Thomas. Mr and Mrs Saddiqui and their children, a boy and a girl, both in their early teens. Average. No clue, except that Mr Saddiqui was an elder in his temple and a local councillor.

In his professional life Tom had come across a range of things people could do to each other, many of them mind-numbingly disgusting and most of them seemingly to do with sex, though Tom himself was of the post-Jungian school rather than the post-Freudian, and probably more influenced by R. D. Laing than either. But his doctorate work in the pathology of criminal psychology had been filtered through a lively inclination to believe in the redemptive possibilities of a higher power.

And, occasionally, through a very un-Christian hope that Hell was hot. Many of those latter thoughts arose out of contemplating what people were capable of doing to each other, of a sexual nature. But, realistically, there was nothing immediate in that line that a man could do with several great slabs of explosive secured round his waist like a kilt.

Exertion, then.

He pressed the button on the handset, breaking contact for an instant. 'Did he take anything in there with him?'

'Dunno.'

'Find out.'

It went against the grain to initiate conversation, but, 'I take it you have convictions yourself, then, Mr Thomas?'

'Convictions! Good word. Yeah, I got convictions!'

So Sigmund was right about subconscious association, if nothing else. You idiot! thought Tom. You sodding idiot, Fowler! You're not here to turn the screws on him. Yet.

He pushed the button; broke the connection. 'Anyone mention a criminal record?'

'Nah. Not under that name.'

So, Mr Thomas, you've been born again.

'They've got a photo, though. They're checking. That's where the chief superintendent is – down at the command wagon looking at the computer.'

'Do you belong to a local church, Mr Thomas?'

'Universal. Know what I mean?'

'No, I don't think I do.'

'We're everywhere, Fowler; we're the Universal...'

Two policemen arrived together, the sergeant who had gone off to find out what Thomas had been carrying – but he stood no chance against the chief super, self-importantly full of information from the police computer network. 'He's Martin Henry Perrott. Builder from Brixton. Killed two Jamaicans outside a church in South London five years ago. Claimed they were infidels, polluting the country with ungodly religions. Got seven years less remission. Let out just over a month ago – Tuesday, April 15th.'

'Easter Tuesday.'

'Apparently he was upset about that. Should have come out a week earlier. Procedural foul-up.'

'I see. And what did he take in with him?' Tom turned to the sergeant.

'Wood and a tool kit.'

'Wood. What sort? Twigs? Sticks? Planks? Boards? Branches? Beams?'

The sergeant opened his mouth to reply when the cross came out of the window. It came out of the upstairs bedroom window and it shattered the whole bay window casement. It was not a small cross and when it landed in the front lawn it buried its foot deeply but still stood more than six feet high.

Long before the cross had landed, however, Tom Fowler had whirled to the side of the Special Forces man. Just for an instant, just for the blink of an eye as the window exploded outwards and the great cross fell, there was a clear sight of Martin Henry Perrott framed in the window as though he himself was crucified.

'*Shoot*,' spat Tom Fowler.

The soldier obeyed at once. A single shot cracked out. Perrott jerked back out of view.

At the very instant that the cross landed, upright, in the front garden, the rest of the window it had come through was blasted out after it by a massive explosion. The roof went up like a flock of starlings and everybody in the roadway dived for cover.

Ten minutes later, a bevy of police men and women were leading the family out of the wreck of their house. They were lucky that they had been secured downstairs when the explosive – not quite five pounds after all – had detonated upstairs. They had been doubly fortunate, reckoned Tom, mopping a head wound from a sharp shard of roof tile. For there was no doubt in his mind that Mr Thomas – the late Martin Henry Perrott – had meant to make them an intimate part of his own martyrdom in a few minutes' time.

'I'll put in a full report as soon as I've had this head-wound seen to,' said Tom to the chief superintendent as they walked slowly back towards his debris-strewn Rover.

'You had it all sussed out, didn't you?' The chief super was a friend if not a fan.

'Pretty much, towards the end.' Tom was feeling sick and beginning to wonder whether he should be driving after all.

'Easter I understand. And I was listening when he said he was looking down on you, but what tied it all together?'

'The name. They choose a new name and they choose one that gives it all away. They do it every time; you'd think they'd learn.'

'Thomas? What? Tom, Tom the Piper's Son?'

'Most amusing. Usually it's Thomas for John Thomas – from those who have heard of *Lady Chatterley's Lover*, at any rate. But not this one.'

'Not Thomas the Tank Engine?'

Tom Fowler looked across at the chief superintendent and for a moment there was about him nothing at all of the absent-minded professor. 'Try Tomás de Torquemada,' he said. 'You should know all about him. Founder of the Inquisition.'

He was just reaching for the handle of the Rover, feeling quite pleased with his last remark, when the sergeant called out, 'Wait,

Professor Fowler, there's a phone call for you. Switchboard says its from someone in Hong Kong...'

Edgar Tan looked down at the two bodies on the hotel floor, then up at the slightly sheepish, deeply sickened face of the police inspector at his side. The bodies were less repulsive so he looked back down. Both bodies were naked, and the feminine body at least had a great deal to recommend it – other than the bullet wound, of course.

'Why don't you run me through that again,' said Tan. As soon as he said it, he paused, aware that his phrasing of the simple question was all too obviously influenced by American English. Singapore was a society which had made it all but illegal for citizens to follow his profession, that of private investigator. The authorities knew that Edgar was not his Christian name; so, as one of the rapidly decreasing number of professional detectives in the city-state, he needed to be careful even though he was long established and well respected in his profession, not least by the authorities themselves. He specialised in small stuff. Divorces. Missing persons. Corpses were out of his line.

'I mean to say,' he continued gently, 'I was hired by Mrs Sawa to find out what exactly her husband was up to. She thought maybe a little extra-marital liaison or whatever. She didn't suspect a bloodbath. I didn't suspect a bloodbath. Tell me about it, Sung.'

The policeman shrugged. 'Who would have thought it, Mr Tan? It was one of those things which nobody could predict.'

Tan looked at the portly corpse of his client's husband and agreed with the policeman wholeheartedly.

There was a sudden stir behind them. It was the hotel manager, enquiring when the police unit envisaged releasing his third floor and the guests who had been sleeping on it when the incident occurred. Inspector Sung looked at him until he went away again, but he never stopped talking to Tan.

'The gentleman, Mr Sawa, apparently was concerned to maintain absolute secrecy. He must have been aware that his wife was beginning to suspect something.'

Tan nodded. It was possible, he could see that.

'And – I'm surmising here – the lady in question...'

'Miss Fa. His secretary.'

'Miss Fa was the sort of a bed partner who makes repeated, individual, and very loud noises at particular times. So they had the television on quite loudly in order to cover the noise they were making. Unfortunately for them the walls in the hotel are thin and the guests on either side were tired and impatient. It was unfortunate, too, that they were using a gangster film to cover up what they were doing.'

Inspector Sung stopped, as though assuming Tan would be able to work it all out from there, and Tan was just about to ask one or two pertinent questions in order to make sure that he had, in fact, got everything clear in his mind, when the policeman started to speak again.

'After four repeated complaints, the manager phoned the room but there was no reply. The complaints persisted, mentioning screams and sounds of violent fighting, so he called the police. The officer who answered was young, inexperienced; eager. He came to the door and he, too, heard repeated screams, shouted threats and, at the moment he knocked on the door, a gunshot.

'At once, the officer drew his pistol and charged the door with his shoulder. The doors in this hotel are, as you can see, as flimsy as the walls and it burst open at once. At this; point, he says, he called the caution as required, but I doubt that anyone heard him.

'Mr Sawa and Miss Fa were on the sofa which, as you will have noticed, has its back to the door. The people and the television were all, therefore, concealed from the officer who ran into the room to the sound of a shot being fired and believing an act of violence was being perpetrated. Mr Sawa then popped up, stark naked, from the sofa. The officer shot him. The bullet went straight through his heart and then through the television, causing it to explode with some violence. At this point Miss Fa, whose screams, one assumes, were rapidly moving from the ecstatic to the terrified, also popped up.'

'He's a very good shot, this young officer.'

'Champion marksman.'

'What's the phrase?' asked Edgar Tan idly, thinking of something philosophical like 'In the midst of life, we are in death'.

'*Coitus interruptus*,' answered Inspector Sung, whose mind was moving along different lines.

And that seemed to sum it up, really. Except that Edgar Tan still had a phone call to make to a client who had been plotting a divorce and now had to plan a funeral instead.

Helen DuFour, senior executive of Heritage Mariner, looked across the table at the committee. There were six of them, all looking like retired rugby coaches – solid, square, slightly battered. Their suits were well-cut though and their eyes, though weary, were intelligent.

Behind them this particular window of the Kremlin gave a spectacular view of Red Square which for some reason was even more busy than usual today. Wearily, for she was as exhausted as any of them after the weeks of negotiation, she wondered whether she should start going through things again. But the chairman prevented her.

'We had assumed, you see,' he said in his technically flawless, richly accented English, 'that the incident in Chechnya would have pulled the republics together. President Yeltsin at that time, you will understand, was concerned about the manner in which gangster elements were moving into the most powerful positions in some of the governments of the republics and it was always his contention that this was the case in Chechnya.'

'I see,' temporised Helen. This was old news but a new ploy. She glanced left and right at the rest of her little team. They too were frowning with concentration. Perhaps, after all, their persistent patient probing had at last worn through the bullshit.

'You can imagine in general terms, I am sure,' the chairman rumbled on, 'with what horror the government here viewed the possibilities of such a thing. Whole republics being run by gangsters, drug barons, smugglers, answerable only to their own greed and the orders of their bosses further up the Mafia chain. Imagine if Siberia was run like that!'

Helen tried to imagine the man who ruled Siberia taking orders from an old-age pensioner somewhere in Sicily. But the chairman's point was well made, and it was relevant if he was telling the truth and President Yeltsin had been driven by such nightmares. And it suddenly broke upon her that, after Chechnya, the brigand ruling Siberia would know all too clearly that he didn't have to take orders from anyone. Including, in fact, the Kremlin.

'You have been locked in negotiations with us for nearly five years now over the matter of decommissioned warheads,' said the vice-chairman when the chairman himself fell silent.

'With you and your predecessors, yes. We are the only people who can guarantee to move the warheads safely when they are decommissioned and to dispose of them properly.'

'We recognise that. And, indeed, that if properly carried out, the business might be done to our mutual profit. But . . .'

There was the briefest of silences as the chairman reassumed his authority. 'But it all turns on one simple thing. The guarantee that the republics will give up the warheads as agreed. And after Chechnya . . .' He stopped, and shook his head.

'It is almost two years since Chechnya,' observed Helen with all the courtesy she could muster. Which, after all this time, was not a lot. 'Why do you bring this up now?'

'Because now is the time when we have to admit that we cannot guarantee the obedience of the republics in this matter. We cannot guarantee your supply because we cannot control what is going on out there.'

Helen looked at him, flabbergasted. It had been in the backs of all their minds, of course, for there was obviously a weakening of the political grip from the centre. But if the chairman of this particular committee, with its contacts not only in the civil nuclear programme but also in the relevant sections of the armed forces, was prepared to admit that they were losing control, then things must be at a pretty pass indeed.

'Of course, one is aware of the amount of material coming out illicitly through Europe, through Germany particularly.' she said sympathetically.

And the chairman actually laughed.

Helen stopped, surprised, for the Russians were never rude when sober, except on purpose. Her eyes slitted and her mind raced.

'My dear lady, I am sorry. I meant no rudeness. But you are talking about the little trickles which go west into a high-security situation with thousands on the watch – security forces, police forces as well as news agencies, newspapers, reporters of all kinds trying to get hold of it and publish what they have found. And where is the market there anyway? A few ersatz terrorists? Gaddafi? No. I am afraid the haemorrhage that we fear is flooding out, even as we speak, far beyond our ability to control it, to the east and to the south. China, Korea, India, even Japan – the powers around the Pacific Rim. It is all to play for there, as the English say, and that is where the stuff is going now.'

And just at the moment when the chairman made this admission and effectively brought to an end nearly five years of intense negotiation, there came a knock at the door and a secretary peeped in. 'There is a call for Madame DuFour on line one,' he said quietly. 'I understand it is from Hong Kong.'

Helen looked up, suddenly aware that everyone in the room was looking at her.

Charles Lee sipped the green tea with every evidence of enjoyment, watching Xiang Lo-wu through narrow eyes. This was the point when the game turned. This was the moment when all that could be done was done and everything else was down to joss and ancestors. The tea lay bitter on his tongue as he waited for the next word, and grains of dust from the cooling liquid ground between his teeth to warn him that his jaws were working with tension.

A warm wind rattled the ill-fitting windows and more dust puffed in round their edges. The thickness of a spring sandstorm obscured for a moment the thoughtfully smiling face of Mao Zedung as he gazed down from the Gate of Heavenly Peace across the Square of Heavenly Peace, also known as Tiananmen Square.

Most of the negotiations had been held here, although this was by no means the most important of the government offices. Nor was it the easiest to reach from the Beijing Hotel. The rest of the negotiation had been held out in the government suburb of Zhongnanhai, as was only right and proper. It was hard to estimate which section of the negotiations was the more important. He suspected that the words in this room were the vital ones, however. This was the reason they had chosen to speak them overlooking the site of his destruction – well, the destruction of his plans, at any rate.

The Chinese government negotiator was in no rush to speak, however. He seemed to be enjoying the bitter, grainy tea. And there was a paper he wished to consult, invisibly, in his Western style executive briefcase which lay, like Charles's, on the table between them. Had either been an aficionado of Western cinema, they might have been put in mind of gamblers, or of gunfighters facing up in a saloon.

'When,' began Xiang Lo-wu at last, 'you bribed a whole generation of our most promising students, what did you hope to gain?'

Always expect the unexpected. Who said that? Some unsubtle Western thinker, or writer. But it was a good lesson. He had been so entranced by the unsubtlety of negotiating in this place that he had taken his eye from the reason *why* they were negotiating in this place. Well, never bluff a bluffer. 'To gain power and influence.'

'When you financed the student reform movement which met its end outside this room, were you seeking power for yourself individually? For your family, your company or your country?'

'For myself first, then for my family. If the Lees are powerful, then our businesses will thrive and Xianggang,' he calculatedly used the Chinese name for Hong Kong, though he was more used to the Western one, 'Xianggang will join its near-neighbour the great city of Guangzhou and its other powerful sister, Shanghai, in taking the real financial power in the Pacific Rim and the world away from the Americans and the Japanese.'

'You believe that this can be done?'

'I do.'

'But you do not trust us elder brothers in government to do it for ourselves?'

'Beijing is a long way from Guangzhou, and it is even further from Xianggang. We do not always even speak the same language.'

'You insist on speaking with such a . . . *Western* accent.'

'Are we, then, to return to the days of the Quing Empire and look for ever inwards? You know what that led to, elder brother.'

'You believe that there will be another, what would you call it? Opium War? And that, once again, we would lose it?'

'There are companies in Japan and in America, and even in Europe now, who see business as war without end. You are familiar with the writings of Sun Tzu?'

'*The Art of War . . .*'

'They use it as a training manual for business executives. They have done so for many years.'

'But not Heritage Mariner?'

'In Heritage Mariner, I am the only senior executive who has read Sun Tzu, as far as I am aware.'

'You are uncertain?'

'There is one with whom I shared a course, a professor, twenty years ago at Johns Hopkins...'

'This one?' Xiang Lo-wu took a paper from his briefcase and placed it in front of Lee. On the front page was a picture of Richard Mariner and Lee's eyes leaped avidly down the page to the headlines and stopped. The newspaper was printed in a language he did not understand. He looked up at the Chinese minister, betraying – against all his inclination, breeding and training – surprise.

Xiang Lo-wu took back the paper and looked down at once, seeming not to notice his victory.

And Charles Lee did the only thing he could do under the circumstances: something equally unexpected. So unexpected was it that it even surprised Charles himself. He laughed.

He laughed at the ridiculousness of finding himself here, negotiating with a man who had used tanks to slaughter his unarmed teenage student friends. He laughed at the pointlessness of even expecting to walk away from here alive. And he laughed at the simple, dark joy of having been bested so elegantly at such an unexpected but perfectly chosen moment. It was very Western laughter, utterly un-Chinese.

Xiang Lo-wu looked up, surprised. And down again, impressed.

'No,' said Charles Lee after a moment or two. 'No, not him; his wife.'

'Really? His wife?' asked Xiang, apparently surprised again. He paused for an instant. Then, 'This person, perhaps,' and he presented another newspaper, this time with Robin's picture on the front. And this time Charles could read the writing; 'SHIPPING MAGNATE ACCUSED OF MASS MURDER'.

Then the paper was gone again, into the briefcase. Charles felt a little less like laughing. 'Yes,' he said quietly. 'That person. Robin Mariner may have read Sun Tzu.'

'And is it your opinion that this person is the sort of business executive who would learn from what she has read? And practise what she has learned?'

'Oh yes, definitely.'

'In that case, Mr Lee, why is she not here in your place? Must we assume that the position for Heritage Mariner which you are trying to negotiate is of secondary importance to the company?'

'No. The opposite. It was felt that, if I succeeded in approaching the relevant ministers, I would be in a position to negotiate hardest and to learn most. Sun Tzu commends highly the importance of precise intelligence.' There was more than a touch of wryness audible to his own ears in the admission.

'Indeed.' It was not a question.

Perhaps Xiang Lo-wu had also read *The Art of War*, thought Charles in the silence which succeeded this exchange. But the thought was short-lived, drowned in a welter of speculation about the meaning of the newspaper headline.

'But the fact is, if something were to occur which kept these other persons occupied, shall we say, then power would pass to you, as elder son?' purred Xiang Lo-wu.

Charles was by no means certain that he did hold the position of Crown Prince behind the Mariners in Heritage Mariner. The family held all the stock at the moment, and Helen DuFour was nearer family than he was for she was all but married to Sir William. But now was not the time for hesitation.

'Yes, that is indeed so,' he said firmly.

'Then you will wish to keep a close eye on events, I should imagine.' Xiang Lo-wu slid the paper with Robin's picture on it across the table with every appearance of solicitous courtesy.

As Charles's eyes devoured the story below the headline, a quiet chirruping noise insinuated itself above the bluster of the sandstorm outside. Xiang reached into his briefcase and pulled out a personal phone. '*Wai?*'

'The caller from Hong Kong is trying to reach Mr Lee once again,' said the politician's elder son and confidential secretary. 'Should we allow the call through?'

'Not at all.'

'Very well, sir. But how long will it be before he finds out what is going on?'

'He is learning something at this moment.'

'Then surely he will wish to return to Hong Kong as soon as possible.'

'Conceivably.'

'Would we be willing to restrain him? How could we then continue to negotiate with him?'

'There will be no need to run the risk. We will anticipate his wish and meet him halfway.'

'Halfway?'

'More than halfway. Inform my office that we are going south. All of us.'

'Of course, sir. May I enquire where in the south your destination is?'

'Guangzhou.'

Chapter Twenty

Robin was sitting in Andrew's swivel chair with her feet resting on a couple of law books up on his desk, to all intents and purposes sound asleep. She was not quite the same build as her solicitor and what with one angle and another, all that kept her decent was the fact that she was wearing jeans. Andrew looked down at her pale, dark-ringed face and up again at the chart on the wall opposite.

The chart was on white paper more than a metre square. It had been broken into four sections by two slashes of a red marker. Each section represented a week to the trial date. Each had days and dates marked in columns down one side and each of them was full of different people's handwriting in various coloured inks.

The writing in each of the four sections represented a set of targets to be achieved. These included obvious things like 'Clear desk' in Andrew's own handwriting, 'Mine too' in Gerry's and 'Settle Mandarin & find me a service flat ASAP' in Robin's. They also included running directives, like 'Visit Richard' which was repeated and repeated, except that, from tomorrow's section, a note was added to 'See Richard with Tom Fowler'. Finally, there were one or two more cryptic directives like 'Get Maggie and 'Call Helen'.

They were all aware, however, that there existed in Robin's head a list of targets which could never be written on the wall open to public view. This list included such things as 'Find some way to contact Twelvetoes' and 'Get back to Ping Chau' and, urgently, 'Break into the computer disk'. 'Test the Ping Chau paper' was one of a number of targets that had been met already. The paper was utterly unremarkable. It betrayed nothing unusual at all and was currently wedged into the corner of the mirror in Robin's new bedroom. Most of the targets on the first section of the chart were in fact crossed out because they had been met – indeed, the whole week was crossed out because it was long gone – but a couple had yet to be achieved and had been carried forward into the second section, with asterisks marking them as being increasingly urgent. It was a messy system but it was effective. It allowed them to keep track of what was going on, to see the patterns in what needed to be done, to make more assured plans and to use the increasingly short time to maximum effect.

Down the whole side of the second section, in Gerry's square script, was 'Go through prosecution with Thong's people'; Gerry was currently cross-checking every fact that had been alleged by Mr Po, Lee, Huuk and the rest with a young man from Edward Thong's office. They knew that Maggie DaSilva would be out to join the team soon and Thong was happy to prepare the ground for her and to assist her in court.

In Andrew's handwriting this section also said 'Go over S.Q. with Robin', and that was what he wanted to do next. As soon, in fact, as Robin had met her own deadline of 'Press conference' which she was due to hold immediately after lunch. This would bring them almost up-to-date, except that, in Robin's beautiful, rounded hand, beside urgent asterisks, it still said, 'Contact Charles', 'Do disk' and, perhaps most disturbingly, 'Find Wally Gough'.

'Well, Robin,' Andrew said gently, 'we've done an enormous amount and it seems to me that once you get the news conference over we can take the computer disk out to the *Sulu Queen* and slip it back into their system while we're going over everything else.'

'You're right,' she said without opening her eyes. 'It's our best shot. Two birds with one stone. And, after I've gone over it, then our own experts come in and double-check the evidence in the same way as Gerry's double-checking the facts.'

'That's about the size of it.'

'It's going to be another busy week.'

'A mistress of understatement. Look, do you want to grab forty winks? You look all in.'

'Mister Charm!'

'I wouldn't mention it, but you want to look good for the press, don't you?'

'Innocent boy,' she said with a dry laugh. 'Why do you think I brought my overnight bag up from my flat in Repulse Bay? When I'm finished I'll have a make-up job that'll still look good on camera after I've been dead for six months.'

'Well, if you don't want to sleep, why don't you eat something? No matter how good you look, it'll be fatal if you pass out on us.'

'Sure as hell didn't do President Bush any good. Pity; I liked him.'

'That's right.' He forced himself to be brutal. 'And look what happened when your father had his seizure on television.'

But she was not to be drawn. Surprisingly, she gave a wicked little chuckle. 'Maggie DaSilva gave him the kiss of life and knocked twenty years off his age.'

'She must be quite something.'

'Brother, you have no idea.'

It was a completely different Robin who sat beside Andrew two hours later. Her make-up was a little heavy for his taste but it transformed her from the wan figure in his office to the powerful chief executive who had almost got in to see Richard on her first night here. She was back in the sloppy top and jeans, however, for they were coming away from the news conference and heading up towards Kwai Chung.

'I think that went quite well, don't you, Andrew?'

'Very well. You managed to cast doubt on the prosecution, their case, their leanings and their preferences. You threw into very grave doubt the Crown Colony, its police force and its naval complement. I think some of what you actually said may be libellous, but it was certainly effective.'

'Helen DuFour will report in later this evening about how it went down in the City on the lunchtime news. It's such a relief to have her back in Heritage House. And I have friends in New York who will check in when it comes out there,' said Robin.

Helen had been back in London for two days now and was overseeing the extra work arising from the tragic events and liaising with the authorities who were supporting the families of the dead and missing, including Brian Jordan's young wife and two daughters, Charles Macallan's aged mother and an extremely worried Phylidda Gough in Budleigh Salterton. Robin had asked her about the disk and the China Queens network word processing function – but the senior executive had been unable to help. The inquiry which Helen had instituted on Robin's insistence had established only that the information needed was probably somewhere in the China Queens office in Singapore. Sir William had come back down to London and the twins, in seventh heaven, were with Richard's parents in their house called Summersend on the edge of the Lincolnshire fens, overlooking the sea. It was a good arrangement, for Richard's mother, tied to her wheelchair, needed his father's assistance at all times and so neither of them could come out to the colony; and there was nothing for them to do but sit at home helplessly and worry. The grandchildren were a distraction which was more than welcome.

Andrew already knew about Robin's friends and family. Messages of sympathy and support, offers of advice and help had come in from all over the world during the last ten days. Every day had been like Christmas as far as the post had been concerned, and there would be another pile waiting for them when they got back from the container terminal. Each call, message, fax, E-mail message, card and letter had been filed for immediate or eventual response. Robin had done it all herself, on top of everything else, including getting herself moved down to the leave flat he had found for her at the bottom of his hill in Repulse Bay and getting settled in there. He had never seen anything like it.

'And Maggie will be here for the next one.' There was a great deal of contentment in her voice as she made this observation.

'Is that so important? You handled them like a seasoned pro. Some of them had tears in their eyes towards the end.'

'Crocodile tears!'

'No. You were open, honest, impressive; noble, almost.' He hesitated, embarrassed at having gone too far. But she knew that the best way to take a compliment is in companionable silence. 'I just don't see,' he said emphatically, 'how she could do it any better.'

'Once she's here I can focus properly, Andrew. I won't have to be looking over my shoulder all the time and measuring my words. Maggie will run interference for me until I'm all but invisible. And she'll present a cracker of a case.'

'She'll present the case we give her,' he said with some asperity.

Robin chuckled. 'She will take whatever we give her and she will transmute it into legal gold.'

'Well, I'm not convinced.' He had an attack of gallantry. 'And I don't think anyone could make you seem invisible.'

'You wait. You'll see. I'll be able to forget about the cursed make-up bag. I could go onto camera stark naked beside her and nobody would notice a thing.'

Andrew gave a bark of laughter and shook his head. He had supposed that women were jealous of other women more lovely than themselves, but not Robin, apparently. Probably not any women, actually. That was a piece of wisdom he had gleaned from books and bar talk, he realised with a flash of dangerous insight. He did not, he realised a little sadly, know a hell of a lot about actual women at all. He put the Vantage into top and took her screaming over the speed limit to compensate.

Sitting at the foot of *Sulu Queen*'s gangway was a silver Honda Accord. 'Huuk's aboard,' warned Robin as soon as she saw it.

'Will that be a problem?' asked Andrew.

'Might be. I don't know. I'm not allowed to hit him, am I?' Robin had not seen Huuk since Richard's transfer and felt she had something of a score to settle with him. Andrew laughed, thinking she was joking, but in fact there was so much rage and frustration building up inside her that she genuinely had no idea what she would do when she next saw Huuk; hitting him seemed the least violent of the preferred alternatives. Andrew parked the Vantage beside the Accord because there was nowhere else available near the ship. Every space nearby was occupied, and there were even a couple of coaches parked among the cars.

When the Chinese officer met them at the top of the gangway, Andrew was suddenly suspicious that Robin might not have been joking after all when she threatened to assault him. The big solicitor abruptly felt an urgent need to step between them, such was the hostility crackling in the atmosphere. He was acutely aware that Huuk was backed up by two guards, both fully armed, and he had a feeling that Robin did not give a damn about the fact.

She managed to hold herself in check. Huuk himself hid behind a mask of Oriental inscrutability and from his demeanour during most of their visit aboard, it would have been hard to guess that he had ever met either of them before. Except for one brief instant right after they arrived on board. One of the guards said several words *sotto voce* to the captain; all Andrew heard clearly was the phrase 'body search' and he tensed, ready to protest. But Huuk spat a negative. Just for an instant, however, his long eyes dwelt on Robin's body and Andrew was not a little disturbed by what he thought he saw in them. And then the shutters came down.

'I have been ordered to give you full access to all areas, all equipment, and all existing records,' Huuk said as he led them up the empty deck towards the bridgehouse. His voice was tranquil, distant. Andrew filed what he thought he had seen in a compartment of his memory. He would examine it and test it later on. But it would be interesting, he thought, if the prosecution's chief witness had developed a romantic inclination for the mainspring of the defence.

'All existing records?' queried Robin at once.

'There were no official logs, movement books, lading books or ship's records found on the bridge,' Huuk explained. 'And, although an extensive set of records was kept in the ship's computer network, a flaw seems to have developed in the system and we cannot retrieve all the files.'

Robin's hand surreptitiously brushed the pocket containing the little disk. Her step lightened a little at the thought of breaking into it at last.

'Of course,' continued Huuk, apparently unaware, 'we have computer experts working on the system now so we may be able to give you more information in due course.'

'Thank you,' said Andrew, as though he was grateful.

They spent the next two hours going through the bridgehouse, with Robin making careful, knowledgeable observations and Andrew recording them. The process was detailed – they were not likely to have the time or the opportunity to do this again – but it was also oddly noncommittal because Huuk accompanied them every step of the way.

In fact, the ship was so busy that he need hardly have bothered. The whole vessel was one massive crime scene and although it was now more than two weeks since the crime itself had been committed, experts of all sorts were still checking and double-checking, testing, taping, taking, bagging, measuring and photographing. So busy were some sections of the bridgehouse that both Robin and Andrew began to wonder whether much of the activity was actually being staged for their benefit, to emphasise the range of dedicated expertise standing against them and to undermine their confidence. If this was the intention, it failed signally.

At the end of two hours, at half past five, the visiting experts all came to the end of their working hours. With much cheerful badinage they packed up and went ashore, some swiftly, some slowly; some laden, some empty-handed; just like a shift clocking off at a factory, they all began to go their separate ways. This was a crime scene to dream about, huge, complex, challenging; and absolutely secure.

Robin watched them from the bridge wing, deep in thought. Most of all, at that moment, she thanked God that Mr Feng and John Shaw had managed to make alternative arrangements for the shipping of the cargo – as soon as it was released from bond. The cargo – which Andrew and she would go over tomorrow – would not be held right up to the trial date. The ship certainly would. And then, of course, she would need to be completely re-crewed before she would sail.

Still, if the worst came to the worst, the *Seram Queen* was due in Hong Kong in a month's time. She could take on anything still outstanding – if that rude bastard Captain Sin consented to take an order, for a change. And thinking of Sin and his rudeness brought the computer disk back to the forefront of her mind. It looked as though the computer experts were leaving with the rest. Robin had been keeping a covert eye on them and was not really convinced that they were doing any serious work on the network. She was almost certain that, even if nobody else was, they were window-dressing put there to deny her access to the system. But now they were gone. She might get a chance to try it after all. If only she could think of a really good excuse to go back to the first officer's cabin. If only she could get rid of Huuk for a while.

The first challenge proved all too easy. She had seen a fair number of computer monitors around the bridge, but only one printer. The one in the first officer's cabin. 'You promised us some records,' she said to Huuk. She had not hit him; she had not been courteous to him either.

'Yes, we did. They were printed out earlier. I believe they are still by the printer in the first officer's cabin.'

'Good. I'll go down and start looking through them.'

'Of course.'

Andrew was standing on the navigation bridge looking at the watchkeeper's chair with a slightly sickened expression. As they went past him, Robin, who had been saving this suggestion for just this moment, said to him, 'Andrew, would you mind looking over the radio room for me? I know the communication logs are missing but I never met a sparks in the commercial service who didn't keep his own private record.'

She swept on across the navigation bridge as though unaware that Huuk was hesitating. In the Navy they never allowed radio officers to keep independent records – and they did not, in fact, usually allow them to do so on Heritage Mariner ships either; but Huuk did not know that, and Robin's request sounded reasonable. The captain's defences were split. Which should he oversee? The woman who was going through records that he knew all about or the man checking for something whose existence he had never suspected until now? Robin didn't think she was taking too much of a gamble.

'Right-ho,' said Andrew amiably and turned towards the cluttered little room. Robin did not deign to look back but she knew Huuk was following him, not her.

With excitement bubbling in her, Robin ran down the stairs towards the first officer's cabin. Still she would not allow herself to touch the little disk in her pocket – just in case. The cabin was just as she remembered it. She had been worried that they might have removed all of the furnishings, the books and the computer itself for testing, but no. It was all still there, except for the file of little disks. They were safely under lock and key somewhere until the computer network was up and running – always supposing it had really crashed in the first place, as Huuk had said.

Robin settled in front of the machine. There were several things she had to be certain of before she proceeded. To begin with, she had to be certain that when she used this machine, the rest of the other machines did not light up as well, as they had the last time. Secondly, she had also to be certain that the machine was not, in fact, faulty. If Huuk was telling the truth and if she put the precious disk into it, she ran the risk of wiping it clean and of losing all the information it contained.

At least the power was still running and the machine was on. By the look of things the computer was loaded up and was holding the directions from the network in its stand-alone memory. It was certainly a much more powerful machine than any of the others on the network. Holding her breath, she pulled the network circuit plug from the back. Sitting down again, she was relieved to see that the screen was still alight and asking for directions.

She wondered if Huuk's men had gone through the bookshelves as thoroughly as she and Twelvetoes had done. She checked; they had. Even the disk behind the family photograph was gone.

Robin unbuttoned her pocket and slid the disk out, noting as though for the last time Brian Jordan's schoolboy hand on the bright label, the numbers beneath the title, the little air bubbles trapped beneath the paper. Then she slipped it into the machine in drive A.

PRESS ENTER TO PROCEED said the screen.

She watched it as though it was a venomous serpent poised to strike her. Nothing happened. She raised her hand. She pressed ENTER.

The screen went black and all hell was let loose. She sprang back, upsetting the chair, such was the unexpected brutality of the noise the machine emitted. One of Huuk's computer experts had rigged the machine so that the action of pressing ENTER would trigger an alarm. Nor was that all. When she pressed the release button, trying to retrieve the disk, it soon became apparent that this had been tampered with as well and the little grey square of plastic was not going to come out again at her command. And in the meantime, the siren wailed and wailed.

Huuk himself was there within moments, his face like stone. He gestured to her to get out and she obeyed. She did not see what he did, but the wailing stopped and when he came out into the corridor where she was waiting he was holding the disk.

'Lieutenant Jordan had a system,' he said. 'All the disks were numbered as well as labelled. We knew one was missing from the time you last visited the ship. Thank you for returning it to us.'

'Can I at least take the records you printed out?' she asked a little desperately, just as Andrew puffed up beside her.

'Of course. They are defence copies. Is there anything else?'

She looked at Andrew. 'No,' he said. 'Nothing else.'

Huuk nodded. Silently he turned, stepped back, picked up the pile of print-outs and returned with them in his hand. He gave them to Robin with something of a gesture, like a duellist saluting a gallant but lesser opponent. Then he escorted them to the gangway and watched them as they walked down to the Vantage.

'Was it worth it?' asked Andrew as they settled into the massive sports car.

'Wait,' she said. 'I'm half convinced that devil Huuk can still hear us. Do you suppose he's psychic?'

'God knows.' He turned the starter and the engine crashed into life. He pulled off before Robin fastened her safety belt, but it was not until they reached the main gate that she reached down and pulled a second disk out of her shoe. She put it up on the dashboard and the last of the evening sun glinted on the side with sufficient force to show the tiny traces of adhesive which remained where the label had been carefully removed.

As she was strapping on her seatbelt with a secret little smile playing around her lips, Andrew reached into his jacket pocket. 'Brilliant idea, that, checking the radio room,' he said. 'Look what I retrieved from under the main transmitter while Huuk was downstairs dealing with you.'

And he threw a little black-covered notebook onto the top of the dashboard beside the disk.

Chapter Twenty-One

It was nearly midnight when Andrew said, 'Look, Robin, you've got to go back to your own flat now and get to bed. Think of what you've got to do tomorrow. You have to meet Professor Fowler, brief him and take him in to see Richard. It's going to be hard enough even if you're bright-eyed and bushy-tailed. It'll be hell if you've had too little sleep.'

'Sleep?' she said in a tone of voice he hadn't heard her use before. 'You think I sleep?'

'Listen to yourself, Robin. You're exhausted. You want me to run you down the hill in the Vantage?'

'What, wake up that monster simply to drop me somewhere I can get to in a five-minute walk?'

'Well . . .' he shrugged a little helplessly.

'You're sweet. And you're right. I'll go at once. Do you want a hand with this stuff?' She gestured vaguely at the leftovers from a takeaway Sechuan feast.

'No. The *amah* will tidy it up in the morning,' he said. And she was too tired to argue.

At the door he took her coat down and then reached for his own. 'No,' she said gently when she saw what he was doing. 'I'll be all right. I want to walk slowly and finish thinking this through. You get some rest yourself.'

He was glad enough to obey, but as he turned back to switch off the lights after closing the door behind her, he saw the mess in the dining room again and found himself going through and tidying it away after all.

Robin walked slowly down the hill. The roadway was well lit and the town at the foot of the slope, a couple of hundred metres distant, was still bustling. The walk could not have been safer, and she was aware that if she gave in to offers like Andrew's of a lift home too often she would soon become reclusive and useless. And she had not been spinning Andrew a line. She did want to wander along slowly, thinking on her feet.

The black book Andrew had discovered contained some interesting information. Robin had worked out the cryptic notes without too much trouble; it was their precise meaning she wanted to think through, and some of that meaning was hidden between the lines. She had to think it through – to her own satisfaction at the very least. And she had to do it tonight for, regretting already the rush of blood to the head which had made him steal it for her, Andrew proposed to hand it back to the authorities tomorrow. She could hardly blame him, and in any case it did not seem to her to add to the case against Richard. Andrew continued to suggest most strongly that she hand back the disk as well, but somehow she could not bring herself to give that up. It contained a secret file marked for her eyes only, after all, and she could not bring herself to trust Commander Lee or Huuk.

In essence, the black book was a simple record of calls which had been made between the captain of the *Sulu Queen* and the company secretary in the China Queens office. Robin suspected there would be no record of these calls in the radio log itself if it were ever found. The calls were regular but at odd times of the night; and they were far longer than company rules stipulated. What was exercising Robin's mind was the fact that the calls stopped just a little less than a month ago, on the very day that Richard had sent her the postcard of Raffles to show that he had arrived in Singapore. The book had been kept beyond that time, for there was a series of neat ticks against the days and one or two personal notes, but no further radio calls were recorded.

And the most likely reason that Robin could think of why the captain of the *Sulu Queen* should stop making his regular radio calls was if he was no longer there to do so.

Which might explain what Richard had been doing aboard in the first place and certainly explained why Wally Gough wasn't listed among the dead found aboard *Sulu Queen*.

But, if Wally wasn't on board his command when she left Singapore, where the hell had he got to?

Robin had just become fully alive to the urgency of switching rather more of the investigation to the city-state of Singapore at the earliest opportunity when she realised that she was no longer alone. A tall figure, dressed in black and almost indistinguishable from the shadows, was moving at her side. She jerked in her breath to scream but recognised his chuckle just in time. 'You are hard woman to catch alone.'

'I really need a way to get in contact with you, Twelvetoes.'

'I will think of something. But I am always closer than you think.'

'You don't know how reassuring it is to hear you say that.'

'You have more friends than you realise – '

'That's very—'

' – and more enemies than you know.'

'Enemies?'

'What did you find on Ping Chau Island?'

'Containers. Empty.'

'Perhaps not as empty as you think.'

'Perhaps not. I didn't have time for much of a look. Can you get me back there?'

'No. But I will send someone on your behalf, quickly and secretly.'

'Why can't I go?'

'Did you know Daniel Huuk has issued orders to send a launch back to check again? They sail tomorrow ... No? He did not mention that this afternoon? Well, there are many things he does not want you to know; that is another of them. But I doubt the Navy will find anything this time. What you did was ... *unexpected*.' There was a smile in his voice on the word. He sounded a little like a proud parent.

The pair of them were almost at the light of the first intersection now and, although they were walking more slowly, Robin was all too well aware that her time was strictly limited. What did she want to ask Twelvetoes now that the Ping Chau matter was settled? Her mind raced, but nothing solid would come. She would wake up in the middle of the night berating herself for not thinking more clearly, she knew. 'Twelvetoes,' she said, desperately, 'do you know what is really going on?'

'Of course not, Little Mistress, or I would tell you!' The laughter had died in his voice, replaced by a tinge of indignation.

'Is there anyone who does know?'

'Not that I know of, or I should be asking him.' The way in which he said that made her pause.

'But someone must have some idea!' she almost cried.

'There are, I believe, several people who know part of what is going on. They are Daniel Huuk, of course, and Victor Lee; a man I will not name who is the leader of the White Powder Triad; another who shall again remain nameless, who leads a family of pirates in Manila; two diplomats, I think – St John Syme and a man called Xiang Lo-wu who is currently entertaining Charles Lee from your company – did you know that? No? Believe me, it is true.' The smile was back in his voice but the sound of it was becoming softer and softer as though he was fading away altogether.

'Then there is yourself, your solicitor and Captain Walter Gough.' The thread of his words persisted, though he himself was lost in the shadows again. 'You all have a fairly clear idea, I think, of the section of the pattern you are involved in, though I suspect that Captain Gough only knows as much as Anna Leung will allow him to know. I myself see enough of the pattern to suspect where the rest lies and as soon as I know more than you will too. But other than we few, I think there is only one person who has seen the grand design.'

'And who is that? Who is that, Twelvetoes?'

'Why, Richard, of course.'

It was impossible to guess the motives behind Twelvetoes' information, its nature and its timing. What was certain, however, was that a good night's sleep for Robin did not feature in the old man's plan. She tossed and turned, sifting his information, testing it against her own knowledge and trying to use it as a lens through which she could examine what was going on from new perspectives and so gain new insights. But it all kept slipping away from her and ultimately she knew she would have to settle for the immediate targets she had agreed with Andrew. Only by sorting things out little by little and one step at a time could she have any realistic hope of clearing Richard's name. And that was the overall goal, after all. Everything had to tend to that end. In one month's time, plus however many more days the trial took to come to a conclusion, Richard had to be exonerated, declared innocent of all those terrible charges and free to come home with her. That was Robin's only target. Any other pattern of motives, involvements and events which Twelvetoes Ho chose to talk about was relevant to her only if it helped her get Richard free.

The first major step on this quest was to meet Professor Tom Fowler of the world-famous psychiatric section of the Maudsley Hospital in London at the airport next morning, but his flight wasn't due until ten o'clock local time, so she had time to clear up a little niggling irritation first. She was at Andrew's door at eight thirty and the pair of them were in his office by nine. She was on the phone to Singapore at five past. There was still no reply from the China Queens office. Enough was enough. She asked the operator to put her through to the Singapore authorities.

So it was that at 9.15a.m. on the morning of Tuesday, 27 May, Robin found herself in contact with Inspector Sung of the Singapore police.

She explained who she was and what her problem was.

Inspector Sung was good enough to inform her that the disappearance of Miss Anna Leung was already the subject of a police enquiry there. There had been some question of financial impropriety, not to mention moral laxity; and in any case co-operation had been sought by Commander Lee of the Royal Hong Kong constabulary.

Exhausted, under enormous stress, extremely irate and mentally cursing herself, Robin announced that she would very much like to support the authorities in this matter and asked whether the inspector could by any chance give her the name of a reputable local private investigator.

So Inspector Sung told her about Edgar Tan who, he happened to know, was not working on a case just at the moment.

Tom Fowler's plane had come into Kai Tak, and, even after the time it had taken to clear immigration, collect his baggage and come through Customs, he was still as pale as the woman who had come to meet him.

'How do you do?' she said. 'I'm Robin Mariner. Can I help you with any of that?'

He handed over the briefcase and hung on to the suitcase. He rarely travelled and never travelled light. 'I've organised a taxi to your digs,' she said. 'You'll be staying with my solicitor if that's acceptable. We can check you into an hotel of you would prefer but things are getting pretty busy now that it's only a month or so to handover. Lots of people who don't have to be here coming in for a visit; lots of people who can't go anywhere else trying to do so, just in case. Very busy indeed.'

'And not exactly the best time for a trial,' Tom observed.

'The worst.'

He had stemmed the flow of information and he had not meant to do so. 'But you have a trial date and are preparing the defence,' he prompted.

'That's about the size of it. We have a little more than two weeks left. Our barrister is due later in the week. She's flying out from London too.'

'Are there no competent barristers here, then?' He was surprised enough to ask an indelicate question.

'On the contrary, the people here are extremely competent. The same is true of psychiatrists, of course. This barrister is something of a good luck charm, though.'

'You think you need luck?'

'I believe in luck and I'll take all I can get.'

'Very wise.'

They had arrived at her taxi now and they handed the cases to the driver. 'It's a lovely drive to Repulse bay,' Robin said. 'And it's long enough for us to start making some plans.'

'What I need to know first,' said Tom as the taxi headed out of Kai Tak, 'is exactly what you require.'

'What do you mean?'

'Obviously I stand to be corrected as I get to know the case more intimately, but from what I understand at this point we are dealing with a case of complete dissociative amnesia, taken to the point of loss of personality. There is a closed head injury involved—'

'Closed head?'

'What it sounds like – the head was not cut open. Quite. And there has been a history of amnesia.'

'Richard lost his memory once a few years ago – another closed head injury. He fell out of a crashing helicopter and caught his head on some deck furniture.'

'That incident lasted how long?'

'A couple of days.'

'That's quite long.'

'But nowhere as long as this time.'

'That's right. But we'll have a look at the pathology of the case when I actually talk to your husband. We'll take for granted that, for whatever reason, he cannot remember what has happened to him up to and including the time he spent on the ship *Sulu Queen*. In the meantime, let's talk about what you want me to do.'

'We've come round full circle here and I still don't see exactly what you're driving at.'

'Do you want me to work on the area of retraining your husband in the basic memory skills?'

'Teach him how to remember?'

'Yes. Teach him how to progress from this point onwards, building a new memory and, if need be, a new sense of himself?'

'Is that what you do?' She sounded horrified.

'In some cases, yes.'

'God, no. I want you to try and make him *really* remember. Make him remember who he is and what happened on the *Sulu Queen*.'

'But it may well be that he does not wish to remember what happened on the *Sulu Queen*,' Tom warned her.

'What do you mean?'

'You must know that lengthy loss of memory through a simple knock on the head, no matter how hard, is quite rare. Fugue states such as this most commonly arise because the mind cannot accept what has gone on. In rejecting what it cannot accept, however, it sometimes rejects everything else as well. The result of this is that the patient has no memory of anything, even of their own identity. And sometimes they even damage their ability to use memory at all. They retain a range of skills and some basic general knowledge but they can lose the ability to concentrate. Sometimes they need to be reminded about new facts. It is rare but it has been known. Wars have furnished a good few classic examples; violent incidents, accidents, murders. There are well-documented cases, and almost all of them have involved people running away from something which they have found themselves absolutely unable to face.'

'Well, it wouldn't be too surprising if that is what we're dealing with, would it?' she observed bitterly. 'Richard was the only person found alive on a ship full of forty recently butchered people and five Vietnamese who had been dead for a few days longer. No matter what happened, he isn't really going to want to remember it, is he? Would you?'

'If people were trying to prove I had killed them all and I hadn't actually done so, then I most certainly would want to remember, yes!'

Robin looked at Tom and gave him a dazzling smile; he realised he had been outmanoeuvred. It was the price of allowing the conversation to drift into quasi-medical areas as he tried to explain some general principles to someone who did not possess the vocabulary needed. But being outmanoeuvred was a small price to pay for that smile. 'Right,' she said. 'That's exactly the situation Richard is in. We have to help him remember. *You* have to help him remember.'

'Very well,' he capitulated. Secretly he smiled a little himself. Robin Mariner had a much more positive air about her now. That was all to the good: he did not want her to be added to the list of his patients. And when it came right down to it, as a fully trained doctor, he would go through the set routines and make up his mind for himself no matter what possibilities he was willing to discuss now.

'What I would like you to do,' said Tom gently, 'is to try and tell me the absolute truth. Whatever it is. At all times.'

'Right-ho,' said the *Sulu Queen*'s survivor. He smiled up at the doctor and the expression in his eyes was as bright, and as shallow, as sunlight on glass.

This was an extremely bad beginning, thought Tom. But immediately he wiped such preconceptions from his mind. Watch and record; don't judge. He smiled supportively. 'Good,' he said. He sat down opposite his patient and put a small personal tape-recorder on the plain, painted wood. 'Do you mind?'

The survivor shrugged amenably but silently. The sudden cessation of spoken communication was not lost on Tom either. He remembered all too vividly the way that Thomas, the religious fanatic with several pounds of commercial explosive had also been playing mind games, apparently without reason, while he was building himself a cross. Tom switched the machine on and watched the little tape spool running for a moment while he cleared his mind again. Then, 'Just for the record,' he said, apparently casually, 'could you tell me your name?'

Robin was fit to explode, but she saw the logic in Tom Fowler's asking her to stay away from the first interview at least. After dropping him off at the hospital, she took her taxi on down to the Heritage Mariner office. She had lots of things she could be getting on with the first of which involved Mr Feng. Mr Feng was slight and bald. His whole head was dominated by an enormous pair of black-rimmed spectacles. The impact of this eyewear was intensified by the fact that the thick lenses were light-sensitive and even in cloudy conditions or shade, they remained darkly tinted. He had the appearance and furtive air of a night creature caught out in the day. John Shaw drily suggested that night was a time when Mr Feng came into his own: he and Mrs Feng had ten children, though he was sending the eldest ones abroad to relatives all over the world just at the moment, in case things went badly here after the handover.

But the fact was that Mr Feng was a well-connected, astute and efficient businessman and even though he kept short and precise office hours, he did a first-rate job. Robin was impressed. It seemed to her that she had to expend so much time and energy to get anything done at all that the effortless ease with which Mr Feng performed made her shake her head and sigh to herself.

In the absence of half of their China Seas fleet, Mr Feng had perforce moved the focus of their operations into brokerage and he was currently engaged in finding cargo space for a whole range of goods which he could no longer fit on the *Seram Queen* whose holds would be fully laden when she passed through Hong Kong in the wake of her stricken sister. Further, a great deal of extra work had landed on his desk because of the absence of Anna Leung and the effective closure of the China Queens office in Singapore. And even more work had been heaped upon his frail shoulders by the fact that Robin wished to set up a far more efficient and comprehensive series of communications channels between Hong Kong, Singapore and head office in London. She had seen all too quickly that the offices here regarded themselves as subsidiary members of Heritage Mariner only very distantly indeed. If communications had been better, she would have been in possession of a full itinerary of Richard's movements.

But the communication she had come to check on had been moving the other way down the newly-cleared channels to London. Slowly spooling, page by page, out of the fax machine on Mr Feng's desk was the whole of the bulky Heritage Mariner file on Richard. The last time she had looked at it, that file had been nearly fifty pages long, comprising as it did a whole series of documents accumulated in the range of companies and situations Richard had worked his way through. Helen DuFour had also sent Audrey, the night secretary from Crewfinders and one of their oldest friends, down to Ashenden. The result of Audrey's research was that, as a kind of appendix, there was a whole pile of family stuff – birth certificates, wedding lines, letters and photographs – which traced Richard's life from his earliest years as the son of a country vet who had done his war service in the Navy, married the daughter of a Morningside solicitor, and set up an idyllic practice in the village of Bolingbroke at the heart of the Lincolnshire fens.

Unable to stop herself, Robin picked up the last sheet which had spooled out of the machine and found herself looking at the photograph of a small, vibrantly excited boy dressed in shorts and a T-shirt standing outside a long, low-fronted stone building. In her neat, precise writing, his mother had written 'Richard arrives at Summersend, August 1950'. He was as proud as a king, the glow of his joy emphasised by his halo of near-white hair.

His hair had become so black that Robin sometimes forgot that he had been blond as a child. As, indeed, were her own two children.

Summersend, the Mariners' big old bungalow overlooking the North Sea, was where the twins were now.

She looked at the ceiling, refusing to sniff or sob, and let the hot tears run back into her hair. Mr Feng concentrated absolutely on the records he was typing into his computer and for a moment there was quiet in the office. Then the phone began to ring.

Mr Feng was concentrating so hard on his computer that Robin answered. 'Mariner.'

There was that slight time lapse which tells of very long distances, then, 'Robin? It's Audrey here. Are all the faxes through? The last sheet I sent was the picture of Summersend.' Audrey could not really bring herself to trust these machines for all they sent automatic confirmation sheets.

'All here, thanks, Audrey.'

'Good. There's something else, too.'

'What?'

'You might want to check the China Queens office again. After all this fuss, I've been trying at odd hours. It gives me something to do during the long night watches. Well, I don't know how important this is, but I finally got through on the number you gave me. It must have been about eight thirty in the morning Singapore time.'

'And?' Hope sprang up in Robin's heart. Perhaps Anna Leung was back after all and she could put that whole section of the business firmly out of her mind. She looked automatically at her watch. Three hours ago.

'I got this nice policeman who informed me that the China Queens offices were now under police guard pending an investigation. Is that important?'

'We knew about the investigation, not the police guard. Thanks.'

'Yes, Mrs Mariner, that is correct. The office is under police guard.' Inspector Sung choose his words carefully. 'It is not accessible to anyone. Should a senior executive of the company require entry, that would be taken under consideration, of course. But in the meantime the office has been closed and sealed.'

'But why?'

'As part of our investigation into the disappearance of Miss Anna Leung. As I have said, there is a question of financial impropriety.'

Robin abruptly wished that she was calling from Andrew's office; it would have been useful to have had access to a solicitor at this point in the conversation. But she had no one to refer to except Mr Feng.

'Just a moment, please, Inspector. Mr Feng, when is the *Seram Queen* due in Singapore?'

'Ten day.' She noticed that he did not even have to refer to his computer for the information.

'Might I ask, Inspector, whether this investigation is simply a missing persons case, or is there some suggestion that Miss Leung's financial improprieties might involve the whole company?'

'Too early to say. The paperwork in the China Queens office will guide us further, I am sure.'

'Thank you, Inspector.' She hung up, deep in thought. 'Mr Feng, what is the name of the China Queens solicitor in Singapore?'

'China Queens a respectable company, missy. No need solicitor in Singapore!' He sounded genuinely outraged at the suggestion.

She stood, wrapped in thought. So there was no company associate in Singapore that she could contact in order to look after their interests and find out what was going on. And she needed to know for certain in ten days' time or they could lose the *Seram Queen* as easily as they had lost access to the China Queens office. And, she muttered grimly to herself, when things are already this bad, you really have to plan on them getting worse.

'Mr Feng,' she said, coming to an unwelcome decision, 'where is the telephone number of that investigator in Singapore? What is his name? Edgar Tan?'

Chapter Twenty-Two

The problem with preparing for the worst, thought Robin glumly, was that you didn't always know which direction the worst was coming from. She had no sooner set Edgar Tan onto the trail of Anna Leung, the facts about what had happened during those lost days in Singapore, and some kind of an estimation as to whether *Seram Queen* would be allowed out of the port again, than Tom Fowler called. They met in the coffee bar on the ground floor of the Queen Elizabeth.

'It's very much as we discussed,' he said, stirring his coffee slowly with a biscuit and choosing his words with the utmost care, every inch the absent-minded professor. 'He seems to have no clear idea of personal identity. He certainly has no memory which he can access for any part of his life before he woke up in hospital here.' He pulled the biscuit out of his coffee just as it was beginning to crumble and sucked on it meditatively.

'His general knowledge is quite wide, but I have no idea how wide it was before. Equally, he knows an awful lot more than I do about ships and shiphandling, but again, I don't know how that measures up against his original knowledge. There are no personal memories there at the moment. No matter how far back I went, there was nothing we could get hold of. Business matters came and went. I can sense a pattern there, but I can't see it. No real grasp of political events, nothing current about the cinema or television.'

'He doesn't watch much television as a rule.'

'No, indeed.' He reached for another biscuit and slid it into his increasingly lumpy coffee. 'But it's a standard indicator, you know.'

'I have his whole file in my briefcase here. All sorts of stuff from home.'

'Good. The problem as I see it is, that we don't know exactly who got shot in the head.'

'What do you mean?' Robin felt an obscure sense of outrage as though Richard's truthfulness had been called into question. As though her most basic beliefs were being challenged.

'I'm sorry, I phrased that badly.' He sucked on his biscuit again. This time his timing was not quite so good. As he pulled it out of the cooling liquid it began to crumble. A fair amount of it landed on the table, looking like rusks and baby food.

'Well,' she asked, slightly mollified, 'what did you mean to say?'

He gave no appearance of having heard her. 'What I meant to say,' he popped the rest of the biscuit into his mouth and chewed, 'what we have to ask – though I cannot at this moment begin to wonder where we will find an answer – what we have to ask is, was he already in some kind of hysterical amnesia when the captain shot him in the head?'

There was a brief silence.

'You brought up the question yourself almost as soon as we met,' he continued. 'And that's what it seems at this stage to come down to. Was Richard Mariner shot, a fully sensible, perfectly functioning Richard Mariner. In which case this is a relatively simple case of post-traumatic amnesia resulting from a severe closed head wound. Or was the person who was shot in the head already in a state of hysterical amnesia and no longer your Richard at all? In which case we have ... duck soup.'

'What?'

'An impenetrable mess.'

'A bit like the mess you have in your coffee cup?'

'A sickeningly accurate comparison. But it presents us with a further conundrum which you should be aware of.'

'What's that?'

'If the duck soup theory is the correct one and at the moment when he received the blow to the head which began the post-traumatic amnesia...' he tailed off.

'Yes?' she prompted.

'If, at that moment, your husband was already in the grip of hysterical amnesia brought on by the unacceptable intensity of whatever experience he had been through...'

'*Yes?*'

'Well, in that case we will have to be very careful about how we proceed because, you see, it might, in the worst case, be possible just to jump him back not into full knowledge of himself, but into that moment when he first switched off. We could bring back not your Richard but the madman with the .44 calibre pistol whom Captain Huuk says he had to shoot in self-defence.'

That gave Robin pause, but not for long. 'I don't believe Captain Huuk,' she said. 'And even if I believed he thought he was telling the truth, I reckon he probably panicked and misinterpreted what he saw in any case.'

'So, even if there was hysterical amnesia, there was no madman with a pistol.'

'No. Never.'

'OK. I'll go along with that. In the meantime the first thing we have to establish is how badly Huuk's anti-personnel round damaged Richard's brain. Then we can begin to estimate the relative strengths of the conditions he may be suffering from.'

'So, how do we find out?'

'Someone somewhere nearby already has a good idea, I think.'

'What do you mean?'

'This is a fine hospital, well equipped and modern. Richard is under close arrest here but even so he is owed a duty of care. He can't remember having had one, but they must have done a brain scan on him and someone in this hospital must have seen the result. There must have been a series of careful clinical tests done on him and, again, someone here must have the results – probably the same person.'

'Dr Chu!' she said.

'I beg your pardon?'

'Chu. I think that's his name. Richard's doctor here. Dr Chu. But surely all these records should be made available to us. Andrew Balfour said—'

'Experience with the British police and the Crown Prosecution Service suggests that they all will, eventually. But I would like to see the records as soon as possible, and talk to the doctor too. I will need to do all that before I see your husband again, I think. And ideally I should go through the records you have brought with you.' He leaned forward urgently and his professorial demeanour disappeared for the twinkling of an eye. 'It will all take time, you understand, even after we agree on a course of action. Recovering his memory, getting some sense of what was lost particularly while he was on board the ship, recovering his past life and personality may be only the beginning. Further treatment may well prove necessary and will take time. You do realise that?'

'What do you mean, agree on a course of action?'

Tom sat back. He picked up the cold cup with its coffee-coloured gruel and sipped appreciatively. 'I don't know how hard the people here have been digging, trying to reconstruct his memory. They may not have been punctilious in passing on the records of standard treatment, but I assume they would have had to get permission to try anything else. And the only persons they can approach for such permission are his defence or his legal next of kin; in other words, you. Therefore it should be safe to assume that they have not used drugs or hypnosis yet. But we can't be absolutely certain until we ask.'

'Drugs?' she said with something akin to horror. 'Hypnosis?'

'If they haven't, then we must,' he warned. 'Either one, or a combination of both, is the next step. It's the only way, for a start, that we have any chance of accessing the memories of what happened on the *Sulu Queen*.'

'But he doesn't remember.'

'Oh yes he does. He just can't access the memories, or bring himself to get in contact with them, that's all. If I can put him in a deep hypnotic trance then I will be able to access them for him. But it isn't something we want to rush into. We have to prepare the ground. There's a lot we don't know. A lot we desperately need to know. What was the name of this doctor?'

'Dr Chu.'

'Right.' He emptied the last, thick contents of his coffee cup down his throat with every evidence of enjoyment and put it down with a decided *chink*. 'Dr Chu. He'll be here somewhere. Let's go and find him.'

Dr Chu was striking in several ways. His hair was incredibly black, thick and lustrous; so heavy that it seemed to weigh his head down. His body was bird-like and slim, so that his white coat flapped like wide starched wings. His skin was a peculiar, almost smoky shade, as though he spent several hours each day soaking in a bath of strong tea. And his accent was purest Oxbridge.

'Even from the simplest medical viewpoint this is a fascinating case,' he was saying, alive with academic enthusiasm. 'The subject was so dissociated when he first arrived that I really thought his scan would show massive damage. But no – well, not *massive* at any rate. Certainly nowhere near the amount I would have suspected in the face of such a condition.'

'Hmmm . . .' said Tom Fowler, studying the scans with gimlet eyes.

'How was he when he first came in?' asked Robin.

'Ah . . .' Dr Chu was caught on the hop by having to speak to a non-specialist, and one to whom he might accidentally give the sort of information Inspector Lee had warned him against discussing. 'He was awake . . .'

'So I would hope,' said Tom, insidiously. 'How many hours after he had been shot?'

'Oh, only ninety minutes, I understand. They brought him in by chopper, you know.'

'Even so.'

'Well, awake but not really coherent. Classic dissociation, it seemed to me at that stage.'

'Ah,' said Tom, apparently appreciatively; much as a Rolls-Royce aero-engineer might appreciate the opinion of a Skoda fitter.

'I did a thorough physical examination but really it was only the head wound which merited attention.'

'Quite so.'

'As soon as I was satisfied that there were no immediately life-threatening conditions – he had of course received paramedical attention in the helicopter – I put him in for the scan and a series of function tests and then a further series designed to demonstrate his current brain functions.'

'You were of course concerned about both areas of damage to the skull.'

'The damage at the back, naturally, but I could discover no damage to the occipital bone itself, or to the atlas or the joints in the area, even though it was almost as though he had been rabbit punched by the stairs on the way down. We still get a lot of martial arts combat victims, as I am sure you realise—'

'Quite. No damage there except superficially to the scalp. But this damage to the temporal lobe...'

'Much more interesting. It seems to be exactly over the top of an old injury. I would dearly love to know whether that original injury was also associated with any significant memory loss...' Dr Chu looked hopefully at Robin and she was about to tell him what she had told Tom Fowler about that very injury when Tom cut in before she could open her mouth.

'And the actual tests you tried were?'

'Well, the function tests were the ones you would expect, ECG, liver and blood. The patient showed no sign of excesses of alcohol or any drug at all at that stage.'

'He's tee-total,' interjected Robin. 'He hasn't had a drink in twenty years. Doesn't smoke either.'

'Quite so,' said Tom approvingly. 'But you say you did some memory tests as well, Dr Chu.'

'Well, I did an old Wechsler adult intelligence test. The results were below average, but of course I don't know how he might have scored originally.'

'High, I would have said. It's a broad spectrum function intelligence test, Robin. Very standard. Anything else, Dr Chu?'

'Well, I'd read up on the work Lehermitte and Signoret did—'

'Twenty-five years ago.'

'Well yes, but, well, I did some spatial and temporal tests such as they—'

'Right. Well, if you will let me have a glance through your notes, I'm sure they will make very interesting reading. Now, I would like to make some arrangements to try a series of my own tests. I am sure you are aware that it will be an integral part of the defence's case to try and restore Captain Mariner's memories of the actual event so there is a legal basis for my access and for my work.'

'Of course, Professor. Anything I can do to assist. I need hardly say that I am an employee of the hospital here. I am not by any means directly associated with the police or the prosecution.'

'Quite, quite. Finally, Dr Chu, has your patient demonstrated full memory of basic functions? There has been no soiling? He remembers how to wash and bathe? He has been able to dress and undress himself at all times?'

'Oh yes. There has never been any trouble with anything like that. He had been cleaned up by the time he came in to me so I can't speak for the actual shooting incident itself.'

'Has the accused been examined by another doctor, a police surgeon?'

'Only on the helicopter. There was a police surgeon there with the paramedic, I understand. But he gave no real treatment. Simply cleaned up and applied a bandage or two. I was the one who did the full battery of tests. All the tests were my responsibility. One of the reasons I had to be so careful with my range of tests was that the police wished to interrogate him at the earliest opportunity.'

It just so happened that Tom was close beside Robin when Dr Chu made this innocent admission and the psychologist's hand caught her arm and restrained her into silence.

'Naturally. Standard procedure. And what form did these interrogations take?'

'Standard question and answer, except that the answers weren't standard, of course.'

'Of course. Many interrogations?'

'Oh yes. Detailed and persistent, mostly by Commander Lee, but often by Captain Huuk.'

'Were you present at all of them?'

'Oh yes.'

'And he has never been taken out of the hospital?'

'Yes. Once.'

'Back to the scene of the crime?'

'Yes. But there was no reaction whatsoever.'

'Very frustrating. Did you use Pentothal?'

'Not at that time, no. But I have used it on two occasions since.'

'On police authority and without the knowledge or agreement of next of kin, I assume.'

'I did what I was directed to do. Twice.'

'So it has now stopped?'

'Oh yes. We haven't used any Pentothal for more than a week now. The prisoner is routinely interrogated for an hour every morning, but I think they are beginning to see that he isn't bluffing and that he won't remember any more than he does at the moment for the foreseeable future.'

Only Tom's steady grip kept Robin from interrupting. She was beginning to see for the first time how little real protection she had been to the man she had flown halfway round the world to help.

In the corridor outside the little office she exploded and Tom let her talk uninterrupted as she got her bitter frustration out of her system. She didn't stop until they reached the lift.

'So,' said Tom, on the way down in the lift car. 'They don't really know what to do with him, do they? They can't work out whether they want his memory back or not, so they're hesitating while they think. While they get some more legal advice, I shouldn't wonder. Treating him medically if not psychologically, treating him very well, in fact, and waiting for things to jump back into perspective, as they usually do.'

'But they've drugged him! Taken him to that ... *place*!'

'You must see that they had to try both of those approaches. Almost all police cases are based on some kind of confession. All they're getting from Richard is "I don't know" and it simply isn't good enough for them.'

'It isn't good enough for us either, though, is it?' She was beginning to calm down now, seeing where the conversation was leading.

'No, that's right. It isn't good enough for us either. And all we can do is to try what they tried, but do it better. And do it soon. A man who says "I can't remember" may be said to be pleading not guilty according to the law, but it won't carry nearly as much weight as if we can make him say, "No, I didn't do it and here's what really happened". And at the moment the only way we can get deep enough into his memory to stand any chance of reaching the truth is to take him back aboard *Sulu Queen*, to use Pentothal and, with your permission, to try a little hypnosis.'

Robin dropped Tom off at Andrew's office, handed him the pile of records Audrey had faxed out to her and then she and Andrew went back up to Kwai Chung to look through the *Sulu Queen*'s cargo.

In the car, they talked through what Dr Chu had told her and Andrew agreed to get hold of the transcripts of any interviews which had taken place so far as a matter of urgency, especially those held while Richard had been drugged. 'I'm not sure that confessions elicited by the use of truth serums would stand up very well in court in any case. The same is true of statements for use in defence and anything Richard says while he's under hypnosis. You do realise that?'

'I didn't but I'm sure Tom Fowler does. He works with the police quite a lot. That's why I wanted him in on this.'

'True. Still, I'd better be there too, just in case.'

It took them four hours to go through the cargo and they found nothing untoward. The slow, tedious task gave time for Robin's temper to mend, however, and she was in a better mood by the end of it. On the way back she asked Andrew if he had handed back the black notebook and he had the grace to blush: he had put it in a plain envelope and posted it anonymously, he admitted.

Much amused, she asked if he had thought to wipe their fingerprints off it.

Of course he had, he informed her, surprised that she should have doubted it.

She was still laughing when they got to Repulse Bay.

After dinner at the Stephensons' – Dottie's speciality of sweet and sour stuffed chicken with baked rice and Chinese vegetables – they split up and each pursued their own further researches. Andrew and Gerry were wading through the first pile of papers that the police had given them and Tom was still going through Richard's past with a fine-toothed comb. Robin wandered back down to the leave flat. She sat in the window seat going through the print-outs of the records which Daniel Huuk had surrendered yesterday, glancing up every once in a while to look past Tin Hau's temple over the busy crowds and into the thickening gloom. There was nothing helpful in the print-out and she went to bed at midnight dissatisfied – and unsatisfied – in every way.

As she was still awake at three, she put a call through to Summersend where the twins would just be getting ready for bed. She talked to them and to her adored parents-in-law. Then she called her father and talked to him for half an hour. She slept like a log for four hours, greeted Su Lam the *amah* as Su was on her way in and she was on her way out, and was at Andrew's door, bright-eyed, by half past eight as usual.

'Your parents send all their love, darling,' she told Richard at ten, having insisted on some private time before Tom started his first preparatory session. Dr Chu's revelations of yesterday had redoubled her resolution to see him as often as possible, preferably immediately after the morning interrogation so that she could look for bruises and needle marks. But of course there were none. 'They're both very well indeed and the new chair-lift down the front steps is just what your mother wanted. Much smoother than the old one. She's quite happy to work it herself so she can potter around down at the front just as she does out at the back. And your father says she needs to! The twins are having a wonderful time and are being as good as gold but they've set up a cricket pitch on the front lawn and you know how thin the grass is on that sandy soil down at Summersend, and as for the bushes on the boundaries...'

It continued as a daily routine during the rest of the week, varied only by occasional – apparently casual – questions about what had happened on *Sulu Queen* and what message he had put onto the disk. Even though he answered none of her questions, it became as therapeutic for Robin as it was supposed to be for Richard. This was especially true as her immediate involvement in the preparation of the case moved out of the centre. There were no new facts to uncover, no new adventures to be had. There was only the slog of checking statements and depositions, of cross-checking facts and allegations, of testing and reinterpreting evidence. And in this Richard himself moved into the centre of things, for by the end of the week it became obvious that the only evidence left for them to collect in or around the Crown Colony lay locked inside his head.

'All right,' said Robin, handing the papers back to Dr Chu.

Tom Fowler nodded and reached for Richard's hand. Richard gave it to him as easily as Robin had given over the disclaimer forms which the hospital required from them – though not, apparently, from the police. Richard's eyes dwelt on her, except for the moment when the needle actually entered the vein in the crook of his elbow.

'Are you all right, darling?' she said gently as Tom steadily depressed the plunger, squeamish on his behalf.

'Fine thanks,' he said with that endless cheerfulness which came near to making her scream. 'What is this stuff? Is it the same as he used?' The bright eyes flicked to Dr Chu.

'Yes,' said Tom, folding the sleeve of Richard's pyjamas and dressing gown back into place. 'Just sit there quietly for a while. It won't take long.'

Richard looked brightly around the room, smiling cheerfully at the assembled faces. Dr Chu, Tom and Andrew all smiled back but none of them could think of anything to say.

'I've ordered you some new night things,' Robin told him gently, to fill the silence. 'I'll bring them in tomorrow. Is there anything else you want?' She always asked; he never answered – unable to imagine the detail of what was available out there, she supposed.

But by this time the drug was beginning to take effect so he told her the truth. 'Yes,' he said. 'I want to go home.'

She opened her mouth, but Tom held his hand up and silenced her.

'And where is your home, Richard?'

'With her.' Richard pointed and smiled. This time his smile was not so bright and shallow.

'And who is she?'

'I ... I ... It's on the tip of my tongue, but it slips away. It slips away.' he shook his head, with unnecessary force, as though hoping to shake his memory back into place.

'Don't worry about it,' soothed Tom. And Robin smiled supportively until the violent motion stopped. 'Now,' continued Tom quietly, 'I'm going to ask you some questions, then we'll proceed a little deeper. All right?'

'All right.'

Half an hour of gentle probing established that Richard could tell time, understood right and left (and port and starboard), could use his fingers dexterously and could stretch them to a width that Rachmaninov might have envied. That he knew where he was and where the hospital was situated. He had a clear idea where Hong Kong was situated but had no idea of its history or immediate prospects. He realised that he was English but had no idea who the people were in a photograph of his parents. He did not know who the current Prime Minister was, or who was President of the United States. He failed to recognise a range of famous film titles and popular television programmes, but he knew who wrote *Oliver Twist* and admitted that he preferred *Macbeth* to *Hamlet*, but he liked *Antony and Cleopatra* best, probably because it had good sea battles in it. Tom went on to prove that Richard could focus on a series of objects at various distances away from him. That he could hear equally well in both ears. That he could remember a list of unfamiliar television programmes given to him ten minutes earlier.

At last, Tom put in front of his subject the one piece of equipment he had not used so far. It was a little flat disc about the size of a side plate mounted on a spindle which stood up from a motorised base so that the disc would spin like a little wheel. On one side of the disc was a simple spiral design in bright, almost fluorescent colours. 'Have you ever been hypnotised?' asked Tom as he set this up on the table in front of Richard.

'No. Never.'

'It's nice to see you so certain,' said the psychologist. 'Have you any basis for the certainty? I see you are becoming a little agitated. Have you actively avoided being hypnotised?'

'I don't like . . .'

'Don't like what?' Tom was a little more challenging. Richard's agitation was more obvious now. There was even some perspiration on his brow.

'I don't like to lose . . .'

Tom changed tack abruptly, and let the confrontational tone drop. 'You don't like to lose what?' he asked more gently. 'Your socks? Your tie? Your trousers?'

'Control,' said Richard. 'I don't like to lose control.'

'Very good,' said Tom, his tone of voice betraying that he was genuinely impressed by this statement. 'But you needn't worry. You won't lose control, I promise. We're all here to make sure of that. Robin will make sure of that.'

Richard's eyes fastened on her with agonised intensity. 'I promise,' she said, her voice as full of intensity as his had been. 'Nothing will hurt you, Richard, I promise.'

The signs of his agitation began to ease. He nodded slightly, his lips tight and pale, his chin square and resolute.

'Look at the disc,' said Tom and he pressed a switch on the base of it which activated the motor. The motor was absolutely silent, turning the disc so that the pattern began to spiral into the centre. In motion, it resembled nothing more than a whirlpool and the others on that side of the room had to be careful to keep moving their eyes away from it or they, too, would have succumbed.

'All I want you to do is to look at the centre of it,' said Tom softly and flowingly as though his voice was part of the whirl of the disk. 'Look at it right in the centre and try to keep your attention on that spinning point. You don't have to keep your eyes focused. If they begin to blur, don't worry. Your mind can still pick up on the movement of the pattern – that's why it is designed with that combination of colours. The less your eyes focus, the more the colours blur, the more your mind interprets the movement. And, as you keep watching, you begin to see that there is a little hole right at the centre of it and that little hole begins to spread in an odd kind of way. Sometimes it throbs with the rhythm of the movement and sometimes it grows and grows and grows under its own steam until it just sucks in the whole of the disk and there's nothing there to see but a huge black hole and there's nothing left to do but to fall. Just let go and fall now, just let go and trust us to catch you. Don't you worry now, we're all still here and Robin's here. Robin won't let anyone hurt you. We'll catch you and we'll hold you safe. Just let go now, just let go.'

It came as a shock to Robin to discover that Richard's eyes were shut. She had gone along with this but had never really thought that her strong-willed husband would succumb. Almost in panic she looked across at Tom and he smiled reassuringly at her. He raised his right hand in a sign demanding silence and with his left hand he turned off the machine.

Richard sat, apparently asleep, entranced.

'Richard,' said Tom gently, 'Richard, are you there?'

Silence.

'Richard?'

Silence.

'Who are you?' asked the psychologist.

'Survivor.' The word was slurred and hard to understand.

Tom asked, 'Who am I speaking to, please?'

'Survivor,' said the survivor of the *Sulu Queen* more distinctly.

'Hello, Survivor. I have a simple instruction for you. Will you be able to remember it?'

'Yes,' said the survivor.

'What I want you to remember is this. When I clap my hands, you will wake up. Do you understand?'

'Yes. When you clap your hands I will wake up.'

'Good. Now I'm going to start by asking you some questions. Is Richard there too?'

'Richard hurts.'

'But he is there?'

'Yes. Richard is here. Richard hurts.'

'I understand that. But can we speak to Richard?'

'Richard hurts.'

'Can we speak to him?'

'Richard hurts too much.'

'I see. Can you tell me this then. Why does Richard hurt?'

'They shot him.' The hands on the table jumped spastically and lurched up through the air towards the gauze-bound temples.

'Where does Richard hurt?'

'In the head.'

'Why does Richard hurt in the head?'

'They shot him in the head.'

'Who shot Richard in the head?'

'More pirates.'

'Why did they shoot him?'

'Pirates kill. That's what pirates do. Rob and kill.'

'Just rest there for a moment. Relax now. Is that correct, Dr Chu? Were Huuk and his men disguised a pirates when they went aboard?'

'I have no idea. How should I know?'

Tom's eyes met Andrew's. The solicitor gave a nod: he would find out.

'Now then, Survivor, I would like you to take us back. Please do not move or gesture. That's right, just rest your hands back on the table there, and relax. Now, I want you to describe what you can see. Start with the man who shot you.'

'Pirate. Gun. Massive gun!'

'So that's all you really noticed about him? His gun? What are you doing, Survivor?'

'Watching!'

'What are you holding in your right hand?'

The subject's head moved, as though he would have looked down – had he not been forbidden to do so. His right hand, on the table, twitched. It was clawed round something only he could see. 'A gun.'

'What sort of gun?'

'I don't know. Big.'

'Where did you get the gun?'

'Took it. *Took* it!'

'Who did you take it from?'

'I took it from him!'

'You took it from the pirate who shot you?'

'No. Other! From him. *Him!*'

'Him? Does *he* have a name?'

'No. I don't know.'

'A member of the crew?'

'No. Yes.'

'Which is it?'

'Yes. No.'

'And what did he do when you took the gun?'

'He screamed. He died. Richard hurts.' The voice was shaking now.
'He died?'
'He died. Richard hurts.' A break in the voice made it clear that the pain to Richard was real and extreme.
'How did he die?'
'He died. Richard hurts too much!' There was childlike simplicity, an absolute trust in the way in which these words were said. The pain was too much now and they had promised to stop it. She had promised.
'You have to stop this,' said Robin. She started to clap, as though applauding the show. The psychologist paid no attention to her. Neither did his subject.
'*How did he die?*' snapped Tom, his voice raised. After the quiet and calm so far it was as though he shouted, but he did not.
'Richard . . .' came the choking answer. The hands on the table were shaking now, the one holding the phantom gun jumping up and down convulsively, trying to reach the agonised head.
'*Stop!*' screamed Robin.
'Richard killed him!' grated the agonised survivor, his voice breaking as though the confession was being tortured out of him. 'Richard killed him. Richard killed him. Oh Robin, it hurts. Make it stop, make it stop!'
Robin was sobbing now, beating her hands agonisingly together and watching her poor lost darling with flooding eyes, rapidly going over the edge of her self-control into a pit of pure hysteria. But when Tom snapped 'Stop!' she obeyed.
The instant that there was silence, Tom slapped his hands together once, and it was as though a switch had been thrown in Richard's head. All the pain was gone in the instant. The survivor sat back smiling slightly, absolutely relaxed, once again at peace.

Chapter Twenty-Three

The new airport of Chek Lap Kok was open and accepting regular flights now, though there would be some weeks yet before they began the process of closing down Kai Tak. On the afternoon of Wednesday, 4 June 1997, the arrivals hall was bustling with a surge of last-minute tourists here to see Hong Kong in its last days as a Crown Colony. Among them was Andrew, growing more and more irritably impatient as he waited to meet this much-hyped, lucky-mascot London silk of Robin's.

The number of tourists was augmented by those brought in by the promise of a solid month of festivities from the middle of June to the middle of July. The festivities were going to be lavish and continuous. They were designed to emphasise the continuity of everything which was important in Hong Kong as it passed from being a Crown Colony of Great Britain to a Special Economic Zone of the People's Republic of China. In spite of all the efforts made by the Chinese government, a lot of people were still pulling out and the trickle of migrating companies and individuals that had begun more than five years ago was something of a flood now. Andrew knew himself to be lucky. He wouldn't find it too hard to get a job back home if things got too grim here. He was in contact with a firm of solicitors in the City of London who were interested in his particular areas of expertise. He had somewhere to go; and the right and ability to go there. There were millions and millions trapped here with nowhere to go at all. As he watched the bustle of people passing through the new airport, he found himself wondering how many of these arrivals were going to stay; and how many in the departure hall were going to come back.

Where was this bloody woman? he wondered. What time was it now? Just after two. Ye gods! He had been hanging around here for the better part of an hour!

Then he looked down from the clock and there she was: Magdalena DaSilva, in all her glory, striding out of the Customs hall like a tiger exploring new territory.

It was as if he had been winded. He just stood there and gaped.

She had no idea that he was there; she swept out of the Customs hall behind a glowing Chinese porter who was wheeling her luggage as though it was the Crown Jewels. Andrew noticed the porter with surprise; he had never seen a porter bother with only two cases – or a Chinese smile like that before. Behind Maggie, he later discovered, came Lata Patel with shoulder bag and briefcase. Maggie, too, was carrying her briefcase but he did not notice that.

She was wearing her Burberry travelling coat open so that her simple black suit could be seen between check silk wings whenever she moved. Her blouse was white, with a high, plain collar and a profusion of ruffles dancing down across her bosom. High though the collar was, her neck rose enough to carry her chin far above it. She struck him as being taller than she really was, perhaps because the glorious ebony excess of her hair was mostly up on the top of her head. Her chin, nose and cheekbones were long, her lips were full and dark, and her forehead pale and high. It was all there to be remembered, except that the image was dulled, somehow; knocked out of focus by the power of her impact. But he never forgot the size, the colour, the honeyed depths of her eyes.

'How will I know her?' he had asked Robin two hours earlier as he set off to meet her, almost like a sulky schoolboy, making it obvious that he didn't really want to go at all.

'You'll know her,' Robin had assured him cheerfully, refusing to notice his mood.

And he did know her. There was never any doubt in his mind. Nor was there any of his usual shy hesitation in his approach of her, once he could get his legs to work again; though he felt like a bit of a clodhopper in her presence at first.

He walked to the barrier and stopped, hoping to catch her eye as she approached. She looked at him, he caught his breath; she looked on past him and he wilted a little. 'Hello?' he said. She looked back at once. He pulled himself up again, living through his eyes. Tiny lines deepened at the corners of her eyes. He found that his mouth was watering, so he swallowed. 'Ms DaSilva?' he said. The deepening of the tiny lines became a smile. 'I'm Andrew Balfour,' he said. 'Robin sent me to meet you.' And the smile turned into a grin. He had never imagined that teeth could gleam so perfectly whitely.

He stuck out his hand and she came up to the barrier, still grinning, to take it. Her eyes were all he could see. The contact between their fingers was like an electric shock and her grin flickered slightly as she felt it too. Andrew gasped and was introduced to the scent of Obsession.

'A pleasure to meet you, Andrew,' Maggie growled, shaking his hand, firmly, once, and letting it go. Immediately his hand felt cool, as though her flesh had somehow warmed it. 'This is Lata Patel, my junior.'

It had never occurred to him that a voice could embody the notion of smoke. And not just any smoke – the smoke of joss sticks, of burning sandalwood, dusky, distant, exotic.

'How do you do, Ms Patel?' He felt her take his hand and shake it but he did not look at her and would not have done so, in all probability, had Maggie not moved. She did so, however, and he found himself face to face with a serious-looking, studious-seeming young woman. Her face was devoid of make-up and her hair was swept back severely. He would have guessed her to be in her late teens, which gave him a twenty-year superiority over her, from the safety of which he observed that she seemed to have taken a dislike to him. This may have had something to do with the expression on his own face. He was conscious of trying to adjust his expression to his most irresistible twinkle as he walked beside them the few steps to the end of the barrier and relieved the porter of the baggage. He discovered then that the porter didn't seem to like him either.

'Now I love this!' was Maggie's reaction to the Aston Martin. He opened the passenger door and reached in to rock the seat forward.

'Will you be comfortable on the back seat, Ms Patel? he asked, glowing with pride at Maggie's throaty compliment. 'Robin didn't think there would be room in there for two, that's why she didn't come, but perhaps one – sideways?'

Ms Patel said nothing. With her nose in the air she somehow still managed to stoop low enough to climb in. He went round to the back, opened the boot, and thanked God the two women were travelling light.

'What is this beast?' called Maggie as she pulled the passenger seat back into place and climbed aboard.

Had anyone else called the Vantage a beast he would have been outraged. From Maggie it was a term of endearment.

He closed the boot and went to the driver's door. He told her what the car was as he climbed in beside her.

'I love fast cars!' she informed him, her voice loud, as though she knew how much noise the starter was going to make.

'And what about you, Ms Patel?' he asked, ever the gentleman, meeting her eyes, the colour of dark chocolate melting, in the rearview.

The edges of the eyes crinkled. 'I have never ridden in a really fast car,' came the gentle voice from the rear seat.

'Well,' he said, to both of them, 'this is an extremely fast car. But I won't drive it too quickly, I promise.' He engaged reverse and was actually very careful about his speed.

'First things first,' said Maggie as they pulled out onto the North Lantau Expressway. 'How are Richard and Robin?'

Quickly and concisely, he brought her up to date on Richard's current physical and mental state, and spent a moment or two describing yesterday's experiment with hypnotism. 'We're taking him out to the ship itself tomorrow, to see if that triggers anything, but it's hard. Hard on Richard, of course; I've never seen anything like the psychic pain he was in yesterday but Tom says we have to discount it and break though it if we're going to get any further. It's harder still on poor Robin, though.'

'How is Robin?'

'Exhausted, depressed; getting desperate. She's increasingly trapped. Everyone knows she's here now and the papers are after her all the time. She had a nasty experience in the Cat Street market ten days ago and since then she only pops out once in a while to pick up stuff for Richard. She goes to the Heritage Mariner office sometimes when she thinks the reporters won't be waiting for her there, but the rest of the time she hides in my offices if she's in Hong Kong or vegetates down in Repulse Bay. Just about the only relaxation she's had was at the start of this – what she called "shopping as therapy". She hasn't even got that now. I really don't know how she keeps going.'

'Is there anywhere we can send her for a week or so? Anywhere distant but relevant?'

'What do you mean?'

'Somewhere where she's not so well known, somewhere she can get a bit of peace. If I know Robin, she won't leave her Richard to our tender mercies unless she's doing something important to help his defence along. Is there anywhere like that? Anywhere at all?'

'Well...'

'Should we try and talk her into going back to London?'

'No, she's got things well sewn up there, I understand and the twins are with Richard's parents.'

'Well, we'll just have to do a little more thinking, that's all. Now, talking of Richard's defence...'

All the way back into Hong Kong town and then out to his office, he was careful about the speed at which he drove, but even so he pushed at the upper edge of the limit while engaged in a lengthy legal discussion with his passengers. He updated them on everything that had happened so far and gave them the benefit of his experience and of the best of his guesses as to what might happen next.

'So,' Maggie summed up as they came out of the tunnel and turned into the snarl-up heading east, 'they have charged Richard with the murder of everyone else aboard the ship, but they have no confession. They believe he might have done it on his own and can prove that he was close to some of the victims when they died and that he handled all of the murder weapons at some time or other. But they have not yet actually proved that he fired the fatal shots or chopped the fatal chops, and they don't know whether he did it all on his own or in confederacy with someone who has since disappeared. And they aren't sure what to do with him next.'

'That's about the size of it,' Andrew admitted, impressed by her summation.

'So their case really rests upon the fact that he was the only survivor of the incident and they have no other suspects.'

'And his loss of memory.'

'No, not really. The fact that he can't remember anything seems to be incidental. If he was in perfect mental health and saying he was asleep when it all happened or was struck on the head at the outset and only woke up afterwards, then they would still be holding him and trying to prove that he was lying.'

'It's more complex than that, surely,' said Andrew.

'Well, perhaps. But I think that's still the bottom line. He's in the frame because he was in the picture. He was the only one in the picture, in fact. But what precisely is it a picture of? Is there anything else going on here? Anything political? If Richard didn't kill all those people, who do you suppose did? And why?'

'That's a question we haven't even begun to address,' admitted Andrew. 'We have absolutely nothing to go on, so we've concentrated on working with Richard himself. Except...'

'Except?' purred Maggie.

'Do either of you know anything about computers?' For some reason his eyes met Lata's in the rearview as he asked this.

And she answered for both of them. 'No. Why?'

'Never mind,' he said. 'Our first objective had been to find out what did actually happen. And our best source of information is Richard. We're working on the assumption that he will prove to be innocent of all charges, though while under hypnosis he has apparently admitted to one slaying.'

'I won't ask about circumstances at this point, it would be a waste of time. We can't deal with evidence gained under hypnosis, so the circumstances of the alleged slaying are irrelevant.'

'Yes, that's what Tom said.'

'Tom?' she asked with a quickening of interest.

'Tom Fowler, the psychologist,' he said.

'Ah yes, I've heard of Tom Fowler...' Her voice trailed off.

'The case of the suicidal Christian,' prompted Lata. 'What was his name? Perrott? And the plane full of explosives at Heathrow last Easter.'

'Yes, I remember. So Robin's got Tom Fowler out here.' The purr of intrigue in her voice made Andrew unaccountably jealous.

'She told us that. Didn't I mention it to you?' asked Lata gently.

'Not that I remember,' answered Maggie shortly.

Maggie's arrival gave Robin a shot of badly-needed adrenaline. The brilliant barrister swept into the team mentally as well as physically and shook them all up with her electric energy. They had been feeling pretty glum, especially after the trauma of that interview with Richard –

though Richard himself had no memory of the event at all – but Maggie assured them that even as they stood they had a strong case. Without any more ammunition at all, she reckoned she could blow enough holes in the prosecution's case to give Richard a fighting chance. But, that being said, it was always better to be safe than sorry, so they were to keep working just as hard, and keep looking for that one vital clue. And that, of course, meant that they had to continue Tom's exploration of Richard's battered memory.

They needed two cars the next day when they went to pick up Richard because there were so many of them now. Andrew felt that he should be there as he was, after all, in charge of this section of the defence.

Maggie went too. It was unusual, she admitted, for a barrister to be this closely involved in the preparation of a case at this stage, and she hoped Andrew would tell her at once if he felt she was getting under his feet. He would rather have died. Maggie cheerfully explained that she was used to being briefed by a solicitor at a much later stage and only meeting the accused on a couple of occasions before they came to court. But she was out here now and working exclusively on the case and she would put her shoulder to the wheel as forcefully as anyone else. Where Maggie went, Lata followed.

Tom had to be there; he was going to be master of ceremonies. And Robin, of course, had to be there too. That went without saying in her own mind, but the others were not so sure and the idea that Maggie had planted in Andrew's brain was rapidly flourishing into a fullscale plot to get Robin out of the spotlight for a few days at least, while they all went to work on her behalf unhampered by worrying about her.

At the hospital they were joined by Richard, Dr Chu, Daniel Huuk and a two-man police escort, so it was almost a convoy, led by a police car and completed by an Aston Martin, which pulled up beside the gangway up onto the *Sulu Queen*.

It was at once obvious to everyone that Richard was very nervous about going aboard. 'Was he this upset the first time you brought him down?' Tom asked Dr Chu.

'Not at all. He showed no sign of nervousness at all.'

'Maybe we knocked something loose with the hypnotic session. Has his behaviour varied at all during the last forty-eight hours?'

'Not until now.'

'Well, let's go on. Slowly and carefully. One step at a time. Captain Huuk, will Captain Mariner be escorted by those two guards at all times?'

'We will see, Professor. For the time being certainly. Now, are we going aboard or not?'

'After you, Captain—'

So Huuk went first, followed by Richard and his guards who urged their captive on while he clearly wished to hang back. Then Tom and Robin, followed closely by Dr Chu, and all the rest in a bunch.

Are you going to try hypnosis again?' asked Robin as they followed the nervous man onto the deck and paused there.

'We'll see. He tapped his pocket. 'I have some Pentothal here too.'

'I'm worried.'

'Yes. Richard's very disturbed. That's a hopeful sign, I think. We may not need to do anything other than get him to talk us through his thoughts as he walks around the bridge.'

Tom's words were meant to be helpful and bracing to her, but they did not put her mind at rest at all. In fact, by the time they arrived at the main door into the bridgehouse, she was almost as agitated as her husband. It became obvious that they would have to give Richard a shot of the Pentothal in order to sedate him a little, or the guards would have to carry him around the bridge by main force. 'Wait here a moment,' ordered Tom as they gathered outside the doorway on the narrow section of the deck there. 'Is there a chair nearby?'

Huuk vanished for a moment and returned with one of the library chairs. Richard sat on it while Tom gave him an injection. He was much calmer within a few minutes, but Tom decided to take the opportunity presented by the pause to put Richard into a hypnotic trance. 'I know what I said,' he told Robin quietly, 'but it will give us more control. He will be all right, I promise.'

He turned to Huuk. 'What I propose is this. I want to walk through the bridgehouse with Captain Mariner, once. You and your men will escort us, of course, but I want to be close enough to guide the captain if need be. I suggest that you, Robin, take his left arm and be prepared to guide him as well. Andrew, you need to be sure you have clear sight of anything that happens and be in a position to take note of anything said. I will be taping everything myself. Dr Chu, you will wish to stay close at hand as well, of course. Maggie, you will have to follow along as best you can. Not a situation you are used to, I dare say, but it's the best we can do for the time being.'

Tom's suggestions were taken up by everyone, which was fortunate because the companionways and passages within the ship were narrow and there would have been a great deal of confusion otherwise.

'Richard?' said Tom, forgetting for a moment that it was Survivor he was speaking to.

Silence.

'Survivor?'

'Yes?'

'I want you to open your eyes, please.' The eyes opened. They seemed to Robin absolutely flat, like tiny panes of stained glass.

'What can you see?' asked Tom.

'People. Deck. Door.'

'Is anything you can see familiar to you?'

'I've been here before. With them.' He turned his head, looking with his steely gaze at the huddle of Huuk, Chu and the guards. 'Richard didn't like coming here with them.'

'Is Richard here?'

'Richard hurts.'

'All right. Don't worry for the moment. Can you stand up?'

'Yes.'

'All right. Stand up, please.' The long body unfolded from the chair. The movements were fluid and sure although seemingly under Tom's control; there was nothing stiff or robotic about the way Richard moved. And, when she came close to take his left arm as directed, Robin was surprised by the warmth and power in the limb. It was as though, with Richard's mind locked away in whatever secret section of his brain it occupied, she had assumed that his strength and grace would have vanished too. But this was not the case. Quite the reverse. She felt nervous suddenly, hoping poignantly that she would only be required to guide him. If she needed to try and restrain him, she would stand no chance. She glanced around, to see where the guards were positioned, but before she could make eye contact with anyone, Tom had stepped through the door, called, 'Follow me,' and they were off.

Robin's perception of the others in the group vanished almost immediately. Her concentration became absolute and centred on the muscular limb she was holding. After a while it felt to her that everything she was experiencing was being filtered through that arm – except, perhaps, what she could see. For it soon became obvious from the play of the muscles and the jerking movements which neither of them could quite control that he could see very much more than she could, and was reacting accordingly.

Someone somewhere had made an observation which struck her now: lunatics do not behave in an illogical manner, they react logically to a world which is almost unimaginably different from ours.

There was no power on, but the afternoon was bright and humid. The bridgehouse was airy and cool with hardly any shadows. Yet it had an atmosphere of fearsome horror about it, as though it contained miasmas from countless haunted graveyards; strange that it should strike her now, on her third visit here. But then she realised that it struck her now because she was feeling something of what the man whose arm she was holding felt.

No sooner had they followed Tom over the door sill than the long limb tensed. She felt the muscles from elbow to shoulder writhe into rock hardness. 'It's all right, darling,' she whispered, as though to one of the twins. 'It's all right. I'm here.' He paid no attention because, as far as he was concerned, she was not there at all.

Slowly, with the others trailing a little despondently behind, they walked forwards to the foot of the first internal companionway. As soon as they got there, Robin found herself being jerked backwards like a rag doll.

'Stop!' ordered Tom. And was obeyed. 'Tell me what you can see.'

'There's a man! With a gun!' Richard's right arm tore itself out of Tom's grasp, pointing up the stairs to the first landing. 'He's going to shoot!'

They all looked up as though they expected to see the gunman there, but the little landing was empty.

'I'm going to count to three,' said Tom. 'When I get to three, the man with the gun will have vanished. Do you understand? One ... two ... three. Can you still see him?'

'No. He's gone now.' Robin felt the muscles in his arm and shoulder relax. She noticed that as they mounted the stairs, however, he was careful where he walked, as though someone was still standing in his way. In the next corridor up, there were no sudden surprises, but she could feel the muscles begin to tighten again as they came towards the doorway into the first officer's office. Relentlessly, Tom guided the three of them towards the door, which was closed. As he turned the handle, Tom said quietly, 'There's no need to be disturbed. There's nothing here to harm you. Just tell me what you can see.'

'Brian!' shouted the survivor, his voice shaking with mingled sorrow and disgust. 'Chas...' He was fighting to turn away, bound by the rigid muscles as though by a strait-jacket.

'It's all right,' soothed Tom.

Robin had the momentary impression of the others crowding round and craning to see in, but there was nothing for them to see. The room had been stripped; even the linoleum was gone now. It was a bare, metal-floored shell, with only two slight indentations to show where the dead men had lain. Two slight indentations in the bare grey metal, looking oddly like empty eye sockets.

'I want to take you back,' said Tom quietly, insistently. 'Come back in time with me.'

'Back...' there was deep concern in the voice.

'One day back. Think; look into this room one day before you saw the bodies there. Tell me what you see.'

'One day back. One day...'

The tone of voice in which this was said struck Robin as being so odd that she looked up at the profile so close beside her, just in time to see all expression there switch off.

Now he was like a robot. No, not a robot, a mannequin, a dummy.

'Come forward again,' insisted Tom. 'Come forward twelve hours.'

Still that vacant stare, mouth slightly open, eyes like glass balls. She would have thought he was in some kind of seizure except that the arm to which she was clinging was relaxed. Almost soft, as though he was empty somehow. An empty shell. How could he still be standing up?

'Tom?' she said.

'Six more hours,' soothed Tom. 'Eighteen hours forward ... Yes, Robin?'

'Can't you feel it?' she whispered. 'It's as though he's empty.'

'I feel it,' said Tom, his voice was calm and quiet still. 'I'm going to count you through the last six hours, Survivor. Nineteen hours forward. You're coming back to us now ... Twenty hours ... Twenty-one ... Twenty-two ...'

The body under her hands jumped. The muscles went rigid. 'NO!' came a great bellow.

'What can you see?'

'Dead, they're ... DEAD!'

The massive body began to swing from side to side and Robin suddenly realised he was shaking his head again with terrible force, so fiercely she expected to hear the neck muscles tearing, the neck bones breaking apart.

'Where are you?' bellowed Tom. 'Tell me where you are.'

'Richard hurts!'

'Tell me where you are and what you can see!'

'Richard *hurts*!'

'One thing! One thing that you can see and I will bring you out!'

'*RICHARD HURTS!*'

He tore loose from them then and it was only the shaking of his head that stopped him running amuck. He reached out, as though holding on to the sides of an invisible doorway, and hung there while his head shook, perspiration spraying right and left like rain.

'All right,' called Tom piercingly, 'when I clap my hands you will wake up. One, two, three!'

This time when his hands came together, Richard's body pitched straight forward onto the floor and lay there as though he had been shot.

Someone said, 'Jesus Christ!' Someone else was sobbing hoarsely.

Robin slowly realised that Maggie had spoken, but it was she who was sobbing.

She reacted with an anger which reflected her agony in its intensity; not a quiet anger, therefore, but a blazing rage teetering dangerously near to hysteria. She managed to control it during the silent ride back to the Queen Elizabeth, but she could feel it simmering inside her and not even the sight of Richard, fully restored and apparently unaware of what had happened, could calm it down.

It exploded the moment they arrived back in Andrew's office, and it was all aimed at Tom. 'How could you, you *bloody* man! My God! What you put him through! And for what? What did we learn from all that *agony*? Not one useful thing! Not one thing! Jesus Christ, I could weep when I think . . .' She was, in fact, weeping already.

Maggie began to cross the room, coming to support her friend, but she met Tom's eye and stopped.

'All right, Robin,' he said. 'I'm sorry. But you do know it has to be done. If you want Richard back, something has to be done.'

'But . . . *God!*'

'The best treatment is rest and relaxation. He should be in hospital, tucked up in bed, warm and calm and sedated if need be until he manages to re-orientate himself. It's only a question of maybe a month or two until he begins to come back to himself.'

'Oh, come on, Tom!' It was Maggie who said this, unable to stay out of a fight for long. 'We haven't got months. We've got weeks. And not too many of them, either.'

'Precisely. You know that, don't you, Robin? You remember what this is all about? If Richard's mind is still blank on the trial day then he'll have lots of time to recover properly. But he'll be locked away in a prison hospital, probably up at Siu Lam; or perhaps at Broadmoor with the Yorkshire Ripper. And then, when his memory comes back, we can start all over again, trying to get an appeal put together, organised, fitted on some judge's calendar in some court somewhere, maybe in London, maybe out here again. Unless we run out of time, of course, and he's executed under Chinese Basic Law.'

This time Maggie did not stop when she crossed the room to Robin.

'You really have to get a firm grip on this, Robin,' Tom went on relentlessly. 'Richard's on trial for the brutal mass murder of forty people. This won't go away. We can't assume his innocence is absolute and will be obvious to a jury even if Maggie can find a jury of seven people here who haven't made their minds up already from reading the bloody papers. We have to *prove* it. And the first place to start is with his version of what really went on during that last voyage, and especially during the final days. And we've made a good start, believe me. We made excellent progress today.'

Had Maggie not been holding her, Robin would probably have collapsed under the weight of the truth in what he said. She knew he was right, but she went down fighting hard. 'And what, for heaven's sake, did we learn that was important today?'

He came across to her as Maggie helped her into Andrew's big old swivel chair. He smiled at her question. 'You know very well,' he said, as though he were chiding a wilful, beloved child. The tone of his voice was not intimate or patronising, it was supportive, almost uplifting. 'We have now established that Richard suffered his breakdown on seeing something really terrible less than four hours before Huuk and his men came aboard. But by the time they did, Richard had been replaced by this half-formed personality calling itself the Survivor.'

Much of her anger was gone by the time she was seated comfortably. And of course he was right. She knew exactly what he was talking about. 'And it was the Survivor who got shot in the head,' she concluded. 'So it is the Survivor who has amnesia, and as he's only four hours old, he must be confused as merry hell. Richard is in there somewhere, but he's still locked far away and we have to get past the Survivor to get to him.'

Clear-eyed as always, Robin saw more than that. She saw how wrong she had been to be so angry, and she also saw the reason for her anger and the fact that she could never hope to control it well enough to leave them be and let them do their jobs unhampered. And that meant she was more of a hindrance than a help here at the moment.

Andrew arranged for a cup of tea and they all gathered round his desk to eat gingernuts, discuss their progress and make their plans. It gave Robin a chance to calm right down, admire the quality of the team which she had created, and realise just how much of an outsider she had suddenly become.

Chapter Twenty-Four

Edgar Tan turned out to be a dapper man of middle height who favoured conservative slacks, slip-on brown brogues with tassels instead of laces and rather more flamboyant shirts. He didn't need a jacket; it was coming up to 30°C. His skin was the colour of teak and his eyes and hair were equally dark, though the hair was short while the eyes were long. He hung his head slightly, pushing his pointed, elfin chin forward, and he almost danced on his feet, seeming to lead with his shoulders like a boxer. He may, indeed, have been a boxer in his youth – his pock-cheeked face was battered enough – but Robin recognised his blood and antecedents at a glance. His forefathers had all to a man been *orang laut* – men of the sea.

He recognised her from her photograph and crossed the arrivals hall at Changi with a grin and a wave, calling her name like an old friend, as he might just as well have been – they took to each other at once. They shook hands, sizing each other up and liking what they saw. 'We've got a lot of ground to cover,' he said. 'You want to freshen up or go at once?'

'Let's go.'

He glanced down at her weekend case, measured its weight like a bellboy and her strength like a trainer, decided she didn't need any help and didn't offer any. With a kind of amused distance, she watched him doing this and, taking strength from his aura of restless, relentless questioning, she hefted the bag and slung it over her shoulder. Then she settled the handle of her briefcase in the other hand and followed him.

He led her through to the car park and showed her to an elderly but sturdy Nissan Bluebird. She would have expected something less conservative and considered asking about it; but she didn't feel she knew him well enough yet. As she was all too well aware, cars can be as personal as underwear with men. She sat in contented silence, therefore, as he drove aggressively but safely along the East Coast Parkway. Once she got used to his particular style of driving, there was nothing much to distract her – the grass on either side of the highway was vividly green and perfectly tended. It was as though they were driving across a massive bowling green.

'What do you want to do first?' he asked.

A sensible person might have said, 'Check in to my hotel', but Robin was far beyond that stage by now. This was the late morning of Monday, 9 June. Richard's trial was due to start one week today, one calendar month from the transfer, as Stipendiary Magistrate Morgan had ruled. Richard was due to be tried in Court Four of the Supreme Court Building before Mr Justice Fang. Robin had less than a week, therefore, to find out what had happened to Richard here, to check up on the China Queens Company, to try and trace Anna Leung and find out why Wally Gough had not sailed with his ship on that fateful day little more than a month ago – and what had happened to him since. In a few days also, the *Seram Queen* was due, and Robin had in her case that frustratingly impenetrable little computer disk, ready to slip it into the ship's network at the earliest opportunity. The ticket in her wallet was an open-ended return, but she proposed to use it next Sunday evening after she had visited the *Seram Queen* and decoded its message.

'It's a long while since I've been here,' she said, 'and I never stayed for long. Singapore is not a city I know all that well. You know what we've got to do, you know what you've covered so far. Where would you start, Mr Tan?'

'Well...' Tan drew the word out as he thought. 'I've checked at the Port Authority. They have the correct registration of the *Sulu Queen* arriving – Master: Captain Walter Gough, and all that sort of thing. And they have the same for when she left, so if your husband did go aboard here—'

'He must have done.'

'Yeah, I guess. But if he did, he didn't notify the Port Authority. I've checked down there. No record. End of story.'

'Well, that's important, Mr Tan, and I don't think it can be the end of the story because when the *Sulu Queen* was found, the only person aboard who held the correct papers to command her was my husband. There was no trace of Captain Walter Gough, Master and Commander; and the Port Authority here could not possibly have let a ship sail without a qualified captain in command of her.'

'I didn't realise that.'

'No reason that you should, Mr Tan. It's the sort of thing that would occur to a sailor or a shipowner, though. I need to talk to the pilot who took *Sulu Queen* out into the roads. He should be able to tell me who was in command.'

'And we'll find him down at the Port Authority, will we?'

'Yes.'

'So, I guess that's where we'll start,' concluded Edgar Tan. 'I'm glad you left this decision to me.'

They came in along the eight-lane Parkway, over the bridge onto the land extension and down through the massive road complex at its end into Keppel Road, heading for the World Trade Centre, past the ultra-modern, computerised Tanjong Pagar container terminal. As they drove past, Robin strained as though some magical exercise of her eyes could help her see into the big, square hangar-like buildings and into the great handling yards beyond, which fronted Keppel Harbour itself. They swung on up onto the Ayer Rajah Expressway and off towards Pasir Panjang, Port Singapore and the Authority building itself. Robin was familiar with most of this through conversation with her friends and captains, and through maps and charts, sometimes unfolded to settle a point, as often as not drawn in some more or less alcoholic liquid on a table top. But she had a vivid imagination and had travelled enough to make these travellers' tales come to life accurately when they were told to her.

They had no trouble discovering which pilot had taken *Sulu Queen* out after her last stop-over, but he was taking another ship out now and would not be available for interview until tonight.

'We'll be back,' said Robin to the accommodating Port Authority clerk and turned to Tan once more.

'Check in to your hotel?' he suggested.

'No. Let's go to the China Queens offices first.'

'You're the boss.'

'Seventy-four Kandahar Street, then. Wherever that is.'

'Orchard South.'

'Off we go, then.'

Robin had brought the spare keys which Mr Feng had kept in the Heritage Mariner office and she was also armed with documentation prepared for her by Andrew. She did not want to have to start getting legal advice arranged here as well if she could possibly help it but she was well aware that Singapore had its own peculiar legal system, and if she had to deal with it at any level other than the most cursory, she had better get a local solicitor involved.

But, as it happened, Andrew's papers were more than sufficient to get them past the policeman guarding the door into the China Queens office. He leafed through the papers, scanned her passport, and then with a curt nod opened the door for them.

The first thing Robin saw when she entered the little suite of offices was a computer. With hope welling in her heart, she switched it on and provided an operating system as requested. There was a standard word-processing package which auto loaded. As it did so, she opened her briefcase and lifted out that increasingly battered little book-shaped parcel wrapped in Mickey Mouse paper. It had gone beyond being a perfect hiding place now – it was almost a good luck charm. Just for a moment as she looked at it, Robin thought that she had better get some matching paper and rewrap it before she sent it on to the little girl for whom it was destined. No, she decided. She would not just send it, she would take it herself.

As she thought these thoughts, she slid the disk out of the wrapping paper and placed the present back in her briefcase. Then, heart in her mouth, she slipped in the disk from the *Sulu Queen* and asked for the index. The tiny red light at the drive port flickered on as the machine consulted the disk, looking for a program it recognised. The screen on the monitor flickered and went blank.

'You got nothing on that disk at all,' said Tan helpfully, looking over her shoulder.

'I've got a lot on this disk. I just can't find a program that's compatible with it, that's all. You know any computer experts?'

'No. We could try the Yellow Pages.'

'Not with this one, it's too precious.'

'If you won't trust experts to get into it for you then you're looking at a long haul before you find out what it says. There must be thousands of programs on the market. And even the new ones which are compatible with each other aren't compatible with the older ones.'

'I thought you said you weren't an expert,' she said, popping her disk out of the machine and slipping it back into the wrapping.

'I'm not. I keep up to date because I keep promising myself I'm going to buy one some day, but every time one I like comes along, something even better's in the shops before I can raise the purchase price.'

'You've got to buy them on hire purchase.'

'Never get into debt. This is a low-return business at the best of times.'

'Wise man. Now, I'll look through the computer files here. You look through the rest of the offices.'

'OK. What am I looking for?'

'Anything which throws any light on Anna Leung or Captain Walter Gough, their relationships, and their disappearance. Records about the crew of the *Sulu Queen* – here's a list. Anything about the China Queens Company which doesn't feel right. Hard copies of any records, especially lading records of the cargo carried most recently by the *Sulu Queen*, origin and destination.'

'OK,' he said equably. 'But do you think the police will let us take any of this stuff away with us?'

'Depends on the case they're trying to prove, apparently. My advice is from my Hong Kong lawyer so some of the detail may not quite fit in with the local scene but I have enough documentation to prove that this is my company and therefore my property. Shouldn't be too much of a problem.'

'Unless they want to charge you with anything that this Anna Leung has been up to. Anything that the company itself is actually responsible for, in law.'

'It's a risk we may have to take. But it's pretty remote, my solicitor tells me. And if the worst comes to the worst and Ms Leung has been involved in fraud of some kind for which the whole company is legally responsible, then I can start getting that sorted out in short order and there'll be less chance of them holding the *Seram Queen*.'

'And that's important too, is it?'

She glanced across the room to where he was going through a tall filing cabinet slowly and carefully as they talked. 'Heritage Mariner is a big company, but we've never been that wealthy as companies go. If *Seram Queen* is held for any time at all, then the China Queens Company folds. Heritage Mariner, as parent company, will become liable for all debts and losses. We could go down too.'

'Sounds important to me. Ah ... Gough, Walter. Captain.' He slipped out a fat file and began to pore over it.

Robin's deft fingers danced across the keys of the computer, exploring the company records on disks which the system could read.

Inspector Sung arrived while they were still working, but Robin had been expecting that. It was all very well for police constables to allow access to places they were guarding but no constable in his right mind would do so without alerting his seniors.

Sung was urbane, cheerful and friendly. He already knew Edgar Tan, of course, and seemed quite amenable to chatting with Robin, watching closely as she worked and answering her questions with apparent candour.

'Can you tell me whether there are, in fact, any charges outstanding against Miss Leung?'

A glance passed between the two men, a flickering of the eyes and nothing more. It was so quick that Robin was not really certain she had seen it but it alerted her to be careful from here on. There might be just a little more happening than immediately met the eye. She decided to try some subtle interrogation of Tan at a later stage. For now she concentrated her eyes on the monitor as she scanned file headings and her ears on Inspector Sung's gentle voice. 'No. There is nothing specific against Ms Leung at the moment. Let us say that she has been mentioned in connection with another, ongoing, investigation.'

'If her name has been mentioned, then this company must have been mentioned, if only by association. And the company itself is clearly under some kind of investigation too.'

'In a very general way. This company has always stood far above suspicion, you understand. But during the last five years, since Ms Leung took over as company secretary here, there have been ... questions.'

'Five years is a long time to be asking questions.'

'That fact alone should tell you how nebulous those questions were. In any case, it was one of those general investigations which is always running in some form or another.'

'You mean like investigations into drug running, smuggling, that sort of thing? You mentioned financial irregularities. Is this an investigation into white-collar crime, then, like the investigations run by our City watchdogs back in London?'

'In the past, many shipping companies of more or less solid reputation have found themselves caught up in smuggling adventures of all sorts, though in my experience most drug smuggling has been done by individuals. And, yes, we do have ongoing investigations into fraud involving shipping concerns, but only because they are companies like any other, and the same crimes of fraud, improper dealing and so forth can be run through them. But the ongoing investigation which currently involves Ms Leung – by name if not in fact, yet – is none of these. It is one which we are running in association with colleagues far to the north and south of here, but it is centred here. It is an investigation into piracy.'

Robin stopped typing and sat, her eyes apparently focused on the screen in front of her. 'There are many different types of piracy,' she observed.

'Indeed. Everything from the old-fashioned, traditional type involving going aboard ships with teams of armed men and stealing goods and valuables to the more modern type involving the creation of a container and a package which seems to be the product of a famous factory when in fact it is a cheap imitation. In this part of the world both of these types overlap more completely than in any other. And they are augmented by that other great piratical tradition, smuggling. Inevitably so, since once you have created your cutprice Chanel perfume, you still have to move it to market, do you not? And, of course, if you can move your suspect goods through the good offices, shall we say, of a well-respected shipper, then you will have less trouble in passing it off as the genuine article. That is why shippers of established reputation, such as the China Queens Company, are a particularly tempting target for pirates of all sorts.'

'I can see that. But by definition, then, your investigations must focus for some of the time on companies which have the best of reputations.'

'Indeed.

'Companies which deserve their reputations because they have never, in fact, done anything illegal.'

'True. But we do not look at companies as monolithic institutions. We look at them as collections of individuals. And, no matter how great or good the company itself may be, individual people are fallible, lazy, self-serving, greedy, desperate, open to blackmail.'

'And which of these was Anna Leung?'

'Oh, Miss Leung is none of the above, as far as we know. No, she is far more interesting than any of those.'

'Then what is she? Apart from missing?'

Inspector Sung actually laughed. 'I'm not sure that she is even missing. You see, what is so interesting about Ms Leung is that she never existed in the first place.'

The public records of Singapore went back, uninterrupted, to the year 1819 when Raffles himself had arrived. There was a range of people called Leung, and several of them, in that melting-pot of a society, were called Anna. But the Anna Leung whose details were on record at the China Queens Company had never been born in Singapore or christened there, in spite of the fact that the China Queens records were very specific about her original nationality and held the number of a current Singaporean citizen's passport for her. They also checked the immigration files. No one called Anna Leung had ever arrived, by any legal route, in the city-state of Singapore. The only record of an Anna Leung of the correct birth date and birthplace was accompanied by a record of death a little less than three years later.

'We didn't pick up on this, you see,' explained Inspector Sung, 'until after she disappeared. No one has actually reported her as missing, and we might never have noticed that anything was amiss except for the enquiries arising out of your husband's case in Hong Kong. Commander Lee is our direct liaison on the piracy investigation and Captain Daniel Huuk is our liaison with the Royal Hong Kong navy contingent.'

'But she must have bank accounts, rooms somewhere.'

'Not in the name of Anna Leung. She ran the offices here alone, had done so long before Heritage Mariner became involved. She paid herself a salary in cash, according to the records. Apart from that, everything seems to be quite above board. She took her cash each week and effectively vanished. Who she really was and where she actually lived, we have no idea yet.'

'And that's all there is? An invisible woman?'

'That can't be all there is, can it? Nobody would set up a front like this and run it for five years without good reason. A good *illegal* reason. But if she wasn't fleecing the China Queens Company, then what was she doing? And why has she disappeared?'

'Goodness knows. But surely it has to have something to do with what happened to the *Sulu Queen*, whose captain has also disappeared. God, I've got to think this through!'

'Keep me up to date with anything you work out – and anything you find,' requested Inspector Sung.

Five minutes later, Robin and Tan hesitated on the steps of the Public Records Office.

'Where do you want to go in order to think things through then?' Tan asked.

Robin glanced at her watch. 'It's still too early to go back to the Port Authority. I need a cup of tea.'

'Kill two birds with one stone,' suggested Tan. 'The Raffles serves good tea, so I've been told.'

'Back to Beach Road, then,' she said. 'Lucky this place is no real size at all.'

An hour later they were side by side in a corner of the Long Bar. Robin poured the tea.

'One lump or two?' she asked.

Tan would have preferred a Singapore Sling but it was early and they had a lot of work to do. 'No one's ever asked me that before,' he confided.

'You're joking!'

'No, really.'

'Well, I'm glad to have added to your education, Mr Tan. Now, how much sugar would you like? It's Darjeeling.'

He shook his head in befuddlement. This was way beyond him. 'Milk,' he said. 'Just milk. Thanks.' But when he sipped, he smiled. Afternoon tea was not really his line but this was the best he had ever tasted.

'Now,' she said. 'Let's try and make some sense of this so far. Two years ago, flush with some profits made because we were able to pull an iceberg to the west coast of Africa on behalf of the United Nations, Heritage Mariner was looking to expand a little. One of our senior executives, Charles Lee, who was born and raised in Hong Kong, suggested we look East. A wise decision based on sound judgement. He came out here himself, did a lot of networking and research and bought the China Queens Company, lock, stock, barrel and Ms Leung. Assets, two ships in good working order, fully crewed – one crewed with men we already knew or knew of. Going concern with much local standing and good will, running a circular shipping route round the outer edges of the China Sea. Office here, apparently ticking over perfectly. We set up a subsidiary office in Hong Kong to run in full co-operation. Which it did. No problems at all. Good profits. No trouble.

'Until six weeks ago. Six weeks ago, something important happened. My husband, Richard, was called out here. I don't know why or by whom. He arrives, sends a postcard which I get. He writes a letter which gets destroyed. He makes a call or two which get wiped off my answerphone. *Sulu Queen* comes in, unloads, loads, apparently as normal. You have checked that for yourself. Richard goes aboard. Somebody, and I am quite sure it was Richard, makes some notes in the ship's network, addressed to me. For some reason they don't reach me;

they just stay in the computer's memory until I down-load them onto a disk I can't get back into. Richard stays aboard. We don't know what Wally Gough, the registered captain, does – but we'll start to look into that when we talk to the pilot later this evening. Somewhere in its run up towards Hong Kong, the *Sulu Queen* comes across some Vietnamese boat people and takes them aboard but they are all dead. Murdered, by the look of it.

'Within ten days of Richard's arrival, Anna Leung has vanished, the offices here are closed; *Sulu Queen* has been attacked and everyone aboard killed except for Richard. Something among the cargo may or may not have been removed. Some containers she may have been carrying later end up empty on Ping Chau Island just off the Chinese coast. But, if that is so, then someone else must have gone aboard *Sulu Queen* at some time, taken the containers, at the very least, and come off again, leaving no real trace. And that does present some problems because it is almost impossible to surprise a well-guarded ship and get your men up into the bridgehouse without an emergency being sounded over the radio. There has been no question, as far as I am aware, that there was anything wrong with *Sulu Queen*'s radio, though I'd better double-check.

'*Sulu Queen*'s most economic cruising speed is about eight knots. So the run up from Singapore takes a week. One week after she departs, there she is, drifting without power into Hong Kong waters with everyone aboard her butchered, except for Richard. And the team who go aboard, who construct the case and who are preparing to take him to court for mass murder, are the colony's specialists in piracy. And that is interesting too because piracy keeps cropping up here, doesn't it? It's there, but in the background as far as I can see. Who but pirates would go aboard and then come away again without leaving any traces? Who but pirates would want to smuggle containers off and carry them to Ping Chau? Who but pirates of some kind or another would want to fill these containers with contraband in the first place? Who but pirates with a really far-reaching, well-organised plan could move the containers off Ping Chau within days of their first discovery?'

'And who but pirates,' wondered Edgar Tan, 'would have killed all the Vietnamese you mentioned just now?'

Late tea turned into early supper, two culinary jewels joined by the irresistible string of a Singapore Sling or two – though Edgar Tan, too well aware of the Singaporean drink-drive laws, was careful with his second one. Robin, who had eaten nothing but Chinese food for a month, and little enough of that, insisted on the Elizabethan Grill and gorged herself on rare roast beef from the silver trolley. Edgar, concerned about the possibility of physical action later, was happy with a little sole. They were finished by seven thirty and piled contentedly into the Nissan to return to the Port Authority building.

* * *

The pilot's name was Ram Seth and he was of Indian extraction. He was a solid mahogany ball of decisive energy who bounced on his feet even when at rest. He had thin black hair which he wore slicked back with a pale-floored parting on the right. On his forehead and on his ebony crown there remained the line where his uniform cap had sat. He wore gold-rimmed half-glasses for reading, but his distance vision was perfect. 'Now,' he said, his accent deepening the vowel, allowing it to sit deep in his throat as it rolled over his tongue, 'what can I tell you about the *Sulu Queen*? Well, as chance will have it, I can tell you quite a lot.'

He ran his hand back over his forehead, pulling his perfect hair flat as he thought. 'There were two captains aboard. Captain Gough and Captain Mariner. Captain Gough was in command and Captain Mariner proposed to come ashore with me in the pilot's cutter once the ship was out in the roads. But that is not what happened at all. As we were pulling well out, Captain Gough fell violently unwell. Oh yes. It was most unexpected. And it was most upsetting for everyone. It was the advanced stage of appendicitis, I understand – what is that called?'

'Peritonitis,' suggested Robin.

'Yes, even so: peritonitis. One moment he was on the bridge standing beside the helmsman Wing Chau, the next he was on his knees on the deck clutching at his side and screaming. It was most unsettling, I can tell you. I crossed to him. "Captain Gough, are you quite well?" I asked. He fell onto his side. He was grey. You understand – his face was white. He was extremely unwell. I had no alternative but to call the first officer. His name was, let me see...'

'Brian Jordan,' Robin supplied.

'Even so. I called Lieutenant Jordan and he, as medical officer, diagnosed peritonitis and suggested that I must take the captain ashore at once in my cutter. But he did not have the papers to assume command, you see. So I suggested that the ship should return to Singapore at once. Then Captain Mariner showed me that he had the papers for command. He said that he would take the ship to Hong Kong and arrange for a new captain to be put aboard her there. I saw the papers. I made the regular checks. Everything was quite satisfactory. I have to tell you, however, that I did not dally over this. Time was extremely short and it seemed to me that Captain Gough was expiring even as we went through the procedures. It was, fortunately, a calm, clear night, and there was no trouble in carrying the stricken captain to my cutter and bringing him ashore. Naturally, we had radioed the China Queens office and were fortunate in being able to contact the secretary there, Miss Leung, if I remember correctly. Miss Leung was waiting at the quayside with an ambulance. It was taking my responsibility a little far, perhaps, but I rode in the ambulance with them to the Singapore General Hospital. In the ambulance I gave Miss Leung an envelope from Captain Mariner, and she assured me that she would make arrangements for all the correct procedures to be followed and notifications to be given. And that was that.'

'Captain Mariner gave you an envelope?' asked Robin at once. 'Have you any idea what it contained?'

'Not particularly. It was not a letter, I think. It seemed to me to be a hard square thing, perhaps a little more than three inches square. One can tell these things by touch, through the sides of an envelope.'

'Indeed. And did this envelope have an address on it or anything like that?'

'No. A name only. He had assigned it to himself, I believe.'

'How do you mean?'

'He had written on it "To Captain R. Mariner". I remember particularly, you see, because it was such a strange thing to have done.'

'In any case, you gave the envelope to Anna Leung and saw Captain Gough into the hospital.'

'Yes. That is correct. Except that I did not actually go with him into the hospital, you understand. I felt that I had done my duty and so I went straight round the corner and got a taxi back out to the Port Authority. I do hope the poor fellow is better now. I hoped Miss Leung would inform me – she promised to do so, but she never did. And I have thought of him often during the last few days, after I heard what had become of his command . . .'

Tan drove slowly back along the highway towards the centre of Singapore. 'That's a bit of a poser,' he said.

'Why is that? It could explain what happened to poor Wally at least. Peritonitis. That's where your appendix actually bursts. It's incredibly dangerous.'

'Yeah, I guess, except for one thing.'

'What?'

'Hospitals and morgues were the first things I checked. It's routine. Nobody called Walter Gough has been taken into any hospital in Singapore during the last five years at least.'

Chapter Twenty-Five

The *Seram Queen*, inbound from Jakarta, fully laden with a range of goods all safely stowed in her sixty-five containers, came picking her way carefully through the narrow, reef-infested Selat Durian under the last of the light, four days later, while the first gentle puffs of the south-west monsoon began to blow behind her. The monsoon was a little late this year and allowed one last great thunderstorm to welcome the cargo vessel to Singapore.

The temperature all day had been in the high thirties and the light winds had augmented a vertiginous tumbling of the local air pressure resulting from the sweltering heat. The waters of the Singapore Strait, and the Malacca Strait flowing into it, seemed to steam, giving up their lightest, hottest, most highly-charged and least stable water molecules into the humid air. And the air, puffed listlessly hither and yon, began to rise ever more powerfully, sucking up more and more of the water vapour as it went. By mid-afternoon there was a thickening overcast as the upper air met the cooler troposphere above, but this cool air with its thickening cloud was trapped at the top of a column which kept rising ever more fiercely from below. The clouds thickened, took more and more forcefully the towering anvil shapes of thunderclouds, and hovered, as though trapped helplessly, against the southernmost point of the Malaysian Peninsula.

The first, hesitant puffs of the monsoon swept more vapour into the swirling storm factory and very soon it became clear to even the most mediocre watchkeeper that the wind was not so much blowing north-east as being *sucked* north-east. And sucked ever more powerfully towards the writhing static-charged hearts of the huge, black, square-shouldered clouds towering above the jewel brightness of the city.

It was a Friday afternoon, 13 June, and passing through four o'clock. Everyone who was able to do so left work at once and headed away through the humid oven of the afternoon, hoping to make it home before the storm broke. Rush hour started early and snarled up quickly. The MTR became crowded and people, usually placid, became fractious and impatient. The hawkers who peddled their wares in little stalls along the tourist-packed roadways of Chinatown, Little India and Bugis Street looked at the restless sky and checked the lashings of their frail premises, muttering.

Robin and Edgar were working in her suite in the Raffles. The main entrance to the hotel was on Beach Road but Robin had been given one of the suites on the southernmost corner so that her window looked out across Bras Basah Road, past the War memorial, over the Singapore Club and the park to the marina itself. It was not a view which gave her a great deal of seascape to look at, the Raffles is no high-rise, but it gave her an excellent view of the sky. Looking up at about four thirty, she caught her breath at what she saw.

'Hey, Edgar. Come and look at this.'

On their right, the Westin Plaza Hotel stood immediately across the road but the taller Westin Stamford loomed close behind it and rose so high that the upper floors seemed hidden by the thickening haze. Away beyond the bright-windowed skyscrapers was something even more breathtaking. It was a solid cliff of cloud. Seemingly as massive as the coal face it so strongly resembled, it stood apparently only a couple of kilometres to the south and only two hundred metres up above the arch of the expressway. As they stood silent, the only sound in the room the steady rhythmic pounding of the fan, the black cloud seemed to move relentlessly closer and lower. It looked disturbingly like the jaw of a black vice closing inexorably down to crush the city. 'I've seen storm clouds in my time,' said Robin quietly, 'but I've never seen anything quite like that.'

Edgar's narrow eyes almost disappeared. He looked down at his watch. They had made no specific plans for this evening and he was wondering whether he could get across town to his modest little high-rise flat before Armageddon began.

Seeing the movement and correctly reading the thoughts behind it, Robin said, 'Edgar, why don't you call it a day and try to get home before this lot breaks.'

'No,' he said. 'Look at the snarl-up out on the expressway there. I'll give it another half-hour and see. There's some stuff here I can tidy up.'

Fifteen minutes later they were both engrossed in the paperwork again, though every now and then one or the other of them would glance unbelievingly out of the window to where the Stygian sky seemed to be trying for a new world record in natural darkness before exploding into the storm.

The telephone rang.

Robin picked it up, dipping her head slightly, as she always did when answering the phone, to clear her golden curls out of the way. 'Hello?'

The line crackled. Her hair swung back against her knuckles and gave her a considerable static shock. She hissed. 'Hello?' she said again.

'Hello, Captain Mariner, this is Ram Seth. I am calling from the Port Authority building. The *Seram Queen* has just requested pilotage into Singapore harbour. I will be going out to her in one half-hour. Would you like to come?'

'Would I ever! I'm on my way at once. Meet you at the Port Authority building, main entrance in twenty-five minutes at most. Oh, and Captain Seth?'

'Yes, Captain Mariner?'

Robin glanced back over her shoulder to where Edgar Tan was sitting, apparently still absorbed in the papers before him. Her hair crackled with static electricity as she moved and the line did the same. 'May I bring a friend?'

Edgar Tan's forebears through several generations may have been *orang laut*, men of the sea, but they had passed to him their blood, not their stomachs. As soon as he stepped into the pilot's cutter, the detective knew that he had made a mistake. The boat was powerful; and quite well fitted, with a big, comfortable cabin equipped with a range of comforts, from microwave ovens to coffee-making machines. Edgar liked the look of these things but found them far beyond anything he wanted to use once they got under way. From the moment the cutter began to move, all he wanted to use was the leeward rail. And he only knew to use the leeward rail because Robin took him up and explained it to him, very quickly and very clearly.

They had managed to reach the Port Authority building before the storm broke, though the oppressive feeling of high humidity and static electricity made everything everybody did almost impossibly stressful. There were several major accidents on the parkways and innumerable shunts on the lesser roads, each one surrounded by a tight knot of viciously ill-tempered people, so that they were lucky to make their rendezvous on time. 'You're late,' snapped Seth irritably.

Robin shrugged accommodatingly and Tan apologised. 'Traffic,' he explained.

The cutter was waiting for them at the bottom of the Authority steps, ready to go. At the sight of it, Edgar froze. 'I thought you used helicopters nowadays!' he exclaimed.

Seth gave him a tiny, tight grin. 'You don't think they'd risk a helicopter in this weather, do you?'

The wind was gusty as they pulled away, and the lowering sky felt as heavy as an avalanche upon their shoulders, but the cataclysm had not yet begun. As they looked south-westwards through the cutter's clearview, it seemed as though the sky was going to close down against the surface of the sea before the first bolt of lightning ignited the whole pyrotechnic process. There was the thinnest band of clear blue sky ahead of them. Under the black weight of the clouds, it was a dazzlingly blue colour – blue enough, in fact, to remind Robin of Richard's eyes.

Edgar Tan, who had done most things and thought he had seen all there was to see, was fascinated. He had always retired to his flat and hidden when the thunderheads began to build. Never in his wildest dreams had he thought that he would ever be out in one of Singapore's famous deluges, let alone in a small boat rushing across the harbour and out through the roads. The sight of the sky overcame the uneasy signals emanating from his stomach and, to begin with at least, he stood up by the helmsman looking out along their course. He saw the black sky close down inexorably, seeming to squeeze more blinding brightness into the narrowing strip of sky ahead. And then, just when he thought that the horizontal line of brightness along the horizon which gave the quadrant its name could not become any brighter, a truly blinding bolt of lightning leaped down vertically into the sea immediately ahead.

Tan staggered back, his eyes closed, with the circle of his blind vision precisely chopped into four by the afterglow of the intersection of two lines of brightness. The helmsman called something to the pilot, a warning perhaps, then everything was lost in the holocaust which followed. As though that one bolt of lightning had been sufficient to tear the guts out of the monster above them, sheets of rain were released at once. The immeasurable forces unleashed by the falling of so much rain summoned up storm-force winds in a twinkling, and big seas came with them, pitching the little cutter wildly hither and yon. It was at this moment that Edgar Tan wished most urgently to become acquainted with the deck rail, and Robin took him outside into the driving maelstrom and made sure that whatever he did he did downwind.

Out on the foredeck, the awesome power of the storm was enhanced by the impact of the noise it was making. The thunder seemed to be continuous. Edgar's vision was blurred by wind, rain and spray at once but Robin was treated to a display of lightning jumping down onto the water all around them. As Edgar heaved his last few meals out over the leeward rail, the experienced captain was aware that they were badly at risk out here. If the lightning was exploding down to the sea surface so close ahead, then it was only a question of time before it began to hit the cutter. 'We'd better get in,' she said to Tan. 'Let's go below!' She saw his face clearly in another blue-white bolt of light. 'I'll get you a bowl,' she said, just as the greatest crack of thunder yet seemed to split the air, making it doubtful whether he heard her.

Half an hour later, the pilot's cutter pulled into the wind shadow under the lee of *Seram Queen*. A Jacob's ladder was unrolled and flapped restlessly against the side. One of the cutter's crew steadied a light on it and Seth crossed towards it, with a halo of rain exploding off his wet-weather gear. Robin looked at her briefcase and knew she would never be able to get it up the ladder. She looked down at Tan and knew he would never be able to get himself up there either. She opened the briefcase, slipped the gift-wrapped package into her pocket and then left the two pieces of excess baggage side by side.

It was a hard climb, the weather had hardly moderated, though it was difficult to imagine that it could possibly maintain this fearsome intensity for very much longer. As she ran, sure-footed, along the slippery deck, hurrying to catch up with the little group formed by the pilot and the officer sent to welcome them aboard, she nevertheless took the opportunity to glance around. She was in the lee of the containers, though she could hear the wind screaming through the gaps between them like an army of banshees. The containers seemed perfectly loaded and well secured. Certainly, she had no sense of danger as the weather crashed against their far side, trying to blow the whole lot over on top of her.

The two men waited for her in the shelter of the port bridge wing and then they all stepped through the big door, over the high sill, into the relative tranquillity of the A-deck corridor.

The pilot bustled on ahead, shaking off the water as though it had personally insulted him. Robin found herself walking alongside a tall, spare man of indeterminate Eastern origin. He could have originated from anywhere – Malaya, the Philippines, Vietnam; it was impossible to tell. Robin looked up into the slightly woebegone skull of his face and smiled. 'I'm the owner,' she said firmly. 'And you are?'

He could have been any crew member; beneath his black oilskin, his white overall was innocent of badges of rank or responsibility. 'Wai Chan,' he said. 'Secor roffis, *Sera Quee*. You berra comalomg, missy see captir now.'

'After you, Second Officer Chan,' she said.

As they waited for the lift to return from delivering the pilot to the bridge, Robin took the opportunity to ask, 'Is the first officer better now? I understand he had malaria.'

'For roffis worsa naow. Maybe send hospitar. Captir say. Afir turraroun Singapore.'

I hope the captain's English is better than this, thought Robin as the lift came.

His English was; his temper was not. 'Mrs Mariner, what are you doing aboard here uninvited?' demanded Captain Sin as she crossed the bridgehouse towards him. He was a fat little man, hardly taller than the pilot but without Seth's rubber-ball hardness. Captain Sin seemed soft, self-indulgent. There were big black bags under his eyes and his skin was ivory-pale. He affected a small moustache. Designed no doubt to bristle and swagger, it drooped like a black caterpillar which had crawled there and died. He gave an impression of slight oiliness and sloppy dissidence, even though he wore a well-pressed uniform of dark blue cloth and a white-crowned captain's cap. 'I'm sorry to hear your lading officer is so unwell,' she said, offering her hand. 'That will be inconvenient. It may even slow you down.'

Sin disregarded her hand. 'First Officer Lau has malaria. It is an old ailment. He will be up and about in time for turnaround.'

'I can go down and take a look at him if you like. I have treated many cases of malaria. I have served as medical officer on several ships and my first aid certificates are all up to date. Is he on penicillin?'

'I...' Captain Sin stopped speaking. His face grew rigid as his mind all too obviously raced. Then he turned towards her and reached for her hand after all. Close to he had a personal odour compounded of sweat, cinnamon and Old Spice. His breath smelt of something minty when he spoke. 'I would be very pleased if you would take this trouble, Mrs Mariner. We have put up a day bed in his office to save him dragging himself up and down all the time.' He smiled his most charming smile. The gesture revealed two gold canine teeth of unusual length and brightness, separated by a range of uneven greyish incisors, and did not have the effect he clearly intended.

Robin smiled back, disengaged her hand and glanced around the bridge one last time. Pilot Captain Ram Seth was quietly in command and they were moving towards the distant lights of the city through the still whirling heart of the storm. As she looked, entranced by the beauty of Singapore's waterfront illumination, bright even beyond the columns of the lightning bolts, she saw the riding lights of the pilot cutter pulling away ahead, bouncing up and down as the little vessel dashed from one wave crest to the next. Poor old Edgar Tan, she thought. Another rough ride home. But the thought was an automatic one, far at the back of her mind, for her eyes were searching for something other than the distant gleam of the lights. And she found it. A computer monitor. It stood in precisely the same place as the one on *Sulu Queen*'s bridge and looked to be of exactly the same type. Great. She was really in business now.

Concentrating on taking the main chance and getting the little disk into the first officer's computer at the earliest opportunity, she ran lightly down the stairs towards his day room. But she was distracted at once by the obvious weakness of the first officer himself. He was tossing feverishly on the narrow little cot that had been set up for him. His skin was like rice paper stretched over the angular bones of his unexpectedly youthful face. So much like rice paper was his skin, in fact, that it seemed as though his very flesh was dissolving in the perspiration that was soaking him.

Robin had not been lying to the captain when she told him of her qualifications. And she had taken in more information during her visits to this room in the *Seram Queen*'s sister than she had realised. One look at the man in the truckle bed sent her striding purposefully across to the cupboard which she knew would contain the first officer's first aid box. She took out the feverscan first, not wishing to chance a thermometer stem between those chattering teeth and reluctant on such slight acquaintance to check his temperature by any other means. She had some difficulty holding the plastic strip in place, however, and needed to pin him like a wrestler in order to keep his head still. She hardly had time to pray that Captain Sin's diagnosis of malaria was correct and she was not dealing with a plague victim here when the 40°C band lit up and she knew that no matter what was wrong with Chin Lau, she had better act fast if she was going to save him. She cursed Captain Sin, shocked that he had not sent this man back in the cutter and surprised that he had not even sent out a pan-medic warning. But the cutter was gone and there was no chance of getting a helicopter out to them in this, so she was the best hope the officer had.

It was kill or cure to begin with – no one seemed to have kept a treatment log so she had no idea whether he had been given anything and, if so, how much or when. She gave him the biggest dose of penicillin she dared. If it damaged any of his internal organs they would have to arrange repairs later on. Then she began to work on getting his temperature down. All she had to help her there was paracetamol. But it was good enough. By the time the *Seram Queen* came out of the storm and into the Singapore roads, he was quietly asleep, well tucked in and running a temperature of only 102°F according to the old-fashioned thermometer in his mouth. She called the bridge on the first officer's phone, however, and warned the captain that Chin Lau should be ashore and in hospital. The captain was courteous, but he didn't sound all that impressed or convinced. Then Robin turned at last to the computer.

She took the book-shaped parcel out of her pocket and placed it on the table beside the computer itself. The machine was on and the screen was in that familiar bright format. With her eyes on the picture, she pushed the disk across beneath the wrapping paper until she could pull it free. With her heart in her mouth, she popped it into drive A and pressed ENTER.

The following files are available for general access, it told her. *Please use your F keys to select and then press ENTER to proceed.*

Against F10 it said *Enter company code to proceed.*

'Yes!' she said, thumping the desk top, too excited to remember what a hard time she gave young William when he did just that.

Within a very few moments she was back at that same point, with her breathing shallow and her mouth dry. *PLEASE SAVE THIS FILE AND SEND IT DIRECTLY TO MRS MARINER.*

She placed her fingers against each other as though she was going to pray, and bent them back until her joints cracked. She took in a breath and held it while she tried to clear her mind. She separated her hands and held them as though she was a magician performing a spell. Then, with the index finger of her right hand, she pressed ENTER.

Robin – Disregard what I wrote in my letter and said in my last phone call. I'm aboard Sulu Queen *and will be taking her on the next leg of her voyage as acting captain. Poor Wally has just been taken very ill*

and I'm sending him ashore with the pilot. I'll send this message on a disk ashore with him, with a handwritten note asking Anna Leung to send it on at once via the Internet directly to Helen DuFour's desk in Heritage house. Hence the *EYES ONLY* message at the top. It should get to you as soon as you return from Skye. A useful insurance. By the time you get back though I should be just about pulling into Hong Kong. I'll call from there at the earliest opportunity of course. But you must take action at once. There's something wrong here. Something I can't quite put my finger on. I sense it but I haven't really had time to look properly. It was good of Charles Lee to send word that the China Queens were under police surveillance but I haven't been able to get back in contact with him since I arrived. Apparently lines to Beijing are not quite as open as we had expected. In any case I want you to find some way of keeping the *CLOSEST EYE POSSIBLE* on Seram Queen. You may need to pull head office rank and put someone we can trust aboard her – I don't know. You will certainly have your work cut out dealing with Captain Sin – a nasty piece of work by all accounts. I hope Anna Leung doesn't read this before she sends it. She has a soft spot for both of her captains, she tells me! Love to the twins.
RICHARD.

With her mind a whirl, Robin glanced through the screen full of type then she checked the printer and pressed ESCAPE: PRINT, craning across to see that it was in fact coming out onto the roll of continuous-feed paper. It was. She sat back, to think. But even as she did so, her eye fell on the parcel destined for Brian Jordan's daughter. The wrapping paper was dirty, bedraggled and soaking. In her hurry to take the computer disk out, she had torn a hole in the side. Tutting at her clumsiness she picked the thing up and pulled the ruined wrapping paper off it. At the earliest opportunity she would get some more and re-wrap it. But as she stripped the paper away, her movements became slower and slower and her attention was pulled away from the computer towards the video case in her numb hands.

'Walt Disney's classic *SINBAD*,' it said. 'Featuring the voice of Sir Anthony Hopkins in his Oscar-nominated performance as the Sultan of Deriabar.'

As she looked, she remembered a couple of things. She remembered that the vendor in the Cat Street market had said that these videotapes were only just beginning to arrive when she had bought that guilty present for the twins. If that were so, how had Brian Jordan got hold of a copy for his daughter at least a fortnight earlier? And she remembered the tiny strip of paper taken from the inside of the empty container in the cave on Ping Chau Island. She remembered the colour of that piece of paper perfectly. It was exactly the same, unique, fluorescent aquamarine as the cartoon-bright seascape beneath Sinbad's sea-booted, pirated, feet.

The last survivor of the *Sulu Queen* was picking his way slowly through the carnage of the stricken ship's bridgehouse. Wherever he looked there were bodies, frozen in their eternal, never-changing positions. But the survivor was aware of a disquieting tension in his mind, a tension tightened inexorably and agonisingly, by the slow passage of time. Time was a problem to him in all sorts of ways, as a matter of fact. He kept bumping into bits of it which were running backwards. That was a problem which no one else around him seemed to be having and it added to his worries. But the people around him were all caught up in different bits of time in any case. And that was more worrying still. Take that naval man for instance. Huuk. He was there, the survivor knew, with the two uniformed guards close behind his back. And yet the same man, dressed in shirt and jeans and Reebok trainers with that massive gun on his hip beneath the open flak jacket was running down the last few steps towards him! He jumped back as the phantom Huuk swung the huge gun down, colliding with the real Huuk behind him.

'It's all right,' said Tom Fowler, taking a firmer grip on his arm. There's nothing there. Come on.'

And, when the survivor looked up, he saw that Tom was right. There was nothing there now after all. He went on up the stairs, moving forward with his guide and inexorably backwards through time.

BANG! BANG! He looked round. Not even Maggie had flinched at the overpowering concussion of those shots. They came round onto the B-deck corridor. *The whole corridor was a mirror with himself fleeing along towards his own staring face!* How could they not realise what was going on? His phantom self flattened his back against the far side of Brian Jordan's office door. The survivor did the same on this side. 'We've been through this, surely,' said Andrew Balfour's voice distantly. How could he be so unconcerned? thought the survivor. Didn't he know what was in there? His phantom dived in through the doorway. The survivor did the same, tearing himself out of Tom's grasp. Overlapping with that other version of himself, he dived into the day room and froze. Brian Jordan and Chas Macallan lay trussed up and face down, a combination of steam and smoke wafting delicately upwards from the gaping backs of their heads. *There! Just beyond them!*

'Look out!' he screamed at the top of his voice, warning Tom and the others. The noise he made seemed to jerk the two images of himself apart. The phantom image stumbled forward, falling to its knees. The other person in the cabin swung round, crouching, his yellow shirt wide across his yellow chest, his face a mask of shocked surprise and his long arm ending in that great square box of the Smith & Wesson automatic. Then the phantom self was up again, hurling forward across the bodies of his crew mates, squelching through the matter gushing out of them, reaching wildly for the gun.

Only Tom's firm grip upon his arm stopped the survivor hurling himself forward to help his phantom self. So the survivor stood and watched the ghostly body in the blood-spattered overalls swiftly prove more than a match for his wiry opponent. And, as he did so, the survivor realised that when the man in the yellow shirt screamed for help he was by no means the only one to do so. All around the bridgehouse rang with the most horrific cacophony of yells and screams and shots. The sound built up and up in his head until that one place, deep down in the very centre, began to hurt again. The deepest spot in all his reeling brain. The spot where Richard was imprisoned. 'Richard hurts!' he warned, watching the tall figure in the overall wrestle the yellow-shirted man round so that he could hold him safely, arm across a yellow throat, gun against a black-haired temple. 'Come along, you *orang laut*,' said the phantom figure to his captive.

'*Orang laut*,' echoed the survivor, turning to follow his ghostly self, his hands copying the hands that he could see. Right hand gripping the gun while the left folded tight across a scrawny throat.

'What did he say?' asked Maggie.

'I don't know,' said Tom.

'Andrew, did you recognise what he said?'

'Sorry, Maggie,' said Andrew.

'*Orang laut*,' said Huuk. 'It's Malay. It means a seafarer. A pirate.'

'What's he doing now?' asked Maggie.

'I don't know,' said Tom.

The whole conversation was far less real to the survivor than the sounds of slaughter going on all around him. Imitating their every movement he followed his ghostly self and the captive along the corridor. Light kept coming and going. He knew that the alternators were going down. He would have to go down there and check them later. If he survived. He had to keep light and power at all costs.

'One thing at a time,' he told himself. 'Sort this bloody mess out first.'

Now which one of him had said that?

The *orang laut* in the yellow shirt broke away at the foot of the companionway. The phantom in the boiler suit was far too slow to stop him. The survivor watched himself swing round and mirrored the motion, bringing up the great gun, aiming down the stairwell where the man had gone and hanging there frustrated. Too late. 'Too late,' he said sadly. The man in the yellow shirt was gone.

The Smith & Wesson dropped to his side, almost tumbled to the floor, so unbearably heavy had it become. Step by step by step they started climbing to the bridge.

All of them, phantom and real, almost came to a dead stop at the bridge door. The survivor watched himself hesitate on the threshold, summoning up the will to proceed, then, together, bound like body and shadow, they stepped forward.

The bridge was a mess. Wing Chau the helmsman lay in a crumpled heap on the deck but it was the impact of what he saw above which caused the survivor to stagger back. 'The head, he gasped. 'The . . .'

And young Trev Latham groaned. It was the most terrible sound that the survivor had ever heard in his life. He ran to the third officer's huddled body where it lay twitching on the deck. 'How can he not be dead?' yelled the survivor. He knew which one of him had said this for the phantom had been silent as he crouched over the poor boy's hacked and mangled body, looking into the eyes which refused to die, and mindlessly tried to tend him.

The survivor crashed onto the deck, pulling Tom down too, and his hands moved almost helplessly. Only in his own mind did the survivor see himself lay the automatic on the floor and try to put some part of the poor boy back together again.

'Tom,' said Maggie's voice from very far away, 'whatever he's doing, I don't like it. Jesus . . .'

'Huuk,' said Tom, from an equal distance, 'what was here?'

'One of the bodies. Third Officer Trevor Latham. Second Officer John Tong was over there by the door.'

'John,' gasped the survivor. 'God, where's John? It's all right Trev, he said. 'I'll find John Tong. He studied to be a doctor. He'll know what to . . . John! *John!*'

He heaved himself to his feet and staggered across to the bridge wing door. Pushed it open. Lurched out. 'John!'

The tone of his voice told the others all they needed to know. Oh God, John . . .' He went down on his knees again.

'Wait a minute, said Andrew. 'I thought Second Officer Tong was found on that chair inside the door.'

'Wait!' spat Tom. '*Look!*'

The survivor lifted his dead crew mate onto his knees and they stayed together there for a moment as the survivor tried to find a pulse in the great veins of John Tong's armpit. And that was what he was doing when the figure in the yellow shirt burst out through the bridge wing wielding the panga with all his might.

Overcome by horror and surprise, the survivor hurled John Tong's body up, holding it as a shield against those massive blows, pushing it back, step by step, as he forced his attacker back onto the bridge itself.

'My God,' called Maggie, 'what on earth is he doing now?'

'Richard, called Tom, 'can you . . .'

The mention of the name ignited a fearsome agony in the survivor's head but he could not stop for that now. His opponent hacked again at poor John, his blows restricted by the doorway, his face twisted with fierce bloodlust. Survivor was groaning now, his shoulders on fire and his strength all but gone.

'Richard!'

Tom's near scream coincided with a clap of thunder loud enough to throw the *orang laut* in the yellow shirt forward. Tom, unwisely, came between them and metamorphosed into the unfortunate John Tong. The survivor hurled the psychologist back with the last of his strength and he collapsed into the bare metal frame of the watchkeeper's chair.

But the survivor was out of control now, nothing and no one existed except the writhing yellow man with a bullet hole exactly in the centre of his chest.

'Trev!' He hurled himself forward, then froze unsteadily on his feet. 'God, you got him! I'd never have believed! Trev . . . *Trev!*' He hurled himself forwards again, slipping on the slimy flooring, fighting to stay erect.

Once again, he was the only one to hear the thunderclap of the automatic's second detonation.

Tom sat, winded, on the metal frame of the watchkeeper's chair where the hacked remains of John Tong had been found and he watched the great body of his patient hanging there looking down at the grey metal flooring. He recognised the way in which the great tousled head was shaking helplessly from side to side. Behind him the others stood, shaken to the core by the glimpse they had been granted into what this man had experienced here – or at any rate *believed* he had experienced here.

Tom watched as the great splayed hands came up to hold the shaking, grizzled temples. And they all watched as the strength of the knotted hands and arms slowly overcame the shaking of the head.

Tom closed his eyes and sent up a quick prayer. He had arrived now at the very second he had been striving towards for weeks – the moment Survivor was born.

'*Richard!*' rapped the psychologist, his voice at its most compelling and commanding. '*Richard Mariner!*'

The head began to shake again and Tom breathed out, defeated, expecting to hear the plaint 'Richard hurts!'

But no. The great head came up, the wild blue eyes flashed, quickened, deepened. 'Yes?' said Richard Mariner. 'Here I am. But where am I? And who are you?'

Chapter Twenty-Six

It was a weekend of feverish activity for everyone concerned and yet by the time Sunday evening arrived none of them felt that they had made very much progress.

In Hong Kong, both Saturday and Sunday were vibrant with the first series of public celebrations due to mark, during the next lunar month, the last two weeks as Crown Colony and the first two as Special Economic Zone. In the midst of it all, Tom Fowler fought against a general sense of anticlimax, in himself and in those immediately around him, as he took the newly-restored Richard Mariner and tried to rebuild his memory as effectively as he had restored his sense of personal identity.

'It's not unusual,' he explained on a faint line to Robin in Singapore at teatime on Sunday. 'He is almost bound to go through a period of confusion and disorientation as Richard Mariner comes to terms with what happened to send him into a state of amnesia, and with what has happened to him during the month or so since he went under. Even in a relatively uncomplicated case we would have to contend with this confusion, but with the added complication of the closed head injury, it is very difficult.'

'Will it help if I come straight back?'

'No...'

'You don't sound certain. Maybe I should be there.'

'No, I don't think so. He has your picture, and those of the twins, his parents, his childhood. Still no obvious recognition there. He used to know Maggie very well as a close friend, she tells me, but there's no glimmer of recognition there either. If he isn't reacting to photographs or to close personal friends, you'd probably just be wasting your time. Andrew says you think you're on to something important down there.'

'Perhaps. I'm going back on board the *Seram Queen* later. They've almost completed turnaround and are looking for a first officer in any case. Look, can you hand me back to Andrew now?'

Edgar Tan was standing outside the door of his office as though waiting in his own waiting room. He was keeping guard, and under the circumstances he did not feel one bit silly at all. If his phone was tapped, which he said was unlikely, there was nothing they could do about it. But beyond that, Robin wanted to take every precaution possible. She remembered too clearly what Twelvetoes Ho had said to her and she was worried about Triads and pirates and Chinese diplomats – and English diplomats with highly perverse habits, come to that. In her less serious moments, she was aware that what she was most afraid of was her own imagination. This was probably just a small-scale smuggling enterprise which had fallen foul of some terribly violent thugs.

'I can't see that there's much doubt about it, Andrew. It's the only thing that makes sense as far as I can see. I have no idea whether the *Seram Queen* is carrying anything illegal, but *Sulu Queen* certainly was. As far as I can see, she was carrying at least one container full of pirate video tapes of the latest Walt Disney cartoon *Sinbad*. It can't possibly be out on video cassette legally yet, it's only just been released in the London cinemas. I have no idea where these things were originally made, where they came aboard or where they were bound for, but I think they began to turn up in the Cat Street market within days of *Sulu Queen*'s arrival.

'I don't know whether you know anyone who can give you a lead on what sort of turnover can be expected from dealing in this sort of thing, but if you run into any trouble, I suggest you give Helen DuFour a ring. She can use the Heritage Mariner network of contacts. I dare say the International Maritime Bureau would be a good place to start. I have no idea whether this is the only thing that the *Sulu Queen* was smuggling or whether there is a range of contraband which the China Queens Company might have been involved with. Until we find Anna Leung – or whatever her name really is – I doubt whether we can find any more hard facts.

'I think we can assume that whatever Anna Leung was up to, Wally Gough was involved in it. It's early days, of course, but Wally seems to have faked a peritonitis attack just before the ship set sail out of the Singapore roads. There is no record of anyone going by his name in any hospitals here, and he and Anna Leung seem to have disappeared at the same time. It seems likely to me that wherever they are, they are together. But that's just a guess. Edgar Tan is looking into this.

'In the meantime, I have a message which Richard wrote a couple of minutes before *Sulu Queen* set sail under his command, and it asks me to try and keep a close eye on the *Seram Queen*. The best way I can think of to do that is to go aboard her, if the captain will take me. He needs a first officer as a matter of some urgency so I stand an excellent chance of getting aboard. She is due in Hong Kong within the week; and that's what I would like to do unless there is a really pressing reason for me to be there for the opening sessions of the trial. What does Maggie think?'

'I don't know, Robin, I'll hand you over to her.'

'Hello, Maggie? Do you think it will help the case if I'm there at the opening of the trial?'

'Legally, there's no need, of course. You're not a witness to any incidents involved in the trial. You might be relevant as a form of identification or even a character witness at this stage but that's all. On the other hand, if you can come up with evidence that something was going on aboard these ships beyond Richard's knowledge when he became involved with the *Sulu Queen*, anything which might explain what happened in terms other than that he took the weapons held by the prosecution and committed mass murder, then obviously it will help us – if the facts can be proven and supported by independent witnesses and can be presented to the court within the relevant time frame.'

'OK. I'm going back on board the *Seram Queen*, then. It's what Richard wanted, I think, and there's a strong possibility that I can find out what is going on, especially if I settle in as first officer and lading officer. I'll stay in close touch, though. And in the meantime, Edgar Tan will follow up the most important elements here, which means looking for Anna Leung and Wally Gough.'

Robin and Edgar held one last council of war later on that same Sunday afternoon. They were in the Long Bar again, drinking tea. Robin had moved her baggage out of her room and was all set to join *Seram Queen* as she got ready to sail before midnight. 'You'll be able to contact me,' she explained. 'Just use this number and you'll be patched through to the ship's radio room.'

He took the number and folded it into his wallet, thoughtfully.

'I won't be able to do anything or go anywhere for six days. *Seram Queen*'s due at Hong Kong next Saturday and I'll be free to move from then. By that time, of course, I hope to have a clear idea of what is actually going on.'

'You don't think it's just too risky?' he enquired when she stopped speaking.

'That's a good question,' she admitted. 'But I simply do not know the answer. There's a chance that whoever attacked the *Sulu Queen* may have a motive for attacking the *Seram Queen* too, I suppose, but it seems unlikely. What can I say? The rewards seem to me to be worth any risk involved. If I can get a believable, provable explanation for what is going on here then I've got a chance to help Richard. I don't have to prove everything down to the last detail, just enough to make the jury think again. Remember, they have to be convinced "beyond a reasonable doubt" before they can return a verdict of guilty. That's as true in Hong Kong as it is in England. All I have to do is introduce a "reasonable doubt" and we're home free. Think of it.'

'I'm thinking of the risk you're running.'

'I'll keep a good lookout. Anything that doesn't look right, any hint of trouble and I'll be on the radio screaming for help, believe me.'

'But you'll be on a ship which could be up to three days away from a proper port. There's no end to what can happen in three days.'

'No. *Seram Queen* might be three days out of Hong Kong or three days out of Singapore in terms of sailing time, but she'll never be more than two hours' flying time away from either Singapore or Hong Kong – and there's Sarawak, and then the Philippines only half an hour away.'

Edgar saw that she wasn't going to change her mind. 'All right, so there's all those places,' he said. 'And there's this too.'

He placed on the table in front of her a battered, inconspicuous leather case. She tilted her head like a bird surveying an unexpected peanut. 'What's this?' she asked. 'Christmas?'

'This is highly illegal,' he said. 'Take it, please, and I will show you the best way to conceal it.'

She opened the top of the case and gasped. 'What is it?'

'Insurance,' he said, looking intensely at her over the top. 'It's called a Glock. It's so small that it looks like a toy but the clip will hold thirteen bullets and it will fire individual or automatic. The clip is full with one shell in the breach. It is ready to fire once the safety is off. The bullets are called Glazer rounds. Each one will stop an elephant. The funny looking bit on the top is a laser sight. That's for people who can't shoot at all. When the gun is up it shines a red dot and where the dot is, that's where the bullet goes. Almost any range, almost every time. This switch is the sight and this one is the safety. They both go the same way, see? On, off. Other than that, all you have to remember is to hold still and pull hard; it's a double catch. Take it. You might need it.'

'Richard had that big thing, that Smith and Wesson,' she said. 'It didn't seem to do him much good.'

'You don't know that. He's still alive; nobody else is. It may have done him all the good in the world.'

'What can I say?'

'Just get it back to me once you're safely in Hong Kong.'

'Even if I have to smuggle it.'

'You will. You can't just post these things. You're going to have to smuggle it onto *Seram Queen* and hide it. Hide it safely, but close at hand.'

'Right. Thanks, Edgar.'

They transferred all the papers from her big briefcase into the old case on top of the gun which sat snugly in recessed foam. By the time they had finished, it was impossible to tell that the little weapon was there.

'Now what about your part?' said Robin when they had finished. 'You have to find Wally Gough and this Anna Leung character. You know that anything they discover at Heritage Mariner, or anything passed to Heritage House by the International Maritime Bureau, will come into the China Queens office. You have the keys?'

'Yes. I have the keys. I'll check twice daily.'

'And in the meantime, could you keep an eye on First Officer Chin Lau in hospital?'

'I'll be giving him the third degree right there in the ward. I want to know everything he can tell me about the *Seram Queen*, her officers and crew.'

'Be gentle with him. He's had really serious malaria; he's lucky to be alive. And, what else?'

'I'll check Changi Airport again now that I know I'm looking for two people. But I really don't think they left that way. I wouldn't. I'd go by boat.'

'What size boat?'

'Depends on destination,' Edgar answered, aware that he was speaking to a master mariner. 'But it wouldn't take much of a boat to island-hop across the Selat Durian to Indonesia. Then it's wherever you want.'

'Only if you can get across to Padang. Sumatra's a big island.'

'Why do you think they invented the jeep?' he laughed. 'For crying out loud, they've got buses which run across.'

'True. But if you're island hopping anyway, why stop?' she mused.

He shrugged his grudging agreement. 'You could hop islands all the way round to Japan. Jesus, you could probably hop all the way up Japan and across to Vladivostok, if you wanted. And if the pirates don't get to you first.'

'But I thought we thought Anna Leung was working for the pirates.'

'Now there,' he said, his voice like silk, 'I believe you have a point.'

Robin went out to *Seram Queen* with the pilot, but it was a stranger this time, not Ram Seth. The pilot and the cutter crew waited cheerfully enough, however, as she went through the usual procedures, opening Edgar Tan's briefcase with a look of innocence to take out, one at a time, the papers which the authorities required before letting her depart on the waiting cargo vessel. The pilot and the cutter's crew looked strangely at her but she shrugged, elated by her first serious, and successful, piece of smuggling, and reckoning that she might as well get used to this sort of thing now as later. This time she had brought her shoulder bag into which the little briefcase fitted securely. The Jacob's ladder was no problem, especially in the absolute calm of the monsoon-freshened evening.

Captain Sin had not really wanted her aboard, but he had been desperate to get a competent lading officer. There must have been some officers on the beach in Singapore, waiting for berths and available, but Sin would have had to have gone looking for them, and he was falling behind schedule. What with having to send Chin Lau in to hospital – an action he had only taken when Robin and the ailing officer had prepared all the cargo details for the computers and the authorities in the Tanjong

Pagar container terminal – and then having to wait because of damage done to the automatic container loading system by the storm, turnaround had taken nearly four times the usual nine hours, and then he had had to wait until this evening for final clearance. Nearly forty-eight hours all in all. Enough to get even a captain in trouble, these days. It must have occurred to Sin, therefore, that if he had a member of the board as a senior officer, no one was going to hold the delay against him. That was one of the things Robin was counting on to get her aboard and to keep her safe. That and Edgar Tan's gun.

She ran on ahead of the pilot, leaving the gruff official to the tender mercies of the lugubrious Second Officer Wai Chan. Had she been captain of this vessel, she would have wanted her first officer on the bridge and she saw no reason to expect Sin's standards to be lower than her own. She paused at the door of the first officer's day room to sling her weekend case into the space left by the removal of the day bed, and then she hesitated. No, given what it now contained, she had better keep it with her until she could put it safely under lock and key. She carried it with her and slid it safely under the chart table as she reported to the commanding officer.

By the time the pilot arrived, the first officer – of unusual gender and uniform – was standing beside the helmsman looking out, slit-eyed, across the Singapore Strait; ready, willing and able to guide the *Seram Queen* along the course recommended by the *Ocean Passages of the World* and the *Admiralty Pilot* for the South China Sea. She had checked it out this afternoon and she could almost see it stretching ahead of her along the 1,450 old-fashioned nautical miles, NE to Pulau Aur and Kepulauan Anambas; passing NW of the Udang Oilfield and SE of the Charlotte Bank; between the Paracel Islands and the Macclesfield Bank, up the long haul NE, then hard round past the Vereker Bank and into Hong Kong itself.

Everyone had wound themselves up for the next morning but, again, it was something of an anticlimax. Lata Patel had not gone down with Maggie. The Hong Kong bar forbade her to act in this case and although she was happy to be in the Crown Colony and was enjoying her odd combination of vacation and detective duty, she knew that her usefulness ended at the door of the Supreme Court Building. As the tall girl walked up the steps and through that august portal, she felt isolated and suddenly lonely. Andrew was waiting for her immediately inside, however. He swept her along as soon as he saw her. He was formally dressed. This was clearly going to be a very different affair to the slightly shabby Magistrate's Court. But even so, it was quite an ordinary door. It was panelled teak and beside it was a label in beautiful lettering screwed to the wall saying 'COURT FOUR' but that was all.

Andrew opened the door for Lata and ushered her in. Immediately in front of her there was a wall of wood. She paused, confused, until she saw that Andrew was walking away to the left down a narrow passageway between the wood and the wall proper; then she understood that the wood was the solid side of a grandstand. As they had in the lecture theatres in the universities and colleges of her youth – and in the major courts she was becoming used to working in at home in London – the chairs rose tier by tier to look down on the bench at the front of the big, airy room. It was only possible to get a seat by doing what Andrew was doing. You had to walk down to the front where the first row was at floor level, then you had to turn and start climbing, and look for a seat.

Lata didn't have to climb far, but she soon realised she was lucky to find a seat at all in the crowded courtroom. She was removed from the little team down at the front of the room; very much part of the crowd up here in the gallery. Andrew was sitting down in the second row himself, just behind Maggie and Mr Thong who was acting as her junior. Lata felt a poignant twist of envy and took a deep, shuddering breath. Both of the barristers were fully wigged and robed. Before them, on the parquet flooring of the courtroom stood a solid table covered with books and notes – and bearing also decanters of water. Even before Lata could orientate herself further, there was a movement among the officers of the court and someone called, 'All rise!'

The High Court judge, Mr Justice Fang was a rotund little man whose figure was over-emphasised alike by the bulk of his formal black robes and bright white wig. He bustled in, bowed precisely to the court and sat, seeming to give off sparks of intellectual energy. No sooner had he sat than he reached into the breast pocket of his jacket beneath his robe. Lata was reminded forcefully of the way Stipendiary Magistrate Morgan sucked on his cough sweets and she half expected to see Mr Justice Fang pull out sweets as well. But no. He took out gold-rimmed half glasses and settled them on the ivory stub of his nose, then he gazed around the court over the top of them.

Lata also took the opportunity to look around. The lay-out was not dissimilar to a high courtroom at home – in many ways identical in fact, to the court in the Old Bailey where she and Maggie had last worked together. Maggie and Mr Thong sat five levels down immediately in front of her. Away to her right, also at floor level, behind another table, sat Mr Prosecutor Po. At right-angles to the front bench, stretching away on Mr Po's right there was a range of empty benches which, she realised, were desiggned to accommodate the jury. Directly across from the jury box was the empty dock which would, any moment now, contain poor Richard. Further round was the witness box, again empty. Across the front of the court room, opposite the tables of the prosecution and the defence was a wooden platform surmounted by a high, ornate bench behind which sat Mr Justice Fang. And at his feet sat the officers of the court. Lata sat back and began to observe what was going on – it might just be a worthwhile learning experience, she supposed. And with any luck it would be interesting.

Richard's trial in the High Court before Mr Justice Fang got under way, but it began with the selection of the jury. In Hong Kong there was only a seven-person jury, unlike the twelve-person jury in the rest of British legal jurisdiction. Even so both Mr Po and Maggie, under the advice of her junior in this case, Mr Thong, had the right to hear details about each member of the jury.

Richard was held below and incommunicado while the time-consuming process of preparing the court to receive the case was gone through. Maggie was particularly glad that Robin was on the *Seram Queen*. Had she advised Robin to rush back, then there would have been an even stronger feeling of frustrated anticlimax. How could the barrister have explained to the distraught wife that this lengthy process was as necessary as a carefully prepared defence?

It was all settled by the end of the morning's session, however, and Mr Justice Fang rose for lunch in the full expectation that the afternoon would begin with the reading of the charges.

Richard was brought into the court immediately after lunch and his identity was duly established. Then the clerk of the court read the charges against him.

The charges took a mere ten minutes to read, the simple, bland wording almost concealing the seriousness of the crimes.

Mr Justice Fang paused for a little careful consideration at 2.15p.m. as he calculated how much business he might reasonably expect the prosecution, on behalf of the Crown, to complete before the end of business for the day. He estimated three and a quarter hours would amply allow Mr Po to present his opening statement.

And so it proved. Mr Po addressed the court for two hours precisely, describing the circumstances of the slaughter of the *Sulu Queen*'s crew; how they had been discovered, identified, and how the guilty person had been identified, as well as the scientific methods by which his guilt had been established beyond a reasonable doubt. He briefly sketched the manner in which the Crown proposed to establish in the minds of the jury the motive, the opportunity, the evidence and the unassailable guilt associated with the defendant Richard Mariner.

In summing up he touched slightly on the only defence offered by the accused Captain Richard Mariner – that he could not, in the face of the massive weight of this evidence, remember anything.

'I ask you, ladies and gentlemen of the jury, how can this stand as a defence? The accused does not tell us "I did not perform these actions; I have an alibi". No. He tells us that he does not remember! He may have done these truly terrible acts, or he may not, he just does not remember! What sort of an alibi is that? But, at the end of the day, members of the jury, it is a matter for you to decide!

'And there,' said Mr Justice Fang, as Mr Po's ringing words echoed across the crowded courtroom, 'I propose to call a halt for this evening. Mr Po, I know you are keen to call your evidence but I'm afraid you must wait.'

'All rise!' ordered the clerk of the court.

Tom was allowed one hour with Richard at the Queen Elizabeth Hospital between 6 and 7p.m. that evening. At least having Richard himself back gave the psychologist a chance to try and reconstruct memories of the earlier part of the voyage, before the protective carapace of the Survivor had been born. And it was in this most recent area of Richard's memories that the psychologist had to concentrate, rather than on the identities of his parents and details of his childhood home which is where he would have preferred to begin.

Hour by hour through five full days he worked his subject back, but all he received was evasion, inaccuracy, outright refusal to remember, and a kind of running gibberish which made no sense to him at all. Had the psychologist possessed maps and charts, had he been able to cross-check the gibberish against landmarks, hazards, islands and shoals, he might have understood a little more, but he was used to dealing with people who understood London and the Home Counties, as Tom did himself. The names of Richard's apparent gibberish were not the names of roadways and districts or suburbs, villages and stations which might have rung a bell in the Londoner's subconscious. Here, indeed, though none of them realised it, Robin with her seafarer's mind would indeed have made all the difference.

But of course she was not there. She was following the tangled trail of islands, reefs and hazards for herself. All 1,450 nautical miles of it.

Richard was still at the stage of working back from where his mind switched off and his amnesia began. Everything else, including last night and today in court, seemed more like a dream than reality. Unaware that he was tapping a fund of chart-born vocabulary he was utterly ignorant of, Tom was playing word association games with Richard. There were only ten minutes left in the consultation, and Tom was tired and dispirited, but by no means giving up and taking an easy ride. He was recording each word and each association to be checked up and thought through at greater leisure later.

'Five days back, now Richard; I want you to think five days back. Can you do that?'

'Yes.'

'Say the first thing that comes into your mind when I say the following words. Ready?'

'Yes.'

'All right, let's start with something easy and general. Let's say, animal.'

'Tapir...'
'Tapir?'
'Orang Udang...'
'Orang-utan?'
'Orang laut... Orang...'
'All right, calm down, Richard. Let's try something else. Names. Girls' names.'
'Susan...'
'Susan?'
'Mandai...'
'Mandy?'
'Jemima...'
'Jemima?'
'Damar...'
'Damien?'
'Dam... Damn... Damn...'
'All right. Let's try places now. Places.'
'Krakatoa...'
'Krakatoa?'
'Helzapoppin...'
'Helzapoppin?'
'Hell... Hell... Hell...'
'Singapore!'
'Selat Singapore...'
'Singapore!'
'Selat...'
'Singapore!'
'Sulu...'
'Singapore!'
'Argo...'
'Argonauts!'
'Jason...'
'Golden Fleece.'
'Dragon's teeth... *Dragon's teeth*... DRAGON'S TEETH...'
'All right, Richard. We're both tired. Let's call it a night. When I clap my hands you will wake up. All right? One... two... three...'

During that Monday, Robin had settled in as best she could, getting used to being the one officer most obviously in charge of the *Seram Queen*. She had seen the ship out of the Selat Singapore and into the first section of her voyage while the captain had sat silently watching, at first beside the pilot and then on his own.

Then, with a shy young third officer on watch well after 2100 hours, she slipped down and unpacked her stuff in the first officer's cabin. She was in no mood to try and scare up some late supper so she went back onto the long, low poop behind the bridgehouse and, trying not to be overly sensitive to the massive bulk of the poop cargo standing weightily just behind her and moaning in the wind, she looked at the falling, fading lights of Singapore away behind the luminescent wake for the better part of a dreamy hour. Then she went back up onto the bridge and passed some companionable time with the third officer before officially relieving him for the middle watch from midnight until 4a.m. She learnt that his name was Sam Yung and this was only his second stint as third officer. He was terrified of Captain Sin and very nervous of Wai Chan the second officer who was impossible to understand, devious, manipulative and a bully.

Although she discounted any real risk of physical danger, Robin took careful precautions. Before she went to bed she was determined to get a key to her cabin door. The first officer, according to the company job description, was – on top of everything else – officer responsible for security aboard, but it was obvious that the lamented Chin Lau had held no keys. Second Officer Wai Chan glumly and almost impenetrably informed her that he held none either, but he offered her a piece of sage advice which she at first took to be a gratuitous insult.

'What did you say, Mr Chan?' she snapped, her voice rising with anger and outrage.

'Fat Cow—'

'Mr Chan!'

He was alike unaware of her mounting rage as of any cause for anger. But he was conscious that he was not communicating, and he wished very much to do so. His long face folded into a frown of concentration as he tried to force his civilised, Middle Kingdom tongue round the *gweilo* barbarian sounds. 'You ask chief steward, name Fat Chow...'

And so it was that at 04:30 on Monday morning, Robin made the acquaintance of, and earned the undying enmity of, Chief Steward Fat Chow. The skull-like face of this inappropriately named functionary burned in stony hatred as he sorted through his selection of keys under the intransigent gaze of the first officer. It had taken ten solid minutes of pounding at his door to stir him from slumber and it looked as though it would take the better part of a week to find the actual key she sought. But each was carefully labelled and what seemed at first to be chaos turned out to have a sort of order. By ten minutes to five, Robin was holding what she desired even more than she desired sleep. 'This had better be the right one, Fat Chow,' she observed apparently mildly. 'If you have any doubts, you had better bring your whole collection along. Neither of us gets a wink of sleep until I can lock my door.'

'It iss the correct key,' he spat, his voice lent an unfortunately sinister hiss by a set of badly perished brown teeth. 'Iss key to firss offiss's cabin. Iss true, misssy.'

'It had better be,' she said.

It was. And so Robin's routine of sleep became established. Each night at 21:30 she turned the hard-won key in the lock of her cabin door, then wedged it tightly in place so that it could not be knocked free and pulled under the door; and also so that it could not simply be superseded by a master key. She stripped, dumped her dirty washing in the basket for the stewards' attention, then replaced it with fresh clothes carefully positioned within easy reach for emergencies, and slipped into the bunk. Then, covered only by a starched sheet, she fell into a deep slumber until aroused by a combination of her personal alarm clock and a solicitous call from Sam Yung on the bridge to warn her that she was due on duty in one half-hour, at midnight.

For all that it took her away from Richard and thrust her into the petty squabbles and worries of this strange ship with its alien, impenetrable crew, being back at sea gave Robin unexpected relief. Monday dawned clear and fair and the monsoon gusted gently behind them all day as they wandered lazily up the recommended course, well clear of the charted obstacles, with nothing to worry about and not a dark premonition in the world.

While still on that first watch, Robin had seen the ship safely past Heluputan and the Kar Katoaka. Soon after she retired they were sailing lethargically past the islands, points and reefs named Jemaja, Mangkai and Siantan. As she came onto the bridge at 0800 next morning to watch Wai Chan hand over to Sam Yung, away off the starboard bow in the vast blue blaze of the morning she could see the warning signs of the Udang marine oilfield and by the time the lazy day was coming to its blood-red end, off the far port quarter she was aware of the most distant glimmer which was the Tapis marine oilfield.

As she settled onto her middle watch at the end of that first day as Monday midnight teetered over into Tuesday morning, with her mind full of an exact breakdown of the first day in court from Maggie and an all too imprecise report from Tom on the latest talk with Richard, she was most strongly aware not of the most recent impressions of the voyage but of one of the first.

On the verge of sleep, but far to good a watch officer ever to slide off the edge, she sat in the watch officer's chair and thought back to that dreamy hour on the poop looking back across the Selat Singapore along the gleaming wake to the heave of black land lying like a sleeping dragon along the mystic joining of the sky and the sea. Of the thrust of the dragon's head down to its snout at Singapore itself, with all those great soaring buildings jutting upwards, rooted on the coastline, blazing with their own electricity and catching the first light of a low gibbous moon, standing there like dragon's teeth magically ablaze in the night.

Chapter Twenty-Seven

The crew all called Robin 'missy', except for Captain Sin who insisted on referring to her as 'Captain Mrs Mariner' with almost Dickensian formality. Robin didn't think they meant the term 'missy' as any kind of sexist comment, it was simply that they could not conceive of calling a Caucasian woman anything else in formal intercourse – so the term was probably fundamentally racist as well, she supposed. With a wry grin and a mental shrug, she determined to get used to it – she would only have to put up with it for five days at the most. Certainly, she soon discovered, the title – she would not think of it as a mere epithet – was capable of a full range of intonation. Everything from 'You are utterly wonderful' to 'You are a gibbering cretin' could be contained in the syllable and a half they used to say it. She felt patronised and isolated, almost inevitably, but never really threatened. Not until Wednesday, at any rate – though looking back on it she was able to see the pattern beginning to emerge on Tuesday.

But hindsight, as they say, gives 20/20 vision; at the time, even as late as Tuesday evening, she noticed nothing at all.

The first twenty-four hours of duty took her and *Seram Queen* away between the oilfields, and past Point Laut, well out into the South China Sea. The next twenty-four hours took her from midnight – through her watches, and through the examination and the cross-examination of Daniel Huuk nearly twelve hundred kilometres to the north – to midnight once again. And in that time the ship ran through what was, in its way, a commentary upon recent history, through many past glories of the British royal family towards Dangerous Ground. Past the banks named for Queen Charlotte, she sailed, and past others in the Vanguard; past still others named for the Prince Consort and Princess Alexandra until the series, backed by the London Reefs, culminated in the Coronation Bank.

As they passed Prince Consort Bank, just as Robin was relieving Sam Yung for the first dog watch at noon on Tuesday, she was aware that 200 kilometres further west, lurking behind the feature named for Queen Victoria's beloved husband, stood a much more timeless and much larger collection of reefs and shoals named the Rifleman. And she was aware, as which navigating Officer in the area was not, that the Rifleman stood as outer marker to a series of hazards so difficult to chart or categorise that it all went by the name of Dangerous Ground, even on the most up-to-date Admiralty charts. The better part of 15,000 square kilometres of ship-killing Dangerous Ground stood all too close to the west of them, off Palawan Island in the Philippines. Its uncharted reefs and banks and atolls contained myriad tiny islands, home to who knew what pirate fleets of deadly cutthroats. But in the lazy azure blaze of the noon watch it was easy to disregard the dangers which might lie there. Really, there was nothing at all to worry about except the running and the handling of the ship, maintaining the security of the cargo and delivering them all, safe and sound to their port of destination.

'Now, Captain Huuk,' began Maggie, unconsciously curling her scarlet nails like cat's claws, once her first cross-question had been allowed, 'you cannot seriously ask us to believe that this phone call just came in from out of the blue, giving you information like this without rhyme or reason.'

'On the contrary, ma'am. This sort of thing occurs quite often. There were, at the last count, four individual Triad organisations jockeying for position in Hong Kong. We are often used as a blunt instrument, so to speak, in the activities of one against the other.'

'You believed that your information, and what happened to the *Sulu Queen*, was the result of Triad action?'

'I did not say that. I said that Triad action in the area made mysterious phone calls quite a regular occurrence in my office. In this case, we were not aware of any associated Triad action, but...'

'But, Captain?' Maggie's gaze on the unusually hesitant Huuk did not waver.

'Well,' said Huuk, 'I was going to say that of course the Triads are as aware as the rest of us that Hong Kong will become part of China in less than a fortnight now, and while no doubt they have made their plans, they must know that the People's Republic has no intention of allowing the sort of Mafia-style activity which is said to have characterised some sections of the Soviet Union during the last few years.'

'And so, Captain? I am afraid I do not altogether follow your reasoning.'

'The result of this has been a combination of increased Triad activity as the foot soldiers jockey for position, and a breakdown of traditional associations and systems as many of the senior, traditional, figures – the godfathers, if you like – move away to San Francisco, London – America and Europe in general.'

'Let me be quite clear about this. You were not surprised to receive this phone call because such things are increasingly common now that you can no longer trust the Triads to police themselves?'

'Effectively, yes. With the big boys away, there is a lot to play for among the ambitious middle-rankers left.'

'And so you went out to the *Sulu Queen* in disguise because you feared that you might be getting involved in a Triad war?'

'Yes and no.'

'What sort of an answer is that?'

'I believed the situation was sufficiently complex and dangerous to warrant clandestine procedures.'

'Because you believed the ship to be involved in Triad activity?'

'Yes...'

There was still just the slightest hesitation in Huuk's voice and Maggie was on it like a flash. 'But you believed something more than that?'

'The situation is complex, and politically sensitive.'

'Oh, come along Captain. You cannot prevaricate with the court. What was it that you suspected? What was it that made you decide to put your men in disguise and take such a range of arms with you? Why such a complicated reaction to a simple telephone call?'

'The ship, the *Sulu Queen*, was reported to us as being just outside our waters. The Navy could not go aboard, we had no jurisdiction. But we could not just leave her there without investigation, so we went out and boarded her at once but took no action until we established beyond doubt that she had drifted into Hong Kong territorial waters.'

'But surely,' purred Maggie, as the full relevance of Huuk's admission hit her, 'if the *Sulu Queen* was not in Hong Kong territorial waters when you received your mysterious call, and perhaps even when you went aboard, then she must have been in the territorial waters of the People's Republic of China.'

'It is possible.'

Maggie let that grudging admission slide for the moment, for she spotted bigger game here. 'So, should you not have contacted the coastguard division of the Chinese People's Navy and asked them to look into this derelict ship?'

'No. The ship was clearly drifting towards our waters and would be in them before any action could be taken.' He took a breath. 'And in any case, the *Sulu Queen* is a Hong Kong registered vessel.' He took another breath. 'And besides, it is common knowledge amongst my command that, apart from Triads and their Filipino associates, the people most likely to be guilty of piracy in local waters are renegade Chinese naval units in any case.'

It was just coming up for 8a.m., British Summer Time, in Budleigh Salterton, Devon, England.

Here, in Scrimshaw, Marine Drive, Phylidda Gough was making her way slowly down to breakfast. She had been awake since before six but she refused to come down until her normal breakfast time, otherwise she found that the days were far too long to handle, filled as they were with speculation as to the fate of Walter, her husband.

Friends and associates from the Heritage Mariner family had been to visit – Sir William Heritage himself had been down. They had given her the facts but explained that Wally was missing and could not be presumed dead yet. And a stiff police man had come in from the local station to inform her that her husband's disappearance was the subject of an investigation in Singapore where he had disappeared and the Crown Colony of Hong Kong where his ship had been registered and where his dead crew had turned up. As captain's wife, she had been den mother to the other officers' families and her duty had been clear to her. She had called the other wives – widows all, now – aware that they had so much more than she to grieve over. She had posted a birthday present to Brian Jordan's poor little girl. And she had waited for news.

Her son, called Walter like her husband and a junior deck officer with the Heritage Mariner shipping fleet, had been home for two weeks' compassionate leave after Walter senior's disappearance, but Phylidda found that, with no news of any kind, having him there upset her routines and got on her nerves so that he was as much of a hindrance as a help. A beloved hindrance, but a hindrance nevertheless.

She had set up a routine for herself and she stuck to it, following it religiously every day, from that first cuppa out of her old Breville Teasmaid at 6a.m. through breakfast television – with Classic FM to fall back on when the antics on the screen bored, irritated or shocked her – to wrapping up in her dressing gown and coming down at eight. She would sort through the letters – and there had been so many letters – and make herself some toast before returning upstairs to wash, dress and prepare to answer the most pressing correspondence.

But not this morning.

This morning, 8:05a.m. BST found her standing, stricken, on the doormat, looking at her left hand as though it had just turned leprous For there, tucked between the gas bill and another bloody letter from her bank was a postcard, well-travelled and dog-eared, bearing God alone knew what sort of a stamp, written in close-packed, slightly smudged, scrawling, shaky writing which could only belong to one man in all the world – her errant husband Wally.

Five minutes later she was on the phone and dialling – not the police; oh no – dialling the old, familiar number of the twenty-four-hour secretariat on the top floor of Heritage House.

Not even Maggie DaSilva could extract more gold for the defence from Captain Huuk under cross-examination. She tried, but either the Judge would not allow her question or, when she asked it, Huuk had an answer which seemed acceptable to the jury. The captain, bloodied but unbowed, stepped down at 4.25p.m. local time, just at the right moment for the judge to direct that the court rise for the evening, the jury take care not to discuss what they had heard with any person, and to demand that they should all reassemble here by 10a.m. on the next day, Wednesday.

The defence all stood up, exhausted, as they had on the previous evening. Richard was taken back to his secure rooms at the Queen Elizabeth and Tom followed him for another consultation.

Maggie and Andrew pulled their papers together and retired to his office in order to discuss how today had gone and to prepare their strategy for tomorrow.

Isolated, lonely, ignored and a little jealous, Lata Patel followed them, like a younger sister sent as chaperone on a courtship. She ended up carrying most of the papers out of the court. She had to struggle to get the papers into the briefcase, while the other two discussed the case with more passion than was absolutely necessary beside the Aston Martin in the underground garage. She was directed – somewhat dismissively, she felt – to put the papers in the boot and to put herself into the back seat. And later she had to listen as Maggie admitted to her that she was as smitten as the solicitor. Maggie treated her junior much as though Lata was a younger sister, discussing her feelings for and interest in Andrew Balfour as the pair of them dressed for the evening in the rooms they had taken in Robin's leave flat down the hill from the solicitor's home, looking out past the temple of Tin Hau, goddess of the sea.

Lata had been invited, very much as an afterthought, and to add a third to the dinner table so obviously designed to be *tête à tête*. Andrew had booked a table at Saigon on Lockhart Road, Wanchai, for he and Maggie were both interested in Vietnamese food. Not a little angrily – though neither of the would-be lovers noticed her pique – Lata declined, saying she would meet them back at the flat in two hours' time, and wandered off down Lockhart Road to find some cuisine more suited to her own palate.

It was early in the evening and the busy road was bustling. There was a lively, potent sense of excitement abroad. Long before Lata had been born, the Wanch had been *The World of Suzie Wong*, known worldwide as one of the most romantic areas which lonely men could visit; haunt of the mythically understanding bar girls. But such things were hardly on the minds of the bustling crowds this early in the evening and so Lata could wander, unmolested, along the roadway, entranced by the luminescent fruit stalls which reminded her of Berwick Street Market at home in the Soho she had come to know and love since leaving her family home in Edgware and settling into her bachelor flat off Wardour Street.

And, now that Lata looked around, she saw the Chinese food shops so familiar from Gerrard Street and Little China, the second-hand bookshops so reminiscent of the Charing Cross Road. So it was that she settled happily into the seedy, familiar air of the place; even the redlight clubs and the over-endowed, too easily available girls fitted comfortably into the familiar ambience. So at home here was she, in fact, that when the tall man dressed in black fell in beside her and showed every sign of trying to engage her in conversation, she was not even faintly embarrassed. She was on the point of telling him to leave her alone and go talk to the dark girl with the brass-blonde hair and the enormous chest across the road when he said, in a soft and cultured voice, 'Miss Patel, it has been my ambition for the last week or so to engage you in some conversation and, perhaps, to offer you a little food.'

Lata stopped dead. 'How do you know my name?' she snapped. 'Who are you?'

One or two of the *amahs* nearby, obviously out doing a little late shopping, paused as the tall man stopped and turned courteously towards his young companion. 'My name is Ho. You may have heard the nickname Twelvetoes used. I am a close friend and sometime associate of Richard and Robin Mariner. It was Robin who mentioned your name when we were talking one evening a week or so ago. Please may I buy you dinner? I have a thought or two which might be useful to Ms DaSilva's case and it would be so churlish to approach her directly this evening, don't you think?'

'Well . . .' Lata hesitated, and wisely. He was unknown to her though his name was familiar enough. Goodness knew what she might be risking, going off somewhere with a strange man in such a strange city. All the wise words of her mother, all the direst warnings of her father, rushed into her head.

'Somewhere public, needless to say,' he continued, as though reading her mind. 'Somewhere full of tourists where a simple word from you would call up all the aid you might require in an instant. I had thought the SMI Curry Centre close by which serves world-class Indonesian and Singaporean curries; but, if you would prefer something closer to home, there is the Maharajah just round the corner on Wanchai Road itself.'

That won her over. The Maharajah was a little further away than she had imagined but there were only two turnings, one to the right and another to the left, and Lata was never in any doubt as to the way back. As they walked, they chatted and it was no time at all before Lata found herself relaxing in Twelvetoes' wise and witty company, and even beginning to take him a little into her confidence. He told her how he had met the Mariners because he had been chief steward on the company ships. How he had earned the name Twelvetoes because of his uncannily sure footing on even the slipperiest and most agitated deck. How each of the Mariners at one time or another had saved his life. How they had returned him to Hong Kong in possession of a fortune which he could never in his wildest dreams have hoped to amass by legal means. And she reciprocated by telling him of her life, of her family, her current employment and her ambitions. So wrapped up in their conversation was she that she did not notice the pattern of women who followed them facelessly along the road, nor the manner in which her host was welcomed into the restaurant and shown to the perfect spot, where their conversation could not be overheard but they could be overseen by the wide range of tourist clientele, and the little group of Chinese women who, unusually, decided to dine here too.

Like many people of slight build, Lata was a considerable trencherman. While she carved her way ecstatically through prawn puri and paratha, Twelvetoes nibbled on a plain poppadom. Then, while she ladled chicken korma onto a fragrant bed of pilau rice, and added to it a selection of mixed vegetable bahjee and one small stuffed paratha, he nibbled contentedly on a plain naan and asked for a bowl of undressed rice. And their conversation switched to business.

'What do you know of the container trade?' he asked.

'Nothing, except what we have prepared for the case. That is that containerisation means that shippers can fill boxes of an agreed size with their produce and list the contents in the expectation that it will only rarely be checked. That ships are designed to take set numbers of containers below decks or on deck – forward deck or poop deck. That places like the Tanjong Pagar facility in Singapore and Tilbury in England can be run by computer, unloading and reloading these things without much human interference because they are all the same size, they all weigh effectively the same, and they all fit together like sections in an old-fashioned Rubik's cube. Somewhere like Tanjong Pagar can turn a ship round with a standard sixty-three container load in about nine hours flat. Which is what it did with the *Sulu Queen* before Captain Mariner went aboard.'

'Exactly so; a fine summation,' purred Twelvetoes Ho. 'But I ask you to consider this. What if a ship, let us say the *Sulu Queen*, had been especially designed to take not sixty-three containers of standard size but sixty-five containers, each one almost imperceptibly smaller than the normal? The standard handling equipment at most ports along her route might remain unaware of the small variation. Even the computerised lifting mechanisms at Tanjong Pagar must have an element of variation built into their programs. Human beings, alas, are not always as invariably reliable as machines.'

'Yes? And so?' asked Lata, pausing in her flight to gastronomic heaven while she considered his carefully-weighed proposition.

'So that, passing around the edges of the China Sea, in the hands of the China Queens Company, there would be two almost full-size containers on the *Sulu Queen* and, who knows, perhaps even on the *Seram Queen* as well. Two phantom containers which nobody knows are there. Two containers which are never declared on the manifest, never officially loaded or unloaded, never checked by the authorities. Two containers which can carry anything at all from anywhere to anywhere. Two phantom containers travelling between, let us say, Vladivostok and Sapporo, with summer excursions as far north as Magadan. Let us suppose that two containers which nobody knows about travel down to Fukuoka, to Naha and T'ai-pei, to Manila and General Santos, to Manado and Ujung Pandang, to Jakarta and Singapore, to Hong Kong, allowing contact, let us say, with Saigon – as it was – and Da Nang, Haiphong on occasion, and perhaps even to Guangzhou, past the coastguards like Daniel Huuk and up the Pearl River. Then on to Shanghai and perhaps Tianjin, allowing access to Beijing, and across to Seoul and down to Pusan and out again to Vladivostok. Can you imagine the worth of two containers per ship, two unknown, unchecked, unsuspected containers which could be taken between the Soviet Union, Japan, Taiwan, the Philippines, Java and Sumatra, Malaysia, Vietnam, the Peoples' Republic of China, and Korea? Imagine what could be carried in two such containers. Weapons-grade nuclear material; revolutionary computer parts of motorcar components; the new genetic materials; pirated goods of all sorts, from perfumes, shirts, watches and footwear with spurious brand names to CD-Roms and videotapes; drugs from the Golden Triangle; Western delicacies for the greedy mandarins of the People's Republic. Imagine what such a cargo would be worth. Imagine, should its existence become known or even suspected, what some people would do in order to obtain it . . .'

Chapter Twenty-Eight

'This is very bad,' said Maggie two hours later. 'I need to go through this again in some detail. It makes the case against Richard so much stronger that it is very bad indeed.' Her voice was rough, her tone abrupt. Perhaps she was unsettled by the manner in which Lata had interrupted her increasingly intimate *tête-à-tête* with Andrew a little under an hour ago. Certainly it was difficult for both of them to change back from lovers to lawyers in an instant as required by the new situation.

'Afraid I can't see that,' said Gerry Stephenson quietly. 'How exactly does it make the case against Richard stronger?'

Maggie glanced up. Her golden gaze swept around the three other faces in Andrew's office. Gerry was clearly speaking for them all. They had caught him working late when they arrived three-quarters of an hour ago full of exquisite food, deep in the throes of a burgeoning affair – Andrew and Maggie were, at least; Lata was as coolly demure as ever – and all agog with Twelvetoes' revelations.

Almost unconsciously allowing her eyes to dwell on Andrew's open, boyish, irresistible countenance, she tapped with one long red fingernail against the Tables and Index volume of the famous law-book *Archbold Criminal Pleading Evidence & Practice* which lay piled on Andrew's desk in front of her. Then she began to growl an explanation. 'In the absence of confession or witnesses, the prosecution case should be built on four main things: motive, opportunity, forensic evidence and benefit. There is no doubt that Richard had the opportunity to kill everyone aboard the *Sulu Queen*. Someone killed them all and he was there while they did it. We think it was pirates who came aboard and then vanished leaving no discernible trace. We guess it must have been the *orang laut* that Richard was apparently fighting with when Tom took him back aboard *Sulu Queen*. Huuk was worried that the Chinese coastguards may have been involved somewhere along the line. But that's not really relevant now. What's important is this: the prosecution have got a point. Richard did have the opportunity to do it. And they have their experts all tooled up to explain the forensic evidence in such a way as it appears possible that Richard was associated with all the recovered murder weapons in some way or another. We know that. What they don't have, or didn't have up until now, is any sort of idea of motive or obvious benefit. In spite of everything they can prove, why on earth should Richard bother to kill thirty nine people on board a ship he owned? What reason could he possibly have? What good could it conceivably do him?'

'What reason could anyone have for killing so many people?' mused Andrew, his mind clearly on other things.

'The same reason most people have for killing anyone. Profit. Gain. Money.'

'Fraid I don't follow you...'

'Imagine that what Twelvetoes Ho told Lata is right. Add it to the things he told Robin just before I arrived. Look at what it means. Two phantom containers going round and round the outer edge of the South China Sea, able to carry any contraband at all.'

'Yes,' said Andrew, frowning with concentration. 'I accept that, but...'

'Now, what do you think the White Powder Triad would want to ship in those containers?'

'Well, drugs of course. Cocaine, probably, but...'

'Have you any idea how much two container-loads of cocaine would be worth?'

'Millions and millions, I suppose.'

'Maybe billions. Enough to be worth killing a few people to get hold of?'

'My God! Yes, certainly!'

'Bingo! We have a motive.'

'Yes, but wait a minute, there's still no benefit. Richard hasn't got them! He hasn't got the drugs or the money! He doesn't even have the containers. They were on Ping Chau Island.'

'Some containers were on Ping Chau. For a while. You know they were gone when Huuk got back again. But there was nothing to say that they were *the* containers, was there? And who says Richard hasn't got them? Richard or his associates?'

'Associates? What associates?' asked Gerry, surprised by the sudden turn of the argument.

'Walter Gough and Anna Leung, of course!' explained Andrew, his eyes on Maggie. She gave him a tiny, intimate smile of congratulation.

'Good Lord,' said Gerry, quietly. 'How on earth are we going to handle this? You think it'll come out in court, Maggie?'

'Certain. Probably tomorrow. Where are the notes on Commander Lee's evidence? Like I said, I have to go through it all again with these new facts in mind.'

'Listen,' said Gerry apologetically, is it something that you can do without me? I have to get back. It's coming up for two a.m. now and Dottie's not all that well...'

'That's all right with me,' said Maggie. 'It's a one-man job anyway, Lata, why don't you go home with these two? Andrew, is there a bed out back or anything? It's been a long night so far and it's nowhere near over yet...'

'Bedroom with shower *ensuite*,' said Andrew. 'All made up and ready to go. I use it quite often if I have to work late.'

'That's fine then. Show me where the papers are and leave me to it.'

Andrew followed the other two down to the underground car park but then he walked across to Gerry's car. Lata followed the two men. All three of them crossed the echoing chamber in silence. They hesitated at the side of Gerry's big Daimler as though uncertain what to do next. Then, with the possible exception of the speaker, no one seemed particularly surprised when Andrew said, 'Look, Lata, Gerry ... why don't you two go back down to Repulse Bay together? I can't really let Maggie slog through this all on her own. It's just not on. I know where everything is. I'll stay in case she needs a hand or anything...'

'That's her junior's job,' snapped Lata, possessively.

'Perhaps ... But you're not acting with her on this one are you? I couldn't possibly haul poor old Thong out of his bed at this hour. And anyway, as I said, I know where everything in the office is filed. What if she wants to consult any other sections of the prosecution notes? I know where to look – you don't.'

Lata still hesitated, until Gerry said quietly, 'Come on old girl, Maggie can look after herself. What do they say – nobody messes with Maggie unless Maggie wants to be messed? If I know that, you must know that.'

With one fulminating look at the sheepish solicitor, Lata got into Gerry's car and slammed the door. Gerry hesitated as though he too were about to say something, then he climbed aboard and the big eight-litre saloon purred into motion.

Andrew stood and watched the sleek car pull away into the exit lane then he turned and strode purposefully across to the Aston Martin. He pulled open the door and slid into the driver's seat, but he allowed the force of his movement to carry his head and shoulders across until he could reach the glove compartment. He unlocked it and pulled it open, rummaged around in it for a few moments, then took out a plain-wrapped little package. He pulled himself upright and looked at what he had found for a moment more, then he said, quite loudly, 'That's one I owe you, Jeremy, old man,' before slipping it into his jacket pocket. Then he climbed out, locked up and marched back towards the building.

'It's only me,' he called as he opened the door, and walked through into the office. 'I thought I'd come back and give you a hand.'

Maggie gave no appearance of having heard him. She had kicked off her shoes and put her feet up on his desk before burying herself in the papers he had found for her. He saw at once that she painted her toe nails.

He had not noticed that before – but he had somehow always known that she would do so. Then he noticed a great deal more than her toes. When Robin Mariner had sat in that position some uncalculated time earlier, just before going to her press conference then on out to Kwai Chung, her modesty had only been protected by the fact that she was wearing jeans. Maggie was wearing a short black silk skirt and no tights or stockings. And it so chanced that her legs were of a length to guarantee no modesty was left at all. Andrew stood, suddenly quite breathless, much struck by the manner in which the almost syrup-golden skin on the insides of Maggie's thighs had a strange, smokey hue somehow reminiscent of her voice. And the higher up those honey columns he allowed his eyes to wander, the smokier, the softer, did that strange, seductive hue become. Perhaps it was the subtle contrast between the flesh itself and the white silk of her underwear that made the topmost curves of her thighs, just where the soft rolls of skin nestled up against the taut web of fabric, seem so much darker and so much more tempting than all the rest.

When he looked up, her eyes were on him and it was as though the air between them were filled with electricity. 'Now what are we going to do about this?' she whispered, and he knew she was not talking about Lata's information and Lee's testimony.

'I suggest we make love at once, several times, and see whether that helps,' he said.

She made a sound somewhere between a chuckle and a growl. 'That sounds like a perfect start,' she agreed. One naked foot reached up languorously onto the pile of *Archbolds* with the Hong Kong bar notes lent them by Mr Thong. The skirt's taut hem slipped up past her hips. She allowed her right arm to fall out on the hinge of her elbow apparently moved by its own weight, and she dropped the testimony of Commander Lee onto the floor. The tip of her tongue caressed dark-shaded lips and her nostrils flared.

Andrew began to shrug off his jacket but somehow his legs would not keep still and his arms could not wait to hold her. As he came towards her she swung round and opened one thigh for him like a turnstile so that he found himself half sitting on his desk, reaching down for her as her legs closed up around him.

It was she, therefore, who slid the jacket back over his shoulders as he did the same for hers. She was lithe and strong enough to keep her lips glued to his even though the chair back was far behind her. He was self-controlled and calm enough to unbutton her blouse without his fingers trembling into clumsiness but they had to break apart for an instant to get rid of his tie because the knot tightened inexorably under her fingers. Then he simply tore his own shirt off, buttons flying, and hurled it aside. The feel of her breasts against his chest, clothed as they were in a still-crisp mesh of lace was the most exciting experience he had ever enjoyed. And it was but the beginning.

She was surprisingly substantial – her chest was deep and powerful for all that her waist was slim – but he straightened with her in his arms easily and she came up towards him, one foot still firmly on the *Archbolds*. Then, with her arms fastened tight around his neck and her lips still pressed to his, she held herself still while he unzipped her skirt and eased it down below her bottom. When he put her down, she broke her grasp and kicked off against the desk. The big old chair rolled backwards on its castors so that she could kick her skirt free and reach forward for his belt all in one fluid motion. As his trousers came down he reached behind him for his jacket, pulling out of his pocket the little packet from the glove compartment. 'These were put in the Vantage by a bloke I know called Jeremy,' he said. 'He meant it as a sort of a joke.'

'I love a good joke,' she said softly. 'Let me put one on for you.'

When she had done this, she leaned back again, hooked her hands onto the arms of the chair and her feet onto the edge of the table, gimballing up her hips so that her buttocks rose out of the seat of the chair. Andrew reached down and took the waistline of the white silk panties in gentle fingers. As he drew them down she breathed in languorously, hollowing her tummy so that the peaks of her hip-bones stood proud. Then she lowered her hips and pulled one knee close to the other for an instant allowing the silken loop to slide free of one long limb. He pushed the warm, damp material along her left calf thoughtlessly as he pulled her back towards him, and for the next few moments it lay, cooling, across the august black, gold and ox-blood cover of Mr Thong's *Archbold*.

Mr Thong's *Archbold* was on the defence's table in Courtroom number four of the Supreme Court bright and early next morning, Wednesday, and beside it lay the typescript of Commander Lee's evidence with copious annotations in Maggie's decided hand. How these notes had been made and under what circumstances, only Maggie, Andrew and *Archbold* knew, and none of them was saying anything.

Andrew sat, still dazzled, full of energy, more intensely alive than he had ever been, in the second row, slightly elevated, immediately behind Maggie. Lata fulminated up in the gallery far behind, all too well aware of the subtle changes in Andrew's and Maggie's body language – and what these changes revealed. Maggie herself had that rare facility of being able to exclude from her immediate consciousness everything except the matter at hand. And the matter at hand was Commander Lee's testimony.

'So, Commander, you are in command of an on-going investigation into smuggling and piracy centred in Hong Kong?'

'Yes, Mr Po. That is correct. The investigation is centred here, but the smuggling and piracy under investigation take place all around the South China Sea. Some of it right around the Pacific Rim.'

'So a range of authorities is involved?'

'Authorities here, in Singapore, in Japan, Indonesia, Malaysia, the Philippines, Washington – and London, obviously.'

'No more?'

'Oh yes, many more. But not on quite such a regular basis.'

'Very well. Could you please detail this investigation for the court – so far as you are able without compromising it.'

'Of course. Our investigation has been centred on all the major ports around the South China Sea. We have, during the last decade, placed informants in Hong Kong, Bangkok, Jakarta, Brunei, Manila T'ai-pei, Fukuoka, Kanzanawa, Sapporo, Vladivostok, Pusan and Singapore. It has to be said that the information we gathered in the first few years has all been put in the shade by that which we have managed to gather since nineteen ninety-four. During that time we have observed the collapse of the Soviet Union and the increasingly wide availability on the market of nuclear material up to weapons grade. We have observed the somewhat hesitant process by which North Korea has been accepted into the international system, and its demand for just such fissionable material. We have observed the manner in which China has moved back into the centre of the international arena; with its attempted annexation of the Spratleys, its pressure to make Shanghai the city of the twenty-first century, its, shall we say, individual relations with the United States. We have seen the burgeoning growth of a range of pirated materials from Rolex watches to Rolls-Royce engine parts; from Filipino tobacco to a range of hard-core pornography; from counterfeit currency of all sorts and denominations to small arms and claymore mines dug up in North Vietnam; from Walt Disney videos to the latest designer drugs.'

'My Lord?' Maggie rose, apparently deep in thought.

'Ms DaSilva?'

'If I may . . .'

'Of course . . .'

'Thank you My lord. Now Commander, how, do you believe, this contraband is transported around such a wide area?'

'Well, I . . .' Commander Lee was thrown off his stride and not a little flustered by the unexpectedly abrupt question.

'Yes, Commander?'

'Our information posits the existence of a series of ghost containers which move from port to Port but are never checked by customs officials.'

'Posits, Commander?'

'We have never actually got hold of such a container with the contraband intact.'

'But unless it contains contraband, one container is like any other, surely?'

'Indeed.'

'So, after the better part of a decade of investigation, you now tell the court that you guess that among the millions of containers moving around the Pacific Rim, there may be a couple which might contain contraband?'

'More than a couple. On a regular basis. As part of a pre-prepared smuggling network. And we are amassing proof.'

'A smuggling network being run by Captain Richard Mariner?'

'Well no...'

'But you believe that the China Queens ships were somehow involved?'

'Yes.'

'And do you have any proof of this?'

'Not at the moment.'

'You have impounded the cargo of the *Sulu Queen*. Are the containers anywhere in this cargo?'

'No, they are not.'

'So you have no proof that the *Sulu Queen* was ever carrying these supposed containers.'

'We have not.'

'But you are suggesting that the containers were aboard when the ship left Singapore.'

'Yes.' The Commander was sweating now, more than a little bemused by the speed at which Maggie was moving.

'So you must suppose that someone came aboard and removed the containers before Mr Huuk and his men went aboard.'

'Yes.'

'So why can it not be the case that these people committed the murders of which my client stands accused?'

'The forensic evidence proves that the accused was intimately involved with the murders.'

'And therefore with these mysterious pirates who came aboard and removed the containers.'

'That is so.'

'You are asking the court to believe that Captain Richard Mariner, a pillar of the British shipping community is closely associated with China Seas pirates?'

'Perhaps not the accused himself. Not directly...'

'Then, perhaps by his associate known as Anna Leung?'

'Well...' There was something in the Commander's tone which made Maggie look up, her eyes bright with revelation. She caught her breath.

'Thank you, Commander,' she said, and sat.

Mr Po frowned as he stood to resume his examination, for he could not quite see what Maggie had gained from her cross examination. He would have frowned more deeply, perhaps had he been privy to the message Maggie passed to Andrew. 'Anna Leung was probably a police informer. Tell Robin on the noon radio link.'

* * *

At noon on Wednesday, Robin was sixty hours into her 120-hour voyage, and feeling very much on top of things when Andrew's information on their midday radio contact turned everything upside-down. In that intense, five-minute conversation he redirected her attention to the containers and their contents and revolutionised the way she thought about the mysterious secrecy of the China Queens Company. She had spent most of her time so far settling in and reacquainting herself with the ropes – literally as well as figuratively – and had made only a relatively cursory exploration of the ship and its cargo, so far, but she had found opportunity to be in most places aboard and to check most things. She had checked the outsides of all the containers easily reached and planned to try and get inside one or two as soon as she had the chance. She reckoned she had done as much as might reasonably be expected of a busy first officer with a full range of duties, catching up on a certain amount of missed sleep.

Robin had, in fact, enjoyed two good nights' sleep so far, in so far as the catnaps she had been able to fit round the 00:00 to 04:00 watch counted as a good night's sleep. As with most first officers in her situation, she tried to sleep between 21:30 and 23:30, then from 04:30 to 08:30. Perhaps this did not count as a good night's sleep in the head, but in the heart it certainly did. It was incredible to her just how quickly she stepped back into the old, familiar shipboard ways. In fact she had not felt so well-rested since she had slept like a baby, alongside her own babies, on the Isle of Skye.

Robin loved the middle watch for she could sit there, alone, at the centre of the illimitable night, observing the slow spin of the constellations, keeping careful lookout for signs and signals of danger nearby and making up the careful logs of the state of sky and sea. These watches were balm to her troubled soul on Sunday, Monday and Tuesday nights as the *Seram Queen* ploughed carefully north-west across the South China Sea. The British Admiralty *China Sea Pilot* (Volume 1) warned her against scorpion fish, stone fish, stingrays, barracudas 'considered the most dangerous of fish', sharks, moray eels 'particularly dangerous in April to May, their breeding season' – an uplifting thought this early in June – and 'a species of jellyfish, whose sting can cause death'. Robin was not looking forward to the first lifeboat practice which would probably bring her into all too close association with these particular dangers.

The Pilot also took time to describe the beautiful bioluminescence which had followed the ship, and occasionally surrounded her, on the voyage so far. But it had not mentioned the silver-sided tuna which could leap – individually, or in shoals which looked like the surf on an uncharted reef – out of the water around the bow. It did not mention the gleaming, oiled-steel dolphin which sported in the bow wave then peeled away like Battle of Britain Spitfires to hunt the gleaming tuna. Alone to think, and glad enough of the unaccustomed leisure, Robin turned recent events over and over in her mind, trying to look at it all from a new perspective, one which would give that extra gleam of light which would unearth a hidden clue like a diamond hidden in ice.

And, each dawn, when she awoke again, still locked safely in her cabin, still stark but cool though more often than not wildly entangled in the now twisted rag of a sheet, she moved to put her thoughts into the first stages of action. Her days were apparently full of the normal bustle which filled the routine existence of any first officer. She had safety checks to make – she was responsible for all the lifesaving equipment and needed to be sure that it was in full working order for the strict series of drills Captain Sin never quite bothered to call. She saw that the quietly competent Sam Yung had completed all his duties, though he seemed mildly surprised when she checked his emergency lists and lifeboat disposition lists twice. Wai Chan remained grudging if not quite obstructionist in his reaction to her checking on his work. It was with him that she went through the pre-set channels on all the two-way radios aboard, and checked that they were in place, powered up and working at optimum.

She was also responsible for the safe bestowal of the cargo, above decks and below. As lading officer, she had to ensure that the weight of the cargo put the hull in no danger and guaranteed its most economically efficient movement through the ocean. She was also responsible for ensuring that nothing in one container could possibly contaminate, or otherwise damage anything in any neighbouring containers. The sickly First Officer Chin Lau seemed to have been an efficient lading officer – if his records actually accorded with the disposition of the containers. The only way to check that was for Robin to choose a random selection and open them for inspection. In most ships she had served upon, and on any ship she had commanded, the captain would have insisted that the lading officer completed these duties in very short order, for the captain was ultimately responsible for the safety of the hull and the economic consumption of bunkerage. But Captain Sin was somehow uninterested, or otherwise engaged, or he simply didn't care to have his strange first officer poking around in the cargo.

Robin filled her days with doing immediately important tasks, being casually careful to give priority to those which allowed her to explore. She kept expecting to fit her activities into the routines dictated by the captain, but Sin seemed to be a hard man to pin down. By the dog watches on Tuesday afternoon, Robin was actively seeking him out. The ship should have gone though a full lifeboat drill but it had singularly failed to do so. This was worrying. Although the individual pieces of equipment, from the boats themselves to the lines on the davits, all checked satisfactorily, the only way to check them properly was to test the system as a whole, and that meant using it. But even though she was ship's security officer, only the captain could call a lifeboat drill.

As lading officer, Robin needed at the least to inform her commanding officer that she had checked every single container aboard from the outside – except for the series of containers carried in the deepest section of the hold. She needed to apprise him of the fact that she proposed to open some containers and check that their contents actually agreed with the manifests.

In her attempts to reach the elusive captain, Robin came up against the intransigent and unsettling Fat Chow, chief steward. When at last, on that sultry Tuesday evening, she hammered on the captain's cabin door, it was the chief steward who answered, like a cornered rat turning on a terrier. Or, better, like a cobra confronting a mongoose. 'Captain not available, missy,' she was informed. 'He ssend hiss orderss through me. You do what I ssay, misssy. Yess?'

'Fat Chow, are you familiar with the phrase "In your dreams"?'

'No misssy.'

'Keep this up, and you'll get to know all about it. Now, I need to see the captain. I accept orders from no one else. Do you understand?'

'Yes, misssy.'

'Good. Do I get to see him?' She pushed against the door. The wiry man holding it was surprisingly strong. There was no way past him other than to fight him.

'Captain sick, misssy.' Their eyes locked. He was simply not going to let her past.

'Really?' If force would not work, maybe cunning would. 'Then perhaps I should inform you that I am ship's medical officer – and, indeed, acting captain if he's too sick for command.'

'Chow?' called the captain's voice from inside the cabin. The chief steward shot her a fulminating glance and slammed the door. As soon as the door was closed, the key turned in the lock. 'Well done, Fat Chow,' said Robin, loudly enough to be heard if he was listening. 'Two keys in two days. That must be some kind of a record.'

So it was that running a ship she didn't know with a cargo she hadn't properly checked, a crew she had never met, and safety equipment she had not had a chance to test took up all too much of Robin's time. The long middle watches were her only unpressured time, the only time in which she could think, plan and question, but it was in the busy dog watches that she expected to achieve her first real breakthrough, for it was then that she was up and about, searching, looking and checking, militantly unaware of the cold eyes of Fat Chow, Wai Chan and the mysterious Captain Sin, which were all focused on her back.

In the event, the first of the answers came not during the workaday dog watches but in the quiet middle watches, so that at first, when the way began to come off the ship at 02:36 on Thursday morning, Robin believed that the strange sensation she was experiencing must be part of a dream.

As soon as she realised that the strange sensation was actually a sudden cessation of engine vibration, Robin pulled herself out of the watch-keeper's chair and crossed to the long shelf of equipment which reached under the clearview windows across the front of the bridge. There were no alarms ringing. Nothing untoward seemed to be happening – except that the automatic log showed that the ship's speed was falling rapidly away from the eight knots she had maintained since Singapore.

Robin's first action was to call the captain. Such a loss of propulsion had to be reported immediately. Her call was answered at once by a wide awake and very irate Captain Sin; she had half expected to be talking to Fat Chow. Inform Chief Engineer Chen Hang, she was instructed by the miraculously fit and clear-thinking commanding officer, and tell that lazy individual to get his act in order.

The chief, too, answered on the first ring and grudgingly agreed to assemble his engineering officers and find out what was going on.

By the time there was a full showing in the engine room, it was the better part of 03:00 and the *Seram Queen* was dead in the water, except that a sluggish current was pulling her fitfully north-eastwards along her plotted course, towards the Paracel Islands which lay perhaps seventy kilometres dead ahead. There was, Robin calculated as senior navigating officer on the bridge, no real danger at present. *Seram Queen* was well over the Herald Bank which stood, at its height, 235 metres below the keel. To the starboard lay the Bombay Reef and to the port, Discovery. But one was thirty kilometres distant and the other more than forty. Not even the warning light on the tall tower on Bombay reached this far. On this course with the currents charitable, the vessel could drift for the better part of a week before there was any real chance of coming dangerously aground on Woody Island of the beautifully named Amphitrite Group, north-east of the Paracels, or on Lincoln Island further west, which already stood with one great wreck so obvious there that it was a recommended radar beacon. So it was with very little immediate disquiet that Robin dialled the engine room and asked the chief for a prognosis.

'Engine broken,' observed the gruff Chen Hang. 'Take time to fix.'

'Yes, I understand that, Chief; but may I tell the captain how much time? One hour? Two?'

'No ideas until I find problem, missy. Maybe one day.'

The word 'day' hit her like a slap in the face. 'One *day*?'

'I do not know. You get off the phone and maybe I be able to find out, missy! Yah?'

The captain was hardly more courteous and Robin recognised that she was caught in the unenviable position of being the lubricant which kept two rough but important parts of the crew from rubbing each other raw.

Her lips thinned. She had gone well past this situation in her normal professional life. Nowadays she had people to act as lubricant for her! She was a ship's captain and a senior executive. She owned this tub, for heaven's sake, every stick and every soul aboard, she shouldn't be greasing egos, she should be kicking butt and pissing people off left, right and centre!

The thought was as wry as it was inaccurate. Rarely, if ever, had Robin rubbed anyone raw. Even those who failed to give satisfactory service were exhorted and uplifted to improving their performance. Not even the most intransigently idle or cross-grained had proved able to resist her dogged excellence of example for long. But she was all too well aware that she was not in any position to pull this crew round; only Captain Sin could do that.

The rest of the watch was filled with a quiet bustle of activity. Robin called Sam Yung out of his scarce-warm bed and summoned the grumbling Wai Chan to her side as well. The navigating officers had much careful work to do. The relatively modern navigational aids available to them – and efficiently functioning as long as the ship's power continued independently of her main motors – established the ship's position with near-perfect accuracy. But only as long as power was maintained. Only a fool would have failed to act on the assumption that they might go blind, deaf and dumb at any moment. Radio Officer Tso was called up too, but the captain refused permission to send a distress signal or even to alert head office. Robin understood that, at least – she would have kept quiet for a while too. *Seram Queen* stood in no danger and Robin's navigating team was perfectly capable of checking, almost to the centimetre, how close any stood, on either hand, ahead and below. But as the long night waned, Robin realised that Chief Engineer Hang had meant what he had said. The engines were not going to come back to life immediately. As dawn crept up, promising a scorchingly bright, high-pressure, monsoon-cooled day, she handed over to Wai Chan and dismissed the comatose Sam Yung to grab a few hours' sleep, as she herself proposed to do.

After a couple of hours restless slumber in the all too quiet environment of the powerless ship, Robin awoke with the irresistible impulse to test the emergency generators in case the maladies currently affecting the engines should spread to the main alternators, as she had half expected them to do last night. In the cold light of day – even a hot, calm day such as this – her fears of the coffin watch now looked even more unsettling. If the chief was right, then there would be no power tonight either. Drifting towards the jumble of banks, reefs and islands of the Paracels wide awake with full electronic warning of any danger nearer than ten kilometres was one thing. Going in blind as well as powerless was something else again. Going into the Paracel Islands powerless and blind might be very dangerous indeed. And once she had arrived at this thought, she felt an equally irresistible urge to institute the lifeboat drill which Captain Sin had neglected to hold so far.

Rolling out of her bunk, still half asleep, Robin climbed into the ready-folded, easy-to-reach uniform which she had taken out of the 'clean' drawer last thing last night. With everything pulled on, tucked in, hooked and buttoned, Robin dragged a long-bristled brush through the golden riot of her curls and crossed to the door – and froze.

Her fingers grasped the cold brass door handle but her eyes were fixed on the empty keyhole. A frantic search through her dirty laundry proved that the key still lay in its usual shirt pocket and Robin wracked her brains for a moment, trying to remember whether she had turned it in the lock and popped it back in the pocket without thinking. One turn and pull on the handle revealed that she had collapsed into her bunk and left the door unlocked. Mentally she cursed herself. Her sleep had been short but deep. Anyone could have come in and done more or less anything. The very thought made her flesh creep. She swung back impulsively and was just about to check her shoulder bag and Edgar Tan's priceless gun when the emergency alarm shrilled.

The noise of the alarm was so unexpected and so loud that it made her start with surprise. She turned, hesitating between the gun and her duty, her mind a turmoil. She looked at the chunky watch she had worn for so many years – though it looked thoroughly inappropriate on her slim wrist. It was 08:07 local time. Wai Chan was on the bridge. She and Sam Yung had enjoyed little more than two hours' sleep after all, and now they would have to face God knew what. As these thoughts raced through her head, she forced herself to be calm. Perhaps this was the lifeboat drill she so much wanted the captain to hold. Whatever it was, she could not possibly waste time looking in her case now.

Within five seconds of the alarm's first sound, she reached for the handset of her bedside phone. There was no reply from the bridge or the engine room. Well, even in the absence of contact with the captain and the chief, her duty was clear enough, and defined by Sam Yung's emergency lists which she had been so careful to study. She caught up the two-way radio from her bedside table and slipped it into her pocket. She crossed to the door once more, glanced around the room from the threshold and locked the door on the way out. Then she was pounding up the corridor to her emergency station, adrenaline lending wings to her heels. It was possible that this unannounced emergency was more serious than a drill – on this ship, almost anything seemed possible.

As Robin ran out onto the deck her eyes were busy amid the bustle of crew, trying to find the captain. He was nowhere to be seen down here, but a couple of figures loomed on the port bridge wing high above. That ought to be the captain and the watch officer. She pulled out her walkie-talkie. Thumbed the open channel to the bridge. 'First officer on the main deck,' she said. 'Please explain the nature of the emergency. Over.'

As she waited for a reply, she looked around her, glad that this was a crew of small-bodied Orientals amongst whom she stood tall.

'... Drill,' said her radio. 'Proceed to ...'

'First officer understands this is a lifeboat drill. Proceeding to my designated position. Over.'

Teams seemed to be forming at the lifeboats and she crossed to her place and began counting the faces, knowing she could never hope to remember all the strange names of the men who should be there. Still too busy to feel isolated or even faintly at risk, she walked briskly down the line, counting. Further down the deck, she could see Sam Yung doing exactly the same thing. On the far side of the bridgehouse, the senior officers in the boats which should have been commanded by the captain and the second officer would be doing the same, she knew. 'First officer. All present, over.'

'Proceed.'

Her eyebrows rose. The man might have been sick but he was certainly making up for lost time now – a full drill. Well, OK.

'Swing out,' she ordered. As though the team had been practising every day so far, they swung into action, hitting the trigger lever and standing ready for the gravity davit to swing out. The long arms moved, then hesitated, then stopped altogether. This was just what she had been afraid of. The pivots were salted solid. Mentally berating herself for not having done more, Robin strode forward, pushing her men aside, to get a closer look at the problem.

It was the wrong thing to do, more risky than she could have calculated. But she was tired, under more strain than she cared to admit and at the far end of a chain of circumstances which could not have been better designed to undermine her solid grasp of professional sealore if it had been worked out with care and on purpose.

Just as she came under the davit, before she could crouch to inspect the apparently frozen pivot, the whole thing lurched into motion once again. No one moved a muscle or called a warning. Perhaps the disaster happened too quickly, too unexpectedly, catching them all unawares.

The keel of the lifeboat came down like a guillotine blade exactly across the crown of Robin's head and laid her out cold on the deck, curled up against the upright of the safety rail, as the boat lurched on down into position with a thunderous scream.

Chapter Twenty-Nine

So important was the package from London that the courier was sitting waiting with it when Edgar Tan arrived at the China Queens office for his regular morning check-up at ten thirty Singapore time on Thursday, 19 June. 'What's this?' Tan asked the delivery boy.

'Urgent package from London,' answered the courier. 'They said I had to wait and hand it over personally.'

The detective let himself into the office so that he could show his identification and letter of authority to the young man. The envelope was padded and, in spite of its directions, Customs stamps and senders' details, it looked brand new, as though it was ready to send not as though it was at its destination, half a world later. And it was so light, he discovered as soon as he had signed for it, it might almost have been empty.

He turned it between his long fingers, wondering whether to open it at once or whether to listen to the answerphone messages first. Fortunately he listened – so that he could think a little more – before he acted. It was the second message which told him what he needed to know.

'William Heritage here. I understand that in my daughter Robin's absence I will be talking to the detective Mr Tan. Earlier today, Wednesday, we came into possession of a postcard apparently posted last week by Captain Walter Gough, somewhere in the Philippines. We have taken all the details we can here and will try to work out whether he really sent it or not, and if he did, where exactly he is at present. In the meantime, I have sealed the card itself in plastic and sent it by courier directly to the China Queens Office. If it hasn't arrived yet it will do so imminently and you are advised to wait for it. I have notified Hong Kong of my actions and they agree that Singapore is the better place for the card to go. It may well be that local people there with you will be able to discover more about it than we can at this end. I would strongly advise some sort of contact with the police if that is possible. At the very least you will want to check it for fingerprints, I am sure. We have no record of Captain Gough's fingerprints, I am afraid. Nor have the British authorities, as far as I can ascertain. But there might be others and they might be germane. We are certain that the writing is his, and so is his wife. There seem to be several obvious conclusions to be drawn at once, even at first glance. This is especially true if the photograph on the card is a picture of the captain's current whereabouts or anywhere nearby, as seems to be suggested in the message. But these thoughts will be best discussed at a later date, I think. If you wish to talk things over do not hesitate to call me. If I'm not here myself I guarantee that there will be someone competent to pass on my thoughts and those of the International Maritime Bureau with whom I have been in touch. Signing off now.'

'What does it say?' mused Inspector Sung, looking down at the plastic-wrapped message while various of his underlings assembled to operate upon the little square of cardboard as though it were a murder victim at a post-mortem.

Tan took the question literally and read out the message. 'It says "I'm fine, don't worry. Policies all activate within six months. Death or disappearance – standard for sailors. Should start to pay by Xmas if you tell no one. Mortgage should hold till then as company continue to pay OK under HM personnel rules. Bri Jordan will advise if any trouble. He knows. Don't tell Wally. Too much for him. The picture is what I see each evening. Never stopped loving you – started to hate the life. Sorry, sorry, sorry." It's unsigned but there's apparently no doubt.'

'Yes,' said Sung, 'but it actually tells us much more than that, doesn't it? Much more than that this is a message from a desperate man at the end of his tether who has run away and yet cannot bring himself to make a clean break.'

There was a brief silence as the two men looked at the writing on the card, and then at the spectacular sea, sand and sunset picture on the other side and then at the writing again.

'He has no idea about what happened to the *Sulu Queen*, has he?' said Edgar Tan at last.

'It doesn't look like it,' agreed Sung.

'There's a supposition here that First Officer Jordan will be alive to advise Mrs Gough. And a supposition, therefore, that Jordan is the kind of person who won't mind joining in a little fraud. Gough sounds pretty confident about that.'

'He obviously assumed Mrs Gough would join in on a fraud, too,' said Sung, 'and he was wrong there. But he wasn't absolutely sure. Otherwise why say "if you tell no one"? You would have supposed that he would know his wife well enough to be certain whether or not she would be willing to join in or not after all their years of marriage. Twenty, was it?'

'Twenty-two, according to the China Queens personnel file,' agreed Tan. 'But it isn't a simple fraud any longer, is it? Even if she was the kind of woman to close her eyes and collect the insurance payments, she's den mother to an awful lot of widows all of a sudden, including

Mrs Jordan. And the man who owns the company responsible for her income until Christmas is being accused of all these murders. She can't close her eyes to that.'

'So, if Gough was right about her, he was probably right about his first officer too – is that what you're saying, Tan?'

'First Officer Jordan, a man to trust with something a little less than legal. Interesting. And what was there to hate, I wonder, about sailing in a big circle round the South China Sea, putting in his last couple of years and waiting to retire to Budleigh Salterton?'

'Beginning to realise that there is more to life than Marine Drive? Beginning to get a bad feeling about exactly what the less than legal Jordan might be up to? Being apart from the nubile Anna Leung?'

'She certainly seems to have started coming on board very much more regularly during the last couple of years. It's all in the files – apparently routine.'

'Coming on board. I like that. Is she nubile by the way?'

'Do you know, that's a very good question. You may not be surprised to hear that her personnel file seems to have gone and there are no photographs of her anywhere that I can find.'

'Even so,' said Sung, 'whoever heard of a sailor running away with an ugly girl.'

'There's only one way to find out isn't there?'

'Go with the obvious, you mean? It's what we policemen do all the time, Tan. But in this case you would go, and I would guarantee to update you if the experts here find anything unexpected or revealing.'

'You're right. Even if you find sand from a beach you can identify or spores from a fungus which only grows in one place on earth, there's no guarantee they didn't rub off another postcard going to the next house down Marine Drive in Budleigh Salterton. When you get right down to it, there's no guarantee that anything your experts find on the card didn't get there somewhere en route. No. Captain Gough really expected his wife to read it then destroy it. And even if she didn't, there's no indication on the picture, or the postcard as a whole, of where the original photograph was taken so he probably felt safe on that count as well. Sure as hell he didn't expect her to tell anyone except First Officer Jordan about it. But he obviously didn't know his ship had been hit and his crew killed and what should have been a small-beer disappearance was extremely big news. Wherever this sunset is, it is somewhere so remote it's beyond the reach of television. And he doesn't bother with the radio, so batteries are hard to get hold of or oil for the generators is expensive – or hard to ship. And we can safely assume that he doesn't have any morning papers delivered. He was taking a chance and being more stupid than he knew, but then he never expected anyone to come after him, especially in somewhere this far from civilisation. It's all there on the card.'

'When you're right, you're right,' said Sung. He squinted a little to make out the Italic printing at the top of the left-hand panel. 'Printed by Beautiful Views Ltd, Rizal Avenue, Manila. They have copyright of the photograph and therefore, one assumes, a record of where it was taken.'

'And it was posted in the central post office in Laoag less than ten days ago. What can I say? I'm on my way.'

On Thursday, the evidence presented in Court Four of the Hong Kong Supreme Court was all expert testimony, exact, unassailable and tedious. After Commander Lee had described the smuggling system and the China Queens' alleged position in it, the Crown's experts worked doggedly to link Richard to the violence this smuggling had caused. Section by section, in spite of all Maggie could do in cross-examination, the witnesses called by the Crown built up the case which defined the exact manner in which all the victims had died, and purported to link Richard with all the deaths except those of the Vietnamese women and children.

There was little Maggie could do. The fact was that Richard's fingerprints had been found upon the panga, the semi-automatic and the handgun. There was no question that the clothing he had been wearing when arrested had been covered in blood, sprays of soft body parts and copious traces of gunpowder. All that Maggie could suggest was that Richard had been closely involved with the dead and dying as he sought to bring some measure of relief and that he had certainly been involved with at least two of the weapons as he fought off homicidal intruders.

For the Crown, Mr Prosecutor Po re-emphasised that the sprays of soft body parts found on his clothing had in the past been taken to prove that the accused was immediately proximate to the victim while his life was ended. The accused must have been standing, for example, just beside the victim's head while his brains were blown out. Or immediately in front of the victim while he was being hosed to death with automatic fire. Or just beside the victim while he was chopped to pieces with the panga. The only reasonable explanation for all this forensic evidence, submitted the Crown, was that Captain Richard Mariner had been the perpetrator of all of the crimes of which he stood indicted. And, they insisted, they would support their case beyond any question of a reasonable doubt tomorrow, when they called their final witness.

'Do you really think they have anything hidden up their sleeves?' asked Tom Fowler as they finished the early-evening war council at eight that evening. They would hold another one later, when Tom reported back from his nightly interview with Richard.

'Heaven knows,' answered Maggie. 'What do you think, Andrew?'

'I think they definitely have something. Who is it that they haven't called yet?'

'I have no idea. There isn't really a new witness. We certainly haven't had anyone enter the game who hasn't been playing for a fair length of time already. What do the trial notes say? Just that a witness is coming and they will give us his statement as soon as it's prepared. That could be five minutes before he actually takes the stand. I have no idea who they could call.'

'Well,' said Tom, 'if you think of who it might be, then give me some idea and I'll put it to Richard. We might get a reaction from him. We could certainly do with one.'

'What is the game plan for tonight?' asked Maggie.

'Photographs. Random association. Carefully considered questions. Extension of most recent memories. Truth serum. Hypnotism. Prayer. Black magic. Entrails. Virgin sacrifice. Anything else I can sodding well think of. Same as usual.'

'Right,' said Maggie.

Tom still had no idea how close he had come two evenings ago with his random association. He had mentioned the sequence of words to no one because they had seemed to him to be gibberish. When he entered the little consultation room in the Queen Elizabeth Hospital later that evening, therefore, he had no idea of the progress that he and his subject had actually made and the impact his proposed sequence of moves might have.

The first thing he did was to throw the folder of photographs almost casually across the table at Richard. Richard's great hands came down on the slithering file with a decided *slap*. The long, gaunt face looked up, blue eyes blazing under the slightest of interrogatory frowns. The two of them had become fast friends, even on so few days' acquaintance. Those few days now apparently comprised the whole of Richard's memory. 'What is it, Tom?' Richard still had only the scantiest understanding of the danger he stood in. He was far more concerned about the emotional state of his psychologist.

'Nothing you can't put right, Richard. Take a look through those, would you, and tell me about anything which springs to mind.' Tom got out his notebooks, one full of the notes from previous meetings and another in which he would make notes of this one. Richard watched him in silence for a moment, his face utterly blank, then opened the file and began to examine the photographs it contained.

'Yes, of course. This is me isn't it?'

'It is. How do you know?'

'I recognise it from yesterday.'

'Nothing wrong with your short-term memory, then,' observed Tom, scribbling in his notepad. 'Next?'

'William and Mary. You told me this was taken in London...'

Richard's voice faltered slightly, as though doubting the certainty of what he was saying.

'I told you that under Pentothal...' The psychologist consulted the notes of the last session, just to be sure. 'But not under hypnosis. Even so, an impressive feat of memory.' Tom made more notes.

'Are you going to put me under Pentothal again tonight?'

'If I have to. And under hypnosis. If I have to.'

'I don't like that. I don't like to lose...'

They had gone through this conversation every evening so far and the content had never varied. Tom drew in his breath automatically to finish Richard's sentence for perhaps the tenth time.

'... control,' said Richard, before the psychologist could speak. 'I don't like to lose control. Do you know what I mean?'

'Yes,' said Tom. 'Yes, I do indeed.' He leaned forward and made a note. Without looking up, he said, 'Do you want to continue leafing through those photographs for me, Richard?'

'Yes, of course. These are my parents. That's Summersend, their home. There's Summersend again but...' The tone of Richard's voice was thoughtless, unguarded, open.

'But?' Tom's voice invited confidence but exerted no pressure whatsoever, his pencil poised.

'Well, I don't recognise this contraption down the front steps to the garden.'

'That's because it's a new contraption. The picture is only three weeks old. It arrived earlier today, as a matter of fact. But you recognise the house?'

'Well, yes, of course. As a matter of fact...' He turned over the next photograph and his speech stopped.

'You recognise those two?'

'Well...'

This had been carefully calculated by Tom. The photograph in front of Richard was a recent one of the twins which he could never have seen. He had looked at pictures of William and Mary, but never any so recent, never any which showed the twins as they were when he last kissed them good night or goodbye.

'Well, of course. It's the twins.'

'You didn't seem too certain.'

'They look so grown up.'

'It's a recent picture.'

'It must be. I mean, there's that cut on Mary's leg. She did that tackling William just before ... just before...' Richard's voice faltered, the unconscious certainty beginning to slip away.

'Well, never mind. It'll come back later.' Tom's tone was dismissive but his pencil was busy. 'Turn over again, why don't you?'

'All right. Well, that's easy. That's Ashenden. I can't remember how many of those I've seen...' And he stopped once again, with the next photograph half revealed.

'You recognise her then?' asked Tom casually. His senses were really beginning to quicken now. All his responses were on full alert. He switched over to shorthand and began to record things verbatim.

'Yes, of course. I've seen more pictures of her than I can count since I woke up properly. This is my wife, Robin.'

'But it seems that you really do recognise her. What do you feel?'

'I feel... *alone*...'

Tom was startled. He had phrased the question uncalculatingly. Richard had not been drugged or hypnotised yet. Now here they were suddenly into word association and truth games.

'Why? Do you think she has left you?'

'She was here, wasn't she?'

Tom could have danced. This was the first evidence of communication between the Survivor and Richard himself, for Robin had only spoken to the former since this episode began, never the latter.

'Yes, she has been here. Often. The next picture is of her, too. Does it bring anything to mind?'

'Well, she's in uniform... She is very beautiful, isn't she?'

'Very. And?'

'Well... I know the uniform, of course. It's my uniform. My captain's...'

'It's her uniform too, Richard.'

The ice-blue gaze switched up to Tom's face, disturbingly like a searchlight beam. 'Her uniform? She's a captain? A master mariner?'

'Amusing, when you think of it. Kind of a pun, really. Mrs Mariner is a master mariner...' Tom's wise eyes noted that Richard had placed the two pictures side by side, face up. As he talked, Richard was leafing through the pile and pulling out all the other photographs of Robin. There were five more. 'She's at sea now. That's why she's not here.'

'At sea.' Richard's voice was dreamy with concentration as he moved the pictures of Robin from one pattern to another.

'At sea, under your orders.'

'What? How?'

'You left her a message, don't you remember?'

'Message?'

'On a computer disk. With a copy on the ship's network.'

'*Sulu Queen* had a network?'

'That's right, Richard! Well remembered. You left her a message on the *Sulu Queen*'s computer network telling her to go aboard the *Seram Queen*.'

'I did? I did that?'

'I can show you a copy. She faxed it over to us before she went aboard.'

'I sent her aboard the *Seram Queen*?'

'I'll bring in the message tomorrow. We'll talk about it then.' Tom, still looking down, made a last note in his book before moving on to the next phase of the interview. He looked across the table. 'Now...' His voice trailed off. Richard's hands were beginning to tear the first photograph of Robin into pieces. His face was set like stone, his blue eyes burned with almost unearthly intensity and tears streamed down his gaunt cheeks. 'Richard!' said Tom. 'What are you doing?'

'I sent her aboard. *I* sent her aboard!' said Richard, his voice hoarse and deeply troubled; and he reached for the second photograph across the torn ruins of the first.

Charles Lee lowered the folded page of the latest edition of the *Yangcheng Wanabo* newspaper and looked thoughtfully away across the Zhujiang which the Western invaders called the Pearl River, down towards Xianggang which the Westerners called Hong Kong, little more than a hundred kilometres distant.

Charles had been in the Middle Kingdom for six weeks now and was feeling increasingly remote from Western society, and from Heritage Mariner. So remote did he feel, in fact, that he had started thinking of himself by his Chinese first name Cha-ho instead of the Westernised equivalent he had taken in the early seventies.

Charles/Cha-ho was well aware that what he was allowed to see and hear was carefully vetted – only a barbarian would use such a blunt word as censored – and he was beginning to wonder whether he was the unwitting subject of some sort of mind control as well. His communications with Heritage Mariner head office were all conducted via telex and he had spoken to no one directly, even in the early days here when he had been desperately trying to get more information about Richard's predicament, Robin's position, Helen DuFour's plans and Sir William's ability to hold things together for a while. Elder Brother Xiang Lo-wu never had any trouble with his portable phone, but apparently that was because he never tried to call outside China itself. All the lines Charles wished to use were unfortunately malfunctioning.

But that first telex from Helen had been reassuring. Richard was in good hands. Everything was being done that could be done. Helen was in control at head office and Sir William was back at Heritage House. Charles's work was too important to interrupt and if he felt he was making progress he should continue. And, of course, he was the one man on the inside if things should go wrong and Richard's case became involved with the Chinese legal system and Hong Kong's new Basic Law. Indeed, Charles felt that this appraisal of the case was correct. His relationship with Xiang Lo-wu was progressing so satisfactorily that there was no longer any irony in their use of the familiar forms of address 'elder brother' and 'younger brother'. It might be that Charles was in a position to do Richard some good – though he had no idea of the actual power enjoyed by Xiang. Twelvetoes Ho might have an idea that Xiang Lo-wu was destined to be senior executive of the Special Economic Zone which would include Hong Kong in ten days' time, but he neglected to inform Charles of the fact. The business executive remained in blissful ignorance, therefore, and concentrated on business rather than politics – or believed that he did at any rate.

There had been three telexes a week each way, and the company news had remained satisfactory in spite of the adverse publicity attracted by the trial. The judge in Hong Kong had apparently called for a news black-out now, but there was still speculation in every quarter of the media all over the world. It had been the international news section in the *Goat City Evening News* which Charles had been reading just now, and it gave some details of the testimony delivered today. Naturally so. Guangzhou would be the regional capital of the Special Economic Zone when it came into being next week; and in British terms, Hong Kong would start playing Liverpool to Canton's London. That was the theory, as far as it went.

But there was already a kind of infection spreading outwards as the pre-unification publicity made the millions in the province look Westwards more acutely than ever. Charles had been here a month. He had needed no time to settle in – he knew this city well; or Lee Cha-ho did. He had spent all too much of his childhood running contraband up through the Tiger Gate and along forty secret kilometres of the Pearl River into the hungry markets here. Xiang's men had put Charles in the old colonial White Swan Hotel on Samian Island, but Cha-ho would have been comfortable anywhere. Even more than London or New York, this was his home from home. Which was why he noticed at once how much it had changed. From the beginning he had been aware that there was a powerful slide towards Westernism here.

Like Xiang Lo-wu Charles wore simple shirts and plain denim suits. His Saville Row tailoring had soon felt out of place in sand-swept Beijing and he was content to wear clothing which was light and comfortable, especially now, in this sub-tropical climate. But the first local official he had met here sported a Lacoste sport shirt a Sergio Tacchini leisure suit and Nike Air trainers – even to a business meeting.

Xiang seeing Cha-ho's expression, had said gently, after the interview was finished, 'You should not be shocked, younger brother. After all, was it not you, in the days of your misspent youth, who smuggled the first rock and roll record into the floating market here?'

Charles had laughed wryly. Xiang had become used to this Western way of expressing surprise, and he lowered his eyelids accommodatingly, seeming to overlook the loss of face. 'Indeed,' admitted the Hong Kong shipping merchant. '*Bat Out of Hell* by Meatloaf. An icon of its time. A gleaming tower of Western culture.' Charles had been so amused by the weary acceptance in Xiang's voice that he came dangerously close to adding that he had not been alone in the enterprise. He almost revealed that he had enjoyed an extremely active contact with a local entrepreneur called Huw Pei-chun – Paul Huw as he had preferred to be known.

'You were the vanguard of an invasion,' stated the government official.

'I think not, elder brother,' Charles answered warily. 'There were others before me and they brought the Beatles, Levi 501s and Coca-Cola.'

'So that now the Memorial of the Martyrs of the Shaji Massacre is overlooked by a McDonald's and there is a Taco Bell on Sun Yatsen Street. Guangzhou is becoming like any town in America, alas.'

'It is the price of opening the Tiger Gate to that market, elder brother. These things make the tourists feel more comfortable as they pass their hard currency into your purse. But McDonald's is not the only player in that game, you must admit. In Tsimshatsui, Hong Kong, near where I was brought up, there is a McDonald's on Nathan Road a block down from the Chinese People's store Chung Kiu. On Hankow Road, McDonald's is right next door to Chung Kiu. They are just two competitors on the same economic stage. There's a McDonald's across the road from the Royal Shakespeare Theatre in Stratford-upon-Avon in England. William Shakespeare and Ronald McDonald – again two more competitors, one stage. If you want the dollars, you carry the freight. There is no alternative, elder brother.'

There was a brief silence then, at the end of that first meeting, as Xiang seemed to be considering Charles's enthusiastic words.

Here in Guangzhou, little more than a week before Hong Kong became Xianggang and reverted to Chinese control, the elder brother from Beijing was out of his depth. There was a rising tide of Westernisation sweeping in from Hong Kong. In the old days, it would have been rigorously suppressed and those who spread the infection, like Charles himself and his friend Paul Huw, would have been torn down root and branch. But this infection which was so threatening to the past was in fact the germ of the future, and Xiang Lo-wu recognised this. Regretted it, but recognised it. And the gentle, quiet, infinitely devious elder brother was looking for a way to get along with it. No, to go further – to turn it to the Middle Kingdom's advantage. For, to take the analogy to its logical conclusion, if a part of China could catch the germ of Westernism and survive, then its experience could be used as a kind of vaccine to protect the health of China as a whole. And the final elegance of this proposition arose from the fact that Westernism had made the West itself relatively weak.

In terms of global economics, China was surrounded by greedy self-indulgent societies with flabby economies dependent on restrictive practices and trade protectionism to protect their lazy, greedy work forces. In a world like this, a lean and hungry China, ready, willing and able to produce anything for which there was an appreciable demand, proof against the excesses which had torn the USSR apart, with a work force of mathematically infinite size and illimitable potential, would be a tiger in a chicken run. And, Charles was beginning to realise, there was a strong possibility that Elder Brother Xiang Lò-wu wanted him to be the medical consultant in all of this; the consultant who would deliver a controlled dose of Westernism to the body of Sechuan through the hypodermic of Hong Kong. But where did that put him with regard to Heritage Mariner? And where did the current court case place Heritage Mariner with regard to China?

Such were the thoughts which occupied the business executive's mind as he looked southwards towards Hong Kong on the early evening of Thursday, 20 June, with the *Yangsheng Wanabo* idly between his fingers.

The square figure of Xiang loomed darkly across his view, blocking out the prospect of Hong Kong suddenly.

'What brings you here, elder brother?'

Xiang looked down at him with an absolutely expressionless countenance. 'We noticed that in your stay here, your lengthy stay here, you have not ventured into the Quingpinglu.'

'I have had no need of the market, elder brother, nor desire to explore.'

'Oh, but surely, for old times' sake. So much of your merchandise used to turn up here, almost as much as used to arrive in Cat Street, Xianggang.'

'No, really...' Charles suddenly felt ill at ease. The man he saw before him now was subtly different from the Xiang Lo-wu with whom he had been dealing this last six weeks; someone more decisive, more dangerous. But perhaps that was just a misapprehension arising from his earlier thoughts. 'Well, why not...'

Side by side Charles and Xiang walked across the bustle of the afternoon city rush hour towards the market area. The rush hour in Guangzhou was a matter of pedestrians and cyclists, buses and the occasional tram. There were few, if any, cars involved. And, as the hour of departure from work was upon them, this was the most popular time for business at the market. As the two businessmen walked in silence along Renmin Road, they became subsumed in a bustling tide of humanity, all intent upon leaving work, buying something tasty to take home and getting home to prepare, share and eat it. Some, who did not harbour the parochial desire to cook for themselves, lingered at the roadside snack stalls, dipping pieces of lightly stir-fried, ginger-stuffed carp into little bowls of light soy sauce and then slipping them down their throats. No matter what was done, it was done with a busy intensity which Charles had seen in few places beyond downtown New York.

'Are we going anywhere in particular, elder brother?' Charles asked eventually as Xiang turned purposefully into Nurenjie.

'Yes, we are. I wish to show you some local industry. The attitude is, I believe, instructive.' Even as he said this, Xiang arrived at a tall wooden door which stood behind a row of stalls. The stalls themselves specialised in the sale of framed prints. On paper, plastic and silk, pictures of lotus blossoms and humming birds were reproduced in a range of inks. Mountains, islands, dragons and tigers stood beside them, with the occasional monkey for good effect. And the premises into which Xiang led Charles Lee were all too obviously the origin of these wares. Row upon row of illustrators sat, each one specialising in the creation and recreation of exactly the same picture. Lotus after lotus and lily upon lily. Each one perfect. Each one identical to the one before. Each one the result of a few minutes' work, repeated and repeated. 'This is most commendable,' said Charles, feeling a little out of his depth. 'Are you suggesting, elder brother, that there is a ready market for these artefacts in the West?'

'Unfortunately not,' answered Xiang, abruptly, almost roughly. 'But there seems to be a ready market for this!' As he spoke, he pushed open an inner door to reveal another room, almost as big as the first and every bit as busy. Here, however, the pictures were not representations of flowers, animals, birds or natural scenes. Here, time after time, were perfect representations of Chanel check, the Givenchy logo, Burberry check, the Gucci colours, Harrods gold and green.

'There is more,' said Xiang, his voice heavy with disapproval. He proceeded, pushing through to a deeper, darker area. Here, men and women were concentrating absolutely on the reproduction of product identification tags – Rolex, Hi-Tech, Reebok, Cartier, Alfred Dunhill. Like Virgil leading Dante downwards, Xiang led Charles to a deeper circle of this industrious little Hades. Here they were reproducing company-guaranteed part-identification stamps: Rolls-Royce, Pratt and Whitney, British Aerospace, Westland, Bell, Sikorsky, Harland and Wolff, Mitsubishi Heavy Industries; Ford, Rover, General Motors, Ferrari, Lamborghini. In the face of this, Charles remained silent; he knew what damage could be done by a part of an engine identified as being genuine but actually a fake.

There was more yet. In a dingy little back room saved for last on moral as well as economic grounds, a team of illustrators were producing pictures for the pornography market. From a basic series of pictures of naked forms in various revealing poses, the artists were reproducing drawing after drawing of women and a few men undergoing a mind-numbing range of trials and tribulations, most of which would have resulted in an agonising death had a real person been required to experience them.

'Where there is a market, you see, we can supply the demand more cheaply than anywhere else. Any market. Any demand.'

Charles was beginning to feel badly wrong-footed now. He had articulated part of his economic credo and this was the result. Or, as he began to realise, the first part of the result. For Xiang swept him back out into the market. With his eyes attuned to what they were looking for now, he began to see it all around him. On the stalls which lined the narrow roadway were piles of contraband. Yves St Laurent shirts, Reebok footwear; leisurewear by Tacchini and Lacoste. Perfumes by Chanel and Kalvin Klein. CDs and videodiscs by Paramount and Philips. Computer software by IBM and Apple. Games by Sega and Nintendo. Videos by Amblin, Virgin and Disney. The two men walked through the bustling black market as though unaware of the increasing tension in the air around them. It was not until they reached the end of the narrow roadway that Charles realised the reason for this atmosphere. Drawn up across the street was a line of uniformed men.

'It is the job of the Excise officers to control such activities,' said Xiang. 'And this contingent is just about to close down every stall in the market which deals in illegal merchandise, and the factories which supply them. We will not, you see, Comrade Lee, deal in such stuff. Now or ever. But first, perhaps you will allow me to introduce you to the officer commanding these Excise officers. He is with the Navy of the People's Republic and acting coastguard commander for this province. His name is Huw Pei-chun.'

And so the two old friends, Charles Lee and Paul Huw, stood face to face at the end of Renmin Road, within arm's reach of one another for the first time in more than twenty years. And if they recognised each other, neither of them showed it.

Charles Lee realised that he had perhaps underestimated everyone and everything around him, even if this climactic meeting with his childhood partner in crime was a coincidence. Most especially, Charles had underestimated Xiang Lo-wu and the mortal danger he was in.

Robin woke up with a crippling headache and the flesh-crawling feeling that she had been intimately interfered with. She sat bolt upright in a strange bunk on the *Seram Queen*, even as Charles Lee stood riven in Renmin Road, Guangzhou, away to the north of her; and Richard, despairingly, began to tear up her photographs in the Queen Elizabeth Hospital on Wylie Road, Hong Kong, not quite so far north but a little further to the east. And, far to the south and west, Edgar Tan was standing impatiently in the offices of Beautiful Views Ltd, on Rizal Avenue, Manila. Robin's first action was to clasp her hands to her head, which throbbed with a piercingly intense pain. She was wearing a rough skullcap of padded gauze through which her hair seemed to be poking in an uncontrolled riot, like briars through a wicker fence. The next thing she did, prompted by the strange feeling on her burning skin, was to bring her hands down to her shirt. The buttons were largely undone. Her shorts seemed to be awry. When she looked down, she was confronted with a gape of crumpled cotton, a couple of generously exposed lace cups and a great deal more cleavage than she had shown at any time since her wedding night.

'Where in hell's name...' she said aloud, looking around at last. There was some relief here at least. As acting medical officer, one of the first facilities she had checked out was the ship's medical room. And that was where she found herself to be, in the one bunk which comprised the rudimentary isolation ward.

She sat for a moment, a sailor before she was a woman, turning her bandaged head from side to side. The slight movement she felt revealed that the ship was still drifting slowly through a near calm. The silence spoke eloquently of continued failure down below by the chief engineer and his team. Narrowed eyes judged the time of day by the fact that the whole room seemed to have been washed down in blood a day or so ago. The surgery itself, with windows out onto the weather deck, looked as though it had been washed with blood a moment or so ago. It was sunset and the shadows of the north-facing bridgehouse dictated the colours reflected in here by the ruby sky, the red and grey deck cargo and the green-brown deck itself. Please God it was sunset Thursday, she thought. Even sunset Thursday would mean that she had been out for more than eight hours. She did not care to think what her insensible body might have gone through in a longer time than that, especially as the alternative would seem to be more than thirty hours.

Robin swung her legs over the side of the bunk and stood up. The action required some fortitude, for her head swam and her legs shook while her knees threatened to buckle and all sorts of internal bits of her threatened to revolt – each in its own revolting way. She took several deep breaths, an action which served to remind her of the state of her clothes. But she did nothing to put it right, for she found herself crossing to the door as though in a dream. As though in a nightmare, she discovered that the door was locked. She shook it and battered on it but there was no response. Her head continued to swim and her ears to ring.

The sensation of woozy almost inebriated disorientation was so strong that Robin drunkenly checked her arms for signs of needle marks, half believing that she had been drugged. Certainly her current state put her forcefully in mind of experiments with a strange-smelling cigarette during her days at the London School of Economics and with an odd little pill at Johns Hopkins. She wiped her forehead and found herself looking dully at the back of her hand, wondering whether the liquid there was so vividly red because of its natural colour or because of reflection. Looking at the floor down a body which seemed to have grown dizzyingly tall, she watched her feet place themselves one after another, increasingly heavily on the linoleum flooring as she walked back to her bunk. Here she stood for a while, catching her breath and collecting her thoughts. Then she set herself in motion again and managed to cross as far as the doorway into the surgery. Here again she paused, hanging crucified between the uprights, gasping for breath and feeling the perspiration running down the outside of her ribs and the inside of her thighs. The surgery was not a large room. There was a basic operating table in the middle of it and glass-fronted cases of medicines on two walls. There was a secure cabinet for sharp instruments and a safe for drugs. On the wall opposite the open doorway were square windows which currently looked out onto the variegated wall of the containers on the deck.

Robin crossed to the operating table and paused again with her hands spread over the smooth plastic surface, her wrists close together, leaning her short ribs against her elbows. Eventually she summoned up the strength to swim across the thick red air towards the window and look out across the deck. When she reached the window, she found she had to lean against it with her hands spread and her arms straight in order to remain erect. For this reason, she remained at arm's length from the thick glass, and the extra element of drug-enhanced distance gave the scene which met her eyes then the quality of utter unreality which she for ever afterwards associated with it. All but insensible with fatigue, stress, painkillers and concussion, she saw the first of the natives come up over the side. He was tall, dark-skinned and stark naked apart from a necklace of shells and a headdress.

All the books Robin had read during her youth and teens had been to do with high adventure in far-flung places. She knew, therefore, exactly what was going on when *orang laut* came stealthily aboard a powerless freighter drifting helplessly through the South China Sea. Given strength by a sudden, giddying, surge of adrenaline, she turned and prepared to stumble back to the door. She must give the alarm, no matter what. The phrase 'play up and play the game' fled through her mind like a blazing bonfire rag borne aloft by a November wind. But a further movement caught the corner of her eye and swung her head back again before she moved her feet. Behind the naked man came an invasion of further figures. All equally naked, all very obviously female. Not even the most xenophobic of the late-Empire adventures had ever suggested that a stark native, up to all sorts of unsportsmanlike skulduggery, would be accompanied by the contents of a seraglio, stripped and ready for action. But that was probably because such works were usually sexist as well as racist. Only the Greeks had ever come up with the idea of a race of warrior women and, according to the Victorian cannon, the Greeks had been deeply suspect to a man.

As Robin stared, the deck seemed to be inundated with a flood of lightly-oiled *café-au-lait* flesh. The gleaming curves flowed like liquid, mesmerising, seductive; they turned to reveal brief muscularity, pulling this and that aboard. Robin strained to see the darkening ocean beyond the safety rails but the deck obscured the water – and the long canoes which must be hurrying to and from the ship. Robin shook her head like a punch-drunk boxer fighting the count. What sort of invasion was this? How would she go about stemming that gleaming, irresistible tide of naked bodies? What sort of weapons had they brought aboard? Who was there to stand against the invasion with her?

As Robin lingered, indecisive, the deck lighting came on. Each curve of rib, buttock, thigh and breast, each point of finger, toe, nose and nipple was thrown into stark relief at once. And there came Captain Sin, no longer sick; Wai Chan, no longer on watch; Chief Chen Hang, no longer working on the engines; Fat Chow, no longer preoccupied with supporting the captain and spying upon her; and even Sam Yung, no longer quite so boyish after all. They took in hand the naked, nubile native girls and vanished with them into the cinnabar shadows.

Robin hung there, supported by her left hand against the window, looking back across the sickroom, away from what was all too clearly happening so close at hand. 'Watch the wall,' she told herself, quite loudly and extremely ironically. 'Watch the wall, my darling, while the gentlemen go by.'

Chapter Thirty

Edgar Tan stepped out of the early-morning bustle of Rizal Avenue and into the offices of Beautiful Views Ltd. It was a little after 8a.m. on the morning of Friday, 20 June, and the detective had already had a bad day. He had arrived at Ninoy Aquino Airport at 5a.m. on the Red-eye out of Singapore and his luggage had been lost by 6. He thanked the Lord that, knowing Manila International of old, he had kept anything of any real importance in his pockets or in his briefcase. He had waited for half an hour before a cab had turned up and then he had watched in growing disbelief as the driver, obviously lost, took him on an unwanted tour of the south of Manila. They ended up on Santos Avenue instead of Rizal, miles away from where Tan wanted to be, and he very nearly had a fight with the driver over the exorbitant fare. In the end, perversely glad he did not have to worry about his heavy suitcase, he had caught the rush-hour Metro up to Don Jose Station, exited with a crowd which seemed to comprise about half the population of the city, and walked.

At first glance, Beautiful Views was unpromising. It lurked behind one of those narrow, slightly tatty shop fronts which can be found in any city. Its one mean window was filled with a display of views which Tan himself did not find particularly beautiful, for all their anatomical precision. The gamely smiling women on show were in almost every respect at the furthest possible end of the spectrum from the genuinely beautiful view on the postcard still wrapped in plastic in the briefcase. And it was quite a shock to find one of these game women, fully clothed, standing behind the counter in the dingy, dust-smelling little shop.

Tan put his briefcase on the counter. 'Good morning,' he said in English. 'I would like to see the manager, please.'

The woman looked at her watch. 'He be in by ten, maybe.'

'Well, perhaps you can help me.' Tan opened the case and extracted Captain Gough's card. 'Can you tell me which of your photographers took this picture?'

The woman's long eyes dwelt on the plastic-wrapped photograph. She seemed almost surprised to see the long swell of sand coloured like the flank of a sleeping native woman; the chiaroscuro palm trees leaning down towards the wine-dark sea etched against the orange and rose-coloured sky. Tan astutely surmised that his was not an unusual question, it was just unusual for someone to be asking about a sunset.

'Why do you want to know?' she asked.

Tan, correctly, guessed that this question actually meant, how much are you willing to pay?

A pair of well-practised hagglers, they switched into negotiating mode. Each polite phrase carried a financial undertone which both of them recognised.

'I am conducting an extremely important investigation,' he said. I haven't time to haggle – name your price.

'It is an old photograph, I am not certain...' It's going to be expensive.

'This is an extremely important investigation. I will be very glad of any help you can give.' I don't care how expensive.

'I could look at the records, of course. Are you in a hurry?' You want speed, you'll have to pay even more.

'Records? Perhaps I should wait for the manager.' Don't push your luck or you'll have to share.

'No, no. I'm sure I can find what you want without waiting for him.' OK. Point made.

'In that case,' said Tan, closing the deal, 'perhaps I could offer you a little remuneration for your trouble...' And he named the sum the cabbie had demanded for taking him to the wrong address.

The woman's jaw fell, and Tan realised a little ruefully that he had overpriced the market. He could have had the information, a couple of hours with the woman, carnal knowledge of a couple of her friends in the window and a great deal of change. But he had named his price and he would stand by it.

She gave him the address of a studio out on Santiago in Quezon City without consulting the records after all, and he handed over the money. As he crossed to the door, however, he asked, 'How come you didn't have to check the records?'

'We have only ever had one photographer. He is my husband. He starts work at nine. He will be in the studio all day today. My name is Consuela, Consuela Lopez. His name is Jorge. Tell him I sent you; I will call him and warn him you are coming otherwise he will not let you in, I think. He has his girls around today.'

This time, Tan found a taxi driver who knew the city and understood the charging system. The detective was outside the address Consuela Lopez had given him by nine thirty. His persistent ring at the bell was answered after a few moments. The door opened a little and the face of a teenage girl peered enquiringly round its edge. 'My name is Edgar Tan. I have come to see Jorge Lopez,' Tan said. The girl seemed to understand nothing more than the photographer's name but she gestured him in. He stepped through the door and stood, rooted to the floor with shock, as he realised that she was wearing only panties and a towel clasped to her chest. 'Jorge Lopez,' he said again and she nodded, smiling, closed the door and led him deeper into the house. He followed her through a dark corridor, too surprised even to admire the way in which her long pale back dived, divided and spread into the seat of her tiny white cotton panties.

She pushed open a door and called something impenetrable in Filipino. Lopez, recognisable because he was the only person in the room with a camera, the only man, and the only person fully dressed, called, '*Mabuhay; sandali lang!* You wait please, Mr Tan. *Halika dito*, Conception.' The girl dropped the towel which had so modestly concealed from Edgar Tan the bosom she was all too obviously about to display to the camera, and dived among the other girls on the bed beneath the studio lights. There was much giggling and wriggling.

Faintly embarrassed to find himself standing in the shadows watching three eighteen-year-olds wrestling each other out of their underwear, Tan began to look around. Jorge Lopez's studio was ramshackle and tacky. The photographs pinned to its walls reflected the intense young Filipino's range as a photographer. Certainly, the girlie shots in the window of Beautiful Views were far more artistic than the basic hard-core stills on the walls.

The detective stood at the back of the squalid little studio, wearily wondering how anyone could find anything new and exciting in the pale, partly-clad bodies lying increasingly graphically revealed on the bed. From the look of it, some of the more nubile students at the university were supplementing their grants. But at least it was only more girlie stuff. Had Jorge Lopez been working on anything stronger, like the stuff up on the walls, Tan would have probably lost his lunch. Yesterday's lunch; it was coming up to twenty-four hours since he had eaten. But then, unexpectedly, one of the naked young bodies reminded him of the dead secretary he had seen the week before this case had started – what was her name? Miss Fa? – and he began to feel nauseous after all.

Then again, thought Tan, trying to clear his mind of the images from that sad little hotel room in Singapore, had the photographer been doing anything more graphic than this, he would never have agreed to see him. Though he had no doubt that the main reason he found himself here now, watching the show on the creaking bed and waiting to speak to the photographer, was the fact that the redoubtable Consuela, calling from the shop, had told her husband that the foreigner was incredibly rich and could be taken for large amounts of money with hardly any trouble at all.

When he saw how little the photographer handed to Conception at the end of the session Edgar realised just how very generous he had been with his initial bribe and deep in his heart he swore a dark revenge against that first taxi driver, whose fare had been his yardstick, if ever their paths should cross again. But he summoned up an accommodating smile as Jorge patted the girls paternally on the head and sent them off to dress.

'*Magandang umaga*, Mr Tan. What can I do for you?'

'Good morning, Mr Lopez. It's about this postcard. Do you recognise the photograph?'

'*Aywan ko*...'

Here we go again, thought Edgar; he spoke enough Filipino to know 'I don't know...' and he knew that tone in any language.

'*Sayang*,' he spat. What a pity! He began to put the card away.

'*Sandali lang*,' said Lopez, thrown off balance: just a moment.

'*Opo?*' Yes? Tan was fast running out of vocabulary, but he was also out of patience and that was a big advantage.

'*Sige*,' said the photographer: OK. There was defeat in his tone; he was not a shadow of his wife when it came to bargaining. He held out his hand and Tan gave him the card.

'Did you take it?' he asked.

'Yes.'

'Do you know where?'

'Yes.'

'Tell me where and how to get there and I'll give you five thousand pesos. Come with me and I'll give you ten thousand.'

'When?'

'Now.'

'But it's too far...' As he spoke, Conception, the eldest of the models, popped her head back round the door. She had slipped on a silk shirt and tied it instead of buttoning it. The bright material cradled the cleavage which had just been so starkly on show – making it very much more appetising. '*Tayo na*, Jorge,' she said: let's go, Jorge.

The photographer wavered. There was sweat on his narrow, intense face. His eyes remained fixed on the postcard, however, and the fortune which it promised him. '*Alis diyan*, Conception!' he said at last. Get lost, Conception!

And Edgar Tan knew that he had won.

'And finally,' said Mr Prosecutor Po, 'the Crown calls Mr StJohn DeVere Syme.'

It was ten thirty in the morning of what Maggie would later come to recall as one of the longest days in her life. Notification of exactly who Crown were going to call, together with the notes of his testimony had arrived at Andrew's office at 8a.m. It was only because Andrew and Maggie were effectively living there that they got such early warning of the development. They read the testimony, naked, over breakfast then had to rush through their shower and ablutions before his secretary arrived to catch them 'in flagrante'. The notes made depressing reading, but nowhere near as depressing as the testimony itself. Maggie sat back, as alert as a hunting tiger, looking for an opening for cross-examination.

'You are StJohn DeVere Syme of twenty-three Montpelier Place, London?'

'That's right.'

'You are an under-secretary at the British Foreign Office, with special responsibility for liaison with the Hong Kong police during the period leading up to the handover?'

'That is correct.'

'And your most recent specific area of interest has been to do with smuggling in this area?'

'Smuggling and piracy. Yes.'

'And, Mr Syme,' said the apparently mild-mannered advocate. 'You first became aware of an association between the China Queens Company and this nefarious practice when?'

'Five years ago. It so happened that the China Queens Company was advertising for a company secretary. We caused one of our operatives to be put in place. She was accepted into the company and awarded the post.' Maggie at least had the satisfaction of writing 'Bingo' on her trial notes.

'Why this particular company, Mr Syme?'

'We understood – and when I say we I mean the Crown Colony police, the Singaporean police, and other authorities involved with the investigation – we understood that the China Queens Company was a front for a Triad smuggling enterprise run at that time by the White Powder Triad operating out of Tsimshatsui, Hong Kong.'

'So this person was placed undercover?'

'Yes.'

'With the knowledge of all the authorities involved?'

'With the knowledge of the authorities in London and Hong Kong only. Least said, soonest mended, so to speak.'

'And yet you admit to her presence now, in open court.'

'The operative vanished more than a month ago. There has been no contact. We believe she is, in all probability, dead.'

'Why do you believe that, Mr Syme?'

'Apart from the breakdown in usual procedures, for the first time in this operative's history, there is the fact that everyone else involved with this particular incident is dead also. Apart from the defendant, of course.'

'This particular incident, Mr Syme?'

'The operative in question has kept us informed of the movement of various sorts of contraband over the years, some carried by the ships of the China Queens Company, some by other ships. We have informed the authorities of all of this information, needless to say, and they have seen fit to intervene on occasion.'

'But never against the China Queens.'

'No, indeed, Mr Po. We needed to protect our source.'

'Then what happened some two months ago, Mr Syme?'

'Two months ago we received word that an enormous amount of crack cocaine was being prepared in the Philippines to be shipped by the China Queens container vessels.'

'And how is this information relevant to this particular case?'

'Little more than a year ago, the China Queens Company was purchased by Heritage Mariner, London, of which the accused is a senior executive officer.'

'Forgive me, Mr Syme, but why should the Triads part with a successful smuggling system such as this company seems to have represented?'

'The imminent return of Hong Kong to the People's Republic has caused a great deal of concern among the business communities, both legitimate and otherwise. Put at its simplest, if a pillar of the legitimate business community such as Jardine Matheson were willing to move out, the White Powder Triad were never going to be too far behind. So they got rid of their apparently legitimate business fronts.'

'And so the China Queens Company was sold to Captain Mariner?'

'Not quite, no.'

'Please explain, Mr Syme.'

'The company was sold to Captain Mariner's opposite number in the boardroom. A local man. The brother of Commander Victor Lee, officer in charge of this investigation.' At this bland assertion, both Andrew and Maggie jumped with shock. It was such a common name here – Victor and Charles might as well have been related to Bruce Lee as to each other! But Mr Po persisted.

'By definition, therefore, a man of repute and standing, a man above suspicion.'

'Unfortunately not. As Commander Lee will admit, I am sure, a man who made his reputation as a smuggler and inciter of civil unrest. Mr Charles Lee of Heritage Mariner was noted in this neighbourhood as the man who opened the Tiger Gate to smuggling in the late sixties and who fomented the student riots in Beijing in the eighties. His reputation here is anything but savoury, I'm afraid.'

'And where is Mr Charles Lee now, if I may ask?'

'The last report delivered to my office before I came east was to the effect that Mr Lee was in Beijing. But—'

'Hearsay, My Lord,' interjected Maggie.

Mr Justice Fang nodded. 'Mr Syme, even an official report must be regarded as hearsay. Unless you have direct personal knowledge, then I cannot allow this testimony.'

'No, My Lord'

'Very well. The jury is asked to disregard Mr Syme's assertion as to the probable whereabouts of Mr Charles Lee. Please proceed, Mr Po.'

'Thank you, My Lord. Let us return to the company itself, Mr Syme. There is no question of the probity of Heritage Mariner or any of its other officers except, perhaps, Mr Lee, surely?'

'No. Well, not until—'

'Please, Mr Syme,' interrupted Mr Po before Maggie had time to object. 'Explain what you mean concisely.'

'Less than forty-eight hours before her disappearance, our operative in Singapore sent one last message.'

'And what did it say?'

'I have no precise idea. It was a fax and it was addressed neither to her control nor to Queen Anne's Gate. It was addressed to Captain Richard Mariner. We knew about the message because all her communications were monitored as a matter of routine; but we only covered a part of this final fax. It was an urgent summons demanding that the captain come out at once to Singapore, and mentioning a shipment which we had been keeping an eye out for during the whole of the spring.'

'The shipment of crack cocaine from the Philippines.'

'Yes, two full containers' worth.'

'I thought you said that the White Powder Triad had sold the company on, to Heritage Mariner, through Mr Charles Lee.'

'Indeed they had, but clearly they wished to make one last great killing. And the pipeline was still in place, even though the company had changed hands.'

'I see. So Captain Mariner, in receipt of a fax about drug smuggling aboard his vessels, reported this contact to the authorities?'

'He alerted the Foreign Office to the fact that he was travelling abroad and came to Singapore, arriving within twenty-four hours of receipt of the fax.'

'What did he do then?'

'He checked into the Raffles Hotel and contacted our operative at the China Queens Office. He did not know, of course, that she was working for us.'

'And what transpired?'

'We do not know, and neither do the authorities here. The operative had vanished within twelve hours. It seems that they spent some time together and yet neither of them passed any information on to the authorities either in Singapore or here – or in London, come to that. Though we have reason to believe that Captain Mariner communicated at some length with his wife. Whatever they talked about, and whatever communications resulted from their conversation, nothing was communicated to the authorities, a fact which we regarded then and regard now as having possibly sinister implications. Captain Mariner was the last person to see our operative alive, as far as we know.'

'My Lord, this is mere innuendo.'

'No, Ms DaSilva, I think we have a report of fact here, which the jury may choose to interpret as they will. Please proceed, Mr Po.'

'Thank you, My Lord. So Captain Mariner talked at length to your operative at the China Queens Company. She then disappeared. The authorities remained in ignorance of anything untoward in the offing. What then?'

'Then the *Sulu Queen* arrived at Singapore, Captain Mariner went aboard as soon as the ship was turned around, took over command and sent the original captain, Walter Gough, ashore. Captain Gough had also vanished within a matter of hours. We believe both Captain Gough and our operative are dead.'

'What evidence do you have for supposing that they are dead?'

'The fact that, with the exception of Captain Mariner and Mr Lee, everyone else involved in this incident seems to be dead. Except for the Triad members, as far as we know. And Mrs Mariner, though of course her personal involvement seems to have come later, after Captain Mariner's communication reached her.'

'Could you enlarge upon the involvement of Mrs Mariner as you understand it?'

'My Lord!' Maggie was up, trembling with outrage at this unexpected turn.

'Ms DaSilva, are you wishing to infer that Mrs Mariner has not been involved in this case?'

'No, My Lord, but—'

'Then I can see no grounds for an objection at this point. You may hold yourself ready to cross-examine, of course, Ms DaSilva. In the meantime, Mr Po?'

'Thank you, My Lord. Mr Syme?'

'Within eight hours of her husband's formal arrest, Mrs Mariner was on her way to the Crown Colony. She was interviewed by myself and one of my operatives on the plane on the way out and she reacted extremely negatively to assurances that no special treatment could be guaranteed for her husband. Immediately on her arrival here, Mrs Mariner was in contact with a local solicitor and had acquired the services of an eminent local barrister. I am talking about a woman who has come halfway round the world to a strange city and achieved all this in less than twenty-four hours. Mrs Mariner achieved something close to a miracle of organisation within the first twenty-four hours. Within the next twelve she was seen in the company of Twelvetoes Ho, the last major Triad leader left in the Crown Colony. The last of what we call the

469s left here. And Mr Ho has been seen in her company since. Indeed, he has been seen dining with defence counsel's friend Ms Patel.' Both Maggie and Lata reacted to this testimony – but there was little they could do other than to brindle and blush.

'On that point,' prompted Mr Prosecutor Po before Maggie could think of an objection, 'might the jury be shown exhibit Number Twenty-One?' This was the first photograph the jury had seen since the photographs of the corpses and the places where they had died. Many jurors reacted with horror at the thought of another one, but this picture simply showed a restaurant table laden with curry at which an elderly Chinese man was in animated conversation with a young lady whose bloodline clearly reached back to the Indian subcontinent.

'So, within thirty-six hours of her arrival in Hong Kong, Mrs Mariner was in contact with the leading Triad member in the colony, and he has remained in close contact with the defence team.'

'Yes.'

'What else do you know of Mrs Mariner's movements that have a bearing on this case?'

'During the course of my investigations into the most likely places in the colony where drugs might be obtained in order to discover what had happened to the crack cocaine I believed the *Sulu Queen* had been carrying – guided, of course, by one of Commander Lee's men – I visited the club here where cocaine is usually available and to my surprise saw Mrs Mariner, looking very much at home.'

'My Lord! I must protest!'

'Mr Syme, please confine yourself to answering the questions put to you.'

' I apologise, My Lord.'

'Very well. Please proceed, Mr Po.'

'Thank you, My Lord. So Mr Syme, within a few hours of her arrival here Mrs Mariner was in the company of a leading Triad figure and within a few days she was observed by yourself where, precisely?'

'In a club noted for cocaine dealing.'

'Is this club the sort of place a tourist lady might find herself visiting innocently?'

'It is called Bottoms and its cabaret specialises in what I believe is called bondage. People are tied up and subjected to various sorts of more or less painful abuse. It is not a place which any *lady* would ever find herself visiting. Unless she had business there.'

'My Lord!'

'Very well, Ms DaSilva. The jury will please disregard Mr Syme's imputation. Please take more care, Mr Po.'

'With respect, My Lord, the point was carefully made. If I may expand just a little further.'

'You have just a tiny bit of latitude, Mr Po.'

'Thank you, My Lord. So, you suggest that your researches have led you to believe that, with Captain Richard Mariner's memory damaged, Mrs Mariner was checking on the likely destination of the missing cargo, just as you were?'

'She had been to Ping Chau Island. She had risked her life in order to get into the caves which she had apparently discovered and look closely at the containers which no one else had ever suspected might be there. She had consulted with a Triad leader. Now she was checking the market here. It was always clear to us that such a vast quantity of cocaine could never simply be destined for the Crown Colony.'

'If not here, then where, Mr Syme, according to your expert estimation?'

'The People's Republic of China.'

Chapter Thirty-One

Life as he had grown used to it during the last six weeks ended for Walter Gough at 13:45 on the afternoon of Friday, 20 June 1997. As soon as he heard the thud-thud-thud of the helicopter blades grow loud enough to drown out the grumble of his generator, he knew it was all over. If the truth were told, he had been waiting for the idyll to end ever since it had begun. He was too much a product of a particular place and time to believe, deep down, that Anna and he would ever get away with it. He had done nothing to deserve Anna other than to love her, and he came from a society which could never bring itself to believe that love was all that mattered.

No. Wally had suspected, right from the start, that they were doomed. He had broken too many promises, shirked too many responsibilities, let too many people down, told too many lies. He had been careful not to probe too deeply, but he suspected that Anna had paid a similar price for her freedom. Perhaps it had been a kind of masochistic, self-destructive impulse which had made him send the card to poor Phyl, though all he had been aware of consciously was a burning desire to fulfil that last responsibility and see her safe and sound. And to look after the boy. He had continued to love his son long after he had stopped loving his wife. In spite of what he had written, he had secretly hoped she would tell young Wally he was all right; he had kicked over the traces and gone native like that chap in *The Moon and Sixpence*, but he was out there somewhere, and all right, something of a romantic figure, to be looked up to and fantasised about.

Anna came in to the little house at a run, her face white, in stark contrast to the sun-darkened expanses of her naked body. There was white sand like sugar cast over the upper swells of her breasts, gleaming in the luxuriant black wool of her pubic hair – and only the rotors of a hovering helicopter could have kicked it up on a calm day like today. Wally never found out whether she was pale with shock or with embarrassment. Like him, the first thing she did was reach for swimwear. They said nothing, like guilty murderers discovered in the act, made silent by the burden of their guilt. In those long moments during which the thud-thud of the rotors echoed thunderously around the tiny island, their heaven became a hell. They dressed like strangers, embarrassedly, back to back, and ran out to meet their fate, not quite side by side, as though they just happened to be here together by chance.

The helicopter had floats as well as wheels and, having circled the tiny island, it settled like a dragonfly in the shallows just beyond the beach. The wind of its rotors lifted the palm-frond thatch on their hut like a typhoon. No sooner was it firmly on the restless water than the side door opened and a slight, active man jumped down into the foam. Grimly – angrily – he waded ashore, wildly out of place in his two-piece suit and city shoes: all soaked. He carried a briefcase which also got drenched by the spray from the slowing rotor blades.

The wiry stranger slopped up onto the sand. For the first three or four steps, clear water gushed out of his stretching shoe leather onto the yellow shore. The soaked material of his trousers clung to his muscular calves. His thick, blue-black hair stuck up wildly. His rage burned and when he shoved his dark, pocked face towards Wally and snarled, 'Captain Gough, I presume?' Wally merely nodded, unable to reply, all too aware how skimpy and tight his swimming trunks were.

'What do you want?' demanded Anna, her voice scarcely more accommodating than their visitor's.

'And you must be the mysterious Anna Leung.' He made it sound like an accusation – which it was.

'Who are you?' faltered Anna, her world beginning to crumble, like Wally's already had.

'My name is Edgar Tan and I've come to take you back.'

'And why should we come with you?' she shrilled, her voice betraying how near to hysterics she was.

'Anna, old thing—'

'Shut up, Wally. Just let me talk to this *creature*!'

'I say, old girl . . .'

'Why should we come with you, Mr Tan? Why should we listen to you for one cold second and why should we even dream of giving up this paradise which we have made for ourselves? Give us one good reason!'

Edgar Tan drew himself up to his full height and looked at the pair of them. They seemed such nice people. Misguided and a little naive, perhaps, but *nice*. It caused a poignant ache in his heart to do this to them, for he had a sneaking respect for what they had achieved and he hated to bring destruction to a fantasy so close to his own heart. It was this as much as his exhaustion and the shocking price it had cost to hire the helicopter which made the detective so uncharacteristically enraged. But the unlikely lovers seemed to have no idea of the full implications, or of the tragic consequences, of their romantic actions. He looked at their faces, watching so much die in their expressions; he looked at their tanned bodies in the skimpy swimwear and he saw them begin to sag with sudden age as they waited for his word. He realised how a judge must feel, pronouncing a sentence of death.

It was lunchtime in Hong Kong. The court had closed early on the completion of the prosecution's case, and Mr Justice Fang had given permission for a slightly extended midday break to enable Maggie to prepare her opening. Maggie and Andrew sat on the same side of his big desk. Lata, Gerry and Mr Thong sat opposite them. On the desk itself, amid the litter of papers, well clear of the pile of *Archbold* volumes, lay the remains of a light takeaway lunch.

'So,' Maggie was summing up, 'the cross-examination established that although Syme and Lee have both been working on this case and Anna Leung was their operative, none of them actually came up with a completely waterproof reason why Richard was involved. That is especially true with Ms Leung now vanished. That's the weak link in the prosecution's case. Even if they can prove that Richard was closely involved in the deaths and that he handled all the weapons they still haven't quite made it to the line, have they?'

'Only the jury can tell us that,' warned Mr Thong. 'You know how unpredictable juries can be.'

'I agree,' warned Andrew quietly. 'We can't take this for granted, Maggie.'

They were well established as lovers now and it was with some hesitation he ventured – for the first time – into an area of possible disagreement. But, characteristically, she reacted in the least predictable fashion. 'You're quite right,' she admitted. 'We have to take the jury back to the basics here. There is no doubt that the prosecution has covered the weakness in its case very well. They have called an impressive Naval officer, a senior police officer and a senior civil servant. Just their presence adds enormous weight to what they have said. And it does make a kind of sense. It is just conceivable that Richard has grown desperate enough to gamble everything on pirating a shipment of cocaine. Perhaps it is possible that there was a link via the old-time smuggler Charles Lee with the more questionable elements of the People's Republic and their criminal coastguards. Perhaps Twelvetoes Ho has got a secret plan which has allowed him to manipulate us all the way along the line. God knows, he could still be manipulating us even now. Maybe Anna Leung was involved way over her head. Perhaps we can imagine that she and Walter Gough are somewhere together – either in a safe haven with the money or the cocaine – or at the bottom of Singapore harbour.

'No, we have to keep plugging on with the facts that Richard is genuinely amnesiac – that he isn't putting it on. And we have to keep clear in the jury's mind that even the prosecution are half convinced that someone else did in fact come aboard . . .'

'It was clever of you to get Commander Lee to admit that. I don't think he even realised what he had said...'

'Thanks darling. The bottom line is this, however: if we don't find some way of undermining the case the prosecution have made, then Richard could be in bad trouble.'

'We were right to push for a quick trial,' murmured Andrew. 'I'd hate to be in this position a fortnight from now.'

'Certainly. There's no appeal from an execution.'

'Don't,' said Lata. 'It's too horrible even to think about.'

'Even so, we need to push hard. Let's pray Tom can come up with something when he goes through things with Richard now.'

'Either that or a call from Robin. How long has it been now?'

'More than a day. We haven't talked to Robin directly since we passed on the information about Anna Leung and the containers. What was that? Wednesday noon. And it's Friday now. God, how time flies. It's not unusual for Captain Sin to break off radio contact as he goes through the Paracels, according to Mr Shaw, but I must say I'm a bit worried. Lata, would you and Mr Thong pop down and see if you can get any further information from the Heritage Mariner Office, please? But take care, Lata. I think Mr Shaw is weakening towards you in a big way.'

'Very funny, Maggie.' Lata rose and crossed to the door. Thong followed her and paused at her shoulder as she turned to look at her friend and colleague. 'See you in court, Maggie,' she said. It was an old battle cry – their version of *Geronimo*.

Maggie looked up and favoured her with a glowing grin. Against her better nature, a little like a sulky child, Lata smiled back. And it was a smile which lingered after she left the office. Maggie's happiness was so contagious that Lata could resist it no longer; they were friends again.

Gerry bustled off immediately behind them. Balfour Stephenson had not stopped serving the wider community just because one partner had been subsumed so completely into this case.

As Gerry's footsteps echoed off down the corridor, Andrew wound his arm around Maggie's shoulder and turned her head into the crook of his elbow. On every occasion they had found themselves alone during the last few days they had made love. 'Anything I can do to relax you, darling?' he asked suggestively.

Her smile of answer was tinged for the first time with regret instead of sensuousness. 'Yes, love,' she answered, picking up the papers from the top of his desk and dusting off a grain or two of egg fried rice. 'You can go through this opening with me.'

Commander Lee and Dr Chu had allowed Tom Fowler to have some time alone with the accused, and this time Tom had thought to bring a chart with him. It lay spread on the table between the men now, and the psychologist was guiding the ship's master along the route of the *Sulu*

Queen's last voyage. But to the Londoner's untutored ear, the names of the hazards still sounded nothing like the gibberish of the word-association exercise a few days ago.

'So, you came out of Singapore and through past this thing here called Horsburgh.'

'It's a lighthouse. The Horsburgh lighthouse...' Richard's words were unthinking at first but coloured by growing wonder on the repetition as he realised that he had remembered something without help, drugs, hypnosis or appreciable effort. And what he remembered was correct – deep in his bones he was certain of that.

'Right, out past the lighthouse into the Singapore Strait.' persisted Tom as though he had noticed nothing. 'What's this thing here?'

'Wreck. Swing south a little, towards Heluputan.' Richard's eyes were half-closed now as though he hardly needed to consult the blue, white and sand-coloured paper.

'Yes, I see that,' said Tom, his voice low. 'Then what?'

'Beware of floating islands.' Richard's eyes were closed now. This was information not displayed on the chart.

'Isn't that a kind of pudding?' asked the psychologist, sidetracked by surprise.

The master mariner opened his bright eyes and looked down on him from an ineffable, unamused height. 'They can be big. Fifteen metres long, five metres high. Trees, animals, you name it. Make a nasty mess of you. They come south out of the Mekong. You have to sail almost due north into the flood of them as they come south out of the Mekong.'

The repetition made the psychologist prick up his ears but he still had no idea how close he was to pushing things through the barrier in Richard's memory. 'So, you go north, through the outwash of the Mekong, depending on the season, past this place called Krakatoa...' Now that sounded familiar, Tom thought. Why did that sound so familiar?

'Kar Katoaka,' corrected Richard gently. 'Yes, that's right. "Kar" is short for "karang" or reef. It's shallow water but we keep well clear and swing round here towards Pulau Jemaja, with the Pulau Mangkai light at its north-western point. Once past that, we sail on up due north past the Udang oilfield. There are two platforms, a storage tanker and a radio station, but it's nearly thirty kilometres south-east of us. We've nothing to worry about until we come up towards the Charlotte Bank and Scawfell. We run north-west past Alexandra, south-east of the Julia Shoal and the Catwicks, keeping an eye out for mines south of Dao Phu Qui.'

'More hidden dangers from Vietnam, eh?' asked Tom.

Richard flinched. The psychologist began to realise how close they were to making some kind of breakthrough. But he did not fully understand how, or why.

'After that,' he persisted, 'it looks to me like plain sailing until the Paracel Islands.'

'Clear, up to the Paracels,' agreed Richard, his voice dreamy. He sounded to Tom as though he was on Pentothal and under deep hypnosis, but he was not and they had only been talking for a few minutes.

'Then, once you come through the Paracels, once you come up past these – what do you call them? Lights. Once you come past these lights at Woody Island and North Reef, then you're set fair for Hong Kong. Nothing more to worry about. Not even your nightmares from Vietnam can get at you up here.'

The observation was inspired and its effect cataclysmic. Richard rose, his face dead white, his wide eyes staring across the table at Tom.

'Tell her!' breathed the terrified man. 'You have to tell her.' His face twisted in a mixture of rage and fear. 'Get through and tell her at once.' His tone of voice took on a terrible earnestness; a depth of concern which made Tom, for the first time, genuinely fear for Richard's sanity. 'You have to warn her about the Vietnamese. The Vietnamese! Don't you understand? They're not all dead. Oh God! They're not all dead.'

Less than an hour later, at 13:30 local time, Lata Patel found herself sitting beside John Shaw in the Heritage Mariner office on the fourth floor of the Jardine Matheson building as the young Chinese punched in *Seram Queen*'s call sign on the company radio frequency. They were alone together now, for Mr Thong had gone back to court. 'They checked in at nine thirty, a little later than usual,' he was saying to her. His dark eyes were fixed on her face but he was having trouble stopping himself from examining her breasts. 'They did not report any trouble at that time. It was a standard "fair weather, calm voyage" report. *Seram Queen* is well clear of the Paracels now, and behind schedule because of some trouble with the engine yesterday. They reported that last evening. It is a bit of a nuisance, but nothing unusual. Nothing to worry about apparently. They will proceed a little above maximum economic speed to try and catch up but we have moved her booking at Kwai Chung to allow for a slightly later ETA. It has all been routine.' John Shaw surrendered to his lower instincts and dropped his gaze. Her white blouse was tight and the space between the buttons gaped slightly, revealing a web of white lace.

'I expected an update this morning,' he continued, his voice quieter, more seductive, in spite of the bland words. 'But they will probably save it for later. They are due to call back at sixteen hundred and I'll reconfirm then. Those are her call times, nine in the morning and four o'clock in the afternoon Hong Kong time. But Captain Sin doesn't approve of detailed reports. If there is anything wrong, he usually waits until he can report in detail in person at the next port of call. It is to do with his face as captain. Do you understand about face, Miss Patel? I sometimes think Captain Sin would have to be going down with all hands before he authorised anything more than a standard progress report.'

Lata seemed not to have heard John Shaw's brief lecture on the captain's sense of personal pride; and thankfully she had not noted the direction of his hot gaze. Instead of answering him directly, she said, in worried tones, 'Tom Fowler was quite specific. We have to warn them about some Vietnamese people. Beyond that, things aren't quite so clear. Does it normally take this long to get through?'

'No, not usually. I mean, it is lunchtime out there the same as it is here, but there should still be a watch officer on the bridge even if the radio officer is eating.'

'Whose watch should it be?'

'The first officer's.'

'That's Robin. I can't imagine her skipping out on her duty.'

'No, there's no question of that,' said John quickly, abruptly concerned that he might appear to be accusing Robin Mariner, for whom he still harboured some indulgently lustful thoughts. He stopped examining Lata's bosom and raised his eyes, frowning with concern, 'And anyway, Mrs Mariner has been putting in a regular midday call to keep up with the progress of the captain's trial and to pass on her thoughts, but she has not been in contact for a couple of days now. Still, you must know all that. Let's try this again . . .'

John Shaw went through the simple routine again. Then, 'Vietnamese, you say?' he asked, to cover his increasing embarrassment and loss of face at failing in such an easy task before the attractive young woman.

'That's right. Tom Fowler says Captain Mariner is well on the mend but he still doesn't make absolute sense, especially when he feels that something is particularly vital.'

'This sort of thing happens to us all,' said John Shaw. 'I am often forgetful of names. And the more I try to remember who someone is, the less chance I have of getting it right.' An admission of a small, common social failing covered his much larger failing with the radio, and helped him save face.

'I'm just the same,' said Lata, frowning into the dumb instrument as John Shaw completed the call sequence, again with no success. 'There's something wrong, isn't there?'

'Something is not working properly, that is certain. It may be that this radio is broken. Or the radio on *Seram Queen* has developed a fault in the same way that the engines did yesterday. But I do not believe there's anything actually *wrong*. They have emergency equipment. If there was anything actually wrong, they would contact us via the open distress channel available to the lifeboat radios, of which she has four. She is an old ship, but she still has a supply of open-channel emergency beacons. There are many ways for them to alert us if there is anything badly wrong.'

'But in the meantime we can't actually warn them about these Vietnamese.'

'Well, no. But I bet they will be on again as usual at sixteen hundred hours.'

'Unless Captain Mariner's mysterious Vietnamese have struck in the meantime.'

'Is that a joke?' John asked with an air of innocent enquiry, as though trying to comprehend a cross-cultural experiment in communication. He turned towards her again and let his gaze settle downwards one last time.

'No,' said Lata, suddenly cold with foreboding. 'No, I don't believe it is.'

They had come for Robin twelve hours before this conversation took place. She was more than one hour late for her midnight watch, but they had let her sleep on for reasons of their own. The last of the natives had departed, bowlegged and laden, soon after midnight, and the thoroughly sated crew had begun to sort out their ship once again. The chief engineer found the strength to restart the engines and give the ship some steerage way. Third Officer Sam Yung took up his watch late, and stared dreamily ahead, his eyes scarcely focused, his mind full of libidinous memories and his back and private parts full of a thoroughly satisfied ache. He had no idea at that stage that the parts in question were also full of a painful and embarrassing social disease.

Down in his cabin, Captain Sin, who found his satisfaction in different ways, was carefully counting the money which he had earned in the little personal enterprise which the orgy on the foredeck had been designed, so successfully, to disguise. The Captain had no clear understanding of the very much larger contraband cargo carried by his ship; the secret, extra containers were carefully hidden and were accessible from on board only through the use of the deck gantries. The lading officer knew that all was not quite right, but even he – still lying comatose with fever in Singapore – had done little other than to look the other way when he realised that the computers at the automatic container ports loaded or unloaded a couple of extra boxes, apparently by accident. Their existence was concealed in his records just as they were hidden at the heart of the cargo on the deck. Only the unfortunate Brian Jordan, ever a man with an eye to the main chance, had looked deeper than that.

And so, on the bridge, Sam Yung stood, almost as comatose as the distant, hospitalised Chin Lau, at the shoulder of the steersman as *Seram Queen* gathered way into the small hours, with the Woody Island light swinging through the visible quadrant away to port, on his left.

Sam had just enough intellectual energy to ensure that their course kept them well clear of the Dido bank low on the starboard. And then he collapsed back into the watchkeeper's chair and fell asleep as the ship surged up out of the island chain and, apparently, out of danger at last.

In the ship's surgery, Robin slept deeply, under the influence of shock, exhaustion and painkilling drugs. In spite of all her foreboding, she had little to fear from Captain Sin and his crew. Even Chief Steward Fat Chow was less fearsome than he seemed. They were rogues, perhaps; and they were none of them above taking advantage of easy money and easy virtue; but they were not murderous – or desperate enough to dream of attacking her, or even of harassing her in any particular way. They fantasised about her – or Sam Yung certainly did – but that was all. She was, after all, the wife of the man who owned the company. And if he was mad and she was eccentric – both true as far as the crew of the *Seram Queen* could see – nevertheless, if any harm came to her then they would all be out of a job in very short order. This job was a very cushy number, with automatic loading and unloading in most of the major ports, the chance of a little profit from personal enterprise, and a regular orgy on the Paracels every time they came through. The risky plan of knocking her out with a lifeboat had been no more than an attempt to make sure she knew nothing about their dealings with the islanders that Thursday night. And, as far as any of them knew, it had all worked perfectly well. There would be a little more treatment, a lot of apologies and a sad farewell in Hong Kong. Mrs Mariner would leave the ship none the wiser, leaving everyone richer, more satisfied and secure in their jobs.

It never occurred to them that what had happened to their sister ship would happen to them as well. The two crews, although they worked for the same company, were not close. No friendships had been formed; no professional links forged. The deaths of their colleagues, the disappearance of the captain and the accusation of his stand-in all seemed distant events, irrelevant to their placid existence. Even the disappearance of Anna Leung touched them not at all now that their jobs and their pay seemed to be set fair to continue.

No one aboard was aware that it was *Seram*, not *Sulu*, which was carrying two containers full of crack cocaine belonging to the White Powder Triad of Hong Kong and destined for a specific market in the People's Republic of China, as the less legal business concerns in the colony tried to go one better than Charles Lee and his friends in gaining influence after the colony was handed back. It was well understood by the leaders of the White Powder Triad that such a cargo would attract attention, which was why they had let it be known that the cargo was on the first of the ships. This ploy had led to the wrong ship being attacked but, like the authorities in Hong Kong, the Triad had no precise idea who had actually carried out the attack. If Captain Mariner had killed everyone himself, that was all very well by them. Unlike the police, the Triad knew that the missing cargo was not a fortune in drugs; but if the Triad knew what had actually been in the crates later discovered on Ping Chau Island, then they were not about to act on their knowledge. They were saving themselves up to deal with the next offloading of a China Queens ship at the container port of Kwai Chung. And so, while she was at sea, they had no real way of protecting the second ship or the priceless cargo she carried. Since no one, except the men involved, knew exactly who it was that had come aboard the first ship six weeks earlier and, failing to find what they sought, had carried out an orgy of frustrated revenge, no one, not even the White Powder Triad, knew for certain whether or not these men would return and try again. No one knew for certain but, as Twelvetoes Ho had observed, Richard Mariner knew more than most, if only he could remember what he knew.

It was the itching which aroused Sam Yung. He had not had the opportunity of showering before coming up on watch and the whole of his body seemed to be crawling as his perspiration dried. He looked up at the ship's chronometer above the steersman's head and noted dreamily that it was a little after 1a.m. Scratching thoughtlessly and easing his clothing as he moved, he crossed to the side of the lone man at the helm and peered ahead. The limitless night gathered in front of him, gulping down the deck long before the furthest pile of cargo. There was just enough overcast to wipe away all trace of moon and stars. The quiet sea was not agitated or populated enough to give off any luminescence. Apart from the dully glowing bank of instruments below the clearview and the ghostly reflections in it, Sam might just as well have been blind. It was a lowering thought, and in the grip of an epic bout of post-coital depression, he wondered whether he was in fact losing his sight. 'I'm going out onto the bridge wing,' he informed the helmsman, and crossed to the door.

The night wind outside was much warmer than the air-conditioned bridge, and his itching returned with a vengeance as his sweat glands became active again. He leaned up against the forward rail and strained to see ahead. Slowly, his eyes became more used to the near-absolute darkness and he began to make out the lines of the ship below. Idly, he wandered across to the observation post at the outer corner. Here there was a stand for a pair of night glasses. They were kept in a weatherproof pouch nearby. Sam pulled them out and clicked them home on the stand so that he could scan ahead. As soon as he put them to his eyes, everything for half a kilometre ahead became a kind of luminous green and even the heave of the waves became visible, though slightly out of focus. Little by little Sam extended the range, checking the figures of the range finder up the right edge of his magically enhanced vision, watching with lazy fascination as the green brightness of the multiplied light slowly surrendered to the cloudy black distances a full kilometre ahead. For a while, like a child with a new toy, he stood, trying to make out the detail of anything lying just on the visible edge of his vision.

When the flare ignited almost exactly a kilometre ahead, according to the automatic range-finder, it was precisely in the middle of his vision and it blinded him for some moments while he hopped clumsily about, mumbling in agony and rubbing his eyes. Only when the discomfort began to subside did he realise what the signal must mean. He ran back to the night glasses and scanned ahead again. The flare had gone out while he had been dancing, swearing and rubbing his eyes, but as he peered past the bright area in the centre of his vision, he began to make out the outline of a half-submerged boat. It looked like a Vietnamese sampan but it was hard to tell because little more than the poop and the thatched house halfway along its length were showing above the sluggish green-black surface of the water.

Captain Sin was obviously not best pleased at being woken, but he grudgingly agreed with the third officer that some kind of attempt should be made to check aboard the little craft. A flare obviously meant someone was alive down there, and everyone knew that when the Vietnamese fled, even the meanest of them were likely to come laden with a life's collection of valuables and trade goods. 'You had better wake up the first officer,' commanded Captain Sin. 'This sort of thing is her job; and in any case, she should have been on duty for the last hour.' He went back to sleep, chuckling quietly to himself at his cunning, for he still had no idea that Robin had seen the native traders and their women come aboard.

Neither the captain nor the third officer was particularly struck by the coincidence of two derelict boats being discovered by the two sister ships in more or less identical locations – there had been little reporting about the Vietnamese corpses on the *Sulu Queen* when there were so many other more interesting bodies to write about. There had been no logs recovered to record exactly where the first boat had been found and there had been no radio report of the discovery, for *Sulu Queen*'s equipment had began to malfunction almost immediately after the rescue.

Sam Yung went down to the sickbay and knocked respectfully. There was no reply. Had he known the first officer better, he would have realised that the '1812 Overture', the section where the cannons fire, played on quadraphonic equipment at 600 watts per channel, at full blast, would not make her stir now. Only word of an emergency or the smell of teak-dark breakfast tea could do that. He went in when there was no reply and found her curled on the sickbay cot, fully dressed and dead to the world. He shook her firmly by the shoulder. She snored. 'Mrs Mariner,' he called loudly. She wriggled over onto her other side and snuggled down. She presented a sight he would have enjoyed more had he not used up all of his libido earlier in the evening. 'Number One,' he said, quite quietly, 'there's a wreck ahead and I think there are some survivors aboard.'

'How far ahead?' Her eyes opened as she asked the question.

'Less than a kilometre.'

'Tell the captain.' She was sitting up now, her steady grey eyes firmly on his own.

'The captain sent me to get you. It's your watch.' At his word she looked down at her wrist. The movement of her head made her wince and her hand came up to the gauze bandage.

'It's been my watch for more than an hour.'

'We were going to let you sleep. You had a nasty bang on the head.'

'Who patched me up? The second officer?'

'Fat Chow. He's ship's medic.'

'He seems to have done a good job.' She heaved herself to her feet and tottered. 'Get back onto the bridge and bring the speed down. I'll follow you up in a minute. In the meantime, we'll need a dead stop as soon as possible and the ship's cutter crewed and over the side. If you're on the bridge, I'll want Wai Chan with me. And get Fat Chow too; we may need a good medic.'

In the sickbay's tiny head, Robin tried to organise her thoughts and rationalise her priorities as she allowed her bladder to catch up with more than twelve hours since her last visit. She would have to confront Captain Sin, but she expected little more than a series of more or less plausible excuses for what had gone on during the last twelve hours – nubile natives and all. She would let it ride for a little while and see what had actually resulted from the exploits before risking a confrontation. And she would discuss it with Richard, of course, when...

She flinched as though struck. Richard! She would be lucky to be discussing anything with Richard for a good long time to come. Perhaps the bash on her head had knocked her memory loose too. It was as though she had forgotten Richard's plight and was learning of it for the first time now. That indeed caused her to reassess her priorities.

Christ! How long had it been since she last called in? Her watch informed her that it was after 1a.m. on the morning of Friday the 20th. She had last checked with Hong Kong at noon on Wednesday. Anything could have happened! She took a deep breath and focused on the job at hand, her thoughts lent urgency by the change in the engine note vibrating through every surface around her.

Her first port of call was the bridge to check what Sam Yung had told her, and sure enough, there, gleaming with a ghostly light, was the sampan floating in the night glasses' range. She checked the figures at the side of the display. Half a kilometre out. 'You did well to see it a kilometre away, Sam,' she said to the young officer at her side.

'There was a bright light, some kind of a flare, I think. It nearly burned my eyes out.'

'Really? That's unusual. Isn't it?'

'You can never be sure out here. There's never any telling what will come out of Vietnam. There's so much stuff buried in there still, even twenty years and more after the end of the war, that there's no way of guessing what will come out next. I understand there is a healthy trade even now in mines, ammunition, all sorts of materiel, left behind or just left buried.'

'Even so,' she said, 'you still did well to spot it. Let's hope that whoever lit the flare has the strength to hang on until we can get to them.'

'Right,' said Sam, following her back as she strode across to the bridge proper. 'But take care, please, missy. You be very careful, *yah?*'

Sam Yung's words reawoke her concern about her position here, especially after what she had seen last night. But, typically, she would not let her nervousness slow her down. She would meet each problem as it arose – no sense crossing bridges until she came to them. So, thrusting aside all paranoid suspicions that this might be some elaborate way of getting rid of her, she hurried back down to the weather deck, slipped on the life jacket waiting for her by the rail and then clambered handily over the side, swarming down the Jacob's ladder and into the waiting cutter with a minimum waste of time. Wai Chan and Fat Chow were both waiting for her in the bow and neither of them looked particularly happy with the duty she had handed them. But she was in no mood to put up with ill temper; the pair of them had better jump when she ordered them to move or they would get the rough side of her tongue.

As the cutter pounded out towards the distant derelict, Wai Chan peered ahead through another pair of night glasses and kept up a desultory conversation with Sam Yung who had a better overall view from fifteen metres up on the bridge wing and could guide them to their goal. As she watched and listened, Robin tightened the straps on her life jacket and then lashed a line securely round her waist. Then she took the walkie-talkie and spoke to Sam herself, discussing the circumstances with him and agreeing a course of action. They worked well together. The young third officer was unexpectedly competent in a crisis. Robin handed the radio back to Wai Chan, hoping the lugubrious second officer would prove as reliable.

The current was taking the sinking sampan across the bow of the *Seram Queen* and away to the east. They would never be able to get a light on her from the ship's deck, so whoever went in after the survivors would have to do so in the dark. Robin reached back and caught up a powerful electric lantern. That meant her, of course, and alone at first, until she had discovered the lie of the land, so to speak. Once she was happy that the lantern was working properly, she gave a concise series of orders to the men holding the rope looped round her waist, then a supplementary set of directions to Wai Chan and Fat Chow.

As they came up behind the sampan, Robin shone her lantern onto the dark wood of her waterlogged poop, wondering inconsequentially whether Richard had done the same thing six weeks earlier. It was an idle thought, no more than that; none of them had any idea of the importance Richard's damaged memory attached to his experience of this incident. In fact, it was with no sense of foreboding at all that Robin leaped aboard the little sampan. With nothing beyond an inevitable nervousness about going into a dangerous situation full of imponderable possibilities, she slithered down the deck into the ramshackle shelter amidships. It was typical of her to go charging in, for she believed in confronting fear when she felt it; lingering on the poop would only draw out the inevitable and make the whole thing worse.

The warm water came very nearly up to her waist, but she was too busy with the job in hand to worry about any shark or barracuda which might be cruising close by within it. The lantern's orange beam showed a basic construction of shelves on the walls on either hand and, between the forward part of them, a simple net. On the shelves stretched along their full lengths lay two figures. On the net, caught like fish half out of the water, lay two more. It was immediately obvious that the two figures on the net were dead. They were both women, and they seemed to have suffered some violence. Both were staring fixedly and one of them had her face half under the surface of the water. Robin took a deep breath and started retching as the fetid sweetness of putrefaction washed into her nostrils. Then she turned her lantern onto the nearest figure lying on the right-hand shelf. It was a man of indeterminate age, lying face down. His arm reached off the wooden platform and trailed across the netting. The position gave mute but moving testimony to a failed attempt to support the nearest woman, the one with her face in the water. Robin did not touch the still figure, but thrust her ear close to the half-turned head, hoping to catch the sound of breathing, or the cool draught of a breath upon her cheek. There was nothing. With a sinking heart, she crossed to the fourth figure, the one on the left. This, too, was a man, a young one, scarcely more than a boy. He lay on his back, apparently as lifeless as the others. His face was swollen, as though it had been punched repeatedly. His cheeks were full, but their skin was pale, waterlogged. His nose was flat. His mouth thrust out like a monkey's, the lips encrusted with salt sores. But there was telltale black on his half-closed fist which told of a flare, held until it burned him and he dropped it. His eyes were closed, but in the sudden brightness of the beam, they flickered.

Robin put the walkie-talkie to her lips and said, 'Please come aboard, Mr Chow. You have some work to do here.'

It was 03:00 before the dead women had been respectfully put in the cold store which some practical ship's architect had designed to sit behind the main refrigeration unit but to open into the back of the sickbay. The two men, at death's door but still just alive, were safely in that same sickbay so recently vacated by the watch officer herself. Fat Chow was indeed a good medic and the sun-scorched, salt-burned, dehydrated bodies had been bathed and dressed. Their dry, parched, salt-raw mouths had been rinsed with distilled water, but they had been allowed only the tiniest amount to drink for fear of inducing vomiting. They were on glucose and saline drips, resting securely as their bodies soaked up liquid and nourishment directly through their veins.

The captain, informed formally by Robin that they were safely aboard and informally by Fat Chow that there had been no valuables worth salvaging, suggested that the morning would be soon enough to try pan-medic calls though Robin doubted it would come to that. If they lasted the night, then the emergency would be past; if they did not then it was too late to bother with a doctor anyway. She made up the logs, wondering whether to be vexed with Captain Sin or not. Pan-medic calls could come very expensive indeed, and the survivors showed no sign of having insurance. Robin was all too well aware that *Seram Queen*'s insurance was unlikely to cover a call-out under these circumstances – Sin could well have saved the company many thousands of pounds. But the exercise was not cynically Thatcherite. She had heard Fat Chow reporting his belief that the men, miraculously, would pull through; and she was inclined to believe him. They both seemed to have been beaten up and subjected to many days without food and water, and they both were suffering from severe exposure, but their hearts seemed strong and neither of them was having any trouble breathing.

What had happened to the women, however, she did not wish to guess. Their physical state was very much worse and as she arranged the bodies, she could not help noticing several deep wounds which no doubt explained the almost total lack of blood in the bodies. This was unusual and it triggered another association in her memory. The Vietnamese women on *Sulu Queen* had been virtually bloodless as well. But it was only an association, not an alarm. The state of the women's bodies was so unpleasant, it spoke so graphically of an agonising and protracted end, that their bloodlessness seemed relatively unimportant.

Fat Chow agreed to keep checking on the patients and to post a permanent nursing watch if need be. Robin went up onto the bridge and made up the logs. Somnolent with the shock of finding and handling two corpses and with latent concussion as well as the effects of Fat Chow's drugs, she kept her watch until Wai Chung relieved her, as agreed, at 06:00. Then, with the morning watches dogged instead of the evening ones, she went to bed and slept like the dead until 10:00.

It was during this sleep that Captain Sin himself oversaw the morning radio report to head office in Hong Kong and ensured that nothing untoward was recorded, although Radio Officer Yuk Tso warned him that, because of his interference, the broadcast was going out half an hour behind schedule. Captain Sin calculated that if he established that everything – apart from the temporary breakdown in the Paracels, already written up in the engine room log as water contamination in the fuel jets – had gone quite normally, then even if Mrs Mariner had noticed anything yesterday evening, he could always say it was some kind of hallucination. He and Fat Chow had discussed this and it seemed like a good idea.

Such was the captain's desire to establish absolute normality of progress, therefore, that he decided four Vietnamese boat people could wait to be reported too, especially as two were obviously dead and the other two seemed very little more than dead – though both men had survived so far. Of all the mistakes he made on the voyage as a whole, this, seemingly the slightest, was by far the most disastrous.

Robin awoke at 10a.m., clear-headed, though with a lingering headache which centred itself on the crown of her skull whenever she moved too quickly. She showered and dressed, then for some reason she would never understand, she checked that the gun Edgar Tan had given her was still safely in place. Having done so, she washed her hands assiduously, twice, fearing that the odour of gun oil might give the game away. She was hungry as a horse, and so she reported to the galley first, on the lookout for some late breakfast. The ship was run to a clear timetable. Breakfast was long past. But it would take a brave chief catering officer to argue with a first mate as determined and as ravenous as Robin. And, for once, the chief steward was not around to back him up.

By 10:45 local time, with her tummy full of fried egg sandwiches and her temper in better repair, Robin went in search of the captain. He was not on the bridge. Sam Yung was, however, sound asleep in the watchkeeper's chair and alone as, with daylight, the captain had ordered the automatic steering gear switched in. Robin shook the young officer increasingly fiercely until he roused, sleepy and grumpy, trying to scratch his crotch without making it too obvious. Robin promised to relieve the third officer in due course and plunged below to see the captain. She had half expected to be greeted by Fat Chow's snarling face at the door, but no. Captain Sin was in his day room, and he did not have the fortitude to keep his first officer out without his chief steward's support.

'What is it that you require, Number One?'

'Tell me about yesterday evening, Captain.'

'What you mean?'

'You know very well what I mean. By sunset last night this ship was awash with natives from the Paracel Islands. They were wearing very little and making a lot of very close friends amongst your crew.'

'I do not know what you mean. This was, I am sure, some kind of an hallucination. From the blow to your head.'

'Oh, come on, Captain!'

'Or from the painkilling drugs with which you were treated. You ask Fat Chow. He warned me something like this might happen.'

'You mean to tell me that Fat Chow said, "I'm just going to give the first officer some painkillers now, Captain, but don't be surprised if she suddenly thinks the ship is full of naked Paracel islanders bonking the brains out of the crew"?'

'You find Fat Chow; you ask him, missy!'

'Well, Captain Sin, I think I shall do just that!'

But Fat Chow was not so easily found. After a cursory search for the chief steward, Robin became sucked into first officer duties and by midday she was back up on the bridge, relieving Sam Yung for the afternoon watch. It was only after he had thundered down to get some lunch that Robin realised the obvious: if Fat Chow was nowhere to be found in his usual haunts, then perhaps he was still tending the Vietnamese men. Perhaps he had even set up his own nursing watch on them.

Robin at once called the sickbay on the internal phone but there was no reply. She stood the first hour of her watch, brooding over the fact that she might have misjudged the grumpy little chief steward and the fact that she had definitely been derelict in her duty. As first officer it was she, and not the chief steward, who was ship's medical officer. She should have been in charge of the treatment of the sick men, or at the very least fully apprised of what was happening to them. She should have arranged a round-the-clock watch on the sick men herself and a regular pattern of reports on their welfare.

By 13:00 Robin was so restless that when the unfortunate Sam Yung, also unable to find Fat Chow, came onto the bridge to ask a question about personal itching, she handed over to him instead of answering him, and vanished below. But Fat Chow was nowhere to be found in the sickbay.

Now that she was here, Robin thought to salve her conscience a little and check the patients for vital signs. Although they both remained comatose, their heartbeats were strong, their respiration seemed normal and their dark eyes reacted to light when the lids were rolled gently back. The only thing which seemed to have gone wrong was that the young one, the one with the burned hand, had pulled his drips loose. Although he was lying perfectly still now, he had obviously been restless at some time. She reinserted the needles into his arm and fastened the tape over them. Then, with a glance around the little room, she went about her business again.

Sam Yung obviously wanted to chat about something but she gave him no chance. As soon as she reached the bridge again, she sent him below with the specific mission of finding Fat Chow and setting up with him a regular watch on the Vietnamese. Or, if the chief steward remained hard to find, to select six sensible sailors and arrange a watch himself. The third officer went with an ill grace, and Robin served out the rest of his watch. There was a lot to do. She made up the logs, leaving a space in which she would in due course insert the goings-on in the Paracels; detailing the rescue of the Vietnamese, and describing the condition of the two survivors. She wrote up their position and their progress since the engines had been fixed. She plotted their exact position at noon, and duly assumed her own proper watch. And, now that normality was re-established, she crossed to the radio shack at 12:10 precisely to put through a call to Hong Kong and find out how her beloved husband was.

By 12:15 Robin began to suspect that there was something wrong with the radio, but it was nothing as simple as a loss of power. The set seemed to be on and to be operating normally; had she not been trying to use it she would probably have noticed nothing untoward. But no matter what combination of buttons her practised fingers pushed, no matter what dials and displays she checked and reset, the radio would not respond to her. Doggedly, increasingly irritably, she kept this up until 12:30 when she gave in and sent for Radio Officer Yuk Tso.

Yuk Tso spent much of the rest of Robin's watch fiddling with the equipment, tutting with confusion. He went through the same routines which Robin had already tried, with her standing at his shoulder telling him she had tried that and she had told him so. Then he went through a rather more complex series of routines, still with no result. Finally he took out the manual, and Robin knew that this would take some time. She returned to her watch out on the bridge and busied herself about her duties while Yuk Tso took bits of the radio out and checked them; he removed one or two down to the workshop, but nothing he could do seemed to make any difference. 'I don't know what it is,' he admitted to her at last. 'Could anyone have come in here and fiddled with this stuff?'

'Who?' asked the irritated Robin. 'Why?'

'I do not know, missy. But this just not right.'

'There's been an officer on watch in here at all times.'

Yuk Tso shook his head. 'Something wrong somewhere. But I can find nothing...' By 15:00 he had stopped fiddling with the equipment and began to trace the wiring. He double-checked all the power lines, then he began to trace the aerial conduit round the room and up to the port-side wall. 'Well,' he announced at 16:00 as Wai Chan appeared to take up his watch accompanied by the captain who was ready to oversee the evening radio link, 'the radio is still dead, and I can find nothing wrong inside.'

'Maybe something's wrong outside?' suggested Robin, and wished at once that she had held her tongue.

From 16:15 until sunset she accompanied the deeply confused radio officer as he traced the aerial conduit up the outside of the bridgehouse. Privately as she fumed over landing herself with such a tedious and time-consuming duty, she thought that if there had been any damage done out here then it served Captain Sin right for filling the ship with natives in the night. At no time did it occur to her that the Vietnamese might have been involved. It was a long, long time later before she put together the disappearance of the chief steward, the loose drip feeds and the damaged equipment. But by then so much else was going on that her discoveries seemed hardly important.

In the meantime she toiled up the bridgehouse, helping the radio officer as best she could, doing a job which the meanest of the GP seamen would have been able to do as well as she. By 18:30 the pair of them were right up at the top of the radio mast, the better part to twenty-five metres above the surface of the water as the evening closed down through sunset, salmon-pink and rose, massive, calm and breathtaking. Standing on the little platform, perhaps four metres square, with her back to one narrow set of steps, looking at Yuk Tso standing atop another set, fiddling with the last few metres of aerial, she had ample opportunity to look around, savouring the dusty grey tones filtering into the French blue of the sea and sky, watching the way in which the last of the sunlight bled out of the air on one hand while the indigo armies of the shadows massed on the other, pulling the dark horizons in towards the ship like a massive tidal wave.

Just as the dark seemed to break over the ship and Yuk Tso announced that there was nothing more to do and they should give up and go back down, Robin saw, somewhere out to the south-east of them, away at the very foundation of that rushing wave of night, a bright burning light which flashed and was extinguished, as though some secret ship was signalling there, just on the very horizon. And, for some reason she could not fathom, the sight of it made her hair stir and her blood run cold.

Chapter Thirty-Two

Maggie rose majestically, at ten past one next afternoon, Friday, 20 June.

'My Lord,' she began, 'ladies and gentlemen of the jury. It is most fitting, I believe, that here and now, in the last days of the rule of British law in the Crown Colony, we should see it functioning in its purest form.

'As you are aware, the adversarial system which stands at the heart of British common law is based upon an ancient and elegantly simple premise, that the prosecution and the defence present evidence, witness and testimony to a jury of clear-thinking men and women such as yourselves; peers, as it is said, of the accused. Each advocate seeks to present these things, to prove, to explain and to interpret them in such a way that the jury can have little or no doubt of the innocence or guilt of the accused, subject only to direction by the learned judge on relevant points of law. The jury then must decide their verdict, unanimously and, as the celebrated phrase has it, beyond a reasonable doubt.

'But of course life is never that simple. There are often conflicts within each case. These will often be revealed, indeed, by the process called cross-examination. Evidence may not stand up to scrutiny; expert testimony can be called into doubt; witnesses can be shown to have misremembered and on occasion they can be proved to have perjured themselves.

'Most notably, also, the explanations given by the accused and the victim to the jury can weigh very heavily in their minds, more heavily than all the testimony and evidence adduced elsewhere. And, finally, the appeal to their critical and logical faculties made by the prosecution or the defence can vary for any number of extraneous reasons. The whim of tabloid editors and programme presenters; the race, the gender, the profession, the social standing of the accused; his dress, his looks, the colour of his eyes or hair.

'How fortunate we are, therefore, to be dealing with a case where there is almost no dispute about the major facts, for, as things stand, there will be no direct evidence from anyone actually involved in these events at all. Even the accused man, Captain Richard Mariner, having been severely wounded in the head by those men who might have been assumed to be his rescuers, has no current memory whatsoever of the dreadful events which make up the case against him. Everything, therefore, depends, purely and absolutely, upon the interpretation you, the jury, put upon the facts – largely undisputed, as I say – and the manner in which these facts may be interpreted.'

Maggie paused here, looking round the court, letting her golden gaze settle on each juror, before she turned and glanced at the judge.

'Ladies and gentlemen,' Maggie continued, 'what you are asked by the prosecution to believe is this. That Captain Mariner went on board the *Sulu Queen*, perhaps with the desire in his mind to kill everybody aboard. That, during the voyage towards Hong Kong, he decided that he definitely would kill everybody aboard. And that, finally, on the night of Thursday, 8 May, he acted with the full intention of killing or grievously wounding everyone aboard.

'All of the weapons he used, ladies and gentlemen, we must expect him to have smuggled for the purpose either out of England or in from Singapore, one of the most carefully controlled societies in the world with regard to the supply and smuggling of guns. Or perhaps the prosecution is going to ask you to believe that, coming aboard with these murderous thoughts harboured within his breast, Captain Mariner was fortunate enough to find this striking range of weapons already concealed on the ship and convenient to his hand. Or even – though I find my own credulity beginning to stretch quite painfully here – the prosecution may ask you to believe that the captain arranged for a gang of mysterious confederates to appear out of the night, supply the weapons, perhaps even aid him in his gruesome task, and vanish again leaving no discernible trace. For, I ask you to recall, ladies and gentlemen, in fact I ask you never to forget, that in order to prove their case of murder, the prosecution must establish that Captain Mariner *planned* to do these things, *meant* to do them, saw an *opportunity* to do them and then actually *did* them; in cold blood and while of sound mind, with or without help. Each murder as charged, with each or all of the weapons named, must have been done by him or on his order. It must have been planned to some extent beforehand, it must have been done on purpose, not by accident, and it must have been done with full intent by a man of sound mind. If the actions of a person accused of murder do not fit into these categories, *all of these categories*, then he is not guilty of the crime. The prosecution ask you to believe one of the propositions I have already put to you, or something very like it; they ask you to believe that there is no other explanation, and that, beyond a reasonable doubt, Captain Mariner stands guilty as charged.' Maggie, her throat dried by her carefully calculated oratory, reached down to the table behind which she was standing and took a sip of water. Once again, her eyes were on the jury. She was not addressing these remarks to anyone other than them, and was taking the opportunity to establish eye contact and a basic relationship, hopefully a sympathetic one, with each of them. With her eyes fastened on the plump, perspiring face of a particularly susceptible young man in the front row, she continued her opening address.

'But what are the actual facts with which we are dealing here? They may be simply recounted. A little less than two months ago the Mariner family set off for a spring holiday. Captain Mariner stayed behind to finish some business while his wife drove up to Carlisle with their twins, six-year-olds, a boy and a girl. They all planned to meet up at her father's home near Carlisle and to drive north in a day or so. Instead of her husband she received a brief message that he had been called to Singapore on business and would contact her. That contact failed to materialise or was destroyed.

'Although he has no memory of what actually called him out, or what he did when he got there, we have established that, within a day of his arrival in Singapore, Captain Mariner was aboard the *Sulu Queen*, a ship owned by his own company who have recently acquired control of the China Queens Company which has run this ship and her sister ship for some years in the local area. On the very moment of sailing, *Sulu Queen*'s original captain, Walter Gough, was carried off, apparently with peritonitis, and vanished from Singapore General Hospital.

'Captain Gough appears to have vanished from the whole of Singapore, in fact, apparently in company with the secretary of the China Queens Company. This lady, who worked under the alias of Anna Leung, was a complete mystery until earlier testimony explained that she was, in fact, an undercover police operative. Her motives remain a mystery to us – as does the reason why she failed to deliver a range of important messages.

'Within days, as she came north towards Hong Kong, the *Sulu Queen* was out of radio contact. We know that somewhere along the line she picked up some Vietnamese people, women and children – dead women and children. There the facts we know about activity on the *Sulu Queen* herself, stop.

'But then we learn of a mysterious message to the naval contingent coastguards section here in Hong Kong telling of an apparently derelict ship drifting without power into Hong Kong waters. The Navy disguises itself, no doubt to avoid any chance of diplomatic incident with your near neighbours the People's Republic of China, and goes aboard. And, as we know – as the whole world now knows – the Navy finds aboard some forty-five corpses. They find only one man alive in that charnel house and so they shoot him in the head and destroy his memory. Then, while he is unable to enter any plea of his own because of the damage they did to him, the authorities accuse the survivor of murdering everyone else. Except, that is, for the unfortunate Vietnamese!

'And so we stand here ready to consider this case with almost none of the facts disputed, with much of the evidence agreed and with no witnesses – without even one word of testimony from the accused – to cloud our deliberations. But while the defence disputes almost none of the facts in this case, we do most certainly dispute almost every interpretation the prosecution has put upon those facts. We absolutely and bluntly refute the charges the prosecution alleges arise out of those interpretations, and it is our hope and our belief that we will cause you, ladies and gentlemen of the jury, to doubt those interpretations also and to dismiss these ridiculous charges out of hand.'

There was a ripple of something very like applause as Maggie took another sip of water, but a glare from Mr Justice Fang brought silence swiftly back. Then Maggie looked up, took a deep breath, and opened the defence case proper.

'First, My Lord, I would like to call Dr Thomas Fowler, Consulting Psychologist to the Psychiatric Unit at the Maudsley Hospital, London.'

As Tom made his way to the stand, Maggie DaSilva stood, apparently the personification of cool confidence, trying to disguise from the jury the fact that she was feeling a little faint.

'Now, Dr Fowler,' Maggie said after having established Tom's identity and credentials, 'I would like you to describe the mental state of the accused as far as you understand it.'

'Captain Mariner is emerging from a state of hysterical amnesia. He already seems to me to have emerged from a deeper state of physiological amnesia caused by a blow to his left temporal lobe.'

'Lets be absolutely clear about this, Doctor. Captain Mariner was originally the subject of a physical amnesia caused by a blow to his head?'

'That is correct. There was a large bruise in his left temple, with a great deal of short-term tissue damage immediately behind it.'

'And we have heard in evidence already that this was caused by an anti-personnel round, fired during his arrest,' Maggie slipped in.

'I am not competent to comment on that though I understand that this was indeed the case,' concurred Tom solidly.

'But the captain has now recovered from the effects of this blow?'

'I believe so.'

'And yet, in your expert opinion, Doctor, he is still subject to amnesia?'

'I believe that the captain was already in a state of hysterical amnesia, almost a fugue state, when he was hit on the head. Even though he has recovered from his injury, he is nevertheless still subject to the psychological state.'

'Could you please clarify the terms "hysterical amnesia" and "fugue state" for the jury.'

'Hysterical amnesia has nothing to do with the popular conception of hysteria. We are all, I expect, familiar with the Victorian idea of the hysterical woman who only needs a good slap to calm her down. Hysterical amnesia is very much more complex and dangerous than this. It occurs when a subject experiences something so terrible that he or she simply cannot accept that it has happened and refuses to remember anything about it or anything to do with it. In such a state the patient usually retains a sense of personal identity, his own general and expert knowledge and all his high motor functions.

'In a fugue state, however, not only is the specific memory expunged, but so is all memory of personality, of past experience and acquaintance, much past knowledge and some higher functions of the brain. The fugue sufferer classically simply vanishes from his old life, assumes a new identity and makes a new life somewhere else. Cases of fugue state, popular though they are in fiction, are in fact very rare but those few fully documented have only been discovered when someone in the fugue state, who has assumed a new life and a new identity, suddenly recalls his original identity and finds himself in a place he does not recognise among people he does not know even though he may have been known to them in his new identity for years.'

'So fugue states may in fact be more common than we realise simply because a high percentage of people simply never come out of the fugue?'

'It is tempting to assume this, especially given the number of people each year who vanish without trace. But we have no way to test such an hypothesis. It seems to me, however, that Captain Mariner, certainly in the grip of hysterical amnesia of the sort familiar from the battlefield and from road accidents particularly, may have formed a new identity, that of the Survivor, shortly before he was hit in the head by Captain Huuk's anti-personnel round. He was technically in a fugue state, therefore, when he suffered damage to the left temporal lobe of his brain and lost his memory for the second time.'

'Have you ever come across a case like this before, Doctor?'

'When a man who is already suffering a psychological loss of memory is hit on the head and suffers a physiological loss also? No, not personally. But there are known battlefield cases like this and in Captain Mariner's case, it is the only hypothesis which fits the circumstances.'

Lata sat in the public section of the court and watched her colleague work. She had been so closely involved in the construction of the case that each twist and turn, each stop along the golden thread of logic, came like the line in a familiar play – expected but oddly striking – exciting. While she had been a part of the construction of the case, however, there had never been any question of her representing Richard in court – the Hong Kong bar had found it hard enough to swallow Maggie herself. And yet Lata felt she was performing an important function. In the midst of the audience to this terrifying piece of theatre, she was able to keep her finger on the pulse of public reaction – to report back to Maggie her thoughts on how testimony was being received; and, perhaps most importantly, to stand as an obvious point of contact should Twelvetoes Ho have anything further to add. For they were all acutely aware that, useful though Twelvetoes' help was, there was no way for them to bring anything he told them into court.

'Now, Dr Fowler, you have said that hysterical amnesia and the fugue state most commonly occur when the individual in question is confronted with something which he simply cannot accept. Does the unacceptable vary, in your opinion?'

'It certainly does. Effectively, it varies from person to person.'

'And, in your expert opinion, what is most likely to prove absolutely unacceptable to Captain Mariner?'

'The captain seems to me to be possessed of a classic dominant personality. It is most likely, therefore, that the unacceptable is likely to arise from some overwhelmingly horrific circumstances over which he has no control.'

'Such as a number of people coming aboard his command, for instance, and killing his crew in spite of his attempts to stop the slaughter?'

'Indeed. Precisely so.'

Even Andrew was aware of the stirring in the court as Tom answered this question. This was the first crucial point – the establishment in the jury's mind that other people may indeed have come aboard – as the defence team were now convinced they had. He dragged his gaze away from Maggie's reed-straight form and looked across to Mr Justice Fang who was looking, narrow-eyed, at the beautiful barrister, clearly calculating whether to let the assertion stand. Surreptitiously, Andrew wiped suddenly damp palms against his trouser-thighs. Maggie had paused for a heart-beat. Now she plunged on.

'Is it possible that the loss of control was actually a loss of *self*-control? I mean, if he is mentally running away, is it not possible that he is running away from a situation created by his own loss of self-control?'

'I would have thought that extremely unlikely. It is the strength of his self-control which makes the captain so firm in his control over everyday situations.'

'Are you aware, Doctor, that the captain was diagnosed as being a potential alcoholic more than twenty years ago?'

'Yes, I am.'

'How are you aware of this, Doctor?'

'I have examined all the medical notes which form a part of his company file for Heritage Mariner.'

'And how is that knowledge relevant to this case, Doctor?'

'The captain cured himself by exercise of his self-control. According to his notes, he has not had an alcoholic drink since nineteen seventy-four.'

'So, Doctor, if we rule out any breakdown in his self-control, then how can this cataclysmic loss of control over the situation be explained?'

'In my opinion, only by the exercise of some extremely powerful external influence. I can see no other explanation.'

Andrew rubbed his palms on his thighs again as both Po and Fang looked up. The prosecution had been in possession of transcripts of this evidence for a while but no one in the prosecutor's office had calculated the emphasis Tom was going to place on that word *external* influence. They were back to the theme of pirates slipping aboard. And, with Twelvetoes' conversation with Lata to go on, they had sight of a reason *why* the ship might be attacked. But even as these thoughts entered Andrew's head, so they were driven out by thoughts of Maggie herself and of the glorious body which lay beneath the shapeless, formal High Court robes. His hands stayed moist but his mouth went dry.

Maggie, her nerves at full stretch, worked harder than she had ever done to wring from Tom's rock-solid performance every ounce of material her case could use, alert to every objection Mr Po might raise, anticipating every weakness the prosecution might exploit. Four thirty came and went, and even Maggie was beginning to wilt when a bit of a stir was caused by the arrival of a newcomer to the defence benches.

No doubt because his office hours were over, but glowing with excitement for all that, Andrew Balfour's partner Gerry Stephenson arrived. Grudgingly allowed onto the defence benches by the court officials, Gerry drew the ire of Mr Justice Fang by holding an animated if whispered conversation with Andrew. Long practised in courtroom etiquette, however, Gerry had finished his conversation before the judge felt compelled to rebuke him. At once all the eyes in the crowded courtroom switched to Andrew as he began to gesture in an increasingly urgent pantomime, trying to attract Maggie's attention.

'So,' she was saying, 'in your expert submission, Doctor, the fact that the accused is supposed not only to have handled the three murder weapons but to have used them during what must have been an extended period absolutely rules out the Crown's supposition of a cataclysmic loss of self-control.'

'Just so. Indeed it does.'

'In short, it would require a full and calculating maintenance of self-control to take a handgun and shoot several people, then to exchange it for a semi-automatic weapon and slaughter many more, then to take a panga and finish off the rest before reclaiming the original handgun and preparing to attack Captain Huuk and his men with it?'

'Undoubtedly so. There is no question in my mind but that these actions could not possibly have been completed by Captain Mariner under such circumstances as the Crown suggests.'

Maggie, her throat raw, reached down for a drink of water. As she stood, the glass to her lips and her eyes on her opposite number, a strange sort of Chinese whisper swept through the defence bench until it came to her ear.

After a moment, Maggie replaced her glass with a *click* which brought every eye in the courtroom upon her. She turned towards Judge Fang.

'My Lord,' she said quietly, 'I apply for leave to introduce the testimony of two witnesses who have just contacted the defence.'

'My Lord...' Po was up, but the judge overrode him.

'What witnesses, Ms DaSilva?'

'Captain Walter Gough and Miss Anna Leung, My Lord. I am informed that they will be here in Hong Kong within the hour.'

A stunned silence filled the courtroom. Mr Justice Fang looked at the two counsels standing before him. He looked across at the jury and then up at the faces in the public gallery. Then he looked at his watch. 'It will be too late to hear any more testimony tonight, Ms DaSilva,' he said, dropping every considered word like a stone into the well of silence. 'But under the circumstances, and with apologies to the ladies and gentlemen of the jury, we will reconvene here at nine thirty tomorrow morning.'

Tom Fowler was like a wet rag by the time he got to the little consulting room for that evening's session with Richard. This time, he was not surprised to observe, Dr Chu and Captain Huuk were going to keep him company and to take careful notes. 'Well,' began Tom, spreading the chart across the table once again, 'that's certainly good news about Wally and Anna turning up, isn't it?'

Richard looked at him, narrow-eyed, as though trying to assess whether the doctor was serious or not.

'You do remember who they are?' asked Tom, smoothing out the chart.

'Walter Gough, captain of the *Sulu Queen*,' recited Richard as though by rote.

'So, you remember the testimony about him. But do you remember the man himself? You've known each other for a while, by all accounts.' Tom's eyes flashed up from the chart. 'Has he got blue eyes or brown?' he demanded.

Richard shook his head. His whole body seemed to slump a little. He was clearly giving up the effort to remember. Tom felt sympathetic. He would have liked to have given up himself. But neither of them had the option.

'What about Anna Leung, then? Nobody can give us much of a lead on her. There are no up-to-date photos. Apart from Walter Gough, you're the only one to have seen her. Black hair?'

'I think so.'

'No prizes for that one, old chap. With a name like that she's not going to be a Nordic blonde is she? Eyes brown?'

'Yes. I...'

'Broad cheekbones, medium height, wide nose?'

'*Yes!*'

Tom's gaze flicked across to Daniel Huuk and Dr Chu. 'I bet this rings a bell with you two as well.'

Neither of them said anything.

'So, we've narrowed the description to any one of a quarter of a billion Asiatic women. Wally's hair brown?'

'White.'

'Anna wear much personal jewellery?'

'Jade ring.'

'Wally a tall chap, like yourself?'

'Shorter. Five ten. I...'

Neither Huuk nor Chu moved or made a sound, but Tom's concentration faltered and the impetus went out of the inquisition. Richard, who had begun to pull himself upright, his face coming alive with the realisation that he was *remembering*, started to sag once again.

Watching the blue eyes lose their sparkle and the great shoulders begin to hunch, Tom gave himself a swift mental shake and hit his client with everything he had.

'I have bad news,' began the psychologist again. '*Seram Queen* is out of contact. We haven't been able to get through to her with your warning and she hasn't made her usual routine contact at four o'clock.'

Richard's face was stunned, as though Tom had hit him physically instead of mentally. Tom persisted, hoping to knock things loose with his brutally jolly words. 'Still, she's only twelve hours out; or rather she would be, except that she lost nearly twelve hours when she broke down in the Paracel Islands on Wednesday. Did I tell you about that? That would put her about here.' Tom's finger prodded the chart to the north of the Paracel Islands where a big circular compass rose was marked in fine purple print.

'No!' Richard's face was white. The word was more than an answer, it was a horrified denial. His eyes were fastened on the white chart as though something truly dreadful were figured there.

'That's right. She must still be, what, twenty hours out.' Tom made a rough measurement by stretching his fingers apart. 'John Shaw has her booked into Kwai Chung at four o'clock tomorrow, apparently,' he continued. 'Just in time for us to catch up with what Captain Sin would have said on his normal afternoon broadcast. Just in time for you to have a nice cup of tea with that lovely wife of yours.' Once again the psychologist's wise eyes looked up from the chart, catching Richard's open, honest, anxious stare. 'Of course I did tell you we haven't heard from *Robin* since Wednesday?'

'NO!'

'No, of course, there wasn't an opportunity last night, was there? And we had better things to talk about this lunchtime. Still, I expect she's all right. Captain Sin was on this morning, just before the radio went down, and I'm sure he would have mentioned if anything had happened either to her or to the ship. No mention of Vietnamese, either, alive or dead. But it's odd that the radio just went off like that. We've checked the equipment at our end, of course. No problem there. And I know Captain Huuk's people have tried to contact *Seram Queen* too, haven't they, Captain?'

Richard swung round, his face working, taking in the Chinese captain's presence for the first time. 'We tried,' said Huuk. 'No joy. Their equipment is down all right. But on the other hand, we've received no distress calls either.'

Richard's eyes stayed fastened on the Chinese officer's face. 'You won't,' he said, with dull defeated, certainty. 'There'll be no calls from *Sulu Queen*. No calls from *Sulu Queen*.'

'No,' said Huuk gently. 'You're confused, Captain. We've had no calls from the *Seram Queen*. And no mysterious phone calls about her either, yet,' he added in little more than a whisper.

Richard's face was folded in a frown. Guessing that he was having trouble separating the two ships in his still faulty memory, Tom repeated what Huuk had said. 'Not the *Sulu Queen*, Richard. *Sulu Queen* was your ship; *Seram Queen* is Robin's. *Sulu, Seram*. See?'

'*Sulu, Seram. Sulu, Seram. SULU, SERAM*!' Richard's voice rose in agonised distress.

The three other men in the room rose, fearing that the massive patient was about to slip into uncontrolled violence, but instead Richard sat, shaking, only his self-control keeping his massive torso still, like a strait-jacket. As the three men looked down at him, the great, long-fingered, square-knuckled hands closed like talons on the chart, crushing the thick paper as though it was tissue. '*Sulu* and *Seram*,' he said more quietly. '*Seram* and *Sulu*.' He turned, slowly, forcefully, like an unstoppable automaton, thrusting out the crumpled chart towards Huuk, the only other sailor in the room. There was a truly terrifying intensity on his face, but when he spoke, his trembling, forceful tones imparted something which at first sounded like little more than a child's doggerel. 'The ships are the same. *Seram. Sulu*. You came aboard at the Wenwei Zhou!'

'What is that?' demanded Tom, his voice scarcely less intense than Richard's. 'What is the Wenwei Zhou?'

'It's a light. The light off Macau. The first light going into the Pearl River estuary, up towards the Tiger Gate and Guangzhou,' said Daniel

Huuk, his voice filling with wonder. 'And he's right. He's remembered perfectly. That's exactly where I went aboard the *Sulu Queen*, somewhere south of the Wenwei Zhou.'

'And he thinks that what happened to the *Sulu Queen* there is going to happen to the *Seram Queen* as well. Can't you see that?'

'But it can't though, can it?' said Huuk, his voice like thistledown. 'Because *he* won't be aboard her, will he?'

Robin was on the bridge at nineteen thirty, at about the same time as Huuk made this accusation. She was craning over the circular bowl of the collision alarm radar with Second Officer Wai Chan at her side. 'There was something out there, I'm certain of it,' she said. 'Down there on the south-eastern horizon. It was just a flash of light, but it was so intense. Can we put this up to maximum range?'

'The outer rimit become furry on maximum, missy. You be fortunate to see a supertanker at that range.'

She tried anyway.

'What is it you see?' he asked.

'No idea. Something bright, like I said. Maybe a signal; maybe a reflection. There aren't many lights down there.'

'Woorry Island?' he hazarded. 'Noff Reef?'

'I don't think so. Further east. Hainan Dao?'

He hissed his disbelief. She tended to agree. They were too far from the great island in the Tonkin Gulf for her to see the Beishi Dao light off its nearest coast. Either way, there was nothing to be described on the radar. To all intents and purposes they seemed to be utterly alone out here. And that thought, in the circumstances, was so unsettling that when the emergency siren blared, she nearly jumped out of her skin.

She crossed straight to the telephone and dialled the captain's cabin.

'*Wai?*'

'It's the first officer, Captain.'

'I call lifeboat drill.'

'Very well, sir. Is there any specific reason?'

'Still no sign Fat Chow. Fat Chow taken afternoon off before, but Fat Chow never missed bringing my evening meal at nineteen thirty. Never before. I call lifeboat drill then "Man Overboard" maybe.'

Robin took a deep breath. If Fat Chow had gone overboard, he could have gone as long as ten hours earlier. Calling Man Overboard now was not going to help anyone, least of all the chief steward. Ten hours. He would be, quite literally, shark bait. If the barracuda hadn't got him first. Particularly as, she now remembered all too vividly, the man had cut himself quite badly looking for valuables in the Vietnamese sampan. 'Captain!' she snapped.

Robin's thoughts had flowed so fast, Sin was still hanging on. 'Yes?' he answered.

'Do you want the men in the sickbay moved to lifeboats? They haven't been assigned places yet.'

'No. Leave them. Everyone else up and out.'

'Yes, Captain.'

Alone of all the crew, except for Wai Chan who was on watch, Fat Chow did not show up at his lifeboat place. If he was aboard, he was incapacitated somehow. 'Organise a search,' ordered Sin.

'Yes, Captain,' answered Robin at once. I will order Wai Chan to keep his watch until the search is over. The engineers will search their own areas and the cargo decks below. Sam Yung and I will take the GP seamen to search the weather deck and the bridgehouse. We will report back to you as soon as we are finished, Captain.'

'Thank you, missy. Please to proceed.'

She had to rely very heavily on Wai Chan and Sam Yung to detail reliable teams. Although she had the experienced officer's facility for remembering names and faces, it was far beyond even her capacity to differentiate between all the dark-haired, broad-cheeked, long-eyed Asiatic faces after only four days. All the seamen and most of the officers were at first glance indistinguishable, a collection of wiry men in white boiler suits. But, taking the advice of her number two and number three officers, Robin soon got things sorted out and for the next hour or so the whole place was a bustle of men working singly, in pairs and in teams, hurrying hither and yon in their frustrating, fruitless search.

Within the hour it was clear that the chief steward was nowhere obvious aboard. Robin accepted reports from the other team leaders and then reported to the captain herself. Captain Sin was strongly of the opinion that they should declare Man Overboard, but Robin persuaded him that it would be useless to do so. On the other hand, in order to seal the bargain, she had to agree that, as soon as her men had gulped down a late supper, she should take them out again, to search all the places which had not been checked so far; for this was a large ship and there were many places in which a small man might end up hidden, either on purpose or by accident.

Robin herself did not get the chance for a sedentary supper. Grabbing a sandwich, she went along to the sickbay. If Fat Chow had been missing for more than ten hours, then she herself must have been the last person with any medical expertise to check on the Vietnamese. She was not unduly worried for she knew that Sam Yung's nursing watch would have alerted her if there had been anything to worry about. But when she reached the sickbay, she found the two patients unattended. They were both still comatose, but they had clearly been looked after in her absence. Full bedpans had been placed in the surgery in front of the doors of the cold storage containing the dead women. The beds showed signs of having been disturbed and hastily remade. Both men seemed to have had their drips replaced again and she checked the needles once more. The crooks of both arms were bleeding slightly, but neither showed any great evidence of blood loss. 'You ought to be waking up soon,' Robin told the men as she bathed their torsos with cool water and wet their lips with distilled water once again. Then she went in search of Sam Yung to ask about the nursing watch.

The third officer was on the bridge, having at last relieved Wai Chan. He told her that the two men he had found who were competent to do the nursing work had both reported to the lifeboat drill with everybody else and he had not made a point of telling them to return to the duty.

'I'll look after things up here,' said Robin. 'You go and find them, would you? Those poor Vietnamese have been very lucky to make it this far and I think they've pulled through in spite of what we've done rather than because of it. If Fat Chow has gone by the board then I'm in charge of the sickbay now and I want a round-the-clock watch until they wake up, or until we come into Kwai Chung. Is that clear?'

'Yes, missy,' said Sam Yung and thundered off to carry out her orders.

Alone on the bridge, Robin first glanced up at the ship's chronometer above the vacant helm. It was well after twenty-two hundred hours now, less than two hours before she was due to take over the middle watch. How on earth was she going to arrange a decent search for Fat Chow now? Idly, she crossed over to check the log. Feeling slightly out of place because she was really only minding the store and was not really on watch or in charge, she fiddled with bits and pieces of the equipment, checking the probable distance to Kwai Chung, getting an update on the weather, looking morosely in at the useless radio. While she did this, it occurred to her that she had better sort out one of the lifeboat radios. They would need a radio in the morning in order to call up the Hong Kong port authorities, if nothing else.

It was strange, Robin mused, how they had managed to settle nothing in the last twenty-four hours – get nothing fixed, explained or sorted out. It was almost as though they were being manipulated, somehow, for some sinister purpose. With a shiver, she wondered whether Richard had felt like this eighteen hours out of Hong Kong, just before everything had blown up in his face. Even now, in spite of all that had happened, she still could not bring herself to believe that everything was just about to blow up in her own face. The thought of Richard's dilemma took her across to the collision alarm radar. Unusually, it was switched off, and the round bowl was absolutely dark. In the dim light of the bridge, she felt for the little switch which activated the machine and depressed it. At once, the bowl glowed green. The bull's-eye circles reached out, and the straight lines of the directional grid sprang to life. And there, in the south-eastern quadrant, shockingly close behind them, was a pattern of tiny bright green dots. The collision alarm made one urgent, strangled chirrup and the whole machine died. Robin jumped back as though she had been stung. She looked around the bridge as though disorientated and wondering where she was. 'This is simply not happening,' she said aloud, then she crossed to the internal phone. After an instant's hesitation, she punched in the captain's number.

'*Wai?*'

'First officer here, Captain. I'm on the bridge. The collision alarm radar . . .'

'Why you not conducting second search for Fat Chow? Why you disobey my order?'

'I'm not disobeying you, Captain. I'll be conducting the second search in a few moments. I'm on the bridge keeping watch while the third officer arranges a nursing watch on the patients in the sickbay for me. In the meantime, I called to warn you that the collision alarm radar has just gone down.'

'Why you tell me? You tell Sparks. He fix same as usual. Is pile of junk anyway. He fix radio yet?'

'No, Captain.'

'Is other pile of junk. You get him up and out. He fix radio and fix radar, pretty damn quick. I not going into Hong Kong deaf, dumb and blind, missy!'

Robin found herself nodding – her own thoughts of a moment before. 'If the worst comes to the worst, I can sort out a shortwave two-way from one of the lifeboats for you, Captain. It would have more than enough power. But in the meantime, just before the radar went down, I was certain I saw some signals on it. Vessels, quite close behind us. It could have been a fishing fleet, but I'd like your permission to post lookouts all around the ship. After *Sulu Queen*, we don't want to be taking any chances at all.'

'You find Fat Chow then you post lookouts, missy! I want lookouts on forecastle if the radar's down in any case and you had better cut speed. Go to Slow Ahead.'

'Slow ahead, aye, Captain.'

'But you remember, missy, no lookouts and no nurses until you complete one more good search. But you get Sparks up first, and that lazy Chief Chen Hang to look after motor while we go on low revolutions. You tell Sparks to fix all that lousy junk equipment up there pretty damn quick! I not taking my ship into Hong Kong Vessel Traffic Management System using only lifeboat radio! I should bloody think!'

'Aye aye, Captain!'

She punched the chief engineer's number. 'Chief, the radar has just gone down and the captain wants the revolutions cut to Slow Ahead. He wants you on watch until we can go up to our usual speed.'

There was a reply, but she pretended not to hear it.

She punched in the radio officer's number. '*Wai?*'

'Sorry, Yuk Tso; the captain wants you up and out. He wants you to take another look at the radio, and the collision alarm radar's just gone down too.'

Yuk Tso made a hawking sound and muttered something about Japanese junk. 'I come on up right now, missy,' he promised.

Sam Yung returned, closely followed by the radio officer. 'Just before the radar went down,' Robin said, as she and Yuk Tso looked down into the dead black glass bowl and Sam Yung wrote up a new section of the log, 'I thought I saw some signals quite close behind us. Could that have been a ghost of some kind? Part of the fault which closed it down?'

Yuk Tso looked at her as though she was insane. 'What you think, missy?' he said derisively. 'If the radar shows you contacts, then is because there are boats out there.'

With the disturbing vision of that ant colony of green dots clustering close behind the ship on her mind, she arranged for the more detailed second search for Fat Chow. But she was her own woman with her own agenda. She led the search but dictated the areas she herself examined. Firstly, she had the lifeboats winched down and checked in them. The radios were not kept in the boats themselves, but in secure storage in the bridgehouse, ready to be brought aboard as part of any emergency procedure. There were emergency beacons in the boats, however, which would broadcast a broad band, high-frequency distress call incorporating the ship's call sign. The beacons were just about the most up-to-date things on the ship. She slipped one into her pocket.

Fat Chow was not in any of the lifeboats. There was nothing untoward in any of the lifeboats, in fact. Except that in the one which hung nearest the A-deck door out onto the main weather deck, there was a white suit, such as they were all wearing. It had been bundled up and stuffed out of sight, only to fall free when the boat was moved. Robin looked at it with hardly a second thought. Seamen could be a sloppy lot, she thought; someone simply too lazy to take it to the laundry. She folded it automatically, as though it was a piece of Richard's clothing, or William's or Mary's, ready for washing. And that was how she noticed that on one sleeve, just where the crook of the elbow might have been, there was a bright trace of fresh blood. But, preoccupied with the bright dots on the dead radar and the need to post watches in spite of her orders, she sent it down to the laundry without another thought.

Next, she led her longsuffering little team onto the poop deck. There were two high piles of containers here, with a walkway round to the after rails and the little flagpole there. Although it was soon obvious that Fat Chow was nowhere back here either, Robin lingered, looking into the absolute darkness behind them. She strained her eyes, and ears but there was nothing to be seen and, apart from the rumble of the motors, the grumbling thrust of the big single screw and the hissing tumble of the wake, nothing to be heard. 'You two,' she said decisively, pointing to a pair of pale figures visible largely because of their white boiler suits, 'I want you to keep watch here. I'll have you sent something to eat and drink, and a couple of walkie-talkies as well. You'll be relieved in an hour or so.'

The two men shrugged accommodatingly and went to stand where she directed.

Back in the bridgehouse with her depleted little team – which would have been nonexistent had it not contained the two men Sam had detailed for the nursing watch in the sickbay – Robin organised the last quick search while she pounded up to the bridge and asked the tired and increasingly grumpy Yuk Tso to send walkie-talkies down to her watchkeepers on the poop. He would do so, he said, just as soon as he was finished here – or, more to the point, as soon as he gave up here. 'This stuff couldn't be more dead,' he said bitterly, 'if some bastard had killed it on purpose!'

It was coming up to midnight, so Robin popped down to the meeting place she had arranged with her exhausted team and dismissed all but two of them. These last two she took to the officers' galley where she found some food and filled a thermos with hot chocolate for the men on the poop. She checked briefly on the patients and pounded back up to the navigation bridge. Before she dismissed Sam Yung, she gave him strict orders to rearrange a watch on the sick men and a relief for the watch on the poop before he turned in.

By twelve thirty she had dismissed Yuk Tso with orders that he supply her poop-deck watch with walkie-talkies as promised, and was all alone on the navigating bridge, drifting exhaustedly in the wash of all the activity which had so suddenly come to a dead halt. Of all the things she had planned to do this evening, she had omitted to get a lifeboat radio up here to replace the main set tomorrow if push came to shove. Well, she had better just bustle about early and get it sorted out before breakfast. John Shaw would have alerted the authorities and warned Kwai Chung, but the Hong Kong authorities would still demand a detailed report – name, flag, tonnage, draught, call sign, length, contents and state – a good many hours before they were due to dock.

She signed in on the log, and began to pace restlessly, feeling disturbingly alone at the heart of the vast night. She was struck, not for the first time in her twenty-odd years at sea but more poignantly than ever before, by how big and how empty the accommodation and navigating areas could become late at night. Once Yuk Tso had given the walkie-talkies to her watch men and turned in, she would effectively be all alone up here. The bridge was five decks high. Each deck contained more than ten rooms – galleys, saloons, offices, cargo-handling rooms, sickrooms, day rooms, rest rooms, bars, library, video room, recreation room, cabins, chart rooms, radio rooms, the navigation bridge itself. Immediately abaft the bridge was more accommodation – storage rooms, cold rooms, all the rest. Aft of these were the upper engineering areas around the thrust of the funnel itself. These areas all interconnected in one way or another. All available to a man who wished to hide, or who was lost or hurt, and all of them except the cabins empty now.

The crew were packed two or sometimes four to a berth on A deck, four huge decks down from the navigation bridge. Then, on the next deck up, B deck, were the junior officers, navigating and engineering. On the third deck, C deck, were the cabins and day rooms of the senior officers, including her own cabin, although her office was down beside the cargo handling room at main-deck level. On D deck, immediately below the navigating bridge, were the cabins and day rooms set aside for the captain and the chief engineer, the owner and one important guest. Two of these spacious suites were empty too. There were forty people – thirty-nine men and herself – in a block of flats which on land would easily accommodate one hundred and fifty. Never had the bridgehouse seemed so huge, so lonely.

When the walkie-talkie in its pouch beside the watchkeeper's chair squawked, she jumped. 'You're getting far too nervy, my dear,' she told herself out loud as she crossed to it.

'Bridge,' she snapped. 'First officer here.'

'Radio officer here. Where did you say you had placed your watch?'

'On the poop. By the stern rail.'

'They gone, missy. Nobody here.'

'What—' The bridge phone rang. 'Wait.' With the walkie-talkie still to her ear, she crossed to the shrilling instrument. 'Wait a minute, Sparks.' She lifted the handset of the internal phone. 'Bridge.'

'They've gone, missy!'

'What? Who is this?'

'Third Officer in the sickbay. The Vietnamese men have gone.'

She closed her eyes then. Her mind should have been racing but it was not. The truth of their situation was absolute and obvious. So obvious, it was as though she had always known it. She saw dead women drained of blood so that they would not attract shark or barracuda to the live men on the sampan. She saw two men miraculously alive in spite of impossible odds, able to signal to the approaching ship. Two men who had not been properly watched except by Fat Chow who had vanished. Who showed signs of moving and slipping the needles out of their arms in spite of their near catatonia. She saw a crook of ivory-skinned elbow with a pool of blood in it. She saw an ill-concealed, all too anonymous boiler suit with a trace of blood on its crisp white sleeve. She saw a pattern of green dots on a radar bowl which was broken, which stood beside a radio which had been sabotaged. And she remembered how devastatingly effective the Wooden Horse of Troy had been, also the brainchild of a cunning sailorman.

'Get up here, Sam. Drop everything and get up here right now.' She put the phone down and pressed SEND on the walkie-talkie. 'Sparks. Get up here. Now.'

She put the walkie-talkie down on the equipment shelf beside the automatic steering equipment. She took a deep breath, then she hit the Emergency siren. As the first piercing notes blasted out, she hit the tannoy button. 'This is the first officer speaking. All officers and crewmen report to the navigating bridge at once. I say again, all officers and crewmen report to the navigating bridge at once. This is not a drill. The ship is under attack.'

Chapter Thirty-Three

The final day of Richard Mariner's trial, Saturday, 21 June 1997, began as early for the prosecution as previous days had begun for the defence. And it began badly. Po Sun Kam, unmarried if highly eligible, lived with his mother and had promised, perhaps unwisely, to escort her to the People's Celebratory Party on Shek O today. Although the old lady was fiercely ambitious for her son, the disappointment resulting from Judge Fang's decision to continue the trial on a Saturday had upset her considerably and amends had been time-consuming and expensive. Only the fact that Po had beggared himself to get a pair of tickets to next weekend's even greater party on the Peak itself had mollified her and allowed him to get back to his work.

As Po pored glumly over today's trial papers, such as they were, he kept one eye on the clock, all too aware that Mr Justice Fang had ruled the proceedings would open at nine thirty, probably because the judge himself wanted to get to Shek O for the party too.

By nine fifteen, the prosecutor was in the robing room of the Supreme Court getting ready. When he got out into court he knew he would find there a range of officials, including Captain Huuk and Commander Lee to whom he would have to express his regretful opinion that their case would not stand up for very much longer. He had tried to get them both on the telephone before he left his office, but neither was immediately available. He hoped that he would get a chance to talk to one or both of them before things got properly under way. Magnanimous withdrawal would save a lot more face than ignominious defeat.

But when he went through into the court, neither man was there and he felt unsupported and alone, especially when the defence team swept in like a small army. He felt every eye in the packed public galleries boring into his back like so many daggers, and every hissed comment and stifled whisper seemed aimed at him.

The conversation intensified as the prisoner was led to his place. Po could not remember ever having seen him look so alert, so intensely alive. From the prosecutor's point of view, it was all intensely depressing.

The clerk of the court arrived. 'All rise,' he demanded, and Po, an aficionado of Western culture, glanced across to his stunning opposite number, and thought to himself, it's showtime, folks!

Mr Justice Fang took his position, bowed, sat. The court officials bowed and sat in their turn. Just as they did so, Commander Lee bustled in and took his place. 'Sorry to be late,' the stolid policeman imparted, *sotto voce*, 'but just as we were leaving, Huuk got another of his funny phone calls. It's *Seram Queen* this time.'

Po's mind reeled. This seemed like the final nail in the coffin of the Crown's case. They had proceeded on the assumption that the accused, Captain Mariner, was solely responsible; that he had undertaken a range of killing, beginning with two deaths in Singapore, in order to secure a fortune for himself or for his company; that the whole thing had been a desperate half-sane one-off. And now, just as the two original victims had come all too conveniently back to life, the same thing was happening all over again to the sister ship.

But the Commander had not finished speaking. 'It's probably a hoax,' he opined. 'I'm getting Huuk to check it out thoroughly before we even dream of taking it seriously.' Then he sat back as Maggie rose for the final time.

'I would like to call Miss Anna Leung, company secretary to the China Queens Company,' she said.

Anna Leung looked exhausted and nervous as she came to the witness stand. She was all too well aware of Commander Lee's cold gaze. She would be lucky not to be standing in the dock next time she came here.

'You are Anna Leung, of the China Queens Company, Singapore?'

'I am known as Anna Leung, yes.'

'That is not your real name?'

'It is an alias I adopted at the behest of the Royal Hong Kong Police's Criminal Intelligence Division.'

'So you are, in fact, a police officer?'

'I was, but I have resigned my commission. I am a private citizen now.'

'Very well. Now, if we can turn to the matter in hand. For what purpose did you assume the alias of Anna Leung?'

'So that I could investigate smuggling as it was carried on through the port of Singapore. More specifically through the Tanjong Pagar computerised container terminal. It was understood by my superiors that the China Queens Company was involved in such smuggling. When the operation in which I was involved began, the China Queens was owned by a front company ultimately run, we believed, by the White Powder Triad. Although they used it for their own business occasionally, they also had a lucrative sideline in hiring out the container space to other concerns who wished to transport merchandise invisibly and without the inconvenience of Customs inspections.'

'I see. So the Criminal Intelligence Division arranged for you to be put in a position where you could monitor this?'

'Yes, but in fact things rapidly became more complicated than we had at first calculated. When I first went in, it was assumed that the White Powder Triad would be using this system for a limited number of spectacular shipments which we could include in a series of cases which would close down the whole operation and perhaps even bring to book the senior echelons of the Triad itself.'

'But things did not work out that way?'

'No. Firstly, they kept their operations small. It was as though they were being warned of our intentions from inside. Secondly, they started, as I said, to let the spare container space, almost as a legitimate business would, and it became increasingly difficult to focus on what was their contraband and what was being shipped by other people. Thirdly, where we had expected confrontation and violence, there was none. The system ran simply and bloodlessly – up until the *Sulu Queen* incident. Goods were smuggled into the terminals at Singapore, here, wherever, in small quantities and slipped into the crates. A tiny adjustment to the loading programme on the computer, a bit of a backhander to a couple of lading officers and that was all.'

'And you reported all this back to your superiors?'

'Little by little, as I discovered it. But you must understand that there was never anything big. Certainly nothing big enough or priceless enough to make it worth springing our trap and closing down the operation. And it took nearly three years to get all the groundwork in place. Furthermore, I was in a perfect position to pass on wider information about the ongoing investigation into piracy of all sorts in this immediate area.

'Then things became more complex still. With the nearing of the date for the handing back of the Crown Colony to the People's Republic of China, the senior Triad members began to move their power bases and their business enterprises out of Hong Kong. The China Queens Company's headquarters were there and both of the ships are registered there, but their main shipping offices were in Singapore. It was a perfect situation for the Criminal Intelligence Division but it was that which let us down. The White Powder Triad put the company on the market. As the company which owned the business was seemingly quite legitimate, it found a legitimate buyer.'

'Heritage Mariner, of London.'

'Just so.'

'So, if Heritage Mariner are legitimate, why were you left in place in the Singapore office?'

'Because the system continued to function, as far as we knew, under the aegis of the White Powder Triad. Although they no longer owned the ships, they still had full control over the ghost containers.'

'Now, please be quite specific about this, Miss Leung. What evidence did you have that Heritage Mariner themselves were involved in this enterprise?'

'In the smuggling? None whatever.'

'Which officers of the company have you met, Miss Leung?'

'Of Heritage Mariner? Mr Charles Lee and Captain Richard Mariner.'

'And what evidence did you find that they, either individually or in concert, were involved with the smuggling?'

'None whatsoever.'

'Surely, Miss Leung, with the company now in legitimate hands, you made representations to your superiors that it was time to recall and reassign you?'

'No. As I said, the containers were still being used, though without the knowledge of Captain Mariner or Mr Lee, as far as I am aware. Furthermore, I heard a whisper that the White Powder Triad were going to try one last huge operation just before the handover of Hong Kong, before the Chinese authorities moved into the Crown Colony. I heard that they were going to ship two containers full of crack cocaine out of the Philippines. It was just the sort of operation which the Criminal Intelligence Division were looking for.'

'The sort of operation you had been specifically placed to warn the Criminal Intelligence Division about?'

'Just so. And so I stayed in place.'

'But you had a stronger reason even than duty to keep you in place, did you not, Miss Leung?'

'Yes. I did.'

'And what was that?'

'I had fallen in love with Captain Walter Gough, master of the *Sulu Queen*. We had planned for some time to run away together. We had been saving up what we could towards buying the home in which your Mr Tan discovered us yesterday morning.'

'Please explain that plan to us, Miss Leung.'

'The last time Wally was due to come through Singapore, he was going to fake peritonitis. He had had a grumbling appendix for years. He had to take care to know all the symptoms in case he had an attack at sea and so it was easy for him to reproduce them to order. He would be rushed into hospital and then discharge himself as soon as his ship had sailed and we would run away together.'

'And how did Captain Mariner become involved in your machinations?'

'Well . . .' Anna Leung took a deep breath and continued to look at her hands as they writhed against each other on the edge of the witness box in front of her. 'Wally decided that this run had to be the one. But he knew nothing about my real involvement or about the consignment that the White Powder Triad were apparently planning to move. His first officer, Brian Jordan, was the only one who took back-handers on the *Sulu Queen*.'

'I see. So?'

'Brian Jordan was an adequate first officer but he was by no means qualified to take command of the ship if the captain fell ill. But we couldn't risk having the *Sulu Queen* sitting in Singapore while a new captain was found. To begin with, such a situation would slow down the movement of both ships and put the whole Criminal Intelligence Division investigation at risk. And...'

'And?'

'And it would make it absolutely impossible for Wally and me to vanish in the way we had planned.'

'I see. So what did you do?'

'Wally suggested I should think up some reason or other to get Richard Mariner out. They had known each other socially on and off for years. Captain Mariner was the chief executive of the company which now owned the ships and he had made his reputation with his own company Crewfinders which specialises in replacing sick or injured officers on ships all over the world. It seemed to us, therefore that there would be no question that he would be able to take over the ship straightaway. It was a very good idea. It solved all our problems. I agreed to do it. I sent Captain Mariner a message which I believed he would find irresistible. I warned him that his ships were being used for smuggling purposes and were the subject of an investigation. I warned him not to contact the authorities until after he had spoken to me directly. He knew me. He came. At once. Without question. It broke my heart to betray such a man.' Anna Leung glanced up briefly. Her gaze met Richard's for a second and then fell again.

'What then?' Maggie persisted, an edge in her voice.

'I timed my information so that he would arrive mere hours before the *Sulu Queen*. I took him to Tanjong Pagar and let him see what happened during the turnaround. He went aboard the ship to find out what was going on and to inform the authorities in Hong Kong. Wally faked his attack and came back with the pilot. He gave me a series of messages Captain Mariner wished me to send. Some were letters and some were electronic messages on disk for me to send on the Superhighway. I sent none of them. I destroyed them all.' Once again, she looked across at Richard and this time their gazes locked for a longer period as his face worked with growing revelation.

'Miss Leung?' Maggie's voice cracked like a whip and the exhausted witness jumped as though she had been struck.

'Wally and I left for Manila later that night, exactly as planned,' she concluded sadly, her voice beginning to break and her eyes to fill with bitter tears. 'For nearly two months we have been living on an island which has no contact with the outside world. We visited Laoag only once and I now see that this was a fatal mistake. We knew nothing of what happened subsequently until Mr Tan told us yesterday, and would still know nothing of it now had Wally not sent that postcard to his wife.'

There was a moment of silence as the desolation in the woman's voice echoed around the court.

Then Maggie said quietly, as though she were not in open court at all, 'Well, that just about does it for me.' She turned, and her voice echoed also as she said straight to Mr Justice Fang, 'My Lord I invite the prosecution to consider their position because on the basis of this evidence it appears their case has collapsed. There is nothing left for my client to answer, except perhaps how he came to handle the weapons left by the pirates who killed his crew, believing that they were smuggling cocaine when they were in fact unknowingly smuggling pirated videotapes and while the authorities stood by and waited to make their sure-fire case against the mandarins of the White Powder Triad.'

'Mr Po?' asked the judge gently. 'Has the Crown anything to add?'

Mr Prosecutor Po looked over his shoulder and Commander Lee simply shook his head. The young Chinese barrister rose as though he had been stricken with arthritis during Anna Leung's testimony. 'No, My Lord,' he said quietly. 'My learned friend has expressed the situation to perfection and the Crown has nothing to add. Under the circumstances, we will offer no further evidence. Captain Mariner has nothing more to answer. He is an innocent man, My Lord.'

Someone in the gallery started clapping and even Mr Justice Fang's glaring demand for silence was overcome in the ovation like a drop in a downpour.

Ten minutes later, Richard, dazed by his sudden freedom and by the memories which Anna Leung's testimony had reawoken in his head, was led out into the corridor outside the courtroom. He was escorted by Andrew on one side and Gerry Stephenson on the other. Maggie swept before him with Lata at her side, the women clearing a way through the cheering crowd more effectively than a squad of policemen could have done. Behind him came Mr Prosecutor Po and the square bulk of Commander Victor Lee. They had progressed no more than four steps when Daniel Huuk came running through from the reception area and, looking past the tall, disorientated figure of the man he had shot seven weeks earlier, called out to his immediate chief in a voice of agonised suspense, 'Commander! It's the *Seram Queen*! She's just been spotted drifting to the south of the Wenwei Zhou. *And the pirates are still aboard!*'

Robin Mariner sat on the tiny platform at the top of the radio mast like Jim Hawkins in *Treasure Island*, pointing Edgar Tan's pistol down the ladder between her widespread ankles and waiting for the first pirate to try and climb up after her like the evil Israel Hands.

Far below her, the main deck was a bustling hive of industry as the topmost containers were winched off the piles of deck cargo and swung out over the starboard side to be dumped in the restless water among the bodies floating there. It was a glorious morning, just coming up to noon, and the sun beat down upon her unprotected head and shoulders, causing sweat to run uncontrollably into her tired eyes, but her concentration did not waver. She had ten bullets left and was determined to use them all. The platform itself was four square metres of thick, bulletproof steel and it could only be overlooked from a helicopter. As the pirates did not seem to have a helicopter, the only way to get her was to come up the ladder after her. It was a long ladder, coming up to a square trapdoor. The trapdoor was too small to shoot through from anywhere below. She hadn't seen any heavy artillery or rocket launchers. The platform was too small and too high a target to make a lob with a grenade even remotely feasible. No. If they wanted her, they would have to climb the ladder to get her. But the ladder could only be climbed by one man at a time. The first ten men to start at the bottom would never make it to the top. Number eleven would lose his teeth and his eyes on the way through the trap. And then she would wing it. In the meantime she was safe and she was set. Now for part two of her cunning plan.

Letting go of the pistol's stock with her left hand, she pulled the emergency beacon she had taken from the lifeboat a lifetime ago last night out of her pocket and switched it on. It had a range of more than fifty kilometres from up here, and by her best calculation the ship was less than ten kilometres south of the Wenwei Zhou. This thing should ring alarm bells everywhere from here to HMS *Tamar*. She put it beside her on the steel platform, and, while she waited for someone somewhere to answer its urgent summons she thought back over the last eleven all too active hours.

Captain Sin had been the last man onto the bridge in answer to her alarm. This was because – like any captain sensible of his position – he had dressed before leaving his cabin. 'Now just what the hell you up to, missy?' he yelled across the milling crowd of night-dressed crewmen who were packed nervously into the open space of the navigation bridge waiting for her detailed explanation.

'I believe the men on the Vietnamese boat are pirates and they came aboard in order to put the radio and radar out of commission so that they can help their pirate colleagues come aboard. My evidence for this is the fact that the men have been up and about in secret. The equipment in question is out of commission and my two watchmen, as well as Fat Chow, have vanished.'

'This is a dream! You make this up. You hysterical woman, missy!'

'No Captain! I saw a fleet of small craft immediately behind us before the radar went down. I saw blood on a boiler suit which could only have come from the arm of one of the men in the sickbay. I posted two watchkeepers on the poop and they are gone. I asked Fat Chow to keep an eye on the survivors and he is gone. I tell you all, this is the way it must have started for the *Sulu Queen* but they didn't know what we know. What have you got aboard worth killing for, Captain Sin? What are you smuggling?'

'You mad woman! You make this all up. I have you clapped in iron.'

'Come on, Captain! This isn't the *Bounty*! What have you got hidden aboard? I'm not talking about the small-time stuff you smuggle into the Paracels and then trade with the local moneymen while the crew here are getting screwed in all sorts of ways. I'm talking about the big stuff. What have you got in the two ghost containers, Captain? What's hidden in your deck cargo? Have you any idea at all? Something from the White Powder Triad, perhaps? Something scary enough to frighten First Officer Chin Lau off the ship and into hospital?' She had gone far beyond anything she was certain about, she was just guessing desperately, throwing out some of the ideas which had been spinning around in her head and some of the names given to her by Twelvetoes Ho two weeks ago before she had come south to Singapore. But she hit the mark.

'What you mean, missy?' Captain Sin's voice was horrorstruck.

'Don't bluster, Captain. Your men know. There's something aboard worth stealing and there's a fleet of pirate ships pulling up behind us now who will stop at nothing to get it. We have to organise and we have to do it fast or we'll all end up like the crew of the *Sulu Queen*!'

The crew of the *Sulu Queen*! Robin's words echoed like doom in the ears of the crew of the *Seram Queen*. They didn't like them, they didn't get on with them, they didn't socialise with them, but they all knew what had happened to them.

'First off, are there any arms aboard?'

Shit! she thought as she asked the question. She had forgotten Edgar Tan's gun! All this and pirates coming aboard and she had forgotten the bloody, bloody gun. *You stupid bloody woman!* 'This is no time to be coy,' she added. 'No one's going to take your name or dock your pay. Quite the reverse, in fact. If you can get a gun or a knife or a club up here we'll all stand a much better chance of staying alive. Just as soon as we stop talking here I'm going to get *my* gun!'

She looked across the range of frightened, intensely concentrated faces until her eyes met those of Captain Sin. His mouth was working, but no sound was coming out of it. She felt a stirring of sympathy. 'Captain. Have you anything to add, sir?'

'Radios?' he suggested.

'Aye aye, sir! I'll take a team at once and see whether we can liberate a lifeboat radio before anyone comes aboard.' Before anyone *else* comes aboard, she thought, thinking of the so-called Vietnamese fifth columnists already working to clear the way for the rest of the pirates.

'In the meantime, is there anyone here who has arms aboard?'

There was some shamefaced, hangdog shuffling which she took to be the affirmative. 'If you have any weapons aboard, go and get them now, please. Catering Officer, go down to the galley and get all your biggest knives, and while you are down there, you should get all the food and drink you can carry just in case this thing becomes protracted. Captain, have you no ship's weapons aboard?'

'There is a strongbox in my cabin. One pistol. One rifle. I have key here in my pocket.'

'Wai Chan, can you go and get them, please. And don't forget the ammunition. Remember, all of you,' she said as the men began to move, 'there are two spies aboard who have probably disguised themselves to look like you and who have probably killed three people already. Take care.'

They would have to keep an eye out for those two even if the main force had not boarded yet, Robin thought as she prepared herself for action. It was not likely that people capable of planning something like this would send aboard anything other then their best, most dangerous men. And these men would have been as fully alerted as the rest of the crew by her sounding of the alarm. Indeed, the whole fleet of pirate ships so close behind the *Seram Queen* might have been alerted. But there was no help for that now. The most likely results on the pirate strategy would be to hurry the fleet up, bring the boarding closer, and pressure the spies into taking a closer look at what was going on. The spies had already proved their reliance on disguise; a successful stratagem was likely to be repeated. She had better choose a team of men whose faces she knew well, therefore. She did not want a spy in a boiler suit joining her team without her knowledge.

Robin was not standing still as she entertained these thoughts. She was pushing through the milling crew, picking out men as she went. The last team member she selected was Sam Yung and when he joined in behind her there were five of them in all. Thinking feverishly, she stopped an instant after Sam fell in behind her. 'Pop out onto the bridge wing and get me the night glasses, please, Sam,' she ordered *sotto voce*. He nodded and was gone. Then she was in motion again.

At the door Robin turned and paused, waiting for Sam to come back with the night glasses. She was close to Captain Sin now and she did not have to raise her voice, but even so her words carried clearly as she tried to motivate the stunned man into rapid and decisive action. 'Captain we have to assume that the ship will be invaded by a large number of men who will stop at nothing. If we are going to survive, we must make the bridge here our defensive position. You need to do two things immediately while waiting for the others to come back with their armaments. You need to check that there are only *bona fide* crewmen here and that every face is familiar before you let anyone back in here. Secondly, you must put up some kind of barricades at the points where attacks could be mounted and post watches at those points. With my team, I will go and get my gun. Then I will try and get a lifeboat radio and any flares I can get hold of too. Finally I will go and spy out the after sections with the night glasses and a walkie-talkie so that I can warn you when the pirates begin to come aboard. The more we know, the safer we will be. Do you agree?' Inconsequentially, she wondered whether Captain Sin had read Sun Tsu. The more people among the crew who knew about *The Art of War* the better.

'Yes,' acceded Captain Sin. 'If you are correct and we are about to be boarded, then we must make our defences.'

'Good. I will stay out for as long as I can and pass on as much information as possible. But I won't be taking any silly risks. Neither should you. Anyone coming aboard will simply be looking to steal whatever they can either from the accommodation areas or from the cargo. No one is going to want to risk a pitched battle. If you are all safely barricaded in then, it is highly unlikely that you will even be attacked.'

As she said these bracing words, Robin was joined by a breathless Sam Yung. She took the glasses from him and led her little team out onto the first stairwell. As the five of them, with herself and Sam in the lead, went down the stairs on tiptoe, her mind was full of tactical considerations so that as she moved, with every sense concentrating on what was immediately around her, her thoughts remained preoccupied with the layout of the bridge above their heads. On the face of it, the crew should have no trouble barricading themselves safely in the navigating bridge. The bridge itself was a long room with a wide window forward overlooking the deck and another aft looking out into the main lateral corridor. At each end of this corridor were massive iron doors out onto the external companionways. Once these were secured shut, there was no way in through them. On either side of the bridge itself were two slightly lighter doors leading out onto the bridge wings. They, too, were capable of being secured and, once closed, would keep any invaders safely outside. Even the glass panels in their upper sections were double-strengthened and effectively unbreakable.

Leading aft from the bridge on the port side were the chart room with the captain's watch cabin behind it – scarcely more than a cupboard with a bunk – but it was secure. On the other side was the radio room, out of order but also secure. Aft of the lateral corridor were two internal companionways and a lift shaft going down. All they had to do was to jam the lift and barricade the top of the companionways and they were impregnable. Especially if they had enough weapons to put a protracted wave of fire down the steel-walled, steep and narrow companionway wells. It would be a classic siege situation. The pirates could stop the engines and cut the power, but unless they had some skilful big-ship men working with them, they could not turn the ship off her course, so their time would be severely limited. Even drifting, *Seram Queen* would start to attract official attention early tomorrow morning and the Hong Kong coastguards would probably be aboard by noon.

By the time they were at the foot of the second set of steps, the team had formed itself into a line of overlapping pairs, as though they were all carrying guns with which to protect each other's backs. They proceeded silently down the corridor towards Robin's cabin, three against one wall, two against the other, eyes everywhere, ears on full alert. Although she did not clearly recognise the fact, all the men were keeping a special watch on her, each one tensed, coiled, like a steel spring, ready to run to her aid. But the corridors through which they were creeping, the companionways down which they were tiptoeing like a patrol in enemy territory were empty and, apart from the sullen grumble of the slow-revving engine, silent.

But in a siege situation Robin was thinking, with two sets of forces in an intractable position, it was likely that intelligence would be of the first importance. In order to ensure their survival, Robin's crew would need to have as clear an idea as possible what the pirates wanted, how far they would go in order to get it, how they would react to the unexpected situation, and what sort of timescale they would allow themselves to get the situation resolved. The pirates had put two spies aboard. Robin could not hope to put any spies in the pirates' camp but she could try to overlook their positions and report back with some idea as to what they were doing. Mentally, she began to list all the highest points aboard which would allow an observer to watch without being seen. At the back of her mind, however, sat Sun Tsu's heartening observation, '... he who occupies the field of battle first and awaits his enemy is at ease...'

At the door to her cabin, she stopped and signalled the three crewmen to keep watch, then she unlocked the door and, with Sam Yung at her back, she went into the dark room. All the curtains had been drawn at sunset, as was standard practice, but even so, Robin did not want to risk turning on the light. In the shaft of brightness from the open door she pulled the briefcase from under her bed and knelt beside it, opening it and turning it so the broad beam showed the contents. Under the papers and documents, the little moulded foam compartment lay snugly filled with cold metal. With a silent sigh of relief, Robin pulled out the weighty little gun and held it in the brightness so that she could see what she was doing. It was the work of an instant to push both the switches forward, and a bright red dot appeared on the wall above her rumpled bunk.

Robin moved like a ghost through the shadows to the back of her office beyond. Here she caught up the walkie-talkie on her desk, knowing where it was even in the absolute darkness back here. She pressed it to her lips and pressed SEND.

'*Wai?*' The answer was loud enough to make her jump and shorten the heart-lives of her men by quite a bit.

'First officer, Captain. Proceeding to the second leg now. Will contact you in due course.'

That red dot led the way downwards through the bright, silent bridgehouse as she took her team on the next leg of their mission. They had no time to hang about. She kept a close eye on the slowly elapsing minutes although she had no way of estimating whether the main body of the pirates could be expected in five, ten, or fifteen minutes. At the very most, she reckoned, they had twenty minutes' grace, and seven had elapsed already. But she would not hurry. The red dot went round every corner and swept along every corridor, probed every stairwell, before the rest of them followed it.

At last they came to the A-deck door out onto the main deck. Behind here where the corridor came to a dead end, there was a secure weatherproof box. And in that box, checked every day, fully charged up and ready to go, was an emergency radio. On either side of the radio was a set of flares. On top of it were two big battery-powered lamps such as she had used on the sampan last night. Robin undid the security lock and opened the front. The flares slid out silently and were handed back to the nearest seaman. The lamps came out also and were handed to the next. The radio she handed to Sam Yung. This was neither the time nor the place to test it, so she simply motioned with her hand and took point position again.

They made it back up to C deck before fifteen minutes in all had elapsed. Here, the team broke up. Robin gestured that Sam should take the radio on up towards the navigation bridge from where the sound of barricade building was coming. Another gesture informed him that she herself was going out onto the exterior companionway here. As he understood that she was proposing to go out onto the deck behind the funnel which overlooked the poop and set up her observation there, Sam shook his head and handed the radio to the nearest of his men. Then in pantomime he informed the first officer that he would accompany her on this foolhardy mission. She nodded and gave a tight smile at once. Of all the crew, Sam was the man she would most like to have watching her back in a tight spot. Two final gestures directed the men with the flares and the radio upwards and ordered her deputy observer to follow her outside.

The door onto the exterior companionway was open for only an instant as the two of them slipped out into the night, but even so, Robin was intensely aware of how much of a signal it would be to anyone watching the bridgehouse. They did not linger but ran as fast as was safe down the metal steps of the open companionway and onto the decking on the port side of the funnel. Keeping in the darkest shadows, regretting poignantly that they had not had an opportunity to change out of their white boiler suits, Robin led Sam back towards the aft rail overlooking the poop deck two decks below. Here they cast themselves down on their stomachs and looked downwards. Everything was absolutely quiet and still. So still, in fact, that Robin found herself wondering whether she had panicked needlessly after all. The two piles of containers stood immediately below them, so close as to be a seemingly easy jump away. Beyond these, it was just possible to see the pale end of the company flag fluttering maybe a metre out beyond the aft rail. But the rail itself was hidden by the tops of the containers. A whole army could pull itself aboard over the after rail and they would see nothing. That much was obvious even without resorting to the glasses. Hissing with irritation, Robin turned to look at Sam and explain the problem to him when she saw the shadow just behind him rise into a human shape. Without thought, Robin rolled back, putting the glasses and the neck they were slung round severely at risk. She was holding the gun in two hands and she pointed it by instinct up towards the charging shape. The limbs of the shadowy shape waved and worked distractingly – it was only on cold reflection later than she realised the man was swinging a panga – and for a horrific moment she could see no dot at all. The gun was unexpectedly heavy and even though she held it in both her hands, it began to pull her arms down at once. Sam, seeing what she was doing, reacted physically, beginning to rise, and it was on his shoulder that she first saw the dot. 'Down!' she spat and, on her word, he flattened. She saw the dot leap out over Sam's prostrate body onto the attacking pirate. The dot was more or less in the middle of his charging shadow and wavering downwards as the weight of the gun caused her hands to sink, so she pulled the trigger with all her might. The explosion of the shot was shatteringly loud. The muzzle flash in the darkness was blindingly bright. She did not see what happened to the man she had shot but when she blinked her eyes clear, he was gone. Sam rolled away for a moment, then, before she could bring herself to move he was back. Now he was holding a panga. 'Thank you, missy,' he whispered.

The leap out onto the top of the containers was as easy as it looked and that was as well, for Robin's legs were none too steady as the impact of her first killing hit her system. Not only was standing difficult, an urgent visit to the toilet seemed to be called for. And – if her respiration and heart rate were anything to go by – an iron lung. With her stomach cramping, threatening to squeeze all sorts of liquids out of either end of her, Robin crawled forward over the rough, ridged surface of the container top until she had a clear view of the after rail. Here with Sam keeping close watch with the panga, she at last put the night glasses to her eyes. And as she did so she caught her breath.

It was worse than she had supposed. Out there, bobbing in the wake of the *Seram Queen*, there were at least ten boats, all clustering in under the overhang of the counter, like leeches ready to fasten onto the ship's lifeblood. Working feverishly, given extra impetus by the sound of the shot no doubt, one figure was throwing ropes over and out. And even as Robin got the glasses focused and brought the green-tinged scene into proper perspective, the first of the pirates swarmed aboard. She continued to observe closely, until the first figure on the poop, with a growing group around him, turned and gestured with uncanny accuracy towards the exact spot where Robin and Sam were hiding. As the men moved to obey his directive, Robin saw all too many metallic gleams. Knives, pangas, handguns – perhaps the odd rifle. It was not a pretty sight.

'They're coming up to check on the shot,' she breathed. 'I think it's time to go.'

'How many are coming aboard?' asked Sam, his voice little more than a breath.

'Ten boatloads.'

'That could be more than a hundred!'

'Too true.' Robin pulled the walkie-talkie out of her pocket and pressed the SEND button.

'*Wai?*'

'First officer here. There may be as many as one hundred pirates and they are coming aboard now. I suggest you get your defences ready and your sentries out as soon as possible.'

'All done, missy. You come back now.'

'Aye aye, Captain!' She lifted her thumb and spat at Sam, 'Let's move!'

Getting back up onto the mid-deck was unexpectedly difficult, especially for Robin who found the night glasses round her neck and the walkie-talkie in her pocket added immeasurably to the weight of the gun in her hand. In the end Sam leaped first and hung onto the outside of the railing there so that she could hurl herself across into his waiting arm. Then, side by side, they scrambled over the top and onto the deck. Running back towards the external companionway, Robin nearly tripped over the sprawled legs of a supine figure on the deck. So it was that she saw the results of her handiwork with the gun for the first time.

Stricken, Robin faltered in her flight, looking down at the dead man, but as she did so, Sam grabbed her by the arm and pulled her into motion once again. It was fortunate that he did so, for as they slipped back in through the door and through to the C-deck companionway they heard, perhaps one deck below them, the sibilant rush of bare feet. Running for their lives they sprinted up the three half-flights of stairs until at the last turning Robin had the good sense to pause. 'First and third officers coming up! Don't shoot,' she bellowed.

'Yes, missy,' called a nervous voice from above and the pair of them were in motion once again. At the top of the stairs was a solid-looking wall made of planks of wood, sections of shelving, bits of chairs and heaven knew what else. The captain's bunk, the chart chest, all the instrument housings and much of the spare shelving from the radio room seemed to have been used. The wall was perhaps a metre and a half high, extending the top step, and looked quite imposing, topped as it was with a motley range of weaponry.

And it was as solid as it looked Robin discovered, as she threw herself up on it and was hauled over it into the relative safety of the navigating bridge. The corridor behind the bridge was clearly designed as the arsenal. Here a range of guns and knives, meat cleavers, rolling pins and ammunition were piled against the low wooden wall ready to hand. Beside the weapons were the packets of flares and the powerful flashlights she had sent up with the radio.

No sooner was she safely in the corridor than she walked down to check that the second barricade was equally solid. It was. And it was equally well manned. Having satisfied herself on that account, she checked on the lift – but someone had been quick-thinking enough to put it out of commission. There was no way for the pirates to get onto the bridge, and no way for the rest of them to get off, for the time being. And in spite of what she had said about intelligence being so vital in this position, she knew that only a lunatic would venture over the wooden walls out into Indian territory tonight.

No sooner had Robin completed her cursory inspection of the defences than the lights died. The auxiliary lighting clicked in at once, glowing dully. Then it, too, died. At once the searchlight beams of the torches speared down through the shadows to the first landing in each stairwell. Robin looked at her watch. It was surprisingly late – after two already. Well, in little more than four hours it would be dawn; then things were bound to look up. Picking her way carefully, she moved onto the bridge proper and crossed to the radio room where Yuk Tso was trying with no great success to raise some traffic on the lifeboat radio she had liberated.

Robin crossed back to the watchkeeper's chair which held the somnolent form of the captain. Although he seemed to be asleep, he roused at once to her presence and they discussed the limited number of tactical alternatives open to them. In spite of his initial unwillingness to accept the danger of their situation, Captain Sin had taken charge quite adequately during her reconnaissance mission. The sentries had been split up into watches and everyone had some kind of duty to perform somewhere along the line. As the dark hours passed, the watches changed and the trapped men felt that they had some kind of control over their situation, and this boost to morale was important, for the sounds of destruction from below made everybody up here think of treasured or valuable keepsakes which they would never see again. As the hours ticked by, the sounds of the destruction slowly came closer but no one ever put his head round that last little turn of stairway into the torch beams or the fields of fire.

Sometime after five, when dawn was beginning to threaten, Sam Yung shook Robin by the shoulder just hard enough to rouse her from her restless, nightmare slumber full of dark figures spinning slowly away from the deadly flashes of her pistol and gestured towards the nearest bridge wing door. There was just enough light to see that its handle was turning, slowly and silently. The third officer was all too ready to go and interfere with whatever was going on, but Robin held him back. The door was tried, silently, but it would not yield. There was the faintest scratching, as of someone testing whether a lock might yield to a pick; then a slightly heavier scraping, a sound like the blade of a panga might make, testing the strength of hinge and jamb. But these sounds stopped. Whoever was out there gave up and went away as stealthily as he had come.

And that was all. Robin had no doubt that the door to the starboard bridge wing must also have been tried, and the doors at the ends of the corridor, but they did not yield and nothing more came of it. No doubt, too, naked feet went scurrying across the upper deck immediately above their heads, but there was no way in here from up there. And she suspected the lift shaft would have been examined from above and below. But the pirates needed an ingress which they could force in large numbers by surprise and there simply was no such thing. So, in the end, they were content to leave the navigating bridge alone. But that very fact, Robin was to think later, should have alerted them to something.

So much else might have been tried. With the light and power, the air conditioning had gone. It would have been easy enough to build a couple of fires in the stairwells and smoke them out. It would have been dangerous but feasible to swing weights down from the deck above, smash the clearviews and then come in like an army of Tarzans, sliding down ropes. In the final analysis, they could even have got a couple of battering rams and come in through the bridge wing doors the hard way. But they didn't. And no one thought to wonder why.

After an hour of effort, Yuk Tso gave up on the radio, deciding to conserve battery power until there was more traffic about in the morning and, when Robin blinked herself into wakefulness at a minute or two before eight next morning, the first thing she heard was the radio officer's monotonous repetition of the distress call. As with any self-respecting radio officer, Yuk Tso kept the radio room well stocked with electric equipment, including a kettle, but without power there was nothing for breakfast except sandwiches and water. For a while it seemed that the worst thing the pirates had done to Robin, apart from the nightmares of the killing, was to rob her of the morning tea without which she found life all but impossible.

With the coming of morning, the crew began to stir and a feeling of battle camaraderie filled the stale, hot air. It was as though they had come through the most testing military campaign together and stood victorious now. Men who had done nothing but huddle down fearfully and sleep fitfully began to move around as though they were heroes and the hum of conversation rose to a confident babble. Over which, a little after nine o'clock, Yuk Tso called exultingly, 'I have a signal! Quiet please. I have a signal!'

'Good morning, *Seram Queen*, this is the coastguard. How can I be of service to you?'

'Hello, coastguard, this is *Seram Queen*; handing you over to the captain now.'

Sin took the microphone and pulled himself erect, full of importance, like a victorious general reporting to his emperor. 'Good morning, coastguard, this is Captain Sin of the *Seram Queen*. I have to report that we require assistance urgently, please. We were overrun by pirates in the night. There are several crewmen dead and we are barricaded in the navigation bridge without power and propulsion. Can you help us, please?'

'Of course, *Seram Queen*. Can you continue to hold out for an hour? We will be with you in an hour at most.'

'We have held out through the night. We should manage one more hour. I should warn you, however, that there are more than one hundred pirates, according to our best intelligence.'

'That many, Captain? You and your men have done very well to hold out. Congratulations, sir.'

'So you need to come out fully armed, coastguard.'

'Very well, *Seram Queen*. We have a fix on your signal. You are five kilometres south-west of the Wenwei Zhou light. We will be with you in one hour and will warn you of our approach. And we will be fully armed. Over and out.'

Captain Sin put the microphone down and walked with solemn stateliness to the barricade at the top of the stairwell. 'Do you hear that, you pirate scum?' he called at the top of his voice. 'The coastguards will be here within the hour. Cut and run, you bastards, cut and run!'

There was no reply; in fact there was no sign of life at all. Within fifteen minutes, the bridge wing doors were open and the first crewmen were creeping carefully out into the bright morning, eyes everywhere, ready for attack. But the bridge wings were clear. And, from the vantage points of their outer edges, it seemed that the forward and the poop decks both were clear also. With mounting confidence, Captain Sin asked Robin to lead a small commando of heavily armed men down to get things ready for the coastguards when they came aboard. Reluctantly, she agreed. The barrier was raised and, accompanied by Sam Yung armed with the ship's old Webley Scott six-shot service revolver and two others armed with rifles, she went slowly down the stairwell, step by step. In the bright sunlight, it was hard to see the faint red dot, but; she followed it nevertheless in an agony of suspense. The bridgehouse was a mess. Everything which could be stolen seemed to be gone and anything which remained had been smashed. Although they tried to move silently, their feet crunched on broken glass and splintered wood. Absolute quiet was impossible. The four of them stuck to the corridors, keeping well clear of the wrecked rooms. Coming out of the C-deck door, they ran onto the after deck in the shadow of the funnel and looked down onto the poop, which was empty, and away across the seemingly empty sea. There were no boats to be seen and no pirates either. Even the corpse of the man Robin had shot last night had disappeared.

She put the walkie-talkie to her lips. 'Captain?'

'*Wai?*'

'No sign. Looks as though they might have gone.'

'Good. Coastguards here in fifteen minutes, they say. You let down ladders portside.'

'Very well, Captain.'

With increasing confidence the four of them went down onto the main deck and did as they were told. The white coastguard cutters were well in sight now, and Robin wondered whether she should wait at the head of the boarding ladder to welcome them aboard. But even as she wondered this, Captain Sin himself came bustling out onto the deck. Behind him came the rest of the crew. It was all so natural, so inevitable, that something about it made Robin very nervous indeed. 'Wait here, Sam,' she ordered, and ran up the deck towards the approaching men. Captain she called urgently. 'Captain, take care!'

'What is, missy?'

'You're all being too quick about this. We haven't searched. The pirates could still be aboard!'

'What we care? Coastguards come now.'

'Yes, but—'

The conversation was cut off by the thud of the first coastguard cutter thumping against the ship's side. At once Captain Sin thrust Robin aside and strode off down the deck bursting to welcome the coastguard aboard and explain their heroic actions to him. The rest of the crew surged after him. Robin stood back, her breath bated, and watched them go. And nothing happened. No screaming horde of pirates came out from behind the containers. No wave of cunningly concealed boarders broke up over the edge of the deck. Only a tall, white-uniformed coastguard came up onto the deck with a line of white-kitted men behind him, all armed to the teeth, as the captain had suggested.

You stupid woman, said Robin to herself, turning away to go back into the bridgehouse. And as she did so, she heard the one sound she was not expecting. The sharp *snap snap* of a squad of automatic weapons being cocked. She whirled round in the doorway looking back. She was just tall enough to see Captain Sin's head beside the coastguard's. Then there was a loud report and the captain's head was gone. She whirled again and took to her heels as the crisp report of the firing squad echoed that first shot. The sound of the firing loosed all hell. Behind her, she heard yelling and screaming, and more shots. The regular controlled firing of well-drilled soldiers firing into a body of ill-prepared men.

She came round the corner of the stairs up onto C deck and bumped into her first pirate. He was stepping in through the door from the deck which she had visited last night and this morning. He was dressed in jeans, trainers, a bright red T-shirt and a balaclava. He had a long panga which he raised as soon as he saw her. Then as she stood, frozen, he charged down the corridor towards her. She raised her gun. If he saw it he did so too late to stop his charge. But his shirt was red and she could not see the dot. She blinked once, trying to focus her terrified eyes, then pulled the trigger because it was far too late to do anything else. The detonation, in the enclosed space, made her ears ring. She did not close her eyes this time, and in the brightness the flash was by no means blinding. She saw the man's solid body, which at one instant had been hurling towards her, reverse its course magically and fly backwards along the corridor, arms and legs waving. Then he sat down. His shoulders hit the wall behind him. His eyes burned fiercely through the hole in the balaclava and then they rolled up.

The bridge itself was empty. Through the clearview, she could see down the length of the main deck to where the disciplined squad of white-uniformed coastguards were dumping the bodies of the crew over the side. One glance was enough, then she was in motion again, her mind racing wildly, wondering what in hell's name she was going to do now. Some deep instinct drove her higher still. She ran out onto the starboard bridge wing, on the far side of the bridgehouse to the coastguard boarding party, and hopefully out of their sight. At the aft section of this bridge wing was an exterior companionway leading up to the deck above the navigating bridge itself. Almost blindly, she ran for this and swung onto it, her breath given ragged, panicked voice by the terrified sounds her throat was making. She went up the steps two at a time and ran out onto the topmost deck. And into the arms of the pirate at the top of the stairs.

Robin hit the pirate so hard that she knocked him back two steps and this gave her some respite. She whirled away from him and bounced off the railings like a pool ball rolling along a cushion. The deck beneath her reached out into the metal awning above the starboard bridge wing and she found herself rattling down this dead-end pulpit while the pirate, overcoming his surprise, prepared to come after her.

At the end of the awning, Robin turned again with the railing across the small of her back and beyond that a fifteen-metre drop into the sea. She forced her eyes to look at the man who was advancing towards her and she gasped in recognition. It was the younger of the two survivors from the sampan. He was wearing a loose pair of shorts and a bright shirt that was too small for him. Grimly, Robin took in the peacock colours of the shirt: the last time she had seen it, Fat Chow had been wearing it. She raised the gun. 'Stop there,' she said. He raised his hands and smiled accommodatingly. But he continued to move forward. 'Stop!' she said again. His grin widened slightly. He stopped. But he was positioned exactly across the end of the pulpit. There was no way past him. Almost all the shooting and screaming had stopped below now and she knew she was running out of time. In her mind, she started swearing to herself, more and more viciously and obscenely. Her eyes flickered away from him, searching desperately for a way out. But there was no way out. And when she looked back at him he was closer still.

Suddenly, unaccountably, she found that she was crying. Perhaps it was shock. Perhaps it was rage. The pirate took her tears for defeat, and as soon as she blinked to clear them from her eyes, he charged. He had taken three steps and he was on top of her. She pulled the trigger at once. One second he was so close she could smell him, the next he was sitting, stunned, against the uprights of the deck rail. His face was absolutely white. On the breast of Fat Chow's shirt were three small red dots, she noticed. Then he rolled onto his side. She walked across to his hunched body. Behind and below it, the sea stretched anonymously. She put her foot against his shoulder and pushed with all her might. He rolled under the lower rail and fell outwards into the water. He didn't even leave a bloodstain.

Robin turned and looked up at the radio mast, her mind racing wildly. She had to have a plan. It was her only chance for survival.

Chapter Thirty-Four

Outside the Supreme Court it was bedlam. The street was full and everybody in it seemed to want to talk to Richard. Richard, however, had been galvanised by Daniel Huuk's words and all he wanted to do was to get down to the sea and into a boat which would take him out to Robin at once. Huuk and Lee vanished and there was no doubt in Richard's mind where they had gone. He burned to go with them but he was held back by the crowds. At last, wild with frustration, he turned to Andrew. 'Where's your car?' he yelled.

'Down in the official car park.'

'Let's go.'

'Where?'

'Wherever I can grab a fast boat or a helicopter. I have to get out to *Seram Queen*. Robin's aboard her!'

'I know that. But you're... Well, you're not well enough!'

'Then we'll take Tom too. For Christ's sake, let's get moving!'

Such was the intensity of his client's command that the solicitor found himself pulling Richard through the crowd. Head and shoulders above everyone there, Richard had no trouble in spotting Tom, and by good fortune they had to push their way past him to get to the car.

The psychologist didn't take too kindly to being grabbed by the shoulder, but conversation was impossible and so the three men just linked up like a kabaddi team and pushed on through. The security guard on the car park gate let them through into the relative calm of the car park and it was possible to have a bellowed conversation as they ran across towards the great crouching shape of the Aston Martin.

'Where do you think you're going?' yelled Tom.

Richard told him.

'You must be mad!' said the psychologist.

'You should know. Do you want to come?'

'Think, man! How can you hope to pull this off? You're just out of custody. You have no money, no identification. No friends, no influence. You haven't even got a proper memory. Where will you go? What will you do?'

'Tamar first. That's where Huuk and Lee will be going. Not the new one out on Stonecutter's Island, the dock down by the Prince of Wales's building. They might give me a lift. They owe me a favour or two, I think.'

'They won't. You know it!'

'You never know till you ask. Coming?' Richard was holding open the Aston's passenger door. He was sparking with frenetic energy and the psychologist was suddenly put in mind of someone leaping from brain damage to complete nervous breakdown by way of wild hyperactivity. It was all too common in his experience. The sudden access of partial memory making the patient burn all too brightly, like a bulb about to fuse. 'Come on!' bellowed Richard. The psychologist climbed aboard. Richard folded himself into the front seat and Andrew hit the starter.

Once they were free of the traffic round the courthouse, they had a relatively clear run down the hill and they were pulling in beside the Prince of Wales's building within twenty minutes. As Richard had surmised, Huuk's powerful-looking coastguard cutter was sitting at the bottom of the steps and as the three men hurried across the road, the two officers clambered aboard her. Richard skidded to a halt at the top of the steps. Huuk looked upwards and their eyes met. The white-uniformed figure shook his head and yelled an order. The powerful boat surged forward and out into the open waterway. Richard slapped his open hand against the bollard at the top of the steps and turned, racked by frustration, momentarily at a loss. Up on the roadway behind, a taxi pulled up and a tall, white-haired figure pulled himself out of the back. Hurrying down the side of the Prince of Wales's building, the figure came close to a run. 'What do you want here, Wally?' called Richard as he recognised the anxious face of his erstwhile friend.

'Richard,' the old captain panted, 'I'm sorry. I had no idea, I swear. My God, I . . .' He came up beside Richard, his open face marked by sorrow and his open hand held out.

After a moment, Richard took the open hand. 'It wasn't your fault, Wally. You were only trying for a little happiness. Phyl's going to have your guts for garters, though.'

'How can you be remembering all this?' called Tom, overcome by the knowledge his patient was suddenly displaying.

'God knows,' answered Richard. 'What I still don't know, however, is just how the hell we're going to get out to the *Seram Queen!*'

But even as he spoke, the answer came nosing up to the bottom of the steps in the shape of a long, black sampan. The door at the back of the low, coffin-shaped house amidships opened and Richard found himself looking into the calm, still face of another old friend. 'Going my way, Twelvetoes?' he asked.

'I have an account to settle with the men on the *Seram Queen*,' said Twelvetoes quietly. 'And I believe you do too, old friend.'

'Coming?' Richard asked the others, throwing the question over his shoulder as he sprang into action; but Andrew and Tom held back. 'Fair enough,' snapped Richard, acting as though all the slow hesitancy which had marked his demeanour during the last weeks had just invested more and more vigour to be held against this moment.

Halfway down the steps, he turned and looked up again. 'Wally? You have some scores to settle out here too.'

Wally nodded once and was in motion.

'Aw, what the hell,' said Andrew. 'It can't be any worse than rugger.' Halfway down the steps he turned. 'If I don't get back,' he said theatrically to Tom, 'tell Maggie I died with her name on my lips.'

'Tell her yourself,' said the psychologist, and followed the solicitor and his patient down onto the sinister-looking boat.

The sampan looked to be old and battered but its lines were lean and aquadynamic. What seemed to be a venerable, lethargic transport was actually anything but. The sides were high and the keel narrow and deep. There was a deep step down into the body of the boat and a right turn into another deep step down past a tiny but hyper-efficient wheelhouse packed with enough instrumentation to guide a destroyer into battle. Beyond the wheelhouse, down in the depths of the coffin-like cabin, was a long open space with benches on either hand and high, wide ports which let in lots of light.

As soon as the four Englishmen had stepped aboard, the vessel surged forward with a thoroughly deceptive access of naked power. 'Good God!' said Andrew, as the full impact of the acceleration hit his system. 'This thing pulls away like my Aston. What do you think, Tom?'

'I think I ought to make an appointment to examine the pair of us. This is utter lunacy,' he said bitterly as he followed the rest of them down past the wheelhouse into the depths of the cabin.

But no one was paying any attention to him. Twelvetoes and Richard were crouching over a long box which stood open along the middle of the narrow cabin, made narrower by the fact that a round dozen of fiercely-armed young men and women were seated down each side with their knees pointing inwards. Richard glanced up from what he and Twelvetoes were doing. 'Want a gun, Wally?'

'Got a Webley? That's about my speed.'

'Not by the look of it. Smith and Wesson revolver any good?'

'Richard,' said Andrew urgently. 'This is all terribly illegal. If you don't get killed, you really are running the risk of ending up back in prison. And not in any cushy hospital room this time, either. Stanley, Shek Pik or even Sieu Lam. Bad news. You don't want to think about it, believe me.'

Richard looked up at him, blue eyes dazzling. 'It's like this, you see, Andrew. My wife Robin is on the *Seram Queen*. You've met her. You know what she's like. I still only remember bits and pieces about the life we had before I went on the *Sulu Queen* but since I met her six weeks ago, I've fallen in love with her all over again. I know that she will have found a way of staying alive if there was a way to be found. She'll probably be waiting and hoping for help. And I'm going to help her the best way I can no matter what. I won't hang about and I won't hesitate. I won't go in unarmed and I don't care who I have to kill. I'm going in to get her and I'm going to bring her out, if I can, no matter what it costs. Do you understand that?'

As a matter of fact, Andrew had understood relatively little, up to now. But now he understood all too well. And what he understood was this: he was trapped aboard a high-powered, probably unregistered sampan with a small army of Triad soldiers, a considerable and certainly illegal arsenal, a senior Triad man and a lunatic. And the only person he could ask for help was caressing a Smith & Wesson revolver and looking fiercely ahead across the water. Suddenly the bravado of his last words to Tom struck him like a lead balloon coming down on his head as he realised that, with or without Maggie's name on his lips, he might well die here. Really and genuinely die here. Perhaps he should take a gun after all, just to be on the safe side.

Andrew ended up with a gun not dissimilar to Robin's, equipped with a red-dot laser sight. It was the best gun Twelvetoes could supply for a man who had never shot. Then, after he had accepted it, Andrew followed Richard up out of the doors at the front of the long cabin and up onto a pointed forecastle head. Here, with the air thudding past them and the spray sheeting up on either hand as the lean vessel powered forwards at the better part of thirty knots, Andrew spent the better part of half an hour trying to hit bottles and cans which were thrown over the side as target practice. To begin with he missed everything, but by the time the half-hour had passed, he was hitting one in three. He was quite elated when he went back down below.

They could not convince Tom, however. 'I'm a doctor, for heaven's sake, Richard! I know we don't actually *take* the Hippocratic oath, but I'll be damned if I'm going to run around slaughtering people!'

'That isn't the point,' said Richard steadily, his eyes almost white with intensity. 'The point is that when we get on board the *Seram Queen*—'

'If we get aboard.'

'All right, if we get aboard, then we will in all probability find a small army of men who will not think twice about killing us. All of them will be armed with pangas at the very least. Many of them will have handguns and some of them will have automatic weapons. I . . . I . . .' but the wild certainty died. Richard had run hard up against the edge of his damaged memory.

'There's something else?' asked Tom, overtaken by professional curiosity. 'Something else important?'

'Where do pirates get automatic weapons?' grumbled Andrew.

'From the Philippines,' supplied Twelvetoes.

'What are Filipino pirates doing this far north?' demanded Wally, deeply offended by the unsporting nature demonstrated by Filipino pirates hunting outside their proper territory. 'Surely . . .' his voice tailed off, and he frowned.

'Precisely,' said Richard, his eyes narrow. 'There's a good reason for it, I just can't remember what it is.'

'You will, old friend,' said Twelvetoes quietly.

The sampan was raging along at near full speed but not quite at full throttle, for, as the lawyer in particular was all too well aware, it was following in the wake of a flotilla of much more official vessels. Ahead of them and on the right – 'Starboard!' bellowed Richard – raced an arrowhead of three white naval launches from HMS *Tamar* and a blue-sided police cutter. 'They're never going to let us get involved anyway,' said Andrew with considerable satisfaction as forty-five minutes of the wild voyage ticked by and noon came up on his watch.

'That will depend upon what they are doing themselves, will it not?' asked Twelvetoes and Andrew found himself running out of charity with the Chinese's cryptic observations pretty quickly. But that might have been something to do with the tension he could feel cranking itself up towards terror in his breast.

He opened his mouth to say something cutting to Twelvetoes but just as he did so, the young man in the wheelhouse leaned down into the cabin and yelled something to Twelvetoes instead. The Chinese looked across at Richard for an instant, but Richard was unaware of the calculating gaze. 'OK,' yelled Twelvetoes in reply and the young man disappeared again.

'Are you going to stay aboard the sampan, Tom?' Andrew asked conversationally.

'I'll plan to be wherever I think it's safest,' said the psychologist.

'Wise move. Except that you left the safest places far behind when you got on board this boat,' observed Andrew drily.

'Must have been a rush of blood,' admitted Tom. 'And I wanted to be with Richard when he burnt out.'

'I'm not going to burn out,' said Richard.

'I wouldn't bet on it.'

'But then I bet you're not a betting man, Tom.'

'That's true, Richard.' Tom forced himself to keep his tone neutral, accommodating. It was a standard phase of treatment that the subject should start to experience negative thoughts towards the psychologist but Richard was going through too many standard phases in too rapid a succession for Tom's peace of mind. Still, when you came right down to it, all he could do was watch and wait.

'How much longer?' asked Andrew, really beginning to regret his bravado now.

'Not long. You should try some more target practice. One hit in three isn't really good enough,' said Richard.

'It is if you're going to avoid shooting at anybody.'

'True.'

On Richard's slightly mocking monosyllable, the young man in the wheelhouse leaned down and called through to Twelvetoes in an impenetrable babble of Cantonese.

'We're nearly there,' said Twelvetoes. 'The man says there are three boats there, the *Seram Queen* and two smaller ones.'

'Is he sure he's got the right ship?' asked Richard.

'Oh yes. We have been following the beam of a ship's emergency beacon for some time now. Since noon, in fact. The beacon broadcasts *Seram Queen*'s call signal.'

'Two other boats,' mused Richard. 'Big boats?'

'Large cutters, perhaps,' suggested Twelvetoes calculatingly.

Richard's face went blank and for a moment Tom feared that all his worst fears had come true and Richard had burned out.

But no. 'Cutters!' said Richard, his voice scarcely more than a breath. '*Coastguard* cutters!' His eyes ignited. Tom had never seen anything like it in his life. It was as though a pair of magnesium flares had gone off behind panes of deep sapphire. It was as though beams of brightness shone out of the lean, angular face. The effect was most unsettling. But that was nothing as compared with the tone of his voice. 'Of course! That was it!' His spread hand came up to slap his forehead with stunning force. Tom winced, but Richard did not seem to have hurt himself. That terrible, hate-filled voice grated on. 'The pirates set us up and the coastguards all but wiped us out, then the pirates came back and finished the job. The Chinese coastguards.'

'I don't understand,' said Andrew. 'What are you talking about?'

'They have an arrangement! An agreement. The pirates send out a half-wrecked sampan full of corpses with a couple of their men apparently at death's door in among the genuine Vietnamese. The two men shut down the radio and any other equipment they can and help the pirates aboard. The pirates go through the ship but the crew as likely as not makes a bit of a fight of it. Then next morning, bright and early, the Chinese coastguards show up and drive the pirates away. The crew comes out and the coastguards arrest them. Lock them away. Any argument and the coastguards kill them. Then the coastguards load whatever they want onto their cutters and leave the last pickings to the pirates. It was so ... so ... neat. We didn't stand a chance, Wally. And when they discovered the containers weren't carrying what they wanted, they all just went mad. Pirates, coastguards, the lot. I've never seen ... I've never seen ... And, God, Robin will fall for it all the way down the line. Robin will fall for it all ...' Richard's voice faded away, and Tom realised with a visceral shock that his patient was actually remembering. Actually remembering everything which had happened on the ill-fated *Sulu Queen*. Facing everything he had run away from for the last seven weeks.

Remembering because to do so was the only way he could hope to help his wife if she was trapped in the same situation now. It was a massive act of will, far in excess of anything Tom had ever considered possible. But, then, Tom had never actually been in love.

Much struck by this melancholy thought, Tom went out onto the forward deck to have a word with the one other man aboard who he knew to be deeply in love: Andrew.

As soon as the psychiatrist was gone, Richard swung round to focus his blazing glare on Twelvetoes. 'And I think I can see where you fit into all this, too,' he spat. His tone was cool enough to render the Chinaman's still gaze faintly speculative.

'Indeed. I said to Robin that you would be the first to see the whole pattern as soon as your memory returned.'

That gave Richard pause. 'You talked to Robin?'

'Twice. And to Miss Patel. I offered such help as I could and such information as I knew. As much as was safe.'

Richard's lips narrowed; so did his eyes until they were as deeply slitted as the Oriental's – the bright pupils still burning behind them like the last of the sky beneath the storm clouds off Singapore in that instant before the lightning struck. 'Do these people speak English?'

'Perfectly, all of them; but you need not hesitate to talk in front of them. They are my sons and daughters.'

Richard did not even hesitate to consider whether Twelvetoes meant that literally. He plunged on, pulled by the power of his awakening reason, adding what he had heard in evidence during his trial to what he had known before Huuk had shot him, carried away by it all like a novice astride a runaway horse. 'It was all yours, wasn't it? You have a Triad of your own and you concentrate on smuggling pirated goods, discs, CD Roms, software, videos. The White Powder Triad let it be known that the ghost containers were full of cocaine in order to cover the fact that it was the next shipment which would contain it. In the meantime the containers were really full of your goods. All those videos of Disney's *Sinbad*; they were coming to you. *You!*'

'And if it is true?' whispered Twelvetoes.

Richard hardly seemed to have heard his old friend. He plunged on, his words falling over each other, scarcely making sense at all. 'And they took it all. They went through the containers until they found the marked ones – up on the top right out in the open – and then they went mad. They were expecting cocaine and they found *Sinbad* instead. Of course they went mad, But they took the containers nevertheless. And it was your shipment all along.'

'I admit nothing, of course,' said Twelvetoes more firmly. 'But if it were true, then what?'

'Then you have some scores to settle too. My God do you have some scores to settle.'

Twelvetoes nodded once, a precise, chopping movement of the head – uncharacteristic in a man whose movements were always so fluid. '*Hai*,' he said. 'Then let us find the Little Mistress and settle our scores shoulder to shoulder, old friend.'

There was a moment of silence while the two of them remained face to face, mere centimetres apart; then Richard pulled back with a bark of laughter. 'Tell me you haven't planned this, right from the start! he said. 'As soon as you heard what had happened to your shipment and discovered what had happened to me, it all became part of your plan!'

And Twelvetoes gave the ghost of a smile.

The helmsman leaned in again and yelled, '*Ngah fan!*': five minutes. Richard and Twelvetoes climbed back up into the wheelhouse, and as they did so, a gabble of conversation through the radio became audible. There were no familiar voices but the overlapping conversations were all in English and it was plain at once that they were coming from transmissions aboard the cutters and launches to starboard.

'... Chinese coastguard cutters still in position ...'

'... Cutters not responding ...'

'Come in, Chinese coastguard. You are in Hong Kong waters ...'

'... I have to inform you that you are in Crown Colony jurisdiction. Please reply or we will be forced to board you, over.'

'Last container being winched into place ...'

'... Men in uniform coming off the freighter now, sir ...'

'... First cutter pulling away now, sir ...'

'Chinese coastguard cutter, heave to, please. I have to inform you that you are under arrest ...'

'Second cutter pulling away now, sir ...'

Then a familiar voice, tough and decisive. 'This is Commander Lee. All Crown Colony vessels pursue Chinese coastguard cutters. I say again, all Crown Colony vessels pursue Chinese coastguard cutters. These vessels must not be allowed to escape!'

The group of stunned listeners on the sampan looked away to the right as the arrowhead of official vessels swung away to the starboard and began to pursue the vanishing Chinese boats. And, dead ahead, the good ship *Seram Queen* lay dead in the water. Dead and, to all intents and purposes, deserted.

They were all out on the forecastle by the time the sampan came in under the high counter of the quiet ship and began to nose in towards the lowered accommodation ladder, gently pushing its way through the first of the floating corpses as it went. It was lucky that the sampan was substantial and the accommodation ladder was fully extended, for the water was heaving. It would not have taken the sharks long to find the bodies of the stricken ship's crew even had they not been chopped about by the blades of the fleeing cutters' propellers. The presence of the boats and the activity going on around them had kept the ravening fish away until a few minutes ago and there were no large numbers yet and nothing like a feeding frenzy so far – but the water was clearly a lethally dangerous place to be and everybody aboard the sampan was well aware that they would have to be extremely careful how they moved.

'Had we better do one full circle before we go aboard, just to scout things out?' asked Wally, harking back to his long-past Navy days.

His answer came in the sound of a single shot from high above. They all looked up as though their heads were moved by a single impulse. And as they did so, the port side of the sampan slid up against the platform at the bottom of the accommodation ladder. Twelvetoes leaned down into the long cabin and spat an order. At once the forecastle of the long boat was full of his soldiers. They held the boat in place as the first team of five went over and up, moving like a jungle patrol with swift, silent, shadowy liquidity, forming overlapping pairs and vanishing onto the deck. Another order was called, another patrol vanished upwards. 'We go next,' said Twelvetoes. 'They take the point but we lead the main attack. We will not rush along the deck, however. We will form up at the head of the accommodation ladder until we are joined by the other two contingents, and wait for each *wu* to report. We will not proceed without intelligence.'

'That sounds sensible to me,' said Tom.

'Like hell it does,' said Andrew. 'It sounds like that man is getting ready to go to war. We're all going to get arrested. If we're lucky enough to survive until the police get back.'

'Oh, come on!' said Wally. 'You want to live for ever?'

Andrew thought about all the things he wanted to say to – and do with – Maggie DaSilva. 'Yes,' he said feelingly. 'Yes, I bloody well do!'

But this conversation was being continued as they all hurried down the length of the sampan and by the time Andrew came to his heartfelt conclusion, he was stepping across onto the platform at the foot of the accommodation ladder.

Then, in silence, they all ran up the ladder and tumbled over onto the deck in a group, except that Richard and Twelvetoes somehow seemed to be in the lead. Andrew and Wally followed, and Tom came up behind them. Although Tom was no military strategist and had no idea he was listening to the precepts of Sun Tsu, Twelvetoes' words had made it sound as though things would be well-organised and relatively safe up here. And one look at what was happening in the water beside the ship had put the psychologist off any ideas of staying below.

The deck was littered. The Chinese coastguard had not been too particular about the way in which they unloaded the containers and, although some had been dumped over the side, others had been dropped onto the deck, leaving a jumbled terrain of smashed wood and wildly spewed contents.

The command team ran forward half a dozen steps into the shelter of a half-container with a jagged top. Then, while the others crouched hard against the reassuring solidity of the wooden wall, Richard and Twelvetoes looked between the pointed crenellations as though over a castle wall. All the way up the length of the deck there was a mess of ruined, burst containers – plenty of cover. But, what was cover for them was also cover for their enemies. As they watched, they saw the ten Triad soldiers working their way swiftly up towards the bridge – a series of shadowy movements, no more – surveying the terrain as they went.

'If it is clear between here and the bridge then we will move forward and re-form in the A-deck corridor,' said Twelvetoes gently.

'We're not likely to be dealing with a well-organised force,' agreed Richard, 'but it wouldn't take much of a general to let your first *wu* past and then blast us from the upper decks of the bridge when we begin to follow them up the deck.'

'In difficult ground, we will press on. It is conceivable but I would not base my calculations upon such a remote possibility.'

As he finished speaking, there came a brief buzzing sound and from the pocket of his black tunic the old man pulled a tiny walkie-talkie. He pressed it to his ear. There was a gabble of sound. 'We go,' he said at once.

Side by side, with two more groups of five running beside and behind them, the group of men went up the deck. Breathlessly, they jumped in through the open door into the A-deck corridor. Immediately in front of them the two teams of five were waiting, keeping the area safe until they arrived. At the instant of their arrival, the two forward teams were off again. 'I'd send one team at least aft,' said Richard, his voice low. 'If there are many pirates aboard, they'll be grouping on the poop.'

No sooner had he stopped speaking than Twelvetoes gestured and one of the two remaining teams of five vanished to check Richard's suggestion. No sooner had they gone, however, than a shot rang out just above their heads. It was followed by a loud, wavering scream which was abruptly terminated by a second shot.

'We have contact,' said Richard. He swung round. 'Right, you three. It's make up your mind time. I'm going up there. I have to find Robin if she's aboard and this is the best place to start looking. Twelvetoes is a good general. He will check ahead and progress from citadel to citadel. It should be as safe a way of getting around this ship as there is. You can come with me or stay with him and his staff here.'

'I'll stay,' said Tom at once.

'Me too,' said Andrew.

'Very wise. Wally?'

'I'm with you, Richard.' The old man cocked the Smith & Wesson to show that he meant business.

'Right,' said Richard. 'Got a spare walkie-talkie, Twelvetoes?'

Twelvetoes gestured at the leader of the last five-man unit and the young man handed over his walkie-talkie without question. As Richard took it, he realised with a slight shock that the young warrior was not a man at all but a woman, little more than a girl.

Richard checked the tiny, state-of-the-art instrument and slipped it in his breast pocket. At no time did it strike him as incongruous that he was embarking on what was to all intents and purposes a guerrilla war dressed in the white shirt, paisley tie, dark pinstripe suit and suede shoes purchased by Robin in Cat Street market for his court appearance. He checked that the boxy grey Smith & Wesson automatic he was carrying was cocked. He patted his left-hand pocket like a man checking his keys before leaving the house. But it was not keys that he was interested in, it was spare magazines. 'Do you remember how to do this?' he asked Wally quietly.

'Navy days seem a long way away now but I trained with Special Forces for Korea,' admitted Wally. 'Standard high and low?'

'I'll go high and I'll go first.'

'Right you are.'

The conversation had hardly risen above a monotone and was over within seconds but when the two men vanished into the stairwell moving upwards, they left behind a telling effect.

'Who'd have thought it?' muttered Andrew. 'Maybe we'd have been safer with those two.'

'Oh no,' said Tom feelingly. 'No, I think not.'

Robin had seen the Chinese coastguards load the containers onto their boats with increasingly frenetic haste. In spite of the heat, which was giving her the mother and father of all headaches, she had seen the chevron of official-looking boats come speeding over the horizon and she'd seen them peel away like a squadron of fighters in pursuit of the fleeing, container-laden cutters. She had seen the long black sampan come nosing through the carnage in the water but had not recognised it as the one which had taken her out to *Sulu Queen* all those weeks back. Frankly, she had not liked the look of it, and this jaundiced first impression had been compounded by the fact that, no sooner had it come nosing under the flare of the forecastle head than a pirate had rushed wildly across the deck below her and started to try and climb up the radio mast.

At first, when the top of his head, shaded with a bright headcloth, had appeared at the bottom of the ladder, she had been stricken with indecision. He did not seem to know she was there. He was simply climbing up to hide, the same as she herself had done. But then, by sheer good luck from her point of view and bad luck from his, he had looked up. Their eyes had met. Twisted by surprise, anger, some terrifyingly powerful emotion, he had snarled at her. Actually snarled, like a fierce animal. She had shot him without a second thought then, sending a bullet through the red dot on the upper slope of his chest to knock him down and away like a fly being swatted. Her only real regret was that the body lying immediately below her on the deck gave her position away to anyone who wanted to do a little thinking. But thought was a commodity in short supply aboard the *Seram Queen*, she thought bitterly.

She saw a surge of movement up over the edge of the distant main deck, then a dark ripple of movement along its littered length. Then she stopped paying attention, for a series of much closer sounds began. She wondered whether it was worth the risk to climb down from her safe haven and move the body away. But that lack of thought apparently saved her from further molestation for the moment. A small group of men, apparently friends of the deceased, came scurrying across the green deck below her and, finding him stretched out there, made quite a pantomime of looking for the source of the shot. Right and left then fore and aft they looked, but none of them looked upwards. Then, a couple of decks further below, there came a shot and a heartrending scream followed by another shot. The little group of pirates jabbered excitedly to each other and then fled away across the deck again, heading down into the bridgehouse. More in order to ease the unutterable tension of her neck and shoulder muscles, Robin sat back and looked around. So it was that she saw the Chinese coastguard cutters surging away towards the northern horizon with the three white Crown Colony cutters close in their wake. And she saw that the blue-sided police launch had turned away from the chase and was heading back towards the *Seram Queen*.

Richard and Wally came across the first corpse in the middle of the B-deck corridor. It was the corpse of a Chinese coastguard, dressed in white uniform, complete with starched shorts. He had been shot messily through the belly, just above the groin, and neatly through the heart. Whispers of movement all around them told of black-clad figures searching the wrecked rooms and clearing the decks one by one going up, so that Twelvetoes and his command centre could move upwards one step at a time without fearing attack, if they chose to. But Richard particularly wanted to proceed a little more quickly than that, no matter about the increased risk. He had a private mission and would not be satisfied until it was fulfilled in one way or another. The two men danced past the dead Chinese and whirled into the next companionway, vanishing upwards like wraiths, Richard going high and Wally going low at every turn.

Richard and Robin often teased each other that they were psychically linked. They would start conversations together, pick up each other's meanings halfway through phrases. On at least one occasion, only the knowledge that if one died they both would die had kept the pair of them alive. But if they had really shared any kind of psychic link, Richard would have picked up the lingering warnings that Robin had left on C deck, knowing as she did that the C-deck door out onto the companionway and the rear deck beside the funnel was the pirates' favourite method of ingress and egress. As it was, Richard picked up no warnings at all as he and Wally whirled round the corner, high and low, scanning the corridor. It was all quiet. They moved, dancing out into the corridor itself and preparing to run on up towards the navigation bridge. Just as they did so, in that moment while both of their guns were pointing up the stairwell towards the next landing, the door at the end of the corridor burst open and half a dozen pirates spilled in. Both men spun round, their guns levelled. There was a fraction of a second's hesitation. Neither Richard nor Wally wanted to start a gunfight and the pirates in all probability could not believe that they were confronted by a couple of men dressed in dark suits, as though on their way to a funeral. But the hesitation lasted only a split second and then the pirate nearest the back, protected by the bodies of his crew mates, shot first. His bullet went wide and sang away down the corridor, ricocheting off the steel walls, but the sound of the shot was enough and the ricochet was lost in the hail of fire which followed. Richard, going high, was half in the stairwell with his left shoulder behind the steel wall. Wally was half a body's width in front of him so that Richard's right side was behind his old friend's left. Richard shot and shot and shot over Wally's shoulder, not really picking his targets, and certainly not trying for the double-tap he had been taught in the Gulf, but emptying his magazine into the mass of enemies at head height, blasting them backwards as hard as he could, trying to give them no real opportunity to reply.

Wally, too, was firing as fast as he could but the old revolver was a very different weapon to Richard's automatic and he found it hard to get the double action flowing smoothly. There was a great deal of shouting and screaming going on here, he thought, and he hoped he wasn't doing any of it himself. And then there came the most God-awful pain in his side and he found himself sitting down suddenly. He couldn't focus his eyes and his gun grew terribly heavy. Richard stepped over and past him, the remorseless hammering of his pistol never letting up as he walked towards the men crouching – no, lying – at the door. At least the screaming seemed to be dying down, thought Wally; that was something to be thankful for.

Then there was silence, though Wally still had the strangest ringing in his ears. A sort of hissing, whistling ringing. And he couldn't catch his breath because of the pain in his side. Richard loomed over him suddenly and he realised he must have slipped from sitting to lying without noticing the change in position. God, his side hurt. And he knew exactly why, of course. He had always feared it and now it had happened. How ironic, he thought. 'Sorry, old man,' he said. 'My bloody appendix has exploded. Always knew it would. No use to you any more, I'm afraid. No use at all.'

Richard looked down into the great ragged wound left by the makeshift dum-dum round fired by the dead pirate. He couldn't even see a way to staunch the blood hissing out onto the floor because the wound was so enormous. That's all right,' he said gently. 'Just you wait here. Twelvetoes' people will be up to check us out in a moment. You'll get sorted out then.'

He had hardly finished speaking before they arrived in a silent rush. Five of them all at once. Calm-eyed, intense, terrifyingly efficient. Armed to the teeth. All girls. Richard hadn't realised that they were all girls. Wally pulled convulsively at his sleeve. 'I say, if I don't make it to hospital this time, just tell the old girl that I love her, would you? And the boy. Mustn't forget the boy.'

'Yes, of course,' said Richard automatically, then he opened his lips to ask a question, but as he did so he saw the light die in Wally's eyes and he knew he was too late, and he didn't know which old girl Wally was talking about.

Richard took a deep breath, breathing in until his ribs felt as though they were going to burst apart. Do any of you speak English? he asked the girls, only just managing to keep his voice under control.

'We all do,' said one of them so quietly he had to strain to hear.

'Are you the leader?' He dropped his voice to echo her tone.

'Yes.'

'Can you spare me one of your team? I need another partner.'

The calm eyes regarded him from under the deep lids and the high black arches of the eyebrows rose just the tiniest of fractions.

'You know where you're going, Captain? she asked. He was asking to borrow one of her soldiers – it was a reasonable question.

'I'm going up,' he answered. 'You and the others are checking deck by deck, I know, so if my wife is in any of the rooms in the bridgehouse you will find her and you will tell Twelvetoes and he will tell me. But I need to go first into the places you might not be searching and I need to go quickly. Time may be limited. The only shots we have heard since we came aboard that you or I did not fire came from up there. I must go up!'

The leader's eyes narrowed until they were invisible behind the thickness of her black lashes. And she nodded once. 'Su-zi,' she said.

The smallest of the team stood up; scarcely more than a teenager by the look of her and certainly nowhere old enough to be holding a gun that size. As far as Richard could tell, it was the identical gun to his own massive Smith & Wesson .44 Magnum. 'Right,' he breathed. Then he pulled out the empty clip and replaced it. The sound this made was the loudest sound that had occurred in the corridor since the shooting had stopped. 'If it's all the same to you, Suzy,' he whispered, you go low and I'll go high. And I'll go first.'

High and low they went, round the next corner and up the stairs, and round the next corner. Were it not for the fact that they were being extremely careful, they would have died then, for that last corner brought them round into the well of the last set of stairs up to the navigation bridge. At the top of this stairwell was the barricade Robin had caused to be erected a little less than fifteen hours earlier and behind it was a bunch of extremely nervous pirates whose fear had been wound to fever pitch by the sounds of shooting they had just heard from immediately below their feet. At the first intimation of movement, the pirates let loose a volley of shots and Richard spun backwards, knocking Su-zi out of the line of fire as he went. He fell clumsily and rolled down the stairs to land on his hands and knees in Wally's blood. Su-zi landed like a ballerina beside him and looked down expressionlessly as he began to pull himself up. 'OK,' he said, just audibly, 'point taken. I'm sorry.'

The rest of Su-zi's *wu* had gone, and so had poor Wally. The dead pirates were still piled against the bullet-pocked door, however. 'This way, I think, said Richard, gesturing with his chin. Su-zi gave a minuscule nod and they were off, out onto the external companionways.

The two fusillades of shots gave Robin some hope. If whoever was coming her way through the bridgehouse was fighting the pirates then they might well be willing to help her. What was the old saying? 'My enemy's enemy is my friend.' But if they were coming up through the bridgehouse deck by deck, as they seemed to be doing, then they would in all probability drive the pirates up here first. So she was likely to have at least one more hard fight before she met her enemy's enemy. Still, she had nine shots left, her back was not quite against the wall yet.

But no sooner had this bracing thought entered her head than pandemonium broke out on the deck below. Up one side of the deck came half a dozen white uniformed Chinese coastguards and up the other came a similar number of pirates. Whether the tension of their situation was simply too much for them, and panic took over from reasoned thought, Robin did not know, but as soon as they saw each other, both groups opened fire. At once, Robin's confidence that the platform she was sitting on might prove bullet-proof was also challenged as bullets came singing up past her in screaming ricochets. The two groups seemed to be past any kind of human reasoning. Instead of finding cover and sniping at each other from relative safety, both groups, like pointlessly suicidal Kamikazes, ran towards each other, screaming wordlessly and firing with all their might. Almost inevitably, the two waves of men met halfway across the deck, exactly at the foot of her radio mast. Down there, immediately below her, a wild and terrible shoot-out took place, for none of these men in their hand-to-hand fighting was using knives or even pangas, they were simply standing almost breast to breast emptying bullets from handguns into each other at point-blank range.

They could not keep it up and none of them could survive such an onslaught. At last there was only a jumble of twitching bodies lying at the foot of the ladder below her. And, on the top, one man still alive, facing upwards. Robin knew he was still alive because of the electric jolt which slammed through her system when their eyes met. He lay on his back, on the top of this pile of bodies with his white uniform shirt torn and stained with what looked like blackcurrant jam. And he looked up into her wide eyes and he smiled. His body began to twitch and writhe, and Robin thought perhaps he was trying to get up, but then, suddenly, incredibly, she saw that he was pulling his pistol up and taking aim at her. Frozen with the inconceivable insanity of his action, she sat and watched him pull a huge, old-fashioned revolver up and, with his face locked in an agony of concentration, push it up towards her into the firing position. It was only the sharp click as he pulled the hammer back which galvanised her. 'No!' she screamed at the top of her lungs and she pushed her own gun down towards him. The dot flared brightly on his breast and she squeezed the trigger with all her might. The gun exploded and his body slammed back into the soft pile beneath him as though the dead men had been mere cushions. She raised the gun until it was pointing at the sky. Then she realised she was still screaming down at him, and she choked herself into silence.

Richard slammed back against the wall outside the C-deck door, his eyes raking the deck beyond the companionway and then flicking out over the sea. In an instant of vision he noted that the cutters, Chinese and Crown Colony, were very nearly hull down now, and that the police launch was very very close indeed. He wondered for a split second why Commander Lee had commanded his men to bring him back – probably so that he could put any surviving pirates under arrest. But then Richard's thoughts were wiped away by a screaming, thundering fusillade of shots which seemed to come from immediately above his head. Such was the overwhelming noise of the battle, he and Su-zi had no need to worry about moving quietly and so they pounded up, past the closed doors protecting the passage ends behind the fortified bridge and onto the topmost section of the deck. Here, piled round the foot of the radio mast, was the result of all that shooting. And even as Richard's great body froze, with Su-zi by his side, taking stock of the carnage, so the topmost body on the pile thrust his arms upwards, taking aim, and a voice screamed 'No!', only to be drowned out by the explosion of a gun. The body on top of the pile jumped as a bullet hit it, and the cry went on and on.

And Richard recognised the voice. The sound of that cry echoed within him as though it would cause him to explode. He tensed himself to run forward but Su-zi's hand fastened on his arm, restraining him.

'It's my wife,' he said, still talking in the near-whisper of combat. 'It's Robin.'

'She safe,' breathed the wise warrior. 'We take care.'

'I've got to go to her!'

'One step at a time. You no good to her shot in the back.'

She was right. Silently, but as swiftly as they possibly could, the pair of them began to pick their way across the deck, checking that all the silent, bleeding men were actually dead. It was the action of perhaps ten minutes before they were absolutely sure that it would be safe to approach that central pile. I go in first,' said Richard. 'You cover me.' With his heart in his mouth, he walked forward across the deck, his eyes fixed on the square trap in the steel floor of the little platform high on the radio mast. He walked slowly, knowing that she would be able to see him long before he could see her, but by no means certain that she would be able to make out exactly who he was and wondering whether he should call out to her. His head was whirling with such a wild range of speculation that he wondered whether or not Tom had been right and he was just going to burn out before he could let her see that he was free, that she had pulled it all off and rescued him.

Richard stopped at the outside edge of the pile of bodies, peering up, still not able to see anything beyond the square edge of the trap. 'Robin?' he called, but he couldn't get his voice to work and no sound came out. He tried to clear his throat. 'Robin?' he said again.

But the sound of Richard's word was lost in the sound of a single gun shot. Richard whirled, raising his own gun. 'Too late, Captain Mariner,' called a mocking, familiar voice. There, with his arm round Su-zi's throat and his service revolver moving back to cover her head, stood Commander Victor Lee of the Royal Hong Kong Police. He was little more than seven metres distant, and for a wild moment Richard thought about risking a snap shot – but the girl's body was held too close and covered too much of Lee's to give him any realistic chance.

'Too late for what, Commander?' called Richard, his voice betraying his amazement that the man was here, and behaving like this.

'Too late for you, too late for your friend Twelvetoes Ho, too late for his daughter Su-zi here. You did not know? I see you did not. But there is so much you did not know, Captain. It is too late for the good Captain Huuk who, I fear, will never catch his Chinese smugglers now. Perhaps even too late for the People's Republic of China who think they will come and take away my country and my home and all my life's work. I have started another Opium War, Captain Mariner, and I have done it in spite of everything you have tried to do to stop me. Now, put your weapon down, please, and be quick. There is little time.'

At the sound of the shot, Robin jumped awake. It was as though she had been in a trance since she shot the man at the foot of the ladder. She had noticed nothing of the new arrivals on the deck and it came as a stunning shock to her when she heard Richard's voice. Fighting back an impulse to stand up and call to him, Robin instead peered carefully out of her little eyrie. She could not see Richard at all, but she could see the fat policeman holding a frail girl round the throat.

But then she heard Richard's voice again, speaking slowly, addressing the words to Lee but actually speaking to her.' Little time for what, Commander? What have you got planned this time?'

'You'll never find out, Mariner. I'll keep you alive as insurance until my men have cleared things up below and then this time you're going to meet an unfortunate end.'

'Your men? Is that the pirates or the Chinese coastguards?'

'What do you care? Coastguards, pirates, policemen. They all work for me. All they need now is some organisation to stop them slaughtering each other like those imbeciles you were looking at. Then we'll see what next week will really bring to Hong Kong!'

Down below, a fierce fusillade of shots broke out, but unlike the others, this was not a short burst. This was a pitched battle.

'Right!' screamed the Commander. 'You lose! I win!' He pushed the gun into Su-zi's ear and for a moment Richard really believed he could see the red light of insanity in the man's eye. Then half of Lee's head flew apart and he whirled backwards, throwing Su-zi and the gun both wildly away. Richard ran forward, crouching, to snatch his own gun off the deck but by the time he had straightened, the fat policeman was nowhere to be seen.

'Richard?' called a wavering voice from the platform halfway up the radio mast. 'Richard, are you all right?'

'Yes, darling,' he called back. 'Yes, I'm all right now.'

And as he spoke, the northern horizon lit up in a huge fireball. The lower sky seemed to catch fire and waves of force came flashing out towards them. And, following the first blinding wall of light, before even the thunderous rumble of sound, there came a lone aeroplane, silver, sleek, deadly, bearing the markings of the Chinese People's Air Force. And as it passed at zero feet over their heads, it slowly waggled its wings and the sun caught the empty clips which had held its air-to-surface missiles. Dazed, the three of them waved up at it – Ho Su-zi from her knees on the deck, Richard, standing, shaking in the blast, and Robin, wedged up in her safe haven high up on the radio mast. They waved, and they began to cheer as the fighter circled the ship.

Commander Lee's Opium War was over before it even began.

Epilogue

Charles Lee folded the *South China Morning Post* and put it reverently away in the drawer of his big business desk. Then his eyes lost their focus as he looked out of his office window and across the teeming waterway towards Kowloon. That same edition, some months old now, had detailed the historic passing of Hong Kong from British jurisdiction to Chinese; the heroic destruction by the People's Air Force working in co-operation with officers from HMS *Tamar*, of the White Powder Triad's load of crack cocaine; and the facts in the death of his unfortunate elder brother.

How much his world had changed in the last three months, Charles mused, moved to philosophy. It was as though his long stay in Beijing and Guangzhou had opened in his mind doors which his education in England and America had only served to close in spite of his revered father's good intentions. And what would that wise, essentially gentle old patriarch have thought of the naked hatred with which he had infected his eldest son and the tragic lengths to which that hatred had been stretched? The new more philosophical and gentler Charles Lee could scarcely imagine.

Well, Charles would certainly still be here on the Festival of the Hungry Ghosts next year, and he would bring all kinds of food and sacrifices to put his brother's troubled spirit to rest. There would be time and there would be sacrifice; there would be atonement and, eventually there would be peace.

Charles felt most poignantly the need to make peace with his brother's hungry ghost, for in a strange way which could only make sense here, in the People's Republic, the sins of the elder brother had atoned for the sins of the younger. When Xiang Lo-wu had understood at last that it was Victor Lee's dark plans which were funnelling contraband in through the Tiger Gate – in the all too familiar methods of the younger Charles – he had at once released the Heritage Mariner executive, sending him downriver and across the border into Hong Kong for the last days of Crown rule. And here Charles had been able to meet up with Richard, Robin, Andrew Balfour, Maggie DaSilva and the rest and to enjoy the non-stop party through the last week in June and the first week in July. Though he, like all of them, had found the festivities tinged with his own personal sadness.

But, alongside the sadness there had been happiness too – happiness and stunning surprise, for on the last day of June, he, Charles Lee, had received an invitation to attend the ceremony in which the new People's Governor of Hong Kong would assume power on behalf of the People's Republic. All unaware, he had turned up on that bright auspicious morning, with Richard and Robin who had also been invited. Side by side the three of them had walked into the main reception room of the Governor's Palace and taken their allotted places. Amid all the pageantry they had seen a range of familiar faces. The last Governor of the Crown Colony; the Prince of Wales; the Foreign Secretary; StJohn Syme. Daniel Huuk was there in full dress uniform, as part of the last-ever honour guard. And a slight figure almost invisible amid all the pomp and circumstance, Charles's friend Xiang Lo-wu.

Charles had actually been looking around the dazzling room, wondering where the People's Governor was and why he was so late to this incredibly important ceremony when he realised that the People's Governor was there and had been there all along. And no one applauded more loudly than Charles as Xiang Lo-wu accepted his duties and responsibilities as the first People's Governor.

As Charles was folding his *South China Morning Post* and placing it reverently in his desk drawer down in the new Heritage Mariner office on the sixteenth floor of the old Jardine Matheson building, Richard Mariner was standing a couple of hundred metres behind him and eight storeys higher.

The Mariners were fortunate that the suite on the corner of the twenty-fourth floor of the People's Mandarin Hotel was available and they moved in with the twins. They had no intention of staying long on this occasion, but it was difficult to be sure about the future. It seemed most likely that Charles Lee would be the executive to settle here long-term. He was the man with the background, after all. And he was the man with the contacts – and the good sense never to take them for granted.

There had never been any question of giving Heritage Mariner an unfair advantage, in spite of everything, but there was no doubt that they had their foot in the door now. Here and now. Richard felt himself filling with all the old excitement which he thought had long since gone. There was so much to play for and the rewards of success would be simply breathtaking. He was put in mind all too vividly of the feelings he had experienced on assuming his first command. He had gone from being the busiest man aboard to the most powerful. It had seemed, then, that even life and death had lain within his hands. And he had the same feeling now. They were stepping up from senior office to command. They were joining the front rank. Becoming world-class.

Robin came through into the sitting room from the main bedroom where the twins were bouncing on the great teak bed. She found Richard out on the balcony beyond the French windows, leaning pensively over the railing and looking across the near gridlock of Connaught Road, past Jardine House and away towards Kowloon. The waterway was abustle with shipping of all sizes, through which the Star ferries were weaving their busy way. Robin, with the association still so vivid in her mind wondered about Twelvetoes, for she had seen nothing of him since he had dropped them all back at the Prince of Wales's steps after the problems with the pirates on *Seram Queen* had all been tidied up. Remembering the gentle smile on his wise old face, she could not bring herself to think that anything bad had happened to him – or would happen to him under the new system here. He had been the man who dealt in the cleanest of the contraband, and while there was a market for St Laurent shirts and Reebok shoes and Rolex watches and Walt Disney videos which were not quite what they purported to be, then Twelvetoes would continue to make a living. And so would all his daughters – and his sons, if he had any.

Robin stepped silently up onto the balcony and wrapped her arms round Richard's slim waist. 'Penny for them,' she said.

'Oh, I was just thinking,' he said gently.

She folded herself over him so that her chest was flat against his back and her chin rested on his right shoulderblade. In this position, it seemed to her, she could follow his gaze out across the busy waterway. A big ship was pulling out past the Ocean terminal just at that moment and she supposed it must have taken his eye. 'You promised, darling,' she chided gently. 'No more vanishing down to the seas again. No more commands.'

'I know,' he said equally gently. 'I'm getting too old now. I'll leave it to the younger chaps.'

The quiet admission caused her heart to swell painfully within her but this time she had no fear of falling lifeless onto Connaught Road and leaving her darlings parentless. 'Come here,' she said throatily, and she pulled him upright. He turned towards her and she swept him into her arms, thinking how much easier life would be now with Richard working nine to five in Heritage House and the family wandering contentedly between Ashenden, Summersend and Cold Fell. Thinking how little she would miss the adventures the separation, the stress.

And, as she thought these contented thoughts, Richard swung Robin round and locked her in his arms. His face swooped down and their lips crushed together. In a cocoon of contentment, she closed her eyes and allowed the sensations of love and security to wash over her, and the feeling was utterly glorious.

But even as he kissed her, Richard's eyes were tempted away. Just across the road stood the great skyscraper of Jardine house. During the last few weeks the Heritage Mariner offices had moved up from the fourth floor to the sixteenth. Where would they move during the next few years? Here was the most exciting business community in all the world and he and Charles Lee had got their foot in the door. True, everything was under new management, but here was a company ready to play by its rules.

The old Noble House had made its fortune, its face and its position out of the prosecution of the first Opium War. Why could the next one not establish its beginnings in the destruction of the second Opium War – Victor Lee's Opium War? Richard crushed Robin to his chest and crushed his lips most passionately to hers. She pulled away for an instant to whisper, 'You promise? No more ships? No more commands?'

'I promise, darling,' he whispered back, but he hardly heard what he was saying.

For Richard was looking past Robin's tumbled, golden curls and he was thinking, we can do it; we have the position, the time, the opportunity. The next Noble House. The first Noble House under Chinese rule. Good Lord, they even sound the same: Jardine Matheson – Heritage Mariner! We can do it, I know we can! God, it was so exciting!

Acknowledgements

The Pirate Ship is quite long enough without the addition of Authorities and Book Lists – but I cannot complete it without a short list of acknowledgements. It is the longest book I have ever written and it took the longest to plan and research. Firstly, therefore, I must thank those intrepid travellers who went where I could not: Richard Atherton, Kendall Page and Anne West all selflessly and shamelessly rifled tourist booths in Singapore and Hong Kong on my behalf. The amount of literature they amassed is largely responsible for such vividness as I have been able to bring to my descriptions of those two vibrant cities. I must thank Ursula Price the librarian at the Hong Kong Government offices, for her help and advice. I must also thank John Murr for boldly going through the Channel Tunnel on my behalf to bring back literature and detail about the experiences which Robin could expect. Of my colleagues at The Wildernesse I must particularly thank Ron Herbert, not as Headmaster but as the A Level Law tutor for guiding me through the system which Richard could expect to experience. I must further thank Peter Scurfield who was, in effect, my armourer and supplies officer. Every piece of hardware in *The Pirate Ship* came from him, I believe; and much of the information as to what, precisely, such hardware might be expected to do to people. It was also his edition of Sun Tsu to which I referred at all times. Finally I owe an enormous debt of gratitude to Richard Atchley who read the typescript (all 192,000 words of it) in the middle of an extremely heavy work-load in a range of courts and found time to annotate it in great detail, steering me right on legal and technical terms, and every piece of procedural minutiae that might be expected to happen in the process of arresting and bringing to trial a man such as Richard Mariner accused of such a crime in such a place at such a time. Once again, Richard, I really could not have done it without you – or your *Archbold*. Half a case was nowhere near enough!

Peter Tonkin, Sevenoaks, 1994–1995.